GIDEON AT WORK

J. J. Marric

GIDEON
AT WORK

Three Complete Novels

**GIDEON'S
DAY**

**GIDEON'S
WEEK**

**GIDEON'S
NIGHT**

HARPER & BROTHERS, PUBLISHERS, NEW YORK

Gideon's Day

1 . Gideon's Wrath

THE wrath of Gideon was remarkable to see and a majestic thing to hear. Among other things, it transformed Gideon himself. From a massive, slow-moving, pale man with a quiet voice and unassuming, almost modest manner, he became as a raging lion, cheeks reddening and voice bellowing. Such times did not come often; but as Gideon was a Superintendent at New Scotland Yard, whenever it did, it made many people uneasy, and set them searching their consciences for evidence of things undone or badly done. All the sins of omission and commission noticed by Gideon but not used in evidence against his subordinates became vivid in the recollection of the offenders; on any one of these, Gideon might descend. The first cause of the storm often suffered lightly compared with others. One consequence was inescapable: a shaking up. The thin, chill, sardonic reproof of the Assistant Commissioner, the curt disapproval of the Secretary, even the cold or hot wind created by the induction of a new Commissioner, were petty trials compared with the wrath of Gideon, for he was the Yard's senior Superintendent, and regarded by many as its Grand Old Man.

Yet Gideon was not yet fifty.

On the occasion under discussion the first signs of the wrath to come were visible when Gideon drove too fast into the approaches to the Yard, swinging his new-looking black Wolseley off the Embankment at Flying Squad pace. He squeezed between the A.C.'s Daimler and Mr. Millington's Riley at fully twenty-five miles an hour, and had only a foot to spare on one side and six inches on the other. He brought the car to a standstill with its bumper a bare inch off the wall, more by luck than judgment.

Quite evidently, this was going to be Gideon's day.

Five officers, all uniformed, read the signs.

By the time Gideon reached the foot of the stone steps leading to the main hall of the C.I.D. building, the news, in the form of a "get everything under control, G.G.'s on the warpath" warning, was on its way through the Yard, *via* a one-armed lift attendant, two plain-clothes sergeants and a telephone operator named Veronica (who was engaged to one of the sergeants). It quivered along telephone lines, cut into large offices and small, like a draught of cold wind; it reached the canteen, the divers departments from the laboratory to ballistics, and made the men on radio-control duty much brisker in the Information Room. In fact, by the time Gideon reached his own office, it had reached the ears of the Secretary, that almost anonymous personage who knew practically everything that went on.

The Secretary grinned.

Few others found it even slightly amusing, for even at the Yard a completely clear conscience is a rarity. Chief Inspector Lemaitre, who shared Gideon's office, had two minutes' notice of the storm. That was time in which to straighten his tie, put on his coat, empty the seven cigarette stubs out of his ashtray and then, for appearances' sake, pick up two and put them back. He also had time to stack the morning's reports on Gideon's desk, under three headings: New Inquiries, Inquiries Proceeding, and Investigation Closed. That done, he trundled back to his own desk, lifted the telephone and called B1 Division; he considered it wise to be on the telephone, for that would give him time to judge the likely effect of the tempest on him. Lemaitre was just a year younger than Gideon, a thin, lanky and laconic man, showing to all except Gideon a confidence which suggested that he was sure that he could never be wrong. In fact, he was prone to the mistakes which usually follow overconfidence.

He was holding on for the call when the door opened, banged back against the doorstop, and admitted Gideon. It was rather as if an elephant had changed its slow, stately progress for the furious speed of a gazelle; except that Gideon was not even remotely like a gazelle.

He looked round at Lemaitre, who raised a hand and gave a bright smile; and allowed it to freeze on his lantern cheeks, as if he had received no warning.

Gideon pushed the chair behind his own desk into position, so that it banged against the wall. He dropped into it, and stretched out for the telephone. He looked across at Lemaitre, his big, gray eyebrows thrust forward, his lined forehead narrowed in a scowl, hooked nose quivering slightly at the nostrils, as if under the influence of an unfamiliar smell. In his big way, Gideon was distinguished looking, with his iron-gray hair, that nose, arched lips, a big, square chin. His looks would have been an asset in almost any profession from the law to politics, and especially in the church; as a detective, they occasionally helped to impress a jury, especially when there were several women on it.

"Give me Foster," he said into the telephone.

Lemaitre thought of a youngish, up-and-coming detective, spruce looking but unpopular. What had Foster done to cause such a storm as this? Lemaitre speculated hopefully; then his call came through but the man he wanted wasn't in. That was an advantage after all.

"I'll call him later," he said, and rang off. He smiled brightly. "Morning, George."

Gideon nodded and grunted, but obviously was thinking of the telephone. A faint murmur came from it, and Gideon said: "Come and see me, Foster, at once."

He put down the receiver, so heavily that the bell sounded. Then he placed both hands on his desk, fingers spread, and kept them very still as he looked at Lemaitre. The Chief Inspector probably had more experience with Gideon's wrath than anyone else at the Yard, and was quite sure that the cause of this was really serious. Gideon seldom if ever let himself go so utterly unless he had been given grim cause.

"What's up, George?" Lemaitre asked.

"Blurry fool," Gideon said. "Blurry crook, if it comes to that. I haven't felt as vicious as this for years. You get out, Lem, tell you about it afterward. Get out as soon as he comes in."

"Okay," promised Lemaitre.

There was room for nothing else in Gideon's mind, another ominous sign; and when he talked of a C.I.D. man as a crook, it was more than ominous—it was alarming. Lemaitre felt uneasy for a deeper reason now.

The "blurry" instead of "bloody" meant nothing. When these two men had first met, nearly twenty-five years ago, Gideon had commanded the vocabulary of a trooper who had served his apprenticeship in Covent Garden market. He had always known exactly when to use it, and had first started toning it down precisely twenty years ago this spring.

He'd been a detective sergeant then, with the same promise as young Foster. "Blurry" had been his first substitution, uttered to Lemaitre's open-mouthed astonishment. Lemaitre, then also a detective sergeant, hadn't been even slightly nervous of Gideon, although he had willingly conceded him best in most aspects of detective work.

"What's got into you?" he had asked. "Toothache?"

"Toothache be *blowed*," Gideon had said, and grinned fiercely. "Sent young Tom to Sunday School yesterday for the first time. When he came back, Kate and I asked him how he liked it. Know what he said? 'Bloody good,' he said, so we weighed into him about wicked words, and know what he said then? He said it was what *I'd* said after seeing a film the night before. I had, too. From now on, I've got to mind my language if I don't want trouble with Kate. The kid's too young to start, anyway."

Lemaitre hadn't heard Gideon swear for many years.

He'd had good enough reason for watching his language, of course; young

Tom had been the first of six, and the youngest child was only eight now. Or was it ten? Lemaitre was not quite sure.

There was a tap at the door. "Come in," Gideon called, and the door opened and Foster came in smartly. He dressed well, was tall, well built, and had quite a name in amateur Rugby and tennis circles. Age about thirty, Lemaitre thought, and if he didn't think himself so clever and put on airs, he would be rated high.

Lemaitre stood up.

"Just going along to Records," he said, "won't be long."

Gideon grunted.

Foster said "Good morning, sir" in just about the right tone and manner. He did not look puzzled, apprehensive or guilty. Lemaitre even wondered whether the whisper of the wrath had reached him: he looked almost too bland for that. His dark hair was brushed flat down and straight back from his forehead; his rather bold eyes and nose told the discerning that he would be too interested in Number One. Lemaitre went out, reluctantly, and subdued the temptation to stand at the door and listen. He strolled off toward the canteen for a cup of tea, calling on Records en route in case Gideon telephoned him there. They would say that he'd been and gone. The fact that Lemaitre thought that a necessary precaution was an indication of the awe he felt at times for Gideon.

In the office, the detective sergeant looked down at the Superintendent.

Gideon's hands were still on the desk, palms downward, skin a leathery-looking brown, fingers and nails big and strong but not at all ugly. The cuffs of a clean white shirt showed. He wore a suit of navy blue and a blue-and-red-spotted tie, all of good quality.

His eyes were slaty blue, big, with heavy, sleepy-looking lids—but there was nothing sleepy about them now. He was a man burning with anger. Foster, at first completely at ease, began to look less self-confident. That became worse because he had to stand in front of the desk like a schoolboy before an unpredictable master; after a few seconds he actually moistened his lips and broke the harsh silence.

"You—you sent for me, sir?"

"Yes," Gideon said very heavily. "I sent for you, Foster. I sent for you to tell you a thing or two." His voice was deep and rather husky; just now he gave the impression that he was trying not to raise it. "I sent for you to tell you that you're a living disgrace to the C.I.D. and the Metropolitan Police Force generally. In all my years on the Force I've met some fools and a few knaves, and here and there a rat, and you're one of the big rats. I ought to put you on a charge right away and make sure it sticks, and I'm not sure that I won't. We make mistakes here at the Yard, and occasionally let a rogue in, but you're the first of your kind I've come across, and I'd like to break your neck."

All Foster's blandness had vanished. His thick, full lips were red and wet, where he kept licking them. His cheeks had no color left, and his almost black eyes couldn't keep steady. When Gideon stopped talking, Foster gulped, tried to find words, but couldn't. Gideon sat there, motionless, damning, as if challenging him to say a word in his defense.

Foster gulped again and eased his collar.

"I—I think you ought to be—to be very careful about talking that way," he said thinly. "You've no right to—"

"I've sent Chief Inspector Lemaitre out of the office," Gideon cut across the protest abruptly, "so we can have this interview between ourselves, without witnesses. But I can get all the witnesses I want to prove that you're a skunk. Only 'skunk' isn't the best word. You're a renegade and you're a traitor, and if you were in the army you'd be shot and I'd be glad to pull the trigger."

Now Foster went red.

"Who the hell do you think you're talking to?"

"At the moment, to Detective Sergeant Eric Foster, of the Criminal Investigation Department," Gideon growled, "but you won't be able to call yourself that for long."

Foster still tried bluster.

"What's this all about? What are you accusing me of doing?"

"If you want it in simple words, I'm accusing you, as an officer of the Criminal Investigation Department, of accepting bribes and so deliberately failing to carry out your duty. I know who's been paying you and I know why, and I've a pretty good idea how much money you've had over the past three months. Like to know how I know?" The big hands didn't move, the gaze of the slaty blue eyes didn't falter. "Because an *honest* crook told me. He said that he didn't mind cracking a crib or doing a smash-and-grab job, but when it came to feeding dope to kids in their teens, he drew a line —and he thought I ought to, too."

Foster exclaimed: "He's lying! There was no dope—"

He broke off, and all his color died away, leaving only his shiny dark eyes.

Gideon said heavily: "That's right, say that you didn't know that they were selling reefers, or that one of them had a hypo and was selling shots of the muck for a guinea a time. Say you thought it was just a question of selling intoxicating liquor after hours—how much better policeman are you for that? You've got a job to do, and if you'd kept your eyes open you would have known what was going on. Even I can't believe that you knew about the dope. You—"

"Of course I didn't," Foster put in quickly. "I—I didn't know about selling drink after hours, either."

Gideon shook his head, slowly, deliberately, massively.

"Foster," he said, "you haven't even the sense not to lie about it. I suppose you've got to lie. It's the only way you might be able to save your skin. So you'll try." Much of the power had gone from Gideon's voice, as if what had happened had exhausted him. "And Chang will lie, too, because if he admitted it, he knows his club would be closed up and he wouldn't be allowed to open up again in London. I don't doubt that you're paid off in a dark corner, that no one sees you meet and no one else knows anything about it—or so you think. Or you *thought*." The sneer was devastating. "Well, now you know better. Now you know you can't get away with accepting bribes. From this day on, you'll know what it's like to realize that thanks to you, some kids have become cocaine addicts, and that it's ruined their whole lives."

Foster said between clenched teeth: "If kids want dope they'll find a way of getting it. And whoever told you that I've been taking bribes is a liar. You say you got a squeak—I want to know who from." He paused. "I know the kind who squeal about things like that. I know the kind who squeal to *you*, too." Foster's sneer rivaled Gideon's; in fact, it was uglier. "Old lags, blackguards who ought to be inside and would be if you did your job properly, but you let them keep out, so that you can get them to squeal on others. Think I don't know? Think I don't know that the name of Gideon stinks in the West End?"

When he stopped, it was almost fearfully, as if suddenly afraid that he had gone too far. But Gideon did not move; just looked at him as he might at something unclean. Foster ran his tongue along his lips.

"I—I'm sorry, sir, I didn't mean that. It's been a bit of a shock. I withdraw that remark, sir. But I assure you, you've been misinformed. I give you my word, Chang hasn't bribed me. I—er—I've been a bit too friendly with him, perhaps, but I think he's a decent chap at heart, and—"

"You'd better go, before I break your neck," Gideon said. "I don't think you're worth hanging for. As from this moment, you're relieved of all duties. You can protest to the Secretary or the Assistant Commissioner, but it won't make any difference. Stay in London, because we might want to see you at short notice."

"Look here," Foster said thickly, "at least I've got the right to speak on my own behalf."

"Every right," Gideon conceded, "and you'll get it, when the time comes. At the moment I know what you've done but I can't prove it in court. I'm going to look for proof at a time when I've a hundred other urgent jobs that need doing. I'm going to have to waste time on a job like this, and perhaps a murderer or two will get away as a result of it. That ought to make you feel happy."

Foster said thinly: "You can't prove what isn't true."

"That's right, too," said Gideon. He closed his eyes for a moment, as if he were very tired. "All right, get out."

Foster turned toward the door. With his fingers on the handle, he hesitated, and glanced over his shoulder. Gideon was no longer looking at him, but out of the window which overlooked the many windows of a wall on the other side of the rectangular yard.

But he spoke.

"Foster," he asked, "what made you do it?"

"I didn't do it," Foster said, viciously angry. "You'll be wasting your time all right. Be careful what you say, or I'll get you for defamation of character."

He went out, and slammed the door.

2 . Gideon Walks

LEMAITRE sat on the edge of his desk, bony legs crossed, cigarette drooping from his lips. All this was safe now, as the rage was spent. As he listened, he thought that Gideon was tired and showing signs of more years than forty-nine. It was always a strain, being a Yard officer, and Gideon took his responsibilities more to heart than most. He lived his job day and night, in the office, in London, in his home. They all did, up to a point, but few so thoroughly as Gideon.

"The filthy swine," Lemaitre said at last. "I never did like him; he's always been too smooth. Can you pin it on him?"

"Not yet," said Gideon. He was pulling at his empty pipe, a rough-surfaced cherry wood, which was almost a sign of affection.

"Who put in the squeal?"

"Birdy."

"Well," Lemaitre said, "you can trust Birdy."

"That's right," agreed Gideon, "you can trust Birdy, especially on a job like this. His own daughter got to like reefers, and he buried her at nineteen. She'd been a pro for three years, and a dopey for two. That makes Birdy the most valuable contact man we've got in the Square Mile on all kinds of dope peddling, and we can't afford to lose him. So I've put a man onto him, and had him warned that he must look out for trouble. Because Foster will tell Chang, and Chang will try to find out who squeaked. He may not have any luck, but if he does—well, we won't go any further than that. Chang will clean up the Chang Club, too; after this morning you'll be able to run a vacuum cleaner over it and not find a grain of marijuana or any kind of dope."

"He'll do that," agreed Lemaitre. "That's what puzzles me, George. Why did you smack Foster down when you did? Why didn't you raid the place first? You might have picked Chang up and put him inside for ten years." He looked puzzled, but he grinned. "But being you, there's a reason, you cunning old so-and-so." That he could talk so freely was conclusive proof that he felt sure that Gideon was his normal calm self again. "After the suppliers?"

"Partly," Gideon said. "I went for Foster and took the chance of warning Chang because I want to drive Foster into doing something decisive. He'll have to go to Chang; if they're watched closely they'll probably be seen together. And we need proof."

Lemaitre wrinkled his nose.

"Sounds more like me talking than you," he remarked. "Couldn't you have watched Foster, without telling him what you suspected?"

Gideon let himself smile, for the first time that day.

"I've had Foster watched for two months," he said, "and even you didn't know. Got nowhere. The thing that got me this morning was the dope. I can understand a man having his palm oiled, but—" he broke off, and ruminated. Then: "I also think Chang's big time, and on his way to the top. I'd like to watch him now that he's had a smack, and see how he tries to cope."

"Cunning as a fox," Lemaitre mocked. "I'd be inclined to put him away before he became big time."

"That way, we wouldn't know who was climbing in his place," said Gideon. Unexpectedly, he smiled again; it gave him the kind of look that all his children loved to see. "You may be right, Lem, this could be one of my mistakes. I think I've started something, and I'd like to see where it goes."

"Going to report Foster to the A.C.?"

"Unofficially," Gideon said. "We can't make a charge. Foster will soon discover that, and he's bound to resign. He's got the makings of a very bad man in him. Can't possibly give him a second chance, of course; if he won't go by himself, we'll have to find a way of getting rid of him, but I don't think that will cause any trouble. Now, what's in this morning?"

He turned to his desk and the three files.

All Scotland Yard knew that the wrath was over, and that it had fallen on the sleek head of Detective Sergeant Foster; none found it in themselves to be sorry, because Foster, being a know-all, was without close friends. One or two casual friends tried to pump him, without success, and he left the Yard a little after eleven o'clock.

By that time Gideon had run through the three groups of cases. Inquiries Proceeding held his attention more than either of the others, and he skimmed through the new cases quickly. Nothing seemed of exceptional interest. Inquiries into several robberies in central London looked as if they were petering out: a jealous ex-lover had thrown vitriol over his love, a woman had been found murdered in Soho. The newspapers would make a sensation of it, but as far as a woman could ask for murder, she had. There was a forgery job building up; it might become very big before it was finished, but he needn't worry about that now.

The Inquiries Proceeding took most of his time, and the report he studied longest was one on the last mail-van job, now ten days old. If the Yard had an Achilles' heel, it was that; mail-van robberies had been going on for three years, and there was plenty of evidence to show that it was the work of one group of crooks; there was nothing about their identity. That worried Gideon because it had become a challenge to the Yard's prestige as well as to its skill.

It wasn't the only challenge.

There was the constant one of drugs. Close up one distribution center, and another would open. Judging from what he now knew, at least twelve were open all the time. None of them was big, none threatened to become extensive or to affect the lives of many people except those who were already on the fringe of crime; it was a kind of running sore. Sooner or later, a duke's daughter or an M.P.'s son would become an addict, and then it would be made into a sensation. The Yard would be prodded from all sides, and Gideon would get as many of the prods as most. He seldom revolted against this form of injustice, for he knew well what some people seemed unable to grasp.

There was a never-ending war between the police and the criminals, a war fought with thoroughness, skill, patience and cunning on each side. With a few exceptions, the big cases were not the important ones in this unending war. A man who had never committed a crime in his life might suddenly commit murder and his trial become a *cause célèbre,* but the chief impact of the big case upon the Yard would be to keep some of the men away from their daily struggle against the run-of-the-mill vice and crime.

Now and again Gideon would say all this, earnestly, to a friend or to a new policeman or even a newspaper reporter, and shake his head a little sadly when he realized that they took very little notice.

There was dope, then; there were the mail-van robberies; there were the thieves who worked as industriously as any man at his job or profession, taking the risk of a spell of prison life as another might take the risk of bankruptcy. Crime never stopped. Big robberies and little robberies, big thieves and the little sneaks, a few gangs but little violence, one fence sent to jail here, another discovered there—oh, the trouble with being an officer at Scotland Yard was that one lived in a tiny world, and found it hard to realize that ninety-nine per cent of the nation's citizens were wholly law-abiding. Gideon's greatest worry, and constant anxiety, were the formidable and increasing evidence that many law-abiding people would readily become lawbreakers if they had a good chance and believed that they would not be found out.

Foster was a painful case in point. . . .

Inwardly, Gideon was worried in case he had been swayed too much by his fury when handling Foster. Ninety-nine times out of a hundred he would have waited to cool off before tackling the man; this time he hadn't been able to. Every now and again he erupted as he had this morning in a rage which perhaps only he knew was virtually uncontrollable.

Well, it was done. With twenty-odd years' experience of the Square Mile behind him, he could afford to play what some people would regard as a hunch—this time, that it was wise not to pull Chang in. It was policy to keep hunches even from Lemaitre and certainly from the Assistant Commissioner, although sometimes he thought that the A.C. knew.

The A.C. took the report on Foster very well. No eruption of shock and shame, just a calm acceptance of the fact that they'd picked a bad one when they'd taken Foster on, and an almost casual: "Sure of your facts, Gideon?"

"Yes."

"All right, let me know if you think he's going to try to whitewash himself." The A.C. didn't smile, but was almost bland. "Nothing else outside?"

"Not really," said Gideon. "Four of those mail bags were found floating in the Thames last night—from the Middlebury Road job, by the markings, when they stole the van and all. Ten days ago. Just a chance that we might be able to find out where they were thrown into the river; the River coppers are trying that now. Otherwise—" Gideon shrugged.

"If there's a job I want to finish before I get moved on, it's the mail-van job," the A.C. said quietly, "but I needn't badger you about it, I know how you feel. All right, go off after your bad men." This time he smiled, and then added as Gideon stood up: "How did that girl of yours get on with her examination?"

Gideon brightened perceptibly.

"Oh, she got through, thanks. She says she was lucky, she happened to know most of the questions, but—"

"Modest, like her father," observed the A.C. "Guildhall School of Music, wasn't it? I had a niece who used to think she could play the piano, too. Your girl a pianist?"

"Fiddler," said Gideon. "Can't say I'm a devotee of the violin, but she passed her exam, all right, and can take a job tomorrow—if she can get one! Won't do her any harm to find that jobs don't grow on trees, though. Hard to believe that there's a musician in the family." Gideon went on, with barely subdued pride, "I can't sing a note without being flat, and my wife— well, never mind. Will you be in today, if I need you?"

"I'll be at lunch from twelve-thirty to three."

Gideon kept a straight face. "Right, sir, thanks." He went out, letting the door close silently behind him, and shook his head. "Two and a half hours for lunch, and I'll be lucky if I have time to get a bowl of soup and a sandwich from the canteen." But he said it in no resentful mood. If changing incomes with the A.C. meant changing jobs, he would stay as he was. Nice of the old boy to remember Pru. Well done, Pru. Eighteen—

He remembered Birdy's daughter, buried at nineteen. He remembered how easy it was to become in need of reefers or of any of the more dangerous drugs; you might have your first taste without knowing it, but you'd still be eager for a second, anxious for a third, desperate for a fourth—and there were precious few cures for addiction.

At half-past eleven, he was walking from the Yard into Parliament Street, soon to turn right toward Whitehall and Trafalgar Square. It was a crisp morning in April, no rain was about, the look of spring was upon London and the feel of spring was in Londoners. In a vague sort of way, Gideon knew that he loved London and, after a fashion, loved Londoners. It wasn't just sentiment; he belonged to the hard pavements, the smell of petrol and oil, the rumble and the growl of traffic, and the unending sound of footsteps, as some men belonged to the country. They could be said to love the soil. The only time that Gideon was really uneasy was when he had a job to handle outside of London or one of the big cities. The country hadn't the same feel; he felt that it could cheat him, without his knowing it, whereas here in London the odds were always even.

He walked almost ponderously, six feet two in spite of slightly rounded shoulders, broad and striking enough to make most people look at him twice, and some turn and stare. He was sufficiently well known for a dozen men to nudge their companions and say: "There's Gideon of the Yard," and sufficiently well liked and trusted to get a grin and a "Hi, guv'nor!" from the newspaper sellers and one or two familiars who knew him in the way of business. Very few people disliked Gideon, even among those he put inside. That was one of the reassuring things, and it put the seal to his oneness with London. He supposed, in a way, that it was the common touch. He could think the same way as many of these men thought; they were as dependent on the throbbing heart of London as he.

Dope, gangs, thieves, murderers, prostitutes, pimps, ponces, forgers,

blackmailers, coiners, con men, big-time crooks and little squealers, frightened men and terrified women, vengeful old lags like Birdy who had suffered
from the parasitic growth he had helped to put upon the body of London.
Here they were, all together, practitioners of every kind of crime, side by
side with every kind of goodness, clean crime and "dirt," too. Somewhere,
Foster was licking his wounds or talking to Chang or plotting revenge out of
his hurt vanity.

Nothing happened that hadn't happened before.

Now, Gideon was going on his "daily" rounds; in fact only once or twice
each week could he afford the time to do this, and the years had taught
him as well as those who employed him that the time he spent on his
rounds was well spent indeed. He was going without any specific purpose,
and he didn't think about Foster or crooks all the time. Twice, a young girl
he passed, bright with the beauty of youth and touched with the eagerness
of innocence, reminded him of his Prudence. Once he told himself that he
thought more of Pru than he did of Kate, and supposed that all couples
who had been married for twenty-six years lost—something.

When he got back to the Yard, it was just after twelve. Except that he
had shown himself to many people who needed reminding that he was
about, it had not been an eventful morning. For the past hour he had hardly
given Foster a thought, which meant that his fears of having used bad tactics
didn't go very deep; it would be all right.

Two or three senior officers made cryptic remarks as he went along the
wide corridors, but it was Lemaitre who waited with the stunning news.

"Hallo, George, you heard?"

Gideon put his hat on a corner peg. "Heard what?"

"Foster's dead," Lemaitre said. "Run over by a car that didn't stop."

3 . Foster's Sister

GIDEON did not answer as he went round to his chair, moved it gently so
that the back did not scrape against the wall, and sat down. He picked up
his cold pipe, and ran his fingers over the corrugations in the cherry bark.
Lemaitre waited until he was sitting back, before adding: "They rang up
from Great Marlborough Street, full of it."

There was another long pause. Then: "What beats me," said Gideon,
making himself keep very matter-of-fact, "is that anyone could knock a chap
down in London and drive off and get away with it. Or did anyone pick
up the number of the car?"

"No," said Lemaitre. "Well, not yet."

Gideon picked up a pencil, and spoke as he wrote down his first note, which read: "General call for anyone who saw moving car near fatal spot." Aloud: "Was he killed instantaneously?"

"Pretty well."

"Anything else?"

Lemaitre looked at a clock with big dark hands on the wall over the fireplace. It was ten past twelve.

"I should say it happened at eleven fifty-five," he said. "If you ask me—"

"In a minute, Lem," Gideon said, and pulled a telephone toward him, asked for the Chief Inspector's room, then gave instructions: it was simply a call to find witnesses of the accident, all the usual routine; he said everything in a tone which was almost eager, suggesting that these hoary measures were fresh, interesting, even exciting. "And let me know what you get, will you?" he added, and put the receiver down. "What's that, Lem?"

"If you ask me," repeated Lemaitre, "Foster telephoned Chang, Chang got the wind up, and put him away. And don't tell me I'm romancing, they don't come any worse than Chang. Just because we've never been able to put him inside, it doesn't mean that he's a lily-white—"

"All right," Gideon said, still feeling the rough bowl of the pipe, "I know all about Chang. I'd like to find out if he did know about Foster being suspended—hmm. I think I'll go myself. Wonder what time Chang gets up." He was muttering, might almost have forgotten that Lemaitre was still in the office with him. "Hell of a thing to happen. Could have committed suicide, I suppose, or else been so steamed up that he didn't look where he was going. Car didn't stop, though. Looks ugly." He stood up, thrusting both hands into the baggy pockets of his jacket, still holding the pipe in his left hand. "Anything else in?"

"Nothing much. There was a go at a mail van in Liverpool Street at half-past ten, the railway police stopped their little game, but the three men involved got away."

Gideon's interest in that seemed sharper than it had in the news of Foster's death.

"Description?"

"No. Masked, until they'd got away."

"You know, Lem," said Gideon, "if we had as much nerve as some of these johnnies, maybe we'd get results quicker. They're quick, they're smart and they're full of guts. That the lot?"

"All that matters, I think," said Lemaitre. "There's a flash about a girl's body found in an apartment near Park Lane, nothing known yet—could be natural causes or accident. Patrol-car flash, just before you came in."

"Um," said Gideon. "Well, let me know." He went to the door.

"George," said Lemaitre strongly.

"Yes?"

"Be careful with Chang."

Gideon's slaty eyes lost their brooding look, and for a moment he smiled.
"Don't be a blurry fool," he said. "Snow wouldn't melt in Chang's mouth
today, never mind about butter!" He gave that quick, paternal smile again,
and went out.

On his way for the morning perambulation, he had gone almost ponderously. Now he wasn't exactly brisk, but took long strides and passed
three plain-clothes men moving smartly toward the lift. He reached it first.

"Hear about that mail-van attempt at Liverpool Street?" asked one of
them, a middle-aged Detective Inspector.

"Yes," answered Gideon briefly.

A white-haired detective sergeant said: "I've got another six months in
this cowshed, and if there's a job I'd like to see finished, it's the mail-van
job. How many robberies is it now?"

The D.I. said: "Draw it mild. This wasn't one."

"Not often they miss."

"Thirty-nine in three years and two months," said Gideon, "and don't ask
me whether they're all organized by the same man. I don't know. But I'll
bet some of them are. Picked up some of the bags from the last job in the
Thames," he went on, in the way he had of talking freely to subordinates
whenever it was possible. "They make pretty sure we can't trace 'em back,
don't they?"

"They'll slip up," the D.I. prophesied.

Gideon rubbed his chin. "It wouldn't worry me if we caught 'em before
they slip up," he said. "Nice if our results weren't always governed by
frailties on the part of the crooks, wouldn't it, boys?"

He sounded positively paternal.

The lift stopped, and the others made room for him to get out first.

"Thanks," he murmured, and was walking toward the steps and his car
a moment later, apparently forgetful of the others.

They watched him.

"Funny thing," the elderly sergeant said, "he came in on the rampage
this morning. Foster went off with a flea in his ear, and now Foster's been
run down. Next thing you know, Gee-Gee will be blaming himself for it."

Gideon—his Christian name of George made Gee-Gee inevitable—
squeezed into his shiny car, turned on the ignition and let in the clutch, reversed until he could swing clear, nodded to the two men who saluted him,
and drove at a moderate pace onto the Embankment. He turned right, heading for Whitehall, then Trafalgar Square, then Lower Regent Street—the
main road route to Great Marlborough Street. Inside the car he looked massive, and rather dull. His driving was automatic, yet he wasn't careless and

was usually a move ahead of other traffic; he changed gear smoothly, and gave no sign that he was thinking about Foster.

He was wondering whether this would have happened if he hadn't blown his top with Foster. The earlier, uneasy fears—that he might have done the wrong thing—were darker and heavier in one way, worrying him. In another, he was relieved. There was no longer the certainty of scandal, the newspaper headlines, sneers at the Yard, and God knew, things were difficult enough without that. Still, it was a worry. It did not harass him enough to make him careless, or forgetful of the main task: to find out whether Lemaitre's guess was anywhere near the truth. He found himself thinking of Lemaitre with a reluctant kind of disapproval. Over the years, Lem had made the same kind of mistakes, due to impetuosity. "If you ask me, he telephoned Chang, Chang got the wind up, and put him away." Lemaitre was still capable of talking like that without a tittle of evidence, of looking upon a possibility as if it were a probability. The years of being proved wrong hadn't cured him; it was why he would never become a Superintendent, either at the Yard or one of the Divisions.

Never mind Lem!

Gideon stopped at the police station in Great Marlborough Street, and had a word with the Divisional Superintendent by telephone from the duty sergeant's desk. Nothing more was known about Foster's accident, no news had come in about the car. The body was at the morgue attached to the police station.

"Want to have a look at him?" the station Superintendent asked. It was on the tip of Gideon's tongue to say "no," and then he changed his mind.

"Yes, thanks, mind if I go in on my own? I'm in a hurry."

"Help yourself," the other said.

There were two other bodies in the morgue; only one light was on, over a stone bench where one man lay and two others worked. Gideon moved among the stone-topped benches, until he reached the workingmen, and saw that Foster lay there. They'd almost finished, and didn't look up until one of them drew a white sheet over Foster's body, up as far as the chin. From where Gideon stood, he had a foreshortened view of Foster; he realized that he had been a strikingly good-looking man.

One of the others, a police surgeon with black hair and a bald patch, looked up.

"Hallo, George."

" 'Lo, Harry."

"He went out as quick and clean as a whistle," said the police surgeon. "It's always a help when you know that. Cracked the back of his head, and crushed his stomach, but the face is hardly damaged. Worked with you sometimes, didn't he?"

Gideon nodded.

"Married?" asked the police surgeon.

"No," said Gideon. "One sister, no other close relatives." Asked about any of the men who worked with him regularly, he could have given an answer as promptly and as accurately. "Well, there we are." He turned away, and walked with the police surgeon toward the door of the morgue.

They didn't say much.

Back in his car, Gideon waited long enough to pack the pipe loosely with a mixture, and to light it. Two loose pipes in the morning, two in the afternoon and as many as he wanted in the evening were his rule. He brushed a speck of glowing tobacco off his trousers, then moved off.

It wasn't far from here to Winter Street, Soho, where Chang had his club.

There was no room to park. Gideon drove round twice and then spotted a constable.

"I'm going to leave this here, double-parked," he said. "Keep an eye open, and if it blocks anyone who wants to get out, move it for me." He took it for granted that he was recognized, handed over his ignition key, and walked toward Chang's, which was just round the corner.

For a district in the heart of the biggest city in the world, this was a disgrace and degradation. It was almost the only part of London Gideon disliked. The buildings were mostly dilapidated, none was impressive; it was like a shopping center in the East End, except for the masses of cars parked bumper to bumper. Most of the shops looked closed. A laundry, a shop advertising: WE MAKE NEW COLLARS FROM SHIRTTAILS; a butcher's shop open, with a woman with brassy hair and talonlike red nails, smoking a cigarette and talking to the butcher, showed a glimpse of Soho life as it really was. Gideon knew the woman; she'd been up before the magistrate at Great Marlborough or Bow Street regularly for the past twenty years. She lived close by, and bought her groceries, her meat, her milk, all the things of daily life, from these small shops. Well, why not? She had to live somewhere. A corner shop was filled with dark-haired men and women, all shorter than the average Londoner; they were southern French, Italian and Spanish—and mostly Italian, Gideon knew. In the windows on the shelves were delicacies brought from the ends of the earth—literally from the ends of the earth. If you wanted a specialty of the Chinese, the Japanese, the Javanese, of India, Brazil, the south of Spain or the north of Italy, from Yugoslavia or from Russia, you could buy it here. Inside, everyone was chatting, all were dressed in black, and Gideon scented a funeral party preparing for the meal to come.

The pavements were dusty, the gutters littered with chaff, pieces of paper, cigarette ends, bus tickets. Dust carts and street sweepers could come through Soho half a dozen times a day without ridding it of this hint of squalor in the worst streets; and Winter Street was one of the worst.

By day, Chang's looked harmless.

The name, in mock-Chinese lettering, was on the fascia board, and the weather or years had worn it so badly that most of the "h" and part of the "g" were obliterated. Chang had been here a long time. It was a double-fronted shop, and the windows were blotted out with dirty-looking muslin curtains, but the bill of fare, showing what Chang had to offer in an English hand which would have suited a Billingsgate pub, looked clean enough. It was a restaurant by day and a club by night.

Gideon went in.

He knew that he had been seen approaching; probably when he had driven past here he had been recognized. Word spread in Soho as quickly as it did to the Yard. He knew that the broad smile on the face of the diminutive Chinese who came toward him, hands covered in the folds of his snow-white apron, hair shiny with oil, and expression one of friendliness and delight, could hide anything from thoughts of murder to honest curiosity.

"Good day, sa, you like good lunch?"

"No, thanks," Gideon said. "Is Chang in?"

"Chang, sa?" The slit eyes widened, the hands performed strange gyrations, still beneath the apron. "I find out, sa, name please?"

"Gideon," said Gideon. "Never mind, I'll find out for myself."

He walked across the sawdusted boards, past several Chinese eating English food, a Malayan couple eating rice and an Indian woman in a pale pink sari, sitting in front of a metal tray with several metal dishes on it, and pushed open a door. Beyond was the kitchen; this was spotlessly clean, with two Chinese women working in the steamy heat. Beyond again was a staircase. Gideon went up the staircase, without hurrying. The boy would have warned Chang.

Gideon sniffed.

There was a strong smell of paint, and it became more noticeable as he approached the landing. The narrow stairs creaked. A strip of hair carpet ran in the middle of them, and along both passages at the top. One door, closed, was marked: OFFICE. The other door, open, was marked: CLUB. "Club" had never been more than a name used so as to obtain a late liquor license, and until recently Chang had done nothing to invite being closed up.

Two painters were busy in the clubroom, one lanky Englishman with a sniff, the other a sturdy, handsome youngster, obviously not English. "A Pole," Gideon thought, as he spoke to the lanky man.

"When did you start this job?"

Wary, watery eyes turned toward him.

"S'morning."

"When did you get the order?"

The lanky man's eyes were now narrowed so tightly that they were nearly closed. The Pole was working steadily, using a small brush fat with crimson paint. The big clubroom stank of oil paint and distemper.

Gideon heard the other door open, although it made little sound.

"None of yer bus'ness," the lanky man drawled nasally.

Gideon didn't argue. "I'll know you again," he said, and turned round.

He wasn't surprised to see Chang in the office doorway. He was surprised to see the woman behind him, standing up and looking somehow unsure of herself, like someone who'd had an unpleasant surprise. She was quite a good-looker. Gideon had once danced with her at a police ball.

She was Foster's sister, and her name was Flo.

4 . Chang

CHANG was smiling diffidently.

Flo Foster wasn't really smiling at all, just looking bewildered. Gideon did not start guessing what she was doing here; it was better to find out for certain. He felt sure that something Chang had said, perhaps about his arrival, had startled her. She was not the type to look bewildered for long, and Gideon had another thought, the kind he would pigeonhole and bring out for examination whenever he felt it necessary. Only a sharp shock would have affected her like this. She came from the same world and had much the same poise—overconfidence—as Foster himself. He did not know her well enough to wonder whether she had the same capacity for error as Foster. "Error" was one word! He judged that she was quite free from the taint of drugs, heavy drinking or any kind of debauchery; she looked not only handsome but wholesome and healthy. She was undoubtedly touched with arrogance.

All this took only a second or two to pass through Gideon's mind.

Chang was moving forward, hands held a little in front of his chest in a gesture which was already self-deprecatory. He had a big, wide forehead and a small, shallow chin, and his face tapered down in the proper proportions from his forehead. One first noticed his face, which was as smooth as yellowed alabaster, and then his small ears, which stuck out almost at right angles and seemed to thrust a way through his dark hair; his hair, like that of most Chinese, was as straight as a woman's in need of a perm. The rest of Chang was not, perhaps, important. He had the facial characteristics of the Oriental, but only those who knew the Orient well could have said whether he was Chinese, Javanese, or one of the other races. His small mouth was faintly pink, a dirty pink. His eyes were dark and pinched a little at the corners; that didn't stop them from being blackly bright. His nose was slightly flattened and the nostrils were dark. For the rest, he was beautifully tailored in pale gray, with a discreet blue tie, a blue handkerchief making a triangle in his breast pocket and, almost certainly, blue socks to match.

He was not effusive. His English was good, with more inflection than accent. He had been born within five miles of this spot, and knew no other language; but he could use pidgin English effectively at times, and pretend not to know English fluently.

"Mr. Gideon," he said, "how unexpected. A pleasure indeed." Now his hands touched at the tips, and he gave the slightest of bows. "You are most welcome. I was about to show my previous visitor the stairs, you will forgive me?"

"That's all right," Gideon said.

"Perhaps you will wait here for me." Chang thrust a hand, fingers crooked and palm upward, toward his office, showing the natural grace so many of his kind had. His smile was not overdone.

"This way, please," he said to Foster's sister, and stepped in front of Gideon, making no bones about wanting the woman to go.

Gideon showed no sign of recognition. Flo Foster now looked away from him, and moved quickly, as if anxious to get out of his sight. She looked good, but not necessarily in the sense of goodness. Her two-piece suit of mustard-color tweed fitted well, and she had all black accessories—gloves, bag, shoes—with a touch of quality.

Gideon inclined his head, ponderously.

When Chang had started down the stairs with Flo Foster, Gideon went into the office. He left the door open. The lanky painter was staring at him, his brush hanging in the air; the Pole was still working, now on distemper with a big brush. Gideon didn't sit down, but stepped to the window and then to a spot out of sight from the surly painter. He touched nothing, but looked about him quickly and intently, missing little. Gideon was a man who, playing the parlor game of "what were the articles on that tray" would invariably win, and would seldom miss even a single item. All he saw here were a few papers, neatly arranged, a big locked safe in one corner, a carved sandalwood box containing cigarettes. The desk was a cheap walnut pedestal one, with a tubular steel swivel chair behind it, and a square of brown carpet centered on the floor had a green linoleum surround.

Chang came back quietly, shut the door and hid the English painter.

He smiled with the familiar reserve, and went round to his chair. His hand moved out again.

"Please sit down."

"Thanks." Gideon sat on an upright chair which looked and felt too flimsy for him. He did not say that he had recognized Foster's sister. Chang's expression was bland: his lips didn't close completely, and showed a glint of white teeth. The silence and the protracted stare probably put him on edge, but nothing in this world was likely to make him show it.

"What can I do for you, Superintendent?"

"Has Foster been here today?" Gideon asked flatly.

"Foster, Superintendent? Who is Foster?"

"You know," said Gideon.

"I am afraid that I do not understand," Chang declared. "Foster, Foster." He let the name float in the air, and so declared his tactics: flat denial of everything. He did not know Foster, he had never bribed Foster, he had not heard that day from anyone named Foster. At the end of this series of mute denials there was defiance, as evident although as mute: "And you cannot prove that I know Foster."

Gideon was convinced that Chang knew everything, now felt that he could go all the way with Lemaitre, although there was still no evidence. By his denials, Chang not only showed his hand but also made it clear that he did not think there was anything to worry about.

Confidence had always been his strong suit.

Overconfidence? Like Foster.

Gideon said: "I mean Eric Foster, a detective sergeant at New Scotland Yard, who's been taking money from you for some time, Chang."

"It is some mistake," said Chang very smoothly. "Perhaps you forget I am not the only Chang in Soho, Mr. Superintendent."

"No," admitted Gideon, "I don't forget." He changed the subject but not his tone. "What are you having the clubroom painted for?"

"But *that*?" asked Chang, and smiled now with greater readiness; a stranger, seeing him for the first time, would have been greatly struck by his open face, the apparently friendly smile, the charm. "I have many clients and I do very well, Mr. Superintendent, and so I am giving them something more pleasant than before."

Gideon didn't answer. Chang did not wilt or even waver slightly under the ruthless scrutiny.

"Chang," said Gideon, suddenly, heavily, "I want to tell you a thing or two. In this country, crimes catch up with you. You ought to know that. Murderers get hanged, thieves get jailed, all criminals get punished sooner or later. We may miss them on one job but we always get them on another.

Don't ever think you're safe. You've been doing some of the foulest things a man can do, and we're after you. That means we'll get you."

Chang's smile became broader, perhaps grew a little tense.

"It is a pity," he said carefully. "I have always liked to be friends with the police. And I shall always be ready to be friends, Mr. Superintendent, but now you talk in hostile mysteries. How can I help?"

"You can't help yourself or us," Gideon declared flatly. "You've gone too far." He got up and moved toward the door, wondering whether to use his only bullet or whether to keep it. He used it: "Who was that woman in here just now?"

"My visitor?" Chang was not even slightly perturbed. "A charming lady, one Mrs. Addinson. She is a painter who would have liked to paint the walls of the club but"—he gave a charming little shrug—"she would also like too much money." He moved toward Gideon, finger tips touching. "So nice to have seen you again, Mr. Superintendent. I hope soon we shall be friends once more."

The smell of paint was almost overpowering on the landing. The lanky painter had lit a fresh cigarette, and seemed to be pouring thinners into a tin of paint. The Pole was slapping distemper onto the ceiling, standing on a square packing case in order to reach up. Gideon didn't look at Chang again, but went deliberately downstairs, glanced into the kitchen, was escorted to the street door by the grinning youth, whose hands still hid themselves beneath the snow-white apron.

Gideon walked back to his car. The policeman was at hand eager to be of help.

"Have you seen Birdy Merrick about today?" asked Gideon.

"No, sir, haven't set eyes on him."

"Well, if you do, tell him to keep out of Chang's reach for a bit," said Gideon. "Noticed anything unusual at Chang's today?"

"Well—in a way, sir."

"What way?"

"He had a visitor—a nice-looking young lady, sir. He often has visitors, but not that kind and they don't usually come in the morning, they're nightbirds. Saw her at his window. She's left now, sir."

"Hmm. Thanks. Anything else?"

"No, sir, but then I've been on my rounds most of the time."

"Any friends round here who might know what's going on at Chang's?"

"I think I could get someone to tell us, sir."

"Get them to, will you? Who left Chang's place this morning after eleven o'clock, say. Especially anyone with a tough reputation. Chang knows plenty of them."

The constable said worriedly: "They *usually* come at night, sir; it's not easy to recognize them."

"We're looking for the exception," said Gideon, and smiled to encourage. "Always worth trying. G'by."

He got in his car, but didn't drive off immediately. Instead, he picked up the radiotelephone, flicked it on, waited for the humming sound to tell him it was alive, then called the Yard. The man who answered from the Information Room knew his voice.

"Yes, sir, two messages for you. One of the three men who tried to rob a mail van at Liverpool Street Station this morning is under charge, being brought to the Yard now, sir, should be here in ten minutes or so. The child found dead in Hatherley Court, London, W.1 was murdered—strangled and interfered with, sir. Chief Inspector Suter has gone over there, and will report as soon as he's had a look around. That's all, sir."

"Hmm," said Gideon. His nose was wrinkled, his mouth turned down at the corners. Most men had a secret horror: his was of men who could first ravage and then kill a child. Nothing, not even the Changs with their dope and devilry, could make him see red so quickly, and as always, he distrusted himself when he saw red. "All right, I'll come straight back."

"Very good, sir."

Gideon started off. At the corners, men and women loitered. The first of the pros were beginning their ambling, more people were in the shops, a brewer's dray with a big engine instead of the horses of yesteryear stood outside a pub while barrels were dropped down the chute into the cellar. A normal enough scene.

Gideon began to feel angry about that child and sour because he couldn't go straight to see Florence Foster. She had to be told about her brother, the job would be left to the Yard, and he couldn't see anyone else doing it willingly. He found himself thinking again that if he hadn't torn Foster to shreds in the office, it might not have happened. It was that blurry hunch—the kind of thing he'd dress Lemaitre down for, but there it was. The Square Mile was his beat, and some pulsating sixth sense told him that this wasn't the time to go for Chang, but the time to start squeezing. When you squeezed a slug, it was surprising what oozed out. Chang with his diffident smile, his charm, his courtesy and his grace, with as foul a mind—

Gideon slid through the traffic and began to argue with himself.

Half the trouble with men like Chang, whether they were Chinese, English or American—it didn't matter what nationality they were—was that they had no sense of doing wrong. They were as the slave traders had been a century ago, as the white slavers of North Africa were today. To them, nothing was sacred, nothing inviolate. He knew of a dozen men, respected, wealthy, perfectly honest by the legal codes, who rejected all moral values.

Foster had said the thing all these would say: if girls didn't get dope from Chang, they would get it from someone else. So it was no crime to make money out of giving it to them. Orientals especially seemed to lack a sense of morality, but hell, some of them were pretty strict in applying moral rules to their own families. That wasn't the point. The point, Gideon decided as he turned carefully into the gateway of Scotland Yard, was that most Eastern countries bred a lot of callousness; the people were fatalists, and if they came to England and turned against the law they were deadly because usually they had good minds and no scruples.

"Something," Gideon said suddenly and aloud, "in a Christian civilization." And then he scowled. "Still, what about Foster?"

He parked the car with more room to spare, and went up the steps. If he cared to count the number of times a week he went up those steps, he would be astounded. Some Superintendents spent most of their time at the desk; some people said he didn't spend enough. He didn't trouble about the lift, but went up the stairs two at a time, nodding at the many who passed him. His own office was empty, a disappointment. Before he sat down, he pressed a bell for a sergeant. Then he dropped heavily into his chair, and squinted down at a penciled note Lemaitre had left: "Mail job man's talking, main waiting room. Lem."

There was a tap at the door and a sergeant in plain-clothes came in, absurdly young in Gideon's eyes.

"Yes, sir?"

"Get the Secretary's file on Detective Sergeant Foster, will you? Put it on my desk. Check whether his sister Florence still lives with him. Lived. If she has a place of her own, find out where it is, find out where she worked, what she does. Don't take too much time about it. See if you can pick up anything from the other sergeants in Foster's office."

"I could put up a bit myself, sir."

Gideon, looking through other messages as he talked, glanced up into gray, eager eyes.

"All right, Miller, what?"

"Still lives—lived—with his sister, sir. I was on a job with him two days ago, he was moan—he was saying that he would have to get a place of his own; his sister didn't like his off-duty hours. He was a bit tetchy. I gathered he'd had a row with her."

"Hmm. Anything else?"

"They live Chelsea way."

"Yes. Check everything you can, thanks, Miller. If I'm wanted I'll be in the waiting room with that mail-van chap." Gideon nodded and hurried out, thinking of the Fosters quarreling and Flo Foster's (Addinson's) surprise, and a man who'd tried to rob a mail van being in a talkative mood.

The main waiting room was on the floor below. Gideon was there in thirty seconds, and opened the door briskly. He heard the words of a man speaking in a cultured voice:

". . . I tell you that's all I know!"

The speaker was young, probably in his late teens. Take away his thin mouth, and he would be a nice-looking lad, with fair, curly hair, cornflower blue eyes, a look of innocence; full of a kind of charm, like Chang. As he stared at the door, he looked scared, and caught his breath sharply at sight of Gideon's burly figure. Lemaitre and two sergeants were in the room with the youth; one was from Liverpool Street, the other a Yard man taking notes. The youth was neatly dressed, well groomed.

"Anything?" asked Gideon.

"Nothing that won't bear repeating," Lemaitre said, "and I should say he's conveniently forgetting a hell of a lot."

"That's a lie!" the youth burst out.

"All right, calm down," said Gideon. He looked at the prisoner's fingers, stained dark with nicotine, then at the thin, unsteady mouth, and wondered when Lemaitre was going to grow up. He took out a fat, old-fashioned silver cigarette case and proffered it; the youth grabbed, as some kids would grab a reefer. He snatched a lighter out of his pocket.

"Thanks." He drew fiercely.

"That's all right," said Gideon, "no need to get steamed up, it won't make any difference, and if you play your cards right you'll probably get off more lightly than you deserve. Mind telling me all about it again?"

In the pause which followed, he glanced at the sergeant's notebook, and read the name: Lionel Tenby.

"Well, Tenby," he went on, in an almost comforting way. "What about it?"

"I've told them!" The words came with a rush, a spate followed. "I don't know the names of the others, it was all laid on by telephone. They knew I could drive a damned sight better than most chaps, so they paid me twenty-five quid to do this job for them. All I had to do was to drive up in front of the van and wait until they told me to get a move on."

"Payment in advance?" asked Gideon.

"Yes." Tenby's gaze flickered toward a table where oddments lay in neat array: a pocket watch, a comb, wallet, keys, silver coins, copper coins and a small wad of one-pound notes.

Gideon's hopes began to fade; this wasn't the first time they'd caught a very small sprat.

"And you didn't know them?"

"No."

"Pity. What else?"

"I asked them how they knew it would be worth doing, and they said that someone had tipped them the wink," Tenby declared. The cigarette was nearly finished, and he seemed to look at it anxiously, as if nervous of what he would feel like when he had to stub it out.

"Tip from where?" asked Gideon.

"How the devil should I know?"

"Hmm," said Gideon. Yes, it was disappointing; if things went on like this, it was going to be an unsatisfactory day. "All right, get that statement typed out, sergeant. Have Tenby read it and if he agrees that it's what he said, have him sign it." He looked at Tenby patiently. "But don't sign it and then start squealing to the magistrate that it isn't what you said. If you're not satisfied, write it out yourself in longhand."

Tenby winced, because the cigarette, now burned very low, stung his fingers.

Gideon gave him another.

"Throw the stub in the fireplace," he said. "You can have some cigarettes; it'll be deducted from any money belonging to you. Fix it, sergeant."

"Yes, sir."

"Anyone you want to know about this?" Gideon asked sharply.

Tenby's eyes glistened; he was very young and he wasn't one of the bad ones—just a young fool.

"No."

"Girl friend? Parents?"

"*No!*"

"Been in before on a charge?"

"No, I—I wish to God I'd never listened to those swine! I'd dropped a bit on the gees, and—" he broke off, biting his lips. Bring his mother into the room at this moment, and he would burst into tears, Gideon surmised.

"Well, listen," Gideon said, "your relations have got to know, and it's better from us than from the press; you won't get much change out of the press. Let us tell your parents or the girl friend, and have them—"

"*I said no!*"

"All right. Let him suffer. Come on, Lem," Gideon said, and led the way out. "Not much there," he added almost absently, "the story we've had a dozen times before. The P.O. people pick their drivers well. Like to know if it's directed by one man or not, there's a lot of similarity. When he's calmed down a bit, get repeat descriptions of the two men. Play him soft, though. Get hold of his people, if you can, and let them come and see him here. Mother, preferably. Blurry young fool." He changed the subject but didn't alter his tone of voice. "Hear about the Mayfair flat job?"

"Nine-year-old kid," said Lemaitre. "I could tell you what I'd do to them if I had my way."

"Thing that worries me with those jobs is the risk of another," Gideon said. "We really want to bring the house down after the chap."

"I'll say!"

"I'd better go along to the Back Room," Gideon said, as if he wasn't quite sure. "The press will be on their toes. If they play up the child murder and the frustrated mail-van robbery, they won't have much room for anything else." They were at a corner, where they would go different ways. "Saw Chang, by the way. Smooth as ever, denies everything." He didn't say anything about Flo Foster (Addinson). "And the clubroom there is being redecorated. The smell of paint and distemper makes sure that no one with a sensitive nose could ever pick out the marijuana they've been smoking."

"You know what you've done, don't you?" Lemaitre said, with a sniff.

"What?"

"Driven Chang somewhere else. It won't stop the kids from getting the weed, and—"

"Nearest thing I know to a certainty is that Chang won't do anything he shouldn't for some time," Gideon asserted, marveling that Lemaitre should think anything different. What limitations even able men had! "We could draw all our dogs off him and he'd still behave like a learner priest, what-do-you-call-'em? *Acolyte*, isn't it? It's beginning to look as if he did hear from Foster, and got a move on. Might have had a row with Foster, though, and so made Foster walk across the road in a rage, not looking. Nobody ever thinks they could be knocked down in a street accident."

"The car didn't stop," Lemaitre insisted. "Don't you want to believe that—"

Gideon was suddenly sharp; almost harsh.

"No," he said bluntly. "No, I *don't* want to believe that Chang had Foster killed. I don't want to think that Foster knew so much about Chang that it was worth killing him. But that's probably what happened, and if it is we'll get the killer and we'll get Chang!" He switched abruptly. "Any news in?"

"We've picked up a girl typist who was looking out of the window and says she saw it happen. She was on her own, her boss was out, and when she saw someone come along the street to Foster's help, she just sat back."

Gideon flashed: "Any squeal of brakes?"

"Eh?"

"Did she hear—never mind, where is she?"

"On her way here."

"Oh, good," said Gideon, "that's fine. By the way, there's a painter chap at Chang's, very thin, six feet one or two, thin, big Adam's apple, watery eyes, probably blind or half blind in the right, it's hazed over. Flat-footed, and pretty sly. I'd like his name and address and anything we can find out about him. There's a copper on duty over there, P.C. 10952; he seemed to have his head screwed on the right way and he's finding out if anything worth knowing happened at Chang's this morning. Send someone out to have a word with him about this painter."

"Okay," said Lemaitre.

They were outside the office. Lemaitre opened the door and Gideon went inside, looking at the carpet and wearing a half frown, one more of preoccupation than of annoyance or worry.

"Well, we didn't get much out of the mail-van chap," Lemaitre said. "Nearly always the same; if we do pick anyone up, it's a young fool who doesn't know anything. But there was a tip-off again. That's the worrying thing, George, isn't it?"

"Hm?"

"A tip-off from the post office."

"Oh, yes."

"I'll tell you what's going to happen one of these days," said Lemaitre. "They're going to kill a copper or someone who tries to stop them and then our noses are going to be rubbed right in the dirt." His own thin nose wrinkled disgustedly. "Anything goes wrong, they blame us, but whose fault are these mail-van jobs? We're understaffed, could do with dozens more at every station in London, the P.O. don't use half enough detectives, seem to think that every van is protected by some spirit."

"Okay, Lem," Gideon said, "it's everybody's fault but ours, and we've got the job of stopping it."

He sat down at his desk, grunting.

On it was a note—a penciled report on an official buff form.

Telephone message received from 7Q Division 12:55 P.M.
Killer of nine-year-old Jennifer Gay Lee at Hatherley Court believed to be Arthur Sayer of 15 Warrender Street, Ealing. Ealing Division has been telephoned, general call asked for Sayer, description and photograph on way to us by special messenger.

Lemaitre was standing by the desk, looking down.

"What's this?"

"Old Tucker at 7Q thinks he can name the swine who killed that kid," said Gideon. "As soon as the photograph and description arrive, put out a general call, ports, airfields, everything, just for safety's sake. I wish—"

The telephone bell rang.

"Gideon," he grunted into it, and then brightened. "That's good. Keep her down there, the small waiting room; I'll come and see her at once." He put the receiver down. "It's that typist who saw Foster knocked down. If she heard a squeal of brakes the driver tried to stop; if she didn't, there's the evidence you've been looking for." He gave Lemaitre a quick but rather tired grin, and went out.

Two minutes later, there was a tap at the door. A constable in uniform, except that he was hatless, came in.

"Photograph and description from 7Q Division, sir."

"Okay, I'll have 'em," Lemaitre said. He stretched out a hand, and a moment later looked down at the glossy photograph of a man. "So that's the brute, is it? Okay, ta."

Lemaitre picked up a telephone and started to put out the general call for a certain Arthur Sayer, who was believed to have murdered the nine-year-old girl. As he talked into the telephone he skimmed the report of the murder, and his eyes frosted, even his tone changed, because it was a very, very ugly killing.

". . . and get a move on," he said. "Once that kind's tasted blood you never know where they'll stop."

The door opened, and Gideon came in, eyes bright, manner brisk, as if he were beginning to relish life.

"Seen her?" Lemaitre asked needlessly.

"Nice little kid, a bit scared, but reliable. There was no squeak of brakes; there's the pointer we want, Lem. Was probably intentional. Anything else in?"

That was like a refrain.

"No," said Lemaitre, "but that poor kid . . ." He was brief but graphic in his description of the mutilations on the child's body.

Gideon stood in the middle of the office, like a statue roughhewn out of granite.

"Schools are closed for the Easter holidays," he said abruptly. "Sayer knew this child, and she trusted him. Better check on other children he knows, fast. All right. I'll talk to Ealing."

He almost threw himself at the telephone on his desk.

5 . The Child Killer

CHILDREN swarmed over Clapham Common. Every square yard of grass was worn bare; every yard of the children's graveled playground, with its swings and seesaws, sliding chutes and vaulting horses, had a pair of feet—well shod, rough shod, badly shod, even three children who were barefooted and wearing such rags that others looked at them askance, and some refused to play.

Clapham Common was one of the places where London breathed.

Now, at the tail end of the Easter holidays, mothers were only too glad to shoo their offspring out. The morning had echoed with the same refrains in a thousand doorways and kitchens: "Be careful crossing the road." "Don't go getting yourself dirty." "No fighting, mind." "Don't speak to any strange man, understand?" "Look both ways." The children had listened with half an ear, and found their way safely toward this breathing ground, soon racing, rushing, running, sprawling, giggling, laughing, crying, climbing, shouting, shrieking in the warm air of late spring.

Here, youths of recognized local renown chose sides at cricket or at football; coats went down for goal posts or wickets; bats came out after a winter's storage; footballs looked flat and flabby and gave off a dull sound when kicked, and stubbed strong toes.

On the seats round the edges of the common, the old folks sat, mostly nice, pleasant, sleepy and indulgent, some with a packet of peppermints or toffees, most of the men with pipe and a little tobacco, all drowsy in the sun and the din. There were a few nasty old men, but each of them was known by the common keepers, the local police, and by a few self-appointed guardians of the children.

"Nothing," each harassed mother had said or thought when the children had gone flying down the road, "can happen to them once they're on the common." And most watched until the first roads were crossed and then went to washtub, sink, floors or bedrooms, or dressed hastily to go out shopping, gradually forgetting fears which would return only if the children were back late for the midday meal.

Some knew that their children might be late; most knew that hunger would bring them clattering home a few minutes before one o'clock or before half-past one, whichever was the regular mealtime.

Of these, Mrs. Lucy Saparelli was one.

Mrs. Saparelli, at thirty-seven, was a red-cheeked, bright-eyed, wholesome-looking woman with a spruce figure and a seductive walk, although she had no idea that a few of the louts of the district called her Marilyn. Her husband was a commercial traveler, away three or four nights out of the week's seven. He had only a vague notion that his forebears had been Spanish or Italian, and wasn't quite sure which. He could go back four generations of solid English ancestry, but was oddly proud of his unusual name: *Sap*-ar-elli.

He loved and trusted his wife and he was fiercely fond of Michael, his eldest child, and as fond of Dorothy, his youngest—aged nine—although for some reason, Victor, the eleven-year-old who came in between, always managed to irritate him.

Victor did not irritate his mother, but if one of the apples of her eyes was brighter than the others, it was Dorothy. Boys drew away from their mother as the years passed, but Dorothy would always be with her. At nine, she was—just *lovely*. She had the looks, the plumpness, the naïveté and the natural gaiety which could make a child win approval from everyone. The hug that Lucy Saparelli gave Dorothy each night and each morning was born of the little extra delight the child gave her. "Delight" was the word which mattered, was the thing the girl child brought to Lucy, to Jim Saparelli, to the two boys.

Everyone loved Dorothy.

Arthur Sayer *loved* Dorothy.

Arthur Sayer knew the Saparellis well, because he had lodged with them some years ago, a schooldays acquaintance of Jim's who had been welcome when money had been short. It had soon become apparent that he was ever so nice, except for one thing: betting was his folly. Lucy had been heard to say, almost in tones of wonder, that he never said a word or put a finger out of place. He was rather odd, in some ways, a bit sissy, with long, silky, brown hair and a love of bright colors, but—well, nice.

Lucy was in her bedroom, scurrying round to make the beds and dust before going to the shops, when the front-door bell rang.

"Damn!" she said, and looked out of the window, but saw no van; so it wasn't a tradesman. She peeked at herself in the mirror and straightened her hair as she hurried down the stairs, her skirt riding up over her pretty legs. The dress was a little too tight and one she wore only when doing the housework. She went quickly along the stained boards of the hall, seeing the dark shadow of a man against the colored glass panels in the top of the door. She knew it was a man because of the shape of his hat.

It was then ten o'clock on Gideon's day; when Gideon was still at the Yard looking at reports.

Lucy opened the door.

"Why, Arthur!" she exclaimed, and annoyance faded into pleasure. "Fancy seeing you at this hour of the morning. Come in, do."

Arthur Sayer hesitated, and she stared at him intently.

He was almost one of the family, and more welcome than most of her in-laws. He looked pale, and his eyes glittered, as if his head ached badly; she remembered that he had often had severe headaches, needing absolute quiet to recover from them. He needed a shave, now, and his coat collar was turned up, although it was already warm.

"*You* look as if you've been up all night," said Lucy forthrightly. "You'd better let me make you a cup of tea and give you some aspirins."

He moved forward.

"Thank—thanks, Lucy. I've got one of my awful headaches."

"Why on earth didn't you stay at home?"

He moistened his lips.

"I—I had a row with someone," he said. "Never mind about that now. I—I knew you'd let me rest here for a bit."

"So I should think!" said Lucy. "Look, you go in the front room, draw the blinds, and sit quiet until I bring you a cuppa." She thrust open the door of the parlor. "The only things in there are Dorothy's dolls; she's having her friends in to an exhibition. That child and her dolls! Now, sit you down, I won't be a couple of jiffs."

She left him in the darkened room.

She frowned as she walked to the kitchen, every movement touched with throbbing vitality. She filled the kettle, put it on the gas, washed two cups and saucers from the pile waiting from breakfast, and then shook her head with a quick little gesture.

"The rest'll have to wait until after lunch. I can do all the washing up together. Now he's come I can't get everything finished before I go out." A pause. "I suppose I *must* go out?"

She put the question aloud, but answered it silently. She gave Arthur very little thought as a person, just accepted him as she accepted the ups and downs of family life, the aches and pains of her children. Had Arthur been one of hers, she would have felt worried because he didn't look well; but she'd seen him almost as bad, it wasn't very important.

Jim would be home tonight, and she liked to have a good dinner for him, so she *must* go to the butcher's. If she had to go out, she might just as well do all the week-end shopping and get it over. She would finish the bedrooms before she left. . . .

If Dorothy came back while she was out, Arthur could let her in; she wouldn't have to play in the street.

She bustled round, easy in her mind.

Arthur said very little when she took in the tea, but swallowed three aspirins obediently. His eyes were glittery, and she wondered if he was running a temperature. Dorothy always went pale when she had a temperature, and the boys were usually flushed.

"Sure you'll be all right on your own, Arthur?"

"Yes—yes, thank you."

"Wouldn't like to see a doctor?"

"No!" He almost shouted the word. "No, don't—don't tell anyone I'm here."

"Look here," said Lucy flatly, "what's upset you, Art? You can confide in me, you know. What's the trouble?"

"Nothing! I—well, I—I owe some money, Lucy, I can get it back, but—"

"Why didn't you say so? It isn't as if it's the first time." Lucy sniffed. "I won't tell anyone you're here, and Jim's coming home tonight, perhaps he can suggest something to help. Now I've got to go to the shops. You needn't answer the door if you don't want to, but if Dorothy comes back I don't like her playing out in the street. Let her in, won't you?"

Arthur Sayer didn't answer.

"Art, you might at least answer me!"

"Oh," said Sayer. "What did—oh, yes. Yes, I'll let Dorothy in. Don't worry, Lucy."

She left him alone, but was uneasy in her mind—although not because of Dorothy. That did not occur to her. He had helped to nurse Dorothy, was Uncle Art to her and would be for the rest of her life. She sensed that he was in serious trouble, and came of stock which was easily embarrassed by thought of any trouble which might warrant the interest of the police. Arthur had always been silly with money and gambling, but—

She saw a bus coming along the main road as soon as she reached it, and rushed across to catch it. Some drivers would wait, some were *devils*.

She caught the bus. The only spare seat was next to a girl with a horse's tail tied with pink ribbon, who was reading the *Daily Mirror*. . . .

Dorothy Saparelli stumbled away from the swing, and the hard wooden edge caught her a slight glancing blow on the shoulder. She turned and shook her fist at the bigger girl who had just grabbed the chain, and had made her get off. Nine years is not the age when one admits the justice of accusations of wrongdoing. She had used that swing for fifteen minutes and wanted it for another fifteen.

She brushed back some hair which had somehow escaped from one of the sleek wings which seemed to sweep from a center parting. It was black, glossy hair, tied with scarlet ribbon. She wore a white blouse and a navy-blue gym suit; her plimsolls were dusty but not dirty or torn.

"Mean pig!" she called shrilly, and looked disconsolate.

Three children were clinging to every place where there was room for one; in this playground Dorothy hadn't a chance of another toy. She sauntered over to a group of girls playing rounders, but they were in the early teens, and one snapped her fingers and ordered: "You sheer off."

Further afield, Victor was playing football. She couldn't see Michael, who was probably messing about at cricket. Disgruntled, a little tired and very thirsty, Dorothy made her way along a tarred path toward the roads leading to Micklem Street, where she lived. There was only one main road to worry about, but she could cope with that; when in doubt, wait until grownups were going to cross, and cross with them. That was so much part of training that a child's pride was never challenged; it simply wasn't safe to cross on one's own.

An old man, carrying a walking stick, was coming toward her.

She didn't like him, and moved off the path, but he stood and watched, raising his stick and smiling invitingly. He had no teeth, and a funny, straggly kind of mustache and beard. She saw him take a bag of peppermints out of his pocket and it seemed as if her mother's voice was actually sounding in her ears.

"Never stop and talk to strange men, even if they do offer you sweets."

She skipped past this old man. She wasn't really troubled, and the moment she was past him, he was forgotten, as a dog safely behind a gate would be. It did not occur to her that the uniformed policeman who started to hurry in the wake of the old man was doing so because of that little interlude.

One word of early warning could save a lot of distress.

Dorothy crossed the main road safely behind a woman with a push chair. She loitered on her way to the house.

She was happier here, her troubles quite forgotten, when a black-and-white spaniel puppy frisked up. She was almost outside her own house, Number 24, when she saw a sixpence glistening on the pavement.

A tanner!

She pounced.

Her delight, as she looked at it on the palm of her hand, was the absolute delight of a young child. Her whole world had changed; she held a fortune because this was money she had not dreamed she would have.

There was a corner sweetshop, not far off.

She hesitated, wondering whether to go and spend it now, or whether to tell her mother. Mum would let her keep it, she was sure of that: findings keepings, if you really *had* found it. Seeing a few dirty marks on it, she began to rub the sixpence with the forefinger of her left hand. She looked at the front-room window. The curtains were drawn, but there was a little gap in the middle.

She did not see Arthur Sayer looking at her.

She was *very* thirsty.

She went to the front door, at a hop-skip-and-jump pace, and banged on the iron knocker. She hoped Mum was in because she was so thirsty, but if she wasn't, Mrs. Pommery next door would let her have a drink of water, or—should she buy a *lemonade?* Excitement came again. She imagined the sharp sweetness of aerated lemonade on her cloyed mouth, and the temptation was so great that she wished she hadn't knocked. If Mum was out—

The door opened.

Arthur Sayer opened the door.

Dorothy stared, and then her eyes glowed.

"Why, Uncle *Arthur!"*

She went in, gaily, and he closed the door behind her, heard her chattering, heard the story of the sixpence, followed her to the kitchen, watched her turn on the tap and put a cup under it.

She screamed three times.

Mercifully, that was all.

No one heard her, except Arthur Sayer.

Lucy Saparelli got off the bus with Mrs. Pommery, who lived next door, and was the only neighbor likely to have heard a sound from the Saparellis' kitchen. Each woman carried laden baskets: Lucy Saparelli had one in each hand. Yet they walked briskly, and a spotty youth, a nightworker, lounging against the porch of his home, watched Lucy's swaying hips and gave a silent whistle, then a whispered: "Hi, Marilyn!" Lucy was talking, about the price of food, about Victor, about her Jim being a bit hard on Victor sometimes, about Dorothy's plan to have an exhibition of dolls, a kind of dolls' party, and wasn't it wonderful for a nine-year-old girl to think of such an idea on her own?

They turned the corner.

Lucy changed hands with the baskets, and wriggled her shoulders because of the strain.

Then she saw Victor and Michael, talking to another boy outside their home. She didn't give a thought to the possibility of—horror. Michael had torn his trousers, and Victor had a nasty scratch on the side of his face, but they looked clear-eyed and happy.

"'Lo, Mum!"

"Gosh, I'm hungry."

"We'll have something to eat as soon as I've had time to look round," said Lucy. "Micky, take this bag for me, there's a dear. Victor, you can open the door for me, take the key out of my bag—oh, silly ass! Just knock, and Uncle Arthur will let us in."

"What?" Michael took the laden bag. "No one's in, Mum. I've knocked half a dozen times."

"Well, that's *funny*," said Lucy. "Where's Dorothy, then?"

She didn't speak again, but opened her bag, took out the front-door key, and went straight to the front door. She could not have told the others what had happened to her in that moment; she probably did not realize it herself. It was as if a shadow had fallen; a darkness, hiding something she wanted to see. She did not consciously think of Dorothy. Afterward, to her husband, she said in a stony voice that she thought Arthur might have done himself in.

She pushed the door open, strode in, and called: "Arthur!"

There was no reply.

She looked inside the parlor, which was empty but for the dolls. She went briskly along the passage, high heels tapping on the stained boards, with Michael behind her and Victor just stepping across the front-door mat.

Then she saw . . .

Then she *screamed*.

6 . Manhunt

GIDEON sat at his desk, in his shirt sleeves, the big, blue-and-red-spotted tie undone and ends hanging down, hair ruffled, face pale but forehead damp with sweat. He had a telephone at his ear, and was waving his left hand at Lemaitre, who came across.

"Someone saw him leave on foot, just before half-past twelve, so he didn't get far. Concentrate everything we've got on the south and southwest London area. Right." He waved Lemaitre away, and grunted into the telephone: "Yes, I've got all that, thanks." He rang off, and plucked up another telephone. "Back Room," he demanded, and stretched his shoulders, leaning back so that his head touched the wall. Then, with his free hand, he picked up the first telephone again. "Is Sergeant Miller back yet? . . . Yes, I'll hold on."

The Back Room Inspector spoke into the telephone at Gideon's right ear.

"Yes, George?"

"This Sayer chap," Gideon said without preamble. "Have a go at the evening-paper chaps, ring up the news editors if necessary, ask them to make sure they run Sayer's picture in each edition, getting it in as soon as they can. And give 'em a picture of a girl . . . either of them will do. . . . Yes, I've just had a word with the Old Man, he's okayed it. Thanks." He rang off, spoke immediately into the other telephone. "Hallo? . . . Good, send him in to me."

He put that receiver down too, and took a deep breath.

Lemaitre was holding on to a telephone, but not speaking. He looked across and said: "We won't get any more done if we starve. What about some grub? *Hallo*. Yes, all the men you can spare; pick up photographs of Sayer at 7Q, that's the quickest way."

The door opened, and the sergeant who had been instructed to find out what he could about Foster's sister came in. He seemed touched by the vibrant excitement which affected the others. Neat as a new pin, he entered as if he were daring the lion's den, with Gideon the lion. But Gideon's expression was placid and his voice quiet, in spite of his pallor and the sweat on his forehead.

"Well, what have you got?" he asked.

"Miss Foster's at her home now," the sergeant said. "Incidentally, sir, she's married, and separated from her husband; she's a Mrs. Addinson. She does murals for cafés and night clubs, has a little studio in the Chelsea flat where they—she lives. As far as I know, she doesn't yet know what happened to Sergeant Foster."

"Chelsea, yes," said Gideon. "Hmm." He lived in Fulham, the adjoining borough. "All right, thanks." The sergeant put down some notes, and turned to go. "Sergeant, send someone down to the canteen for some sandwiches and beer for both of us. Ham and beef all right, Lem?"

Lemaitre seemed to be listening to someone on his telephone; but he nodded.

"Beef well done, and plenty of salt," ordered Gideon. "Thanks." He nodded, and looked hard at the two telephones, as if he could not understand why they were silent, neither had rung for nearly five minutes. He wiped his forehead, then his neck, then made a gesture of tightening the knot of the tie, but he didn't do his shirt up at the neck. The once-smooth, starched whiteness of the collar had wilted, and was damp near the neck.

Lemaitre said: "Oke" into a telephone, banged down the receiver, groped for a cigarette, lit it, and glanced at Gideon. "Quiet, all of a sudden, isn't it?"

"It's one of those days," Gideon said. "Two supers off duty, one ill, three out-of-town jobs taken our best C.I.'s. One of these days I'm going—"

One of his telephone bells rang.

He took it up slowly, almost gently.

"Superintendent Gideon here. Who? . . . Yes, yes, go on." His eyes glistened, he grabbed a pencil and made waving signs in the air with it. He jotted down a couple of notes, and said: "Yes, fine, thanks." He let the receiver go down with a bang, and Lemaitre, looking at him, had an odd thought: that Gideon looked ten years younger than he had first thing that morning. "The River boys say those mail bags were dropped into the Thames somewhere near Battersea Power Station. They've been out to look, and found another flapping around a submerged barge; it caught on a nail or something. Footprints near the spot, some tire marks, everything that might help us to get something. I can push that onto B2; pity it's near the Sayer job, but still." He lifted a telephone. "Give me B2 Headquarters. . . ." He waited, rubbing his forehead with the palm of his left hand. Then: "Hallo, Superintendent Gillick? . . . Gideon here . . . No, not Sayer, but that's priority . . . Yes, he's a swine all right. . . . Listen, Gil, the River boys think that some mail bags, part of that last post-office job, were thrown in the river from a spot near Battersea Power Station last night. They've a launch standing by to guide your chaps. Can you spare a couple? . . .

Sure, sure, plaster casts, tire tracks, all the usual, and if we could have them this afternoon we might catch the beggars yet. We had a set of tire tracks and some footprints from the Maida Vale job, you know, be interesting to see if they match up. . . . Yes, thanks . . . Oh, fine, every one of them, noisy brats most of them . . ." He shook his head at Lemaitre, who was grinning broadly, and rolled his eyes. "Yes, the oldest boy's working, thanks, doing nicely . . . Thanks a lot, Gil."

He blew out a noisy breath as he put the receiver down.

"Champion talker on the Force," Lemaitre said. "Why don't you ring off when he starts gassing like that?"

"Might want some special help from him before this is over," said Gideon philosophically, then looked up at a tap at the door. "I'll swear at anyone short of the Old Man," he declared, and barked: "Come in!"

It was the uniformed but hatless constable, with a tray, sandwiches with ham and beef overlapping the bread, and two pint bottles of beer.

"And *wel*come!" Lemaitre grinned.

Downstairs in the Information Room, uniformed men were standing by the big maps spread out on tables in front of them, with tiny model cars and other models on the tables, and croupier's rakes to move them with. There was a continual chatter of low-pitched conversation, some men talking into radiotelephones, some into ordinary telephones, some to neighbors. No beehive would be busier on an early summer's day.

There were more men round one of the boards than any other—that depicting the southwest area. Here concentrations of model cars and of policemen and plain-clothes men stuck on round wooden bases were continually being moved. A report would come by radiotelephone, a car would be moved; a report would come by telephone, and a man moved.

All the Divisional police stations and the substations in the southwestern area of London were reporting regularly. Police in uniform and in plain-clothes were calling on shopkeepers throughout the huge area, with descriptions of Arthur Sayer. Photographs, some prints hardly dry, were already being distributed in large numbers. Special forces were watching spots like Clapham Common, Battersea Park and Tooting Bec—all places where children played.

In Clapham, a Divisional Inspector with a soft Devon burr in his voice was talking to Lucy Saparelli. Lucy seemed to have shrunk, her voice was a hoarse whisper. Michael and Victor were next door with the neighbor, and a sergeant—selected because he had boys of his own—was talking to them about Sayer.

The two o'clock radio program on all wave lengths was interrupted with a description of the wanted man. The next evening newspaper editions carried his photographs as well as photographs of the first child victim, Jennifer Gay Lee. No minute, no second of time passed without someone showing another picture of Sayer, or asking if he'd been seen in the district.

Gradually the search narrowed. Sayer had been seen at Brixton, in the biggest shopping center in the immediate neighborhood.

A policeman who had been traveling on a bus recognized him. He did not give chase, but went swiftly to a near-by police box and telephoned his substation.

"Got off near the Forum," he reported to his sergeant, "same place as I did. Looked a bit dazed, if you know what I mean."

"I'd daze him! Which way did he go?"

"Turned left—yes, that's right, left."

"Well, that's something." The sergeant picked up a telephone, and the message was flashed to the Yard. Instructions went out smoothly and swiftly for men to concentrate in the Brixton area, with the Forum cinema as a focal point.

Then a waitress at a busy café, shown the photograph by a plain-clothes man, looked up at him eagerly.

"Why, he's been here!"

"Sure?"

"'Course I'm sure, I served him, didn't I? Asked him if he had a headache, and he bit my head off. And a tuppenny tip! Not that I expect—"

"Which way did he go?"

"Well, I don't know that I noticed . . ."

"I know the one," said the cashier, leaning out of her box. "Wearing a light brown coat and gray flannels, and one of those pork-pie hats. He turned left."

"Sure?"

"Wouldn't say so if I wasn't."

Shopkeepers, vanmen, road sweepers, traffic-duty police, newspaper sellers, news agents—everyone between the café and the Forum was questioned quickly and comprehensively, and each revealed a little more of Sayer's trail. It always led the same way: to the Forum.

A commissionaire said: "Let's have a better look." He peered. "D'you know, I think that chap's *inside*. Come in half an hour ago. I remember he looked over his shoulder, as if he were scared of being followed; that's him all right. What's he done?"

A policeman explained.

"What?" The commissionaire looked sick.

A cashier said nervously: "We only had about twenty in, and he was one of them. 'Course I'm sure."

"That's him all right," said the usherette on duty at the balcony entrance. "Proper sissy, he looked, and his hands was so cold you wouldn't believe . . . And don't you come it, copper, just happened to touch his hands while I was tearing his ticket in half, that's all."

A sergeant in charge said: "We'll cover all the exits, then telephone H.Q."

The Superintendent at the Divisional H.Q. said: "Good, but don't go in for him yet; I'll phone the Yard."

Gideon was finishing his last sandwich when the telephone broke a glorious period of ten minutes' quiet. It rang sharply, with its oddly imperious note. He swallowed hard, washed the bread and meat down with a gulp of beer, and snatched the receiver up; he moved quickly, as if he felt guilty at having been eating for ten minutes.

"Gideon . . .

"Put him through!

"Hallo, Gordie . . . The Forum, Brixton? . . . Fine . . . I don't know whether he'll put up a fight or not. . . . Only weapon we know he's got is that knife. . . . No, I won't come over myself, much rather your chaps handled him; if he's there I'm sure you won't miss him. . . . Yes, please, the moment you have any news . . . Gordie, half a mo', and don't get me wrong, he might be deadly. He'll know that he hasn't a chance to save himself from hanging, and he could be right out of his mind. I—*God!*"

He broke off.

Lemaitre actually jumped out of his seat.

"Get your men inside that place," shouted Gideon. "It'll be dark inside, and there might be some kids. I'm coming."

7 . Old Woman Alone

AT ABOUT the time that Gideon was shouting into the telephone in a kind of anguish, an old woman sat alone in the parlor behind her small shop in Islington, on the other side of London.

Her name was Mrs. Annie Sharp.

The Islington police, on the lookout for Arthur Sayer, were on the lookout for a lot of other people, too, although with less urgency. None of them suspected that there was any danger for the old woman in her shop. She had lived in the two rooms at the back for thirty years, and had never been known to have a holiday. Her husband had been killed early in the First World War, and since then she had managed alone. Now her five children were married; those neighbors who knew her well knew that only two kept in touch with her, and one of those was now in Australia.

Annie Sharp was a good-natured, friendly soul, and although the shop did not make plenitude for her, it kept her from want. The counter was built so that she could move from the sweets and chocolate side to the to-bacco, matches and cigarette side without trouble, and her small till was on the corner of the counter, immediately opposite the door leading to the parlor.

The upstairs flat was let to a man, his wife and three children, but they were all out. Annie Sharp knew that, but it did not worry her; thirty years without a frightening incident in the same place breeds a kind of confidence which has nothing to do with logic or probability. The district had its tough and its rough spots, but Annie Sharp's experience with crime was limited to a few small bad debts; and although she was a kindly and soft-hearted woman, some shrewd instinct warned her not to let anyone have more than a day or so's credit.

"Don't ask for credit," said a little printed card in a fly-blown showcase, "and you won't be refused." That hint worked.

The two o'clock back-to-work hooter of a near-by factory had finished blowing some time ago. Everyone who came home for lunch had gone back now. Annie knew from experience that she was in for the quietest period of the day. Until about half-past three, when the women started out with their perambulators, the most she could expect was the odd casual customer for cigarettes; or the child who had succeeded in wheedling a few coppers from a parent who was probably feeling desperately anxious to have forty winks. The shop-door bell would wake Annie up.

She settled down, with her feet up on an old, velours-covered pouf, her thin gray hair awry, her head resting on the back of a comfortable old wing chair. She wore carpet slippers, worn shapeless by shuffling, but in spite of her seventy-two years she had a surprisingly tight little figure.

A tap, needing a new washer, dripped in the kitchen, but the sound did not disturb her. After a few seconds, she began to snore faintly. That and the continual dripping of the water into a saucepan made the only near-by sounds. Occasionally someone walked sharply along the pavement, or a car drove past, but these were distant sounds, and did not disturb Annie Sharp.

Then the bell at the shop door clanged.

Her eyes opened, and she clutched the arms of the chair in the same instant. She allowed herself a second or two to wake, then stood up. The shop door, on a black japanned spring fastener, closed slowly.

"Coming," she called.

Then she heard a sound that worried her. It was as if the flap of the counter were being raised, and she allowed no one to come in here without being invited. A child, perhaps, trying to sneak sweets. What children were coming to . . .

She hurried to the doorway.

She saw the man.

He looked young, although it was hard to be sure of that, because he wore a cap pulled low over his eyes, and a brown scarf drawn up over the lower half of his face. He was at the till, and as she reached the door, it went *ting!* sharply.

"*Here!*" she cried. "You get out of here!" She went bustling forward, more angry than scared; but a little scared too. "Go on, be off—"

"Shut up," the youth said.

She saw his narrowed eyes, and didn't like them, but she was still more angry than scared, and snatched up a bottle of Coca-Cola from a case standing on a shelf.

"Be off!" she shouted.

He didn't speak again. His voice had sounded gruff and vague behind the scarf, but there was nothing vague about his spiteful eyes. She raised the bottle, and he struck her hand aside. The bottle dropped but didn't break. He had a piece of short iron piping in his other hand; Annie Sharp saw it, and opened her mouth to scream.

He struck savagely. . . .

He struck again and a third time, but the third blow wasn't really necessary.

He dragged her behind the counter, and then into the little back room. Two children went hurrying past, girl and boy. He pushed the old woman in a corner, where she lay bleeding to death, and then made a quick search of the room. He found twenty-five pounds in an old tea caddy, and a small bundle of notes, which he didn't trouble to count, in a sewing basket. He uttered something under his breath, glanced at the woman, and then went into the shop.

The till was still open.

He took the few pound and ten-shilling notes from the back, grabbed a handful of silver and dropped it into his jacket pocket, then stepped through the gap in the counter, dropped the flap and went to the door.

He pulled down the scarf, bent his head, opened the door—and almost fell over a toddler standing and peering at the sweets, spittle-damp fingers making patterns on the window. He shoved the child aside. A woman, pushing a small-wheeled pram, was coming from the right. The man turned left. The woman stopped at the shop. The killer reached a corner and looked round; the woman was putting the brake on the pram, and going into the shop.

He began to run.

Gideon, with a sergeant beside him, drove down Brixton High Street as if he were on a lap at Silverstone. He succeeded in scaring the sergeant, who until then had regarded himself as fit for the Flying Squad. He seemed to shoulder other cars aside, and had an impudent disregard of the giant buses, the throbbing of petrol and Diesel engines, the wayward antics of cyclists, who thought themselves dangerproof. Seeing the Forum a little way ahead, the sergeant said: "Nearly there, sir, slow down now."

Gideon grunted.

He saw a gap in the cars parked outside the Forum, and performed a miracle of parking, getting into the space and then out of the car almost in one and the same movement. Once out and on the pavement, the fury slackened.

A plain-clothes man whom he recognized vaguely and two whom he didn't were coming out of the cinema. Several uniformed police were about them, like a blue-bottle bodyguard. Handcuffed to a man half a head taller than himself was Arthur Sayer. His lips were parted and trembling; he was pulling against the plain-clothes man, although a second man held his other arm and was helping him along.

Gideon saw the car they were heading for. He went to it. He would have confessed to no one in the world that his heart was thumping painfully, and that he hardly knew how to frame his question.

"Any more trouble?" he asked as they drew near.

The man he recognized said: "Any more—oh, more kids? No. He was sitting just behind a couple, but hadn't started anything. I—you want to talk to him, sir?" The Divisional man suddenly realized who this was and what respect was due to Gideon.

Gideon wiped his forehead.

"Not now," he said. "But we'll want him at the Yard. Better get him there at once, and have a doctor to him." He looked at Arthur Sayer with eyes which had the hardness of diamonds. "Don't stand any nonsense from him."

"Take it from me we won't, sir!"

"All right," said Gideon. He watched them squeezing into a police car, but hardly saw Sayer; he pictured two small girls, and two mothers and two fathers, some sisters and brothers. He trumpeted into his handkerchief, then turned to the sergeant whom he had scared. "Do you know Micklem Street, Clapham, sergeant?"

"Oh, yes, sir, near the common."

"We'll go there."

"Yes, sir."

"And this time," said Gideon, without conceding a smile, "I'll drive according to the Highway Code; you needn't hold on so tight." He got in, and shot a sideways glance at the embarrassed sergeant. "Get the Yard on that radio, will you, and find out if there's anything in for me."

"Yes, sir!"

Gideon drove as a benevolent bus driver might, with far, far more than average care. He heard the sergeant asking questions. He felt a sense of satisfaction from which anxiety wasn't altogether erased. They'd got Sayer, and with luck they'd hang him. The blurry psychological quacks would try to prove that he was insane, though; Gideon could see the shape of their case for the defense already.

He ought to have told that man what doctor to send for.

"Sergeant, tell them that Sayer is on his way—"

"I have, sir."

"And will they keep all doctors away from him and hold off questioning until Dr. Page-Henderson or Dr. Julian Forsyth can examine him. Ask them to pass that request through to the Old—to the A.C."

"Yes, sir."

The sergeant obeyed, and then listened to the radio reports.

"Anything for me?" asked Gideon.

"They've got that tire and footprint cast ready at B2 Division," said the sergeant. "Superintendent Gillick asked whether you'd happen to be passing, so that you could pop in and have a word for him."

Gideon stifled a groan, and then said: "I'll see."

The sergeant directed him to the street where Lucy Saparelli lived. Judging from the crowds at either end, the throngs on the pavement, the cars parked in or near the street, more people were drawn here than by a street accident, and that was saying something. In spite of police help when they recognized him, Gideon couldn't drive right up to the house. When he squeezed out of the shiny car, a battery of newspapermen, many with cameras, came toward him like a moving phalanx. It was almost automatic: ask questions, take photographs with flashlights which brightened even the bright day, and then hurl more questions.

"All right," Gideon said, "we've got Sayer; you can go home and write your story."

They flung more questions. . . .

After two minutes, Gideon pushed his way through toward the front door of Lucy Saparelli's house. He had some idea of what he would find behind the door now closed and guarded by a policeman in uniform. He was not duty-bound to see the mother of the murdered child, yet something urged him to; as it had from the moment of seeing Sayer captured.

The constable had a key.

Gideon went in.

Two women were with Mrs. Saparelli. There were teapots and kettles

and cups and saucers everywhere, untidy as a child's toys. People spoke to
Gideon but he wasn't interested until he saw the mother. He stood, a giant
in the small room, and looked at her, remembering. It was an old story and
a long one, and it still hurt. Kate had asked him not to go on duty, but to
telephone an excuse, because their second child was ill. He'd brushed the
suggestion off, and told her to pull herself together.

The child had died during the night. One of seven, so six were left; but
the gap was still there.

A mother, bereaved, looked like a woman robbed of hope. Kate had; Lucy
Saparelli did.

"I just came to tell you," Gideon said, looking into those strange lackluster
eyes, "that we've caught him."

"Have you?" Her voice was strained; empty.

"Yes, Mrs. Saparelli. We made quite sure of that. Is there anything we
can do to help? Your husband—"

"No," she said, "you've been ever so good, all of you police have, and
Jim's on his way." She didn't look at Gideon as she spoke. "Ever so good,"
she repeated, "but there's nothing anyone can do, now, nothing anyone can
do."

Gideon knew that she wasn't going to cry. He knew that it was going to
be much worse with her than with many women. Kate hadn't cried. He
didn't know why, but he sensed a measure of self-reproach, of self-blame,
in Mrs. Saparelli. He made a mental note to tell a police surgeon to have a
word with the woman's doctor about that, as he said good-by.

It hadn't taken long but he was glad that he had been there, even though
it made him feel more vicious. It wasn't only the crime; the actual offense
for which a man might hang or serve a long term of imprisonment was not
the really deadly thing. That, a living evil, was the effect on those who
suffered. Mrs. Saparelli, with the long years of self-reproach ahead, was now
living in the shadow of death, and thinking: "If only I'd done this . . ."

It was always the same; there was so much suffering; that was why he
hated killers.

The sergeant was at the side of his car, speaking into the walkie-talkie.

"Anything fresh?" asked Gideon flatly.

"Old woman's been attacked, Islington way," said the sergeant. He might
have been reporting a case of shoplifting, judging from his voice. "Alone in
a shop—till robbed, she was battered to death."

"Death?"

"Yes, sir."

"Oh, hell," breathed Gideon. "Hell." It was almost a groan.

"There was an attempted mail-van robbery at Cannon Row Station twenty
minutes ago," the sergeant went on in exactly the same voice. "No one's

been caught but there's a description of the driver of a van, and the car's been held."

Gideon straightened his back. Something happened to him—something quite wonderful—as if he'd taken a tonic, which had instantaneous effect. His dull eyes brightened.

"Where? Cannon Row?"

"Yes, sir."

"Well, well," said Gideon. "Two of the devils stopped in one day, eh? That's not so bad, not bad at all, we're improving." The dark shadows vanished completely from his eyes; there was eager brightness in them as he rounded the nose of the car and took the wheel. "Might get those beggars soon, after all."

He was looking ahead: to Gillick, to the tire and footprint casts, and to the time when he would be able to include in his report one murderer caught and two mail-van robberies averted.

Behind him, there was grief.

About him, there were the crimes being plotted and the criminals preparing: the good and the bad. He did not always realize how wearying it was to be occupied almost exclusively with the bad.

Two young men whom Gideon did not know, and of whom he had never heard, were preparing to play a part in his life at the time that he left the Yard to visit Superintendent Gillick. Neither knew that they would cross Gideon's path, although one realized that there was a serious risk that he would run into trouble with the police.

The name of the first was Alec Fitzroy. He was twenty-seven years old, had a small West End flat, and a private income of about five hundred pounds a year, which wasn't anything like enough for his expensive tastes or his gambling debts. For a long time he had pondered on ways and means of making a fortune quickly, and had come to the conclusion that the most likely way was by theft.

He had two cronies, whose names don't matter.

The name of the second man was Julian Small. He too was twenty-seven years old, lived in two small rooms close to the church near the river, and not far from Shipham's café, and also had a private income of about five hundred pounds a year. The stipend from his curacy at St. Mary's brought in an additional two hundred pounds a year. Of his total income, he spent one-half on his personal needs, and the rest on the needs of the church and the needy of the parish, especially on the Youth Club. He had only been in the parish for a few months. The vicar was venerable and frail, known to everyone in the district rather as a piece of furniture is known in a home. No one ever took any notice of him.

A great many people took notice of Julian Small. He was unhappily possessed of a long, thin nose which was always red. He looked weedy, too, and he took little trouble with his clothes. After the first few weeks, the boys with whom he had tried to cope had discovered that he was not gifted with the necessary authority. He was full of high hopes and good intentions, but was so easily guyed.

Many were cruel, and guyed him.

Julian Small had one thing in common with Alec Fitzroy: education. They had, in fact, been educated at the same school, and had left in the same year. Their background was as nearly identical as a background could be. One had a widowed mother, the other a widower-father.

In every other way they were almost unbelievably different; but they did have similar thoughts that day although the one was heavy-hearted and bitterly resigned, the other was vicious and determined at all costs to get the money he needed.

Julian Small, walking from his flat to the church, turned into the tiny churchyard and the headstones grimed by London's sooty atmosphere, and kicked against a piece of string tied to headstones and stretching across the path. He crashed down. He tried to save his nose, but couldn't; the blow on it was so painful that tears of pain sprang to his eyes. They were not only of pain as he picked himself up and walked blindly along the path toward the church doors. Shrill, cruel laughter followed him, and brought shame and despair to quicken the tears. He was a failure; nothing could ever alter the fact. There were times when he felt that he almost *hated* the people in the district; the children.

"Suffer the little children . . ."

Some of these were devils!

They shouted obscenities after him, and roared with laughter until the heavy door closed on him. They might go away. They might raid the churchyard. They might throw stones through the windows; the stained glass had long since been moved, for it wasn't safe. There was no end to the sacrileges that the children would commit and which many of their parents would condone.

Julian Small was probably the unhappiest man in the East End of London that morning, and when he looked into a small mirror and saw the blood welling up at the end of his nose, he raised clenched fists and shook them at the reflection that he hated as much as he hated the children.

Or some of them . . .

Alec Fitzroy wept no tears of pain or vexation. At the time when Small was pitching forward onto the asphalt of the churchyard path, Fitzroy was in the upper safe deposit of the Mid-Union Safe Deposit Company, in Wattle Street, E.C.3. He had rented a deedbox there a few months ago, when the plan he was expecting to put into operation tonight had first taken shape in his mind.

He had met a youngster, now one of his cronies, who had been fired by the Mid-Union for drinking when on night duty; and the idea had been born then. Since that night Fitzroy had learned all he could about the safe deposit, the upper room and the main vaults; and he had studied the system by which it was staffed and run at night. His crony had given him a great deal of help.

Fitzroy believed that his plot was almost foolproof. All it needed was a strong nerve. He had that; so had his two accomplices, one of them a man whom Fitzroy had met in the air force and who lived in much the same way as Fitzroy: lazily, lustfully, greedily.

Fitzroy telephoned each man to tell him that this was to be the night, and to lay everything on. That was the first direct move in the collision which was coming with Gideon.

Gideon was on his way across the river, to see Gillick.

8 . Tire Print

GILLICK was a big block of a man with a heavy, thrusting jaw and a peculiarly small mouth with a short upper lip. When he talked he appeared to be chewing, and to his cost Gideon knew that Gillick talked a lot. There was no better man on detail in the whole of London, including the Yard, and his failing was his touchiness. When annoyed, and it was easy to annoy him, he could and often would fall back on working strictly to regulation, and on no job in the world were go-slow tactics more exasperating. The days when the Yard asked for urgent information by open postcard had gone at last, but Gillick knew every regulation that he could use so as to be unhelpful.

His big, pedestal desk was so tidy that it didn't seem real. He stood up from it, navy-blue reefer coat open and square corners brushing a single file of papers, a thick red hand held out.

"Hallo, Gee-Gee, haven't seen you for years! Well, months! Nice day. Must say you're looking well. Got that child killer, I hear; quick work, good job we have a bit of luck sometimes. Pity about Foster, nasty job when a man like Foster gets knocked over. What was he doing—making an arrest, d'you think?"

Gillick paused; and his little brown eyes probed; obviously he thought he was onto something.

"Not been suggested, old man," Gideon said comfortably, "I'll have another look at the reports, though. You might have something there."

"Never know," said Gillick warningly. "Fresh mind often helps." He
went off again, each sentence short and the pause after each one barely
noticeable. Any other man would have sounded breathless, but not Gillick.
"Two mail-van jobs stopped today, I see, don't say we're really near at last.
Talking about that, these prints. Footprints not much good. Look."

Some white plaster-of-Paris casts stood on a trestle table against one wall.
On each was a card, neatly typewritten, giving the details. There were
seven casts of footprints, but only one of a complete toe, another of a complete heel. The card near the toe read:

> Footprint, man's right toe, found in mud on South Bank of River
> Thames, Battersea, spot identifiable as three hundred and fifty (350)
> yards from the main loading jetty of the Battersea Power Station.

> Note indentation showing sole sprigged (nailed) on, not sewn. Note
> smooth edge suggesting plenty of wear.

Gideon studied all these, well aware that Gillick was keeping the most
important until the last.

"By the way, old man," said Gillick, "like a spot? Not too late? Oh, well,
cuppa tea? Good, I'll send for it." He picked up a telephone and gave orders
as a martinet would. "Won't be long." He broke off, and turned to the
trestle. "Tire print's better now. See?" He picked up a large glossy print,
showing the tire track, the footprints, other signs of activity on the river
bank; it was an excellent photograph, and showed where a car or light van
had driven over a soft patch of sandy soil; the mark of the tire couldn't
have been made more clearly in plaster of Paris itself. "Michelin make,
and that's something; they don't make a lot of small tires; this was a 5.50 x
16. Almost new, too—see how sharp that impression is?"

He now turned to the prize exhibit—the molded cast of the tire. It was
beautifully made, quite an artist's job.

"You've got a good chap on this stuff," Gideon said.

"Training, my boy, that's the answer—training! Beat hell out of them
every time they turn in a rough job, and they soon stop. It's really something, this is. Any other make of tire and it would be a needle in haystack,
but a Michelin of this size—eh?"

Gideon felt his pulse quickening, in spite of almost instinctive disagree-
ment with anything that Gillick said.

"You're right, Gil," he said. "This may really be something. It doesn't
square up with the other track we got, that was a Dunlop, but we can
get a search made for this." If there were a job in the calendar which really

made him feel deeply at any given moment, it was the mail-van job. Hope of results could always excite. "How many photographs have you got?"

"Dozen. Twelve. To spare, I mean."

"Casts?"

"Three. Two each for you, one for my own Black Museum." Gillick grinned; his little mouth didn't stretch very widely.

There was a tap at the door.

"There's the tea," Gillick said. "Well, hope this bit of work gets us somewhere. Can't say we lost any time . . ."

Twenty minutes later, Gideon left the B2 Headquarters, with Gillick purring, and the casts loaded into the boot of Gideon's Wolseley. He had spoken to Lemaitre by telephone, and details of the Michelin tire were being teleprinted for attention by all London and Home Counties Stations; the quiet, methodical, thorough search for it would begin before dark and go on all tomorrow and for days on end; the eyes of every policeman would be cast down, and every Michelin tire would be suspect. It wasn't really much; but the owners of cars with 5.50 x 16 Michelins could be watched, and their movements checked; and if a thousand, if ten thousand discreet inquiries proved fruitless and futile, there might be one which helped.

The Yard sergeant came hurrying out of the station, wiping his hand across the back of his mouth; there were two or three cake crumbs on his sleeve.

"You had any lunch?" Gideon asked abruptly.

"Just managed a bite, sir; I'm all right."

"Hmm. Well, I'm going to look in at home for twenty minutes; hardly recognize the place when I do get there."

The sergeant smiled dutifully.

"So you drive back to the Yard, get this stuff unloaded, tell the boys to be careful with it, and then come back for me."

"Yes, sir."

They drove over Battersea Bridge, then turned left instead of right—which they would take for the Yard. Gideon took off his hat and enjoyed the cold wind stinging his forehead. He felt too hot in his serge coat and waistcoat; now he came to think, it had been getting hotter since midday and must be near the seventies.

He wondered if Kate would be in. He knew quite well that he wanted to have a cup of tea with her because of the look in Lucy Saparelli's eyes. He wondered whether Kate would be pleased to see him; the youngsters would—no, the youngsters wouldn't!

The three girls were out at a party—Prudence to play in the glow of her examination success, Priscilla to recite, no doubt; she was a wonderful mimic. Well, good. Penelope just to look pretty, and no one could do that more easily.

Pretty Penelope.

Pretty, dead Dorothy Saparelli and Jennifer Gay—what was the first dead girl's name? He couldn't call it to mind.

Prudence, eighteen plus, Priscilla, fifteen plus, Penelope twelve, with Pru younger than her years except in her playing, so they were all good friends. There was a greater disparity in the ages of the boys. Tom, the oldest, was twenty-six, Matthew was fourteen, Malcolm only just eight. Matthew would almost certainly be out playing—he'd probably gone as far as Putney Common, or even to Wimbledon. Malcolm was more likely to be at home with Kate—unless she had taken him out.

Well, at least he'd have looked in.

The sergeant got out of the car to open the door for him. "Thanks," said Gideon. He did not consciously make a note of the man's name or the way he'd behaved, but except for that attack of nerves when Gideon had been driving, he'd done very well. Shorter than most, wiry fair hair, slim waist and no hips to speak of, he was quick moving, quiet, efficient; oh, yes, and his name was Wedderburn.

"Oh, come straight back. I've got another call to make."

"Right, sir."

Harringdon Street, Fulham, was on the "classy" side, north of the Wandsworth Bridge Road, near Hurlingham—still an oddly exclusive district although bordered by some of the poorer neighborhoods of southwest London. The solid houses were all of red brick, two story plus attic, and most of the householders were sufficiently well off to keep them in good repair; painting the outside every third year was a matter of pride. This had been Gideon's third year, and the painting had been finished only a few weeks ago. It was still bright and shiny, black and white as Kate had wanted it, and made him look up with interest and satisfaction; one could still take pleasure in the appearance of one's house.

There were two stone steps, a shallow porch, and a solid oak door—the door put in by Gideon. Most front doors in Harringdon Street had colored glass panels, open invitation to light-fingered gentry.

Not that wood would keep anyone out, if he wanted to get in.

There was a small front garden, neat and attractive, with a postage-stamp lawn, two beds of varicolored wallflowers, daffodils out and tulips not yet in flower. No one was about; the street as well as the house looked empty. Gideon felt a twinge of disappointment, but it wasn't very strong.

They had come to live in the upstairs flat here when he and Kate had married, and over the years they had converted the flats to one house, reversing the usual process. Always handy with his tools and not so busy in those early days as he had been for the last ten years, he had converted the attic so that there had been a playroom and cubicles for the boys. Now Tom had a small room to himself, and the younger boys the cubicles. A corner of the playroom was used for their books and homework.

Pru had now a tiny partitioned room to herself; the younger girls shared the other side of the partition.

Gideon took out his keys, opened the door, and wondered when he had last come back during daylight. Three Sundays ago, when all the family had been waiting for him since noon, a job had cropped up . . .

The hall was narrow but bright and fresh, and well lit from a landing window.

"Anyone home?" he called, and was startled when he heard an immediate response: footsteps above his head, in his bedroom—and Kate's.

"George, is that you?"

"Yes, m'dear. Just looked in for a cup of tea."

Kate's footsteps came hurrying; he could picture her easy walk. Although she was getting rather heavy-breasted and thick at the waist, she was still graceful, and she didn't have to worry too much about her figure. She appeared at the head of the stairs, wearing a black skirt and a fresh white blouse, looking neat and wholesome; her hair was more gray than his, and she improved a natural wave skillfully.

"You might as well shoot me as frighten me to death," she said. "I couldn't believe it was you when I heard the car, and when it drove off again—"

"Don't tell me you took any notice of a car pulling up outside!"

Kate had reached the foot of the stairs. With her broad forehead and high-bridged nose she was quite striking, and she used make-up well; more, these days, than she had a few years ago. Standing on the bottom stair, she was just an inch or two taller than he.

"Don't tell me you've just looked in for a cup of tea," she scoffed. "What did you leave behind?"

"Nothing, honest. I happened to be handy, and thought it would be a good idea to pop in."

"Crime *must* be in a bad way," Kate said.

It was only half serious, only half hurtful; in fact, hurtful was too strong a word. They had six children, the memory of a seventh, a certain kind of mutual dependence, and practically nothing else in common. In a queer way, one Gideon hadn't been aware of for a long time, he looked upon her as he might a stranger—Mrs. Lucy Saparelli, for instance.

"As a matter of fact," he said, "crime's flourishing. We've had a bad one today. Cleaned it up as well as it can be cleaned up, though."

"Oh." Kate moved, pushing past him, and their hands brushed; hers was very cool. "Well, I don't suppose you've got long. Going to wait in the front room while I get it?"

"No, I'll come into the kitchen. Where's Pen?"

"Gone to the pictures with the Odlums," Kate said. "I think Mrs. Odlum knew all the others were out, and deliberately gave me an afternoon off. I was just going to do some window shopping."

They reached the kitchen. It was spick-and-span, and more than that. Kate knew what she wanted, and went all out to get it; and to help she had a little money of her own. That had always made a big difference to them. The kitchen was fresh and bright in pale blue and white paint, pale blue cake tins, pale blue handles on the saucepans. A new kitchen cabinet was painted the same color—the carpentry and paintwork by Tom and Matthew Gideon! Everything had a clean smell. The gas popped. Gideon sat back in an old bed-chair, one of those Heath Robinson contraptions which could be turned into a bed to sleep an extra one, if needs be.

It was Kate's passion for tidiness, contrasting with his habit of coming home and littering the place, that had first really come between them; really contrast of temperaments. Funny thing, to think like that about the mother of your six—seven—children. One married a girl, loved, lived; after a while the intimacies became almost habitual, and since Malcolm's arrival—

The only time he'd known Kate hysterical was when she had known for certain that Malcolm was coming. In this very room she had cried and screamed and shaken her clenched fists at him.

"I won't have it, I won't have another brat, it's all I ever do! Work, slave, *breed*, work, slave and *breed*. And for you! What do you care? You're never in, never got five minutes to spare, and—I tell you I won't have it! I'll get rid of it somehow."

It had been a bad, even an ugly evening.

They had never really recovered from it, although oddly, she was passionately fond of Malcolm, and showed her affection more than she did with the others—showed it to Gideon that was; the children didn't know. If they did, it was because of some sixth sense that he knew nothing about.

"What kind of case was it?" asked Kate.

He sensed what she was feeling; as if this might be a chance to begin to get to know each other again. He'd made a gesture; she wanted to, too. She wasn't quite sure why he had come, and sitting back there and watching her, he wasn't sure either—except that one idea, which hadn't occurred to him before, came into his mind and wouldn't be dismissed. He had come home because he needed her; because the sight of little Dorothy Saparelli's mother had hurt him more than he knew.

The kettle was boiling.

Kate made the tea, and said, in a tighter voice: "Or is that a forbidden subject?"

"No," said Gideon. "No, Kate. Just nasty. A sex maniac, two little girls, and the hell that it's caused to a couple of families. I've just come from one of the mothers. It—well, you know what it is. Sometimes it makes me sick. Sometimes I wish I were one of the average crowd, lost in anonymity, doing a job which didn't make me rub shoulders with all the beastliness and the brutality there is. A man kills a child—and the pain goes on and on and on. By hanging him, you don't make it any less. I'm not even sure that you don't make it more."

Kate was spooning sugar into his cup. The tea was very strong: sweet and strong, the way he liked it.

She took a big cake tin out of the larder; the cake was already on a plate. Knives, plates and plastic mats appeared as if by sleight of hand.

"You look tired, George," she said abruptly.

"Oh, I'm all right."

"You can't give yourself a few hours off, I suppose?"

"Well—well, no, Kate, I wish I could."

She didn't answer.

The fruit cake was rich, too, and good; it had that richness of flavor that made each mouthful something to enjoy and to remember, not just to eat. He had another piece.

"Window shopping where?" he asked.

"Oh, in town! Knightsbridge or Oxford Street."

"How soon can you be ready?" asked Gideon. "I've got the car coming back in twenty minutes or so. Could give you a lift."

"Oh, that's lovely," Kate said in a flash. "All I need is five minutes. I must be back by half-past six; they'll start coming home soon after that—but it will give me a couple of hours to play truant in."

Then Gideon remembered Foster's sister, in Chelsea; he had meant to call on her on the way back to the Yard. The fact came to the tip of his tongue, but he didn't utter it. Kate looked suddenly gay. She was bright-eyed and eager, her gray hair didn't make her look her age. It wouldn't take him long to drop her, and then come back to Chelsea and Miss Foster—*Mrs. Addinson.* . . .

"Thanks a lot, George, that was lovely," Kate said. "You must drop in more often!" Her eyes were bright with excitement, and she was laughing at him; with the children and with others—and at one time with him—she had always laughed easily. She didn't let him get out, but slammed the door and walked off, tall and brisk, something to see in her black suit and white hat and gloves. He was in at the curb, forgetful of the fact that he was in the way of Oxford Street traffic. He picked up the radiotelephone.

Soon, he was speaking to Lemaitre.

"Got something you want to see here, George—couple of good photographs of Foster, lying in the road." Lemaitre paused; a note in his voice suggested that he had something up his sleeve. "Going to be long?"

"Not long. Anything else?"

"Not to worry about. Sayer's made a clean breast of it, and the mystery of that kid in the tunnel out at Ealing isn't a mystery any longer. He did that, too. You know the job, three weeks ago. Haven't got a clue on that Islington killer, except that the chap was medium height and wore a brown suit. Used iron piping, and gloves—no dabs, not very optimistic." Lemaitre sucked his breath. "Half a mo'."

Gideon waited. Buses pulled up almost on the tail of his car, and then swung out. Traffic filtered past; a constable came up looking as if he had nothing in the world to do, bent down, and peered at him.

"Going to be here long, sir?" He bumped his helmet on the top of the window. "Oo!" Praiseworthy self-control. "Holding up the traffic, you know, very bad place to stop."

"Yes. Sorry. Let me finish this talk to the Yard, and I'll move off."

"To the—" There was a closer, sharper scrutiny. "I didn't recognize you, sir! Sorry. Like me to make 'em give you a bit more lee room?"

Gideon chuckled. "No, thanks, I'm all right."

The constable did his best to salute so that the courtesy could be noticed, and moved off. There was the purr, the hum, the roar of engines, the swish of wheels on the tacky road, the perpetual motion of people weaving to and fro, the air heavy with petrol fumes. Gideon eased his collar; his neck was damp.

Lemaitre came again, almost bellowing: "It's a flash from Waterloo, they've knocked off a van with thirty thousand quid in it. One of our chaps caught a packet. Three in one blasted day! Wonder if the others were dummy jobs—be seeing you."

9 . The Mail-van Job

A SMALL but well-set-up-looking man in the early thirties, at the wheel of an Austin 10 saloon, cellulosed black, was drumming the steering wheel with the fingers of both hands, and watching a flow of traffic coming from the one-way street leading from Waterloo Road. Standing a few hundred yards away from him was another, younger man, dressed in drab gray and rather down at heel. He had a motorcycle. Nearer the Austin was a short, stocky man who kept taking a cigarette out of his mouth, looking at it, then putting it back again.

All three had been there for ten minutes.

The stocky man near the Austin finished his cigarette, glanced up and down, and then stiffened, for a red mail van came in sight. It was on its own, clear of other traffic, and moving at a good speed.

The driver's hands stopped drumming. He started the engine. The others tensed, as if for action, although no one noticed them then.

The van didn't swing beneath the dark arches of the wide approach to Waterloo Station, but came straight on.

All three men relaxed; if *relaxed* was the word.

The stocky one came up to the car.

"You must have got it wrong."

The driver said smoothly: "I don't get things wrong."

"It's late, nearly ten minutes—"

"That's your watch, it's fast," the driver said. "Beat it, Ted."

"We can't stay around here any longer."

"What's the matter, losing your nerve? We'll stay as long as we have to. I got the squeak, didn't I? There are thirty thousand quid in that van, being sent down to Bournemouth."

"It'll have a cop tailing—"

"S'right," the driver said, "and we'll fix the cop and scram. Quit worrying. I'll see you at Shippy's, and—"

He stopped, as another mail van came in sight. This time he didn't relax, for he read the registration number.

"That's it," he whispered, and the stocky man shot away from him as the Austin's engine started; then roared.

The Austin 10 was on the move as the van swung toward the archway; as it turned left, the Austin swung right. That was normal enough, for there was access to traffic from both directions.

Behind the van was a Wolseley, with two men in it. Anyone who knew a Yard car would recognize that; there was something unmistakable about the look of the man at the wheel and his companion. They weren't in any mood of alarm—until the man in drab gray, astride his motorcycle, roared alongside and tossed a little, fragile glass tube through the driving window. It broke on the driver's forehead. Ammonia gas billowed, biting at both Yard men's eyes, mouths and noses. The driver grabbed at the gear lever and his foot went down on the brake, but he was going fast, and was blinded before he could stop. The police car lurched across and smashed into the archway wall. The man by the driver's side gave a funny little grunting sound as the door buckled and squashed him.

The car was slewed across the road; no other traffic could get in, and it was a one-way stretch.

The Austin, a hundred yards further on, screeched alongside the mail van. The scarlet of the van's cellulose, bright under the sun, was reflected on the black shine of the car. The post-office driver and his mate glanced sideways nervously, sensing what was happening. Brakes went on, but the Austin forced the van to keep on the inside, drawing just ahead of it. The Austin driver pulled a gun. The post-office men didn't move.

Two youths, bent low until then and wearing black cloth masks, jumped from the back of the Austin. They didn't wait for keys, didn't speak, smashed at the padlock at the back of the little red van and, as the doors swung open, grabbed the registered bags—all of green canvas.

They rushed back to the Austin.

Within ninety seconds they were being driven away at furious but controlled pace, with the motorcycle roaring after them. The post-office men watched them go, and saw the registration plate of the saloon vanish. It had false plates; other plates would drop as soon as the robber car reached the Waterloo Road.

Back in the archway, cars were lined up behind the wreck. One Yard man was leaning against the wall, with tears still streaming down his face. Two men were pushing at the damaged car, so as to get at the driver's companion, who had slumped down in his seat; there was blood on his chin. Someone was calling for a doctor. Two uniformed policemen came hurrying.

The stocky youth, not needed to make a diversion after all, turned away and walked toward Whitehall, whistling.

Gideon switched off the radiotelephone and started his engine. He felt as if he were back where he had started; the all-pervading shadow of the mail-van robberies had become blacker than ever. Whether the two earlier jobs had been to sell the police dummies or not, someone was bound to suggest that they had been, and two or three of the newspapers would have a smack at the Yard for it; and at him.

He was ten minutes' drive from the Yard.

He was fifteen minutes' drive from Foster's flat and his sister, Mrs. what-was-her-name?—Addinson.

"Can't prevent the damned holdup now," he said aloud and savagely, "and if I don't see the woman soon I'll have to give the job to someone else."

He swung round in the road, where there was a clear stretch, nodded to the watching constable, and drove through Hyde Park toward the south-west and Chelsea.

It was then four o'clock.

Florence Addinson, nee Foster, opened the door. At the first moment, she was just an attractive young woman, with features—expression?—a little too bold perhaps, wearing a washed-out blue smock daubed here and there with paint, and poking red-lacquered finger tips through her raven-black hair. Her hair was untidy and piled up on top with one of those ring buns, or whatever they were called.

Then she recognized Gideon.

"Miss Foster," Gideon said, and felt irritated with himself: why use the wrong name when he knew it was wrong?

"I—yes," she said, as if she didn't think it worth contradicting him. "Yes, aren't you—"

"Superintendent Gideon."

"I thought you were." She hadn't moved away from the door, but held on to it tightly. Nervously? "Weren't you at Mr. Chang's this morning?"

"Yes."

"Superintendent Gideon, can you tell me—" she began, and then snatched her hand away from the door. "Oh, what a fool I am! Won't you come in?"

"Thanks," said Gideon.

"I've just been doing some sketching," she said apologetically. "A rush job."

"For Chang?"

"No, he—he changed his mind." She led the way into a long, narrow room overlooking the Embankment.

Had Gideon ever entered this room during Foster's life, he would have quickly started wondering where the money came from. Detective sergeants didn't usually live in luxurious apartments overlooking the Thames; or have dark, almost black oak furniture, *circa* 1600, in a room which was richly paneled and had several Dutch panels on the wall—each worth something more than three figures.

Had they family money?

The woman stood and faced him, and the impression that she was nervous came back. She seemed younger than Gideon had thought, partly because she'd not made up since morning; her cheeks had a scrubbed look. She no longer looked overbold, nor so attractive, if you liked smoothness of line. The smock hid her figure, too, where her suit had emphasized it.

Her eyes were almost black; like Foster's.

"Superintendent, is my brother in any trouble?" The question came out swiftly, quickened by embarrassment.

"What makes you think he might be?" asked Gideon.

"I—I don't know. That doesn't matter. Is he?"

"Yes, he is." Gideon glanced down at her left hand; she wasn't wearing a wedding ring. "It would be pointless to lie to you; the papers have the story, I'm quite sure." He really meant that it would be a mistake to come out with all the truth now, but if he questioned her first and afterward told her what had happened, what would she think of him?

What did it matter what she thought? He had a job to do.

"I'd like to know the truth." She was taut.

"Good. Do you mind telling me why you should think that he was in trouble?" When he chose to exert himself, Gideon could have the charm of a benevolent patriarch, and could inspire confidence even in people who ought to know better. "It might help a lot, in the long run."

She said abruptly: "He seemed worried."

"What about?"

"I don't know. I think—" she paused.

"I'll find out sooner or later, one way or the other," Gideon said, "and I've come myself because I thought it would help if you knew you were dealing with a senior officer."

"Oh," she said, and mechanically added: "Yes, thank you. Well, it's—it's hard to say. I think he was being threatened. He—"

Gideon's big hand now held the fat cigarette case. Foster's sister took a cigarette. He lit it, then shepherded her to a window seat. It was rather a fine view, especially with the sun shining on the broad Thames, the two bridges in sight just far enough away to look fragile, and the plane trees lining the Embankment powdered with light green; husks of the buds were beginning to litter the road and pavement.

The story came out swiftly.

The girl was no fool, and obviously had been worried for some time. At heart, she said, she'd been worried for two years, since Foster had first started to buy new furniture. Some of this was their own, which they'd inherited, but some pieces were recent acquisitions. All the paintings had been bought in the last year or so. He said he bought them at wholesale prices, and she had never voiced her anxiety to him.

Lately, she knew that he'd been worried; he hadn't slept much; he had been at work all day and out too much at night. She had felt sure that he was being put under some kind of pressure.

"Did you suspect anybody?" Gideon asked bluntly.

She didn't answer.

"Nothing you say to me will be used," Gideon said. "I might be able to switch inquiries, that's all. *Did* you suspect anyone?"

She said hesitantly: "Well—in a way. He—he knew that man Chang slightly, and I knew Chang had telephoned him. He always seemed more worried after that."

"Why did you go to Chang's?" Gideon asked.

"I—I thought I might find out something," she said. "Oh, I know it was silly, but I was really anxious. There'd been some talk of mural paintings for the new clubroom, and I got an agency to introduce me to Chang about it. That's why I was there. I could have dropped through the floor when you arrived."

"You recognized me, did you?"

"You aren't a man to forget," she said.

Unexpectedly, that pleased him; she seemed to know that it did, and for a moment she was more relaxed. Then she changed, and her voice hardened.

"What *has* happened? I've tried to get Eric on the telephone several times, but couldn't, and a sergeant I spoke to was most evasive."

"Hmm, yes," Gideon commented. He didn't like what he had to do, and the dislike stiffened his voice. "Rather ugly trouble, Mrs. Addinson. That's why I went to Chang's. I think Chang was bribing your brother to shut his eyes to certain offenses."

She exclaimed: "Eric taking *bribes?*"

"Yes."

"You can't be certain!"

"No," agreed Gideon, "I can't really be certain."

"Where is Eric? What does he say?" She was flushed and very anxious.

"He denied it, of course," Gideon said, and went on very heavily. "Had you any reason to believe he was taking bribes?"

"No!"

Gideon thought: "I don't believe her." Then he began to wonder more about her: was her explanation of her visit to Chang the true one? Had she known Chang before? Was she involved? Were her present fears due to worry about the possibility of being caught out in some crime?

He saw her, now, just as another witness who might become a suspect. If Chang had warned her about Foster's danger from the Yard, it might explain much. The one thing that seemed certain was that she had not heard of the death of her brother.

"Mr. Gideon," Florence Addinson said abruptly, "will you please tell me where Eric is?"

"Yes," said Gideon, "although it's not a job I like, Mrs. Addinson. I hate bringing bad news of any kind." He felt that it had all gone wrong, he wasn't breaking this gently; she was expecting to hear that her brother was under arrest.

He must get it over.

"He was run down by a car this morning," he said, and stopped again. He saw understanding dawning; surprise came first, because it was so unexpected, shock next; and the grief would come afterward. He knew only too well that it was impossible to judge in advance how a woman would react to such news, but there was a one-in-four chance of a burst of hysteria.

He let her have time to get used to the fear which he'd put into her mind, and then added quietly: "It was over very quickly, I'm glad to say."

"*Over*," she ejaculated.

She sat on the cushioned window seat, back to the sun-gilt river, a few wisps of hair blowing slightly in the breeze from an open window. She didn't move. Sitting this way, the smock was drawn down tightly; she had the kind of figure Kate had had twenty years ago.

"*Over*," she repeated hoarsely.

"I'm afraid that's it," said Gideon, and liked the task less than ever. "It's very distressing."

"I can't—I can't believe it!"

It was going to be hysteria. She'd jump up in a minute and keep repeating that she couldn't believe it, and then she would probably call it murder, and she would look round for someone to blame. She was so young; middle twenties at most, thought Gideon. Then he realized that he was letting the emotional side gain the upper hand; he was seeing her as an attractive woman. He had to see her as the sister of a policeman who had accepted bribes, and probably been murdered; as a witness who might lead him to Chang and beyond; to the distributors of drugs which corrupted and killed.

She jumped up, hands clenched.

"It can't be true! Why, he left here this morning, as fit as—"

She broke off.

Her color was coming back, an angry red which seemed to be reflected in her eyes.

Gideon watched her, not quite dispassionately.

He would let the first blast pass over his head, then try to steady her, then he'd ring Lemaitre and have a couple of good men come along here, to start searching. There had to be a quick and thorough probe. She was on edge and likely to remain so; if they could find one little pointer that involved her, they would be justified in trying to make her crack. If she was in the clear, the sooner it was established the better.

He watched her fighting for her self-control; admiration came back; it was impossible to rid himself of the curious sense of personal concern for her.

Then she said: "I hope you'll tell me everything, Mr. Gideon. Everything, please." She paused and then flung out: "Did he kill himself?"

That startled Gideon.

"No," he said. "No, we've no reason to think so. Have you?"

"Just that he was worried. That man Chang. I—" She raised her hands and let them fall. "Anyhow, it's too late to do anything to help Eric now."

Very quietly, Gideon said: "You may be able to help us, Mrs. Addinson. Will you try?"

"In every way I can," she promised.

It was twenty to five when Gideon reached the Yard. He had waited there until Sergeants Wedderburn and Miller, the day's bright boys, had arrived at the flat. By then, Foster's sister had been completely composed, and he found doubts about her hard to retain. The two sergeants would go into figures, study all Foster's accounts, find out who the furniture was bought from, who sold old masters "at wholesale prices." It had all the makings of a nasty job, and Foster's game might have gone on for some time, but for Birdy.

Gideon had been thinking about the man who had really started his day. Birdy Merrick, at fifty-odd, had spent twenty years in jail. His was one of the worst records of any man in London for burglary and breaking and entering, but he had not been able to stand by and watch young girls become maddened with drugs. Good in every man? Certainly Birdy's love for his dead daughter had gone deep.

Gideon's office was empty.

He hung his hat with exemplary care on the peg in the corner, then took out his pipe and tobacco, next took off his coat, loosened his collar and, putting his right foot up on a chair, eased the lace of the shoe; the little toe was pinching a bit.

It was very warm. He sat down slowly, fingering the familiar roughness of his pipe and the smooth pouch at the same time, anticipating a smoke, feeling less tired than dispirited. That was partly due to Foster's sister. He thought of Kate asking him if he couldn't snatch a few hours off. It was so long since he had worked normal hours, and relaxed in the evening, that he had almost forgotten what it was like.

Lemaitre's hurriedly written notes were in front of him. There was one about a patrolman's report on the painter at Chang's; a man known to have a chip on his shoulder, but as far as was known, quite honest; he'd never worked for Chang before, and Chang had tried three decorators before getting one who had been able to come at once. So the painter was out; Chang's anxiety to get the club painted quickly was more firmly in.

Another showed negative results from the inquiry about anyone with a "tough reputation" having left Chang's about eleven o'clock, and this confirmed, incidentally, that a decorating firm's foreman had been in to see Chang but had not been able to do an urgent job at the club. Chang, this report said, had wanted the decorating finished in time to open as usual that night.

The last report, at the bottom, made Gideon's teeth clench. Attached to it was a print of a photograph of Foster, lying dead in the road. He was face upward. The photograph showed that the blood had oozed from his head into the dust of the roadway. It was a brilliant picture—a bit macabre, perhaps, if that were the word, but as a photograph vivid and clear in every detail. Obviously the car had crushed his stomach.

There was death looking at Gideon—

On the curb was a dark patch and a shiny surface: a puddle. It had rained early in the morning. There was something else, and Lemaitre had pointed a red-penciled arrow toward it. Gideon looked closer, and then his heart began to beat fast, he felt the choking throb of excitement.

The arrow pointed to a tire track.

The tire track looked familiar; and was familiar. It was of a new Michelin type, and the size was probably 5.50 x 16.

Lemaitre had written hurriedly: "Same make tire as Gillick took a cast of, size and all; could be the same tire, and if F. was bumped off by the mail-v. boys—how about it?"

10 . Find That Tire

"THE only thing that matters," said Gideon to the Assistant Commissioner, who had come to his office, "is to find that tire. It's one of the first real mistakes they've made, and they probably don't know it. If we can find that tire—"

The A.C. was tall, lean, gray-haired, sardonic when the mood took him, and just now sardonically amused.

"All right, George, I want them as much as you do, but we needn't get excited about it."

"We needn't get—" began Gideon explosively. He held his breath, then put his pipe down slowly. "If you were Lemaitre, I'd have your hide for that remark! I don't mind telling you that there's just one job—"

He broke off.

They looked at each other uncertainly, and grinned simultaneously.

"Seem to have heard that before somewhere," said the A.C. "Where's Lemaitre?"

"Waterloo."

"He shouldn't have gone before you came back," said the A.C. mildly. "Drop him a hint that if he leaves the office empty I'll have *his* hide. I've just been looking through Sayer's statement. We've got a cold-blooded devil there."

Gideon didn't speak.

"And that Islington job, the old woman in the sweetshop," the Chief went on, "that's a bad one, too. Haven't had a chance to look at it much, have you?"

"No."

"More your cup of tea than anyone else's," the A.C. said, "and if it weren't, I've got to send Chatto to Portugal on that extradition job; he's the only one who can speak Portuguese well enough to get by in Lisbon, and I don't trust Portuguese English. Smith's still up to his eyes in the City fraud case, I don't want to take him off. Deering's cracked up—"

"Deering isn't the only one near cracking up," Gideon said, into a pause. "I'm all right, and will be for a bit, but flesh and blood is flesh and blood. We're all being driven too hard, from sergeants up. Had a chap with me today. Discovered he was on until two o'clock this morning, back on duty at six, and still at it. That's the way we make mistakes, and that's the way we'll go on making mistakes. Hasn't any blurry fool got any idea how to get our recruits' strength up?"

"No," said the A.C.

"I don't understand why it's so hard."

"Want your boys to become C.I.D. men?" asked the A.C. dryly. "Several years on the beat first at low pay with some danger, while there are plenty of good prospects elsewhere?"

"I wouldn't want my boys to become C.I.D. men if it made 'em millionaires," said Gideon forcefully. "Oh, I know what you mean, and I still think it's wrong recruiting methods. Bit more glamour, that's what we want. Well—" he broke off. "What brought you in, sir?"

It was a casual, belated "sir"; just as a matter of form.

"Islington," said the A.C. "Have a look at everything, will you? You've got X-ray eyes. And then there's the Moxley case. We don't want Moxley to get off. If ever a man deserved to be hanged, he's the one. Sure the sergeant and the Inspector you've briefed as witnesses are good enough?"

"As good as we'll get," Gideon assured him. "But don't count on a verdict. Moxley killed his wife all right, and he did it because of that tart who gets her face and fanny plastered all over the papers, but it's going to be tough. Not a thing more we can do about it, either. That rape job's up in Number 2 at the Old Bailey in the morning, too; we'll get those little baskets all right. Cor!"

The A.C. said: "Seamy, isn't it?"

"What I want is to get away, have a nice clean breeze running through my hair for a bit," said Gideon, "but it won't be for a few months yet. I— excuse me."

The telephone bell ran. He picked it up, sitting on a corner of the desk. The A.C., a tailor's dummy of a soldier in mufti, stood waiting. Gideon's expression told him nothing; Gideon's voice told him a lot.

"Hallo, Birdy," said Gideon.

He listened. . . .

"All right," he said, "I'll send it over to you in old notes. . . . I don't know, but someone who'll recognize you. Then lie low for a bit, don't get yourself into trouble. . . . Unless you tell me anything more about Chang."

He paused.

"Okay, Birdy," he said, and rang off.

He rubbed his hand across his forehead; both hand and forehead were damp.

"That's the squeaker on Chang and Foster, sir." Here, if ever, was a time for formality. "I'm paying him twenty-five pounds, and it's cheap at the price. Two men are over at Foster's place now; I hope to have some kind of a report before I go off tonight." He sniffed. "Birdy says that there's a call out for him, and he wants to get away." Suddenly the two men, broadside and rapier in contrast, were standing upright and looking squarely at each other; each with genuine respect. "I don't like it, A.C. Foster was probably run down deliberately, because once we found out what he was up to, he might have squealed."

"But Chang—"

"Don't want to make it worse than it is," said Gideon, "but why assume that Chang was the only one he was taking bribes from? I don't say he wasn't, yet I can't see Chang paying out a fortune, and somehow Foster's cashed in pretty big money. Did you know that the tire mark near Foster's body might match up with the one at Battersea—the car from which they threw those mail bags into the river?"

The A.C. said, "No, I didn't."

"Come'n have a look." They pored over the photographs, Gideon's flat but well-shaped and clearly marked forefinger pointing at similarities. "And that blakey settles it," he said. "See where it's embedded in the tire—comes out in the cast and in the photograph clearly under magnification. Look." He thrust a round magnifying glass into the A.C.'s hand.

The A.C. pursed his lips.

". . . mmm. I see what you mean. Well, I'll finish off where I came in—*find that tire!*"

He went out.

Gideon wrote out a chit for twenty-five pounds. He charged it to the Information Account, rang for a plain-clothes officer, and sent him along to cash it. When the man came back, Gideon was staring at the ceiling, and actually smoking; he owed himself an extra pipe, had only had one that morning.

"Thanks. Green, do you know Birdy Merrick?"

"Oh, yes, sir."

"Sure?"

"Little chap with a chirruping voice and a little beak of a nose that's always red. Been inside—"

"That's the chap. Take this over to him—he'll be near the telephone kiosks at Aldgate Station by the time you get there. Don't let him put his hands on it until you've got his signature on the receipt. I like Birdy, but you can guess how far I'd trust him."

Green, delighted at a chance to go out, chuckled with more than polite amusement.

When he'd gone, Gideon sat and pulled at his pipe and looked at a spot on the ceiling. It had been there for five years and he still didn't know how it had got there: a pale brownish spot about the size of a half crown. In it, he had seen many things and many faces. Leaning back in the swivel chair with the strong spring back at just the right angle, he could see it with complete comfort. He'd trained himself to lean back like this, a form of relaxation that was almost complete. In a minute, he would treat himself to a double whiskey; then he would be set for a few hours.

He thought of Kate.

He thought of Foster's sister.

He had his whiskey.

He thought of Lucy Saparelli. Those kids. Sayer. A little old woman with a battered head.

This was one of the bad days, but the newspapers would look much the same as usual next morning; half the headlines in the popular daily press were about major crimes. No one would be surprised. Now and again there was an outcry about unsolved crimes, and so there should be. Only one crime in two, not even as many as that some years, were ever solved. The miracle was that the Yard got so many results. Give them a 10 per cent increase in staff—

The door opened, and Lemaitre came in, brand-new trilby on, slightly at the back of his head, perky of feature and expression, grinning rather smugly.

"Hi!" he greeted.

"When you're going to leave the office empty again, make sure that the Old Man isn't coming in, will you?" Gideon said flatly.

Lemaitre's perkiness vanished; he positively sagged.

"You don't mean to say—"

"I do mean to say, and why you ask for trouble like that I don't know. Rule Number 1—always have someone in the office. If we both *have* to be out, fetch in a sergeant." Gideon grinned. "But it's up to the Old Man to discipline you, you rebellious old so-and-so. Got anything from Waterloo?"

Lemaitre began to look less disconsolate. He took his hat off and twirled it round his forefinger, formed his mouth into a soundless whistle, and then said: "Yes."

That thumping started again at Gideon's chest.

"What?"

"Tire track, believe it or not. Patch of oil on the approach to the station, just where the van was held up. A lorry had a puncture there a few nights ago, and dripped a lot of engine oil. The rain had smoothed it out. One track as clear as a cucumber, unmistakable, too—but if I hadn't gone there it wouldn't have been noticed. All the photographs they took before I arrived were of the mail van. Five minutes more and they'd have trampled all over the oil patch. Now tell the Old Man—"

"No one said you shouldn't go out on a job sometimes; just be your age and make sure someone's here," said Gideon. He had the patience of a schoolmaster with Lemaitre, who had one thing which no one else at the Yard had quite so well developed: a "natural" sense of observation. Lemaitre's eyes did most of his work for him; he'd miss nothing out, and he could check another man's case brilliantly. If he could only restrain his impetuosity, he'd be a genius. "So, what have we got?" Gideon asked.

"Three Michelin tire tracks," Lemaitre said. "One near Chang's—one at Battersea—the third at Waterloo. I know, I know, three different cars could—"

"They probably didn't. Anything else?"

"It was an Austin 10 with false number plates. The driver had black hair, and his cap was pulled low over his eyes, showing his hair from the crown downward. *And,*" went on Lemaitre, voice rising in triumph, "one of those post-office johnnies kept his eyes open although he admits he was scared stiff. The black hair had a white mark in it—scar of some kind, starting just level with the right ear. Now we can look for the car, the tire and the driver, and oh, boy—"

He broke off, because a telephone bell rang on Gideon's desk.

"Yes," said Gideon into it, and then repeated, although looking puzzled: "Yes, put him through." He glanced up at Lemaitre. "It's Green, chap I sent to pay Birdy his blood money. Move your big head, I can't see the clock." Lemaitre moved quickly. "H'm. Five and twenty past six. Been gone twenty minutes." He waited, with the receiver at his ear. Then: "Yes, Green?"

He listened.

He began to look very grim indeed.

"All right," he said at last, "stay there another twenty minutes, and if he hasn't turned up then, come back. 'By."

Gideon rang off, scowled, looked at Lemaitre steadily, and said flatly: "Someone sent a kid to tell Green we wouldn't be able to pay Birdy off tonight or any night. I don't like that at all." He lifted the telephone, a mechanical action. "Give me G5 Headquarters," he said, and added for Lemaitre's benefit, although he sounded as if he were talking to himself: "Better get the Division to keep an eye open for him."

"We can't afford to lose Birdy," Lemaitre said, and meant it.

I I . Birdy

"BIRDY," Birdy's wife said, "they're after you."

"Wife" was not strictly true, in the legal sense, but in all others it was. She was a small, faded woman, who had never been pretty, was balloon-breasted now, but still had small if work-torn hands—the fingers of her right hand were especially rough, for she was a seamstress. She also had beautifully shaped legs and feet. In spite of her weight and her top-heavy look, she moved very easily.

She had caught up with Birdy at the telephone boxes in the approach to Aldgate Station. The traffic in the wide main road was a hurtling, hooting mass, choking the glorious evening. Barrow boys with fruit stalls magnificently arranged shouted whether customers were near or not; newsboys droned. This great mouth of London's East End and the suburbia beyond throbbed with a vitality which it saw only once each day, always between half-past five and half-past six. All London seemed on the move.

Policemen walked: plodding, watchful, patient.

Thieves watched for their chances.

Pickpockets made theirs.

It isn't even remotely true that everyone in the East End, from Wapping to Rotherhithe, or from Bethnal Green to Whitechapel, is a criminal, or even criminally inclined. But ask any London policeman where crime and criminals flourish most, and he will unhesitatingly point to this part of the city. A few might say that at times there was a greater concentration of vice in the West End Square Mile, but very few are sure.

Most of this East End trouble area came within the jurisdiction of G5 Division. The Division had picked officers and picked men, and knew its job inside out. Like every other section of the London police it was under-staffed, but it was more generously treated than most.

Every policeman in the Division knew Birdy, and most of them knew Birdy's "wife." An odd thing about Birdy was that he looked small, mean, sneaky and nasty altogether, yet he wasn't. He had a kind of morality. He had a kind of courage. He acted upon a kind of code. Take Birdy and his "wife"—her name was Ethel—out of the slums where they lived and worked, out of the tiny, smelly hovel with its front door opening onto the pavement, put them in one of the clean sweet-smelling suburbs, and Birdy might be heard to say that his wife was the best woman in the world, and Ethel would certainly be heard to say that they didn't come any better than her Birdy.

He had a slightly hunched back, and was sparrow-thin, but very bright with a Cockney's twang and a Cockney's swift repartee.

Now he looked into Ethel's scared eyes.

"'Ow'd you know?" he asked and caught his breath.

"Murphy's been around," she said. "Someone told me at Shippy's, so I went 'ome. 'E come to see me, wanted to know where to find you."

"Murphy," echoed Birdy, and licked his lips.

"Syd's at one corner, Hicky at another," Ethel went on, "waiting for you."

"Syd," echoed Birdy, "and—" He didn't repeat "Hicky."

"Any—any of the kids in?"

"Dunno."

"Look here," said Birdy, and licked his lips again, "we got to make sure they don't 'urt the kids. You better go rahnd to the Pie Shop, or git Dais to go, or telephone, see?"

"Okay, but what about you?"

Birdy said: "I'll be okay." He twisted his lips into a smile that called for a lot of courage, and did nothing to betray the suffocating fear which made his heart beat with a kind of sluggish reluctance. "I'll lie low fer a bit, don'chew worry."

"But, Birdy—" Ethel looked, felt and sounded anguished.

"You look arter yourself," Birdy urged, "and leave me to look arter myself, Ethel. Scram, ducky." He gave her a slap, then turned away from the surging, growling traffic toward the bowels of the earth and the Underground that swallowed London's millions, gestated, and then spewed them up. A train was roaring down below. It stopped. A great surge of people, all eyes blinking, came up the wide stairs toward the welcoming light. Birdy was pressed against the wall, close to a colorful tobacco kiosk, where a bright-haired woman began to serve as fast as she could.

Then the crowd passed, and for a moment there was calm.

Birdy had only one idea: to get away from here. There was no safety in the East End. There was little safety anywhere, once "they" came after him, or after anyone. He knew, because he had been on the run once before, and it had lasted for several weeks—until the police had cleaned up the gang that had come for him.

He fingered the scar beneath his right eye: a vitriol scar. He still didn't know what had saved him from being blinded.

He reached the top of the stairs. A man wearing a purple muffler, a light-weight, American-style coat with big stains on the wide lapels, was at the foot, grinning up at him. In the distance, another train rumbled.

Birdy missed a step when he saw the man. He did not reason, because panic came too close. The only sound he could hear now was the banging of his heart: painful, frightening. This meant that "they" were out in strength. The Murphy gang was the strongest in London at the moment, twenty or thirty strong. Like all the successful gangs, and those which flourished at all, it restricted its activities, worked mostly within the G5 boundary, and operated mostly against rival crooks. It had cannibal instincts. Its members were brutish, sadistic and utterly without scruple. It wasn't a gang in the sense that it had headquarters or acted in concert, but only in that it accepted Murphy's leadership. He got the jobs, paid the men off, gave them protection; he would hide them, get them alibis, do anything that was necessary to keep them safe from the law—and he would get his man. Now he had been given a job, and Birdy thought he knew who had given it to him.

Chang.

The job was simply to "get" Birdy.

Birdy didn't know any more than that. It might mean to kill him; it might mean to maim him; it might mean to torture him. There was no end to what it might mean, and that was one of the worst fears: the uncertainty. Only two weeks ago, "they'd" gone after that poor little cove, Charlie Lin. Lin, half Chinese, half Cockney, was runner for a fence, and had kept more than his share of payment for a job. He had probably been cheated for years and driven to desperation, running the risks of taking money to the thief and the hot goods to the fence. He'd kept back a fiver, and the fence had hired Murphy.

One part of Birdy's mind told him that the fence wouldn't have done that if a fiver had been the only thing at stake. More likely, the fence was frightened in case Lin squealed.

Lin was in hospital, being well looked after. At least he wasn't frightened any more. They'd amputated his right leg and the fingers of his left hand, and there was some doubt whether he would ever be able to see again. He'd been found in a battered heap in a rubber warehouse, and there was no trace of the brutes who had done it, although the East End—including G5 Division—knew that it had been a Murphy job.

Murphy hadn't laid a hand on him.

No one knew who had—for Murphy would have given the order to four or five of the boys, who wouldn't talk except among themselves. One might have a drink too many and say what he shouldn't, but that didn't happen very often. Usually orders were given at a café in the Mile End Road—a place called Shippy's, after its owner, whose name was Shipham.

"Shippy's" was a byword.

Well, there was Lin . . .

There was the swaggering man with the broad grin at the foot of the steps.

Birdy turned away as a train rumbled in, another one from the West End. This would disgorge its hundreds, too. He hurried, to get out of the station first, and then saw Ali.

Ali was a lascar.

No one knew when Ali had last been aboard ship, and it didn't matter. He was a little Indian who spoke broken English, had smooth, dark skin, beautiful black eyes and beautiful, shiny black hair: a model for any painter. No one quite knew what went on in his mind, no one quite knew what he did with his days, but they knew him for a remarkably able knife artist. Ali could carve patterns on cheek or belly, arm or breast. He was lounging against the telephone kiosk, with his right hand in his pocket.

He was right-handed.

Birdy missed a step.

A policeman, big and genial, and hot in thick serge, came along, saw Ali, and lost his smile. Ali had never been inside, and had never had his prints taken, and it was the oath of every man on the beat in the Division to get him. Ali stared back at the policeman. He didn't smile, either, but looked with an unmistakable impudence which could make a level-headed policeman lose his temper. The temptation to break Ali's neck was sometimes overpowering.

The train roared into the station.

Birdy waited. The policeman walked on, but took up a position as if Ali's expression warned him of impending trouble, and he meant to stop it. Then the crowd surged up the steps, caught up with Birdy and swept him out of the wide open mouth and past Ali. He caught a glimpse of Ali trying to breast the tide of humanity and keep level, but pilgrims bathing in the holy water of the Ganges could not have kept him away more successfully.

Birdy nipped across the road.

No member of Murphy's gang was in sight, as far as he could judge, but he didn't know all of Murphy's gang; no one did. That was another of the factors which made it unspeakable horror to be hunted by the gang. Birdy could go to the police and ask for protection, and he would get it for a while; only for a while. Once he did that, he would cut off all hope of the future. The whole of the fraternity would turn against him, against Ethel and against the kids. They knew he squeaked sometimes, but they also knew that he squeaked only about dope, and that his daughter, by his first and real wife, had been an addict. They didn't blame Birdy for what he did, but if he stepped outside that one form of squeaking, they'd turn on him.

If he couldn't look after himself, they'd have no time for him, either.

He was in this on his own, and the heat was on. His hope was to get somewhere to lie low until it was off. The police might get Chang, and if Chang couldn't pay Murphy, Murphy wouldn't be interested. It was a matter of time.

Birdy turned down a narrow street leading toward Tower Hill. The East End was too hot for him, his best chance was down in the city, in one of the warehouses. One could live there for days, for weeks, without being seen, emerging only after dark, feeding at one of the little coffee stalls at Billingsgate. It would be dark in an hour and a half; if he could keep safe until after dark he would be all right.

There was one other serious worry: Ethel.

Birdy was sweating.

Murphy would know that he wouldn't tell Ethel where he was going, wouldn't he? Murphy was bad, Murphy's gang didn't care whether they worked on a man or a woman, but they didn't waste their time. They'd be sure that he, Birdy, hadn't confided in Ethel—

Wouldn't they?

He reached the end of a narrow road which led to Tower Hill, and saw Lefty.

Lefty was a snowy-haired youth of nineteen, who looked cherubic enough for Leonardo. His strength was the broken beer bottle, thrust into a man's face and twisted. He was one of Murphy's gang.

Had he heard about the hunt for Birdy?

Birdy nipped back into a doorway, but didn't go fast enough. Lefty didn't smile, didn't change his expression, just sauntered toward Birdy. He wore a big, baggy, black jacket and there was a bulge, the kind of bulge likely to be made by a beer bottle with the neck smashed off. This was in his left-hand pocket. He was called Lefty for the obvious reason.

Birdy turned and ran.

Lefty didn't run; he whistled softly. It was only a matter of time.

Gideon looked at the clock; it was just after six. He yawned, but it was much too early to start yawning. This was a day which might last its full twenty-four hours. He knew himself well; what he needed now was a good meal, well-cooked vegetables and some good red meat, a pint of beer and forty winks. Once he'd had all that he would be all right, but he might not have time.

Lemaitre was out again.

The telephone bell rang.

"Gideon," said Gideon. "Oh, hallo, Fred, what's on?"

He listened, turned down his lips, made one or two notes, muttered an unenthusiastic thanks, and put the receiver down. He began to doodle on a blotting pad, and after a couple of minutes told himself that it was further evidence of the fact that he was running down, and needed replenishing.

Lemaitre came in.

"George," he said, as a man with a worry, "I've just been downstairs to see my missus. Remember, I'm a married man? I forgot that I told her we'd go along for a snack to the Troc, and blow me, she's got tickets for the Arthur Askey show. If I can't go, *you've* got to tell her." His anxiety was comical.

Gideon said: "How long've you got?"

"She's come with the handcuffs," Lemaitre said.

"About the only way they'll ever drag us away," Gideon grunted. "Wouldn't be a bad idea if we laid on a campaign. Now if Kate—" he drove the fanciful thought off. "Okay, Lem, I don't know that there's anything to keep you." What he did know was that this would keep him here until the small hours. "Just had a word with Fred Hartley."

" 'Bout Birdy?"

"Yes. The Murphy gang's out."

Lemaitre said: "Oh, gawd! Poor tick's had it now."

"One day we'll get round to Murphy," Gideon said. "Anyway, Birdy's on the run. We're all looking out for him, and if our chaps find him first they'll pull him in on a charge. Not that Birdy'll want that. Still—" Gideon stood up slowly. He felt very hungry, the kind of raw emptiness that affected one's nerves and muscles, made one sag, started the tight feeling at the back of the eyes. "And Fred's worried about Birdy's woman and the two kids. So he's tipped off Black Jo, and Jo's looking after the family. Murphy won't risk a gang fight, I shouldn't think, but Black Jo won't lift a finger to help Birdy, although he'll help the woman. High life in civilized London!" He scratched his chin. "Send for a sergeant, Lem, and then sort everything out so that it's in apple-pie order when I get back."

"Okay. Where you going?"

"Across to the pub to get a square meal, and I'll tell Fifi about her good luck on the way!"

He was smiling when he went outside; he always smiled when he thought of Lemaitre's wife as Fifi, which was her real name. A French grandmother's influence—or was it grandfather? Skittish little blonde, no better than she ought to be, but then, Lem Lemaitre wasn't exactly a one-woman man. The frailty of human nature—

Fifi was in the main hall, and there was an exceptionally good-looking constable on duty there. She was overdressed in a plum-colored suit and a cherry-and-plum hat, and didn't look bored. Gideon told her Lem would be down in a few minutes, and then walked across the yard toward Cannon Row and the convenient pub where he knew he could get a meal that any trencherman would enjoy. He could afford to relax for half an hour or so, too. It was easy to forget that the Yard didn't stop working, whatever he or anyone else did. Thousands of coppers were on the lookout for that Austin with a Michelin tire, and there was just a chance that they'd have some luck tonight.

Odd thing, that tire.

He thought about it a lot during the meal—roast saddle of mutton, mint sauce and new potatoes, with rich, fatty gravy—probably the potatoes came out of a tin, but they had the true Jersey flavor. He ploughed steadily through the meal, refusing to be hurried, making it clear that he didn't want to talk to the other Yard men, the reporters and a couple of sergeants from Cannon Row Police Station who were at the bar.

Chang—Foster—the Battersea riverside—the Waterloo Station job. If it were the same tire, and there wasn't much doubt, this could really lead to something big. But it connected Chang with some of the post-office robberies, and that was a very nasty possibility. The worst thing about the mail-van jobs was the tips that the robbers had in advance. They always knew when a van would have a valuable load on; they knew when it would leave one place and was due at another; and of late, Yard men on duty at key points had been attacked and prevented from going to the rescue. Today's two morning jobs had suggested a break in the system, but now—

Had Foster been one source of the leakage?

Foster wouldn't have known anything about the Waterloo job, would he?

The door opened, and King-Hadden, the Superintendent of Fingerprints, came in. If Gideon had a close friend at the Yard, as apart from a mass of good friends with mutual liking, it was King-Hadden. This man had succeeded one of the most brilliant fingerprint men the Yard had ever had, and he wasn't doing so badly. In fact, what King-Hadden didn't know about prints no one knew. He was a world authority, and in the middle forties; he couldn't get any higher.

"Hallo, George."

"Come and sit down, Nick."

"Thanks." The barmaid's help hovered. "Bessie—double whiskey and not too much soda, please." He dropped down into a chair opposite Gideon. "Got some good news for you, chum," he said.

"Wassat?" Gideon's mouth was full of succulent roast potato, oozing fat.

King-Hadden grinned as he took a small envelope from his inside breast pocket. He was a big, plump, pale, rather shapeless man, whose intelligent eyes usually held a laugh. Coins chinked in the envelope. He opened it, and let three sixpences roll out onto the cloth; two of them were stained slightly, as if with brown wax.

Gideon knew a dried bloodstain when he saw it.

"Prints on two," said King-Hadden, "middle of the thumb, right index finger—could be the left. It depends on what pocket he had the money in."

"Who and what money?"

"The Islington shop job."

Gideon said sharply: "No!"

"Yes. This was found on the pavement at a bus stop this afternoon, the kid who saw it was being watched by a copper. He recognized bloodstains. They fell out of the pocket of a man dressed in a brown suit, who was waiting for a bus at Islington Town Hall. That's five minutes' walk away from the shop where the old woman was killed. About the time of the job, too. The copper kept his wits about him; lot of good to be said for training some of the uniformed boys in C.I.D. work, whatever there is against it. He turned them in to the Division."

Gideon said: "Any record?" as if it were too much to hope.

"Oh, yes," said King-Hadden blandly, "didn't I tell you?" He looked smug and his eyes glistened. "Identified them as the prints of Arthur George Fessell, who's been inside twice for robbery with violence. The call's gone out for him. See—all we do is your work, while you sit gluttonizing!" He glanced up. "Ta, Bessie, I'll drink your health." He picked up a whiskey and soda, sniffed it, and sipped. "Ah, I needed that. Going home?"

"Tomorrow, maybe!"

"Well, I'm off now," said King-Hadden. "I keep my department up to date. Cheers. By the way, there's another little thing that may amuse you. They've picked up that Austin with the Michelin tire you've been making such a fuss about. Parked in Haymarket. Lemaitre's over there, waiting until the driver turns up for it, and his Fifi's giving him merry hell. Cheers," King-Hadden repeated, and sipped again.

Bessie, flat-breasted and big-handed, approached them again.

"Like any sweet, Mr. Gideon?"

Gideon was rubbing his hands together, and looking as pleased as a prize-winner schoolboy.

"I do, Bessie," he said. "Treacle pudding's on, isn't it? Plenty of treacle, remember. And after that a bit of Dorset Blue and some butter. This isn't such a bad day after all," he confided in King-Hadden. "We got Sayer, we've got a line on the Islington chap, Fessell you say? and now this tire—not at *all* a bad day. Let me buy you a drink."

"One's enough before I drive to the danger of the public," said the flabby man. "How's Kate?"

"Fine!"

"Must have a Sunday together again when the weather gets a bit better," said King-Hadden. "Might make it this week end if it keeps like to-day. Meg'd like it. Well, good luck, hope you catch 'em all, but don't forget the day's only just started!" He sipped again. "Be a funny thing if we could sit back now and know in advance what's going to happen tonight, wouldn't it? What's sure to happen? A dozen burglaries, a murder, dopies getting dopier, girls being laid for the first time, someone sitting back and plotting a coup for tomorrow, someone getting rid of the thirty thousand quid they picked up at Waterloo—who'd be a copper?" He finished his drink. "So long, George."

He went out.

Two minutes later, Birdy's wife came in.

12 . Two Tales of Jewelry

GIDEON recognized Ethel Merrick on the instant, long before she saw him. He judged from the expression on the faces of some of the other men that they also recognized her. She stood there, wearing a gray suit and a white blouse, a huge, frilly blouse which was stretched so tightly that it looked as if someone had stuffed it as sausage meat or sage and onions in a turkey. She had on a coat that was too small for her, and strained open at the front. Her small red hat had a blue feather broken at the tip, and her patent-leather shoes had very high heels. No one could fail to see her distress, no one could miss the graceful shapeliness of those calves and ankles.

Then she saw Gideon, opened her mouth, gulped, and walked toward him.

He stood up.

No one else watched now.

"Hallo, Mrs. Merrick," Gideon said, "come and sit down."

He could hear her agitated, bubbly breathing, almost as if she were asthmatic. She was pale, her forehead and upper lip were wet with sweat. Gideon pulled out a chair, and she licked her lips as she sat down, and then eased her coat under the right arm. Bessie, who had a wonderful sense of timing, appeared with the treacle pudding.

"What will you have, Mrs. Merrick?" asked Gideon.

"Oo, thanks ever so!" Ethel caught her breath. "Could I—could I 'ave a gin and It? I need to buck meself up a bit."

"Of course you can. Double gin and a splash of Italian, Bessie," said Gideon. "Cigarette, Mrs. Merrick?" The big case, with one side filled with cigarettes, the other half empty, was held out in front of her.

"Ta," she breathed, and when she had settled down, added gustily: "It's ever so good of you to make me feel at home like this, Mr. Gideon. I wouldn't have come if I wasn't so worried about Birdy." Then her fear affected her words. "They—they're *arter* him!"

Gideon said calmly: "Who is, d'you know?"

"Why, Murphy's gang! Mr. Gideon, I know Birdy's done a lot of criminal things, but—oo, *ta*, dearie." She almost snatched the glass out of Bessie's hand, for Bessie also had a trick of speed when it was necessary, and gulped. "Ooh, that's better. But he's not bad, like some people, like that Murphy for instance. He—"

"Has Murphy threatened you?" asked Gideon hopefully.

"Well, no, not in so many words, but that don't count, do it? He come and asked where Birdy was, said he just had to see him, that's enough for me. Mr. Gideon, can't you pull Birdy in?"

"He's got a clean sheet these past few weeks, Mrs. Merrick."

"Oh," said Ethel Merrick, " 'e 'as, 'as 'e?" She had given up the struggle with aspirates. "Well, it's not that I like squealing on me own ole man, but don'chew believe it. Remember the Marshall Street jeweler's job? That was Birdy! Got some of the rings at home now; 'e—'e 'id them," she added hastily, "I come across them by accident. Ain't that enough, Mr. Gideon?"

It was plenty.

She knew that if she appealed for police help against Murphy, it would do Birdy a lot of harm. She knew that she dared not go to the Division, because it would be reported. She also knew that if the police wanted Birdy for a "job" it would be a different matter. He would get at least three years if he were sent down for the Marshall Street robbery, and she thought it worth sending him down; that was a measure of her fear.

Gideon didn't want Birdy inside, but he'd have to put him there.

"All right, Mrs. Merrick," he said, "I'll do what I can. We knew that Birdy was in trouble and we're looking out for him. Don't worry too much. This'll have to be done from the local station, you know that—"

"So long as you'll fix it," Ethel pleaded.

Gideon went across to the Yard and "fixed it." There was no news of Birdy. There was no further word from Lemaitre. Fifi was probably on her way to the theater by herself now—Gideon hoped she would not pick up a "friend." The only man at the Yard who didn't know most of what there was to know about Fifi was Lemaitre.

Gideon forgot that.

There was the fingerprint job that King-Hadden had done, and now that he saw photographs of the coins, enlarged to ten times their real size, he was able to marvel at the efficiency of King-Hadden's work; the fragment of the fingerprint on the bloodstained coins was so fractional that few men would have tried to identify it. With luck, it would hang Fessell, whose dossier was on Gideon's desk. It made ugly reading.

Gideon began to wonder wryly about King-Hadden's airy talk of the day "just beginning."

Dusk was falling, the day's brightness had quite gone, there were lights at some of the windows across the courtyards, and he could see lights on the cars and buses which passed along Parliament Street; he could see a few yards of the street from the window, too.

What was certain to happen? King-Hadden had asked.

Burglary; robbery with violence; murder—no, it wasn't as bad as that yet; murder was certain once or twice a week, but not once a day. There was the whole range of crimes, from major to minor. At this moment, men were getting themselves into the toils of women who would never let go, blackmail was being nurtured, frightened people were blustering; there were young girls, perhaps completely innocent girls like Penelope, girls much younger than Pru, smoking their first reefer, feeling a terrific excitement and a tremendous kick and not knowing that they were on the way down to hell upon earth.

Somewhere men and women were out at dinner or at the pictures, who would go home and find their houses burgled. People were sitting at their own table at this very moment, not knowing that a thief had broken in and was even now raiding the woman's bedroom above their heads. It was a never-ending cycle. Gideon's one hope was that whatever happened, it would happen in such a way that he did not have to tackle anything new tonight.

His telephone rang.

"Gideon."

"There's a Mrs. Addinson here, sir," the hall sergeant told him. "She would be glad if you could spare her a few minutes."

Foster's sister had made up, and dressed for effect. Black suited her, the white blouse and cuffs gave a touch of purity. Nice-looking, wholesome woman. Only her eyes hinted at strain, and this eased when Gideon made her welcome and gave her a cigarette. No two women could contrast more sharply than Florence Addinson and Birdy's wife.

"What can I do for you, Mrs. Addinson?" He was almost casual.

"I've come because I think I can help you," she said.

Gideon didn't show how that quickened his pulse.

"That's good. How?"

"I've been going over everything that Eric's been doing and saying," she said. "We had a—a quarrel a night or two ago, because he was never in. He used to pretend he was always on duty, but I knew he wasn't. I said so, and—and he flared up."

"I see," Gideon said. He did not intend to help her; just to let it come. There was still the possibility that she was involved, even though her visit made that seem less likely.

"You may not think so, but I really want to help," she said a little sharply. "I'm reconciled to the fact that Eric was—was doing wrong. I'd like to think that whoever made him do it suffers, too."

Gideon relaxed.

"You don't want that any more than we do." He looked almost eager. "Really think you can help?"

"I'm not sure, but something he said might give you something to go on —unless you *know* who bribed him." She added that so quickly and unexpectedly that it was possible to believe that it was the focal point of her visit; that she had really come to try to find out how much he knew.

Would Chang, would anyone, venture such tactics?

Gideon just couldn't be sure.

"We guess a lot," he said, and left it at that. "What was it that your brother said?"

"He was really talking to himself," Foster's sister answered. "As he was going out of the room, he said: 'I'd be a damned sight better off living with Estelle.' I didn't know whom he meant; I'd never heard him talk of a girl named Estelle. But a woman of that name telephoned me this evening."

Now she really sparked his interest.

"Oh? What about? Eric?"

"Yes," Foster's sister said wryly. "She said that Eric had been murdered. She sounded quite hysterical, and rang off before I could get any more sense out of her." Flo Addinson paused, eying Gideon very intently, before she went on: "Was Eric murdered?"

Gideon answered bluntly: "It's just possible."

After a pause, Foster's sister said quietly: "Thank you. I thought you might look for this woman, Estelle."

"Believe me, we'll look for her," Gideon promised. "You've given us a lead which might be invaluable. If there's anything else—"

"There's just one thing," she said. "I'd like to help actively, and I think I might be able to."

Now he was wary. "How, Mrs. Addinson?"

"I could harass Chang," she said. "There's a picture of a dancer outside his office, and her name's Estelle. It could be the same one." How Lemaitre would benefit from some of her caution! "I thought if I went to see Chang, asked him about what really happened, asked about Eric and Estelle—"

"No," Gideon was abrupt, "leave Estelle right out of it; you'd only warn

Chang that we were interested in her. I'll check the dancer, though, that's most useful."

He stopped.

"May I try to harass Chang?" she asked, and added very quickly, almost fiercely: "I don't think anything could keep me away, but if—if you could suggest how to handle him—"

Gideon chuckled.

"Not bad," he said. "Admire your honesty, Mrs. Addinson. I don't think you'll ever be able to shake Chang, but you might be able to try one angle."

She leaned forward eagerly.

"If there was an association between Chang and your brother, and Chang thinks your brother confided in you, he'll be very edgy," Gideon said. "Edgy men make mistakes. Hm." He hesitated. "Hm, yes," he repeated. "Go along and see him, Mrs. Addinson; give him cause to think you know something. He'll probably try to square you, although he might conceivably try to harm—"

"Oh, he wouldn't dare *that*," she exclaimed. "Not if I told him you were having me followed."

Gideon shook his head sagely.

"You've got a head for this kind of thing," he conceded. "We'll follow you, all right. Go home, Mrs. Addinson, and wait for word from us. We won't keep you long."

They shook hands, and he walked with her to the lift. As she went down, he watched and reflected that she was a very fine-looking, finely-built woman.

Five minutes later, he'd laid on inquiries about the unknown Estelle, and made arrangements for Foster's sister to be followed. After that, he was able to work for twenty minutes without being interrupted.

Perhaps it was going to be a quiet night, after all.

He knew nothing of Alec Fitzroy.

Fitzroy was in his West End flat, not very far from Chang's restaurant, but just outside the fringes of Soho. He stood in the tiny bathroom, shaving. His hand was absolutely steady; he was testing his nerve, making quite sure that it wouldn't let him down.

When he had finished shaving, he felt quite confident.

He left the bathroom, lit a cigarette, and looked at a decanter of whiskey. He wanted a drink, but told himself that it might be a sign of weakness, and that he ought not to have one.

He put the temptation behind him by going into his bedroom. He sat on the side of the bed, and went carefully through all the plans to rob the safe deposit in Wattle Street. Nothing was written down, and only he knew all the arrangements for the coup. He did not trust either of his cronies with everything, although they were reliable enough.

It would be necessary to start for the safe-deposit building soon. The others, who had further to travel, were already on their way. The escape car was parked—a car which had been left near the Mid-Union Safe Deposit building nightly for several weeks, so there would be nothing unusual about it tonight—except that when it was driven off it would be carrying a fortune.

He checked over every single part of the plan, and decided again that it was foolproof.

He jumped up, lit a cigarette, and went into the living room. This time he didn't argue with himself, but poured a tot of whiskey, and tossed it down. He felt angry because of the word "foolproof"; he told himself that his attitude was completely realistic, and only a fool would call this a job which couldn't go wrong.

It wasn't likely to, but it could.

If an inspector or official of the Mid-Union Company were to visit the safe deposit, he would be familiar with all of the night staff, and, seeing strangers, would certainly try to raise an alarm. But he'd be bound to ask questions, and so give his own identity away. He could be dealt with before doing any harm, like the other members of the night staff would be.

Perhaps it wasn't foolproof; but it certainly wasn't far short.

Fitzroy went back into the bedroom, knelt down in front of a dressing chest, opened the bottom drawer, and rummaged among the underclothes in it.

He drew out a gun and some ammunition. He loaded the gun, a .32 automatic, and slipped it into his pocket. Then he had another whiskey, and left his flat.

The little widow with whom the Reverend Julian Small lodged watched him as he sat at the table, that evening, toying with his food. She was a woman of mercifully few words, one of the few regular churchgoers in the district, and a familiar if faded figure at St. Mary's. She was fond of the new curate, but knew as well as he did that the task was too big for him; at least, he showed no sign that he would ever be able to handle it well.

He was far too gentle.

She was surprised by that, in some ways. When his luggage had arrived a few months ago, and she had looked through it, she had found boxing gloves and other things to indicate that he was a dab at games and sports. So when the weedy-looking, rather timid man with the narrow nostrils had arrived on the doorstep, she hadn't realized that it was her lodger.

She had given up hope for him now.

Julian Small had almost given up hope for himself.

He had not properly recovered from the fall that morning. His nose was raw as well as red, and painful whenever he touched it, which was often, because he had a slight cold. His bitterness had gone, however, and in its place there was a sense of shame—that he should have betrayed his trust as he had; "suffer little children—"

He could not find the way to their confidence or their friendship. It wasn't their fault; it was his.

He did not wholly convince himself of that, but he had one narrow wedge of hope: the club, tonight. It was officially the St. Mary's Club and twenty-odd years old, but when he had arrived, there had been the bare hall, a few pieces of damaged furniture, a table-tennis top with the plywood warped and chipped, a dart board so badly beaten away by the darts over the years that some holes went right through it. Small had put all this right. There were three new dart boards, a regulation-size table-tennis top with trestles, draughts, dominoes, chess, a small library, and, what he regarded as more important than anything else, plenty of comfortable chairs. Thirty youngsters could sit in upholstered comfort and read books or magazines taken from the club library. There was also a small bar, offering coffee, tea, soft drinks, cakes and biscuits. In fact, everything that a flourishing club of a hundred or so youths could revel in, and—

The club had *eleven* members.

Usually, most of these failed to appear on club nights, Mondays, Wednesdays, Fridays and Saturdays. No one had ever said so to the curate, but he believed that the others had been intimidated by youths who didn't come; or else made to feel ridiculous for having anything to do with him.

There was to be a special effort tonight; each member was to try to bring one new member. Until the string incident, Julian Small had told himself that it might be the turn of the tide, and, as he set out from his lodgings for the hall next to the church, he tried to induce a cheerful mood.

Twenty-two lads and lassies instead of one would make all the difference.

Lights were on in the hall.

It was very quiet.

He realized that this was partly due to the fact that the noises of cranes and derricks were missing. So were all the usual sounds which came from the docks by night. He didn't think much about this, but wondered how many would in fact turn up. Twenty-two was absurdly optimistic. Fifteen? Sixteen? He shivered with a kind of excitement as he drew nearer the hall; fifteen would make it a successful evening, and give him hope for the future.

He glanced across at a light fixed to the wall of a ruined warehouse, nearby. Some movement by it caught his eye, but he couldn't identify the movement. He took no notice until suddenly the warehouse wall light went out.

That made him miss a step.

Tight-lipped, he strode on to the hall. The door was open, light shone out from it, but he saw no one and heard nothing.

He reached it. . . .

He stood quite still on the threshold, feeling almost choked. Nothing was in its proper place. The table-tennis top was in pieces, strewn about the floor; an ax had been used violently. Pieces of a dart board were almost under his feet, as small as corks. Books were ripped open, pages strewed the scrubbed floor like pieces of giant confetti. And the chairs—

There wasn't a whole chair left.

He went in, falteringly. He looked round at this savage destruction of his hopes and at the shocking waste of money which he had needed for himself. He looked round, forgetful of his thin, bruised nose, aware only of disaster.

Then, slowly, he spoke to the deserted room.

"If I ever set my hands on them," he said, "I'll break their bloody necks."

Suddenly, without having been given the slightest warning, he felt in a different mood from anything he had known before. He was savagely, viciously angry.

Also unknown to Gideon, there was Rose Bray.

Rose, at sixteen, was on her first job, and although all of her friends had scoffed when she had said what she was going to do, she was reveling in it. She was a lady's maid. She had a modest but nice little home with her parents, in Acton, and had been to school until she was nearly sixteen. She knew shorthand, typing and was qualified for many other varieties of jobs, but chose to be a lady's maid.

She liked beautiful clothes.

It was not the kind of liking that creates envy. She was content just to see and handle them, to help dress Lady Muriel, who was nice and natural, not at all like she'd expected real ladies to be—so high falutin' and imperious. "Imperious" was a word which Rose's boy friend had used with great scorn when she had told him what she was going to do.

"These rich people," he had added, smartingly, "just a lot of wealthy tarts, that's all they are." And after a moment's pause for research: "Just a lot of *para*sites."

Rose was thinking about her boy friend at the time that Gideon was looking up at the brown spot in the ceiling, without wondering how it had come there. She was thinking that if Dick only knew Lady Muriel and her husband—who wasn't a Lord or a Sir, she didn't quite understand the reason for that but accepted it—he would have an entirely different idea about the wealthy. Certainly they *were* rich. The diamond necklace which Lady

Muriel had left on the dressing table was worth at least fifteen *years'* wages for her father. The value did not intrigue Rose so much as the beauty, and Rose preferred colored jewels to diamonds, which seemed to her so cold.

But more than precious stones, she loved the clothes: the rich satins, the smooth velvets, the tulles, the luxurious silks, the colors which were so beautiful that they often made her catch her breath. There were three large wardrobes, all filled with clothes, but Rose's favorites were in the dressing room: the evening gowns and cocktail dresses.

Sometimes she would open the door, just to look at and to touch the materials.

Many things here had taken some getting used to: this room, for one. It had two doors, one opening into the passage, the other into the bedroom. And across the bedroom—with its two high beds, the rich, soft bedclothes and the twin canopies, each rather like a big baby's crib—was *his* dressing room. Rose did not go in there much; just occasionally to get something if his valet, Forbes, was out.

Rose did not like Forbes. She could not have explained why, but she didn't trust him.

That evening, Lady Muriel and Mr. Simister were downstairs, with friends. About a dozen in all; just a little informal cocktail party, Lady Muriel had said, as she had carelessly selected a dress which had cost over a hundred guineas. Rose was probably one of the few remaining people who could admire such an attitude toward money.

She stood looking at a rich, red velvet gown, and felt irresistibly drawn toward it, longing to smooth the pile of the velvet between her fingers.

She heard a sound in the bedroom.

It did not occur to her that anything was wrong, but she assumed that Lady Muriel had come upstairs for something she'd forgotten. The carpet on the floor of the dressing room was thick, muffling the sound of her footsteps as she went toward the communicating door.

She actually began to open it, and then saw the man.

He was crouching over the dressing table. In his right hand was the diamond necklace. There were other jewels in the trinket box which he had taken out of a drawer, a drawer usually kept locked. He didn't look up. She couldn't see his face, because of the brown scarf which was drawn up over his nose, but she saw that he wore gloves, which looked skin tight.

After the first shock, Rose felt just one thing: fear. It made her want to run away crying for help. Her heart suddenly began to beat so fast that she felt as if she were choking. She knew that her cheeks went chalk white. She watched, hypnotized, as the man thrust the jewels into a small bag—it looked rather like a chamois leather, the kind window cleaners used. She heard the hard stones grate against each other.

She knew what she had to do, if only she could make her legs do what she told them. It was difficult even to turn round. She let the door go, and managed to turn, then stood quite still; her legs simply would not move. Gradually, she made them. She reached the passage door, which was closed, turned the handle and pulled; the door scraped along the carpet and the sound seemed very loud to her.

If only Forbes would come!

She heard no other sound. The big house in Madeson Square, overlooking beech and plane trees and a small grass plot where the people of the square aired and exercised their dogs, was solid and silent. A door closed out sound as well as sight.

The passage was carpeted.

She crept out of the dressing room, and now she found that her legs wanted to move too quickly, wanted to run. She dared not. She must go past that door and then downstairs to raise the alarm; if she shouted or if she ran she would warn the thief and he would get away.

Being out here, with the bedroom door closed, she felt safe; excitement replaced the panicky fear. Suddenly she saw herself as the heroine: the girl who had saved Lady Muriel's jewels. It would be easy! She tiptoed toward the door—yes, it was closed, just as it had been when she had passed. It wasn't far to the head of the stairs, and once she reached them she could hurry down.

She drew level with the door.

It opened, and the thief grabbed at her.

13 . The Thief

ROSE saw the door open, the grasping hand, the masked face, in the same awful moment of fear. She opened her mouth wide, to scream, but the thief slapped her face. He hurt less than he terrified her. She choked back the scream. He shifted his grip, took her wrist and dragged her into the bedroom.

The door slammed.

"Don't make a sound or I'll break your neck," he growled behind the mask.

She could not have made a sound then, even to save her neck. He was hurting her arm, and pulled her across the room, toward the beds. *Toward the beds.* Then he changed the direction, first pulled and then pushed her into a corner. She did not realize that they were safe, here, from the sight of anyone outside, especially the people on the other side of the square.

"Keep your voice low. Have you warned anyone?"

She couldn't get a word out, could only make the shape of the words: "*No, no, no, no, no.*"

"If you're lying to me, I'll—"

"*No, no, no!*"

"You'd better be telling the truth," he said roughly. "Turn round."

"*No!*" That gasp came out.

"Turn round!" he said in a harsh whisper, and pulled at her shoulder. She gasped again, and turned, helplessly. Then something fell over her head; she started to scream until it reached her mouth, thick and muffling; then it was drawn tight, and she could hardly breathe. Next moment, she felt her hands seized, felt tightness at her wrists, and then realized that he had tied her wrists together behind her.

He spun her round again.

"Sit down," he said, and before she could realize what the order meant, he bent down and picked her up, then dumped her heavily on the floor. With her hands behind her, she couldn't get up easily. The scarf or whatever it was still bit into her mouth, and she was struggling for breath.

He left her.

He must have spent another three or four minutes at the dressing table, cramming things into the wash-leather bag. Then he turned away, and took notice of her again. She had not recovered from the first fear, and all this made it much, much worse.

"Now what am I going to do with you?" he said softly. "If you raise the alarm—"

He came toward her slowly. She wanted to cry out that she wouldn't raise the alarm; if only he would go, she'd never say a word to anyone; but she couldn't utter a sound of any kind. He stood looking down at her. He wasn't really very big, but from that angle he looked enormous, and she was absolutely in his power. All the stories of murder she had ever heard about seemed to flash through her mind.

"Get up," he said, as if he had made up his mind what to do, and she cringed away from him. He bent down, took her wrist, and pulled her to her feet. Then he pushed her toward the dressing room. Her legs moved automatically; she thought she was bound to fall on her face.

The lovely clothes were in the wardrobe.

"Just the job," he said, and hustled her forward. "Get in." He meant, "Get into the wardrobe with the clothes." "Go on, Rosie, get in, I won't hurt you!"

She was breathing through her nose, and felt as if she could never breathe freely again, was almost choked. And she was too frightened to believe what he said. Something made him change his mind, too. He stretched out an arm to her shoulder, turned her round, and loosened the scarf round her mouth; it dropped to her neck.

"My, my," he said, "you're quite something; pity we didn't meet some other place."

Suddenly he pulled her to him and squeezed her. She felt his hard, lean body, the thudding of his heart. She felt the surge of desire in him, too, and a different fear began to choke her. She couldn't breathe; she felt his hands—

He let her go.

"Get inside," he said harshly, "and if you open your trap for the next five minutes, you'll wish you'd never been born."

He thrust her back among the luxurious dresses, among thousands of pounds' worth of the most exclusive models by the world's great designers, and then closed the door. She heard the key in the lock. She leaned back against a velvet gown, slipping further and further down, still frightened, and also disturbed in a different way. She could not forget the hardness of his body against her.

Then she slipped down, until she was almost full length on the floor. With her hands behind her, she could turn round. It was blackly dark. She felt herself breathing evenly, but fear soon began to catch up, like the sea sweeping over her in waves.

She shouted, and the sound was muffled; she knew that it couldn't be heard.

She started to struggle and to shout, and was terrified. The blackness became thick, oily, choking, throttling; the blackness became peopled with strange shapes, strange, bright, dazzling, blinding colors. After a while she was screaming without knowing what she was doing. . . .

Then the door opened: "Good Lord!" exclaimed Lady Muriel's husband. "What—here, Inspector, here's the maid, here she is!"

Rose felt much better.

Everyone had been very kind, especially Lady Muriel and Mr. Simister. The police had been quite nice, too. The man Mr. Simister called Inspector was ever so young, really. She'd had some hot coffee, very sweet, and then a weak whiskey and water, and the doctor—Lady Muriel's own doctor—had been and examined her, and said that she wouldn't suffer much harm. Then the Inspector had started to question her, making her remember everything she had seen and everything that had been said. She didn't like it. Twice Lady Muriel asked him if it were really necessary, and in a firm but friendly way he said it was essential.

Then something he said made her remember that the thief had called her Rosie.

"Are you sure?" The Inspector's voice sharpened.

"Oh, yes! Of course I am."

"How often did he use your name?"

"Well, only once, I remember. . . ."

A few minutes afterward, the Inspector spoke to Mr. Simister in a voice which Rose was supposed not to hear but which she heard quite clearly: "If it's someone who knew the name of the maid, it suggests co-operation from your staff. And a key to the trinket box was used, remember? I think I'd better see the staff at once, Mr. Simister, especially anyone who knew this suite well."

Lady Muriel said in a startled voice: "Not *Forbes.*"

"Don't be silly, darling," Mr. Simister said sharply.

There was a moment almost of conflict; then Lady Muriel turned to Rose. "You look tired, Rose, and I'm sure the Inspector won't want you any more now." Her glance at the Inspector suggested that he had better not. "Come along to the morning room, and I'll get you something."

She put a hand on Rose's arm.

It was rather wonderful, Rose thought, walking side by side with Lady Muriel, who was a head taller, very *very* beautiful, and wearing that lovely cocktail gown which was full of rich colors. It was almost like walking alongside a friend.

Behind them, Mr. Simister was talking worriedly to the Inspector.

The office was hot. April was behaving oddly; you could usually rely on a chilly evening, but even with one window open, it was warm. Gideon had his coat off, his waistcoat open, his tie hanging down, his sleeves rolled up. For once his hair was ruffled. He was talking first into one telephone and then into another, putting down and lifting receivers as if he were juggling with Indian clubs. The smooth transition from one case to the next came much in the way that a brilliant linguist can change from one language to another without any apparent interruption in thought.

And Gideon made notes.

"That you, Adams—anything doing in the Madeson Square job? . . . Hmm . . . No, don't bring the valet over here unless you're pretty sure he's involved; no need to put a foot wrong . . . Yes, old chap, watch him if you like. . . . How's that maid, what's her name? . . . Yes, Rose . . . Good. Any prints? . . . Hmm, looks as if the valet's the chief hope. 'By."

There was hardly a pause before he turned to the other telephone, already in his left hand.

"Hallo, Lem, sorry to keep you. Any luck? . . ." He chuckled. "And you stood Fifi up for this? You're going to know all about it! . . . I know it's not funny, calm down. . . . Well, stay there if you like; we certainly want that chap. Think he's been along already and noticed that the car's being watched? . . . Who've you got with you?"

The other bell started to ring. Gideon lifted the receiver and switched to it swiftly: "Hold on, please." He went back to Lemaitre. "Well, he doesn't look so much like a copper as some of 'em. Give it another hour. 'By."

"Hallo. . . . Oh, Fred, thanks for calling. Any news of Birdy? . . . Pity. . . . Found that junk at his house, did you? Well, spread the story round, won't you? Then if we pick him up, his friends and neighbors will know it's because he's wanted; it won't look as if he came to us for protection. . . . No, I know he didn't. . . . So do I."

There was a moment's lull.

"So do I," he repeated, and meant that he hoped that the Divisional people found Birdy.

The hell of this was that a gang like Murphy's could act almost with impunity; *almost.*

He pulled his wad of notes toward him. These were the scribbled notes he had started to make from the moment he'd come in that morning. Everything that had been attended to he crossed off; only half a dozen items remained, and he wrote these out on a fresh slip of paper. They were mostly trifles, and among them was: Check Basil B. about his evidence on the Moxley job.

He lifted a receiver.

"Know if Chief Inspector Boardman's in?" he said. "Oh—ring his home for me, will you?" He put the receiver down and waited; the other bell rang. "Hallo, Gideon here. Eh? . . . Good Lord!" He found himself chuckling, looked as if he were delighted. "Nice work, glad they don't always get away with it." He chuckled again, and then saw the office door open. "Yes, I'll put some dynamite behind them, but King-Hadden's off duty tonight; it's never so quick when—"

The visitor was the Assistant Commissioner, his sleek gray suit changed to sleek dinner jacket, soft cream shirt, small bow tie: a distinguished man indeed.

". . . okay, Basil," Gideon said, and rang off and looked up smiling. "Didn't expect you back," he remarked.

"I had a dinner date I couldn't miss," the A.C. said, "but wanted an excuse to cut the speeches. How are things going?"

"It's like rain," said Gideon, and then corrected himself. "Hailstorm, rather."

"With an occasional rainbow—what's so funny?"

Gideon chuckled.

"Chap broke into a house in Maida Vale an hour ago, a six-footer apparently, and he had a gun. The woman of the house discovered him and chased him out with an umbrella. He dropped the gun! Empty. Evans was telling me; he can always make a story like that sound twice as funny as it is, but—" Gideon chuckled. "Armed gunman chased by angry woman with umbrella—can't you see the headlines in the morning? It'll keep something off the front page."

"The Waterloo job, I hope."

"Not much chance of that." Gideon grimaced, and told what had happened.

"You've always thought that there was organization in these mail-van jobs, haven't you?" the A.C. asked musingly.

"Some sort of," agreed Gideon. "The pattern's always pretty well the same, isn't it? I'd say that there's a clearing house for information, which always reaches the same chap. He passes it on to different people, and they give him a rake-off. First time I've ever been hopeful is today, if Chang—"

He broke off.

The A.C. lit a cigarette.

"I was wondering," he said, sitting on the arm of the easy chair reserved for visitors. "You've thought that it was worth giving Chang rope, haven't you? Any special reason?"

"You mean, when I heard about Foster from Birdy, why didn't I go for Chang straightaway?" Gideon pinched his nose. "I don't know. Don't suppose I ever shall. I just felt it was the wrong thing to do, but I'm not so sure now. But see what's working out. Birdy squealed on Chang. Chang has put a finger on him, through Murphy. That gives a direct line between Chang and Murphy. Now we know that Murphy is nominal boss of a gang, and that among the people who do jobs for him there's every kind of crook, from killer to snatch artist. Well, if Chang is the man who gets the information about mail vans and passes it on to Murphy, Murphy might pass it further down. I don't say it is the answer, just that it could be. The one certain thing about Murphy's bunch is that they're tough and they're smart and they don't squeal. We've been trying to get Murphy for years, have never pulled him in on anything that counted, and haven't thought it worth while putting him inside for a couple of months. Now we've got a half chance of picking up one of the men who did the Waterloo job today, and if we can lead back from him to Murphy we might really have something."

Gideon paused.

"Yes, you would," agreed the A.C. fervently.

"If we could get Murphy and hit him really hard, it would do more good than we've done at one swipe for months," said Gideon, as if he longed for exactly that. "For *years*. Meanwhile, we've started a new line. I've sent out instructions for all known Murphy men to be checked and to find out if any of them have postmen among their friends. I'm having Chang's customers checked, too, to find out if there are any postmen among them. Or bank managers or clerks, for that matter. It's the first time we've thought of Chang or Murphy together or singly as in any way interested in the mail-van jobs. Could be wrong now, but at least it's giving us a bit of pep for the time being."

"George," said the A.C., "I have never suggested that you don't know your job."

Gideon grinned.

"Thanks! Then there's another angle. Foster's sister had a telephone call from a hysterical woman who said that Foster had been murdered." He deliberately ignored the A.C.'s start of surprise. "Woman named Estelle, apparently a sweetie of Foster's. I started to check, and one of the girls who dances at Chang's club is named Estelle."

"Well, well," murmured the A.C. "Talked to her yet?"

"Haven't found her. She digs in Chelsea, but hasn't been home since morning. As soon as we get a chance, we'll tackle her."

A telephone bell rang, almost before he had finished.

"Excuse me," he said, and plucked the receiver up. "Gideon. . . . *What?*" He bellowed the word, must have deafened the man at the other end of the line, and certainly startled the A.C. "Bring him right over," he said, only a little less boomingly; "nice work, Lem! Wonderful!"

He put the receiver down. The Assistant Commissioner, who knew him in most moods, had seldom seen him show such obvious satisfaction; and that could only come from really good news.

Gideon appeared to want to savor it before passing it on.

"We've got the driver of the Austin with the Michelin tire," he said, at last, and his expression said: "How about *that?*" "Young chap with a scar at the back of his head—the Waterloo post-office driver saw a chap like that, remember?" Gideon was more excited than the A.C. had seen him for years, but he fought against showing it. "Lemaitre's bringing him over. Going to sit in on this interview, sir?" He grinned almost impudently.

The A.C. said: "I think I will, George. That's fine."

"But it's late to have that post-office driver in," decided Gideon, and his pencil sped. "We'll have an identification parade at ten o'clock in the morning. I wonder if this could be *the* day." He got up, to stretch his cramped limbs. "I think a noggin's indicated here; going to have one?"

"On principle and in office hours," said the A.C., "I disapprove. But thanks." The telephone rang. "All right, I'll get the whiskey," he said, and rounded the desk as Gideon picked up the receiver.

"Gideon here."

"Oh . . ."

"Yes, all right. 'By." Gideon rang off, and kept a finger on the cradle of the telephone as the A.C. stooped to open a cupboard in one of the pedestals of his desk. "Fire out at Mince Lane, a big fur warehouse. The fire chief thinks it might be arson. I'd better send Marjoribanks over." He lifted a receiver. "Detective Inspector Marjoribanks, please. . . . Hallo, Marj, got nice job for you. Belinda Blue-eyes thinks that there's arson in Mince Lane —pretty well gutted a warehouse, I gather; have a go as soon as you can.

"Thanks," he added a minute later, and then put the receiver down and took a glass from the A.C., who held a syphon in his right hand. "Splash more, I think," he said, and watched the soda water as it squirted and splashed. "Whoa! Ta. Here's to getting a trail back from this to Chang or Murphy." He ran his tongue along his lips. "No more news of Birdy; I'm worried about that. I—oh, *damn the blurry telephone!*"

"If I were you," said the A.C., "I'd get out for a bit and leave a sergeant in here."

"Blurry sergeants! . . . Gideon . . . Eh? . . . Oh, not bad, but he can keep until morning; hold him at Cannon Row, will you? It won't do him any harm to wriggle a bit. Yes, I'll hold on. It's Percival, from London Airport," he told the A.C. offhandedly. "That Foreign Office chap who pinched the diplomatic bag from the sanctum sanctorum's turned up, complete with bag. It's still full, so we do get results sometimes." He scribbled. "Must let the press have that, quickly, especially the *Globe*; it's been screaming about missing diplomats for two years. Or is it three?" Into the telephone he said, "Violent, is he? Well, get some help; don't let him cut his throat. 'By."

He rang off.

"You rather remind me," said the A.C., sipping his whiskey and soda, "of a bulldozer which never stops moving."

"Don't say that in anyone's hearing or I'll be the Bulldozer for the rest of my stay here, which I sometimes hope won't be long!" Gideon grinned.

He rang the Back Room Inspector to tell them about the arrest of the diplomat.

He had time to light his pipe.

He picked up a telephone at the first ting of the bell.

"Gideon. . . . Oh, yes. . . . Oh, Lor'. I hate those jobs. Can you handle it yourself? . . . Yes, you'll have to stop him, I suppose. Fix it with the stations, ports and airports, but soft pedal a bit." He rang off, forgetting to say " 'by." "That was about Eric Rosenthal—he and his wife have been having a tug-o'-war with their kid, remember? The wife got a court order for custody, and Rosenthal snatched her this evening. What will a thing like this do to a six-year-old girl?"

He shook his head.

He thought of Kate.

The telephone rang.

This time it was news with a vengeance. The man Fessell, wanted in connection with the murder of the old woman in the Islington sweetshop, had been seen in Watford. He should be caught before long.

Then Gideon thought of Birdy Merrick.

He didn't think of a man named Fitzroy, for he had never heard of him.

14 . The Murphy Gang Draws Close

BIRDY stood in a dark doorway. Gaslight showed white and pure behind the glass of a lamp fastened to a wall by an iron bracket. Nearby, the ripple of the water of a backwater of the Thames sounded softly and insistently, as if someone were whispering to him. A long way off there was another whisper of sound: traffic on the Mile End and the Whitechapel Roads.

The river traffic was silent.

It was not often silent, like this; usually a tug chugged along, or hooted; or cargo ships laden down to the Plimsoll line sent their short, urgent blasts to tell the Port of London Authority officials that they were on their way to distant lands. Or a police launch barked in its urgent, questing note, and a searchlight swept the dark, dirty water, looking for unexpected things; or else expected jetsam, such as floating bodies.

This silence was accursed. In it, every little sound could be heard, and Birdy knew that two of Murphy's men were near him; listening. Their ears were as sensitive to the night sounds of London as a Bushman's would be for the night sounds of the forest.

No cranes were working.

The silence was so deep that Birdy could have screamed; and screaming brought death or whatever they planned for him.

Why weren't the cranes busy?

Birdy remembered: there was a strike. Not a full-blooded one, but a nasty, mean little strike—no overtime. Birdy had heard dockers talking about it, some for and some against; but they all obeyed. There was no trade union in crime; criminals were self-employed, uninsured and independent. Now that awful hush fell upon dockland, and upon Birdy. He had wormed his way here after seeing Lefty, and waited for the blessed fall of darkness. He had felt that he dared hope, and stood in the doorway, listening for protecting noises which would not come—and listening, too, for the stealthy sounds which might tell of Ali or the Snide.

The Snide was a knife artist, too.

Lefty was a broken-bottle artist.

Down at the foot of the steps at Aldgate Station there had been a razor artist. So Birdy had a good idea what to expect. They were going to cut him up. Chang had given the word because he had squealed, and now Murphy's gang were going to cut him up.

It would be better to kill himself.

He heard a soft, swift footfall.

His hands went up to his breast, clenched fearfully; his ears strained the quiet; his eyes tried to probe the darkness beyond the clear glow of the gas lamp.

It came again—stealthy, nearer.

A voice whispered: "Come on, Birdy, we've got you cornered."

That was the Snide. The Snide had once been an artist in making lead coins, sludge, snide, call it what you liked; but now he preferred that knife. He wasn't so good as Ali, but he was good.

The sneering, mocking whisper came again: "We've got you cornered."

Everything Birdy knew, everything he sensed, worked in him for his own protection now. Thirty years of East End slum life, most of it with one of the gangs or another—not a fighting member, just a hanger-on—had told him plenty. He knew London and Londoners and Ali and the Snide. That whisper was to work on his nerves, to lure him out of his doorway, to make him run *away* from the sound; and if he did that, he would run into Ali. There might be others, too; he had been crouching here for ten minutes, plenty of time for reinforcements to creep up.

"Give it up, Birdy."

"What part of you shall we send home to Ethel, Birdy?"

The Snide always tormented like this; he'd had an education, and liked to demonstrate it.

"Come on, Birdy—"

Birdy fingered a sardine tin in his coat pocket; he'd picked it up from the curb, at dusk, and it was a weapon of sorts: not of attack, but of defense by ruse. He nicked his finger on the torn edge. He didn't wince, but flinched.

The Snide was very near.

Ali . . . ?

In a moment or two, they would rush him.

Birdy raised the sardine tin, moving it round in his fingers until he found a smooth section which he could grip. He made a few silent swinging motions with his arm, and then tossed the can into the air. It made a funny little twittering noise; the others must wonder what it was. Then there was a hush; then the tin clanged upon the road on the other side of the street.

Birdy darted out of his cover.

In that split second, the Snide would be distracted; at least he ought to be. He would look toward the sound, and Ali would probably do the same thing. That would be Birdy's chance, his only one. He darted out of the doorway, and was revealed for a moment in the white glow.

He saw the Snide, a thin face turned toward the sardine tin. He did not see Ali, but guessed that Ali was behind him.

He leaped forward.

The Snide swung round, the knife glittered. Birdy was very close. He felt the knife cut through his shoulder, and then he drove his knee into the pit of the Snide's stomach with sickening force, and with the accuracy of an expert. He heard the Snide give a groan that was torturing in its anguish, in its tale of dreadful pain. The Snide slid away from him, and Birdy raced on toward the corner, the docks, the ships where he hoped to find refuge.

He heard Ali.

He looked over his shoulder and saw the dark shape of the lascar, and his long shadow cast by the gaslight.

Then he saw a man in front of him.

Lefty . . . ?

Birdy's heart seemed to stop.

Lefty.

He swerved to one side. Lefty moved toward him with the extra speed of twenty-one to forty-one. Birdy was sure, then, that he hadn't a chance. He ran on blindly. He felt Lefty's outstretched hand pluck at his sleeve, but tore himself free. Now all he could do was to run until he fell in his tracks. There was no hope, but he had to go on until they fell upon him and carved him up—or tore him to pieces. Hounds after a fox. Hounds—

He became aware of a different, moving light, coming toward him, bright beams sweeping the street. A blue light showed at the top of the car, with the word *Police*. Birdy could just make out the shapes of the two men in the car.

He heard nothing behind him, but he knew that Lefty and Ali had turned away, in alarm. They might help the Snide or they might leave the Snide to be picked up.

Birdy waited until the car had passed him, and then began to hurry toward the docks. He could get into a crane, or sneak aboard one of the ships; he might even swim across to the other side of the Thames. He'd done it before.

That was, unless a Murphy man was watching him now; or waiting for him in the shadows ahead.

Gideon, his tie knotted loosely, coat on, shirt cuffs undone, bloodshot eyes, obviously very tired, and hat on the back of his head, looked at the sergeant who had just come in. He had nothing against the sergeant; nothing against sergeants as a general rule. But you got a fool sometimes, and he had had two or three bright specimens that day: this seemed to be his moment of misfortune.

"Yes, put every message on paper," he said, "and make sure that anything that different sections ought to have reaches them quickly."

The tow-haired sergeant, who was old enough to know better, said timidly: "What kind of things, sir?"

Gideon managed not to swear, tried to phrase what he meant simply, and was almost relieved that the telephone bell rang. He turned back to the desk to pick up the receiver, knowing that he ought to leave this call to the sergeant. Lemaitre and the others were downstairs with the prisoner with the scarred head: a man named Mazzioni. In a fury of checking, the Yard knew that Mazzioni had no record in London, and copies of his prints were being made to send to the provinces. The A.C. was downstairs, waiting for Gideon, and a blockhead of a sergeant—

"Gideon. . . . Oh, hallo, Fred." This was the one call he was glad he'd taken, after all; and he was surprised that he felt really on edge. "Anything?"

"Yes and no," said the G5 Superintendent. "One of my patrols picked up the Snide. He had a couple of knives in his pocket, with traces of blood on one—"

Gideon winced.

"—but Birdy got away," the Superintendent went on. "Our chaps saw him as he headed for the docks. He's as slippery as they come, and as frightened as hell."

"I'd be frightened, in his shoes," said Gideon heavily.

"Who wouldn't?"

"Well, thanks, Fred," Gideon said. "We picked up a chap in connection with the Waterloo job, by the way, and may have some luck."

"Here's to it," the other man said.

Gideon put the receiver down, and looked up at the sergeant, forgetting to glare; the man was at Lemaitre's desk, with a telephone in his hand. Gideon found himself chuckling.

He nodded, and went out. Halfway along the passage, he remembered that the sergeant seemed to be confident enough now, scribbling something in so fast that it must have been in shorthand. A job in hand was a fine nerve tonic.

Now for Mazzioni.

Mazzioni looked tough.

You could pick them out, and it was obvious from Lemaitre's manner that he had picked Mazzioni out, quickly enough. For the man was handcuffed with his hands in front of him. He was hatless, and swarthy—no, olive-skinned; not one of the good-looking Italians. He was either Italian or of Italian extraction, Gideon knew, and when Italians came bad they were often very, very bad.

Mazzioni was shorter than medium height, and not particularly broad; really, a small man, but very upright. It was obvious that he was physically fit; his poise somehow made that clear. He had a broad, flattened nose, obviously broken many years before, fine eyes, thick, jet-black hair and jet-black eyebrows. He needed a shave. His lips were parted, and showed a glimpse of white teeth; he had that caged, criminal-at-bay look which the really vicious criminals had, and Gideon thought he had something else: the look of a dopey.

There was a nasty graze, bleeding a little, on his right temple.

Lemaitre said: "He made a fight of it; that's where he got marked. Plenty of witnesses."

Lemaitre no longer sounded cock-a-hoop; it was as if he knew that Mazzioni wasn't going to be a lot of help. There was the kind who would talk under pressure and the kind who wouldn't, and it was usually easy to pick these out, too. In Lemaitre's words as well as his manner there was a hint of frustration, and a thing which everyone at the Yard or on the Force anywhere suffered from: fear that he would be accused of exceeding his duty. A prisoner with a bruised face was a prisoner with an angry, vengeful counsel. Once convince a jury that a man had been ill-treated, and the odds against a conviction—

Gideon checked himself.

The A.C. wasn't here after all.

"When's the Old Man coming?" he asked.

"Just rang, won't be a minute," Lemaitre answered.

Gideon nodded.

Mazzioni looked from him to Lemaitre and back again. He wasn't sure what to make of this or what they would make of him. He would be happier if either of them talked: this silence, this cold appraisal from the newcomer, were unsettling, disturbing things. And Gideon, looking like a great bear and glowering as if the bear were angry, didn't mind how much he worked on the prisoner's nerves.

Was he a dopey?

There was a tap at the door. A uniformed constable looked in.

"All okay, sir."

"Thanks," said Gideon.

That meant that the A.C. was in position, able to listen to what was being said, and looking into the room through a window which appeared to be opaque from the inside. They were ready to start.

But as he looked at Mazzioni, with his first question on his lips, Gideon

felt suddenly hopeless, although it was hard to say why. It was partly because he was tired; not flogged out, as he was sometimes, but flagging badly;
the day had caught up with him. It was partly because of the ugly look in
Mazzioni's eyes, too, the certainty that this was a tough nut.

This interrogation was going to last a long time.

Lemaitre had his notebook out. Lemaitre, after his burst of triumph, felt
much the same as Gideon; catching your man was only the beginning, and
in this case it didn't look like the promising beginning they had hoped.

Lemaitre had been going to take his Fifi out.

He'd be lucky if he were home by midnight. So would Gideon.

The hell of it was that this was just another day.

Mazzioni didn't talk, but two things made Gideon very thoughtful. A
police surgeon said that he was certainly addicted to cocaine, and at Mazzioni's rooms in Bethnal Green the Divisional police found a packet of
reefers and a small packet of cocaine.

15 . Worried Men

CHANG was worried.

He was in his office, with ledgers open in front of him, for his best love
was to work over the figures of his businesses. Then the news of Mazzioni's
capture reached him by telephone. It was a whispered statement, briefly
made, as if the speaker were eager to get the message delivered and be off.
He put the receiver down stealthily, and there was silence on the line and
in Chang's office.

Chang now wore a dinner jacket, beautifully cut, a white shirt and a
purple bow tie. His sparse black hair glistened with brilliantine. The light
in the ceiling cast soft shadows of his prominent eyebrows and his nose over
his face, giving him an oddly sinister look. His lips were parted but not
visible to anyone who happened to look at him. He sat quite still, a faintly
yellow hand resting on the open pages of the ledger, in which he was keeping records of restaurant trade: or so the ledger's legend said. For tea, Chang
read reefers; for deliveries of tea he read marijuana or hashish, whichever was
available. Occasionally it was dagga from Africa, and the effect of this was
much the same, with dagga perhaps more harsh than the others.

Coffee and cocaine were synonymous.

All this afforded Chang deep amusement most of the time, for he could
safely allow the police to study these records. Until that morning, at all
events, he had felt sure that there was no risk. With Foster at Scotland

Yard, biddable under the twin pressures of greed and fear, with several
key men in banks and post offices throughout London, and with his own
carefully conceived plan to block every line of inquiry which might lead to
him, he had felt that nothing could go wrong.

He was less sure now. Foster's telephone call, his sister's prying visit,
Gideon's call and then a hysterical outburst from the dancer, Estelle, had
combined to give him a very bad day. It was Estelle who had betrayed the
fact that Birdy had found out, and squealed. Now Birdy was on the run,
and so was the dancer.

Murphy was after them both. Chang did not think Birdy could be dangerous, and knew that it had been a mistake to set Murphy onto the squealer.
The police knew about it by now; and Murphy's contact men were unable
to concentrate on the search for Estelle, whose knowledge could be deadly;
could, in fact, hang him. Chang had not realized that Estelle was in love
with Foster.

Chang sat quite motionless in the small, warm office. No sound came
from the café, although a radiogram was playing soft, rhythmic music in
there, and occasionally a crooner sang. No reefers were being sold, the soft
drinks were not pepped up, yet any Yard man who came in, any doctor who
knew the signs, and any victim of the dream drugs would know that half of
the people here were dopies. From their bright eyes, they would have known
that they had recently had a drag or a shot.

Chang did not think of these things.

Chang, in his way, was very like Gideon. He had the same kind of mind,
the same tight grasp of situations and circumstances, the same unfailing
memory and the same intentness. For Gideon there was the reward of doing
his job, for Chang the reward of making a fortune; but to each the actual
task was the very pulse of life. In Gideon the chief thing was the task of
seeking the criminal and hunting him down, of making sure that he could
never strike again to hurt, to rob, to frighten or to maim. In Chang, the
attraction was the plotting against the police, the moves in a game as in a
game of chess or mahjongg—wits against wits, and the amassing of a fortune.

The police had become his natural enemy.

They had suspected him for a long time, but with Foster in his pocket
he had known that he was temporarily secure. Others were also in his
pocket. He was ringed round with men, a few of whom knew that they
served him, most of whom did not know that their instructions came from
him. "Instructions" was too often the wrong word. Hints, tip-offs, suggestions, help in emergency—all of these came through Chang, and for
reward he received a share of whatever profit was made. His share was
passed on to him. Sometimes it was handed over, in cash, at the café; or to
other, smaller cafés, where he had contacts in the East and West Ends, in

Chelsea, in Bloomsbury. There was Chang with supplies for his cafés, all legitimate business on the surface—here was Chang, deeply worried. Estelle was anxiety enough, but he had trained himself to concentrate on one thing at a time, and the greatest anxiety was the captured Italian.

Chang knew Mazzioni personally, and Mazzioni knew him; so he could betray him to the police. The Italian's record was good, because Chang had saved him from a charge several times, but reputation went for nothing once the police were working on you. Mazzioni might crack and talk, to save himself.

Never trust anyone, Chang believed, unless you could compel him to serve faithfully.

Mazzioni was out of his reach.

Mazzioni's wife wasn't.

How should he deal with the Italian? Could he find a way of warning him of the consequences of failure?

No, Chang decided, not that: not yet. Mazzioni was tough and he would hold out for some time; he might hold out for a long time. He took an occasional sniff of snow, but could get along without it. The way to make sure of Mazzioni's loyalty was to promise him help. Help, for instance, for his pretty young wife; then help with the police.

Chang did not know how the Italian had been picked up. He knew that he had done the job at Waterloo, and that most of the money had already been safely salted away; but Mazzioni might have been caught with some of the money on him. The police might find indisputable evidence of his complicity, but they might be taking a chance. If Mazzioni had an alibi, it could make all the difference to the way the case went.

Chang lifted the telephone, dialed a number, and waited. He had to wait for a long time. *Brrr-brrr, brrr-brrr.* It was too long. Possessed of all the calm of his unknown ancestors he began to bare his teeth; but then the call was answered; a man said breathlessly:

"Mayfair 29451."

"Mr. Ledbetter," Chang said softly, "it is urgent that I should see you."

"Who—"

"An old friend, Mr. Ledbetter."

There was a moment's silence; then the man spoke again, in a voice less breathless but quite empty of pleasure.

"Oh, I know. Look, can't it wait? I have some friends here. In the morning—"

"I am sorry, Mr. Ledbetter, it is urgent. Meet me in Room 217 at the Occident Hotel, please."

"But I can't—"

"It is very urgent, Mr. Ledbetter," Chang said.

Ledbetter answered gruffly: "Oh, all right."

Chang rang off without another word. He lifted the receiver again, almost at once. His movement was quick yet graceful, very different from Gideon's grab; and his hand was half the size of Gideon's.

A woman answered.

"Mary," Chang greeted, "this afternoon, between two o'clock and four o'clock, where were you?"

"Hallo, Chin," said the woman, in a deep, throaty voice. "I was at Kingston. Didn't anyone tell you, I'm at Kingston every afternoon? It's one of the places where I work." There was laziness and laughter in her voice; one would picture a big, hearty, fleshy woman, sensuous, good-hearted, quick-witted.

"Understand," said Chang, "you were at Kingston and a good friend of yours was there, also, with you. Mazzioni."

"Maz? Why, he—"

"He was with you, please remember, all the time."

The woman laughed.

"His little sweetie pie won't like that!"

"His little sweetie pie," mimicked Chang, "will not worry about it this time. Now, please understand. He arrived at two, he left at four, there is no mistake. Find one, find even two people to say that also."

"Okay, Chin," the woman said. "Bad trouble?"

"It could be."

"What I do for my men," said the woman named Mary.

Chang rang off. He sat quite still again, until his left hand moved to the inside pocket of his beautifully cut coat. He took out a tiny lacquered snuff box, with a beautiful garden design, pressed, opened it, and took a tiny pinch of white snuff. He put this onto the back of his hand and sniffed it up each nostril; then he replaced the box slowly. He stood up, stretched for his hat, and went out of the office.

A girl was in the little cloakroom on the landing, and the radiogram was playing swing. Shuffling footsteps told of people dancing. The ordinary, clean smell of tobacco smoke wafted toward him.

"Has Estelle telephoned?"

"No, sir."

"I will be back soon," Chang said.

"Okay."

He went downstairs, passing a colored photograph of Estelle. She had long, rippling red hair and a big, white smile and quite beautiful legs. Chang only glanced in passing. Nodding to a flat-faced waiter, he turned into the spotless kitchen, where the Chinese staff looked at him without expression, and he behaved as if no one was there. He went out of the little back door, and slipped swiftly along a passage toward Middle Street.

At Middle Street, he had a shock.

A plain-clothes man was on the other side of the road; and there was only one reason why he should be there.

Chang felt even more worried.

He smiled across at the man, and turned into Middle Street, then made his way toward Shaftesbury Avenue. He was followed, and was worried chiefly because the police were so interested. He would have to be very, very careful.

Had it been a mistake to run Foster down?

If so, it had been Mazzioni's mistake, too; that was the chief source of worry. Mazzioni had been at hand when Foster had telephoned. Foster had been scared, and had talked of squealing unless Chang promised help. In a quick flood of annoyance and alarm, Chang had made his mistake by telling Mazzioni what to do, and Mazzioni had acted too quickly, and too close to Soho.

Chang thought belatedly of other things that had turned out to be mistakes, too: letting Estelle know that Foster was in his pay, for instance; and forgetting that she had been here, for a rehearsal, when he had given Mazzioni his orders.

At Piccadilly Circus, Chang slipped the sergeant who was on his tail, but knew that there might be others on the lookout for him. He was conspicuous, like any Chinese. Piccadilly Circus always had its policemen, its plain-clothes men, its police spies, and if they had been told to watch for Chang it would be dangerous.

Chang got into a taxi. He did not think that he was followed as he was taken to the restaurant entrance of the Occident Hotel. There was not likely to be a detective lurking at this side, but there was sure to be a hotel dick if not a policeman in the foyer.

He went through a service door to service stairs and then up to Room 217. This was reserved in the name of Smith, and a Mr. Smith had come, signed the register, and left the hotel, sending the key to Chang. It would be a rendezvous for a week; then there would be another hotel, another room.

When Ledbetter came, he also looked worried. He was a big, lusty man with iron-gray hair, quite distinguished in his way. He had a very good reputation, was an astute lawyer, and had made one mistake, a little matter of embezzlement. No one yet knew, except Chang and a clerk in Ledbetter's office who was aware that Chang liked that kind of information.

Chang looked very small beside him.

"Well, what is it?" Ledbetter didn't like Chinese, didn't like anyone whose skin was yellow or brown or black. He was as massive as Gideon, well dressed, scowling, resentful. The furrows in his forehead added to the touch of distinction.

"There is a very urgent matter," Chang said. He found it easy to smile, especially at men whom one disliked. "A friend of mine, named Marco Mazzioni, has been arrested by the police. He is a very good friend, and it would be dangerous for many people if he were to be tried. It is believed that he was connected with the mail-van robbery this afternoon, but that is ridiculous—he was at Kingston, with Mary Clayton. You know Mary."

Ledbetter said: "Did he do the job?"

"You have to see him," said Chang, still smiling. "Just see him, and tell him that he need not worry. Mary will tell the truth and say that he was with her from two o'clock until four. You understand?"

Ledbetter said: "I don't like it, Chang. If the police can prove that he wasn't—"

"Then, Mary lied to you," said Chang. "Do not be foolish, Mr. Ledbetter. This is an urgent matter. See your friends at Scotland Yard at once, please." He smiled. . . .

Ledbetter went out, obviously as worried as when he came in, much more resentful, but undoubtedly prepared to be obedient. Chang went to a telephone by the side of the bed. He looked very short. He hesitated for a moment, partly because he was thinking of Ledbetter. He knew that the solicitor regarded him as a yellow-skinned savage; he also knew that Ledbetter was in a very tight fix.

Chang telephoned Mazzioni's wife.

A man with a deep voice answered, almost certainly a policeman; in fact, Chang felt quite sure. He spoke promptly and in a deep voice from which he kept all trace of accent.

"Mrs. Mazzioni, please."

"Who wants her?"

"A friend."

There was a moment's pause; then the mutter of men's voices; then Mazzioni's wife came on the line. Chang knew her for a pretty, fluffy-haired blonde, with a jealous temperament.

She sounded scared.

"Who's that?"

"Of course, you know of the accident to your husband," Chang said, still sounding "English." "But it will be all right, my dear. You will find out that he was with Mary at Kingston all the afternoon; there is no need to worry at all. That is the perfect alibi, you see."

"The perfect—"

"That is the police with you, I believe," Chang said. "They will ask who called. Say I am a friend, to tell you of what happened to Maz. And one other thing, little one—when the police ask if you know where Maz was this afternoon, be angry. Do you understand?" He paused, but only for a moment. "Be *very* angry, say he was going to see that bitch Mary at Kingston." Softly he repeated: "You understand?"

"Sure," said Mazzioni's wife slowly. She was no fool, and she was cottoning on. "Sure, I knew already."

Chang rang off, unhurriedly.

He was still worried, all the same; he did not like having to work at speed, like this, and did not like having to do so much himself. But it began to look as if the real emergency was past. If only he could find Estelle.

He left the hotel, and twenty minutes later, entered the café in Middle Street again. The plain-clothes man he had shaken off was back on duty. Chang smiled at him, politely, but didn't get a smile back.

In his office, Chang sat back, took another pinch of snuff, and glanced down at the figures in the book. It was silent again and he enjoyed the silence.

The telephone bell rang.

He lifted it, and a man said: "This is Murphy."

Suddenly, Chang was acutely anxious; for Murphy never got in touch with him direct unless there was urgent news. Was this about Birdy Merrick or Estelle? Had Estelle been found by the police? That was Chang's fear, that above all else.

Murphy was also an anxious man, although it took a great deal to get on his nerves. Most days, he told his cronies exactly what he thought of the police and how little they mattered to him; and most days he meant exactly that. The police had no terrors for him. He kept his nose clean, didn't he? He had committed no crime of any kind in the past two years except that of a little street-corner betting, peddling some bad liquor, which was hardly a crime at all, and—inciting others to crime. No one named him as the instigator, so that did not count.

Yet Murphy was edgy.

It was worse, because there had been a long, long spell of freedom from fear. Everything had gone so smoothly that he had become dangerously complacent. He had given more orders himself than he should have done, instead of using messengers, and he had gone to see Birdy.

He would not have told anyone in the world, but he was frightened.

The sense of power, which his habit of domination gave him, had betrayed him. He should not have gone to Birdy's house. Now the Snide was in the hands of the police, and the Snide had been seen to attack Birdy. It would be all right if the police just handled the Snide, but they might check on everyone who had been after Birdy that day.

They were out in strength in the district.

Murphy had that nasty, sickening kind of feeling that the police were out for a kill. It was Chang's doing. The orders to get Birdy had come from Chang, even if they'd traveled through three other people before reaching him. Murphy did not propose to handle this with go-betweens; he wanted to talk to Chang. There was the search for the red-haired dancer, too, which had got nowhere, and was wasting men.

So he telephoned the Chinese.

Chang lifted the receiver, heard who it was, and then very slowly shook his head. Murphy just reported, and asked if he should keep up the search for B. and the skirt. Chang was preparing to answer "for the skirt, only," when there was an interruption.

It was entirely coincidence that at that moment the door burst open, but the sudden movement scared Chang, who actually jumped to his feet.

The door banged back.

Foster's sister came into the room, with a scared-looking Chinese waiter behind her.

16 . Sanctuary?

CHANG looked up at Foster's sister. His eyes were lackluster. His mouth was set in long, thin lines.

"Yes, proceed, please," he said into the telephone. "Now I must go." He rang off.

The woman had thrust her way past the waiter, outside, but Chang's expression stopped her, as a physical blow might do. She stood there, the sudden fear evident in her eyes, in the way her mouth opened and her teeth glinted. Behind her, the waiter hovered, hands rolling and rolling beneath his small white apron. Had Gideon seen the way he gazed at Chang, with silent supplication as to the devil, he would have hardened very much against Chang.

Then Chang spoke softly.

"Good evening, Mrs. Addinson. Please come in. Wen Li, please close the door." As the waiter obeyed and as Flo Addinson moved forward, Chang brought a smile from the depths of his self-discipline, then stood up and rounded the desk.

"Please sit down," he said. His voice was more singsong than usual, as if he were fighting against showing his feelings. He touched the back of the easy chair, and bowed. "Can I get you a drink?"

"No," she said. "No, thank you." She moved so that she could sit down.

Chang bowed again, and went back to his desk. Now the mask was on, but she had seen beneath it and she knew what was really there. When she had come in, she had been flushed, as with anger, actually with nervousness; now she was very pale. Her eyes were bright, a shimmery kind of black, suggesting that she had a severe headache. She fumbled in her handbag, and Chang promptly stood up again and offered her cigarettes.

"Please smoke," he said.

She hesitated and then accepted a cigarette. He smiled as he flicked a lighter for her, but it was the smile of a robot. It was a genuine cigarette, too; there was no drug in it, yet the temptation to give her marijuana had been almost overwhelming.

She still wore the good black suit.

"Thank you."

"How can I help you, please?" murmured Chang.

"I came to—to ask you if you know what happened to my brother," she said.

He was outwardly almost back to normal, suave, almost solemn, spreading his hands.

"I was informed this morning of what had happened. Such a sad accident. I am very sorry."

"I'm not sure it was an accident," Flo Addinson said.

"Oh," said Chang, and his lips parted. Now he was in such complete command of himself that he folded his arms loosely across his narrow chest, and sat back in the chair. It was no indication of his feelings. "I do not understand you. He was run down by a car, is that not so? The driver didn't stop."

Chang spread his hands.

"There are so many callous drivers—"

"Mr. Chang," the woman said steadily, "what association was there between my brother and you? Why did he see you so often? Why was he worried because of you?"

She had alarmed him, she knew; he could not hide it, even though he said: "You are making mistakes, Mrs. Addinson, I cannot understand—"

"I must know what Eric had to do with you. The police kept asking me, they've followed me all day. Why is it? Do you know?"

Suavely, he insisted that he knew nothing, that he and her brother had just been acquaintances. But he questioned her tautly, trying to find out what she knew.

He learned little and soon she seemed to tire.

"You have had a big shock," Chang murmured, when she rose to go. "Please allow me to send you home in my car, Mrs. Addinson. It is no trouble. Unless you would like to stay to have dinner here? As my guest. I shall be very happy."

"No!" She jumped up. "No, thank you, I'd rather walk. If you're sure you can't help—"

"If I could, Mrs. Addinson, I would, gladly."

Chang pressed a bell, and the ringing sound could be heard faintly. In a moment, the door opened and the waiter appeared, big, flat, Mongolian face concealing his fear now.

"Show Mrs. Addinson downstairs," Chang said. He rounded the desk. "My very deep condolences. I assure you, I was very fond of Mr. Foster." He did not offer to shake hands, but bowed; and waited until the door closed on her.

Then he moved to his desk, swift as a flash, picked up a telephone, and was answered almost at once.

"The woman now downstairs," Chang said swiftly, "you will follow her, and see if she is followed by the police. You understand?"

A man said, "Yes, sir."

Chang rang off. He didn't sit down, but went to the door and opened it. The music from the radiogram had started again, a fox trot that sounded rather sensuous and slow. The landing light fell on Chang's black hair. He waited until the waiter came up the stairs, and the man with the flat Mongolian face could no longer hide his fear.

No one should have reached Chang's room without a warning preceding them; he had been panicked into forgetting to press a bell.

His feet dragged on the last two steps.

Chang waited until he was close to him, and then struck him across the face. The man swayed right and left under the impact of the savage blows, but didn't try to evade them. Chang did not speak, but turned back to his office. The waiter stumbled toward the narrow stairs. The fox trot moaned on, and the shuffling sound of dancing feet came clearly. Outside, a car horn tooted.

Outside, Flo Addinson walked toward Shaftesbury Avenue, was followed by a small man in a shabby suit, and by a plain-clothes man detailed to follow her.

In his report to the Yard, this man said that Chang had had Mrs. Addinson followed almost to her door.

"You stay and keep an eye on her," he was ordered.

A few miles away from Soho, in a line which cut through the throbbing, cosmopolitan heart of the West End, through the dead city, and into the shadowy ill-lit streets of the East End, Murphy sat at a table in the front room of his house. For a man in his position, virtually boss of a powerful gang, he lived very humbly. The house was small, and the rooms tiny; only a twenty-inch television set, and bottles of every conceivable kind of drink standing on a cheap oak sideboard, suggested a man of means. That—and his wife. Murphy's wife wore real diamonds when she wore rings or jewelry at all, and she aped a refinement which, in this part of London, made her quite the lady.

She was watching the television, and the light reflected from the screen shimmered on the engagement ring.

Murphy, a big, vague figure at the table, was looking at a small man who had only one arm; his left sleeve dangled empty by his side. The screen flickered, a man talked.

"That's right," Murphy said, "you tell 'em all to call it off, leave Birdy alone, see? And don't lose no time."

"Okay, but—"

"Scram," growled Murphy.

"Red," protested his wife, as if her mouth were full, "why don't you shut up or go in the other room?"

"You heard," Murphy said to the one-armed man.

"But, Red—"

"Get out, I said."

Murphy got up from the table. The one-armed man hesitated, then went out. He closed the door softly. Murphy moved across to his wife's chair, which was placed immediately in front of the big television. She had a box of chocolates open at her side, and Murphy took one. Paper rustled. She put her hand over his, and squeezed. He whispered: "It's okay," and began to caress her. They watched the big screen, and listened to the deep voice coming from the set.

Meanwhile, the one-armed man sent the word round to call off the hunt.

What he had wanted to say was that just before he had been called in to Murphy, he'd been given a message saying that Ali and Lefty had cornered Birdy. It was next door to impossible to draw the hunt off in time.

Birdy did not find sanctuary in a ship, or in the docks, although he had run there believing that he could. A shadowy figure had appeared from behind some crates waiting for loading, and turned him away.

Now he was back on his own native ground; in the narrow streets, among the towering warehouses, within sight of the silent river and the silent docks. Some kind of homing instinct had brought him here, after the sickening failure to get clear away on less familiar ground. He knew every inch of this, every hiding place, every hole and cellar; and he now tried to believe that he had more chance to save himself here.

He did not know if he was being closely watched.

He tried to persuade himself that this was his lucky night; the police car had saved him, he'd seen Lefty just in time, he'd beaten the Snide. But there was something else which filled him with terror. He'd left the Snide writhing in pain on the ground, where the police would pick him up. That would fill the others, especially Ali and Lefty, with a vindictive hatred.

He'd hurt one of the gang; in a way, had shopped him. Now it was more than a job for money, it was a vendetta.

In this narrow street, it was very dark. That worried Birdy more than anything else. There should be a light on, jutting from a warehouse wall. Had it been broken? Had Ali put it out, so that he could confuse the hunted man?

Birdy moved quietly toward a corner. Round it, there was the ruin of a warehouse destroyed by fire; it was no use as a hiding place because it was the first spot where the others would look. But beyond the warehouse was a church.

Birdy worked his way toward this.

He knew the church, as everyone did, but he had never been inside. He knew people who had; among them his daughter, before her death. He knew the elderly vicar whose chin was always on his chest as he walked about the parish, as if the dirt, the squalor, the crime, the vice, all the evil incarnate in man and so visible there, had weighed him down and sickened him, so that he served God only on sufferance and with a heavy heart. Birdy also knew the curate by sight, a spindly, unimpressive young man with a pointed nose, already a victim of catcalls and stink bombs, a man likely to be led a hell of a life in his parish.

Birdy was very near the church. He had only to pass the ruins of the warehouse to reach it.

He had been hunted before, but never like this, never to feel in deadly danger. That was why he saw the church as a very different thing; he saw it as a sanctuary, for no one would expect him to go there.

It offered him life, and it was only a few yards away. The doors would be open, as always. No ordinary criminal would go in and break open the offertory boxes; that was a crime which only perverts committed.

There was a yellow light at one window, at the far end of the church.

Birdy wondered who was there.

He reached the yawning entrance to the ruined warehouse, and as he did so, a figure leaped at him.

It came from the warehouse: a dark figure with arms raised, like a great bat. There was a sliding sound, a deadly rush of footsteps. Birdy knew that they had him; both of them were here. His terror seemed to explode inside him.

He screamed.

He leaped forward and kicked against an outstretched leg and pitched forward. The fall drove the wind out of him. He banged his head so painfully that tears stung his eyes. He heard the thudding of his own heart, which was swelling and pounding with great fear. He saw pictures: Ethel, Murphy, Gideon, Ethel; *Ethel*.

He felt the sharp, searing pain of razor cuts in his cheeks; another in one wrist.

He felt a man kneeling on his back, knee grinding into the vertebrae, agonizing, and enough to break his back. But he couldn't think about that, only about razors and knives. He tried to twist round, but couldn't.

Suddenly, he felt the pressure relax.

That was only for a moment.

Lefty, the bottle artist, caught Birdy's right wrist, twisted him, and turned him over so that he now lay on his back. He stamped his heel into Birdy's stomach, so as to paralyze him. Birdy felt hands at his wrists, pinioning him to the ground. These hands belonged to Ali, and they were coming for his face; his throat . . .

Unbelievably, the pressure at his wrist relaxed.

The awful thrust didn't come.

He heard other sounds, gasping, thudding, grunting. He realized that men were fighting, and thought that the police had come again. He rolled over, but couldn't get up; his back felt as if it had been broken.

He groaned and sobbed.

Then he heard the engine of a car, and although his eyes were only open a fraction of an inch, saw the swaying beams of head lamps. Had he been able to see properly, he would also have seen Lefty reeling back against the warehouse wall, and Ali and another man locked together, gasping and struggling.

He did not recognize the spindly curate.

The police car screamed up, men jumped out, a door slammed, a police whistle blew.

Every instinct Birdy had was to try to get away, but he could not even roll over. He was vaguely aware of footsteps and of a man running. Then came sharp, authoritative voices; next, sharp metallic sounds—the click of handcuffs. A man bent over him, and the light of a torch fell into his face.

"Better get a doctor," said the man behind the torch.

"You take it easy, padre," said another man gruffly. "I've radioed for an ambulance."

Birdy didn't know . . .

Lefty had escaped, but Ali was handcuffed and already inside the police car. The ambulance was on the way. The unhappy curate of the church had saved Birdy's life, and risked his own; the news of that would spread, his stature would rise; he might be hated but he had a chance to win respect.

Birdy just didn't know any of this.

He lost consciousness before the ambulance arrived, and while the police-man was giving him first aid for nasty cuts in his wrist and cheeks.

Gideon, looking solid, stolid and unimaginative, was still in the waiting room with Lemaitre, but he knew that it was virtually a waste of time. Mazzioni had not said a word that mattered. Occasionally he said "no" to a leading question, but the main burden of what he had said was simple: he wanted a lawyer.

He'd been charged with complicity in the Waterloo raid, and had every right to legal representation.

The A.C., behind that window, might now have some idea of the frus-tration that the law itself created for the police. They had a man they were quite sure was guilty of a crime of violence and of highway robbery, and all they could do was ask him *questions;* there was no way to make him answer, no way to get past that silent, sullen front.

Then a sergeant came in.

"Can you spare a moment, Mr. Gideon?"

"Yes, what is it?"

"Outside, sir, if it's convenient."

"All right," Gideon said. He looked at Mazzioni, who was sneering up into his face. The Italian's fingers were stained dark brown with nicotine, but he hadn't tried to take out cigarettes, and Gideon hadn't offered him one. Gideon had an intuitive feeling that he was looking at someone really evil: one who could kill and maim remorselessly, who seemed to have no redeeming feature. Nothing in Mazzioni's manner suggested that he was worth a moment's compunction; or a cigarette.

Gideon went out.

The A.C. was coming out of the room from which he had been watching, and the sergeant glanced at him, then back at Gideon.

"Sorry to interrupt, sir, but there's a Mr. Ledbetter at the main hall, asking for—er—Mr. Mazzioni. He asked whether it's true that Mazzioni is on a charge, and insisted on seeing you personally, sir."

Gideon echoed: *"Ledbetter."*

"Yes, sir."

"Hmm," said Gideon heavily. "All right, tell him I'll see him in a few minutes." He waited for the man to walk briskly along the corridor. "Well, they didn't lose much time, did they?"

"Who?" asked the A.C.

"Ledbetter's already done two jobs for Chang, or friends of Chang," Gideon said. "I don't trust him an inch. Hard to say why. Good solicitor, done some first-class work; until a year or two ago there was nothing rumored against him, but now—how did he get to know about the arrest, unless Mazzioni has friends who passed it on? That's what I'd like to know more than anything else. *How* did Ledbetter get to know?"

The A.C. didn't speak.

"Can't stop him from seeing the Italian," Gideon went on gloomily. "I could stall, but it'd be a waste of time. Better let them meet. There ought," added Gideon with feeling, "to be a law against allowing accused and his solicitor to have a tête-à-tête."

He looked and sounded tired and disappointed.

He was much more disappointed, twenty minutes later, when he heard about the "alibi." More; he was angry, feeling quite sure that the alibi was faked. He sensed a hidden nervousness in Ledbetter's manner, too.

He could have used an alternative charge, of being in unlawful possession of dangerous drugs, but he didn't; he could hold it over Mazzioni's head, and it might help in the next day or two. Mazzioni, "cleared" of the mail-van job, was better free to meet his cronies than on a charge.

Gideon tried to bluff by holding the Italian for the night.

"I take the strongest exception to that," Ledbetter said decisively. "There is nothing to prevent you from asking the witness whether she can offer supporting evidence, and if she can, then it's up to you to check it at once. My client was miles away at the time of the crime you've charged him with. I'm sorry you've made a mistake, but I'm more sorry for my client than I am for you."

Gideon looked at him thoughtfully.

"I don't know whom I'm most sorry for," he said. "Yet."

Ledbetter colored. . . .

When he and Mazzioni had gone, the A.C. looked in on Gideon, approved the decision to hold over the dangerous drugs charge, and asked: "Think you can make Mazzioni crack in time?"

"Dunno," said Gideon frankly. "More than anything else, I want that dancer Estelle."

"Any news?"

"Not yet," Gideon said.

The A.C. went off, as glum as Gideon, and Gideon sat back and studied transcripts of Mazzioni's statements, and the record of the woman who'd given him an alibi. He wanted to talk to her, but—

Before he could even think about visiting her, he had to check what reports were coming in. He hadn't yet heard about the night's biggest job, at the Mid-Union Safe Deposit in the City.

17 . The Biggest Job

EVERY part of London had known its moments of crisis that night, every Division received its urgent call for help. The placid men in the Information Room had taken call after call to 999 without fuss, quietly reassuring agitated callers, extracting the necessary information, passing it through to the Flying Squad, the patrol cars of the Divisions for action.

The Yard seemed more alive by night than by day.

The reports were on Gideon's desk, in a thick sheaf of notes written in a bold, legible hand and a welcome economy of phrase; and the sergeant stood looking at Gideon as if he hoped the Superintendent would make a favorable comment.

There were the burglaries: dozens of them. Attacks on women alone in the streets, smash-and-grab jobs, two club raids with fifty-seven names taken. Great Marlborough Street was overflowing with the so-called flower of the aristocracy, most of whom took a raid on a gambling club for a joke, or pretended to.

There was the inevitable crop of charges of soliciting; there were two men accused of attempting to murder their wives. One was still belligerent after being stopped from thrashing his; the other was cowed and frightened, so much so that it was hard to believe that he had ever been brandishing a knife, as if ready to kill.

Three men had been picked up in the Occident Hotel for passing sludge, or forged money. A man who had already served two sentences for fraud was held on suspicion of trying to earn his third sentence; crimes of all kinds and all varieties were committed in the few hours that were left of Gideon's day, but there was only one which held dynamite.

The note read: "City Police glad if you will call them, suspected burglary Mid-Union Safe Deposit."

"Oh-ho," grunted Gideon.

He skimmed through the other notes, and then the telephone bell rang. The sergeant could have answered it, but Gideon's hand was already on the smooth black surface.

"Gideon here."

He listened. . . .

"Are you *sure?*" His voice rose, his face brightened.

"Oh, that's fine," he said. "How badly hurt? . . . Well, he'll get over it. Tell his wife, won't you?" He rang off, and looked up at the door as it opened, and Lemaitre came in, very subdued. "Thought you'd gone home," he said.

"Daren't," said Lemaitre gloomily.

Gideon chuckled.

"What's pleased you?" demanded Lemaitre. "The last I saw of you, you looked—"

"They've picked up Birdy."

"That so?" Lemaitre brightened. "Okay?"

"Cuts on his right wrist and cheeks, and some nasty bruising on his back and stomach, but an X-ray showed nothing to worry about," said Gideon. "They got Ali, too."

"You mean that little lascar swine?"

"He's being held—was caught with the knife on him and in the act of using it. Actually a curate over there stopped it, young chap who's new to the district."

Lemaitre whistled.

"If he hadn't been new, he wouldn't have interfered! Ali would have knifed him as soon as look at him. That's a bit better, anyhow. We've still got the chance of getting somewhere through the Snide and Ali. One of them will probably squeal, and if we could tuck Murphy away for a few years it would be something. What do you think of that crook, Led——"

"Okay, sergeant," Gideon interrupted, "I'll call you when I want you. Thanks—very good job."

"Thank you, sir." The sergeant hurried out.

"Hell, what would it have mattered if I had told him what I thought of Ledbetter?" growled Lemaitre. "And to think what I've done for this night's work—proper mucked things up with Fifi. If you'd seen the way she looked when I told her I had to stand her up."

"Go home, wake her up, and tell her you love her," said Gideon, "and blame me for standing her up."

"'Struth!" exclaimed Lemaitre. "It's bad enough when I wake her if I just get home late. Anything much in?"

"The City chaps want me," said Gideon. "Some trouble at the Mid-Union Safe Deposit. Better call them." He stifled a yawn. "And then come hell or high water, I'm going *home*."

He felt flat again as he spoke. The temporary stimulant of the news about Birdy had faded in fresh gloom about Mazzioni. Ledbetter's part depressed him, too; there were plenty of unreliable solicitors, but they didn't grow on trees. Few of them were crooked for the sake of it; usually they drifted, some were blackmailed.

"I wouldn't mind a bit of action," Lemaitre said. "Got anything?"

He really funked going home.

"Go and see this woman," Gideon said, and tapped the card with the

name and address of Mazzioni's "alibi." "Try to shake her about where she
was and who she was with this afternoon."

"Oke," Lemaitre promised.

Gideon called the City police.

Earlier in the evening, the night staff of the Mid-Union Safe Deposit
Company had settled down to the usual quiet night's work. Most of this
would be keeping records. There would be some business in the early hours
of the morning, when the really sensible, who had taken out jewels for
wear, brought them back instead of taking them home. That "rush" would
last for an hour, and after it there would be nothing until the morning
staff took over. Only three men were on duty; a fourth, usually present, was
on sick leave.

Three could cope.

The building of the Mid-Union Safe Deposit Company was a large stone-
faced one, in narrow Wattle Street, and was sandwiched between a block of
offices let to a hundred different firms—from lawyers to tea brokers, rubber
merchants to shipping companies, accountants and insurance brokers—and
the head offices of one of the largest insurance companies. Mid-Union
actually owned the building, but let off the ground and upper floors, retain-
ing a basement office and two big vaults, each below basement level. The
entrance was through Wattle Street and past a wide doorway which was
protected, when necessary, by a strong steel door.

This was always open.

No one could step through the doorway without sending two warnings
through to the officials on the floor below; one warning was electric, the
other was by secret ray; neither rang a bell, but each flashed a light which
would be seen at once by the men on duty.

These were behind a strong grille, heavily protected, and entrance could
be gained only through a small doorway which was kept locked and unlocked for every fresh customer. No customer was allowed in the vaults
by himself—neither the one at first level, where the more frequently needed
deposits were stored, nor the deep vault. An armed official always accompa-
nied him. By night, it was sometimes necessary to keep customers waiting,
but if they wished they could drop their packets into a night safe—much on
the bank system—and this would be put in a community safe until they
came to put it in their own box.

The staff took the daily and nightly handling of valuables for granted.
On really busy days, a million pounds' worth of precious stones would be
brought in or taken out, and no one thought twice about it.

Except Fitzroy . . .

About the time that Gideon had finished his dinner, one of the three members of the staff had gone into the bottom vaults, to check some entries. That was regular enough, and he should be gone for about half an hour. In fact, he was longer. Neither of the others was worried about this, for some jobs were difficult to estimate.

All the men on duty carried guns, but in the forty-nine years of its existence, the Mid-Union had never had an attempted robbery. This did not make anyone careless; the warning system was perfect, and each night-duty official was trained in the use of his gun. They were selected men with brilliant war records. No one over forty-five was employed by night.

The big general office behind the reception desk was empty by night, too.

When the first man had been gone for forty minutes—by then, Gideon had seen Ledbetter—one of the others went to look for him, leaving only the night manager behind the grille.

The second man didn't come back either.

The night manager, a youthful forty-one, knew his staff well and was quite sure that they were reliable. He was going to find out what was keeping them, when two customers came in. Both were men, both wanted to deposit jewels. They were regular customers, the night manager could not offend them, and he took them downstairs to the first vault, one at a time.

In all, that job took him twelve minutes.

He locked the reception desk door on the two customers, and hurried to the narrow stone steps which led to the lower vault.

Halfway down, he stopped.

Ought he to telephone the police, and make sure that if anything were wrong—

It was too late.

A man appeared at the foot of the steps, holding an automatic pistol. The night manager felt as if death had suddenly knocked loudly at his door. The man with the gun was masked, tall, lean, leathery looking. The gun was very steady. He started up the stairs, and the manager backed a step, but didn't move far. He was in between two alarm bells that would call the police, and his only hope of getting to one was to turn and rush up the steps.

The eyes of Fitzroy, the man with the gun, discouraged notions of heroism.

"Take it easy," Fitzroy said. "You won't get hurt if you do what you're told, but if you try any tricks, you'll get hurt badly. *And* you might not recover."

The manager licked his lips.

Fitzroy was within two yards of him.

If he jumped—

He jumped.

As he moved, he had an awful sense of failure, of doom. He saw the
gunman draw to one side, saw a long leg shoot out. He could not avoid it,
and fell headlong down the stairs.

Another masked man appeared at the foot of them, and picked him up.
Dazed and bruised, he could only think of the gun.

Fitzroy spoke brightly:

"Just do what you're told, and you won't get hurt. Let's have your keys,
for a start."

"No. No, I—"

The second man struck the manager sharply across the face and spun
him round. The keys were fastened to a thick leather belt running round
his waist. The second man used a pair of wire cutters to cut the belt, then
pushed the manager toward the lower vault. The manager was too frightened to think clearly, but a thought flashed into his mind. These men seemed
to know their way about.

Entrance must have been forced from *below*. That wasn't possible, it—

He was pushed into the large bottom vault, where big, solid safes and
rows of metal boxes lined the walls from floor to ceiling. On the floor, lying
on their backs, were the two clerks. In one wall was a hole nearly two feet
square, and by it was a heap of dirt and debris, chippings of cement, everything to show how the "impossible" had been achieved.

Then a man thrust a cloth over the manager's head, tied it at the back,
seized his hands and bound them, and then laid him down.

He did not know what was happening; all he knew was that he was alive.
Fitzroy looked at him, and grinned, then turned to the two men with him,
pulling off his mask.

"I'm going up to the office, to look after the customers." He chuckled
again. "They won't know how safe their baubles are!" He went off, moving
easily and outwardly confident, and he whistled softly as he took the place
of the manager.

The odds had been nicely calculated.

Fitzroy knew that the fourth member of the night staff was away. He
knew that the hour for late deposits was almost past, and that even if there
were more, they would only be for the upper floor. He could lock himself
in with the depositor, see the goods put in the box, and wish the man good
night. His two assistants were expert safebreakers, and if they managed to
open only two of the safes and two or three dozen of the metal boxes, the
haul would be sensational. So he whistled as he sat at the desk, and made a
show of working when he heard footsteps.

A young man came down, and stopped short at sight of him.

"Evening, sir," said Fitzroy, getting up.

"Good evening. Isn't Mr. Ilott here?"

"Downstairs at the moment," said Fitzroy glibly, "but I can send for him if you really want him."

"Well—"

"Or I can help you, sir." Fitzroy looked so brisk and friendly, smiled so amiably, and spoke with such conviction that the depositor gave way. He had his own key. Fitzroy let him into the upper deposit vault, escorted him to his box, and watched him deposit a diamond ring and two diamond drop earrings.

"I always feel safer when they're locked away," said the depositor.

"I bet you do," said Fitzroy warmly. "I would if they were mine, too. I'll tell Mr. Ilott that you've been, sir."

"Thanks," the depositor said, and left with a hearty "Good night."

Fitzroy went back to his desk, and whistled under his breath until the man's footsteps had faded; then he lit a cigarette, and took out a newspaper folded to the crossword puzzle. Now and again he perked his head up, and listened; he had heard imagined sounds from the street.

Down below, the others were working quickly and with great skill.

Two safes were open, and cash, diamonds, jewelry of all kinds and a little bullion were loaded into canvas mail-van sacks. One man was working at a third safe, the other was beginning on the steel boxes. He had a tool which pierced them at the edges, and, working rather like wire cutters or tin openers, tore a big hole. He made some noise, but it did not travel even up the narrow stone steps to Fitzroy.

He opened box after box.

The other man forced the door of his third safe, and, hardly troubling to examine the jewelry in it, dropped it into another sack.

The first man had emptied twenty-one boxes.

"About all we can manage," he said, looking round the vault regretfully. "I hope we haven't missed any juicy ones. They could tell us!" He grinned across at the three prisoners, but didn't go toward them.

He went up to the main floor, and, without showing himself in the office, whispered: "You there, Fitz?"

Fitz called immediately: "Yes."

"We're going."

"Nice haul?"

"Plenty." There was an echo of satisfaction in the man's voice; an echo of excitement, too. Fitzroy got up and went to the head of the stairs, leaving the reception desk untenanted for a moment. He was pulling at a cigarette, and excitement showed in the brightness of his eyes; the other man showed his with a slight quiver of the lips and the hands. "Wouldn't like to guess how much, but not less than a couple of hundred thousand."

"*Nice* work! Off you go."

"How long will you stay?"

"Ten minutes," said Fitzroy, "and then I'll lock the front doors, and any customers will be annoyed!" The shrillness of his laugh was another betrayal of his taut nerves.

He went back to the reception desk. He didn't hear a car stop outside, but for some reason went suddenly tense.

Below, his companions were taking the loot out through the hole they had made.

A man and woman came hurrying down the steps, the man in evening dress, the woman wearing a long dress and a mink wrap. The man produced his key and his card, and said briskly: "Don't want to rush you, but I'm in a hurry."

"All right," said Fitzroy. "I'll be as quick as I can."

There was no reason at all why they should suspect that anything was wrong; no reason for them to believe that anything was. They looked natural, happy. The woman was little more than a girl, and she had a glow in her eyes which suggested that she was not used to hanging onto this particular arm.

Number 413—close to the head of the stairs leading to the lower vault.

Fitzroy, all right until then, became slow-moving, in spite of the impatience of the man; he was drawing attention to himself by his slowness.

He unlocked the door. He knew that it was a matter of custom for the depositor to come in alone, but the girl was like a limpet. A brunette, rather nice, low-bosomed dress, everything. Fitzroy looked at her, and swallowed hard. This was where he could easily make a fool of himself.

He forced a smile.

"Depositor only, please."

"Won't be a jiff, dear," said the young man, and prized himself free.

Fitzroy's fists, clenched until then, unclenched as he closed and locked the door. It seemed a very long way to Number 413, and it seemed as if the man had eyes that could see through the brick walls. Fitzroy's body was aquiver; it was a good thing that the depositor had to unlock his own box.

He did so, took out a string of pearls, left everything else in, locked the box again, and was back at the grille ahead of Fitzroy. Fitzroy breathed rather hissingly. It was over, and he'd kept his head.

After that it was easy.

He did not give a thought to the three prisoners.

It did not occur to him that trouble might lie ahead.

18 . The Tunnel

GIDEON heard the voice of the City Superintendent, warm and friendly, broad in its Scots accent. Gideon was not thinking deeply about this call yet, for he was still preoccupied, although beginning to warn himself that he must go home and get some rest. Only the countless loose ends which came at the end of every day were left undone.

"Hallo, Alec," he said, "what can I do for you?"

"George, man, I'm puzzled a wee bit," the Superintendent said. "You know the Mid-Union place? They keep half the valuables of London there, which is a slight exaggeration but you know what I mean."

"I ken," said Gideon, straight-faced.

"Stop your joking, man. One of the regular customers went there awhile ago and said that he didn't recognize the official at the reception desk. The official seemed to know his way about all right, but he didn't have anyone with him. And that's a curious thing, George. Under the regulations there are always two men on duty at the desk. I've never known it any different. So I told my man to keep a sharp lookout, and just this minute he's telephoned to say that the doors are locked. Now that's not done any night in the year; the Mid-Union is always open. So I'm putting a cordon round the place. I thought you'd like to know."

Gideon said very slowly: "Thanks, Alec, that's good of you." He was thinking more deeply now; worriedly. The City man had probably exaggerated, but the valuables in that safe deposit were worth a fabulous sum. The City police did not want to handle it on their own, and hadn't lost any time asking for help. "All right, I'll put word round and have some support sent along." Gideon went on: "Are you going there yourself?"

"Aye, I think so."

"I'll see you there," promised Gideon.

He still did not, could not, understand how important the job was; but it might be very big indeed. The drive to Wattle Street in the night air would wake him up a bit. If this fizzled out, he could go straight home.

"Lem, hand everything over to Cartwright, will you?" he said. "And then go home. Better forget Estelle; she'll have to keep till morning. Take a chance on getting kicked out of bed."

Lemaitre grimaced, and moved to his telephone.

Gideon went out.

He was in a curiously unsatisfied mood. He could not really complain about the day, and the capture of Sayer had been of first importance. A lot had gone right, too. At heart, he knew that two things had gone very deep: the discovery of Foster's duplicity, and his death; and the face of Mrs. Saparelli. These made the finding of Estelle more urgent, but it would all take time. There were the drugs at Mazzioni's, too—the Italian didn't know they'd been found. He'd probably make a slip—

Gideon telephoned orders to the Flying Squad C.O. to have all available squad cars concentrated on the City area, and then hurried out. Few policemen were about. A squad car was waiting ready for an emergency call, with two men sitting in front. His own car shone darkly under a lamp immediately above it.

Big Ben boomed eleven.

Gideon got into the Wolseley, slammed the door, and then, for some reason, remembered Kate. There was an added cause for his discontent. He could picture her running down the stairs to him, almost eagerly. *Eagerly.* He could picture her bright eyes and attractive face as she had sat next to him on the way to Oxford Street, and the jaunty grace of her walk as she had left him. She hadn't looked back. She'd obviously been pleased that he had taken the trouble to drop in, and to give her the lift. It would have been all right had he been able to go home early, but here it was eleven o'clock, and even if this turned out to be a false alarm, it would be midnight before he was home.

He didn't hurry.

Two squad cars passed him, on their way to the City.

Fitzroy finished locking the door at the top of the narrow steps, and, still whistling, hurried down them to the brightly lit reception desk. The street door was closed, and they were safe. He opened a drawer, and found some loose change and a few one-pound and ten-shilling notes. He stuffed these into his pocket, saluted the drawer, and then looked round quickly, making sure that he hadn't left anything behind. The stubs of three cigarettes were in an ashtray; he emptied this into a piece of paper, screwed it up, and thrust it into his pocket.

Whistling, he went down the next flight of steps to the main deposit room. The three prisoners lay stretched out, and one of them was wriggling.

"You'll soon feel better, chum, don't worry," Fitzroy said, and then hurried toward the lower vault and the hole in the wall.

He saw one of the others, coming back into the vault, *out* of the hole. The man was treading on bits of cement and dirt.

When he saw this, Fitzroy stood stock-still and open-mouthed. No shock could have been greater. He had pictured his accomplices already driving through London to the safety of obscurity. It was like seeing the ghost of a living man. But this was no ghost; it was a youth in the early twenties, looking badly scared.

"What the hell's this?" Fitzroy demanded, in a squeaky voice.

"We—we can't get out," the man said, as thinly.

Fitzroy just would not believe it.

"Don't talk a lot of bull! We can—"

"Police are—are in Hay Court," the man announced.

Fitzroy didn't speak.

The light was good, and he had not put on his mask again. He had pleasant features, an open face, and smiling blue eyes; only they were not smiling now. A new light came into them, cold and ugly.

"We've got to get out," he said. "Where's Jem?"

"Keeping watch."

"Come on," said Fitzroy.

He had to bend almost double, to get through the hole. He took a torch out of his pocket, and it showed the gap they had made in days of patient labor. Now they made grating noises as they moved along, and once or twice Fitzroy bumped his head painfully on the uneven roof; but he didn't stop. Soon bright light glowed.

He reached the cellar of the building next door, one used for storing old files and documents. The night watchman of the building was in his, Fitzroy's, pay; he did not know what they were doing in the cellar, just turned a blind eye and did not come beyond the first cellar level.

The steps leading to that cellar were of stone, crumbling away. Fitzroy went up them slowly. He moved with great caution, while the full significance of what was happening gradually caught up with him.

He reached the ground floor.

There were two ways out of this building; the big, massive front door, which was barred and bolted to prevent anyone from coming in; and a small doorway at the back, leading to a little courtyard and, by a narrow alley, to Milchester Street. It should have been so easy. The only problem was to get the sacks through the alley to the small car which was parked nearby, in a little private parking place. They had studied the time of the police patrols in the district, and had judged the right moment.

Fitzroy went through the deserted building, his footsteps making little sound on the stone floor of the hall; then on linoleum over wide boards; finally over tiles. Soon he saw the faint light against a window. He could not make out the figure of the third burglar, Jem, but heard the faint whisper.

"How many outside?"

"Dunno."

Fitzroy moved toward the window. He shone his torch so that the beam fell upon a chair which he knew one of the others had put into position. He climbed up, and could now peer through a window into the courtyard.

He saw *three* uniformed policemen.

He got down. His heart was thumping, but he told himself that he wasn't really frightened. He had been in tough spots before, and had got out of them. He slid his right hand into his hip pocket; the steel of an automatic pistol felt very cold.

"How many in Wattle Street?"

"Several," Jem muttered. He was the tallest of the three. "Tell you what—"

"What?"

"We could go up the first floor, and climb up, then—"

"Carrying what?" Fitzroy asked sneeringly.

Jem didn't answer.

"We've got a fortune," Fitzroy said, "and we're going to keep it. Stay here a minute."

He turned back, toward the front entrance. He would not have admitted it to anyone, but he did not really know what to do. He had been so sure that this way of escape would be left open, because it didn't affect Mid-Union. He began to ask himself what had gone wrong, but gave that up as futile. He could see the street lights showing against the huge fanlight, but if he went into one of the offices . . .

He tried a door handle; and the door opened.

He stepped into an office. This had frosted glass halfway up the window, but through the top he could see the dark shape of a lamp standard; as he went in, the light outside grew brighter, and the engine of a car sounded. The car swept along the street, the driver changed gear and turned a corner.

A desk stood close to the window.

Fitzroy climbed up, and peered cautiously over the frosted glass into the street.

Two cars were parked a little way along. Men in uniform and in plain clothes were outside the entrance to the Mid-Union building. It wasn't surprising that the police should concentrate on that, but—

How could he get out?

He climbed down and went away from the window as another car arrived, and stopped.

He began to sweat.

They had to get out now. If the police forced their way into the building next door, they would find the hole in five minutes, would be in this building in ten; squeezed between the two forces, Fitzroy and his companions wouldn't have a chance.

"Jem," he said, when back in the rear hall.

"Yes?"

"Any reinforcements out there?"

"No."

"Okay. I'm going to open the door. I'll keep them busy. I'll take a few sparklers with me, that'll fool them. I'll draw them off, and when I've done that, you two get to the car. Take a sack each, and make it snappy."

"But—"

"Think of anything better?" Fitzroy demanded angrily.

"No, but—"

"Then quit crabbing."

"Fitz," the other man said, in a whisper which was hardly audible, "you won't go killing—"

"Who said anything about killing?"

"That gun?"

"What a gutless pair to work with," Fitzroy growled. "Okay, if you want to spend the next ten years in jail, I don't. Do it my way." He didn't give them a chance to answer, but went to the door.

He heard one of them breathing very heavily, then heard the rustle as he picked up the bag.

He opened the door a fraction, mildly surprised that it did open. He knew that the police would be watching intently, and that they hoped that whoever was inside would come out without realizing that anyone was lying in wait.

The light shone on the paving stones of the courtyard; on the frosted glass of the window of offices surrounding it; on a grating; on a drain pipe down which water gurgled. Apart from that, there was no sound.

He opened the door wider.

He saw nothing.

He called in a whisper: "Looks as if they've gone." At heart he did not believe that, but he was desperately anxious to get away, and wishful thinking fooled him for dazzling seconds. "Come on."

He stepped into the courtyard.

No one was in sight, and there were no shadows. Somewhere, high up, the wind whistled, but in this yard all was still. Perhaps they hadn't realized that the door was opening. Perhaps they had gone to reinforce men at the Mid-Union building, not this.

He tiptoed across the courtyard to the end of the alley.

The others were in the courtyard now.

He carried the gun in front of him, but with the passing of every second, the palpitations grew less, for the chances of success were obviously greater. The car wasn't far away; he would lead the way to it, and keep cover while they got in.

Then he heard a gasp: "Fitz!" a man cried.

Fitzroy spun round, saw one of his accomplices stagger, and saw a policeman jumping *down* from a window just above the door.

Other police appeared at first-floor windows, a whistle shrilled out along the alley.

Fitzroy fired at the falling policeman, did not wait to see if he had scored a hit, but turned toward the alley and ran. All hope of loot was gone, escape was his one purpose—escape, with the determination to shoot himself to safety.

19 . The Escape

GIDEON reached the offices of the Mid-Union Company when two police cars and a small crowd of policemen were outside. He slowed down, and a uniformed man with the helmet of the City police came forward, recognized him, and said: "Superintendent Cameron's in Hay Court, sir."

"Hay Court? Where—oh, I know. Thanks. All quiet?"

"Someone inside there as shouldn't be," the constable said emphatically. "The manager's on the way with another set of keys."

"Good," said Gideon. "Thanks." He drove on, not traveling fast, looking for the narrow turning which would take him to Hay Court. He knew the City almost as well as he knew his own Square Mile, but not quite as well. In the West End he could have found his way about blindfolded; here, he wasn't sure, until he saw another tall City policeman at a corner. The man put out an arm, to stop the car: a silent, immutable force, showing all the confidence in the world.

Gideon poked his head through the window.

"I'm Gideon. Is Superintendent Cameron here?"

"Just along here, sir, but I shouldn't take the car if I were you. We've put a barricade up."

"Oh. Thanks. I'll park along here." Gideon drove on a few yards, and climbed out.

The night air was fresh but by no means cold. The sky had a clearness and the stars a brightness which were more common to winter than to spring. Gideon felt not so much tired now, as relaxed.

He walked briskly and with hardly a sound toward Hay Court. At the end of this narrow, cobbled road, he saw a row of galvanized dustbins beneath a gaslight, and grinned at the form of the barricade. Two policemen stood on duty; one peered at and recognized him, and saluted. Gideon passed between two dustbins, sharply conscious of the smell of rotting vegetables.

There was a small square, surrounded by high buildings, and with two recesses holding the doorways to small buildings, and one lane, which led toward Fenchurch Street. He remembered it well now. He saw two policemen climbing up the side of one office building, and watched them in the semidarkness. They were making for a window sill above a door which was closed, and edged their way along.

He saw shadowy figures at one of the windows.

Cameron came up.

"Hallo, George," he greeted, "good to see you." They shook hands. Cameron was a man of medium size; even in this light his fair features and sharp, pointed nose were evident. "We think they'll come out this way; a door opened a few minutes ago. And there's a car waiting not far away, often parked there late, I'm told."

"Any idea who it is?"

"No." Cameron whispered a few other details: that he had telephoned the manager of the Mid-Union Company and been told that the top gates should not be locked. An observant constable had really started this, and a puzzled customer taken it a step further.

Cameron was in a mood for rejoicing; so was Gideon. Usually they were called after the job was done, when the men and the loot were miles away, and the whole resources of the Force had to be called on, straining the men almost beyond endurance. This should be a short, sharp case, and—

"Look!" whispered Cameron.

In the faint light, they saw the doorway open. Then a man appeared, and looked round, cautiously. Had he looked up, he must have seen the policemen poised above him. He hesitated, then went back into the building.

Gideon's big hand closed round Cameron's arm, and gave a silent message. Cameron breathed: *"Aye, a gun."*

Gideon felt his mood changing to one of acute wariness. He wanted to shout a warning to everyone else within earshot, but dared not. He sensed Cameron's increased tension. Then the man with the gun came forward; other dark figures emerged from the doorway.

One of the policemen jumped.

The movement, the gasp and the scuffle of footsteps came quickly, and then the first man swung round, and Gideon saw him raise his arm.

"Look out!" roared Gideon.

But the shot came before his words. He saw the policeman falling, and heard a kind of squeal. Then the men who had come from the doorway all moved together, but it was impossible to tell one from another. A heavy weight fell. Policemen closed with one man, and then torch lights shone out, carving Hay Court into sections of bright light and darkness, showing the pallor of frightened faces, the darkness of clothes, the gun, struggling feet, a big sack.

Gideon concentrated on the gunman.

Fitzroy was free of police for a split second, but another was running at him, and Cameron moved, too. Fitzroy fired, point blank.

". . . swine," Gideon muttered under his breath.

He waited, like a footballer ready to go into the tackle, swaying from side to side. The policeman fell back, then crumpled up.

Fitzroy was free of him—and Fitzroy saw another policeman coming at him.

He fired again.

The policeman swayed to one side, and Fitzroy made a wild leap, passed him, and reached the end of the alley. The gun was waving as he ran.

Only one big man in plain clothes was in his path.

"Now, drop that," Gideon said. He was surprised that his own voice was level and intelligible. "Don't be a fool."

For a second, a long, frightening, deathly second, neither man moved.

Gideon knew that words were useless, only one thing could save him.

He plunged forward, hands outstretched to clutch the gunman's ankles. It was impossible to tell whether the other would shoot at him or not; if he pointed the gun downward and fired, he couldn't miss.

Gideon felt the cloth of the man's trousers in his fingers. He tried to grab the ankles, but missed. A foot cracked against his temple, and there was an explosive sound inside his head; he wasn't sure whether it came from a shot or the kick. He drew his hands in, instinctively, to protect his head. The thief jumped over him, and the sharp crack of another shot came.

Gideon began to pick himself up, drunkenly.

No one came to help him.

He got to one knee. There was a nasty throbbing in his ears, but he knew that he hadn't been shot, because there was no blood. He felt light-headed. Sounds came as if from a long way off. On his feet, he staggered until he came up against the wall.

Someone said: "You all right, sir?"

"Yes. Yes, don't worry about—" He didn't finish, but tried to focus his gaze. The light in the court was brighter and clearer now, coming from rooms in the near-by offices as well as the torches. It was a strange, almost a frightening sight. Men bent over two policemen who lay on the ground, one of them grunting; moaning. Two men, each handcuffed to a policeman, were standing quite still. Sacks near the doorway told their own story.

Then, from some way off, came the bark of another shot.

"I've got a nasty feeling," Gideon said, "that that brute's going to get away."

"You all right, George?" Cameron demanded.

"Yes, thanks."

"What've you done to your head?"

"Just a kick."

"We'll get him," Cameron said, "we'll get him if—"

He didn't finish. Words were futile, rage with himself as well as with the prisoner who had escaped was just as futile. The simple truth was that the man had shot his way out of the ambush, and in doing so, wounded three policemen, one of whom seemed to be in a bad way.

Ambulances had been summoned.

A general call had gone out for the gunman, and at least they knew his name and had a description; one of the prisoners had talked freely; words had spilled out with fear.

It had all happened ten minutes ago, and it seemed like hours. Gideon, his head aching but no longer giddy, had sent out the instructions by radio-telephone, but he felt sick. It wasn't because of the kick or the fall—it was because of the failure.

Could one call it failure?

Already, he was beginning to ask himself questions about it, and his own part in it. Cameron had been in charge, but he needn't have left so much to the City man. The truth was that he had taken this too casually, almost like an exercise; "trapped men cannot get away" had been his axiom, and he hadn't allowed for a killer shooting his way to freedom. Failure as such wasn't the only bad thing. It meant that the Yard and all the Divisions would have to screw themselves up to a high-powered effort, and tension was never-ending. If all three men had been captured, the police could have breathed more easily; only routine jobs need have worried them; jobs like this seldom came up more than once in two or three weeks.

Well, it had to be done.

The night-duty man at the Yard would be doing much the same as he had been doing all day; every policeman in London would be steeling himself. Gideon couldn't explain why, but it was a fact that if a policeman were shot and injured, especially if one were killed, something seemed to be infused into the rest of the Force. They became killer-minded. They would work until they dropped, and they would get this man Fitzroy. But that wasn't the beginning or the end. They could only do one job at a time, and the little crooks who worked by night were quick to sense when the police had a big job on. This was a night when the graph of London's crime would shoot upward sharply. In temporary, perhaps in false, security, the sneak thieves would be out like vultures ready to peck and tear at an unprotected carcass.

Gideon knew all this.

He knew, too, that if he had grabbed an inch closer to the gunman's ankles, he would have brought the man down, and there would have been no
need for the great hunt. That was one cause of his bitterness. He of all men
knew how tightly the police were stretched; and he could have eased the
burden for a little while, but had failed.

There it was.

He heard a bell ringing, shrilly; an ambulance was on its way. In the
distance, another sounded. Then men came from Wattle Street. Next
Gideon and Cameron went through the building next to Mid-Union, and
found the hole which had been made into the lower vault.

Gideon's lips turned down.

"They didn't do that in a hurry," he said.

"Dunno," said Cameron, and bent down to pick up a small electric drill.
"Homemade job, and it wouldn't make much noise." He paused. "You can't
get through there, can you?"

"No," said Gideon.

"See you on the other side." Cameron was already on his knees, ready
to climb through.

Gideon walked back, into Hay Court, along the narrow cobbled road,
into Wattle Street. The door was being unlocked, policemen were waiting
warily, in case other gunmen lay in wait. None did. Gideon and a scared,
worried manager, who had hurried from his home in Hampstead, led the
way down the stairs. The empty reception office, the narrow stairs, the
ordinary strong room—and the three members of the staff were found,
stretched out, two of them struggling with their bonds, the other unconscious.

Outside, the hunt for Fitzroy went on.

Gideon yawned.

It was half-past twelve, exactly fifteen hours since he had stepped into
his office that morning, an age ago. He was by himself for a few minutes,
sitting in his car. No word had come in of Fitzroy's capture, and the hunt
might go on for days. The ambulances had carried off the wounded policemen and one of the Mid-Union staff, who was suffering badly from shock
and fright. None of the victims was likely to die, that was one relief. The
accomplices had told their story, without defiance, as if they had realized
that nothing else could help them.

They were amateurs who'd adapted army-acquired knowledge to the safe-
breaking. If they were to be believed, and Gideon thought that they were,
the idea had been Fitzroy's. But neither of them had raised any strenuous
objections and they had come in of their own free will. These were the kind
who really worried Gideon most. The old lags, the regulars, the confidence

tricksters, the blackmailers, even the dope distributors—all of them were within Gideon's range. He could understand them and he could calculate what they were likely to do. Amateurs were different, and their methods were different. They were likely to be more reckless, and so more deadly. A man like Fitzroy saw this as a great adventure, as well as a chance of making a fortune. A man like Chang saw it as a game to be played with great precision, and Chang would never take such risks as Fitzroy, would never shoot his way out. If he killed, it would be cunningly—as he had killed Foster.

Gideon found his lips twisting in a wry, almost bitter smile.

If Lemaitre had said that, he would have jumped on him. It was still a guess. It might not be a wild guess; there might be some reason for making it, but it was still a guess. He didn't *know* that Chang had killed Foster, tried to kill Birdy, was hunting Estelle down. He could not be sure that Foster had not served some other master, too, whom Chang did not know.

That was the trouble: not knowing.

If only he had known at the beginning of the day what he knew now, how much could have been prevented and how much done. If he'd handled Foster differently, Foster might be alive now, and willingly co-operating.

The thought of that hit Gideon with savage force, and suddenly he understood why he had been so easily depressed during the day.

He hadn't liked Foster, and that was partly why his temper had broken. With almost any other man at the Yard—the sergeant who'd been so nervous and yet so efficient, for instance—he could have talked reasonably, almost as a friend. He began to go over in his mind the things he should have said to Foster, and the line he should have taken.

His head ached.

He wished Cameron would hurry up with whatever he was doing.

He wondered if they'd catch Fitzroy.

He worried about red-haired Estelle.

He heard the radiotelephone buzz, looked at the instrument without enthusiasm, picked it up, and flicked it on: "Gideon speaking."

"How you doing, George?" This was Lemaitre, speaking direct; and Lemaitre with a lilt in his voice as if his Fifi and his fears were all forgotten. Lemaitre speaking like that was a tonic in itself: cold water in Gideon's face. "Like to meet me over at Shippy's place, Whitechapel?"

"Why, what's on?"

"We've made quite a find," Lemaitre said smugly. "See you there!"

He banged his receiver down.

Gideon fought down the momentary annoyance. In some ways Lemaitre would never grow up, and his attitude now was rather like a boy's. But he was highly pleased with himself, and that might mean anything.

Anything. Gideon was getting up when the telephone rang again, was tempted to go out and ignore it, but conquered temptation.

He had never been more glad.

"Gillick here, G.G.," said Gillick, spitting his words out. "Now I have got some news for us, trust B2. Eh, old boy? All right, I'll get to the point. We've picked up that chap Fessell you're after, the Islington sweetshop job. One of my chaps thought he saw him earlier in the evening, and kept a lookout. He was in a hotel, dabs make it certain. Shall we keep him here for the night?"

20 . End of the Day

GIDEON drove through the deserted streets of the City toward the East End, munching a ham sandwich which Cameron had laid on. Cameron was looking after everything at the Mid-Union now, and Gideon wasn't needed any more. Gideon wasn't sure that he had ever been needed, but at least he knew all about it.

Depression at the knowledge that Fitzroy was still at large had gone. Fessell's capture was a fresh triumph, and there was the titillating promise of Lemaitre's manner.

Shippy's was a café nearly of ill repute, in the Whitechapel area, not far from the Mile End Road. It was known to be the rendezvous of most of the really bad types in the East End. Murphy used it, and most of the men who worked in liaison with Murphy. Many ugly crimes were plotted there. Yet outwardly it was reputable, and Shippy, the man who ran it, looked like a citizen par excellence. As a café, it was not only good, it was spotlessly clean. Shippy, or Luke Shipham, was a thin man who always wore a new white apron, a stiff white collar and a gray tie, whose hair was smartly groomed and brushed to a high quiff. He had never been inside, but had been interviewed a hundred times, and always presented the same bland story and the same bland face: "Nothing wrong happens in my café, Mr. Gideon; I can't refuse to serve men because they might be criminal, can I?"

Most people prophesied that Shippy would slip up one day. Gideon wasn't so sure.

Whitechapel was dimly lit, the wide streets seemed derelict, the unlighted houses were drab, deserted hovels. A few neon advertising signs burned in the High Street, but there was a long gap in them, broken when Gideon came within sight of Shippy's. The name was emblazoned in white neon across the front of the double-fronted café. As Gideon pulled up outside he was impressed, as he had often been, by the smart appearance of the place.

Put it in Oxford Street, and it would compare favorably with most restaurants.

A blue sign declared: OPEN DAY & NIGHT.

A squad car was outside, and two uniformed policemen were walking up and down. They came closer to see who it was, and then touched their helmets.

Gideon felt a quickening of excitement as he pushed open the double doors.

The big room with cream-painted walls, blue and red tables and chairs, and the brightly shining urn at the long counter struck warm. There was a smell of ground coffee. Sandwiches in a glass showcase looked more succulent than those which Gideon had been given by Cameron, and far superior to anything ever supplied by the Yard. A youth stood behind the counter, and two plain-clothes men of the Flying Squad were sitting at a table, eating and drinking; they jumped up when Gideon appeared.

"All right," Gideon said, "so long as you pay for it. Mr. Lemaitre here?"

One man grinned; the other said: "Yes, sir," and nodded toward the open door leading to the kitchen and the room at the back of the restaurant. Gideon found himself thinking of Chang; and restaurants generally; and the restaurants Chang supplied with tea and other goods.

Shippy, looking correct and aloof, was standing in one corner of the room. A uniformed policeman was watching him. Lemaitre, hat and coat off, sleeves rolled up over those big, swelling arms, sat at a desk with another Yard man, and on a big, deal-topped table there were wads and wads of one-pound notes.

Gideon caught his breath.

"Mr. Gideon, sir," Shippy said quickly. "I didn't know anything about it. A gentleman asked if he could leave his luggage here, and I obligingly said that he could. Mr. Lemaitre is being extremely rude, and—"

Lemaitre looked up, grinning so broadly that Gideon was infected by a kind of gaiety.

"Hark at him," Lemaitre scoffed. "White as blurry snow! Know what we've found, Geo—— Superintendent?"

Gideon said slowly, and with great, choking relish: "I've got a good idea, Chief Inspector."

"The notes from the Waterloo Station job," said Lemaitre, unable to repress his bubbling elation. "Exactly the same number of packages, and I've counted five, each with five hundred quid in it. Found them in three suitcases." He chuckled. "I'll tell you more when Mr. Shipham isn't with us."

"Mr. Gideon—" Shipham had a walrus-shaped mustache and sad-looking eyes, but they were scared, too, as if he knew that he was really in trouble at last. "I assure you that I knew nothing about it, and I must ask—"

"Just a minute," Gideon said. "Have you made any charge, Chief Inspector?"

"Not yet."

"All right." Gideon was brisk. "You'll have your chance to tell us all about it," he told Shipham. "Now I'm charging you with being in possession of a quantity of treasury notes, knowing them to have been stolen. Anything you say may be taken down and used as evidence. Constable—"

"It's just not right," Shipham protested. "I don't know a thing, Mr. Gideon. In the name of fair play, I appeal to you."

Gideon looked at him coldly.

"Shippy," he said, "in these mail-van jobs, three people have been seriously injured, one of them crippled for life. A man was injured at Waterloo this afternoon. That's only one angle. You'll get your chance to say what you like to the magistrate in the morning, and if you want a solicitor, you can send for him. But not until we've got you at the Yard. Constable, ask one of the officers outside to come in, will you?"

"Yes, sir."

"But my business—" began Shippy fearfully.

"You won't be doing any more business tonight, and in the morning your wife can open, if we've finished searching," Gideon declared.

Shipham didn't argue any more.

Lemaitre finished a count, and then leaned back, taking cigarettes out of the pocket of the coat hanging on the back of the chair. The other man said: "Five hundred here, too."

"Oh, it's the same stuff," Lemaitre said emphatically. "Every penny of it, George. What a bit of blurry luck!"

It was almost too good to be true.

"How'd we get it?"

"When we picked up the Snide he was in a bad way," said Lemaitre. "Knocked silly, you know. He said he must get to Shippy's. No one took much notice of it, it's a meeting place for the mob, but it was reported and I noticed it. So I got G5 to keep an eye on Shippy's. Half an hour before I called you on the r. t. another of Murphy's boys came here empty-handed and went out with a case. The G5 chap stopped him. There was a hell of a schemozzle, and three others tried to get the case away. Then Lady Luck looked in, because a squad car was coming along." Lemaitre chuckled and rubbed his hands jubilantly. "Now we've got a busy day tomorrow, George!"

Gideon smiled faintly.

He picked up one of the bundles of notes. Fingerprint men had already been over them; he could see the traces of powder. Prints didn't show up on the edges of a bundle of notes, but a few might have been handled top and bottom. Shippy would probably crack when he knew that they'd be able to send him down. Was it worth trying to work on him now? Gideon went into a tiny office behind the shop and ran through the papers— bills, invoices, receipts, delivery orders. Then he began to feel a fresh and tingling excitement; there were several invoices from Chang's restaurant, mostly for tea; yet other big packages marked TEA had a blender's name and address.

Gideon had a funny choking feeling.

Small packets with a different label were also marked TEA. One was open at the end. Gideon took it off a shelf and looked inside.

There were cigarettes.

He stared blankly—and then began to smile slowly, tensely, unbelievingly. He took out a cigarette, broke it, and sniffed.

These were loaded with marijuana; these were reefers! If he could trace this "tea" to Chang—

Gideon laid on a raid before Chang could get warning of Shippy's arrest.

Chang wasn't at the restaurant.

The "tea" was.

Gideon drove home through this dark, quiet London, and the events of the day flitted through his mind. It had been a wonderful day; the day of a lifetime; never to be forgotten.

Chang was under a charge, Mazzioni had been picked up again, and there was a chance of breaking Murphy's power, too, although that would take some time.

Thoughts of the Saparelli family, especially the mother, quietened his jubilation, but the police had done all anyone could, and time would help, wouldn't it?

He thought of Foster's sister; of Estelle who was no longer in danger. They hadn't got the man who'd stolen Lady Muriel's jewels; a dozen, a hundred crimes had been committed that day which were still unsolved; some would remain so for weeks, and some forever.

They'd have to find Fitzroy, and there was a case all right. Red-handed prisoners, no problem, just routine. That was how he liked them.

Gideon turned into Harringdon Street and saw a light on at the first-floor bedroom window of his house. He ran the car into the wooden garage at the corner, and hurried back, suddenly anxious; was one of the youngsters ill?

He let himself in quietly, hurried upstairs, saw a light beneath the door of his room, but nowhere else. So Kate was awake. He called out softly: "Only me."

He opened the door.

Kate was sitting up in bed with a pink angora wool bed jacket round her shoulders, a book open in front of her. She looked tired, but her color was good, and her hair neat in a net he sensed rather than saw.

"What's this?" he asked. "Can't you sleep?"

"Malcolm ran a little temperature," Kate said, "and he hasn't been settled for long. I rang the Yard, and they said you were on your way, so I thought you might like a cup of tea." She glanced at a tray on a bedside table, and the kettle on the bedroom gas ring. Under a silver dish cover, Gideon was sure, were sandwiches.

Kate hadn't worried to do anything like this for years.

"Nothing I'd like more," he said, and went to light the gas. But she slid out of bed.

"I'll do it. You look tired out. And what's that nasty bruise on your temple?"

"Oh, nothing," said Gideon. "All in the day's work."

He began to undress, and to talk as he did so, only vaguely understanding that it was a long time since he had talked about the day's work with Kate. It was as if the years had been bridged, so that they were together again. He did not think of that in so many words; he just felt that it was good to be home.

Gideon's Week

1 . Report for Gideon

As GEORGE GIDEON of the Criminal Investigation Department drove from his home to Scotland Yard that Monday morning, a report was being prepared for him. He knew that it would be ready by the time he reached his office, and could imagine the antics of Lemaitre and the others helping to prepare it. He remembered performing similar antics, long before he had become Commander Gideon. This newly-created title irked him a little; in many ways he preferred the old "Chief Superintendent." Still, "Commander" had advantages, and really meant what it said. Gideon, above everything else a human being, enjoyed the warm glow which springs from reaching the top of the tree.

He had a fairly good idea of what would be in the report, too, although no one had telephoned him since he had left the Yard late on Friday evening. In general terms, he would receive a summary of the crimes committed in the Greater London area during the week end, as well as a résumé of what had happened during the previous week; the report would name all the suspects who had been charged and were now on remand; and would also give the names of suspects against whom there was not enough evidence for an arrest. If the Yard had only to stretch out a hand and pick up those offenders who were known to have committed a crime, life would be comparatively easy. Gideon's first mentor in the Criminal Investigation Department had been fond of saying that the burden of proof was the heaviest burden the Yard had to carry. Trite but true.

It was a mild spring morning, welcome after several bitter weeks and snowfalls which had twice dislocated London traffic and had covered most of the British Isles. As a policeman, Gideon liked cold weather. Those members of his erring flock who worked under cover of darkness—and that was most of them—disliked cold winds, cold hands, shivery corners and slippery roads. They had to be quick and they had to be quiet, so it wasn't surprising

that there was less crime during exceptionally cold spells. The one which
had just passed had been one of the coldest and quietest.

Among the things which made Gideon different from most policemen,
and probably the greatest single factor in his early promotion—for to be
Commander of the C.I.D. at the age of forty-nine was quite remarkable—
was the way he looked upon simple facts such as the effect of wintry weather
on those crooks who worked by night. To most police, the cold spell simply
meant that the bad men wouldn't get around so much. So life would be
quieter, the magistrates' courts less busy, the telephone less urgent and the
insurance companies less active. Gideon saw beyond all this. He saw hungry
crooks, their patient wives, their children going to school so close to the
edge of hunger that it might affect them for most of their lives. Gideon
wasn't simply being humanitarian when he recognized the fact that a crook
could be as fond of his wife and children as any copper, and be just as
anxious to keep them well fed.

With so many burglars nearly desperate to earn money, as soon as the
weather broke, there was likely to be a big crop of crimes. The Divisions,
especially the uniformed men, might be off their guard because of the recent
lull. That was a thing to prevent.

As Gideon drove round Parliament Square and was held up by a traffic
policeman first at the end of Parliament Street and then at the approach to
the Embankment, the duty policeman recognized and saluted him. He drove
slowly along the Embankment, hardly aware of the Thames stretching out
so far ahead, dull and flat in the pale morning mist. Nearing the Yard, he
saw a Squad car swing out of the wide gateway, turn away from him, and
go hurtling toward Blackfriars and the City. Something was up, or a Squad
car wouldn't be going at such speed. He watched the driver weaving in and
out of traffic with the effortless control which marked him as better than
average, even for the Flying Squad.

Then Gideon turned into the Yard.

One of the advantages of his new rank was the fact that parking space
was always left for him. True, his name wasn't on it, but neither was the
Assistant Commissioner's C.I.D. on his, or the Commissioner's for that matter. All the same, no one would pirate their place or Gideon's.

He got out and wound up the windows. The car, a black Wolseley, had
a few surface scratches, but for a year-old model it had been kept very well.
He was beginning to feel affection for it, as for a spirited horse. He turned
toward the steps which led into the C.I.D. building, well aware that he
was being watched not only by all the plain-clothes and uniformed men
in sight, some coming and some going, but also by people at the windows
and almost certainly by a sergeant who was now nipping along to his office
and telling Chief Inspector Lemaitre that the Boss was on the way.

What Gideon did not know was that those who had no need to be wary of him were also aware, by a kind of telepathy, that he was here. And of course he didn't really know what he looked like. He realized that he was big; but so were many men at the Yard. It did not occur to him that none of these others had quite his massive hugeness, or his great breadth of shoulder. He was six feet two, and his fondness for the comfort of loose-fitting clothes made him look even bigger than he was. He walked casually, as if out for a stroll, and with a steady rhythm which, given the right circumstances, held a kind of menace. Walking, Gideon looked as if he knew exactly where he was going, when and how he wanted to get there, and that nothing and nobody would be able to put him off his course.

Lemaitre would now be crossing the t's and dotting the i's of the report, he mused, smiling dryly to himself. So the news flashed round the Yard that Gideon was in a sunny mood.

He reached the top of the steps, and the duty sergeant smiled a familiar welcome, while younger men were more formal. At the lift, with its one-armed operator, he found another man waiting to go up, a comparative youngster in plain clothes. This man was fresh-faced, had bright blue eyes, and was dressed in a carefully pressed navy blue suit which looked embarrassingly new. He stiffened when Gideon got in, as if he would readily press himself into the side of the lift.

"Hallo, Joe," Gideon greeted the liftman.

"Bit milder, isn't it?" the liftman said with the casualness of a man who had been taking senior officials up and down for twenty-odd years.

"Morning, sir," the fresh-complexioned young man said, and turned a brighter red.

"Morning," responded Gideon, and tipped his trilby hat to the back of his head; he felt warm. "You're Abbott, aren't you?"

"That's right, sir!" The man was delighted, and that meant one good thing; he was not likely to get blasé or too cocksure—at least, not until he was past the dangerous formative days for a detective officer at the Yard. Looked a nice lad. Twenty-six or seven, Gideon hazarded. He'd been blooded when on the beat in a running battle with two thieves and a stolen car, had come through with a black eye, a sprained ankle and a week's sick-leave, and the thieves were still inside. Gideon, knowing about this as he acquired knowledge about everyone at the Yard, couldn't decide whether or not to mention it. Better not risk giving Abbott a swelled head. It would be wiser to send him off with a different kind of satisfaction.

"Likely to have a burst of bad-man trouble the next few days, if the weather holds," Gideon said.

"Are we, sir?"

Gideon thought: As honest as they come. Keep that way. "Usually do as soon as we thaw out a bit," he went on, and actually found himself wondering whether, in twenty-five years' time, this same Abbott would remember it as an axiom, as he, Gideon, had remembered the one about the burden of proof.

The lift stopped, Abbott kept back, Gideon nodded and went out. Here he was just round the corner from the office which he shared with Chief Inspector Lemaitre. He wasn't surprised to see the door open an inch; that would give Lemaitre and anyone with him the split second of warning they imagined they needed. He wondered if Lemaitre had thought of sending a note round to the Divisions, saying that they could expect more trouble than they'd been having lately. Probably not.

He pushed open the door.

Lemaitre, tall, thinnish and lanky, was standing up by the telephone, coat off, collar undone, red tie hanging down, thin dark hair smoothed flat, a film of sweat on his forehead. Heat struck Gideon as he went in, although all four office windows, overlooking the Embankment and the Thames, were open as wide as they could be.

"Okay," Lemaitre said, and put the receiver down. "Cor," he said, "what a morning! First time we've had the central heating working properly this year, I should think. Trust those ruddy maintenance men to choose the first warm morning. I'd—"

Gideon shut the door.

"Morning, Lem," he said.

Lemaitre grinned.

"Morning, George. Had a nice week end?"

"Bit of all right," said Gideon, "didn't do a damned thing and it toned me up nicely for the week. How about you?" He was already loosening his collar; it was really steaming hot and unpleasant. He glanced at the big radiator; Lemaitre had turned the heat off, so the room should soon cool down.

"So so," said Lemaitre; "it's a funny thing that whenever you have a week end off, all the nuisance jobs come up, or else the things you know most about. They're all in the report. Pretty slack, generally."

"Yes." Gideon sat down behind his big desk, where the report was waiting, mostly typewritten but with the last-minute additions in Lemaitre's almost copperplate handwriting. "What's on this morning? Saw a Squad car go out."

"Safe been blown at Kelly's Bank, Fleet Street," said Lemaitre. "I've told Dooley to get ready to go over there, and King-Hadden's sending over right away. No night watchman, so the job might have been done any time over the week end, cold as a stone now. Still, you never know." There was Lemaitre, doing the thing which would always keep him down to C.I.'s rank—

jumping to conclusions. He couldn't help it, and nothing would now be able to stop him. His manner and his tone told the story clearly: he didn't expect to get much in the way of results.

"Who's the Squad car driver, d'you know?"

"Soon find out," said Lemaitre, and plucked at the telephone as Gideon sat down, coat already off, and perspiration beginning to break out on his forehead. "Only thing of real interest cropped up since Friday is that they've got that kid for the Primrose Girl job."

Gideon looked up quickly. "Sure?"

"Cast-iron. Fingerprints, footprints, his knife, known to have been with her on Thursday afternoon, jealous because she threw him over. Named Rose. Funny, isn't it?"

"What's funny?" asked Gideon almost sharply, but Lemaitre had switched from him to the telephone. Gideon studied his assistant almost as if he were looking at someone he didn't know well, but his tension eased while Lemaitre talked.

"That you, Freddy? . . . No, rest easy, the Boss is in and wants to know who was driving our car on the Kelly's Bank job. . . . Oh, Sammy Brown . . . dunno, hold on a minute." Lemaitre lowered the receiver but asked so that both the Squad chief and Gideon could hear. "Anything wrong, he wants to know."

"He's a good driver, don't waste him on the easy jobs," Gideon said. "I'll have a word with Freddy a bit later on."

He glanced through the nine pages of the typewritten report, and near the end reached the item about the arrest and charging of one, William Sydney Rose, for the murder of Winifred Ethel Norton, known as the Primrose Girl because she had died with a little bunch of primroses clutched in her left hand. On Friday morning, it had been the newspaper story of the week, perhaps of the month.

There wasn't much here. Routine checking had led them to William Sydney Rose because he was known as a friend of the girl's. This was mainly a Divisional job, although a Yard man had been present at the time of the arrest.

"What's funny about it?" Gideon asked.

"Eh? I didn't know anything was—oh, Rose?" Lemaitre grinned. "You slipping, George? The Primrose Girl murdered by a man named Rose, see. *Rose*."

Gideon looked down at the report.

"Hm. They haven't picked up anyone for the Battersea hit-and-run job, have they?"

"No," said Lemaitre.

He gathered from Gideon's manner that this wasn't likely to be a talking session, after all, and he didn't greatly mind. He sat down, lit a cigarette with a lighter which wouldn't work properly, and glanced at the dark, ugly nicotine stain on his fingers. Then he started to work on two or three routine reports that would have to be vetted by Gideon before they were sent to the Assistant Commissioner.

Between nine and ten in the morning the telephone was usually quiet—well, quieter than at other times. It didn't ring for fifteen minutes. In that time Gideon had read the report through quickly and marked certain paragraphs for a more careful reading. There wasn't a great deal. Seven burglaries Saturday night, four last night. Two fires, one with arson suspected. The usual crop of drunk and disorderlies on Saturday, the usual week-end harvest of West End streetwalkers, a bottle-and-broken-glass fight outside a Stepney public house with both protagonists in hospital but neither on the danger list. Expected arrest connected with some currency frauds, a warning from Switzerland about a man now on his way by air, believed to have five hundred watches hidden in his luggage. Nothing really sensational. Nothing to presage an abnormal week, except the mild weather. Nothing to get under Gideon's skin except the Primrose Girl. You could be as tough as you liked, but there were weak spots. He had three daughters and three sons; his second daughter had been out picking primroses in a sheltered spot in Surrey on Thursday afternoon. The Primrose Girl had been out picking primroses in a sheltered spot in Kent the same afternoon; and while she had been there, she had been savagely attacked, with eleven knife wounds in the chest. Gideon had seen photographs but not the body. He had also seen the photograph of the girl's left hand, tight about some withered primroses.

The telephone broke the quiet.

A telephone call to Gideon could be the prelude to anything from a high-powered murder investigation to a summons from the Assistant Commissioner for Crime to go and see him. It could be some routine question or piece of information. It could be from a squealer with information to sell. It could be his tailor, to tell him that his new suit was ready for fitting; it could even be one of his elder children or his wife, although they seldom troubled him at the office. The essential thing, as Gideon knew, was that when he picked up the telephone he should have a completely open mind; and that he shouldn't be preoccupied. One thing at a time was always safest.

He didn't get any sense of impending disaster.

He didn't flicker an eyelid when the operator said, "It's Mr. Ripley, of Manchester, sir."

Ripley was his opposite number with the Manchester City C.I.D.

"Put him through."

Lemaitre glanced up, and Gideon mouthed, "Manchester."

"Could be that slush job; they picked up about sixty-five one-pounders on Friday," Lemaitre said at once.

Gideon nodded, but he didn't share the opinion. Ripley of Manchester wouldn't telephone him about a job that was already known at the Yard. He knew Ripley too well to think that. They had met first during their early days in the Force; and as far as Gideon had close friends, Ripley was one.

There were the usual noises on the line, and Gideon waited patiently for Ripley's voice, with those broad a's and something like t' for "the." Only one thing was certain: Ripley would not ring him on long distance unless he was prodded by a sense of real urgency.

Then a voice that was not Ripley's came on the line.

"Sorry, Commander, but the Superintendent's been called away in a hurry. He'll ring you as soon as he can."

"That suits me," said Gideon patiently, "but what's it all about?"

The other said, "Mass escape from Millways jail, it's keeping us well on the hop up here. Mr. Ripley wanted you to have word quickly. I'll ring you again, sir."

The Manchester man rang off before Gideon spoke.

2 . The Escape

GIDEON put down the receiver slowly, telling Lemaitre what the trouble was, as he did so. Lemaitre got up, fumbled for a cigarette from a packet, and lit it as he was halfway across the office. His eyes were screwed up, and his lips pursed. "*Mass* escape?" he asked; and when Gideon nodded but didn't speak, he stopped in front of Gideon's desk and then perched on a corner. "I'll bet that means Benson's out."

Gideon brought out his dark cherrywood pipe, with the big bowl that was rough on the outside, something to fiddle with at the moment, and not to smoke.

"Lem, why don't you give it a rest? There are over a thousand prisoners at Millways, and I don't suppose more than half a dozen have got away. There isn't any reason to think that Benson's one of them."

Lemaitre had the sense not to argue.

"What beats me," Gideon went on, "is how they've managed an escape up there this week end. All Lancashire had another blizzard Saturday; I was told the place was snowed up, especially out near Millways. Funny business."

"I could ring Manchester, and—"

"Tell you what we'd better do," said Gideon; "get the rest of the work as clear as we can, in case we have to spend time on this job. Not that anyone who escaped from Millways can have got as far south as this. Now, let's get a move on."

"Okay, George," said Lemaitre, just managing to keep the note of resignation out of his voice. "What goes?"

"First, put a flash out to all Squad and patrol cars to keep a specially keen watch today, tell them that now it's warmer we might find some of the boys getting busy. That will spread out from the patrol cars to the Divisions. Then get me the fullest report you can from the Division on the Primrose Girl job. Find out if Birdy's better this morning and carrying on at the Old Bailey; heck of a mess when a judge falls ill and a trial has to be interrupted. Then . . ."

Instructions, suggestions and questions streamed from Gideon as water from a tap. Soon he was sending for sergeants, for Detective-Inspectors and Chief Inspectors to give brief reports on jobs they were doing. He kept his voice pitched low, and did not give the impression that he paid much attention to what was being said, but every man who entered the office knew better than that. In some ways they knew even better than Gideon himself, because they could watch from the outside. In his way he was a fascinating object lesson. He absorbed information so accurately that he seemed to be almost as familiar with each job as the men who were working on it; a kind of C.I.D. Memory Man. If he didn't get a point clearly, he worried it. And he put out suggestions about how to handle a job, sometimes carefully wrapped up, occasionally twisted so that they seemed to emanate from the man he was talking to. It was a form of briefing which Gideon himself had introduced, and had become almost part of the tradition at the Yard. Sometimes it lasted all morning; today it was over in an hour.

Three times senior officers had asked if he knew what had happened at Millways; the rumor was already spreading, and had probably been started by the telephone operator, unless there was a teleprint message in. He checked; he didn't want operators talking too freely. There had been a teleprint, received a little while after he had spoken to the man from Manchester, but it gave only one additional piece of information.

Nine men had escaped. Five were named, but the man Benson wasn't among them. Didn't Millways *know* who'd gone, yet? They'd alert the local police the moment they knew about a break, of course, and nine would take a lot of checking.

"Why don't you call Ripley?" asked Lemaitre.

"He'll ring when he's ready." Gideon was still smoothing his pipe. It was much cooler in the office, but outside the mist was giving way to sunshine; the Thames could look good. Most mornings he would have gone for a stroll round London's Square Mile—his own particular beat, the one he'd walked for years before being planted on the desk—but the hope of an early call from Ripley stopped him.

Lemaitre went out of the office; there wasn't much doubt that he was trying to find out all he could about the Millways break, but Gideon didn't let himself think too much about it and hardly at all about Benson.

If Benson had escaped . . .

He was getting as bad as Lemaitre. As a matter of fact, this morning he was feeling sour toward Lem, although he couldn't really say why. His good mood hadn't developed, and for some reason he was on edge. That Primrose Girl job was under his skin, of course, and he knew that was a bad thing.

Then Ripley came through.

"That you, George?"

"What's the matter up there, Jim, everyone got frostbite?"

"When I've finished telling you what I think of this job at Millways, you'll have frostbite," growled Ripley. "As a matter of fact, George, it was a right smart piece of work; we have to give them that. They took advantage of the snow; in all about a hundred prisoners were involved in it, and nine got outside the prison walls. We've picked up two already. They built a kind of staircase in hard-packed snow, which had frozen hard, and went over the wall. Must have paid a screw to keep his back turned, but—well, that's not my worry now, that's the Governor's, and I wouldn't like to be in the Chief Warder's shoes this morning. Thing is, George, Benson's one of the seven who are still free."

Gideon said slowly: "Oh, is he?"

"When it's all come out, we'll probably find that Benson was behind the job," Ripley said. "There's just one good thing about it: he'll be afraid to show himself even if he does get out of the Manchester district, and there's no certainty that he'll do that yet. But I wanted to tell you in person, you know Benson and his boys better than anyone living, that's why I rang earlier, but the Chief Constable wouldn't wait. Anyway, there it is, George."

"Thanks," said Gideon.

"I know," said Ripley, in reply to unspoken comment, "they ought to have strung him up but they didn't. And I'm not so sure that a man who's been as near the gallows as Benson will give a damn about risking a life sentence. He's been at Millways for three years; it may have tamed him."

Gideon said dryly, "It looks as if it has, doesn't it? Who else got away? Anyone in the same mob?"

"Yes. Jingo Smith and Wally Alderman. The others are all solo workers.

The list's on the teleprinter by now. Five Londoners, just to cheer you up. George, I'm not going to waste your time or mine, I know you'll do everything that needs doing. Let's hear from you one of these days."

"Okay, Jim," Gideon said. "Thanks for ringing."

He rang off, very slowly and thoughtfully.

He drew a pad toward him and made a note of several different people whom he wanted to talk to about the jail break, and steps he wanted them to take. But he didn't put a call in yet. In the brief and blessed quiet, he was able to think without feeling that he was being pushed—a condition which wouldn't last long. The escape of any prisoner meant high pressure until the man was found or else the hue and cry had died down, and Benson—well, this would mean newspaper headlines every day until Benson was captured. It would put fear into the hearts of several people, too. It would mean giving special protection to at least two people, including Benson's wife. All this was a long story, and Gideon, in a way, had grown up with it. The one overriding factor was simply this:

Benson was a killer. He should have been hanged. He was known to have killed at least two people over a period of eleven years, but the "burden of proof" had been too heavy. Finally, the police had got him on an attempted murder charge, but the victim hadn't died. It was hardly true to say that he lived, either; he was a mental and physical wreck and would have been better off dead. But the law didn't allow a man to be charged with murder because he had condemned another to a living death. Benson had been given fifteen years' penal servitude; he'd served three.

The telephone bell rang.

Gideon lifted the receiver. "Gideon."

"George." This was the Assistant Commissioner, speaking crisply, "Can you spare me a minute?" He could have said simply, "Come and see me," but it wasn't his way.

"Yes, I'll come," Gideon said. "Right away." He pressed a bell and stood up; tightened his tie, shrugged himself into his coat, and smoothed down his thick, iron-gray hair. By that time he'd reached the door, and it was opened by a middle-aged, graying sergeant named Jefferson. "Jeff, stay here until Mr. Lemaitre or I get back, will you? I'll be with the A.C." Gideon nodded and went out walking in that characteristic way, not hurrying, and giving the impression that if anything should get in his path he would push it aside.

He heard the hurried footsteps of a man who couldn't move fast enough, and smothered a grin. This was Lemaitre, who came swinging round a corner, eyes very bright. He almost skidded to a standstill.

"It was Benson!" he blurted.

"Lem, there are times when you've got second sight," said Gideon. "Jefferson's in the office, I'm going to see the old man. You nip down to Records and get Benson's file, will you?—and the files of Benson's pals. Wally Alderman and Jingo Smith."

"They out, too?"

"Yes. Get the names of the others, have the files out, then call the five people I've jotted down on my note pad, and tell them to keep their eyes open. If we don't pick up Benson soon, we might run into a lot of trouble."

"It had to break sooner or later," Lemaitre said. "Been too quiet for a long time. Okay. Like a cushion for your pants?"

The A.C.'s office was on the same floor as Gideon's, overlooking almost an identical scene. It was larger, it had only one desk, and there was a communicating door to his secretary's and personal assistant's office. Tall, lean, tough-looking, the A.C. was dressed in a suit of light gray tweed tailored to fit so perfectly that it looked almost too small. He had thin, crimpy hair, parted in the middle with a wide, pale parting.

"Hallo, George, come and sit down. Have a good week end?"

"Fine, thanks."

"About the first you've had in six weeks, but at least you had some sun yesterday. Sit down." Gideon lowered himself into a wooden armchair. "What have you done about the Millways business? Or haven't you had a chance, yet?"

Gideon smiled in the way he did only when he was with someone he liked.

"Not much," he said, "Lemaitre's on the job now. I'm warning the Divisions where the London men came from to watch their homes. I'm having two of our chaps go round to Mrs. Benson's place to keep an eye on her, better not leave that to the Divisions; and I'm putting out a general call, London and Home Counties as from now, to keep their eyes open. Then I'm getting photographs printed of all the men for the *Police Gazette* and for the police stations. If we pick Benson up in a few hours, we'll have wasted a little money and a lot of time. If we don't, then we'll be off to a good start."

"Every now and again, when I get to thinking seriously, I tell myself that I ought to spend more time in the garden; while you're here, this place works better without me." The A.C. wasn't smiling. "Benson was a man I didn't have much to do with, I've only read and heard about him. This is the first time I've ever believed that he was as bad as the report said. You've convinced me."

"No report is bad enough," Gideon told him flatly; "but when you work it out, he hasn't much chance of getting far, has he? The country's snowbound north of a line from the Severn to the Wash. Manchester's picked up two of the escapers already, and there's a sound chance they'll all be in their cells again before the night's out. With a bit of luck, it will all die down."

"All right, let's look on the bright side," agreed the A.C. "But I didn't really want to talk about that—I'd hardly got round to it." His eyes smiled. "This man Rose and the Primrose Girl murder—have you seen the Divisional report?"

"No, just a précis."

"It looks cut and dried," said the A.C., "but Smedd over at H5 has put in reports that make me think." He passed over some papers, including a photograph of William Rose; and a note said that Rose was twenty years old. "Usually, when a kid is caught and held on a job like this and told what the buildup is, he confesses," the A.C. observed. "He retracts afterward, of course, under the influence of a lawyer who tells him he must do better than that, because lies might save him. But this boy just insists that he didn't do it. Smedd says he keeps quite calm—not at all like most youngsters. Comes from a family with a good background; his father died only three months ago. The mother's distraught. He's got two sisters—one older, one younger than he is." The A.C. had a habit of dispensing information like this in a casual, off-hand way, almost as if he felt guilty at having it. "Smedd seems absolutely sure of himself, but I'd like to see young Rose. Will you ring Smedd when you can fit it in? He'd bring Rose here—unless you're going over that way."

"Could do, a bit later," said Gideon. "I'll have a look at it. That the lot?"

"Not quite." The A.C. grimaced. "The Public Prosecutor's wishing a new boy onto us, and he's coming over to have a talk about the case against Edmundsun. It's the new chap's first embezzlement prosecution; and if you ask me, he'll want wet-nursing. Who would you let him talk to? I don't mean Gideon!"

Gideon said thanks, as if he really meant it. Then:

"Cummings," he said, "unless the new boy's too conscious of his position as a prosecutor for the Crown, and must have a C.I."

"He'll have what I give him."

"Cummings knows that job inside out. He's a bit young, but if he sees this through and we put Edmundsun inside, I'd move him up. Not that it'll be easy, Edmundsun's pretty fly. That the lot?"

"Yes. In a hurry?"

"It wouldn't surprise me if things keep us on the go all day," said Gideon. "There's enough on my plate until middle afternoon already."

He went out, without hurrying. He had long passed the time when he paused to reflect that he and the Yard were lucky with the A.C., and yet a conference, as this one, always did him good. He was completely over his sour mood, too. He'd recovered from the sharp blow of the news from Manchester and was moving into a different frame of mind, the attacking one, in which he could really spread himself. And he'd find a chance to slip out for an hour. Much better to see the Rose boy at Divisional H.Q. than it would be here; Scotland Yard had a peculiar effect on many people, especially people on a charge but new to police methods.

Gideon went into his office.

Lemaitre was saying, "Half a mo, here he is." He lowered the receiver and pressed it against his chest as he looked up at Gideon. "Girl downstairs in the hall asking for you, George; says it's important. Won't give her name, but says she's a friend of your Pru, too."

Gideon was almost knocked back on his heels in surprise.

"Friend of *Pru's*, wanting me?"

"That's the size of it."

Gideon said, "Well, all right, I'll go and see what she wants. You haven't finished those calls yet, have you?"

"No one's called me lightning yet," said Lemaitre.

Gideon went out and made his way in the opposite direction, toward the lift. It wasn't often that he was completely at a loss, but he was now. Prudence, his eldest daughter, had a lot of friends in a world that Gideon didn't even begin to know: the musical world. She played the violin well enough to win a place in the Home Counties Philharmonic Orchestra, and he understood that at nineteen that was remarkable. She could hardly have sent this friend to see him, or she would have said so; at least she'd have rung him up and warned him.

The unexpected was always the thing to tackle first.

Gideon had a word with Joe, at the lift, and two C.I.'s, the only topic being the Millways break. Then he reached the hall.

The girl waiting there was about Pru's age, he thought, rather fresh and pretty, with a very smooth complexion, blue eyes and not much make-up. She looked rather familiar. As he went toward her, Gideon thought that if ever he had seen trouble, it was in this girl's eyes. She was nervous, too, although obviously trying hard to conceal it. She recognized Gideon on sight, took a short step toward him and then hesitated, as if she didn't know what to say. To try to put her at her ease, he smiled as he might have at Prudence.

Then he realized why she looked familiar.

She was like William Rose, who had been arrested for the Primrose Girl's murder, like him as a sister might be.

3 . Alibi for Rose?

THERE was a hard streak in Gideon; had there not been, he would never have reached his position. He dealt in facts and had learned to repress any emotion which might entice him to look on facts from the wrong angle. His master was the Law; and he not only served it but knew that if he or anyone else deviated from it he was likely to store up serious trouble. So over the years he had cultivated the hard streak; and there were some who saw this but did not see the other side of his nature, the sentimental side.

This revealed itself particularly where young people were involved. It wasn't surprising, seeing that he had his own brood of half a dozen, but the real explanation lay in the past. There had been a seventh child, a boy who had died while Gideon had been out on a job, although his wife had beseeched him not to go. The tangled emotions, the self-blame, the remorse, the emotional upheaval within Kate, his wife, for long afterward, had made a deep mark on Gideon; but at least he knew that he was most vulnerable whenever the young were the trouble. That was why from the beginning he had been so anxious to know about the Primrose Girl and her murder—and the boy under arrest. Now, he did not doubt that he was face to face with the boy's sister.

She was nervous of him, almost frightened.

He supposed she was twenty-one, certainly not much more. Her brown hair was a feathery kind of cluster, her eyes were honey-colored. She had on only a trace of lipstick, and her lips were set tightly, as if she was afraid that if she opened her mouth the muscles would take control and she would burst out crying.

Gideon knew that the sergeant and a constable on duty were watching her as intently as he.

There might be a lot of doubt about what to do later, but for the moment he had just to set this girl at ease and smooth out that tension. So he hardly paused as he moved toward her, but maintained his pleasant smile and offered her his hand. With two or three words, too, he did the thing which mattered more perhaps than anything: he gave her a sense of his omniscience.

"Hallo, Miss Rose," he said. "I didn't know you were a friend of Pru's, so many things one's daughter doesn't tell one about." Her hand was cold, but the quick nervous pressure told him that he was already making an impression. "I didn't keep you waiting, I hope."

She managed to say: "No, I—no." She bit her lips, and he saw that tears were stinging her eyes. She couldn't find words, now that she was here; all her strength had gone, on finding the courage to come and ask for him.

He took her arm, much as he would Pru's.

"We can go along here and sit down," he said; and as he led her toward a small waiting room just along the passage, he added to the sergeant, "How about some tea, Matt?"

"Right away, sir."

"Say ten minutes," Gideon said.

The room was a small one, with a window overlooking the barracks-like square, where the Squad and other cars were parked. The window was barred, because occasionally they had a tough customer in here. It had been freshly painted, the walls were a shiny green below and yellow above, there were two armchairs, some upright chairs, a table, ash tray, and—the inevitable wall decoration at the Yard—photographs of sporting giants or teams of the past.

The girl probably noticed nothing of this.

The touch of Gideon's big hand and the minute's walk to this room had helped her. She didn't fight so hard to keep back tears, dabbed at her eyes with a handkerchief, and then blew her nose. Was she a smoker? Gideon took out a fat cigarette case, which he carried only to be sociable.

"No—no, I don't smoke," she said, looking at him intently, and speaking huskily but without a quiver in her voice. "How—how did you know who I was? I didn't tell anyone."

"You're very like your brother," said Gideon, "and I remembered your name, from the A.C.'s report: Mary."

That remark stung her, and she had to turn away again, but only for a moment.

"Yes, I am," she said stiffly. "He—he *didn't* kill Winifred."

"Didn't he?"

"No."

"Positive?"

"He couldn't have," William Rose's sister said.

She said it in such a way that Gideon felt a current of warning; this wasn't going to be just the sentimental, emotional appeal which might have been expected. She was a courageous little customer—hadn't she proved it, by getting him to come and see her by using Pru's name?

"If you're sure he couldn't have, can you help us to prove it?" Gideon asked, watching her very closely. She was no longer looking away from him; her eyes were wide open and steady, shining with a kind of defiance. He went on in the same quiet and convincing voice. "The last thing we want to do is to hold an innocent man and make him go through this kind of ordeal."

"That's what you *say*."

"It's what I mean."

"Well, the men who arrested Will didn't behave like that; they took it for granted that he was guilty from the beginning," the girl said hotly. "I was there when they came to see him, and then took him away. The way they talked to me was just the same. They even told me not to waste any time in lying to try to save him!"

Gideon thought: Oh, did they? but he wasn't wholly surprised. The Superintendent at H5 was coasting along toward retirement, and the Division wasn't running as smoothly as anyone outside it would have liked—or many inside it, for that matter. And, as often happened when there was any kind of weakness, two or three of the senior men had become a bit too big for their boots, showing a kind of truculence, a hardness, almost a callousness which didn't do anyone any good. You might talk to an old lag as the police had obviously talked to young Rose, but not to a boy without a record, who was one of a closely knit family, who . . .

"Perhaps they felt quite sure that he did kill this girl," Gideon said quietly.

"But he couldn't have!"

"Why not?"

"I was with him at the time he was supposed to have been with her," said Mary Rose.

"*Were you?*" asked Gideon, slowly.

He didn't believe her; and now he understood why the H5 men had been impatient. If she had attempted to give her brother an alibi, and they had reason to think that she was lying—well, they'd soon get annoyed. Policemen shouldn't, but they did. He could applaud the girl's effort and her spirit and at the same time feel desperately sorry for her, because she wouldn't have a chance to fool him or anyone else. She was as transparent as a mother trying to save the life of her child.

"Yes, I was," the girl said, more tensely. "We went to the pictures together."

It was building up to form. She claimed that they'd been to the cinema at a time when the house was crowded, throngs waiting to go in, no one able to pick out two youngsters from the hundreds of couples who had been moving to and fro. The pattern of this kind of alibi was so clear that Gideon—and the H5 men—could almost put Mary's words into her mouth.

Gideon didn't intend to.

"Mary," he said, and the use of her Christian name startled her again, "have you made an official statement about this to the police?"

"No. No, I . . ."

"Well, you'll have to," Gideon said briskly. "I'll arrange for someone to come and take the statement down, and then you can come back this afternoon, read it, and sign it. I don't want to miss the slightest clue, the slightest piece of evidence; but I can't do all these things personally, you know, and I haven't been dealing with the case myself."

"If only you would!" she cried.

The truth about Mary Rose, Gideon realized as he studied her, was that she was a young woman, not just a girl. Girls didn't have a figure like that: she was almost fully mature. She had the freshness which no man could fail to approve, and a simplicity which carried her to the point of naïveté. In an idle moment he would run his gaze up and down her figure, from her nice legs to her high bosom, and get that rather warm feeling that the sight of someone so young and desirable always gave. He didn't think she knew that her "If only you would!" might have come from the most disingenuous woman of the world; she probably didn't know just how much she seemed to be intent on flattering him.

"Well, the case is under my authority and there's no reason why I shouldn't look into it," he said practically, "but I've got to do what every other detective has to do: look at the evidence. That's the thing that matters, you know—evidence. Like your statement. When you've signed it, we shall have it as evidence, and if this case comes before the judge and jury, then you'll have to stand up in court and swear, on oath, that the statement was true in every detail." This was where she should begin to wilt, of course, but she didn't. "Then, if the jury believes you—well, that would be that. The verdict might depend on whether there is any contradictory evidence: if someone else saw your brother in a different place about the time . . ."

"They couldn't have, he was with me," said Mary Rose, quietly.

For the first time Gideon began to wonder whether he could have been wrong, whether he was doing a Lemaitre by jumping to any kind of conclusion.

"And you'll make that statement and sign it?"

"Of course I will."

"Good," Gideon said, more briskly. "I'll bring a sergeant along; but before I do, tell me why you lied about being a friend of my daughter, will you?"

He looked very stern, then; as he might with Pru.

The girl flushed a little, not very much. "Well—well, it wasn't really a lie," she asserted. Under his gaze, she turned a deeper red, but stuck to her guns. "I do know Pru, slightly. We met at the Guildhall School of Music when I was studying the piano. She used to tell me—she used to tell *us*," Mary corrected, and now her face was almost scarlet, "that she was absolutely sure you wouldn't *lie* about a case. She—well, we used to ask her about you, because you were interesting. *Every*one's fascinated by a real detective.

We used to egg Pru on to talk about you, and—and in a way we—I seemed to know you."

Now Gideon had to hide a smile; she was laying it on with a trowel, yet obviously didn't realize it; and she had a case.

"I see," he said. "That explains it."

She went on very quickly: "And when this awful thing happened and the other police wouldn't listen to me, I remembered everything Pru had said and just had to come and see you. I didn't think you'd see me if you knew who I was, but a friend of Pru—well, I *had* to see you."

"You know, Mary," Gideon said prosaically, "anyone who has a good reason for wanting to see me or anyone else at Scotland Yard can always come. You don't need special influence. And whether your brother is guilty or not, we want to help you and your mother and . . ."

He broke off.

Tears had filled the girl's eyes again, and suddenly she seemed more heavily burdened than at any time since they had come into this room. She couldn't meet his eyes. She just sat there, hands gripping the arms of her chair, head turned toward the barred window, lips so tight together that he knew she was trying to keep back an outburst of tears. She wasn't just a nice kid fighting for her brother; she was a young woman keyed up to a terrible pitch of emotional tension; her nerves were as taut as nerves could be, and something had twanged them. Gideon wasn't sorry that there was a tap at the door, and the constable came in with the tea and some biscuits.

"Put that down here," Gideon said to him, and then in a low-pitched voice: "Have a policewoman here in ten minutes, tell her to bring some aspirins." The policeman nodded, and Gideon turned round to the girl, then poured out a cup of tea, and went on: "Better have this while it's hot, Mary."

Now she looked at him, but made no attempt to take the tea.

"You don't believe me," she said drearily, "no one believes me, but it's true, it's absolutely true. We were at the pictures. Will had had a quarrel with Win and was ever so upset. He hadn't any money, and I—I *treated* him. But no one will believe me."

If she'd added, "And I'm so frightened," she would have told Gideon everything.

It was certainly time he went to see young William Rose.

The policewoman, who wasn't so much older than the girl, took over; she didn't need telling what to do. Gideon sent for a stenographer to take down the statement, and hovered between thinking that he was a fool to be half-persuaded, and that he was a hardhearted cynic not to take Mary Rose at her word. As he left the waiting room, he knew that it had been one of those interludes which would never be wholly forgotten. He'd bring this girl to mind at odd times when he was thinking of Pru, or talking to her. He'd learned a lot, too. Pru, sitting at the School of Music, talking to a group of students, cashing in on being the daughter of a Yard detective! Pru was the one of his children he would never have suspected of pride. But it wasn't all a matter of tolerant, rather smug amusement. There was this girl and her dread; Rose's mother and sister—and the dead girl. Remember, she had been stabbed eleven times with William Rose's knife. Remember, they'd quarreled. And remember there was another family, the Primrose Girl's family, with their grief.

That was the trouble; once you started seeing the sentimental side, it didn't stop. His job was to find the facts. The truth, the whole truth and nothing but the truth, so help him God.

He went soberly upstairs, and by the time he reached his office, he had decided to go straight over to see young Rose, unless something had cropped up while he'd been downstairs.

The only thing he was more anxious about was Benson's escape.

4 . Benson

BENSON was with a man twelve years younger than himself, named Freddy Tisdale.

Their partnership had been decided upon at the time of the original plan for the prison break. It hadn't originated in Benson's mind, but in the agile mind of Jingo Smith, the ideas man for the gang which Benson had led for several years before they had run into trouble, Gideon, and the immutable forces of the law.

There had been an early winter fall of snow, about the middle of December, and Jingo Smith had seen what might happen if there should be another heavy snowfall and a high wind. In fact, he remembered from the previous year that some of the drifts in the prison yard had been so high that, when frozen hard, they made a sloping bank from the yard itself to the top of the wall. The warders, of course, were well aware of it; and at times when there were big snowdrifts, the watch was doubled and the drifts cleared quickly. But Jingo had talked about this to Benson and Wally Alderman, and slowly and patiently they had developed the plan.

It had meant using trusties, of course. It had also meant the connivance of a warder—not to help in the escape, but to give one or two of the trusties special privileges which had enabled the plans to be laid. The conditions required had been quite apparent: a heavy snowfall, a high wind, and a disturbance in one part of the prison to enable the escapers to win their chance. At first they had planned for six of them to break out. Two more had been added to the list; and, at the last moment, a ninth man had discovered what they were planning and had strung along with them.

If they hadn't let him come, he might have squealed. Benson had no faith at all in honor among thieves.

The actual break-out had gone perfectly, conditions being absolutely right. The disturbance had been a fire which had broken out in the laundry, compelling the warders to pay special attention to that part of the prison. The escapers had been in the library, which was on the first floor overlooking the prison yard. A file, smuggled in from the shoemaker's shop, and a cobbler's hammer had enabled them to break the iron bars and the toughened glass. They'd got out, nipping across the six inches of snow and up the slope as swift as antelopes. The librarian and the two other warders with him had been overpowered and trussed up; and no other prisoners had been in the library at that time.

All had gone perfectly.

That was partly because Benson, having accepted the idea, had worked it out.

That day, with Freddy Tisdale, he hid in a house not a mile from the prison.

And he was ravenously hungry.

Benson wasn't a big man, just average. He did not seem exceptionally strong, although he was. He looked hard. He had sharp, chiseled features and pale blue eyes which could look at a man squarely even though everything he himself was saying was a lie. Hoping for the blizzard, he had made most of the escapers avoid having haircuts, on one pretext or another; only the last-minute man had a prison crop. That was the kind of detail that Benson excelled in, and was why he had been one of the most successful criminals in England for nearly fifteen years.

He had overlooked only one detail, the one that had sent him to jail. He had forgotten that his wife, having learned to hate him, might give the police the evidence they needed.

She had.

She was probably the only person in the world whom Benson really hated.

There was no room for strong emotions in him, beyond that. He had always approached every job, from burglary to smash-and-grab, from beating-up to murder, quite cold-bloodedly, being concerned only with what he might get out of it. The two men he had murdered had died simply because they could have named him and brought his career to an abrupt end. He hadn't hated them; he had had no feeling of any kind toward them.

He had never really loved, but his wife's beauty had bowled him over when they had met fifteen years ago. He had been proud of her for some time, until he had taken up with another girl who had no children to look after.

Benson's children, a boy and a girl, had meant little to him. It had never occurred to him that indirectly they had been responsible for his long prison sentence. Anxiety about the possible influence of a hardened criminal father upon the children had been the chief cause of his wife's "betrayal."

Now, Benson was on his way to see his wife.

He had arranged the pairing of the escape party, and had chosen Freddy Tisdale because Freddy had certain qualities which were the envy of almost everyone in the prison, and many hundreds outside. For one thing, he was double-jointed. For another, he was probably the finest locksmith in the country on the wrong side of the law; there was hardly a lock he couldn't force. And for the third, he looked such a kid. In a way, he was: just twenty-four. He was in prison because he and three other men had been caught red-handed in a fur salon, the locks of which Freddy had forced with insolent ease, and all four of them had beaten up a night watchman who had surprised them. They had been caught by police in a patrol car, while running away. The night watchman hadn't been badly hurt, and Freddy's share of the proceeds of the haul had been seven years.

Benson had realized that, behind the boyish, friendly face and the apparently resigned manner, there had lived in Freddy Tisdale the escape bug. You had it or you didn't have it. Nine men out of ten at Millways, the Moor, or any other prison, would no more dream of trying to escape than they would of spitting in the Governor's eyes. They knew that the prisoner was always caught and sent back, that he lost all his remission, made life much tougher for himself, and often faced a longer sentence because of new crimes committed while free. Perhaps one prisoner in ten would ignore these cold facts and long only for escape.

All nine of them had made it this time: a triumph.

Benson didn't know that two of them had already been recaptured when, with Freddy Tisdale, he had reached the house where they were now hiding.

They had made a beeline for this spot because Benson knew that they wouldn't last long in the bitter cold and the snow unless they had some warm clothes, food, and rest. He'd picked the house out, with his dispassionate cunning, from the Houses to Let advertisements in the *Journal,* a local weekly newspaper which was available in the library at Millways, with certain items of news duly censored. Being a chatty, parochial weekly, there wasn't much blacked out, and Benson had made sure that, when studying the advertisement, he hadn't been noticed by the librarian or a warder.

There had been three houses to let furnished, and only one with an agent's name and address; this, Benson shrewdly suspected, meant that the house itself was empty at the time.

Another big advantage of having Freddy Tisdale with him was that Freddy knew the Millways district—every street, lane, and alley, almost every back yard. The police would watch Freddy's home, of course, and his friends; but to Benson Freddy's chief usefulness had been the ability to take him straight to 15 Nortoft Road, a semidetached house in a street not far from the big canal. They had had to take a chance of some kind, and the chance they'd taken was coming here in daylight, with the risk of being seen by neighbors.

As far as they knew, they hadn't been seen. They had been here for several hours, no one had called, and they'd had plenty of luck. The main electricity was still on, and there were two electric heaters, which would not give off smoke or betray their presence in any way. They put the fires in a small room next to the kitchen, where there were armchairs, rugs and a radio which, tuned very low, was on all the time. This room had only one window; the curtain had been drawn when they arrived. They had spent some time blacking this out so that they could put on a light without being noticed.

Benson was quietly congratulating himself. In fact, there was only one thing wrong: he was hungry. In fact, he was so ravenous that it was a gnawing ache inside him. He even felt annoyed with Freddy, because Freddy didn't complain about the lack of food, just took it like a stoic.

The larder had been absolutely bare, without even an old packet of biscuits or any tins of food; nothing. Now, four o'clock that afternoon, when it was still broad daylight outside, Benson felt sick with hunger, but knew that neither of them dared break out until after dark. He had spent a lot of time going over every detail of what had happened, and didn't think that there was any risk of their being discovered that night if they remained in the house. They had been very thorough, and had even stopped near the canal, tied some old sacks round their feet, and shuffled along to the house; this way, there had been no footprints in the snow.

Benson watched Freddy, who sat in an armchair on the other side of the two fires, wearing a big coat which they had found in a locked cupboard upstairs. Each of them was warmly clad now, and the prison clothes were outside in the scullery, drying. During the night, when no one could see the smoke, these could be burned. They had also found shoes, although these didn't fit very comfortably. Freddy's were better, just a little loose on his small feet; Benson's were too tight. That didn't matter now that he could keep them unlaced, but he would have to lace them up when he was outside.

Freddy sat reading, apparently oblivious of background music. He had fair, curly hair, a pale face—everyone in Millways had that, anyhow—and bright blue eyes. He was beginning to irritate Benson a little, because he didn't talk much either and even in these circumstances could become absorbed in a book. Benson wasn't one for much reading, and there were no old newspapers in the house. Freddy had never smoked, but Benson had an unbearable craving for a cigarette. To make it worse, Benson could have had tobacco, but had forgotten to bring any away with him. There were two pounds of it in his cell! The ruddy screws would get it now, and they'd swear they didn't know he had it. They might not even tell the Governor, might just pass it on to one of the trusties and get a cut in the proceeds.

Freddy flipped over a page.

"Freddy," Benson said, "we've got to eat."

Freddy glanced up. "S'right," he said.

"It's nearly dark outside. Must be."

"Got to wait until it's pitch." Freddy was obviously impatient to get back to his book. "Got to find some food that won't be missed. That shop at the corner'll be okay, but it won't close until six. Got to wait until half past six, anyway."

He was right, of course; there was nothing of the fool about him. He was good, and he had a strong nerve. He would go out and break into the shop, and Benson knew he could trust him. But Benson didn't like his cocksure manner.

Freddy turned back to his book. Now and again he grinned, now and again he read so fast that his eyes seemed to swivel to and fro in his head. All that Benson knew was that the book was a Western—and that Freddy might soon begin to get on his nerves.

He got up and went out of the room, going from room to room everywhere in the house. It was still daylight outside, and the sky was gray, but it wasn't snowing. Snow had been swept from the middle of the road and packed into great banks on either side. Lights were on at several houses. Children were snowballing, some with furious enjoyment. In sight of the front-room window, which Benson approached cautiously from one side, there were three snowmen, each in a tiny front garden. Everywhere it was gently quiet, and even the children's voices did not sound through the closed and latched windows.

Benson went downstairs again and sat for a while until, without looking up, Freddy stretched out a hand and pressed a different button on the radio.

The music stopped; instead, a man was talking about the weather. Benson opened his mouth to ask: "What's that for?" and then realized why Freddy had changed the station. The news would be on the Home Service in a minute or two, and they would be "news" with a vengeance. He forgot his momentary annoyance because Freddy was so self-sufficient.

The weather report ended, and the Greenwich time signal came: *Peeep, peeep, peeep, peeep, peeep, peeep.* At last Freddy put down his book. Both men leaned nearer to the radio, which was tuned very low, so that the voice was only a whisper. Foreign news, Parliamentary news, a Royal visit, all of these came in headlines. And finally:

"Three of the nine convicts who escaped from Millways Prison early this morning have been recaptured, two of them within half a mile of the prison walls, the third as he attempted to obtain clothes from a secondhand shop on the outskirts of Manchester."

Benson and Freddy looked at each other, now equally tense. Details would be given later, they would have to listen to all the other news before learning which three had been caught. Benson's nerves were at screaming point, but at least Freddy Tisdale didn't go back to his book. Once the news was over, it would be dark enough to go and get some food.

As he waited, Benson knew how sick hunger could make a man feel.

5 . The Primrose Girl

GIDEON hadn't been able to go straight to H5 Division and see young Rose. Two things had come in, while he had been talking to Mary: a smash-and-grab job in Soho, and a panic about a Foreign Office man who was missing from his home and his office. The F.O. job was rightly the Special Branch's; but everyone was sensitive to the antics of diplomats, and Gideon had hurried along to a hastily summoned conference with the A.C., the Special Branch Chief, and a Foreign Office representative for whom Gideon had little time. He had hardly got back to his office when his telephone bell rang, and he lifted the receiver as he reached his desk.

"Gideon."

"Excuse me, sir," a man said, "this is Detective-Sergeant Cummings. I'm with the gentleman from the Public Prosecutor's office, and there are a few matters I'd be grateful for your advice on."

"Hmm," grunted Gideon.

"If we could come along for five minutes, sir."

"All right, I'll be here," said Gideon. He put the receiver down, scowled, and told Lemaitre what it was. For once he didn't find himself smiling when his C.I. said:

"These new P.P. barristers get on my wick, twice as much trouble as they're worth. Should have thought Cummings could have handled this chap, though."

Gideon said, "They can't all have your brilliance, can they? Did you fix everything for Benson's wife, and all the rest?"

"All done. Sent Old Percy and a youngster to Mrs. B's—Abbott. You remember, he jumped on a car and nearly won himself an early coffin."

"Divisions take it seriously?"

"Everyone takes Benson seriously," Lemaitre said. "Mind if I give you a word of advice, George?"

Lemaitre grinned as he said that. His lean face, with its rather leathery, hungry look, had a drollness which couldn't be missed; and when he grinned it was with one side of his mouth and with one eye screwed up a little—this because he so often had a cigarette dangling from the corner of his lips. He hadn't now, but the mannerism remained. He had sleek, almost jet-black hair, which was brushed back from his forehead without a parting; and although he was as old as Gideon, there was hardly a gray strand except at the temples and the back of his neck. His eyes were brown, restless, and very bright, and he was always on the move. Take his one big drawback away, and he might become brilliant. There wasn't a better man at the Yard on routine, and whatever the situation, there wasn't a man who knew how to get things moving more quickly than Lemaitre, or who could move faster. He was the ideal second-in-command.

Gideon kept a straight face.

"I'm always ready to take advice from my betters," he said.

"And learning, too," marveled Lemaitre. "I know, I know, you'll tell me to keep my big mouth shut, but here it comes. Don't waste your time on the Primrose Girl job, you're going to have plenty to do over this Millways job. Give you three to one that before the afternoon's out we'll have a conference with the Home Office; you know what they're like on a case like this. And if you're not sitting at the end of a telephone, you'll rile everyone except the A.C., and perhaps even him if the Commissioner gets narky."

"Lem, you couldn't be more right," said Gideon.

Before they could say any more, Cummings and a bright-eyed, fresh-faced young man from the Public Prosecutor's office came in. If anything was certain, it was that the P.P.'s man was not being officious. He looked competent, intelligent and amiable, and there was no long-suffering air about Cummings, either. This was a genuine problem about the case against Edmundsun. Within two minutes, Gideon had shaken hands with the barrister, whose name was Harrison, and had put everything out of his mind except the embezzlement case. The prosecution's main hopes lay in one police witness; the great weakness, that the witness might be shaken by the defense. Young Harrison said that he'd read all the statements and studied the witness's statements, and was sure that the defense couldn't shake the witness, who was vulnerable on two points. How could they block the defense?

The session, interrupted by four telephone calls, lasted for over an hour. Cummings, a youngish man who ran to fat, and whose face and forehead were shiny all the time, had a complete grasp of the intricate case; Harrison seemed to have it all under his hat, too. Gideon knew that he had seen the man before, but couldn't say where; probably in court, when the police had been there in strength.

They all stood up, at a little before one o'clock.

"Better have a day to think this over," Harrison said, "we don't want to put Edmundsun in court and see him wriggle out."

"Give me a ring, and we'll have another look at it tomorrow," Gideon offered.

"Thanks," said Harrison, and then gave a boyish grin. He was public school, probably Oxford; he dressed immaculately and expensively, and he got on as well with ex-elementary schoolboy Cummings as he would with the Home Secretary in person. "Mind if I say it's been nice meeting you? The only time we've met before, you made mincemeat out of me."

"I did?" Gideon couldn't recall any encounter with him. "Where?"

"Number One Court at the Old Bailey," Harrison said. "I was junior counsel for the defense of Sydney Benson, and my leader had been called out. I opened my mouth, and you put your foot in it! Never felt smaller in my life—and never been so wrong," Harrison went on, earnestly. "I hear that Benson's one of the crowd to escape from Millways. That ought to make everyone happy—except perhaps his wife."

This man was no fool; in a few years he would probably be a big name; and he could be human enough to think anxiously about Benson's wife.

He went on very slowly: "I was very green in those days, almost believed that Benson was innocent and the police were perjuring themselves, until I saw the way he looked at his wife when she gave evidence. Remember the way he spoke to her, just before she stood down?" Harrison hesitated, then tightened his lips and spoke so that they hardly moved: a good imitation of Benson's way of speaking. "'Okay, Ruby, I'll pay you for this.' If he'd threatened to slit her throat he couldn't have sounded worse."

Gideon said, "So that's where I've seen you. Well, don't worry about Ruby Benson, we're looking after her."

"I didn't need to ask!"

Gideon grinned. "Think we can't take a hint? How about coming down to the canteen for a meal?" he added. "Or we could go across to the pub."

"Wish I could, but I've got to get back," Harrison said. "Seen anything of Ruby Benson since the trial? I used to wonder if she let Benson down because there was a boy friend waiting until he went inside."

"It's a funny thing," Gideon told him, "but I heard something about her only a few weeks ago. She's been working so as to keep the two kids going; made out all right, too. Assistant in a gown shop. Recently she found a boy friend, and you know what suspicious minds we coppers have. The G5 Divisional chaps made sure that she'd never met the man before. He took over management of the shop where she works, only a few months ago."

"What a future," mused Harrison, slowly. "Husband in jail, and when he comes out he's likely to kill you. Work to keep your children decent, have a boy friend who hasn't a chance of marrying you for twelve years or more, and probably not then. Why can't it work out as badly as that for Benson?" That seemed no more than a casual remark, and Harrison went toward the door, adding, "Know any of the other men who escaped?"

"Only one," said Gideon. "Jingo Smith. The others got into jail without any help from me."

He shook hands, nodded to Cummings, who looked pleased with himself, then went back to the office. Lemaitre, who hadn't shown any outward interest in what had gone on, but who had undoubtedly heard everything, glanced up to speak. Before he could, one of three telephones on his desk rang; he plucked it up as the ringing reached full blast.

"Lemaitre . . . Okay, that's fine, ta." He rang off, almost in the same motion with which he had lifted the instrument, and said quite casually, "They've picked up the chap for that hit-and-run job in Battersea; commercial traveler who lives at Brixton. Blood on the mudguard and tires. Better just leave it to the Division, hadn't I?"

"Yes," said Gideon. "You hungry?"

Lemaitre looked suspicious. "What's this?"

"We could send for a couple of sandwiches," said Gideon.

"When it's your public school pals, you take 'em to the pub and stand 'em a meal," Lemaitre jeered, "but your real friends . . ."

Gideon's telephone rang.

Gideon moved toward it, while Lemaitre was still speaking.

"I suppose you want to get all the desk work done so that you can go and see H5 this afternoon. Fat lot of use giving you advice! But you'll regret it, George; I can smell a busy day, and—oh, hell. But what did I tell you?"

One of his telephones was ringing.

"Lemaitre," he barked.

Gideon picked up his own receiver. He did that as he did nearly everything: with an outward appearance of slowness, as if he were giving himself plenty of time to think. It was simply that he had learned not to rush at anything, except in dire emergency, and even then it often did more harm than good. He put the receiver to his ear, and looked thoughtfully across at Lemaitre, who was snapping briskly.

"Gideon," said Gideon.

"Your wife's on the line, Mr. Gideon," a girl operator said; "I told her I thought you were in."

Gideon didn't answer at once; he really needed a moment to get used to the idea that Kate had telephoned him. It was utterly unexpected. He couldn't recall her doing so for years, except in real emergency. That was the result of the early, bitter estrangement between them, and it had grown into habit. Would Kate ring now unless something was the matter?

With Pru, Priscilla, Penny, one of the boys?

"Put her through."

"Yes, sir."

Gideon was kept waiting only a few seconds, but his heart was beating faster than it should. Lemaitre was now barking into his telephone, but Gideon made no attempt to follow what he was saying, just tried to re-assure himself about this call. Then Kate came on the line. He couldn't tell from her voice whether she was really worried or not; she was a remarkable woman for controlling her emotions.

"Hallo, George, I'm glad I've caught you," she said; "I promised Pru that I'd have a word with you. This isn't a bad time, is it?"

"Promised Pru—" began Gideon, and then relaxed and grinned broadly. "You tell that daughter of mine that when she wants to plead for a young man accused of murder, she'd better come and see me herself, not work through her mother."

Kate said, as if astounded, "How on *earth* did you know?" Then she gave a little laugh, almost one of confusion. "I always understood you were good at your job, but not . . ."

"Tell you about it when I get home," said Gideon. "But you can tell Pru that I shall be seeing young Rose this afternoon, or early this evening, and you can also remind her that we still prefer to let the innocent ones go."

He didn't attempt to keep the chuckle out of his voice.

Nor did Kate.

"That'll cheer her up no end," she said. "She read about it in a midday paper; apparently the boy's sister used to be at the school with her."

"That boy's sister is worth cultivating," said Gideon. "She bearded this lion in his den. Kate, I'm sorry but I ought to get off the line, it's building up to quite a day. I'll get home as early as I can."

"I can guess how early," Kate said dryly. "Good-by, dear." And then, in the same breath, "Have you caught Benson yet?"

"No, but we will," said Gideon, quietly. "'By."

He rang off.

Lemaitre was still on the telephone, but scribbling notes; he could write at furious speed and still be neat. The office was now pleasantly warm, and the sun had broken through; spring was here with a vengeance. Vengeance. Spring, and Sydney Benson out of jail, his wife aware of it by now, other desperate men at liberty, and—frightened people. Mary Rose, her brother, her mother, even Pru. Ruby Benson, and perhaps this new boy friend of hers. And who else?

"We will," he'd told Kate, meaning that they would soon catch Benson and all the others, but—would they? It couldn't be much more important.

Lemaitre snapped into the telephone, "Okay, do that." He put down the telephone, and looked across at Gideon; and for a moment Gideon had a feeling that he was also touched with fear.

"Still caught only three," Lemaitre said; "we'd better soon have the rest, or we'll really go to town. Man saw two of them in a railway shed up in Lancaster. He went after them on his own, and they bashed him with lumps of coal. On the danger list. They're checking the coal for prints, don't know which of the six it was, yet, but that's the kind of thing Benson would do, and if they're going to try to stay clear at all costs—well, I can't say I like it."

Gideon said, "I'm holding my sides. Who'd they catch for Number 3? I only knew it wasn't Benson."

"Nicky Bown."

"Did he say anything?"

"Not much, but he did say that the others are in pairs: Jingo Smith with Matt Owens, Wally Alderman with Hooky, and Benson with a youngster named Tisdale, double-jointed customer who helped to beat up a night watchman. Nice setup. One really tough guy in each pair, and you can be pretty sure they've all gone in different directions. Anything more we can do, do you think?"

"Every man we've got is alerted," said Gideon. "So, there isn't, yet. I . . ."

The telephone behind him rang.

It was too often like this: no pause between one thing and another, no time to get his mind fixed on a problem before he had to switch to the next. Today was worse than usual, or else he was noticing it more. The intrusion of Mary Rose, Pru and Kate were factors he wouldn't normally have to deal with, and he was more worried than he showed about Benson's escape. The man who didn't respect Benson's ability was a fool.

He picked up the receiver.

"Gideon."

"George," said a superintendent named Wrexall, "I've got Ruby Benson on the line, but she'd like a word with you. Can do?"

In the past half hour, several things had happened in London that Gideon didn't know about:

In New Bond Street, only a stone's throw from the police station at Savile Row, a small sports car drew up outside a jeweler's shop, a young man got out and calmly smashed a plate-glass window with a big hammer. The noise was so loud that it sounded like a car crash. As the window fell outward, two other men ran toward it, each carrying a sack with a wide, hooped opening. They grabbed silver, gold, jewels, everything in sight; and, as they did so, the man who had smashed the window tossed smoke bombs among the crowd. In ninety seconds, it was all over. The men ran back to the sports car, which roared along the road, the driver ignoring a point duty policeman, who leaped for his life.

As the car swung round the corner, another policeman leaped at it and tried to get at the steering wheel. One thief smashed at his head, another at his hands, but he didn't let go. The car swerved, mounted the pavement, and crashed.

The policeman wasn't seriously injured.

A few miles away, a young constable, hearing cries for help, peered over Putney Bridge and saw a woman and a child struggling in the river. He spoke calmly to two passersby as he stripped off his tunic, put his helmet on the parapet, and dived into the water. He saved both woman and child.

The third thing was not so spectacular. A constable, doing his usual rounds, noticed a familiar face coming out of a big building in Merton Square, W.1. The face was of one of London's most notorious safebreakers, not long out of jail. This man, Lefty Bligh, was known to spy out the lay of the land thoroughly before he did a job.

The constable made his report about this by telephone to his sergeant, who was soon talking to the Yard.

6 . Benson's Wife

WHENEVER he had a mental picture of Syd Benson's wife, Gideon saw a woman in her early thirties, with a figure that a girl of twenty might have envied, and the face of a woman of middle age. It was a sad face, much more sad than anything else, as of one who had given up expecting anything at all from life. During the time of Benson's remand before his trial, Gideon had often talked to her. Every now and again something had animated her, and she'd shown a glimpse of the beauty she was known to have been; but it was faded, as a dying flower. Even at thirty-three, her hair had been liberally streaked with gray.

As Gideon waited for her to come through, that was the picture he had of her.

Then: "You're through," said the operator.

"Hallo, Mrs. Benson," Gideon said quietly.

"Is that"—a pause—"is that Superintendent Gideon?"

"Superintendent" would do, that was how she had known him.

"Yes, speaking. If you're worried about the two men I've stationed—"

"No, it's not about them," interrupted Ruby Benson, in a voice which suggested that she was more agitated than she wanted him to know. "I was told about Syd early this morning, and I expected you to send someone. But I'm not worried about myself, Mr. Gideon."

Boy friend?

"Who are you worried about?"

"The children," she said flatly, "and I really mean that, Mr. Gideon." He could believe her; and he forgot that he had even thought "boy friend." "You're the one man I needn't be afraid to talk to," she went on; "you know Syd, and you know what he can do. I've been thinking it out, Mr. Gideon: I've often wondered what he'd do if he did get a chance, and I don't believe he'd go for me. I think he'd get at me through the children. Until he's caught, I don't want them living at home with me, I wouldn't feel safe."

Gideon said, "Listen, Mrs. Benson, you've nothing at all to worry about today. Syd can't get to London in weather like they've got up north—there's little traffic about on the roads, watching is easy as kiss your hand. So there's no immediate worry. You going to be in this afternoon and this evening?"

"Well, yes," she said.

"I'll come and have a word with you, but I can't promise when," said Gideon. "Not before half past four, anyhow. And if you're worried about the children today, in spite of what I've told you, I'll arrange for a man to go to their school and—"

"No, it's all right today," Ruby Benson said quickly, and her relief sent her voice two octaves higher. "Thanks ever so much, Mr. Gideon. I'll wait in."

She rang off.

She had never had very much to say, and Gideon had often wondered what she really felt and thought. At one time it had seemed as if the years with Benson had cowed her, but she had shown great courage when she had turned on him. Just now, the sudden relief and the vitality in her voice had surprised him.

He pushed his chair back.

"Sandwiches coming up," Lemaitre said. "Going lady-killing today, eh?"

"That's it."

"Well, don't say I didn't warn you," Lemaitre said. "You heard about that chap who stopped the smash-and-grab job?"

"No. Hurt?"

"They didn't detain him in hospital, he's being taken home. Ought to get a medal, he jumped a car while it was doing fifty."

"Then he'll probably get his medal."

"Good day for heroes," Lemaitre said, with a grimace. "Chap out at Putney dived into the Thames and saved a woman who'd jumped in after her kid—kid had fallen in from the towpath."

Gideon felt a warming glow.

"Get me his name and number, will you?"

"It's on the way. There's another thing we ought to do something about," Lemaitre went on with a sniff. "Lefty Bligh's around again, seen coming out of the Carfax Building in Merton Square. What do you make of that?"

Gideon said quietly, "Find out just where he was, Lem. Send someone who knows his habits. Find out if there's anything worth pinching kept in the place, and lay on everything that's needed."

Lemaitre nodded.

It was nearly four o'clock before Gideon left the Yard. He went alone, driving the black Wolseley, and the bright afternoon sunshine showed up the little scratches, the dust and the smears on the glass and the bodywork. He didn't drive fast. He let his thoughts roam over every inquiry that was going through the Yard, and hoped that nothing big would break for a day or two, but he wasn't too sanguine; big things were always liable to break, and they had a trick of coming two or three at a time. Strictly speaking, catching Benson wasn't a Yard job and wouldn't be until there was proof that the man was in the London Metropolitan area, but Benson was Case Number 1.

Case Number 2 was the Primrose Girl.

Gideon had looked through the afternoon newspapers before leaving the office. The mass escape from Millways had driven the Primrose Girl off the main headlines, but there was the story of the arrest of William Rose and a picture of the boy. The telling of the story was typical of Fleet Street: no direct statement that Rose was guilty, nothing that might at any time be construed as contempt of court, but the facts were stated in such a way that nine readers out of ten would feel sure that William Rose was the murderer. The Divisional police had told the Press plenty, including the bit about the boy's penknife; they'd said more than Gideon would have done, so early as this. H5 Division was worrying him, and would soon become an anxiety.

The world would soon think the boy guilty.

And Mary Rose either knew that he was innocent, or was prepared to lie desperately to save him.

To reach H5 he had to cross the river; it was Lambeth way. He drove faster as he got out of the thick London traffic, and it was half past four when he reached the sprawling building which housed the H5 Divisional Headquarters. The district was drab, most of the houses near it were small, and many wanted painting; taken by and large, it was a depressing area. Gideon knew that the Roses lived some distance from here, in a new—well, newish—estate.

He hadn't told H5 that he was going; only Lemaitre knew. That was because he didn't want everything brushed up and made shiny for him. Within two minutes of stepping into the low-ceilinged hall, however, he wondered if he'd made a mistake. The desk sergeant, recognizing him at the first glance and coming almost to attention, told him that the Superintendent had gone home early.

"Got a shocking cold he had, sir."

"Oh. Lot of them about," said Gideon. "Who's in charge?"

"Chief Inspector Smedd, sir."

"Tell him I'm on my way, will you?"

"Yes, sir," said the sergeant. "Right away."

Gideon didn't hurry. The old building had a lot of steep stone steps, and he knew from experience that if he didn't take it carefully he would be breathless when he reached the second floor; and it wasn't good policy to be puffing and blowing in front of the men up there. He now knew that Smedd was the officer who had arrested young Rose, and he knew Smedd well enough to realize that he was quite capable of brushing Mary Rose off. He was a go-getter, and he was a damned good detective and almost as good a policeman; they didn't always mean the same thing. He wasn't a man whom Gideon liked, but they had never clashed. Taken by and large, if Smedd said that a thing was true, it was.

Smedd was at the open door of the Superintendent's room, which he shared with the Superintendent; and Gideon wondered how often the senior man went home early.

"Hallo, Commander—unexpected honor," said Smedd, and gave a fierce smile and offered a vigorous handshake. He was on the small side for a C.I.D. man and, in his early days, must have scraped in by the better part of a hair's breadth, although the five feet ten rule had been relaxed for a long time now. He was dressed in brown, the color just a trifle on the bright side; his tie was colorful; his crisp, almost ginger hair was very oily. He had a raw look: a scrubbed look, rather. His skin was very fresh, and, especially at his nose and eyes, was a mass of freckles. "Come in—sorry the Superintendent's not here, he packed up early. Sneezing all over the place. You kept clear of colds this winter?"

"Pretty clear, thanks."

"Good. Sit down. How about a cuppa? Had one myself, but never say no, you know."

"I won't, thanks," said Gideon. "Lemaitre poured a cup into me before I left." He sat down and looked about him, and knew, even then, that the Superintendent might spend a lot of time at the station, but he had really given way to Smedd; for this place was spick-and-span, everything was in its proper place. Even the Superintendent's roll-top desk, usually a litter of papers, was as neat as the rest of it. Since Gideon had last been here, there had been a new, bigger, flat-topped desk brought in, too. Smedd's?

Smedd went and sat behind it.

"Come about the Primrose Girl job, I suppose. Glad we didn't take long to get the young swine. Kind I'd hang if I had my way."

"Hmm," said Gideon. "Nasty job. Sure he did it, I suppose?" He didn't smile. "Had a morning session with a man from the P.P.'s office, and the chief moan was that I'd put up a case which might not stand up in court, so I'm sensitive."

"Oh, we'll get Rose," Smedd said.

Gideon didn't comment.

Smedd frowned. A quick-tempered man at best, he wouldn't give way to his temper with Gideon, but neither would he be able to hide the fact that he felt annoyed, or at least impatient.

"I'd take the case to court tomorrow. Asking for a week, of course, if that's okay with you; we might as well get it all sewn up before we commit him for trial, but there isn't a shred of doubt. Talking off the cuff, of course, wouldn't say this to the P.P.'s office yet, but—haven't you studied the report I sent in?"

Reproof.

Gideon said, "Yes, but let me have the main points again, will you?"

Smedd's look said, jeeringly, "I'll bet you've read it—I don't think!" He didn't speak at once, but opened a drawer and took out a foolscap-sized manila folder, opened this, and showed a sheaf of papers clipped together; perhaps twenty sheets of paper, some large, some small, some handwritten, some typewritten. He began to read from a typewritten sheet on the top, without looking at Gideon, but giving the impression that he preferred facts to speak for themselves.

"Rose and Winifred Norton had been keeping company for six months. She was always at his house, or he was always at hers. The only quarrels we can find were because he was jealous—he hated her to be seen with other *men*." Smedd sneered the "men." "Recently, she'd been more interested in other men than in Rose. They had a violent quarrel a few hours before she was found murdered. She went to gather primroses, after the quarrel, and—"

"By herself?" interposed Gideon.

"Yes. She told a girl friend where she was going, and said it was to get away from Rose; she was nervous of him. That's the last time she was seen alive. The body was found the following morning, some primroses clutched in her left hand, eleven stab wounds, mostly in the breast. If you ask me, the boy's a monster." Whatever else, Smedd was convinced of that; the words spat out from his lips. "Those are the facts about her. After the quarrel, Rose wandered about on his own. He didn't go home. He didn't go to her home. He says he went to the pictures, but his footprints were found near the body, his knife was found among the primroses, with some of his prints on it, the blade was smeared with blood. She was stabbed through her clothes, so no blood splashed or spurted, and there was none on his clothes or hands," Smedd went on very quickly, "but we don't need that for evidence. Take it from me, we've got that young swine where we want him."

Smedd broke off, as if challenging Gideon to deny it.

"How does Rose explain his knife?"

"Usual story: he lost it, a day or two ago."

"His footprints?"

"Oh, he admits he saw the girl there, but says he left her. And so he did —dead," Smedd added, and the challenge in his manner became even more aggressive.

7 . Ruby Benson

GIDEON had known from the beginning that it would be as difficult to shift Smedd from an opinion as it would to shift Lemaitre. He knew more: Smedd had done a great number of things he hadn't mentioned. He might have overlooked something, but for the most part he would have done a thorough job. And if he, Gideon, started to check, he would only be putting Smedd's back further up, which would help no one. So Gideon did what he would have done with a man whom he knew better and whom he liked. He nodded, in that almost ponderous way of his, and took out his big-bowled pipe. He found himself smoking less and less these days, and then mostly in the evenings. Now, he began to fill the big bowl; and he gave a slow, rueful smile, which obviously puzzled Smedd.

"Well, you've got it all sewn up," Gideon said. "I didn't have much doubt that you would. Pity."

Smedd's green-brown eyes could not have been brighter.

"Pity?" he ejaculated. "Goddamnit, what else do you want?" So he could unbend enough under pressure. "The swine has a row with his girl friend, nice, clean-living girl, only just beginning to spread her wings. Virgin, too—at least he didn't try to interfere with her. She tells him it's the end, so what does he do? Follows her into the woods and then kills her with his knife, stabbing her nearly a dozen times. He must have lost his temper until he was almost mad, and that's what the defense will try of course—insanity plea. But he's no more mad than I am. He's just like a lot of the young swine these days. All right while he gets what he wants, but as soon as something gets in his way he loses his head. And you say it's a pity!"

Smedd paused.

Gideon was still smiling, ruefully, almost apologetically; and now he had finished filling his pipe. There were a few tricks Smedd didn't know yet, and one of them was that Gideon liked the other man to do most of the talking, especially at times like this. Smedd might keep quiet long enough to force him to comment, or he might not have the patience.

Smedd put both hands together, clenching them tightly.

"Don't tell me that you're starting to sympathize with a young brute like this just because you've got kids of your own. I've got three, remember."

Gideon spoke at last. "No, it's not that, although that comes into it in a way. Funny thing, but young Rose's sister, the one named Mary, knows my daughter Pru. Studied music together, or something. So I promised I'd see if there was a weak spot anywhere. I had a sneaking hope you might not be quite certain that it was this Rose boy. Still, nothing to be done, obviously." He paused. "Mind if I have a word with Rose?"

"Sure, have a word when you like," Smedd said. "He won't fool you any more than he did me. See his sister?"

"She stormed the Yard!"

"She tried to storm in here," Smedd told him, thinly, "but I don't stand any nonsense from the kids who think they know everything. And I don't intend to let anyone call me a liar, even if she is a girl who's a bit worked up."

Gideon made a whistling sound.

"She do that?"

"Oh, and a lot more hysterical nonsense," Smedd said tartly. "Either hysteria, or she was trying it on. Anyhow, what we have to work on are the *facts*." He patted the file of papers. "And in that file there are enough facts to convict him twice over. Only worry I've got is this insanity plea. Every time a kid gets off on that, I think that two others will probably kill in the same way, believing they might get away with it. Funny thing, the human mind. Subconscious has a hell of a lot to answer for."

"I'll say it does," said Gideon. "No weak spots, apart from that?"

"No." Smedd gripped his hands again tightly. "I've seen every member of the staff who works at the cinema where Rose's sister says they went, and had them look at Rose's photograph. None of them recognized him. Don't get me wrong," Smedd went on. "I don't believe the sister, but her story had to be checked, even if it was wasting the time of men who were needed on a more useful job. If she sticks to her story, the defense will try to prove that they did go to that cinema, but I've made sure before they start snooping."

"Couldn't be tighter," said Gideon.

"No, it couldn't be."

"Hardly worth my talking to him," said Gideon; "but you know what it's like with these youngsters, I won't get any peace at home until I've been able to say that I've talked to Rose myself."

"Let's go and see him," said Smedd. "I had a word with the A.C. about the advisability of a special court this afternoon, but he agreed that we could wait until the morning. Gave me time to check everything while making sure that the young brute didn't start running, or do any more damage."

"Hmm," said Gideon.

They went downstairs. The cells at the H5 station were in a semi-basement with frosted glass windows and bars; a gloomy, dingy place, quite enough to work on the fears of an innocent man. A sergeant was on duty at a desk. He straightened up when Smedd appeared, then recognized Gideon.

"We're going to see Rose," Smedd said.

"Yes, sir."

Gideon, effacing himself in a way which was remarkable for so large a man, followed the other two along a narrow corridor toward the cells. He wasn't really affected by Mary Rose's plea, but he found himself thinking about young Rose in a way that Smedd certainly wouldn't approve. Here was a boy, aged twenty, with all life before him; and upstairs, in between two thin covers, were twenty or more years in prison. But supposing he was innocent? What was going on in his mind, his sister's, his mother's?

William Rose heard them coming, and stood up as they reached the cell. He was smaller than Gideon had expected, slender and pale. If Gideon had been told that he was sixteen, he wouldn't have been surprised. He was remarkably like his sister, but his coloring was different; he was fair when she was dark, and his eyes were sky blue, a color picked out by the strip lighting. He wore a gray suit, his hair was neatly done, his shoes were polished; a young man who took care of himself.

Smedd barked, "This is Commander Gideon, of New Scotland Yard."

William Rose said quietly, "How're you, sir."

There was a hopeless look about him, which was apparent at once. Gideon had seen it often before, and it was no indication of guilt or innocence. Everything now happening was so utterly different from his normal life, and he felt lost.

Gideon said, "Evening, Rose. Sorry to find you in this predicament." That was the last approach that the boy expected—or Smedd, for that matter. "I don't know how much Chief Inspector Smedd has told you, but you know that in English law you've got a right to a defense, and the right to be regarded as innocent unless you're proved guilty."

The boy said, "That's all very well in theory, sir."

So he wasn't cowed, yet.

"What do you mean, exactly?" asked Gideon, in his slow, quiet way, and his placid expression could have done nothing to make the boy feel worse.

"There isn't a man here who treats me as if I was innocent; they've all jumped to the conclusion that I'm guilty." As he spoke, Rose looked at Smedd; not bitterly, but doggedly.

"Well, aren't you?" Gideon asked, still in that deceptively mild voice.

William Rose said, "I did not kill Winifred, sir, and I know nothing about it. I lost my knife several days ago, and the killer must have found it. I went to the pictures with my sister Mary, after Winifred and I had quarreled. That's the truth, sir."

Gideon was watching steadily. He said, "Know where you lost the knife?"

"No, sir."

"Told anyone else you'd lost it?"

The boy colored.

"No, sir, I didn't. It was a birthday present from my sister Mary, and I hoped I wouldn't have to tell her—or the family."

"Hm. All right, Rose, if you've told the truth, we'll prove it. Won't we, Chief Inspector?"

"We'll certainly establish the truth," Smedd said flatly.

"And that's all anyone wants," Gideon said. "Chief Inspector, I wonder if you could send a shorthand writer here, and let me ask Rose a few questions. Mind?"

Smedd couldn't very well refuse.

Gideon put the questions, mildly, in a manner much more friendly than hostile. The answers came out sharply at first, as if the boy was aware that he was fighting a losing battle. Gradually his tension eased, and he spoke more naturally; by the time the questions were over, he was speaking eagerly and with color in his cheeks.

His statement to Gideon coincided in every detail with two statements he had made earlier. If he was lying, nothing revealed itself by discrepancies in what he said.

"Thanks very much, Smedd," Gideon said, at the door of the police station, as they shook hands. "Sorry to poke my nose in, but you know how these things are. And with youngsters these days, people are so touchy—want to wrap them up in cotton wool. I daren't take a chance that something might have slipped up here; if it had, we'd be in for real trouble. And just between you and me . . ."

He stopped.

He knew exactly what he was saying and what he was doing, but Smedd didn't realize that. Smedd was agog for a confidence. It didn't come for a long time, and when it did it seemed to be almost with embarrassment.

"Keep this to yourself, won't you, Smedd, but there's a rumor that the A.C. might resign at the end of the year. Come into some private money, I hear. And you can't blame me for keeping an eye on the main chance, can you? Surprising how a 'not guilty' verdict rankles in the Home Office mind. One or two would be quite enough for them to pass me over. What with that and my daughter's personal interest—but I've got to be off!"

Smedd watched him go.

Smedd, who knew that Gideon's recommendation was the only thing he needed to be next in line for the superintendency at H5, was almost certainly checking over every detail in his mind, more determined than ever not to slip up. He would test the weakness in his case as thoroughly as any defending lawyer; there was no more risk that he would steam-roller over young William Rose.

Nice boy.

Nice boys sometimes had uncontrollable tempers, and Rose had owned the knife which had killed the Primrose Girl.

It was a quarter to six when Gideon's car turned into narrow, drab Muskett Street, where Mrs. Benson lived. At a corner of the street leading to it, he had seen Old Percy, one of the senior detective sergeants at the Yard—a sergeant because of seniority only; he was utterly lacking in ambition. Percy was a biggish man, with a big stomach; he had won the Metropolitan Police boxing championship for six years in a row, and still had the strength of an ox. One of the soundest men the Yard was ever likely to have, he recognized Gideon but didn't bat an eye.

He was watching the back of the house.

Young Abbott was at the front.

The detective officer was walking toward the car, and was almost level with Number 52, where Ruby Benson lived. He walked with long, deliberate strides, and looked as if he might have given Old Percy a run for his money had they been of an age in Percy's boxing days. Abbott walked more like a policeman on beat duty than a plain-clothes man watching a house—and it would be a long time before he got rid of that walk. Gideon had no particular objection to it; there were times when it was an advantage for a C.I.D. man to look like a policeman. He'd grow out of it, anyway.

Gideon drew up.

Abbott peered at him, saw who it was, and jumped forward to open the door.

"Afternoon, sir!"

"Hallo," said Gideon, as if surprised. "You on this job?"

"I'm being relieved at eight o'clock, sir. Sergeant Lawson—"

"I've seen him," said Gideon. "Anything happened to worry either of you?"

"Nothing at all's worried me, sir." Abbott reported the comings and goings of the Benson children and of two people who lived upstairs in this small house; and gave the description of two callers, one man and one woman, neither of whom had gone inside. Uneventful was the word. Gideon turned toward the house and saw a curtain move; either Ruby Benson or the children were peeping at him. As he reached the front door, he noticed the children inside the little front room: a boy of twelve and a girl of ten. He knocked. The children shouted something, their mother called to them sharply, and there was a scuffle of footsteps. Then Ruby Benson opened the door.

Gideon had a shock.

This was Ruby Benson all right, but she looked unbelievably younger. Changes in people so often had the opposite effect that this was astonishing. It was like looking at her younger sister. Of course she had her hair touched up, and it was no longer gray at the sides; the gray streak in the front was gone, too; but her youthfulness wasn't just due to her hair. Her skin looked clearer, her eyes had lost the long-suffering look he had known before. He could swear that she had fewer wrinkles, too. She was neatly made up, and her eyes were very bright. She wore a white blouse and a dark-gray skirt, and her figure was still the figure of a girl in her early twenties.

Gideon put out his hand.

"Well, well," he said, "you must tell me how you do it. I wouldn't mind knocking ten years off my age, too."

It pleased her, and she smiled. Her teeth were very even, so even that they were probably false, but that didn't matter. She shook hands hesitantly, then stood aside to let him in.

"I don't have the worry that I used to have—well, I didn't until today," she said. "The front room." Gideon knew the front room, turned into it, and had his second surprise. It had been redecorated throughout, it looked larger, and the freshness was in sharp contrast to the district. "Bit different since you were here last, isn't it?" she asked, and followed him in and closed the door. "It—it's ever so good of you to come. They haven't got him yet, have they?" That came quickly, revealing the anxiety so close to the surface.

"Not yet," Gideon had to agree.

"I've got a funny feeling," Benson's wife said abruptly. "I've got a feeling that he'll get down here, Mr. Gideon, and that he'll have a go at the kids. Like I told you. He knows they mean more to me than anything else, and it would just about suit him, that would—knowing I was alive and the kids were dead or—well, crippled or something. There's something I didn't ever tell you," she went on, speaking much too quickly, as she had done over the telephone. "His mother went to see him in Millways, did you know that?"

"No."

"Well, she did. And when she came back, she told me what he'd said to her. He gave her a message, actually, and she didn't understand it. But I did. I didn't tell her, and I didn't tell anyone; but—well, when I heard about Syd escaping, it came over me, Mr. Gideon. I could hardly think because I was so scared."

He could believe her.

"What was it?" he asked.

She said: "He told me to remember what had happened to the Micklewright family. Just that. You wouldn't know them, I shouldn't think. They were pals of Syd's, years ago, and Micklewright used to do jobs for him. He thought Syd pulled a fast one over him. I didn't *know* for sure but I was always afraid that Syd had done it. Now I *know*."

Gideon didn't tell her that she was almost incoherent. He could see how she had been bottling this up inside her; and now it was bursting out, and when it was all over she would feel better. He could see the outline of the picture that she was drawing, too.

She went on:

"The Micklewrights had two kids, see, and they were hit by a car, hit-and-run it was. They were with Micklewright, with their dad. He was killed, and so was one of the kids, and the other's been a cripple ever since. I couldn't ever be sure that Syd had done that; all I knew was that Micklewright died, and—and what had happened to the kids. Then when Syd's mother gave me the message, well—what could I think except what I did?"

Gideon said, very quietly, "We won't let anything happen to your children, Mrs. Benson."

She said suddenly, fiercely, "That's what you *say*, but who's to stop him? It isn't as if he'd have to do it himself; now he's out he could telephone someone down here, he's still got plenty of pals. As soon as you'd rung off this morning, I thought of that. That's why I didn't let them go back to school this afternoon. Mr. Gideon, how can you be sure he won't hurt my children?"

It had become an obsession.

Over the years, fear that her husband had been responsible for the Micklewrights' accident had been buried in her mind, and the message which Benson had sent back had quickened doubt to certainty. While he had been in jail she had felt safe; while he was out, she would live in a nightmare world of fear and dread, which would get stronger and more hideous as the days, perhaps as the hours, passed. Words wouldn't reassure her. The presence of the two policemen in the street wouldn't; in fact, nothing would, except her husband's recapture.

Gideon said, "I can imagine how you feel, but look at it straight for a minute. I'll have men outside this house day and night, until we get him. I'll double the present guard, too, and I'll make quite sure that—"

"You can't be sure," said Mrs. Benson flatly, and then went on deliberately: "Can you sit there and tell me to my face that you know he hasn't telephoned someone in London and told them what to do? *Can* you?"

Gideon said, "Of course I can't."

"Well, there you are, then," Mrs. Benson said. "There's only one way . . ."

She broke off as the door burst open without warning. The way she jumped told Gideon just how keyed up she was, and how she must have fought to keep calm when he had first arrived. But no danger threatened. Instead, the twelve-year-old boy, young Syd Benson, came leaping into the room, with his sister behind him and only a little less excited. Gideon hadn't seen them for over three years. They looked nice kids: just anyone's children who were cared for properly and in good health, and who came from good-looking parents.

"Ma!" young Syd cried and skidded to a standstill in front of his mother. "You know what . . . ?"

"You'll get a slap round the side of your head if you don't go out faster than you came in," said Mrs. Benson. "I told you to stay and watch the television and not come unless I told you. Go on and do what you're told. Liz, I'm ashamed of you, you ought—"

"But Ma!" cried young Syd, standing his ground with a defiance which obviously wasn't unusual. "Dad's coming on television, it just said so on the news. *Had* to tell you that, didn't I?"

8 . The Reason for Fear

YOUNG Syd's voice faded.

He looked into his mother's face, and showed his own shocked reaction to the way she took the news. She lost her color, and seemed to grow older in front of Gideon's eyes. It was only for a moment; then she braced herself, squaring her chin and her shoulders, and fought to throw off the crushing effect of what her son had said and—so much more important—how he had said it. Now, she looked down at him. He was small for his age; the girl was only an inch or two shorter. He was like Syd Benson; no one could mistake those sharp features, the rather thin lips, the chiseled look. And he had his father's light-blue eyes, with the unexpectedly long, dark lashes. He'd come bursting in to tell his mother that his *dad* was coming on the television; and in the way he had said it there was burning eagerness to see his father; excitement; *welcome*. The man whom his mother feared, whom she thought might harm these children, was this child's father; and the three years or more of separation hadn't altered that and hadn't altered the affection the boy felt.

Gideon found himself in the middle of a maelstrom of emotions, in depths which he only vaguely understood.

Then young Syd said, "He *is*, Ma, the announcer said so. Aren't you coming to see him? It's on . . ."

Mrs. Benson said, "Yes, Syd, I'll come. Will you come too, Mr. Gideon?"

"I'd like to," Gideon said.

"Well, hurry," urged young Syd.

He and his sister led the way. Ruby Benson looked once into Gideon's eyes, and then away; she was tight-lipped; and it was only possible to guess what was passing through her mind. Gideon followed her along a narrow passage to the long kitchen-cum-living-room, where the small-screen television set stood in one corner. It was dark outside, and there was no light on inside; the screen looked very bright. There were pictures of a speed-boat undergoing trials on lakes which were probably in Scotland, and the loud roar of the engines throbbed about the room. The children took their seats; two larger chairs were placed so that anyone sitting in them could get a good view of the screen.

"Please sit down," Ruby Benson said.

They sat down.

"Do you know what?" young Syd burst out. "I haven't seen him for over three years!"

"Nor have I," piped up the girl, "and he's my dad, too."

Gideon heard Ruby Benson's sharp intake of breath. He saw that she was biting at her knuckles. There wasn't a thing he could do except sit there stolidly and watch and listen, understanding what was racking her. She hadn't said anything to try to turn them against their father; that was obvious. Right or wrong, she had let them have their own thoughts and memories of him, and now there was the excitement, this eagerness to see him; no sense of shame, no sense of fear.

The picture and the noise faded.

The male announcer came on.

"Now we take you for a brief visit to Millways jail, in the north of England, from which nine desperate criminals escaped this morning, three of whom have now been recaptured."

The announcer's face faded.

The high, gray, bleak walls of Millways jail were shown upon the screen, and there was silence except for the slight hum of the loud-speaker. The shots were done well, and the announcer did not spoil them with a running commentary; he let the prison speak for itself. The walls with the great curved spikes on the top; the small windows with the thick iron bars; the watchtowers; the shots from inside, with the galleries round the cells, the cell doors open, the convicts coming out, the great net spread between the galleries, to catch any prisoner who was fool enough to try to kill himself. Here was everything, with the warders, the gray-clad, gray-faced prisoners, the long rows of cells, the tiny holes in the doors, the inside of a cell with its bed, one chair, one small table, the pin-ups on the wall.

Everything.

The two children were absolutely still.

Gideon felt Mrs. Benson's hand touching his. He moved, so that he could take her hand, and felt the pressure of her fingers. She needed his presence, the warmth and stolidity of his touch, to help her now.

Then Liz spoke.

"I can't see Dad," she complained.

"You'll see him," the boy said. "Shut up."

The prison faded, and the announcer spoke from a screen filled suddenly with the one word: *Wanted.*

"We are about to throw onto the screen pictures of the six men who are still missing, and for whom the police in the whole of England are searching. By the side of the photographs will be a description which will help in the identification of the wanted men, each one of whom has a record of violence. . . ."

Ruby Benson said in a choky whisper: "They can't stay and see this, I ought to have stopped them, I—"

"Let them be," said Gideon, softly.

Neither of the children turned.

First, there was Jingo Smith, with his bald head and button of a nose, quite a merry-looking man; then, Wally Alderman, with his flat and broken nose, a man whom Lombroso would have welcomed as the perfect illustration of criminal type. Then, Matt Owens, small, with pointed features and one eye which twitched a great deal and, in the photograph, looked half-closed.

Then, Benson.

It was a good photograph; prison photographs were getting better. This showed him exactly as he was, and the boy staring at the screen might have been looking at himself as he would be in twenty years' time. Every line and every feature of Benson's face showed, and those thin lips.

Hair: Dark.
Complexion: Sallow.
Eyes: Pale blue.

That was what made his eyes so noticeable: clear, pale blue in a sallow face, the face that was almost olive-skinned.

Height: 5 ft. 9 in.
Distinguishing marks: Brown mole, left ear.
                                 Appendectomy scar.
                                 Tip of little finger of
                                 left hand missing.

Then Benson was taken off.

Freddy Tisdale came on, looking almost cherubic, in spite of the starkness of the photograph. He gave the impression that he might burst into a smile at any moment. Ruby Benson stopped looking at the screen, but still sat there, as if hopeless. Gideon watched the children, and tried to imagine what was passing through their minds, but that was only for a moment. He leaned forward, took a brandy flask from his hip pocket, and unscrewed the cap.

"Have a sip," he said.

Ruby took it, blindly. When their hands touched again, hers were icy; she had gone cold in a few seconds. She choked a little, and Gideon took the flask away as the last picture faded and the screen went blank, then showed the announcer.

"Tomorrow, at the same time, WYN TELECASTING will bring you up-to-the-minute news of events throughout the world. Now there will be an interval of . . ."

Gideon stood up. The children got up, too, and turned toward Gideon and their mother. It seemed very dark now that the screen was blank.

Quietly and steadily, young Syd's voice came.

"And you're the bloody copper who put him inside," he said. "What wouldn't I like to do to you!"

Gideon had built up the case against Benson.

Gideon had broken down Ruby's resistance, and had prevailed upon her to give evidence against her husband.

Now, Ruby heard her son speak like that.

This was a challenge which couldn't be set aside. If Gideon said nothing to the boy, then the hatred would only fester and there would be a new element: birth of contempt for the police. So Gideon had to take up the challenge, without hurting the mother too much, without showing the slightest sign of vengefulness. He had to make an impression which, later, might stand Sydney Benson's son in good stead.

"Come on, let's get out of here," young Syd said, and swung round toward the back door.

Ruby burst out, "Syd! Don't you dare!"

"I got to go where there's some clean air," young Syd sneered, and glowered at Gideon.

The girl stood there uncertainly, looking first at her mother and then at her brother, but never at Gideon. All Gideon did was to watch young Syd, catch his gaze and hold it. The boy tried to look away, but could not. They were more used to the dim light now.

Gideon said, "That's right, Syd, I did help to send your father to prison. But he knew the risk he was taking, and he knew for years that one day the police would catch up with him. They always do. Do you play football?"

Young Syd didn't answer.

Gideon said roughly, "You've got a tongue in your head, so answer me. Do you play football, or don't you?"

"I—yes. Yeh," repeated the boy, with a gulp.

"He's in the school team," Liz put in, as if glad to say something for her brother.

"Doesn't surprise me, he looks as if he's good at sports," Gideon said offhandedly. "All right, Syd, you're in the school team for football, but what happens when you foul one of the other side? The ref blows his whistle, and there's a free kick against you, isn't there? Do it in the worst place, the penalty area, and it's almost certainly a goal to the other side. What does that mean? If you break the rules, if you foul too often, you'll get kicked out of your school team. That's the way it works at school, and it's the way it works outside. We make certain rules. Most people obey them. Some think they can foul and get away with it. They do for a while; but sooner or later, they're found out. Your father didn't play to the rules. If he had, he'd be here with you today. It's as simple as that. I should have thought you would have known it by now, without having to ask a copper to tell you. Got it?"

The boy said, "Bloody copper, that's all you are," and he turned suddenly and ran swiftly toward the door which led to the scullery. In a moment, he was outside in the small yard; and as Gideon hurried after him, he heard the sound of his steel-tipped heels on the concrete of the yard. When Gideon reached the back door, young Syd Benson was climbing over the wall which led to an alleyway running between two rows of houses.

Behind Gideon was Ruby Benson, clutching the hand of her other child.

"Don't let him get away," she breathed, "anything could happen to him, don't let him get away."

The luck could run well, sometimes.

Gideon was outside and giving orders to Abbott and Old Percy, who came hurrying, when a police patrol car turned into Muskett Street. Radio messages flashed to other patrol cars, and in ten minutes young Syd was discovered with half a dozen other boys standing about an old warehouse not far from the Thames. Gideon didn't send a patrol car or a uniformed man to talk to the boy, but went himself. It gave young Syd a chance to show off in front of his pals, but it also gave Gideon an opportunity to find out if there was as much good in the boy as his mother hoped.

"Syd," he said, "you can play the game anyhow you like, but I've told you what will happen if you play it the wrong way. Now show some sense, and time it better. Fond of your mother, aren't you?"

Syd didn't answer.

Gideon swung round on another lad.

"Do you like your mother?" He flashed to a third. "And you? And what about you?"

He won a startled "Yes," an unexpected "She's okay," and a grunt.

"Been happy with your mother at home, haven't you?" Gideon asked young Syd, still roughly. "Come on, the others admit it, why don't you?"

"Ye-yeh."

"Well, she played to the rules, and she's made a man out of you," Gideon said. "If you hadn't a lot of guts you wouldn't have behaved like you did just now. But don't forget that your mother's having a tough time. I'm talking to you like this because I can tell you've got a good mind, and I won't insult you by pretending that you're just a kid who doesn't understand. You understand all right. Your mother's nervous because your father's out of jail; and if he comes and sees her, she'll want help, not hindrance. It's up to you to do all you can to help her, and pay back a bit of the debt you owe her. But if you don't want to, okay, I can't *make* you go back."

He was thinking, "If it comes to a point, I'll have to find some charge and pick the kid up; he'll be safer in a cell than out here tonight."

He turned and walked off, knowing that young Syd was being watched by Divisional men.

He went back to Muskett Street. There wasn't much that he could say, and he wasn't looking forward to the next interview; but he had another surprise. Ruby had controlled her fears and overcome the moment of crisis so well that she greeted him quite briskly.

"I shouldn't have let him watch, I suppose," she said, "but he'll soon come to his senses. The trouble is he mixes with the kids from Syd's old crowd, and there's nothing you can do about it. One of these days he's going to have to choose one way or the other, though I can't *make* him do it the way I want him to. The important thing is to make sure he doesn't run into trouble. You are having him watched, aren't you?" She was very anxious.

"Closely. He'll be all right, and I think he'll come back before long. We've got to decide what to do with him and the girl," Gideon went on. "I could arrange for them to go away somewhere; but if you send them now, you might make young Syd think that we're just trying to make sure that he can't see his father. That won't help on a long-term basis. Like us to put the girl somewhere, and leave you and young Syd here?"

There was a long silence. Then:

"We'd better all stick together," Mrs. Benson said.

Gideon went back to the Yard before going home.

Lemaitre had gone, and Sergeant Jefferson was there, holding the fort before a night-duty Chief Inspector came in; there was always someone in the Commander's office. Jefferson's gray head was bent over a report as the door opened, and he looked up quickly, then stood up.

"Didn't know whether you'd be looking in or phoning, sir."

"Best to look in," Gideon said. "Anything new?"

"Been very quiet, so far," said Jefferson. "Nothing fresh from Millways. That railway-sidings man who was beaten up is on the danger list. If he dies, that'll be a nasty job." Jefferson had a gentle way with him. "They've picked up a footprint near the Kelly's Bank vault, which might help; but in my opinion it's a bit tenuous, sir. Otherwise, just routine. I'm not expecting things to be so quiet tomorrow. Much warmer tonight, isn't it?"

Gideon smiled.

"We old-in-the-tooth coppers can tell the youngsters a thing or two, can't we? Well, I'm going home. Superintendent Fisher on duty tonight?"

"Yes, sir."

"Good. Pleasant dreams," said Gideon, and went off.

He looked in at the A.C.'s office and made sure that it was empty; had a word with Fisher, who had an office along the corridor; took a last look at the Information Room, studying recent teleprints from other parts of the country and the radio flashes. They were coming in fairly fast, he gathered; there had been five burglaries tonight so far, mostly on London's outskirts, nothing yet which the Divisions couldn't handle. He went off with a familiar feeling which was stronger at certain times than others, and was very strong now. It was a sense of anticlimax: a sense that when so much needed doing, he was walking away from it. The theme song of the Yard was unfinished business, and there was the guilty sense of going away at a time when anything might happen. The night held its secrets; perhaps the dead body, not yet discovered; or the killer, striking at this very moment. The burglar at the window or at the safe; the criminal at work everywhere; the never-ending cycle of the crimes committed by night and of the investigations beginning next morning.

He remembered, suddenly, that in the cell at H5 Division was a lad who might have taken the first steps on that long walk.

He, Gideon, was going home—to his wife, to supper and to bed.

Unless, of course, he was called out.

9 . Benson Alone

BENSON did not know that his picture was being thrown onto the television screens all over the country. He stood in the kitchen of the furnished house, unable to hear the faint sounds from the radio in the next room, but hearing a louder, throbbing noise coming from the house next door; that was either radio or television, tuned too loudly. It got on his nerves. Everything was getting on his nerves, and he didn't realize that it was largely reaction to the fact that what he had planned so long and so carefully had actually gone according to plan.

Freddy Tisdale was out.

It was ten minutes to seven, and Freddy oughtn't to be long.

Benson began to wonder if he could trust Freddy.

Freddy had told him to stay here in the warm, there was no sense in their both going out; and that was right. It wasn't as if this job would be dangerous. It was five minutes' walk to the shop at the corner, and it would be child's play to get in, lift a few oddments of groceries, and get out again. Freddy, whose nerves seemed to be much steadier than Benson's that day, hadn't appeared to give it a second thought.

He'd been gone for twenty minutes.

Benson had opened the kitchen drawer and now stared at the knives, forks and spoons inside. His gaze was mostly concentrated on the knives. There was one, a poultry knife which had worn thin in the middle. It was very sharp. There was also a green felt sheath for a bread knife, to stop it from getting tarnished. He kept searching until he found a knife sharpener, took this to a tap and ran cold water on it, and then began to sharpen the poultry knife. Every now and again he paused, so that the grating hiss of steel on steel stopped, and he listened for the sound of Freddy's approach.

He heard nothing.

Freddy was to tap at the back door, three times.

Benson finished sharpening the knife, and drew the blade along his thumb; he just broke the surface of the epidermis. Then he slid the knife into the green felt sheath, tied it near the handle of the knife, and slid it all down the front of his trousers. He fastened the top of the sheath onto a trousers button, so that it would not work down, and then walked about, shifting the knife until it was in the most convenient position.

Now he was smiling.

He stopped smiling, for it was five past seven; Freddy had been gone a long time. He moved to the door, hesitated, put the light out, and then opened the door an inch. He could see the pale night, reflecting the snow. Some way off there were a few yellow lights, but not enough to worry him. He heard nothing.

Cold air swept in.

He closed the door and began to shiver, only partly from the cold.

Three things were possible.

One, that Freddy had been delayed, but would soon arrive with some food. With *food*.

Two, that he had deliberately run out on his partner.

Three, that he had been caught.

Benson didn't seriously consider the second possibility, but he had to consider the last. It made him sweat, in spite of the fit of shivering. He felt the gnawing at his stomach as if it were a sharp pain. Fear made it worse. He knew Freddy Tisdale only through prison life; he couldn't be sure that Freddy wouldn't break down and give a partner away. And the snow, which muffled all sound of approach, could muffle all sound of the police also, if they were coming.

Benson went upstairs, crept into an icy cold bedroom and, still shivering, moved to the window. He couldn't possibly be seen, yet he kept to one side, as if the night had eyes. He peered into the street, the white pavements and the banks of packed snow, the three neglected snowmen, the little houses with lights at the windows and at fanlights, all the front doors closed tightly against the bitter March wind.

He went back to the kitchen; and as he reached the door which led from the passage, he heard a dull sound. He stopped absolutely still, until it was repeated, and this time there was no mistake. *Bump, bump, bump.* This was Freddy; it must be. Yet, as he moved forward, Benson felt his heart almost choking him. Freddy might have been caught and might have given that signal away; he might open the door to a copper.

And Freddy might have returned—empty-handed.

Benson stood to one side, took the knife out and slid it into his trousers pocket, and then, left hand stretched out, he turned the key in the lock. Freddy could hear that. Then he opened the door a fraction of an inch.

"That you, Freddy?"

"Who the hell do you think it is?" Freddy demanded hoarsely. "Let me in, I'm frozen ruddy stiff."

Benson opened the door wider and Freddy came in, so cold that his teeth were chattering and his body shaking. His eyes looked sharply veined and glittery, his nose and his cheeks were blue, but he carried a cardboard carton, and the pockets of his stolen coat bulged.

Food!

Benson closed the door without a sound and switched on the light. He was breathing harshly, now. Freddy moved toward the kitchen table, dumped the box down, and then emptied his pockets; he didn't stop shivering.

"Flicking customers," he said, "there was a couple of women, standing there gassing; the shopkeeper and his perishing wife wouldn't let them go. I stood in a wind that cut like a flicking knife. Here, you dish up, I've got to go and get myself warm."

Benson didn't speak.

Steaming hot soup, ham, cheese, tinned potatoes, tinned peas, and some rye bread in a packet made a meal which might almost have come from the Savoy Grill. Benson and Tisdale hadn't eaten food like it for three years. They ate slowly and steadily for twenty minutes, until Freddy began to wilt. They had hardly uttered a word since his return.

Suddenly Benson said: "All we could do with is some beer. You got any beer?" He gave a tight-lipped grin.

"Like me to go and get some?" asked Freddy, also grinning. His face now had a much more amiable expression.

Benson said, "You're okay, Freddy, you've got what it takes. What are you going to do after we leave here? Stringing along with me or playing solo?"

"You any idea?" Freddy asked.

"We could play it both ways," Benson said. "I'm going south, but let me tell you something. I've got a card index in my head, the best card index there is in the country. I know the name and address of every man and woman they think I might try to get in touch with, and I know the names of some people they won't even think about. I'm going to get in touch with some of those, and they'll do what I want them to do. They'll stake me, and they'll let me lie under cover. I don't need very long. I've got some dough put away, and I'm going to get out of this country just as soon as I've finished one little job."

"What's the job?"

Benson said, "Know who put me inside, Freddy?"

"No."

"My wife."

Freddy said, "Like hell she did! 'Nother guy?"

"I don't think she had one then, but that's one of the things I'm going to find out," said Benson. "There are a lot of things I'm going to find out." He fell silent for a moment, looking at Freddy through his eyelashes, those fine, dark, curly lashes which were reproduced in his son. "You know where you're going?"

"Syd," said Freddy Tisdale, in a quiet voice, "all I cared about was getting out of that place, and all I care about now is keeping out. I'd kill anyone who tried to stop me, and I mean it. And before I let them take me back, I'd kill myself. That's the way I feel about it."

"That's the way we feel about it," Benson said. "This is what we do. We keep together while we go down south; two can do that better than one, see. And I'll send you to a skirt who'll see you all right for as long as you need to lie low. When the heat's off, okay, we can get out of the country. We go it together until we get to London; that okay with you?"

"It's a privilege," Freddy said.

"That's what I like to hear. Now listen," Benson went on, "I don't want to play the luck too hard. We could stay here for three or four days, and then run right into trouble. I reckon we ought to leave here just before dawn in the morning so no one can see us, and then . . ."

Freddy said, "Syd, that would make me nervous. It'll be so cold then, and it's the wrong time of day anyway. Anyone who did see us would notice us, wouldn't they?"

Benson grinned.

"It's okay," he said, "you know the answers. Freddy, is there a big car park near here?"

"There's the one at the market."

"Market open tomorrow?"

"And every day."

"Could we get there around twelve o'clock, say, when the park'll be full, knock off a car, and get going?"

"We got to try something," Freddy said. "Why not that? If we leave here around half past eleven, anyone who sees us will think we've been looking over the house. That okay?"

"That's fine," said Benson. "Freddy!"

"Yeh?"

"You mean what you said about killing anyone who tries to get in your way?"

"I meant it."

"Okay," said Syd Benson. "So did I."

Next morning, Gideon woke up about seven o'clock, and lay for a few minutes looking at the sun shining in at a corner of the window. He heard no noises about the house; the only slight sound was of his wife's breathing, as she lay in the other bed. None of the children was about, then; the older they got, the later they were getting up in the morning. He eased himself up on his elbows; there was no break in his wife's even breathing. He got out of bed, shrugged on a dressing gown which made him look huge, pushed his feet into slippers, and went to the door. He'd bring her a cup of tea, as he often did. He glanced back at her from the door, and found himself smiling. She didn't look at her best, but she was all right; and when she was at her best she was really something. She wouldn't like the way her hair-net was half on and half off, but that didn't matter, either.

Gideon went out, and down the stairs.

This house at Hurlingham was not far from the Thames and the polo ground. The houses were in long terraces, each with two stories and an attic, and he had taken particular pride in his. Years ago, he had turned it from two flats into one house, and now the attic was set aside for the boys, including their sleeping cubicles; and the girls, Gideon, and Kate slept on the floor below. Gideon had done much of the converting himself and still kept the house decorated; if he had a hobby, it was woodwork and anything to do with painting and decorating. He liked to keep the value of his property up.

He had a good night.

Kate had been waiting for him, too, and he wasn't quite used to that. After the death of their son, seven years and more ago, they had gone through a very bad period, gradually growing apart and aloof from each other. At one time, Gideon had seriously wondered whether they would see their marriage through. Then, without quite knowing what had happened, things had changed.

There was no demonstration, but they began to understand each other

again, and to enjoy each other's company. Gideon soon found this new atmosphere much, much better than he had ever hoped. It brought a sense of
excitement even at home. It helped him to get more fun out of his children,
too—their children now, rather than hers or his. The change was still sufficiently fresh for him to wonder at it; and to wonder, also, whether anything
would happen to spoil it.

The truth was that he looked forward to coming home, and got home
whenever he could. At one time, he had taken any excuse to stay at the
office.

He made the tea, just for himself and Kate; it was a rule that the children
could have tea if they cared to make it for themselves—except on Sundays,
when the girls were given a treat.

He thought he heard a tap running, upstairs, and then reached the landing and heard a door open.

Pru stood there in her peach-colored nightdress.

It was a funny thing, thought Gideon, but you saw your own daughter,
day in and day out, from the time she was a toddler to the time when she
was nearly twenty, and it took a moment like this to make you realize that she
was a young woman. Mary Rose hadn't a thing that his Prudence lacked.
He hadn't realized that she had quite such a figure, her mother probably
made her flatten herself a bit in her day clothes. Trust Kate.

Prudence looked young, fresh, pretty—and anxious.

"Dad," she said in a whisper, "what do you honestly think about Will
Rose's chances?"

"If he didn't kill the girl, Pru, he'll be all right."

"Are you *sure?*"

"Positive."

"And you didn't mind Mary going to see you?"

"No, of course not." Gideon hesitated for a moment, and then looked at
her very intently, suspecting something that she hadn't told him. "What's
on your mind, Pru?"

"You really didn't mind?"

"Not a bit."

"Well, thank goodness," Pru said, "because there's something I didn't tell
you. Yesterday morning, Mary rang me up, she was ever so upset, and she
asked me if I'd have a word with you. I said it would be much better if
she went to see you herself, and—well, you know what happened, don't
you? I don't think she would have thought of coming to Scotland Yard if
it hadn't been for me, and afterward I wondered if I'd rather let you down."

Gideon said, "You didn't let me down at all, Pru. Always fight for anything you believe in, and above all fight for your friends. Was she really a
close friend?"

"Well, no. We did just know each other, but she's two years older than I, you see."

"You didn't know her well, then?"

"Not really."

"Like her?"

"Yes, everyone did."

"What kind of reputation did she have?"

"Dad," said Prudence, wisely, "I wish I knew what you were asking me all these questions for. What do you want to know?"

"Whether Mary Rose is a liar, Pru."

Pru didn't speak.

"Did she have a reputation as a liar?"

"No, *everyone* liked her."

"All right," said Gideon, "if she's telling the truth about what she and her brother did on Thursday, she'll be all right and so will he. If she's lying— well, it will do her more harm than good, and it certainly won't do him any good. Now you go and put a dressing gown on. I left a kettle on a low gas, if you want a cup of tea."

"Oh, thanks," said Prudence. "Thanks a lot, Dad."

Kate was awake, beginning to sit up, with the hair-net off and her hair unruly in an orderly fashion; she had pushed it together with her long, thin fingers. It wasn't really surprising that her daughters had good figures! Her eyes were bright, and she had something of Pru's freshness.

"Hear all that?" he asked.

"Yes," Kate said. "I only hope Mary Rose isn't lying."

Gideon got into the Wolseley a little after half past eight. Prudence wasn't going out until the afternoon, but would spend the morning practicing interminably on her fiddle. Penelope, their youngest girl, was still going to school, and had to go in the other direction. Priscilla, now sixteen, had just left school and had a job in a Chelsea office. Gideon dropped her off at the nearest corner to the office and watched her as she hurried, quite the young woman in her high heels and her nylons. She turned and waved, then disappeared. He grinned to himself, but there was a hint of a sigh as he started off again. Prudence first and now Priscilla had made him feel old. But that mood soon passed; and from then on until he reached the office, he was mulling over everything that had happened the previous day. The report was being prepared, as usual, and he grinned at the thought.

He wondered if any more of the escaped prisoners had been caught during the night.

None had.

There was only one change in the scene since yesterday; the quiet spell had ended, and in the Metropolitan area alone there had been forty-nine burglaries during the night, seven arrests had already been made. Fingerprints both at the Yard and at the Divisions were working to their limit.

There would be no time to spare today.

Lemaitre and Jefferson were in Gideon's office, and for twenty minutes they all went through the daily reports and made comments.

The three men from the Bond Street smash-and-grab raid would be up for the first magistrate's court hearing; in all, there were nineteen cases of major felonies up—most of them likely to be dealt with summarily, three likely to be sent for trial.

Lefty Bligh, the safe-breaker, had got himself a job as a messenger to a small firm of office consultants; and, by a strange coincidence, the office was on the same floor as a bookmaker's, where usually large sums in cash were kept in an ultramodern safe.

"Lefty will have a crack at that, soon," Gideon said. "Have two men always on the premises, to catch him red-handed."

"Right," said Lemaitre.

Next, Gideon glanced through the newspapers, which had difficulty in choosing between the Primrose Girl murder and the prison break. They solved their problems by sharing the space equally. There were photographs of six of the fugitive prisoners, including Benson; and there was a photograph of William Rose.

Before he started the usual briefing, Gideon looked through two medical reports which had been made about the accused boy. One was emphatic; he was perfectly sane and showed no indication of mental unbalance. The other, from a man whose name Gideon didn't know, suggested that there were indications of mental instability and recommended that the boy's medical history be carefully checked.

Gideon telephoned Smedd, who would have a copy of these.

"Yes, I'm getting a report from the boy's family doctor and his school doctor," Smedd said at once. "Should have them in today. I'll send you copies."

"Thanks very much," said Gideon. "Mind if I make a suggestion?"

"Very glad to hear it."

"Thanks. If there's a weakness in the case, it's the knife that was used. The boy could have lost it. Will you try to check, with the family, friends, people at his place of work, and make sure he didn't tell anyone else he'd lost it?"

"I'll see to that," said Smedd.

"Fine. Just as well to seal up all the holes," Gideon said, and felt that he'd done his duty by Prudence.

Next, he glanced through reports which were coming in fast from the Midlands and the North, saying that one or another of the escaped prisoners had been "seen." Such statements came from places hundreds of miles from Millways jail, and not one looked likely to stand up to scrutiny. Most of the provincial police H.Q.'s would be bombarded with these for days; and each would have to be checked. London's turn would come only too soon.

Then Gideon dealt with job upon job in the morning briefing, and by eleven o'clock most of the cases were off his desk. He felt that he could breathe again, and spent some of the next half hour checking in the protection plans for Ruby Benson and her youngsters; everything seemed to be in order, and there was a report that both children had gone to school that morning, escorted by two policemen who were waiting at the school to take them back.

"Keep a special eye on the boy," Gideon ordered. "He might cut and run for it."

"Yes, sir." It was Abbott who had reported, and who was still on duty in the street. "Any news of Benson, sir?"

"No," said Gideon, "and you keep a lookout, as if you're expecting him to turn into the street at any moment."

"Right, sir," said Abbott, in a tone which seemed to say: "If only he would!"

Gideon put the receiver down, and it rang almost at once; this time it was the A.C. He listened, scowled, and said, "I'll come along at once," but when he had put the receiver down again, he didn't move. Lemaitre looked up at him, one eye screwed up against the curling cigarette smoke, and asked, "What's that?"

"The P.P.'s still worried about Edmundsun."

"Why don't they learn to take our word for it?" Lemaitre was disgusted.

"They might have something," said Gideon; "and if they have, I'd rather find out what it is for myself, without being told. Oh, well, I'd better go along. Don't interrupt me unless it's about the Benson job."

"Right," said Lemaitre. "The papers have played it up pretty high, haven't they?"

"What else could we expect?" asked Gideon. "Benson's big news."

He spent twenty minutes with the A.C. and a senior official from the Public Prosecutor's office. The Edmundsun case weakness was worrying everyone, and one surprise defense witness, or the discrediting of a prosecution witness, could lose the case and set a known rogue free. But the talk got them nowhere, and Gideon went back to his office. Nothing important had come in, unless the newspaper which Lemaitre had spread over his desk was important. It was the *Evening Sentinel,* with a banner headline:

DID BENSON ESCAPE TO GET REVENGE?
POLICE WATCH ON FAMILY

"Here we go," Gideon said softly.

"Think he'll let himself be captured alive?" Lemaitre asked. "I should say . . ."

Gideon's telephone bell rang; and with that slow, deliberate movement, Gideon lifted it.

"Gideon."

"I've got Mrs. Benson on the line, sir," the operator said; "shall I put her through to you, or to Superintendent Wrexall? He passed her call on to you yesterday, you may remember."

"Put her through," said Gideon quietly.

It was then exactly twelve o'clock on the second day of the escape.

10 . Twelve Noon

GIDEON first heard Ruby Benson's agitated breathing, and guessed from that her frame of mind. It was just possible that she had heard from Benson; that she had received a sharper, closer threat. His job was to calm her down. He did not want to spend too much time with her, unless she had news of importance. Too much was pressing, and he had only two specific jobs: to make sure Benson didn't do her and the children any harm, and to catch Benson if he came down here. Easing Ruby's fear, soothing out the tensions which tormented her, were incidental; he mustn't spend too much time on it.

But he could help a bit.

"Hallo, Mrs. Benson, how are you this morning?" His deep voice had a comforting boom. "And the youngsters, they all right?"

"Yes, they—" Ruby broke off for a moment, and was breathing very hard. "Have you got him yet?"

"Not yet," Gideon said.

He hoped that by going to see her, he hadn't given her the impression that she could keep asking him for minute-to-minute news, and be continually on the telephone. The woman he had known in the past had realized the position, and been hesitant about taking his time, but now she was driven to desperation because of those fears for the children.

She said, "I know I shouldn't worry you, but I just don't know what to do for the best, Mr. Gideon. I didn't sleep much last night because of the worry of it, and this morning . . ." She broke off, almost choking.

"Well, what happened this morning?"

After a pause, she said hoarsely, "I'm sorry to behave like this, Mr. Gideon, but it was such a shock. I knew there was trouble for the children and me, but—well, there's a friend of mine at the shop where I work, I can't help it if you blame me for going about with him, but I've been on my own for so long and I *had* to—had to have some companionship. He's the manager at the shop, and this morning he had a—he had a phone call."

Gideon exclaimed, "From Benson?"—unbelievingly.

"No, not from Syd; he doesn't know who it came from," said Mrs. Benson quickly; "it was just someone who phoned up and asked for him, and—and then asked if he preferred lilies or roses. That's all, but—but it was the way he said it. And who else but Syd would send a message like that?" Her voice shook.

Gideon understood why much more clearly.

"It sounds like one of Benson's tricks," he agreed; "we always knew he had plenty of contacts in London. We'll keep an eye on your friend, Mrs. Benson. We've already got a man watching the shop, I'll have another to keep an eye on your friend—what's his name?"

"Arthur—I mean, Mr. Arthur Small."

"We'll keep an eye on him," Gideon promised. "Still feel that you'd rather have the children with you, or shall we find a safe spot for them until everything's over?"

She didn't answer at once.

One of the other telephones was ringing, and Lemaitre got up and came across to answer it, had a hand stretched out to pick up the receiver, and then heard a telephone ring on his own desk. He scowled as he picked up Gideon's.

"Mr. Gideon's on the other line, hold on." He went back, and was at his desk and speaking again before Ruby Benson answered Gideon.

"That's what's kept me awake all night, wondering what I really ought to do. I know it's silly, but I don't want to part with them now. I—I get a feeling that if I let them go I'd never see them again."

"You'll see them again," said Gideon, but knew that it was empty reassurance. "How's the boy?"

Another pause.

Lemaitre almost shouted into his instrument: "*What's that?*" and looked across at Gideon, his eyes blazing. "*Hurry up!*" he mouthed, and beckoned furiously.

Something big? *Benson.*

"Just a minute, Mrs. Benson," Gideon said, and clapped a great hand over the mouthpiece. "What's up, Lem?"

"Edmundsun," breathed Lemaitre; "got hold of a razor blade, tried to kill himself, they're rushing him to hospital. Might not live the day out, either. Who shall we send?"

"Cummings," said Gideon, without a moment's hesitation and put that out of his mind as he switched back to Benson's wife. "Sorry, Mrs. Benson. What were you saying?"

"You asked me how young Syd was," Ruby said, "and the truth is, I don't know. I knew he was interested in his dad, I didn't think it was right to put him against his own father too much. To tell you the truth I always told myself young Syd would be a grown man and able to think for himself before he saw my husband again, and—but that isn't the point, Mr. Gideon! I don't know what to make of him. Seeing that prison on the television, and then seeing his father's photograph, did something to him. He seemed different last night, older if you know what I mean, as if—as if he'd been thinking, and wasn't so sure of me any more."

Gideon said, "Mrs. Benson, he's a healthy youngster, and he's got everything in him that he'll ever want. He'll pull through after this, you just needn't worry. Now, I must ring off."

"Yes, of course, I'm sorry I bothered you," Ruby said quickly. "Good-by, and—and thanks a lot."

"If you think we can help, any time, call on us," Gideon said. "Don't hesitate."

He rang off, and looked frowningly across at Lemaitre, who was briefing Cummings by telephone. One half of Gideon's mind listened to that. Lemaitre, who knew every trick in the book and every regulation that hampered or aided the Yard, could do this better than anyone else. If Edmundsun was really dangerously injured, Cummings must try to get a statement, but not offend the doctors. Cummings must also check with the Yard as often as he could.

Other things:

"Don't forget to have someone else as witness to any statement that Edmundsun makes. Don't forget to try to find out where Edmundsun salted the cash away . . ."

Throughout all this, Gideon kept seeing mind pictures of young Syd, who was so much like his father. Abbott was watching the boy, so he should be all right. But the problem was no longer a simple one of Syd's physical safety. It was possible to understand a boy worshiping a father whom he didn't know, a man whom his friends spoke of as a hero. It was impossible to foresee the consequences of such hero worship.

At twelve noon, the moment when Gideon was holding on for Ruby

Benson's call, Benson was closing the front door of the house where he and
Freddy Tisdale had spent the night.

It wasn't so cold, but the snow was beginning to melt, and walking was
difficult. Each of them, Tisdale in the lead, was well wrapped up in clothes
found in the locked cupboards in the house; and each had a hat, Benson
a bowler which was a little too big for him. Each had a muffler and gloves,
too. They might have been exactly what they looked: a man from the estate
agency with a prospective tenant who had been over the house. Two neighbors did, in fact, see them leave; neither gave them a second thought.

They walked on cautiously, because the ground was so slippery. At the
corner, they could turn right toward a busy main road, or left, to a short
cut toward the car park behind the market. Freddy turned left. They didn't
speak, and their footsteps went *slsh, slsh, slsh.* Everyone on foot was intent
on where he was stepping, and avoiding a nasty fall; no one took much
notice of Benson and Tisdale. Every other man they saw was huddled up
in clothes in much the same way, and no one was likely to single the fugitives
out.

They had to cross another main road to reach the car park. They turned
into it—and saw a sergeant of police leaning on his bicycle, talking to a
constable. Both policemen were looking toward the corner, and both saw
Benson and Tisdale.

Neither convict spoke or panicked.

Here was a testing time that was never likely to be repeated; they were on
the same side of the road as the policemen, who stood close to a crossing.
The road was busy. The only place to cross was near the policemen; anyone who tried to cross this side of them would invite attention. The two
men had turned toward the policemen, and couldn't turn the other way
without attracting attention, either.

They walked on.

They still watched the ground, picking their steps carefully. Here, outside the little shops, the snow had been cleared in most places, but there
were slushy patches, and walking wasn't wholly safe. Benson, three yards
from the policemen, actually glanced up and looked straight along the road,
while Tisdale glanced toward the other side.

The sergeant wasn't looking at them, now.

The constable was.

Benson's whole body seemed to be screaming. Every muscle was ready,
to move, to take him across the road, to go tearing toward the car park,
but he knew that if he were recognized he would never get away. He
sensed that Freddy suffered from exactly the same screaming tension.

Twenty yards away, a child stepped off the curb.

The mother cried out, a cyclist jammed on brakes which squealed, a motorist hooted. Policemen and sergeant looked round, abruptly, and Benson and Tisdale reached the crossing. They had to wait for two cars. Even when these passed, they didn't hurry. They were breathing into the thick woolen mufflers, and looking out of the corner of their eyes toward the men in uniform, one of whom was moving toward the woman and the child.

Benson started across the road.

They reached the other side.

Neither said a word as they slipped down a narrow alley toward the car park. Here, the thaw didn't seem to have been so rapid, and the snow was much harder. A boy came running toward them, making a slide, and Benson moved to one side. The boy was about young Syd's age, wrapped in a red muffler and wearing a school cap, his eyes a clear blue and his plump cheeks a bright red.

The two men reached the car park.

It stretched a long way in each direction, and beyond it were the canvas-covered stalls of the big market. There must have been three hundred cars in all, side by side, parked as closely as an expert parking attendant could put them. The ground sloped a little in one direction, and there were two big arrows with the words: WAY OUT.

Few people were about.

"One near the exit," Benson said. "Try the doors as we pass."

"Yeh."

The snow was crunchier here, too, because fewer people had walked on it. They passed between two lines of cars. Not far off, an engine started up and a car moved toward the exit, its exhaust fumes thick and smelly. Freddy paused at the back of a small car which had a front window down, and stepped between it and a green Jaguar. The small car's driving door wasn't locked, either.

"This'll do," he called.

"Okay," said Benson.

He slid between the car and an Austin Seven which was parked on the other side. He had difficulty in squeezing in, for there was so little room to spare, but he managed. Freddy was already working at the ignition with a piece of wire he had brought from the house. His hand looked cold, although he had been wearing gloves, and he couldn't get the "key" to work. He began to swear under his breath. Benson watched him, but looked into the driving mirror, and saw a big, fattish man coming toward him—toward this line of cars. The newcomer was talking to someone behind him, for Benson could see his lips moving.

A small, wizened man appeared by the big man's side.

Benson drew in a sharp, hissing breath.

"What's up?" Freddy asked sharply.

"Get it started!"

"Give us a chance. What . . ."

Benson drew in another hiss of breath. Freddy glanced up, saw the tension on his companion's face and the way he watched the driving mirror. Freddy couldn't see anyone in it, from where he was sitting, so turned his head round. He saw the big man going along the line of cars, and the little, wizened man coming toward them.

It was the car park attendant.

Benson had seen the man's face clearly; the gray stubble, the slobbery lips, one eye which watered badly. He had seen the cap, the woolen muffler tight round the thin neck, the bundle of coats he was wearing, and the ticket machine and leather cashbag which was strapped to his waist.

Freddy said urgently, "What's he after?"

Benson said softly, "It's Taffy Jones."

Freddy's breath hissed, as if Benson had said: "It's the Millways Governor." Until a year ago Jones had been in Millways, a prisoner serving a short-term sentence. He should have had ten years, but had squealed on three men who had done a job with him, so he'd got off lightly. He would always squeal; he was a man whom it was impossible for these two to trust.

And he could not fail to recognize them.

He had reached the back of the car, and was pushing his way toward them, the chinking money in the worn leather bag, the bright metal ticket dispenser shining. There seemed to be no particular animosity on his face as he reached the window near Benson, bent down, and looked in. The window was open several inches at the top.

Then, his mouth gaped. His broken teeth showed. He stood like that, half-crouching, hemmed in by the car behind him, one hand at the window, and the other out of sight. His watery eyes, the one half-closed, held an expression of shocked horror. There was no shadow of doubt that he had recognized them.

And he was a squealer.

There was a split second in which none of them moved. Then, two things happened at once: the ignition light on the dashboard panel showed, as the home-made key made contact; and Benson dropped one hand to his pocket, the other to the door handle, the window shot down.

Taffy Jones gave a gurgling kind of cry, and turned, and started to run. The fat man's car started up, drowning the sounds. There was so little room, and the slush running beneath his feet was ankle-deep. He skidded, gave that gasping cry again, and crashed down, slopping into the slush, splashing the cars, splashing Benson as Benson slid out of the seat. Freddy was out of the other door, almost as swiftly, and he looked right and left, but saw no one. Now, Jones was writhing and squealing, and trying to get to his feet, but he had very little time; and the fat man's car was noisy as it moved off. Jones twisted his head round. He looked like a cretin as he did that; the expression in his eyes and the slobbering saliva at his mouth were revolting.

"I woan talk, I woan talk, I woan talk," he moaned. "Doan 'urt me, I woan talk . . ."

Benson skidded, regained his balance, went down on one knee beside the man—and the poultry knife was in his hand. He had used a knife before, expertly. He used it now. It slid through the thick coats, the shirt, the skin, the flesh. It went straight to the heart, and Taffy Jones' moaning and writhing stopped, there was just the rattle in his throat, strangely subdued, and then a quivering into stillness.

Freddy appeared.

"Got to get rid of him quick," he said, "but put his bag in the car, come in useful that will."

11 . Deep Snow

BENSON was getting to his feet, slowly, and wiping the knife on the dead man's coat. He didn't speak. Except that his lips were set more tightly than usual, there was nothing different about him. He bent down, and used the knife to slash at the leather strap which held the moneybag to the dead man's side. He picked the bag up, and the coins jingled; a sixpence fell out and dropped, to bury itself in the snow. Benson fastened the flap, and pushed the bag through the open window. Now, he looked about him, and Freddy Tisdale did the same; but no one was in sight, although in the distance two cars started up, and that meant that they would soon be passing the end of this row.

Benson said, "Didn't I see a car with a plastic cover over it?"

"Little one, left side row."

"Let's push him under."

"Okay," said Freddy. "Can you lift him?"

"Yeh."

"I'll keep a lookout," the younger man said.

When on tiptoe, he could see all over the car park, and to the moving cars which were converging toward the exit from different directions. Neither of them would come near, but either driver might glance their way.

Benson was picking up the dead man.

"Hold it," Freddy said.

Benson stood upright, and might have been carrying an empty sack, for all the strain his face showed; but he felt something wet on his hand. He watched Freddy tensely, until the cars passed and Freddy said:

"Okay now."

Benson moved swiftly, with Freddy leading the way. Freddy reached the little car, finding that the aluminum-colored plastic sheet over it was laden with snow which was beginning to thaw. It was tied to each wheel with tapes. Freddy could have cut these; he didn't, but plucked at one corner with his cold fingers until the knot gave way. He pulled the tapes out and lifted the plastic, but it caught against the running board; this car was twenty years old if it was a day. He eased the plastic up, and then Benson put Taffy flat on the ground by the side of the car, and shoved him underneath, pushing first with his hands and then with his feet. As soon as the body was completely hidden, Freddy tied the corner back again.

But the melting snow was stained with crimson.

Neither man spoke, but each scooped snow off the top of the plastic cover, and dropped it onto the blood, concealing it. Then they went back the way Benson had come, scuffling up snow with their feet to cover the bright red drops. They got back to the car, and the red ignition light still glowed. Freddy pressed the self-starter. It whined. He pressed again, and it whined more shrilly.

"Cold as ruddy charity," he said, and pressed again. The grating, whining sound seemed to echo all over the great park. A car which they hadn't heard start up moved toward the exit, followed by two more. Freddy peered through the windscreen and, in the distance, saw a little group of men; it looked as if something had happened to make them all come into the park together.

"Get it going," rasped Benson.

Freddy was sweating.

"Hold your ruddy trap!"

Benson opened his mouth, but didn't speak. Freddy tried again, and there was just the grating, metallic sound, setting their teeth on edge. The other men were drawing much nearer. Benson could now see them, and he had a hand on the door handle and another in his pocket.

The engine spluttered.

"Got—" began Freddy, and it died again. He began to swear at it in a low-pitched voice, and he didn't stop even when the engine spluttered again, then began to turn more freely. He pressed the accelerator gently at first, to woo a welcome roaring. The car quivered. Freddy eased off the brake and moved slowly forward. He didn't say, and Benson didn't say, that the great fear now was that the car belonged to one of the men heading their way.

They got out into the lane leading toward the exit, and in the driving mirror Freddy saw at least six men, talking and chatting. No one shouted.

Freddy went up a gear, approached the roadway and turned toward the
wide exit. Beyond was a street with a timber yard on one side and a small
factory opposite. A timber truck was backing out, and a man behind it was
holding up the approaching traffic, including Freddy. Freddy flicked the
gears into neutral and waited while the great truck swung round in front of
him. Benson did not glance at him. Three cars came in quick succession
from the car park, one moving very fast. Freddy saw this leaping upon them
in the mirror, and his sudden, hissing breathing made Benson look round.
The car behind pulled up, brakes groaning; but neither man inside got out,
just waited patiently.

"Okay," Benson said.

Ten minutes later they were out of the built-up area, and driving along
a main road leading south. The road itself had been cleared, but banks of
snow on either side were huge and massive; water from them, thawing out,
was running across the road; the wheels kept splashing through it.

Benson turned round, leaned over the back of his seat and picked up the
cashbag. He took out a handful of small silver, mostly sixpences, and began
to count. It took a long time. "Twenty," he would say. "Ten bob"—and
drop that money into one pocket. Again: "Twenty—that's a quid." "Twenty
—thirty bob." Then after a few minutes, there was a note of deeper satisfaction. "Some two bobs and half-dollars in this pocket, 'bout time too."

The counting took him twenty minutes.

"Talk about a day out," he said; "that's five quid all but two bob."

"I'll take the odd money," Freddy grinned.

"Like hell you will. How's the petrol?"

"Half empty."

"Why don't you be an optimist and call it half full? Okay. We drive on
for a couple of hours and then we'll make a change. I want to make a
phone call, too."

After a long pause, Freddy asked:

"Who to?"

"Pal o' mine," said Benson, and now he was smiling. "Pal I can rely on,
too. Knows my so-called wife. Sent me up a message by Jingo's wife a
coupla times. Know what? My wife's got a boy friend, a sissy who runs a
dress shop! How do you like that? Nice-looking *gentleman*, I'm told."

The car went speeding on. No one took any notice of them from the
roadside. More powerful cars flashed by them, splashing the melting snow
onto the windscreen. The sun was breaking through reluctant cloud, and it
was warmer than it had been for three weeks.

"You going to put that right?" Freddy asked.

"I'm going to put a lot of things right," said Benson. "They can only put
me back again. Freddy, you take a tip from me. You do everything you want

to do, while you can. They'll pick us up for the car park job unless we can get out of this flicking country; and if we get out, it's got to be soon." He paused, but soon went on: "I know a man who can fix it for the pair of us. He'll want five hundred nicker—how much can you put your hands on?"

"I dunno," Freddy said; "but if I need five hundred nicker to get my head out of a flicking noose, I'll find it. This chap okay?"

"Yeh."

"There's only one thing we can do," Freddy Tisdale said, "we can try, can't we? I wouldn't like to be the guy who meets me and recognizes me. No, sir!"

He laughed on a high-pitched note.

Then: "We could stop for some fags," he said. "And I wouldn't mind a cuppa."

"We go on until we're ready to ditch this car," said Benson, emphatically. "We want to be within walking distance of a town when we do that, too."

"We want to be in a town," Freddy said, very thoughtfully. "We want to leave this wagon in a car park or some place where no one will think it looks funny. We aren't so far from Stoke. That be okay?"

"That'll be okay," Benson said.

That was at a quarter past one.

At a quarter past two, held up by traffic and by some roads partly blocked by snow, they reached Stoke. They left the car in a crowded car park, shared the money, and walked off together; no one took any notice of them. They had ham sandwiches at a snack bar, keeping their hats on like several of the other people, and finished up with sweet, strong tea. They bought cigarettes and chocolates, and then went out of the café. Walking about in the town, among people dressed in ordinary clothes, was like a dream. They kept together, didn't talk much, and looked like two reasonably prosperous businessmen. Benson's shoes began to pinch, but he didn't complain.

At half past three, he went into a telephone booth, and Freddy watched him from the outside. He put a call through to a Mile End number, then waited, leaning against the side of the booth and watching Freddy and the passersby.

A man came up and obviously wanted to use the telephone. He hung about.

Noises on the line.

A girl operator's sharp voice: "You're through, caller."

Benson said, "That you, Charlie?" He paused just long enough for the man to say yes, and then went on: "Listen, Charlie, I'm coming down to see you, be there in a couple days. Had an unexpected holiday, see. Bit o' luck, wasn't it?"

Charlie said with a gasp, "Yes, yes—it—listen. Be—"

"It's okay," Benson said, "I'm going to be careful. But do something for me, Charlie. I want to see my kid. You know. The boyo. They're keeping a pretty sharp eye on him, aren't they?"

"You couldn't say a truer word," Charlie told him, and then waited, breathing noisily into the telephone.

"Well, get him away from them," Benson said. "He'll be anxious to see his dad, won't he?" Even Freddy, watching his companion's face, realized that Benson's smile was as evil as a smile could be. "Just have him there for me, Charlie, and don't go making any mistakes, you know what could happen if I were to open my trap. Oh, and Charlie?"

"What?"

"Don't forget what I could tell the world about you," Benson said. "Expect me when you see me, old cock. So long."

He rang off.

The man who had waited to use the telephone was staring impatiently. Benson kept his face covered, and the man went straight into the telephone booth and dropped pennies into the box. Benson and Freddy walked off briskly, with danger forever on their heels.

"We going to knock off another car?" Freddy asked.

Benson said, "I don't want to play my luck too far. We want a car that no one will miss until morning, and the way to fix that is lay up in a house until after dark, then take a car out of a garage. Say we pick another empty house, and keep an eye on our neighbors. That okay?"

"Sure," said Freddy.

Twenty minutes later, they found the house they were looking for. They also saw the house, across the road, from which they could probably take a car. At the moment the car wasn't there; but the garage was standing empty, doors wide open. A young woman, quite something to look at, could be seen moving about inside the house, often a silhouette against the light which she had put on early.

Freddy Tisdale couldn't keep his eyes off her.

Soon, it was dark.

The husband came home in a small car, which he drove straight into the garage. The young woman hurried out, and neither man nor wife realized that they were being watched.

"They haven't been married long," Benson said, grinning. "Looks okay."

"Looks wonderful to me," Freddy said. "Maybe I'll give her a nice surprise, and stay the night."

For Gideon, the rest of that day was wholly unsatisfactory. Days came like it every week, sometimes two or three times a week, but there was seldom the degree of urgency and gravity which he sensed now. There was no news at all about the six men from Millways, except the reports, which were coming from a wider area than ever, that one or the other of them had been seen. The Yard, the London Divisions, the Home Counties, the Midlands and the North country police stations were swamped with such reports, and dozens of men were being interviewed; none was really like any one of the wanted men.

Gideon knew nothing of the body under the car in the car park.

He knew nothing of the furnished house or the burgled grocery shop.

He knew nothing about the two men in the empty house opposite No. 24 Wittering Street, Stoke-on-Trent.

The police just weren't getting the breaks. The evening newspapers were adopting a sharper note, there were two editorials about slackness at Millways jail, and with six prisoners still at liberty there was likely to be a lot of public anxiety. Gideon knew how often these things ran in cycles. Once a moan started, there would be the risk of a barrage of complaints, and with the perverseness of fate, or whatever directed the affairs of men, there would probably be a run of poor results. Already, there was Edmundsun's suicide in the remand cell at Brixton to make ammunition for the critics.

It was all very well to shrug one's shoulders and pretend to ignore or be indifferent to these periodic attempts to ginger-up the Force, but they got under one's skin, and could make the difference between doing a good job and a bad one. Gideon wasn't absolutely proof against them, Lemaitre certainly wasn't, and young chaps like Abbott probably keyed themselves up until they were almost nervous. People too easily forgot that policemen were human.

Edmundsun had died without making a statement. He had probably had accomplices in the embezzlement of nearly forty thousand pounds from a big commercial banking house; and for Cummings and the Fraud Squad there was likely to be week after week of slow, laborious research to try to recover the missing money and to find out who had conspired with the dead man.

The evening papers headlined the suicide and the fact that the six escaped prisoners were still at large. Two of them came out with stories about Ruby Benson's fear, and of the police watch on her and the children.

Gideon had at least made sure that everything was moving as it should. In a quiet way, the Yard had geared itself to exceptional efforts, since five of the six men still at liberty were Londoners. Their wives, their homes, their friends, their children, were all kept under surveillance. There was no way to hide the fact that this was being done; and Gideon had the sinking feeling that Benson, at least, would be smart enough not to come home. But one couldn't tell. He might act on the belief that Muskett Street would be the last place the police would expect him to go. Or he might be driven by desperation, hunger, and cold. These factors were more likely to lead to the recapture of the men than anything else.

The police could usually sit back and wait.

They couldn't afford to, with men like Benson and the others.

It was nearly seven o'clock when Gideon checked everything, yawned, saw patient, gray-haired Jefferson making out reports, and then stood up, fastening his collar and tie as he did so.

"I'm off, Jeff."

"Good night, sir."

"Call me if there's anything worth while; I'll be home all the evening."

"I'll try not to worry you, sir."

"I'll be in the sergeants' room for the next ten minutes," said Gideon. He put on his big hat and went out, letting the door close behind him on its hissing hydraulic fixture. The rubber tips at his heels made little sound as he moved along the bare, brightly lit corridors. Two or three junior men passed him. He went up one flight of stairs, and then into the big room where he expected to find Abbott and probably Cummings. Yes, they were there, sitting together at a table, probably exchanging notes.

They stood up at Gideon's approach.

"Sit down," he said, and ignored the other sergeants in the room. "Thought I'd catch you here. How'd things go, Abbott?"

"Absolutely uneventful, sir," said Abbott. "I had a word with the Divisional Inspector who came round just before I was off duty. He says there's nothing at all to report, none of Benson's known friends have heard from him."

"Known friends" was good.

"It's the beggars we don't know about that we're after," Gideon said. "Anything else?"

"Benson's wife looks pretty worried, sir, and there's the man Small—he went to her home tonight. I gather he's going to stay there until it's all over. He looks a bit edgy, too."

"Who wouldn't? The children?"

"The girl clings to her mother. As for that boy—well, sir," said Abbott, with obvious feeling, "I don't know him well enough to be sure, but he looks as if he could turn out to be a nasty customer. He didn't actually say anything to me, but . . ."

Gideon smiled. "Looks could kill, eh? Yes, he might be strongly pro-Dad. Watch him closely."

"I will, sir!"

Gideon concealed his smile, then; the eagerness of a new man always struck him as amusing; pleasing, too. He turned to Cummings, who wasn't so young—in the middle thirties, in fact. It was a pity how Cummings ran to fat; he looked flabby and startlingly pale against Abbott's healthy tan. His gray eyes always had a rather tired look, in spite of his needle-sharp mind. It was hard to believe that he had a genius for figures and could find his way through involved books of accounts which were Greek to Gideon.

"No luck at all with Edmundsun, eh?" Gideon said.

"I was by his side from the minute I reached the hospital, but couldn't get a word," said Cummings. "Just muttered his wife's name once or twice before he died, that's all."

"Any ideas who did the job with him?"

Cummings didn't speak.

"Well?"

"Don't like guessing," said Cummings, winning Gideon's silent applause, "but you know that Mr. Harrison and I were always worried about the chief prosecution witness—the manager of Edmundsun's department, furniture and household hire purchase. Now I come to think of it, it wouldn't surprise me if the manager isn't deliberately being obscure. He's no fool. Used to be a solicitor, and he knows a lot of the tricks. If he worked on the job with Edmundsun, he may have planned to give his evidence so as to get Edmundsun off. It's only a guess, sir, but it could be worth following up."

"What do you think of the chap? Man named Elliott, isn't it?"

"Yes. And he's all right as a person, sir, affable as they come. But that's nothing to go by."

"No, it isn't," Gideon agreed. "Well, I'm going to arrange for you and probably a couple of others to concentrate on the job; I don't like the idea that anyone might get away with forty thousand quid." He scratched his chin, and the stubble rasped. "Edmundsun kept calling his wife, you say. She get there in time?"

"Ten minutes late."

"How'd she take it?"

"Well, pretty calm, as a matter of fact."

"Know what I'd do," said Gideon, thoughtfully; "I'd have a word with her as soon as possible. Don't put anything into plain language; but just make it clear you're sure that someone else was on this job with her husband, and that, if it wasn't for them, he'd be alive today. If she knows anything, that might persuade her to talk. Worth trying, anyhow."

"I'll fix it first thing in the morning," Cummings promised.

Gideon knew that he would.

There was no garage at Gideon's house, and he left his car at a garage nearby, then strolled toward his house, along the dimly lit street. The weather had changed with a vengeance, and he was almost too warm with his heavy topcoat and his woolen waistcoat. As he neared the house, he thought he saw someone lurking in the shadows of the doorway, and, with a caution learned over the years, he slowed down and approached carefully.

Then he grinned.

They were lurking figures all right, boy and girl. Prudence and a lad. Kissing. Gideon coughed loudly, saw them spring apart, saw Prudence look at him in confusion, and the youngster stand stiffly, almost to attention.

"Mind you two don't catch cold," Gideon said. "Hallo, Pru. Hallo, young man."

"Good evening, sir!"

"Oh, Dad, this is Raymond . . ."

Kate was alone in the kitchen; one of the boys still living at home was out, one upstairs in the attic playing with his electric train set. The two younger girls were out, too, one of them at night school, one with friends. Kate, in a royal blue dress, looked fresh and handsome and obviously pleased to see him. That did him a lot of good. Funny, to find the old affection warming up again. They weren't demonstrative and didn't kiss.

"Did you know about Raymond?" asked Gideon.

Kate smiled. "They don't stay young forever," she said, "and now Pru's finished her exams she'll have more time for boys." Then, obviously because she thought of the Primrose Girl and the boy in the police station cell, her smile faded. "Any news?" she asked.

"No change," said Gideon.

That was at half past eight.

Just after nine, the telephone bell rang; and Priscilla, the middle daughter, as fair as Prudence was dark, went hurrying to answer it. Gideon caught Kate's eyes, and realized what she was hinting: that Priscilla was showing remarkable eagerness to answer the telephone.

He raised his hands, helplessly.

"They grow up too fast for me," he said ruefully, and looked round at the door which Priscilla had left open. He heard her eager voice, and then the flat disappointment which came into it.

"Yes, he's in," she said, and called: "Dad! It's Sergeant Jefferson, wants to speak to you."

Gideon, coat off, collar and tie loose and shoelaces undone, got out of his big armchair reluctantly, and strolled toward the little room where the telephone was.

"Hallo, Jeff," he said.

"Thought you'd want to know this, sir," said Jefferson. "Two more of the Millways chaps caught—Alderman and Hooky Jenkins. They were in a Manchester railway yard, they'd traveled on a freight train. Almost certain that they killed that railwayman. Manchester rang through to say they'll do everything they can to find out if this pair knows which way the others went, sir."

"That's fine," said Gideon, quietly. "Thanks for calling, Jeff."

Now there were four, including the worst of them.

He wondered where Benson was.

Soon afterward, Gideon went to bed. That coincided, although he could not have the faintest idea of the coincidence, with the first offensive move of that persistent thief, Lefty Bligh, and a younger man whom he was training in the gentle art of cracking a crib without making too much noise. Lefty used an oxy-acetylene cutter of a special miniature design. They went across to the bookmaker's door, with a fortune inside waiting for the taking.

His companion watched and marveled at the ease with which Lefty got the door open, dismantled the burglar alarm, and made the whole process look child's play. Both Lefty and his apprentice went boldly inside.

A light came on.

"Hallo, Lefty," a Yard detective-sergeant greeted. "Want something?"

Lefty was one of those criminals who did not believe in violence. He looked as if he could cry. His apprentice made a run for it, but was met at the lift by another Yard man, and promptly gave up trying.

12 . Farther South

About that time, too, Benson was staring across at the house where the young couple lived.

He was sitting on a box close to the window of the house where he and Tisdale had taken refuge. It wasn't furnished, and there was no comfort, but the night was much warmer, and they weren't really cold. They'd eaten two hours before, and had enough food left for another day. They'd sat here, watching the couple sitting by the side of a fire in the house opposite, eating supper from a tray. The more they saw, the more they realized that these were newlyweds; the man couldn't leave the girl alone, and she didn't exactly look as if she resented it. They'd gone toward the door, about twenty minutes ago, their arms round each other; then they'd put out the downstairs light. Now, there was a light on in the upstairs front room, and Freddy was actually licking his lips.

The girl appeared near the window.

"What the butler saw," Freddy muttered; "what wouldn't I give for a chance to change places with him?" Freddy sounded as if he wasn't feeling so good. "How about it?"

Benson said, "You've waited three years, you can wait another few days. We stay here until they're asleep, and then we go and get the car. We push it out of the garage and down the road."

"Okay," Freddy said. "I hope we don't disturb their dreams."

Soon, the girl came and stood at the window, with her face in shadow. The man joined her. Suddenly, the girl stretched up and drew the curtains; she made quite a picture. Freddy swore beneath his breath, and watched shadows.

It was twenty minutes before the light went out.

It was another half hour, and nearly half past eleven, when Benson and Freddy left the empty house. They crept into the deserted street. Except for the odd late bird, no one was likely to be about tonight; everyone who had been to the pictures was home. Only two windows in the whole street showed a light, and there was no parked car.

They crossed the road to the silent house.

The drive, made of smooth cement, sloped slightly upward toward the garage. They made no sound as they reached it. Freddy examined the lock and saw that it was just a padlock with a hasp; elementary. He took out a small screwdriver which he had brought from the furnished house, and set to work on it.

Benson watched the upstairs window and the street.

There was no sound.

Only a few street lamps, at intervals of fifty yards or more, gave any light, and suddenly these began to go out, one by one. The sound of metal on metal sounded very loud. Then, the padlock opened and Freddy whispered, "We're okay."

But when they opened the garage doors, one squeaked alarmingly. Both men stood stock-still, watching the upstairs room.

Janice Morency, a bride of only three weeks, felt the snug warmth of her husband beside her and heard his steady, rhythmic breathing. She was just beginning to learn how quickly he could drop off; he would be wide awake one moment, glorying, and fast asleep the next. The house was very quiet. The street was quiet, too.

The glow from the street lamps began to go out, as they always did at half past eleven.

Then Janice heard the garage door squeak.

She went absolutely rigid with alarm, for she knew the sound so well. She heard it every morning when Frank opened the gates, heard it every time she moved the door herself; there couldn't be any mistake at all.

"Frank," she whispered, "wake up. *Frank!*"

For a tense moment after the door had creaked, Benson and Freddy Tisdale were as still and silent as the girl. Then Benson whispered, "Okay, get inside."

"Suppose . . ."

"Inside, close the doors!"

"But supposing they come . . ."

"And supposing they don't," Benson said flatly.

There was just room for them to squeeze into the garage and pull the door to; it didn't squeak when being closed, only when being opened. They stood in the near darkness. There was a window, which showed just a glim of light, and they worked their way round toward it, then stared up at the house. Benson could tell that Tisdale was more on edge than he had been at any time; some people were at their worst late at night. He didn't watch Tisdale, only the house. If a light went on . . .

Freddy said uneasily, "We could be trapped in here."

"If anyone comes down to see if the door's open, we know what to do," Benson said. "We can't lock the door again; if he comes down he'll find the door open, and he'll raise the alarm anyway. Right?"

Freddy muttered, "I suppose so."

Then the light went on in the front bedroom of the house.

They could just see the window from their point of vantage, and they saw the bright light shine out. A moment later, the light got brighter; that was because the curtains were pulled back. There were shadows; and then suddenly the head of a man appeared, turned toward the garage. He could see the doors from here, but couldn't tell whether they were locked.

Could he?

Benson stood quite still, his right hand touching the poultry knife.

Frank Morency, tousled head and broad shoulders out of the window, and his wife pressing close against him at one side, saw nothing but the outline of the garage, the roof of the house next door, the gardens in the street, the dark road and slender lampposts. He shivered as wind cut along from the east, and backed inside.

"You must have been dreaming," he said.

"Frank, I swear I wasn't."

"Well, have a look for yourself," he suggested, "but go and put a dressing gown on, I don't like you appearing in public like that."

He was laughing at her!

"But I heard the sound, I've heard it so often!"

"All right, look for yourself, but—" Morency stopped abruptly when he saw the change in his bride's expression, slid an arm round her, squeezed, and then said, "Like me to go down and have a look round, sweetheart?"

She didn't answer.

"I will, like a shot," he said.

"If you're sure the doors are still shut . . ."

"I'm positive!"

"Then I suppose I must have dreamed it," Janice said.

She didn't really believe that; she was sure that she had heard a sound, but no longer sure that it had been the garage door. They went back to bed, where for a few minutes the warmth and the strength of his body comforted and reassured her; then he began to breathe very smoothly and rhythmically again, and for the first time in her married life she felt a kind of loneliness.

Soon she dozed off.

Freddy Tisdale stood back from the hinges of the garage doors, an oilcan in his hand, thin oil smearing his fingers. He was breathing very softly, and keenly aware of Benson's watching eyes. The bedroom light had been out for half an hour, and the street seemed absolutely deserted.

"Try it now," he said.

"Okay." Benson began to push the offending door, cautiously. When halfway open, it gave a faint squeak, but nothing like the noise it had made before. This time, no light came on.

Soon they were wheeling the car into the street, along the road, toward the main road. With Freddy walking alongside and guiding it, and Benson behind, they pushed until they were some distance away from the Morencys' house. Then Tisdale got in. A moment later, he exclaimed:

"Our night out, Syd—he's left the keys in!"

Benson actually chuckled.

They started off.

Three hundred yards farther on, they came to a main road. They needed to turn left, for London. As they nosed out of the side turning, they looked both ways. No more than half a mile along toward Stoke, on a straight stretch of road, were several red lights, some yellow lights, and the shadowy shapes of men and cars.

"Road block," breathed Freddy Tisdale. "If we'd gone the other way . . ."

"Well, we didn't," Benson said flatly. "We'll drive on the sidelights only;

if there's another block down the road they won't see us coming so far, and we'll have a chance to stop and run for it."

Freddy didn't speak.

With the sidelights on, casting only a faint glow on the hedges, the telegraph poles and the wires, they crawled along at twenty miles an hour. Occasionally, a car passed them; once, one came streaking up from behind, and whined past; it didn't stop.

Freddy knew the roads well, took the byroads, avoided the towns where the police road blocks were likely to be, and by half past five they reached the outskirts of Birmingham.

In Birmingham, Freddy had a hide-out, with a man he felt sure was safe. Or so he said.

Gideon entered the office, next morning, a little more briskly than usual. There was no reason why he should feel in high spirits, but he did. Possibly the overnight news of the capture of two more prisoners had something to do with it. Possibly, eight hours' solid sleep had helped; possibly, too, amused reflection on Pru's high color when she had come in and again when he had seen her at breakfast that morning. She had asked about William Rose, but had her own absorbing personal interests now. Gideon wondered how long she had known this Raymond, told himself that he would have to make sure that the youngster was all right, then thought reassuringly that Kate would make certain of that, as far as anyone could.

He saw Lemaitre, alone at his desk, with the daily report in front of him.

"Morning, Lem."

"Morning, George." Lemaitre was flat-voiced, gloomy.

"What's your trouble?"

"Trouble?" asked Lemaitre, and gave a laugh which had no body in it. "Nothing but ruddy trouble, if you ask me. Had a hell of a row with Fifi last night; she wanted to go out, and I wanted to stay in—George, you don't know how lucky you are."

Lemaitre had graver marital troubles even than he realized; but Gideon didn't see that it was his duty to tell him.

"She'll be all right tonight," he said, soothingly.

"Sometimes I wonder," said Lemaitre, "sometimes I wonder if—oh, forget it. We picked up Alderman and Hooky last night, that's something. Manchester police say there's blood on Alderman's clothes and under his fingernails, mixed with coal dust. We've got them ready for the long wait." That prospect seemed to cheer Lemaitre up. "Twenty-nine spots of bother in London last night, and we've picked up five old pals who'll be in dock this morning. Young Rose will be up at East London, of course—medical reports on him in from Smedd, in triplicate—Smedd's a boy! Nasty job in Soho:

one of the Marlborough Street regulars cut up. The risks these women take at that game. Nasty job out at Wimbledon, too: nineteen-year-old girl going home after a dance; had a tiff with her boy friend and she went alone. Three fellows had a go at her. Sometimes I wonder what makes men tick, I do really. She got home all right, not hurt except for a few bruises and scratches; she put up a hell of a fight. Kept her head better than a lot would, too: described one of the fellows and said he had a foreign accent. The Wimbledon police boys are checking, they think they can put their hands on the trio. Nice morning, isn't it?"

"If you didn't want to know all about the seamy side, why join the police?" asked Gideon.

He looked through the newspapers. As he'd expected, the "negligence" at Millways was being tied up to the "negligence" at Brixton; the escapes and the prison suicide were being run together as clear indications of low-ered standards at the prisons. There was a sly dig at the police for allowing a party of violent criminals to remain at large, but the capture of Alderman and Hooky won a corner in the Stop Press.

Then Gideon read his own daily report.

He made notes and, before he started the morning's briefing, studied the medical reports on William Rose. One was from his family doctor, and it was a long statement; the doctor had known the Rose family for twenty-five years.

Should be reliable.

Gideon read—and winced.

Penciled in red at the side of the report were the letters N.B. Opposite this, there was the blunt statement:

> From the age of six until the age of eleven the boy showed signs of excessive, uncontrollable temper. His mother brought him to me for treatment, but this was clearly not a matter for an ordinary physician. I understand that the boy responded well to psychiatric treatment, be-coming much more balanced. I questioned his mother on a number of occasions in later years, and was told that there were no further outbreaks of this particular trouble.

Well, well; a history of violent temper. Dig deeper, and this would proba-bly show that Rose flew into rages, possibly that he had been uncontrollable; a mother wouldn't be likely to take a six-year-old boy to a doctor unless it was for some quite exceptional tantrums. No wonder Smedd had written N.B. The family doctor's purpose stood out a mile, of course; he was establishing a history of mental unbalance because he was afraid that young Rose had killed the girl, and that the state of his mind would be of vital importance at the trial.

Not good for Pru's "friend," or for William Rose.

And obviously Smedd had no fresh news about the couple visiting the cinema, or about the "lost" knife.

In the middle of the morning Gideon sent for Lefty Bligh, who had been up at Great Marlborough Street, and remanded for the constitutional eight days. Now that he was over his shock, he was smiling.

"Hallo, Guv-ner, now don't you start," he greeted.

"You're a mutton-headed fool, Lefty," Gideon said, "but I don't suppose anything will cure you now. Heard from Syd Benson lately?"

Lefty's whole expression changed.

"Mr. Gideon," he said earnestly, "I wouldn't have no more truck with that man for a fortune."

"How about making us out a list of his friends? It might help you next week if you did."

The little thief's eyes were filled with reproach which would have made any other man than a policeman believe he was of great virtue.

"Now would I squeal, Mr. Gideon? Even if I knew any of Benson's pals, you know I wouldn't."

It had been worth trying; but as an informer, Lefty was a dead loss. So, to Gideon, was the rest of that afternoon. He just couldn't get the line he wanted so desperately; and each hour that Benson remained free increased his wife's danger.

Young Syd Benson saw Abbott outside the house in Muskett Street that afternoon, glared at him, and then walked along the street toward the corner and toward his school for the afternoon lessons. Abbott followed. It was his first experience of watching a youngster, and he was beginning to realize how difficult a strong-willed boy could make the job. Coming from school that morning, Syd had dawdled along, had jeered and derided Abbott in mime, had talked about flaming coppers, narks and flatfoots to his friends, and generally shown off. Annoyed at first, Abbott had gradually become philosophical, accepting this as inevitable.

He'd already told Gideon that he wasn't happy about the boy, and at that time Gideon was Abbott's Hero number one.

Halfway along Muskett Street on his way back to school, young Syd tried a new dodge: he broke into a run.

Abbott saw that, and hesitated for a split second. The boy was off to a flying start, and could run like a hare. Abbott, who hadn't sprinted for years but who still played a useful game of football, lost time in trying to decide whether he should lose what was left of his dignity by running, or whether he should let the little brute get away.

He ran.

There were a dozen or so other children in the street, all heading toward school, several mothers, two men on bicycles, and a milkman's van. Everyone stopped to stare at the pounding policeman and the running boy. Young Syd reached the corner at least fifty yards ahead, and took time off to turn round and put his thumb to his nose. That started a roar of laughter followed by jeers and catcalls.

"Hit one your own size, can't you?"

"Catch him, cowboy!"

"How're your flat feet, copper?"

Abbott set his teeth and ran on, going very fast now, much faster than the boy could. Provided he was still in the street which bisected this one, Syd wouldn't get away. Abbott neared the corner, and then saw one of the cyclists draw up alongside him. The cyclist was grinning, but he didn't speak. He passed Abbott and, a yard or so in front of him, his bicycle wobbled. He made it do that deliberately, but no one would ever be able to prove it. As if trying to keep his balance, he crossed Abbott's path; the detective looked as if he would crash into him.

Abbott saw the danger in time.

He pulled himself up, inches from the bicycle, and managed to spin round on one foot, as he would on the football field if the ball ran the wrong way. To save himself from falling, he thrust out his right hand, and caught the cyclist on the shoulder. He felt the man give way, heard him bellow, saw him leap for the pavement. Something clutched at Abbott's coat, but did no harm. He didn't look round, but heard the cyclist crash, and then realized that the catcalls had stopped.

He reached the corner.

Young Syd was playing marbles with two other boys; he grinned impudently.

Abbott, gasping for breath, could have wrung the boy's neck. He stopped, standing by the wall of a house, hearing a gabble of voices round the corner. From a distance, a uniformed policeman from the Division came hurrying, and if there was anything that a Divisional man enjoyed it was a Yard man being made to look silly.

The crowd in Muskett Street would be after him for this, too. The cyclist would almost certainly try to make trouble. Abbott, trying to put the detective before the human being, saw through all this to his chief job: keeping an eye on the boy. He would have to leave the constable to make a kind of peace with the crowd, but was afraid that from now on he would be jeered at by everyone in Muskett Street.

The cyclist turned the corner, back on his machine. His right hand was bleeding from a nasty scratch. He glowered at Abbott, and said roughly, "Why the hell don't you look where you're going?"

Abbott gaped—and then found the wit to say: "Sorry. Didn't see you."

A woman, just out of sight, laughed—at the cyclist, not Abbott. The man pedaled off; and as he watched him go, Abbott realized what had happened. Just when he'd feared the worst, he'd had a break. If he'd fallen and the cyclist ridden on triumphantly, he would have been the fool; but in Muskett Street as well as in the whole of London there was admiration for the man who got out of a tight corner; and there was an innate sense of fair play.

Abbott felt on top of the world.

A woman turned the corner, then. She was middle-aged, dressed in a bright blue dress of some shiny material, and she wore a black straw hat trimmed with bright red cherries. She had a huge, tightly confined bosom and a surprisingly small waist; a red, beery face and little brown eyes. She swept round the corner, spotted Abbott and then young Syd, and strode toward Benson's son, ignoring the marbles. She caught one with the toe of her shoe, and it went skimming to the other side of the street.

"Now you listen to me, young Sydney," she said in a voice loud enough to be heard up and down the street. "If you was my boy I'd give you a clip round the ear and keep on doing it until I knocked some sense into you. The gentleman's only trying to help you, see? Help you and your Ma and Liz, which is a damned sight more than your father's ever done. If he'd earned an honest living, instead of taking up with a lot of loose women and neglecting your Ma and then going off to prison and leaving her to look after the pair of you, there'd have been some sense. But he never did have any sense, and by the looks of it you haven't got much, neither. Don't you forget it, this gentleman's only doing his duty, and trying to help you."

She stopped, on a high-pitched note.

Syd's bright blue eyes were not turned toward her, but toward Abbott. "I don't want his flipping help," he said, and swung away.

Young Syd, fuming at the way the woman had talked to him, fuming at the way his mother had rebuked him, hating Abbott, resenting everything that had happened to his father, walked on toward school that afternoon. He was alone except for one boy, a big, gangling lad named Simon who, many people thought, should not be allowed near the school. But he was harmless enough, and had short-lived periods of intelligence. Most of his time he spent in a special school, but at playtime he was allowed in here, with the others.

Abbott, following, would not have been surprised had young Syd played truant; but he went on to school. There were only two exits, and the police watched each; it was likely to be a boring afternoon for Abbott.

It wasn't boring for young Syd.

In the playground thronged with a mob of shouting, running boys, he stood watching, brooding, with Simon near him, gawping about with his mouth hanging open. It was one of his bad days.

Another boy came up.

No one but the gangling lad was near, and he was out of earshot.

The second boy said, "Got a message for you, Syd," in a voice which showed that he was swelling with importance.

"You can keep it," said Syd sourly.

"You'll wish you hadn't said that."

"Listen, Charlie, I don't want to talk to you or no one, get to hell out of here, can't you?"

"Okay, okay," said Charlie, and backed away a yard; young Syd could box! "It's a message from my Dad, though, he says it's important. He'd have given it to you himself, only he knows the cops are watching you."

Young Syd's eyes lost their viciousness in a momentary flicker of interest. "What's it all about?"

"Dad wants to see you tonight, without the cops knowing, see. Can you make it?"

"The flippin' busies watch me all the time."

"That's what Dad said," went on young Charlie, "but it's okay. You've got to climb over the school wall into the builder's yard. Someone'll be waiting in a van, you nip inside the van and you'll be okay. Dad says it's important."

Syd's eyes were shining.

"Okay," he said, "okay."

Abbott didn't see the boy, after school. The rest of the children came out, but not Syd Benson. The teachers came out, too. It wasn't until Benson had been missing for over half an hour that another boy was found who had seen him climb into the builder's yard next to the school.

There was no trace of him now.

13 . Clues

GIDEON heard Abbott's voice, low-pitched and completely lacking the bright eagerness which had been there before. From a long-term point of view, this wouldn't do Abbott any harm; it was never a bad thing to have a job go sour on you in the early days, and too long a run of early successes could do a lot of harm. But it was a thousand pities he had to learn his lesson on this job.

Obviously, Abbott had done everything that could be done at short notice.

"All right, and don't forget it isn't the end of the world," Gideon said. "I'll have a word with the Division. We've got a woman watching young Liz, so you switch over to Mrs. Benson and that man of hers, Arthur Small. Know him?"

"Yes, sir, if you remember, I reported last night . . ."

"Oh, yes," said Gideon. "All right. Good-by."

He rang off, and found himself looking down at a photograph, which had come in only a little while ago, of Arthur Small, who was in charge of the shop where Ruby Benson worked. The shop was one of a chain, with a male manager and female staff; there were three assistants junior to Ruby, as well as Small. Small was in the late forties, rather dapper, and in his way good-looking. He was going a little thin on top, and wore horn-rimmed glasses which gave his face a top-heavy look. Gideon, knowing that it was more than just an affair between him and Ruby, wondered how it would end. Even when Benson was caught, Ruby would be tied to him; she and Small couldn't get married.

The reports on Small were all excellent.

He had been questioned, and had said flatly that he was going to stay at Ruby's house from now until Benson was caught, and if the police didn't like it, they could lump it. That showed spirit if nothing else.

But young Syd . . .

Gideon put everything in hand: a widespread search, photographs of the boy to the newspapers, questioning of the schoolmasters and the other boys; but no reports came in. The builder's men were questioned, but no one admitted having seen young Syd. It was a complete blank, and Gideon didn't like it.

Benson might be in London; might have got hold of the boy; might be within a mile or so of the Yard.

Benson wasn't; that night, the third of freedom, he spent lying low in a house on the outskirts of Birmingham, with Freddy Tisdale. It was quite a night, for they had feminine company.

The body still lay under the little car on the cold ground and so far the snow had prevented any serious degree of decomposition.

No one else visited the furnished house.

Reports of the theft of a car from the car park near Millways, and of the theft of a car from a private garage on the outskirts of Stoke, reached the

Yard in the usual way. Obviously, it was possible that one of the escaped men had taken these, but a dozen cars or more had been stolen from the same area during the past week.

Both cars were found within twenty-four hours. There were no fingerprints in either of them; but in the one found in the Stoke car park there was a little roll of parking tickets of the kind used to refill the machines used at Millways Corporation. The fact that the car park attendant was missing had also been reported; the general belief was that he had absconded. During the first and second days of his disappearance, those councillors and Council officials who had opposed the employment of an ex-convict were loud in their righteousness and in the vigor of their "We told you so."

Then, on the fourth morning, a dog, howling and sniffing, led an elderly man to the car park attendant's body.

"My God," breathed Gideon.

Now they had something to get their teeth into. The stolen car was quickly connected with the old lag's murder; it was clear that a pair of the prisoners had got as far south as Stoke, probable that they had gone farther south. Then a man from the Stoke Police Department's Fingerprints Bureau, checking the second stolen car, found not fingerprints but glove prints.

"Pigskin or imitation pigskin, with a cut in the thumb and worn on the inside edge of the thumb," he said in his report, which reached Gideon on the afternoon of the fourth day.

Soon reports began to flow in.

The police knew what they were looking for, had confirmation from Alderman and Hooky that the other four had gone off in pairs, knew that one of the two wore pigskin gloves, and realized that meant that they had probably got hold of other clothes. A Millways C.I.D. man, trying to find out if clothes had been taken from the scene of any local burglary, learned instead that some food had been stolen from a grocery shop near the canal. The shopkeeper and his wife were quite sure, because they had been taking stock on the night before they'd made the discovery, and had counted the half-pound packets of butter and some packets of biscuits. They had suspected a sneak thief, and hadn't reported the missing food until they'd heard that the police were anxious to know about every kind of theft on the night of the big prison break.

Two glove thumbprints, identical with those discovered on the stolen cars, were found on tins of soup and beneath a shelf in the shop. Immediately, this news brought a concentration of police to the canal area. A sergeant who took the routine in his stride collected all the keys of nearby furnished houses from the agents.

Benson's first hiding-place was found, and the report sped to London. "Now we're really moving," Gideon said, and he felt a fierce excitement. "Benson's prints were all over the house, so were Tisdale's. We've a list of the clothes that have been stolen, size of shoes, hats, everything. There was a careful inventory made before the owners left the place empty; we've got the description down to the last detail."

"Spread 'em around," said Lemaitre, and rubbed his hands together. "We'll soon pick the swine up now."

They were not picked up that night, for they were in Birmingham; reveling.

Young Syd wasn't found, either.

The Assistant Commissioner, often a late bird, looked into Gideon's office about half past nine that night, and found Gideon there alone. That wasn't unusual. Gideon had a mass of reports in front of him, and looked up from the one he was reading: a psychiatrist's report on William Rose, the same psychiatrist who had attended him in his childhood. Gideon put it aside, stretched back in his chair, and then bent down and opened a cupboard.

"I know what you're after," he said. "One of these days I'm going to put a fresh item on the expense sheet—one bottle of whisky for official consumption!" He put a bottle on the desk, then a siphon, then two glasses. "If you want to know what I think," he went on, "I think this is one of the lousiest weeks I've ever had at the Yard."

The A.C. looked at the gurgling whisky.

"They all seem like that," he said. "Don't let it get you down, George."

Gideon pushed a glass toward him.

"Oh, it'll pass, but it's like seeing a blank wall every way you look. I did think we'd get something when we found out where Benson had been and what clothes he was wearing, but—well, mustn't expect miracles, I suppose."

"What's really upset you?" the A.C. asked. "Not the newspaper?"

"If I had my way, I'd dump all crime reporters in the sea," growled Gideon, and then unexpectedly he laughed. "Oh, we can't blame 'em! Four violent criminals still free, then Edmundsun, and then young Benson. No wonder we're making headlines. Chap I'm sorry for is Abbott," he went on. "Seems to think it's nobody's fault but his."

"Like Gideon, like Abbott," the A.C. said, and gave his quick grin. "Funny thing about that boy, though. No sign of him?"

"No. I'm as worried as hell."

"Think someone's hiding him?"

"He could have found a spot to keep under cover by himself, I suppose," said Gideon thoughtfully, "but as far as his mother knows, he had only about sixpence on him, and kids get hungry. If I had to bet, it'd be that he went to a place where he knew he'd be looked after. We've checked all of Benson's friends, and haven't got anywhere at all. He nipped over into that builder's yard, and just hasn't been seen since. The yard opens onto the Mile End Road, dozens of people pass it every hour of the day, and we haven't picked up one who saw the kid."

"Think Benson's had anything to do with it?"

"I think Benson's had something to do with everything," said Gideon, savoring his whisky. "But then, I've a Benson obsession at the moment. That man's running round with a knife, and there isn't a better knife artist in the country—the way he killed that poor devil near Millways shows that. One thrust, and it went right home. He wouldn't need long to kill his wife or her beau."

The A.C. said, "That's not like you, George. You know he'll never get near enough."

Gideon shrugged. "Unless he's soon caught, I'll believe that anything's possible. But you're right, of course; it's not reasonable."

"No. What about this Primrose Girl murder?"

Gideon tapped the report he had been reading. "I've never read a case which looked more open and shut," he said. "There's a clear medical history of mental instability when a child, there's all the evidence that Smedd's accumulated, and except for one thing, it looks foolproof."

"What's the one thing?"

"Rose's sister's story. Nothing shakes it. And Rose himself sticks to it, too—as well as his lost knife story. He says he had this quarrel with Winnie Norton in the woods, left her in a temper, went toward his home, feeling like hell, and met his sister; and she treated him to the pictures. There's no doubt at all that if they went into those pictures Rose didn't kill the girl. Death was at about seven o'clock—the broken watch as well as medical evidence proves that. Mary Rose says she and her brother were inside the picture palace before six—and it's pretty certain that the girl really was there. It was a busy evening, there were dozens going in just about that time, and a hundred or so coming out. The girl can describe every film, the shorts, the news, the cartoon and the advertisements—she even remembers one of the tunes on the record player during the interval! If her brother was with her, he couldn't have killed that girl. Smedd says that he's done everything possible to find anyone who saw either the girl or her brother, without result. And that's the element of doubt," Gideon went on. "If someone had seen her without her brother, we'd know where we are. But she *was* there. She'd announced she was going beforehand, and it's as near a certainty as a thing can be. If she wasn't noticed, then the pair of them might not have been."

"See what you mean," said the A.C. "That's all that's on your mind?"

"I've got a lot of stuff going through the courts tomorrow," Gideon told him. "Nine C.I.s, as many D.I.s and twelve sergeants are all scheduled to give evidence in one court or other. Falling over each other. Old Birdy will be back in Number One, and Lemaitre will have to go there. We had a squeak that there'll be a bullion raid at the London Airport tomorrow, so I've sent half a dozen men up to watch. It's probably a false alarm, but we can't take risks. Take it from me, we could have handled the Benson job much better last week; just now we're stretched as far as we can go. And if there wasn't enough on our plate, there's that attempted rape job out at Wimbledon."

"Unrelieved gloom," the Assistant Commissioner observed; but his looks belied him. "What have you been working late on?"

"Had a session with young Cummings," said Gideon. "He says he's got a feeling that the Edmundsun job will spread a long way before it's over. I'm seeing Edmundsun's wife tomorrow. Cummings thinks she might know who her husband was working with . . ."

The A.C. stopped him with a laugh.

"George," he said, "I'm not going to let you get away with that one. I was talking to Lemaitre, and he told me you put Cummings up to it. Think it'll work?"

"From what I can gather, the wife was in love with him," said Gideon, smiling. "Bit of a spitfire, and if she thinks she's got anyone to hate, she'll hate."

"I'll leave it to you," the A.C. conceded. "Now if I were you, I'd go home; it's late."

"Can't grumble about this week," Gideon said. "I've been home for supper two nights out of three, and I'll be home in time for a nightcap tonight." He stood up, and stifled a yawn. "Any truth in the rumor that you're likely to retire?" He smiled as he looked straight into the A.C.'s face. "I've been reading the *Sunday Sentinel*, you see."

"That's one of the things I came to have a word with you about," the A.C. said quietly. "No, George, I'm not retiring yet. I always planned to have seven years, if they didn't throw me out, and I've four to go. That should make you about fifty-three when you take over, and you ought to hold the job down for eleven or twelve years."

"They won't put me in your place," Gideon said flatly.

"They'll be bloody fools if they don't," said the other man and finished his whisky. "Good night!"

Gideon went through the brightly-lit corridors of the quiet building.

Down below, in the Information Room, they would be busier now than at any time during the day; the night's crop of crimes was being reported. In Fingerprints and Records, in the Photographic Division, in Ballistics—in fact everywhere on the C.I.D. section, there would be experts at work, more than at some periods during the day; and yet you couldn't make night into day, the place had a dead look. The clerical staff weren't here, of course, and the administrative staff were out at the pictures or watching television or listening to the radio, at church socials, at their hobbies, or perhaps cuddling. Gideon grinned at himself, and had a sneaking thought that he was getting a bit too prosy.

He drove home at a steady pace.

Kate, Prudence, Priscilla and Matthew were still up, having a hand of whist. Tom, the oldest son, was working in the north of England, and only came home occasionally; Malcolm, the nine-year-old, was in bed. Gideon watched the game, winked at Kate when he saw her play the wrong card and so give Priscilla a trick, and then sat back in his armchair. Pleasant. There were times when this seemed to be the only part of life which wasn't seamy.

Yet William Rose had spread his influence here.

What *was* the truth about that boy?

It was a little before midnight when Gideon went to bed, and Kate looked through the newspapers as he undressed. She didn't pester him, but he could see that she read the reports about young Syd Benson closely. He told her that there was no trace of the boy.

By half past twelve they were both asleep.

At two o'clock the telephone bell rang.

Gideon was in the deep sleep of the early hours, and heard the sound as through a thick mist. Then he felt something stir. Next he felt Kate leaning across him, her breast against his shoulder. He fought to open his eyes, and grunted to let her know that he was waking up. She said something, then switched on the light near the telephone.

"It's something about those prisoners."

In that instant, Gideon was wide awake.

"They got the others?" He snatched the telephone. "Hallo, Gideon speaking . . ."

"*Where?*" he breathed.

Kate saw his expression, the tightening of his lips, the way the muscles at the side of his face worked. His eyes no longer looked sleepy. He said, "Okay, I'll come right away," and put the receiver down. Kate didn't say: "George, *must* you?" but started to get out of bed.

"You needn't get up," Gideon protested.

"I'm going to make you a cup of tea, you're not going out at this hour without something to warm you."

He grunted, "Thanks."

"It isn't Benson, is it?"

"No, two of the others—Jingo Smith and Matt Owens," Gideon told her. "They've been traced to a warehouse and factory near the docks, locked themselves in the laboratory, and threaten to blow the place up if the police don't let 'em go. Blurry fools," growled Gideon, "but it's the kind of thing Jingo Smith would try, he always was a flamboyant fool. The lunatics didn't send for me until the last minute, they've the fire brigade out and half the police force, I shouldn't wonder."

Kate said, "Oh."

"You don't have to worry," said Gideon, and stared at her in surprise, for she looked almost frightened. "Here, Kate, I'll be all right."

From the door she said, "Sometimes I wonder if you know what fear is. Get your clothes on, and don't forget that woolly waistcoat, it's cold tonight."

"Well," grinned Gideon, "you should know, you're wearing nylon and not much else." He tossed her his own woolen dressing gown, and then turned round to dress.

14 . Cornered

THE streets near the warehouse had been cordoned off, and it wasn't until he had been recognized that Gideon was allowed to go through. As he drew nearer the warehouse, he saw the fire engines with their ladders up and two men perched on a turntable that seemed to be a vast distance up in the starlit sky. The shapes of tall warehouses, of cranes and of the masts of ships showed up dark against the stars. There were the sounds inseparable from a massed crowd of people. Uniformed police and several plain-clothes men stood around, and one after another they saluted Gideon. He drove slowly to a point where there was no room to pass other cars, got out, and walked toward a little group of men near the surrounded warehouse. Car headlights and one ship's searchlight shone on the walls and the windows of this place, and the light was reflected from the glass. Not far from the spot where the group of men waited was an ambulance; two men were being given first aid.

Gideon drew up.

"Anyone hurt badly?" he asked sharply.

Trabert, the Yard man who had summoned him, and the Divisional C.I., named Wilson, turned round at the sound of his voice.

"Hallo, George," the Yard man greeted. "Sorry we didn't call you earlier, didn't think they'd be such fools. It depends what you call badly—one chap's got a knife wound in his shoulder and another a cracked skull. Nice lot, those Millways chaps."

"Seen 'em?"

"No. They're in that corner over there." Trabert, a thinnish, graying man whose overcoat looked too large for him, pointed to a corner. "There's a laboratory up there, with steel doors, and they've closed the doors. Only way we can get at them is through the window. They've got enough nitroglycerin to blow the place sky-high, and they could start a fire that would burn out half London. Been talking to the chief chemist, and he says the stuff's there all right." Trabert had always a reputation for being picturesque, and for exaggeration. "I've talked to the pair on the radio with a loud-speaker, and they've got a megaphone up there."

Gideon looked at the window.

"Any of our chaps inside?"

"I ordered them out. If the place does go up, I'd rather we didn't have a lot of casualties."

"Wouldn't be a bad idea if you moved back a bit yourself," said Gideon. He looked at the dim light, and he tried to picture the two men inside. Jingo Smith was as hard as they were made; a good second to Benson. The man with him, Matt Owens, had no record of violence; but probably he knew that if he were caught his sentence would be so long that it was worth making desperate efforts to stay free.

At heart, each man must know that he hadn't really a chance.

But they could do a lot of damage before giving in.

"Don't mind admitting it was my own fault," said Wilson. The Divisional man had a gruff, whispering voice. "I had a flash from one of our chaps, saying they were here, and thought I'd be clever. Didn't realize that Smith and Owens knew they'd been seen, so I thought I'd pull them in, and make you a present. I ought to be hamstrung."

Gideon said, "Who doesn't make a boner, some time or other?" It was the only thing he could say, although inwardly he felt the welling up of bitterness against a responsible officer who had taken risks simply to cover himself, or his Division, with glory. Some men didn't seem to grow up. "Well, we'd better call the A.C. and let him have a word with a big shot at the Home Office."

Wilson said, "Listen, George, let me go and have a try to reason with them."

"In a minute," Gideon said. "Anyone here from the warehouse, to tell us how to get inside from the roof or the back?"

"George," said Trabert, quietly, "there's only one way in now—through that window. We can't break down a steel door, armor plating couldn't be tougher. If you and anyone else try heroics, you'll be crazy. We could try to hose them out, but if we do they might toss some nitroglycerin down. If it comes to that, we might knock a tube of the damned stuff off a bench, and start the blow-up that way. There isn't any way of getting into that laboratory. We'll have to starve them out."

He stopped.

Then a loud voice sounded from the direction of the window. Gideon and every other man stared toward it and the ladder which leaned against the wall near it. No one appeared; but Gideon saw the round mouth of a megaphone, like those used on the docks when foremen dockers needed to make themselves heard above a din.

"Hi there, Gee-Gee!" That was Jingo Smith. "Didn't think it would be long before they got you out of bed. How do you like it?"

Gideon—George Gideon made Gee-Gee inevitable, and he was often surprised that it wasn't used more—put his great hands to his mouth and called back in a voice which was almost as powerful as Jingo Smith's when amplified by the megaphone. At least fifty people were standing, watching and listening; and more were arriving every minute.

"I don't like it at all, Jingo," Gideon called. "I never like to see a man make a fool of himself."

"I'm no fool," Jingo called back. His weakness, the weakness of so many of them, was vanity. Now he was the center of attraction, and having a wonderful time. It was at least possible that he had managed to get drunk, if only on methylated spirits from the laboratory. There would probably be pure alcohol there, too, and he wouldn't lose any time finding out. "They told you what I'm going to do?"

"No, what's it to be?"

"They *didn't* tell you? What's the matter, they gone deaf? This is what it will be, Gee-Gee! I've got a tube of nitro in my pocket, and I'm going to bring it out with me. Anyone who tries to stop me will get it—and that goes for anyone within a fifty-foot radius, too. Any copper want to come to hell with me? Why don't *you* come, Gee-Gee?"

"Give it a rest," Gideon called. "You can't get away, and you know it. Better have a few more years up at Millways than blow yourself to pieces."

"Gee-Gee," bawled Jingo Smith, "we're coming out in ten minutes; and if anyone gets near us, up will go the balloon."

Gideon didn't speak for at least a minute; everyone within earshot was waiting for him; the tension in the street was like an electric current. Then, just as Smith was going to speak again—they actually heard him clear his throat—Gideon tossed back his great head and bellowed:

"Owens, do you want to be blown to Kingdom Come? Hit him over the head, and knock some sense into him! You'll get off lightly if you do."

Silence.

Would Matt Owens have the nerve . . .

Then: "No, you don't!" screamed Jingo Smith. "I'll smash your face . . ."

His voice fell to a whisper as he dropped the megaphone. Gideon didn't need to speak, but led the rush toward the ladder—Trabert, Wilson and two other men following at speed. They heard the scuffling inside. Behind them there was an awful silence; one which might be broken by a blast which could kill the men in the room and the policemen who were so near. Gideon reached the ladder and climbed up it as fast as any fireman. He heard the gasping and the scuffling. He reached the top of the ladder and could see inside the laboratory as he flashed his flashlight beam into the room.

Jingo Smith and Matt Owens were on the floor, rolling over and over. The megaphone lay near them. The light of the torch flashed on the glass of beakers, burettes, glass tubes, bottles, on Bunsen burners, on all the paraphernalia of the laboratory. A dim electric light burned in a corner, near the men.

Gideon thrust the window up.

He heard bottles rattling. He saw a dozen tubes on one of the benches, shaking when the fighting men rolled against it. He didn't know, and couldn't tell for certain, whether there was nitroglycerin in one of those tubes; he only knew that if there was, and it fell, he wouldn't have anything more to worry about.

He slid into the room.

Jingo Smith brought a bottle down on Owens' head, and as Owens went still, jumped toward the bench with his hand outstretched. There was no doubt that he wanted the small, metal tube which stood there, rocking gently, halfway between the convict and Gideon.

15 . Hero

GIDEON knew exactly what he had to do, exactly what the risk was. It was easy, now, to be heroic, for he had no choice. He had to bring Jingo Smith down, and had to stop him from jolting the laboratory bench. The tube was within a yard of Smith's outstretched hands; and he was looking toward it, lips distended, eyes shimmering. Matt Owens lay on the floor, writhing, yet staring at the tube with the fear of death in his eyes.

Gideon thrust out his right leg, huge foot plumb on Smith's stomach, and shoved with all his massive strength. Smith gave a thin squeal of sound and, his fingers only inches from the tube, staggered away from it. He looked like a man who was staggering away from salvation.

He wasn't finished.

He grabbed at a beaker on the bench, trying to slide it along the bench toward the tube. Gideon saw it, grabbed, and snatched up the beaker. Smith, still staggering, went closer to Owens. Owens shot out a hand and grabbed his ankle; and Smith pitched forward, arms waving wildly, and the tube still within his reach.

Gideon got between him and the bench. Smith fell heavily. Gideon, breathing very hard, went down, heaved the man over onto his stomach, and then chopped with the side of the hand at the nape of his neck. Smith lost consciousness as swiftly as a doused light goes out. The only sound was Owen's gasping breath, Gideon's hissing, and a clattering noise as someone else climbed in at the window. Gideon looked round to see Wilson, who was also gasping, and Trabert on the ladder just behind him.

Gideon looked at the tube of nitroglycerin.

"What did we bring the fire unit for?" he asked. "We can do it just as well ourselves. Don't start rocking the boat, or we'll all go under." He picked up the tube, looked round, and saw a small safe with a steel door standing open. Inside it were other tubes like this, as well as containers which held many things he didn't recognize. Without appearing to take exceptional care, he carried the tube to the safe and saw that inside, on the bottom, there were a number of holes into which tubes like this could be placed so that there was no risk of knocking them down. "Funny thing," he said heavily, "people live every day doing a job which would blow them to Kingdom Come if anything went wrong."

Other police were climbing in.

Matt Owens was getting to his feet, and a hefty D.I. grabbed his arm.

"Take it easy with Matt," Gideon said; "if it hadn't been for him we'd all be bits and pieces. Matt, if you go on being sensible, we'll get you off serious punishment for the break. If you take my advice you'll see your sentence out quietly and give yourself a chance of getting along afterward; we'll help you all we can after this. Had any food lately?"

Owens looked desperately tired.

"Hardly a bite since we got away," he said hoarsely; "squeezed into a freight train, been halfway round the ruddy country." He was shivering, only partly with cold, for he wore an old, tattered coat and beneath it what looked like a new pair of flannel trousers. "Jingo was drunk, Mr. Gideon; he put down half a pint of meth and then he found some alcohol in that bottle. He wouldn't have been so crazy if he hadn't been drunk."

"It's a good thing you kept sober," Gideon said with feeling. "We'll get you a square meal before we send you home. Take him across to the café at

the end of the road," he added to two D.I.s. "Keep him away from the newspapermen if you can."

"They don't want Owens," Trabert said, grinning and showing very big,
shiny teeth. "They want you. Didn't you know you're a hero?"

There he was, too.

Every late edition of the morning newspaper, carried a photograph of
Gideon, C.I.D. There were flamboyant accounts of what he had done during the night, as well as what he had done in the past. The headlines about
Edmundsun and the prison escapes miraculously vanished. The *Daily
Globe* spread itself with a leader on the daily dangers which faced the
police, and cited the Gideon capture of Jingo Smith, the policeman who
had stopped the New Bond Street raiders, and the Putney policeman who
had rescued the woman and her child. It was enough to make Gideon purr;
enough to make everyone at the Yard go about grinning, as if a big load had
been lifted from everyone's mind. To help, the weather turned not only
warm but fine. May had come some weeks ahead of itself.

That day, the fifth since the escape of the men from Millways, was one of
the best Gideon had known for a long time. Small things went right. There
were seven cases up for trial at the Old Bailey, with three of them doubtful
in the outcome; the police knew they had the right man but weren't sure
they had a strong enough case. Each went smoothly, each man was found
guilty. Birdy, the judge in Number One Court at the Old Bailey, must have
read the newspapers; he included a few sentences of congratulation to the
police at the end of the case which he'd been hearing for a week. Cummings alone was less happy: he felt more sure than ever that Elliott, Edmundsun's manager, had also been Edmundsun's accomplice, but seemed
less confident that he would ever be able to prove it.

About noon, on that fifth day, he came in to see Gideon.

"Don't really know that I ought to say this to you, sir," he said, "but I
get a nasty feeling about the whole job. A smell, if you know what I mean.
As if Elliott's covered up a cesspit and I can't make him take the cover off.
When are you seeing Mrs. Edmundsun, sir?"

"Why?"

"I don't know that I should leave it too long, they might get at her."

Gideon said very slowly: "You serious?"

"All I know, sir," said Cummings, looking more flabby and pale and ill-at-
ease than usual, "is that I'm not happy about it. I know it's a bit tough
trying to make her talk, with her husband only just buried, but if Elliott or
anyone else is going to get at her, they won't let sentiment stand in the way."

"I'll go and see her now," Gideon promised.

That was easy. The Edmundsuns had lived in a block of flats in Bayswater, comfortable but not luxurious. Gideon went right away, on his own. A maid opened the door and let him in; he waited in a room which overlooked a garden, vivid green grass and wintry-looking trees, until Mrs. Edmundsun came in. He had only seen her from her photographs, and wasn't really surprised that she looked not only different but much more attractive. She wasn't exactly a beauty, but had a figure that didn't come very often, and she had beautiful gray eyes.

"I'd hoped that the police wouldn't find it necessary to worry me again, Mr. Gideon," she said, turning his card over in her fingers; and she left it at that, as if defying him to be brute enough to question a poor, defenseless woman.

"We want to help," Gideon said easily, "and one of the ways would be to clear your husband's name, Mrs. Edmundsun. All through the investigation, he declared that he was innocent—"

"And I'm *sure* he was."

"Well, there's one way to establish it," said Gideon, "and that's by finding the people who are responsible. For the money *is* missing, you know, it was paid out on dummy hire-purchase agreements. Did he ever—"

"I've told the police everything I can," said Mrs. Edmundsun, firmly. "And if you aren't satisfied, Mr. Gideon, then I really ought to consult my solicitor. As if it isn't bad enough to have lost . . ."

Her eyes began to fill with tears.

A woman in black, with a figure which the mourning dress wasn't designed to disguise, and with those beautiful eyes and that soft voice, could be as unyielding as a brick wall. Gideon sensed it, and knew at once what was worrying Cummings. This woman was supposed to have been desperately in love with her husband; all the reports which had followed the news of his death suggested that; yet here she was as cool as if the tragedy had been a year ago, not a few days.

What had caused the change?

Gideon left her, in a non-committal way, with just enough on her mind to make her wonder whether he or another police officer would soon be back. As he reached the square, and the warm sunshine fell upon him, he thought less about her than about Cummings. A man's appearance could count heavily against him, and Cummings had that paunch, that flabby double chin, the pasty face, and those rather vague-looking eyes. Yet he had "smelt" something. Gideon knew, and everyone with a flair for C.I.D. work realized it, that once in a while a man arrived with that "sense of smell"— someone who was sure a thing was wrong but couldn't get his hands on the evidence. Cummings seemed to have it; and if he did, then his appearance mustn't stand against him.

"I'll give him a few weeks on this job," Gideon said to himself; "if he can get anything out of it, he'll be set fair."

When Gideon reached the Yard, Smedd was waiting in his office, shoulders square, ginger hair bright in the sun, freckles showing up more noticeably than ever, brisk and decisive as he would always be. This was the way of it: not one but several major jobs to think about at the same time, everything to be noted and neatly pigeon-holed, ready to be brought out again when necessary.

Gideon shook hands with Smedd, and didn't show the hope that he suddenly felt. Would Smedd come in person, leaving his precious Division, unless he had news that worried him?

"Sit down, and have a cigarette," Gideon said. He wanted the man friendly, and felt better disposed toward him than he had at the beginning of the week: Smedd had finally confirmed that he was really thorough.

"Thanks," he said, and drew a little quickly, almost nervously, at his cigarette; a kind of mannerism. "I thought I'd have a word with you about this development personally, as I know of your interest."

"Good of you," murmured Gideon.

"I've got a witness who can help us about the cinema," Smedd said. "Young chap, about Rose's age, who went to that same performance. I've had a man at the cinema with the box-office girl, she recognized this boy as a regular twice-a-weeker."

"Yes?"

"He said he saw Mary Rose by herself," said Smedd, deliberately. "He swears black's blue that she didn't have anyone with her. Noticed her because he knows her slightly, in fact; I think he's got one of those I-love-you-from-afar crushes." That phrase sounded odd, in the brisk, clipped way in which Smedd spoke. "That's all we want to clinch things, I think. I've asked everyone about that knife, and Rose didn't say anything about it being lost. Can't trace anyone who's actually seen him with it since he's supposed to have lost it," Smedd went on candidly, "but that's not evidence."

Yes, he was thorough.

"Thing I wanted to check with you, Commander: shall I try to break the girl down now, get her to admit she was lying, or shall I wait until later? Rose is up for the second hearing on Tuesday; he'll be committed for trial, of course."

Gideon said slowly, "I think the best thing is to make sure your new witness is absolutely reliable, and then save him for the trial. We'll look for others, too—and mustn't forget that the defense is going to search high and low for someone who saw them both, or for anyone who was told that knife was lost."

Smedd shook his head swiftly, rather like a ventriloquist's puppet.

"Take it from me, the defense is going for insanity," he said. "They'll know better than to try anything else. Thing is, I'd be happier if they weren't going to put the sister up, lays a false trail—you know how it is. I'd like to let her know we know she's lying, before the trial comes up."

"Well, there's plenty of time," Gideon said. "Won't be up until June, end of May at the earliest. You certainly didn't leave much to chance."

"It isn't my habit to leave anything to chance," said Smedd, almost tartly.

Gideon didn't know that at that moment the solicitor who was looking after William Rose's interests was talking to Rose's sister and his mother, in the small suburban house on the outskirts of the H5 Division. The solicitor, an elderly man with a lifetime's experience, a rather tired manner and a shabby gray suit, was sitting in the front room, considering the mother, not Mary Rose. Mrs. Rose, at fifty-nine, looked nearer seventy: old, tired, so very, very sad.

"What Mary must understand," the solicitor said precisely, "is that the police will do everything to discredit her statement that she went with her brother to this picture house on the day and at the time in question. Now we need her as a reliable witness for the defense, we do not want her to be browbeaten by the prosecution and—ah—possibly caught out in a lie."

He shot a quick glance at Mary.

Mary said, in a quiet, stubborn voice, "They can't prove that I lied if I didn't. I met Will in the High Street, and he told me he'd had a quarrel with Winnie and hardly knew what to do with himself, he was so upset. So I treated him to the pictures, because he hadn't any money."

There was a long pause. Then:

"Mary, did you really—" began her mother.

And Gideon didn't know that, just after one o'clock that day, Arthur Small was talking to Ruby Benson in the back of the shop in the Mile End Road. Two other assistants were attending to a customer, the door was closed, and the couple kept their voices very low. They were surrounded by dresses, coats and suits, hanging inside transparent plastic cabinets all around the room. Boxes, flat now, tissue paper and balls of string were on a table in the middle of this room.

"Ruby, try not to worry so much," Small said, pleadingly. "It's making you ill, and what good will that do you or Liz? The police are bound to find young Syd sooner or later, they're *bound* to."

"If you knew *him*," Ruby said in a flat voice, "you wouldn't talk like that. He's taken the boy away from me, he's taken my own son."

Small, moving nervously about the little room, picked up a packet of cigarettes, put a cigarette to his lips, but didn't light it. It got very wet almost at once.

"Ruby, you know how I feel about you, don't you? I love you more than I love anything or anybody, but—but it isn't any use pretending about anything, is it? If young Syd can be turned against you as easily as that, then he was never very close to you, was he? He was always closer to his father." When Ruby didn't answer, Small tried to light the cigarette; it wouldn't draw. He dropped it into an ash tray, and went on, unhappily: "Ruby, I didn't mean to be unkind, but I can't bear to see you torture yourself like this. I—I'll make it up to you, you know that. If we can bring young Syd round, that'll be wonderful; but if we can't—well, we've still got Liz, and you and me together."

Ruby just looked at him.

He was older than he seemed at first sight: nearing fifty. He was rather small and white and precise, as reliable and as trustworthy as a man could be. Behind his horn-rimmed glasses, his eyes were a clear gray, steadfast, pleading. Since she had known him, he had given her not only comfort but contentment.

Now, out of her distress, she said:

"I know, Art, but—but what good am I to *you*? While he's alive I can't even marry you, it's not fair to you. You ought to go away and . . ."

"Don't talk like that!" Small cried; his voice was louder and sharper, and it made her stop. He took her arms, firmly. "Now listen to me, and stop this nonsense. You're getting hysterical. Supposing we can't get married? We can live together and set up house, can't we, and who's going to care whether we've got the marriage lines or not? We've both got every right to happiness, and there's no reason why we shouldn't take it. *He'll* be in prison for at least twelve years, after this, and I don't care what anyone says, it would be criminal for you to live on your own all that time. And—I'm—not—going—to —let—you."

His grip on her arms was very tight.

Then, suddenly, they were close to each other; she was clinging to him desperately, and crying.

Ten minutes later, she looked less haggard. Her eyes were still red from crying, but not so drawn and filled with shadows. He looked bright and perky, with a cigarette at his lips, also damp but at least giving off smoke.

"That's settled then," he said briskly; "we start the day that he's caught, and they can call it living in sin if they like. Now I must go along to see Rubenstein; if I can buy those dresses for twenty per cent less than he's asking we should make a very good profit, and that'll swell the commission." He kissed her again, and went out into the shop. The customer had gone, and the young assistants looked at him knowingly. He nodded to them, and went out. Nearby was a uniformed policeman, he was used to that. Nearby, also, was the plain-clothes man from Scotland Yard, Abbott; Small was getting used to him. There were the usual passersby, two or three of them looking at the window of the next-door shop; and on the pavement on the Aldgate side of the shop was the simple child, Simon, badly dressed, mouth gaping, drooling a little.

No one ever took any notice of poor Simon.

"Afternoon, officer," said Arthur Small to Abbott, "no news yet?"

"Afraid there isn't, Mr. Small."

"Between you and me I'll be glad for your sake when it's over," Small said; "you must find it very boring." He had a bright look in his eyes and a perkier manner than ever, and Abbott guessed that he'd come to some kind of an agreement with Ruby Benson.

"I get paid for it," he said dryly.

They were within a few feet of Simon, when the lad took a small milk bottle with a wide mouth from his pocket. There was liquid in it that wasn't milk, but thick and oily-looking. Abbott saw that. He was near enough to strike the bottle aside, but he didn't—because it was poor Simon, and because he did not even dream that Simon might have been put up to do this.

There were some things that Simon could do well. He swung the bottle, ejecting a stream of liquid toward Arthur Small. That was the moment when Abbott realized what was happening. He cried out, and leaped forward. He felt burning spots on the back of his hand as he struck the boy's arm aside. The bottle fell; and as it fell, Small clapped his hands to his face and began to scream.

16 . Hospital Case

GIDEON first heard the news when he came back from a late lunch in the pub in Cannon Row. He hadn't meant to have a heavy lunch, but Superintendent Wrexall, the senior Superintendent at the Yard, ten years older than Gideon and due to retire at the end of the year, had suggested that they should lunch together; he had a "case" he wanted to talk over. Gideon didn't know anything about this case, but couldn't very well refuse the invitation, and immediately after he had returned from the interview with Mrs. Edmundsun, he went off, leaving a list of *Do At Once* items on Lemaitre's desk. A sergeant was in charge of the office until he or Lemaitre returned.

Wrexall's "case" wasn't exactly a waste of time.

While some Superintendents at the Yard specialized, like King-Hadden, of Fingerprints, most of them tackled whatever job presented itself. In an odd way, however, certain types of job gravitated, as if of their own volition, toward one man. Wrexall's knowledge of blackmail was the most exhaustive at Scotland Yard. He had that sense of "smell." Now, he had picked out something which might be significant from a series of reports covering several months, from different Divisions. Where another man might have read these reports a hundred times and seen nothing in them, Wrexall had picked out two things:

A respected suburban solicitor had committed suicide six months ago, but his affairs were in order; the only surprise was that his estate had been much smaller than expected. Nothing at all was missing from clients' funds. The police investigation, prior to the inquest at which the verdict had been suicide while temporarily insane, showed that he had changed his daily habits a great deal during the past two years, had frequently left his office in charge of a junior partner and, it was believed, had "gone racing"; that was the official explanation of the missing private fortune and the fact that he had left an elderly wife unprovided for.

Two months later, in another London suburb, the manager of a large branch of one of the joint stock banks had been killed in an accident. The police had suspected suicide, but had not been able to establish it, and the verdict had at least been a comfort to his widow and two children. They had little else to comfort them, for a personal estate, known at one time to have been worth nearly thirty thousand pounds, had vanished. There was no certainty about the way in which the loss had been made, but gambling was suspected.

Wrexall, studying these, had seen the similarity of social position, suicide and suspected suicide, and a small fortune lost either unaccountably or in a way which was surprising when one considered the character of the dead man.

"Just made me wonder whether everything was what it looked like, George," Wrexall had said. He had a mane of iron-gray hair and a most impressive manner. "You know what I'm like, nose as long as a snorkel device. So I put young Chambers onto finding out who the solicitor had placed his bets with. Couldn't find anyone, local or in the West End. In fact, I'm pretty sure he didn't have an account with any bookie. Then I checked the racecourses, finding out the days that the chap had taken out big cash sums. Most of them coincided with race days near London, and I tried to find a bookie who'd taken big bets with the solicitor. Couldn't. In fact there weren't any big cash bets on any of those days. Funny, eh?"

Gideon had agreed that it was funny.

"Now if these two chaps were paying out money under pressure and didn't want to show it, they'd fake a reason, wouldn't they?" said Wrexall.

"But I don't like to think that anyone's managed to drive chaps like them to suicide, as well as make things tough for their families. So I've been keeping my eyes open, and this morning there's an interesting little report in from Guildford. Outside our ground, I know, but very interesting. Accountant, this time, tried to commit suicide. Inherited twenty-five thousand quid four years ago, lived a normal married life as far as we can see—and he's almost on his beam ends. It's no use me ringing up Guildford or the Surrey boys, but if you'd have a word with the A.C. and persuade him that it might be worth looking at, he could lay it on with the Chief Constable of Surrey, and—"

"You could have a few nice, cozy days in the country," Gideon had grinned. "Okay, Tim, I'll tell him it's too good to miss. That worth the money you'll pay for the lunch?"

"Don't know what I'd do without you," Wrexall had said. "Glad to sit and watch you eat, anyway. I never could tell where you put it all."

They went back to the Yard at a leisurely pace, Gideon still glowing from the smooth morning, and because so much had gone right; his regret about the way the Primrose Girl case was turning was almost forgotten. He was even philosophic about Syd's continued absence; had the boy been killed, they would probably have found the body by now; he'd turn up. He had no suspicion of what kind of news would greet him until he opened the door and Lemaitre burst out:

"George, Benson's got his wife's beau! Vitriol. Horrible job, hospital case. And Abbott caught some, too."

Gideon stood quite still, with the door open. He felt the old, crushing weight coming down on him again, and when he moved it was more slowly than usual. He closed the door, and the lock snapped. He stood with his back to it, massive and, in that mood, almost frightening.

"How bad's Small?"

"Side of his face and one eye," Lemaitre said.

"Abbott?"

"Right hand only, as far as I can gather; he's not a hospital case, anyhow—on his way here now."

"Benson?"

"A kid did the job."

Gideon almost groaned, "Not young Syd."

"Dunno," said Lemaitre.

Wrexall's suspicions, Cummings and his worry, the Rose family, the newspaper reports—all of these things vanished from Gideon's mind. He walked to his desk, and it was as if he were walking through shadows, not through bright shafts of sunlight which struck and brightened the wall behind his desk. He sat down slowly, loosened his collar and tie, and took out his pipe. He began to finger the roughened surface.

Then, he made himself say, "Anything else in?"

"Not much," answered Lemaitre. "They caught a shoplifter at Marridge's. He made a dash for it, and caused a bit of panic, then fell down the stairs and broke his leg. Two smash-and-grabs—one in Soho, one near Marble Arch, nothing much gone. Two—"

"Sure Abbott's not badly hurt?"

"Yes."

"Mrs. Benson know about this?"

"Bound to. Happened just outside the shop."

Then, two telephones rang at the same moment. Lemaitre snatched his up; Gideon took his more slowly and raised it as slowly to his ear. "Gideon." He heard Lemaitre say something in his laconic way, but wasn't sure what it was. He could see Arthur Small as if he were here in the office: earnest, faithful, well-preserved, well-groomed, with his pale, regular features, his horn-rimmed glasses.

Glasses?

"Detective Officer Abbott is in the building, sir, would you like to see him?"

"Yes. Right away. Send him up."

"Thank you, sir."

Gideon started to fill the bowl of his pipe, and to find that his mind began to thaw out. He was able to remind himself that this might be the most important but it wasn't the only job on his plate, and he must not allow it to obsess him, even for a few minutes. Then, he realized that in fact it had obsessed him. The awful, hideous mask of failure—such failure that it was possible for a man whom they were "protecting" to be disfigured in this way—was one of the most bitter things he had ever had to face. It undid all the good of last night; of this morning. The Press, the Home Office, the Assistant Commissioner, every man and woman at Scotland Yard might make excuses; but he, Gideon, felt just one thing: it should never have happened and it was his fault that it had. He'd met young Abbott in the lift, formed a good opinion of him, and given him a job which should have been handled by a man with much more experience. The whole world would call that nonsense, but he, Gideon, knew the simple truth.

It was a heavy weight, bearing hard upon him.

There was a tap at the door.

"Come in," he called.

Lemaitre was still talking, but was glancing toward the door as it opened, and Abbott came in. He didn't look very good; his face had lost that healthy glow, in spite of the tan, and Gideon knew that he was suffering from shock; he ought to stay away for a day or so. His right hand was bandaged, and there was a patch of sticking plaster on his right cheek, about an inch from his eye. He kept himself erect with an obvious effort.

What the hell was his Christian name?

Ah: Michael.

He looked as if he expected Gideon to breathe fire.

"Hallo, Mike," Gideon said quietly, "come and sit down." He didn't overdo it, but just waved to a chair, and then pushed a pack of cigarettes across the desk. "Glad to see you didn't come out of it too badly."

Abbott just sat there, his shoulders less square, now, the dejection a physical as well as a mental thing. He didn't take a cigarette. He didn't look round. He managed to meet Gideon's gaze, and that was all. Here was a man who could be broken for life; moments like this condemned men, like patient old Jefferson, to a life in which the highest possible ambition was a sergeant's pension.

"What time did it happen?" asked Gideon. If he could once start the man talking . . .

His telephone bell rang.

"Blast the blurry thing," he said, and picked it up more quickly than usual. "Matches?" He tossed a big box across the desk, and it slid off. Abbott had to bend down to pick it up and, with the matches in his hand, he seemed to lose some of the tension, and then picked up the cigarettes. "Gideon here," said Gideon; "switch all calls through to Chief Inspector Lemaitre until . . . *what?*"

He listened so intently that Abbott, the cigarette now between his lips, looked at him almost eagerly. So did Lemaitre who got up and came across.

Then:

"Thank God for that," breathed Gideon. "Eh . . . Yes, he's with me now . . . Not badly hurt, seems to have done a good job . . . Oh, fine. Fine. Thanks, sir."

He rang off and was smiling; not the broad, homely smile which made him so likable and attractive to many people, but a smile which had a kind of glow about it; in a woman, it would have been radiant. It was the last thing that either Lemaitre or Abbott had dreamed of seeing, and it must have done Abbott more good than anything else could have.

"That was the A.C.," he said. "Young Syd's been found. He's not hurt. Been hiding out with Charlie Mulliver, kind of blurry fool thing Charlie would do, harbor him when he knew we were on the lookout for him. Wouldn't I like to put him inside! And Small won't lose the sight of his right eye, after all; he'll have a scar on the side of his face, up round the temple, that's about all. Lem, ring the shop and tell Mrs. Benson, and if she's not in, ring the Division and ask them to tell her—that's if she doesn't know already." Gideon put his pipe to his lips. "Well, things aren't always as black as they seem, Mike," he said to Abbott. "Feel better?"

Abbott gulped; when he spoke his voice was pitched higher than usual.

"Can't alter the fact that I ought to have stopped the Benson kid from getting away, and I ought to have stopped the other kid from throwing that acid, too. Didn't dream of anything coming from him. He's a half-wit near as damnit, I've often seen him hanging about. When I start thinking, I know that Benson must have found a way to get in touch with him, but at the time he was just a kid to be sorry for. You know."

"I know," Gideon said. "Half-wit, is he?"

"Well known round there, too," said Abbott. Now his voice was more normal, as if his throat had been oiled, but he was speaking very quickly. "Named Simon, people call him Si, but whether that's from Simple Simon I don't know. It's a crying shame, a boy like that ought to be in a home, but he even goes to school! He's at the G5 Division now, there's a doctor with him. They think we'll frighten the wits out of him if we bring him here. But even if he knows who told him to do it, there's no way we can make sure that he tells us."

"We can try," Gideon said. "Just what happened?"

Abbott told him; and before the recital was finished, he was talking at normal speed and in his normal voice.

Gideon sent him home.

Gideon did not labor the obvious fact: that Benson had managed to get in touch with the half-wit, and to give him instructions—almost certainly through a third party.

Who?

The dozens of friends and acquaintances with whom Benson might have got in touch would have to be picked up now, and a full-scale interrogation begun. The movements of the hapless vitriol thrower had to be traced. Given the breaks, none of it should take long; but one fact stood out: Benson had headed for London for vengeance. His wife would be in greater terror than ever; so would his daughter. The one good thing was that young Syd was back.

Was it so good?

Gideon got his mind very clear on what had happened, and what he was going to ask the boy—and say to Mulliver.

The man who had sheltered the boy ran a doss house near the docks; beds at a shilling a night, bring your own food, kill your own rats, find your own lice. It was a place that ought to be closed up on grounds of unsanitary conditions, yet by some miracle it managed to meet all the London County Council rules and regulations. Mulliver, a middle-aged wreck of a man, had a good reputation for helping lame dogs, and he got on well with the police. He wasn't a squealer; as far as was known, he wasn't a crook, either.

Had he let young Syd stay with him out of the goodness of his heart, or under some kind of pressure?

From Benson, for instance . . .

That was just a guess; but it was an accurate guess.

Even if he soon became certain of its accuracy, there still lay upon Gideon the burden of proof.

He cleared up everything on his desk and, about half past three, went to the G5 Division. First, he wanted to see the half-wit, to find out what the Divisional people had done; then he wanted to talk to Charlie Mulliver; next, to young Syd.

One thing was certain: as this news spread, and by now it would have reached every Division, every subdivision, every plain-clothes man and every man on the beat in the whole of the London area, the whole of the Metropolitan Police would be geared to a pitch which it reached only now and again.

Every man would feel it his personal responsibility to make sure that Benson was caught before he could harm his wife or her children.

Gideon felt that the responsibility was all his.

Mulliver swore that young Syd had come to him, pleading to be allowed to hide.

"And where was the harm?" the doss-house keeper almost whined. "I couldn't see any, Mr. Gideon, honest I couldn't."

He didn't change his story, but there was much he could have told.

17 . Father and Son

THERE was just one thing about Charlie Mulliver which the police did not know, and which Syd Benson did.

He was a murderer.

He was not a natural killer, in the way that Benson was. In fact he still had a compassion for his fellow men which, in view of the people he mixed with over the years, was quite surprising. If a man really needed a bed and a cup of tea and a hunk of bread, and couldn't pay for it he would get it at Charlie's; a great many people went to his "hotel" in preference to the Salvation Army Hostel or the Y.M.C.A. or any of the other do-good places in the East End of London.

But Charlie Mulliver had killed his wife.

That was five years ago, and the case had long since been left high on the archives of the Yard, not as unsolvable, but as unsolved or pending. Mulliver's wife, in the common phrase, had been no better than she ought to be. At one time she had helped to run the doss house, looking after a women's section, as well as assisting on the other side. She had bestowed her favors too liberally, and in a quarrel Charlie had killed her. At the time, he had been drunk; at the time he had meant only to disfigure her; but if he were ever caught for the job he would certainly be jailed for life.

Syd Benson was the only man who knew who had killed her. Syd had helped to put the body in the Thames. And the police, knowing her habits, had not really been surprised when they had taken it out. They had questioned Mulliver, of course; and at one time the doss-house keeper had seemed the most likely suspect, but they had reckoned without the organizing genius of Benson. Having set out to fool the police for Mulliver's sake, Benson had succeeded brilliantly, by fixing an alibi at third hand and in a way which the police had never seriously questioned.

Mulliver had been a widower for five years, and all that time had known that one day Benson would want something in return for his help and his silence. There was nothing that Mulliver wouldn't do, to drive away even the thought of paying for his wife's murder.

Benson was not only clever and shrewd, but was also a sound judge of human nature. He knew that Mulliver would do whatever he was told, no matter how serious a crime. Like nine criminals out of every ten, Mulliver would feel that whatever he did, he would avoid being found out. All he had to do was pay his debt to Benson; after that, he would have nothing to worry about.

If Mulliver refused to obey Benson however, Benson would make sure that police would know all about the murder of his wife.

So Mulliver really had no choice.

And his life had been spent in the worst part of the East End, rubbing shoulders with vice and crime, with all that was worst as well as some of the things that were best in human nature. No one could have remained a saint for long while surrounded by that atmosphere, and Charlie Mulliver had been soaked in it for forty-odd years; but, the murder apart, he was not a criminal. It was not so much that he disapproved of crime as that he liked to keep himself safe from its consequences. It worked, too; he was trusted by the crooks and tolerated by the police.

Subconsciously, the gift of compassion in Charlie Mulliver was perhaps a form of self-defense. It paid off to have a heart. But he became so used to violence and crime at second hand that little shocked him. Among the hundreds of down-and-outs, drunks, men wounded in fights, sailors, Negroes, lascars, half-breeds and white men of all nationalities who passed through the doss house, dozens were badly scarred by acid, knife or razor. Scars were commonplace. So when Charlie had been told to brief Simon called Si to throw vitriol into Arthur Small's face, Charlie Mulliver had not revolted against the idea; he knew dozens of people whose faces and bodies were scarred by vitriol; and they'd lived through it. And above all things he had to ingratiate himself with Benson. He'd made a start when he had first learned that Benson was out, by telephoning his wife's boy friend.

Lilies or roses?—that would make Benson laugh!

Cunningly, Mulliver did the vitriol job through a third party, so that Simple Si could not possibly give him away to the police. The man the lad could have given away was now well out in the English Channel, on his way to Australia as a stoker on a small tramp steamer, and there was no danger from him either. So Mulliver felt quite safe. If he was at all uneasy, it was that he had kept young Syd here, but he'd received the order from Benson, and he hadn't seriously thought of refusing to obey. He had known of a dozen places where he could hide the boy, and had decided that the safest was in the doss house—in one of the tiny little private rooms where he lived himself. There had been no trouble at all with young Syd when he'd told him that it was his father's instructions.

All Syd wanted was to see his father.

And on the morning of the fifth day, the morning after Jingo Smith's capture, the morning after Gideon had become a hero, the morning which had gone so well, young Syd Benson had met his father for the first time in four years.

Young Syd hadn't realized what was going to happen.

Mulliver hadn't warned him, but Benson had arrived in London the previous night. He had several days' stubble on his lean face, and looked rough and vicious. Freddy Tisdale was still with him. They had come in on a big truck from Birmingham; the journey had been arranged by Benson's Birmingham friends, and they had arrived in the darkness of early morning. They hadn't gone to the doss house but had been hiding inside big barrels in an empty warehouse not far from the spot where Jingo Smith had made his attempt to blow himself and others sky-high.

It was more an oil dump than a warehouse, not far from Charlie Mulliver's place. It was easy for Benson and Tisdale to get across roofs to the doss house and eat, but at the slightest warning they could go back to the warehouse. It was true that if the police searched the doss house they might find evidence that Benson and Tisdale had been there, but to take all reasonable precautions against that, whenever they were there, they wore cotton gloves and so made sure they didn't leave prints.

The doss house emptied during the day; from ten o'clock until five or six in the evening, there was no one there except Mulliver, a drab who did some of the cleaning for him, and occasional visitors.

It was not until the night guests had departed that Mulliver had gone in to see young Syd and said with that tone of simulated kindliness:

"Your dad wants to see you, Syd. Coming?"

Young Syd Benson, unable to realize that he was actually looking upon his father in the flesh, stood on the threshold of the dingy little room where Benson and Tisdale spent some of their time. Tisdale was over at the warehouse; Benson wanted to see his son alone. Mulliver gave the boy a push and sent him further into the room, then backed out and closed the door. He kept near it, however, ready to raise the alarm if anyone arrived unexpectedly.

Father and son stood looking at each other.

Young Syd just saw a dream; a dream which had become real for a few minutes on the television, only to fade. Now it was back. The black stubble made no difference; the thin face made little; the sharp lines at the side of the mouth meant nothing to him. The living part of his father's face was in those pale eyes.

Benson's black stubble made them look much brighter and lighter even than they were. Shimmering. They were fine eyes, too; and the man who stood there, the dream which had come to life, was striking to look at. With his chiseled chin and his sharp nose and the deep eye-sockets, Benson was handsome in a kind of piratical way.

The odd thing was that they stood so still for a long time.

Young Syd was just numbed; unbelieving; and yet rising toward a tremendous exaltation.

Benson did not feel like that, but he felt an emotion which he had never experienced before: a kind of pride in his son, a kind of satisfaction that here in front of him was a chip off the old block. No one could doubt that he was face to face with his own flesh and blood.

"Hallo, boyo," Benson said very slowly. He clenched his right fist as he moved forward, and pressed the knuckles against the other's pointed chin. Young Syd didn't give ground, even when Benson increased the pressure so that it must have hurt. Then: "How do you like seeing your dad again, boyo?" Benson asked in that clipped, grating voice, and he looked almost savagely into his son's eyes.

"It's the only thing I've wanted for a *long* time," young Syd breathed.

Benson took his hand away from the child's jaw and gripped his shoulder. His finger bit deeply, but Syd did not flinch. He shook his son two or three times, making him sway forward and backward, but nothing altered the way that young Syd looked at him, with a light that was almost of veneration in his eyes.

"Well, I don't mind getting a look at you again," Benson said, and let the boy go. "You all right? They been looking after you?"

"Yeh," said young Syd.

"If they haven't, you just tell me."

"I'm okay," young Syd said firmly.

"Sure, you look okay to me," his father said, and grinned. "Didn't expect me to get out of jug, did you?"

"Yes, I did," said Syd flatly.

Benson exclaimed: "What's that?"

"Course I expected you to get out! I used to tell the other chaps that you wouldn't stay in jug all that time," boasted Syd, and his eyes were still radiant. "I was right, wasn't I?"

"You knew a thing or two," agreed Benson, and his eyes seemed to soften. "Well, I'll tell you another thing, boyo. I'm not going to let them take me back."

"I bet you're not!"

"Now I'm out, I'm out for keeps," Benson said, and his eyes narrowed, his voice dropped. "Sometimes to get the things you want you have to do things you don't like, Syd. Get me? You heard about that cove in the car park, up in Millways?"

Syd gulped, and nodded.

"Well, do you know what he was going to do? He was going to shop me, Syd, that's what he was going to do. Couldn't let that happen, could I?"

Syd gritted his teeth and shook his head.

It wasn't because he felt any sense of horror or reproach; it was because the emotion which he had held in check, unknowingly, was beginning to force itself to the surface. Tears stung his eyes; and it was a long, long time since he had cried. He stood there, jaws working, teeth gritting together, and tears glistening in those eyes which were so much like his father's. Benson stopped speaking. He did not understand this behavior at first, and his manner changed; he was resentful, wary. Then, before he could do anything to stop it, the boy had flung himself forward and crushed himself against him, crying:

"Dad, oh Dad, Dad, Dad!"

Benson stood quite still, feeling the pressure of the taut young body, the hardness of his son's head on his chin, the grip of his son's arms round him. He heard the choking, sobbing cries. He felt something he had never known before, something which had not even been within his understanding. His own eyes felt the sting of sharp, unfamiliar emotion—something that he hadn't felt when he had been sentenced, that he hadn't felt for a single moment while he had been at Millways.

The boy began to shiver.

Gradually, he went still.

Benson eased him away, and said with a rough kindliness which was quite foreign to him: "Now take it easy, kid, you'll be all right. Just take it easy."

They waited there, feeling different now, Syd sniffing and rubbing the sleeve of his jersey across his eyes and nose, Benson watching him with that new-found pride and a fierce sense of complete possession. It was not really long, but to them it seemed a long time before he spoke.

"So that's okay, now forget it, see. You want to know something? I've got a plan to get out of the country, go somewhere the bloody coppers can't get me."

"You—you *have?*"

"Sure. South America. You heard of South America?"

Young Syd, still sniffing and still not able to trust himself to speak properly, just managed to nod.

"Well, that's where I'm going. A pal of mine can fix me up on a ship; I'm going as a member of the crew, see. False name and all that, and I don't need no passport. As soon as I'm three miles outside the British waters, I'm free as the air, see. The captain's in the know, but he's a foreigner and he's getting well paid for it, so it's okay."

"That—that's good," Syd said.

Benson thrust out a hand, put his forefinger under the boy's chin, and forced his head back. The eyes were not yet completely free from tears, and were red and swollen.

"Say, what's this? Don't you want me to go?"

"Oh, yeh, course I do!"

"You didn't sound exactly enthusiastic."

Syd didn't try to look away, but said clearly, "I won't see you again for a long time, will I?"

Benson began to grin again; then he relaxed properly for the first time, took out a packet of cigarettes, lit one, and flicked the match across the little, shadowy room.

"So that's the trouble, is it? Don't want to lose me again, eh? Well, you needn't, boyo. They can try to separate father and son, but we know a way of putting that right, don't we? You want to know something? There's just one little job you've got to do for me, and then we'll get aboard this ship together. You come as a cabin boy, like they did in the old days. Okay?"

Syd said gaspingly, "Can—can I really?"

"Think I'd lie to my own flesh and blood? Sure, you can come, I'll fix it. But don't forget that job you've got to do first, will you?"

"Just tell me what it is, and I'll do it!"

"That's the boy." Now, Benson's expression changed again, and the look in his eyes was hard and calculating; much as it had been when he had talked with Freddy Tisdale up in the furnished house in Millways. He stared for a long time, until the child began to shift his feet, uneasy and unsure of himself. "Okay, let's talk," Benson said abruptly. "How's your ma?"

"She—she's okay."

"She never talk about me?"

"Not—not much."

"She try to turn you against me?"

"No," said young Syd, because it did not occur to him that his father might want him to lie. "She only talks about you if—well, if something happens to remind her. Like the escape from the prison. That—Dad, it *was* your idea, wasn't it?"

"Mine and no one else's," Benson boasted.

"I knew it was! I told everybody at school it was you, and there was a chap named Lewis, he said it was Jingo Smith. I didn't half sock him one!"

"That's the ticket," Benson said, with deep satisfaction. "Anyone says anything you don't like, sock him one. It was me who thought up that escape, and don't you forget it. And I'll get the two of us on that ship going to South America, don't you forget that, either. Your ma get those headaches like she used to?"

"Sometimes."

"Still take aspirins?"

"Yes." Syd looked puzzled, but didn't ask a question.

"Just goes on the same way, eh? This guy she's got living with her, you like him?"

"I—I don't know who you mean."

"This Small, Art Small." Benson was impatient.

"Oh, him," said Syd disparagingly. "He don't live at home, but he comes round most nights, so he might just as well. If he don't come home, she goes out with him to the pictures or somewhere."

"Like him?"

Syd answered slowly, as if he hadn't given the matter any thought at all: "Well, no, not exactly."

"Okay, forget him. What about your sister? She okay?"

"Oh, yeh, she's fine."

"Get on all right with you, does she?"

"She's okay," Syd said; "she's like anyone else's sister; you know what sisters are like."

Benson grinned.

"That's where you're wrong, son, I never had a sister. Never had a ma or a pa, either. Orphan brat, that's what I was. Had to fend for myself from the time I was nine, and don't you forget it. That's how I came to know the best way to look after Number One. Now, listen to me, boyo. You're going back home, see. You're not to tell your ma or anyone else you've seen me. Just say you've been holding out in Charlie Mulliver's place, the police won't worry much about Charlie. Just go home and be yourself, see. Don't talk about me to anyone, just be yourself, just look as if you knew you was going to stay there for the rest of your life. You've gone back because you didn't see the pay-off for you if you stayed away. Got all that, Syd?"

The boy was eager.

"Yeh!"

"That's fine. And listen. You say your ma still gets those headaches and takes aspirins?"

"Like I told you."

"That's fine. Well, I'm going to give you some special aspirin tablets, boyo, and you're going to look after them until you get back. First time your ma says she wants an aspirin, you go and get them for her, see, and you give her one of the tablets I'm going to give you. Got that? One or two, makes no odds, but she's to have them instead of the aspirins."

Syd, his eagerness slightly dulled by a kind of bewilderment, asked slowly, "I can do that, okay, but why? Are they better than ordinary aspirins?"

"I'll say they are, son," said Benson; and now his expression was wholly evil, hard, vicious, in spite of the fact that his lips were twisted into a smile. "They're tons better. She'll go right off to sleep, see, and then you can sneak out of the house and come right back here to me. She just won't hear you, that's a fact. We'll get off on that ship for South America right away, then. You understand?"

The boy's eyes held a light which they had never shown before. He could not speak, could only nod. When his father held out a little bottle in which were two white tablets which looked like aspirins, he took the bottle and put it in his pocket without saying a word. He was swamped by emotion again, but not so helplessly as before, and this time he forced it back by his own efforts.

Benson gripped his shoulder with that same painful tightness.

"Okay, boyo?"

"Sure."

"That's fine," said Benson, but he didn't relax his grip. "Now listen, son. The police will ask you a lot of questions, you know what these perishing dicks are like. So they ask you questions. You don't tell them a thing. You didn't see me, you haven't heard from home, you just stayed at Charlie's place, until you realized there was no future in it. Understand?" Now his grip was really painful, and the boy drew in his breath but made no attempt to get clear. "Listen to me, boyo, if you so much as whisper that you've seen me, that trip's off, see. I won't wait for you, I'll go on my own. Understand?"

"I wouldn't tell them if they *killed* me," young Syd said.

18 . Benson Talks

BENSON stayed at Charlie Mulliver's place for an hour after his son had gone, and then slipped along an alley and over some roofs to the warehouse, using a window which appeared to be locked from the outside, but had been rigged so that it could open easily. He had a bag with a packet of food, four bottles of beer, cigarettes, matches, chocolates, and a pack of playing cards. He was through the window in a moment, and stood by it, listening intently for several seconds; he heard no sound of anyone approaching.

He turned round.

There was a strong smell of petrol in the warehouse; thousands of gallons of petrol in forty-gallon metal drums were stored here. There were other fuel oils, too; the place would become a ready-made incinerator if a naked flame got near any of the oils. It was dark and gloomy except near the window, yet Benson did not use his flashlight. He picked his way over the metal drums, kicking against one now and again so that it gave off a deep booming note, but the window was closed and the warehouse was almost soundproof.

He reached a doorway which led to a pair of wooden steps, a big, square freight lift with open ironwork gates, which led to the floors above. He used the stairs and, as he neared the first landing, heard a whisper of sound. He tapped three times on the wooden handrail, and immediately the handrail quivered from Freddy Tisdale's responding taps. Then Freddy called softly:

"Everything okay?"

"Everything's fine."

"Got some grub?"

"Plenty."

Freddy said, "And can I use it!" He was at the first landing, and now he turned away, in the gloom, toward a little room which had once been used as an office but had not been needed for that purpose for a long time. On the floor along two sides of the walls were bundles of rags, making rough mattresses, and there were blankets for the men to throw over themselves at night. There was a small table, two packing cases to sit on, a candle in the neck of a beer bottle, and a safety lamp. The only light came from a small, frosted glass window set very high in the wall, and they lived here in a state of almost perpetual gloom.

Benson put the food on the table. Freddy tore at it, then opened a bottle of beer and tossed it down his throat; the gurgling seemed very loud. Looking at him, Benson saw the line of his neck, almost straight from his breastbones to the tip of his chin. A funny thought occurred to Benson, then: that a knife laid against that throat would make the flesh twang like tightly stretched wire being cut.

Freddy gasped as he put the bottle down.

"That's better," he said thickly; "plenty more where it came from?"

"Enough," said Benson.

They ate; they lit cigarettes; and they sat against the walls, facing each other. Freddy started several different subjects of conversation, but they all fell flat. Then he asked if Benson had seen the kid.

"Sure," Benson said.

"He okay?"

"He's fine," said Benson, "he's the way I like him." There was a new, vibrant note in his voice, a depth of feeling different from anything which Freddy Tisdale had heard before. In spite of the gloom, he could see the way Benson's eyes glistened, and he sensed something of what was going on in the other man's mind.

Then Benson began to talk.

He had never talked so freely as this about any subject; just uttered a word or the clipped sentences, and lapsed into long periods of silence. Now he talked as if whisky had loosened his tongue, but there was no whisky on his breath, there was just the spirit of that boy. He talked, not knowing it, with all the pent-up love that he felt for his son, and all he had ever dreamed for him, all that had lain buried so long in his subconscious mind now came out and took possession of him.

And Freddy Tisdale listened, fascinated at first.

At last, Benson stopped. He picked up a bottle of beer, smacked it sharply against the table and knocked the neck off, and then put it to his lips, as if it did not occur to him that the broken glass would cut him.

He drank deeply.

"That's the way it goes," he said clearly. "That boy's a chip off the old block, and no mistake. Give him ten years and he'll be as good as his father. That boy's got a future, Freddy, you can take it from me. Wouldn't I like to have seen him growing up, instead of letting that—"

He broke off.

He gave the twisted, hateful smile.

"Well, she's got hers," he said.

He stopped speaking, put a cigarette to his lips and then lit it. He watched the match burn out, unwinking. He did not appear to notice that Freddy had gone very still and quiet. Freddy was staring at him; and after a while Benson looked round, saw that, and asked in a harsh voice,

"Seen enough?"

"Syd," said Freddy, and gulped and broke off. Now Benson sat there, with the empty beer bottle in his hand, and the broken neck with its jagged edges pointing toward Freddy; it had once been his favorite form of weapon.

"What's biting you?"

Freddy said, "Syd, you—you haven't been there and killed her?"

Benson stared in turn, and then let his arm fall; he banged the thick end of the bottle on the table and began to laugh. The fact that he laughed aloud the first time since they had broken out of prison told Freddy a great deal about the state of his nerves: how tense they were and how easy it might be to break them.

"Strike me," he said at last, "what do you think *I* am? Go and see the old So-and-so? Me? With Gideon and half the flippin' police on the doorstep? Have some sense, Freddy boy, have some sense!"

"But you said—"

"I said she's got hers, and that's what I meant," Benson told him, "*and* I gave it to her. But not the way you think, son, not the way anyone thinks. Like to know how I fixed it?" He laughed again, but this time there was an edge to the laughter, and it came out slowly, as if he were not quite sure that it was wise to laugh or to talk. Abruptly: "The kid'll fix it."

Freddy caught his breath.

"*Young* Syd?"

"Any complaint?"

"You can't trust a kid like that to croak his own mother; even if he was pleased to see you, he—"

Benson said, "Stow it. He was pleased to see me all right; and if I'd asked him, he'd have fixed her. But he's only a kid, ain't he? Think I'd want a kid to *know* he was going to do a thing like that? Not bloody likely! He's going to give her some aspirins, that's all, just a coupla aspirins. He won't know what's happened to her. Why, the way these doctors and psychologists work these days they won't even tell him what happened, they'll just ask him where he got the aspirins from, that's all—even if they get round to that. Let me tell you something, Freddy. They're soft about kids, these days. The worst that can happen to him is a few years in Borstal, and that won't hurt him. It could do him a hell of a lot of good, the same way as it did me. Syd'll be okay. But Ruby'll know what it's like to be all twisted up inside before those aspirins have finished doing their job. What with her boy friend's face all burned off him, and—"

He broke off again.

Freddy said, in a strangely weak voice, "You know what you want, Syd, don't you?"

"And I get it."

Silence followed, and lasted for a long time. It was uneasy; sullen. The broken bottle stood on the table between them, the right way up; in Benson's pocket was the poultry knife. About them was the gloom of the dingy office, and below-stairs the barrels of petrol and other oils, the bare walls with the great hanging cobwebs, the spiders, the rats, the bats. Outside, just across the alley, was the little window of Charlie Mulliver's doss house, and beyond that the East End and Muskett Street—where Ruby Benson stood talking, not knowing, then, what was going to happen to Art Small that lunchtime.

Then, Freddy said, "Syd, you got everything laid on for that ship?"

"I told you, didn't I? Can't go wrong. The captain's drunk half the time, and he's brought so much snow into the country he daren't refuse me a passage—the five hundred each wasn't for him, it was to grease a lot of palms. Didn't anyone tell you that palms want greasing sometimes?"

Freddy forced a smile. "As if I didn't know."

"You know. I'll tell you what," went on Benson. He became expansive again, sitting back with his shoulders and his head against the wall, and a dreamy smile on his face; it touched him with the gentleness of what might have been. "We'll have a two-berth cabin on board, see? We'll ship as crew, but as soon as we're out at sea we'll be treated like favored passengers—the only two, in the bargain. The ship's carrying machine parts, and couldn't be cleaner. We'll live like fighting cocks, that's what we'll do, deck chairs and sunshine all day long, just a couple of bucks out on the sea voyage for the sake of their health. And when we get to Buenos Aires, o-kay! We find ourselves something to do. We find ourselves a couple of señoritas, too. You remember that skirt we used to know, back along? Spanish, she was, and—oh, boy!"

He stopped.

He didn't go on again, this time, but stayed there with the half-smile on his lips, his eyes nearly closed, just able to see Freddy between his lashes. Soon, with his eyes closed firmly, he looked as if he were asleep, breathing smoothly and without the slightest hint of a snore—a compact, handsome man with that black stubble and the deep lines of suffering and hardship at his mouth.

Freddy closed his eyes, too, but kept opening them again. Every now and again his lips tightened, and he seemed to be looking at Benson for something that he wasn't very sure about, something he couldn't be sure was there. He could not settle to a book, although there were several old paper-backed Westerns here.

Ruby Benson was back at Muskett Street.

A relief manager had been sent to the dress shop in the Mile End Road as soon as the news of the attack on Arthur Small had been reported. He had sent Ruby home at once, full of reassurance and understanding; she wasn't to worry, she was to stay away from business until this period of anxiety was over; she needn't have a care in the world. There was no need for him to provide an escort, for four policemen were now outside the shop; and wherever one looked, on the way from the Mile End Road to Muskett Street, it seemed as if there was a policeman. In fact there were three in Muskett Street, and two of them went into the little house and looked in every room before Ruby was allowed to go in. That was in spite of the fact that the house had been under surveillance day and night for nearly five days.

That had been at two o'clock.

Liz had been on her way back to school, and Ruby hadn't tried to get her back.

At a quarter past two, a policeman came hurrying across the road, and she saw him through the front-room window. She was in there, hardly knowing what she was doing, wishing that she was with Art Small, knowing it would be no use waiting at the hospital. He might lose his sight, and he might die. She did not think consciously of her husband; she was obsessed by anxiety for the man who had brought so much brightness into her life.

Then the policeman outside knocked sharply.

Ruby got up, hesitated, and moved slowly toward the passage, then toward the front door. She knew that this could mean trouble, and it could also mean good news. She felt a sharp pain at her side as she thought of that, and pressed a hand against her aching head.

She had never had a worse headache.

It showed in her glassy eyes and in the twitching nerves at the corners of her eyes. The bang at the front door seemed to go right through her, making the pain much worse. Then she managed to make herself step forward, and opened the door.

The middle-aged policeman standing on the doorstep looked really excited.

Had the police caught *him*? Hope flared.

"Your boy's okay, Mrs. Benson," the policeman said quickly. "He's on his way here now, just turned the corner." His eagerness faded when he saw

Ruby's expression and guessed at the pain she felt, but he went on: "Hope I'm not talking out of turn, but mind if I suggest something?"

"*Syd's* coming back? Young Syd?" Ruby felt a sudden relief, a kind of gladness. So her son could ease the pressure of her despair.

"Nearly here now, Mrs. Benson," the policeman said, "and if you'll take a tip from me you won't go for him too much for running away. Treat him gently now, and it might make all the difference."

She looked as if she hadn't heard a word.

"And he isn't hurt?"

"No," said the policeman, "he's all right, and—" He broke off, giving up his well-intentioned effort, and he watched her as she pushed past him, into the street. Her expression was very different from anything he had expected. Her eyes didn't glow, but there was no anger in them, and for the first time he realized what a good-looking girl Mrs. Benson must have been when she was young.

She stared along the street.

Young Syd was coming toward her, at the side of a plain-clothes man. His head was held high, and he walked defiantly. Ruby caught her breath, for he looked so like big Syd when she had first met him; as if he were prepared to look the world in the face, and nothing could keep him down.

She found herself hurrying.

"Syd, oh, Syd . . ."

He didn't break into a run. He did nothing to suggest that he was pleased to see her. When she bent down and took him in her arms, he didn't yield, as once he had, but kept his body stiff and aloof. She realized that, and it marred the relief of his return. She realized—or told herself that she did— that it would be a long time before she won his confidence again, that she would have to be very, very careful about the way she treated him.

She took him in.

"What's the matter, Mum?" he asked. "You got a headache?"

She wondered if he cared whether she had a headache or not, and couldn't quite understand the sharpness in his voice.

"A bit of one," she said.

"I'll get you an aspirin, I know where . . ."

"I took two just before you came in," Ruby said; "I won't take any more yet, Syd. Syd, where—" She checked herself; questions could come later, just now she had to try to win him over. For although she did not know where he had been, she realized that he had really gone chasing after his dream—that if he could have found him, he would have run off to see his father. "Are you hungry, Syd?" she asked quietly. "What would you like to eat?"

At half past four, Liz arrived, bursting into the house and hugging Syd. At twenty to five, Gideon arrived.

19 . The Truth?

GIDEON had come straight from Charlie Mulliver, and he was a long way from certain that Charlie had told the simple truth. There was something worrying Charlie, and it might easily have to do with young Syd. Gideon hadn't said or done anything to suggest that he was not satisfied that all Charlie had done was to give the runaway shelter, but after he had left he had called the Yard on his walkie-talkie radio.

"Give me Chief Inspector Lemaitre . . .

"Lem, George here. Have a word with the Division and tell them to check on Charlie Mulliver's place, will you? Don't give themselves away more than they can help, but just check who's been in and out of there lately."

"You got something, George?"

"Could have," said Gideon, and rang off.

Ten minutes later, he was entering the little house in Muskett Street. He had the latest report from the hospital about Arthur Small, and it was reasonably good; he expected Ruby to make difficulties when he started to question the boy, but whether she liked it or not, that had to be done.

The sight of half a dozen policemen in the street depressed him; it should not be necessary to have so many; the attack on Small had put the breeze up all of them; not excluding Commander Gideon, although he hoped that no one but Lemaitre had guessed that.

A policeman was just outside the house, another hovering behind the starched lace curtains of the front room. The policeman outside saluted and the man inside called something, and disappeared. A moment later, he opened the door. As he did so, Ruby Benson came hurrying from the kitchen, wiping her hands on a pink apron and then stretching behind her back to unfasten it. Something made her stop. The apron fell, crumpled, about her waist, and she stood squarely in the small passage, looking up at Gideon with the kind of defiance he had half expected.

"I don't want the children to hear what we say," she said; "they've had enough trouble already."

Gideon said, "All right, Mrs. Benson" in his mildest voice. "Where shall we go?"

She pointed to the front room, and followed him in. The constable closed the door. Outside, there was Gideon's shiny car and more policemen and the curious neighbors—men, women and children. Outside, somewhere probably within easy reach of this house, was Syd Benson, the killer, the seeker of vengeance. His wife's face now held all the strain that it had shown years before, at the time of the trial. The youthfulness had faded. Even her hair seemed flat and lifeless, and the sparkle was gone from her eyes. It was a pathetic, almost a shocking sight.

Gideon knew her well enough to know that she was going to fight for what she wanted, no matter what he said: as she had fought before, to make the terrible decision to give evidence against her husband.

She said flatly, "You're not going to pester the life out of that boy."

Gideon held his felt hat loosely in both hands, in front of him. The woman didn't come much higher than his shoulder, and he probably weighed twice as much as she.

His head was only inches from the ceiling, so he dwarfed both her and the room.

"No," he agreed, "that's the last thing I want to do, Mrs. Benson, but I must talk to him."

"That's the same thing."

Gideon said, "I've talked to you. Have I pestered you?"

She didn't answer.

"Listen," Gideon said, "I've six children of my own. *Six.*" He gave a little, wry grin, and she was so surprised that momentarily she relaxed. "Quite a handful. The eldest is twenty-six, the youngest a year or two younger than young Syd. I know children from the nappy stage upward. I know what they think like and what they feel like, and I know that if you start raising your voice at a boy like your son, and drive him into a corner, all you get is defiance and probably lies."

She didn't speak when he stopped.

"He ran away for one of two possible reasons," Gideon went on very steadily, "and the first is probably the right one. The television show upset him, and he was so riled at me and the fact that you seemed to be on my side, that he couldn't stand it any longer. Lots of children take a run like that—good Lord, I don't have to tell *you!* If that was it, then it's over. He's let off steam, and now he's come back under his own. You couldn't ask any more."

She asked, "What's the other possible reason?"

"He could have been to see his father."

Her face was suddenly twisted with alarm. "Oh, no!"

"Well, I don't think it's likely, either," said Gideon, "but we've got to find out, Mrs. Benson, and I think you and I are the people most likely to get at the facts. Think you can tell when he's lying?"

She didn't answer.

She didn't cry, "Yes, of course!" or attempt in any way to spring to the defense of her son. It was an odd thing, Gideon reflected gloomily, that she should be so absolutely honest, so naturally good. What had brought her to marry a man like Benson? The question was as fleeting as the thought.

"Sometimes I'm not sure," she said.

"Well, let's try."

"All right. Do you—" She hesitated, and then turned away without finishing what she was going to say. "We might as well get it over. I was just making some pastry for supper, he likes hot pastry." What a story that told! And so did her tense, anxious plea: "Go easy with him, won't you?"

"You know I will," said Gideon. "By the way, I called the hospital up just before I came. Mr. Small's eye will be saved, and the scarring shouldn't be too bad."

At the closed door, Ruby turned to face Gideon, and there was a different expression in her eyes.

"Listen," she said quietly, "if it hadn't been for that man Abbott, Art would have got it full in the face. I know, I saw it happen. So don't blame Abbott, see."

Gideon couldn't find a word to say.

All the hostility which young Syd had shown toward Gideon a few days before revealed itself again. The boy stood with his face to the kitchen window, so that Gideon could see every feature, every line. He was struck, as everyone must have been, by the likeness between father and son, even to the set of the jaw and the tightness of the lips; and the defiance. Gideon had the uneasiest of feelings: not only that whatever the boy said couldn't be relied on, but that something had happened within him. It might be something that he had experienced while he was in hiding; it might be simply the effect of the television show and what was happening to him now. And his hatred, his resentment, viciousness, because of his frustrated love for his father, might be centered on Gideon.

"I just went to Charlie's," he insisted flatly.

"Why?"

"Knew he'd let me stay."

"Been there before?"

"Done jobs for him."

"How did you get there?"

"Hid in a van."

"What van?"

"Builder's van," Syd almost sneered. "It was in the yard."

"Anyone know you were there?"

"Course not. It stopped down Mile End Road, and I got out and went to Charlie's."

"See anyone else there?"

"You try staying at Charlie's without seeing plenty."

"See your father?" Gideon asked, in the same flat voice.

There was a pause; just a startled moment of hesitation, when the expression in young Syd's face might have been taken two ways: that he had seen his father, or else that he was astounded at the possibility that anyone should have thought he had.

Then: "No!" he burst out. "Course not!"

"Syd," said Gideon very firmly, "that's a lie."

Young Syd said, "You cops, you can't tell a lie from the other thing. You took him away from me, and now you're hunting him like a dog, that's what you're doing. Don't you talk to me!"

"Syd, where did you see your father?"

Young Syd's eyes blazed, his lips quivered, his hands were clenched and raised.

"I didn't see him, think I don't know what you're trying to do? Trying to frame me, the same way as you framed him, that's what. You dirty rotten beast, don't you talk to me!"

"Think he has seen him?" Gideon asked Ruby Benson a few minutes later. She didn't answer at once.

Her eyes were like glass, and the rims were so red that they looked painful. Gideon doubted whether she had had a good night's sleep since Benson had escaped; or would have one until he was caught. He could tell simply by looking at her that she had a splitting headache; the crisis of the past few minutes had made it far worse. She put a hand to her forehead and pressed, as if to relieve the pain, and then said:

"I don't know; that's God's truth, I don't know."

"Is there anyone who might be able to get the truth out of him?"

"If he doesn't want to tell you, wild horses wouldn't drag it out of him," Ruby said; "he's just like his father in that respect. Just like Syd."

The simple boy, Simon, sitting in a comfortable chair at the Divisional H.Q., with a cup of milk and some chocolate biscuits beside him, stared at Gideon without smiling; blankly. Chocolate smeared his lips—lips which were never really dry. His small eyes were pale and weak, and the puffy eyelids were scabby. He had hardly any eyelashes, just a few fair hairs. His fat, flabby face looked as if the flesh was unhealthy, as well as the poor mind.

With him was a short, gray-haired man wearing a brown Harris tweed suit with the cuffs and elbows patched with leather—a master from the special school where this boy went. The master had told the Divisional Superintendent, who in turn had told Gideon, that sometimes Simon could talk so that almost anyone could understand him, but that under any kind of pressure his precarious control of his mind deserted him, and he could do little more than make grunting sounds.

"How long do you think it will be before he'll talk intelligibly again?" Gideon asked, but he felt hopeless.

"There's no way of telling," said the schoolmaster. "I know what I'd do, but you can't possibly do it."

"What's that?"

"I'd let him go home, that's all. He lives with his mother, who's out charring mornings and afternoons, to keep the two going. If he were settled in familiar surroundings, and allowed to go to school again, I think he'd be all right in a day or two. Normal surroundings help him—like the company of normal children. That's why he and two or three other afflicted boys are allowed in the playground of the big school. They don't feel so lonely, then. If Simon is kept here, or anywhere unfamiliar—well, this mental blankness might go on for days or weeks. It's a kind of paralysis due to shock; in some ways he's much more sensitive than the average person."

The schoolmaster seemed to plead.

Gideon said reluctantly, "Well, the best we can possibly do is to have him looked after—can't let someone who's been tossing acid about run loose. He might do it again, might do anything."

"I know."

"Who'd be most likely to know where he got the stuff from?" Gideon asked.

"I don't know," said the schoolmaster. "He was at the special school this morning, so I should think that someone gave it to him when he was going out for lunch. He had sandwiches. I questioned all the school this afternoon, but no one seems to have noticed him talking to anyone; all we know is that he was down by the docks. He often is—he loves to see the ships go out and come in. No one stops him, it's remarkable how kindly people are to someone like him."

"I suppose so," said Gideon. "Well, we'll be guided by what the doctors say; the one thing you can be sure about is that he won't be ill-treated."

"Oh, I know that," said the schoolmaster. They turned and walked away from Si, who blinked after them, and then picked up his cup of milk with a limp hand; he spilled a little onto his trousers and dribbled some down his chin, but he didn't seem to notice. A police nurse, behind him, just sat and watched.

In the next room, Gideon asked the schoolmaster, "Do you know anything about young Syd Benson?"

"Oh, yes, I teach special subjects at his school, and I've taught him for several years."

"What's he like?"

The schoolmaster answered very slowly, "He's got a good mind, as sharp as anyone's at the school. If he likes a subject, he's way out in front. If he doesn't, he makes no effort at all."

"What's his general character like?"

"Tenacious."

"Honest?"

The schoolmaster said painfully, "That's a very difficult question to answer, Commander. What is honesty in a boy like that? What is loyalty? To his mother or his father? I don't know. If you mean, does he actually steal from his classmates—no. If you mean does he fight to get what he wants, and force weaker children to give in to him—yes. We've a dozen children at the school who have a father—sometimes father *and* mother—who aren't strangers to prison. Some of their children are good, some pretty hopeless. The simple truth is that with such a background they acquire different standards of normal behavior—of right and wrong, if you like. No child will ever believe that something his mother or his father does habitually is wicked. The child just assumes that his father is right, and the rest of the world is wrong. That's how you get generation after generation of criminals. Commander—they're bred less by conditions than by the attitude of mind of their parents. As for young Syd—well, I didn't know him much before his father went to prison. I know he was sullen for twelve months afterward, and then seemed to start getting on top of himself. But it was a common thing to hear him talk about 'when my dad comes out'—and could I, could any of the teaching staff, discourage him?"

Gideon said gruffly, "I know the problem."

"I'm sure you do," said the schoolmaster. "I only wish I could help you now. The woman I feel so sorry for is Mrs. Benson; now she *has* had a raw deal. The way she's brought those two children up—well, young Liz is a model example. Sometimes I think this talk of environment and the attitude of the parents is all poppycock, even though I dish it out myself! I begin to wonder whether some children are born with a kink, and others with a natural goodness. There couldn't be two more different children than the Bensons. How *is* Mrs. Benson?"

"Looking as if she'll crack up if we don't catch Benson soon," said Gideon, "but I think we will, Mr. Thomas. Thanks very much for all you've told me."

After Gideon had gone, after supper, during the evening, Ruby Benson sensed that her son's eyes were on her all the time, watching her, lynx-like, as if he wanted to know what she was going to do next.

And three times he asked her how her headache was.

She kept saying, "I've had worse," but that was hardly true. Soon, she would get the children to bed and then go herself, although she knew it would be impossible to sleep. When she lay down, she would have some more aspirins.

Unless her head got worse, then she would have them sooner.

20 . Night

BY HALF past seven, it was pitch dark. Except in the main roads, the East End of London is not well lit.

Patches of bright lights glowing in the sky from the docks, where ships were being worked under arc lights, showed up clearly. The colored lights from cinemas showed up, too, red or blue, green or yellow, bright against the gray darkness of the sky.

It was a cloudy night.

In the little streets, so drab and mean, there was an uneasy quiet, a stillness which wasn't normal. Every now and again there was such a night as this, when the police of the Division had been reinforced by hundreds of men from outside, and the whole of the district was combed. The people knew why. Not more than one in a hundred had ever committed a felony or committed a crime of any kind—but one in five, perhaps even a greater proportion, knew someone who had: a friend, a relation, a husband, wife or daughter, brother or child.

The whole district knew the story of Benson and his wife, of Arthur Small, the missing boy and his return. None of them took Benson's part—except, perhaps, one or two like Charlie Mulliver, who knew which side their bread was buttered on. Benson's record had been widely known long before his trial; most people knew that he had been lucky not to be sentenced to death. The story of the murder of Taffy Jones in the car park had gone through the East End—as through much of the country—carrying with it a shiver of horror. Everyone knew, now, that Benson would kill rather than be taken, and there was a full realization among the people of the East End that he would almost certainly make an attempt to kill his wife.

The police came from other Divisions and from Scotland Yard, not in petty numbers but in their hundreds. They arrived by car, on bicycles, by bus, in Black Marias. They were watched, at certain focal points, by quiet crowds, and the temper of the district was best shown by the fact that there were few catcalls, little derision.

Under instructions from Divisional officers who knew the district inside out, the great search began.

There were private homes by the hundreds where Benson might be hiding, but Gideon and the Divisional people doubted if he were in such a place; someone was likely to squeal, someone would be glad of the few pounds blood money that he would earn. Benson wasn't likely to trust himself to any man unless he could rely on him absolutely—and those on whom he could rely, as far as Gideon knew, were being watched; that night, their homes would be searched first.

Quietly, the police went about their business.

As quietly, there was an exodus from the East End; not so big and not so noticeable, but quite as purposeful. For if this Division was being strengthened by reinforcements, then the neighboring Divisions were being correspondingly weakened, which made a heaven-sent opportunity for burglary. Every man who could force a window or open a door was on the move that night. Next day, the results of all this would show in the report placed before Gideon. And he knew exactly what was happening, but could do nothing about it.

If Benson was in London, he had to be caught tonight.

They searched Charlie Mulliver's place again; there was no result, nothing to suggest that Benson and Tisdale had been there.

They searched every room occupied by known friends of Benson; with no result.

They searched the docks; the warehouses; ships, small boats which were covered up in the backwaters; barges; lighters; dock installations; factories; empty houses and big warehouses away from the river.

They had a master plan of each part of the district, which spread over the whole of a great wall in the basement of G5 Headquarters; and here Gideon and the Divisional Superintendent, Simpson, with Chief Inspector Trabert who had been with them the previous night, watched quietly, saying little, seeing how the police were closing in. It wasn't the first such raid and it wouldn't be the last, but from each one the police learned something. This time, they had started on the perimeter of the district—the river on one side, and the main roads on the other, and went through it methodically. A second cordon was placed round this whole area on a wider radius —on the other side of the river, for instance, where anyone who sneaked across in an unlighted boat was bound to be noticed. But the river police were not patrolling openly; that was in the hope of luring Benson to the river if he was driven out of his hiding place.

No one could be sure whether Benson knew about the search or not; but even if he didn't know, he might guess.

As it happened, the old warehouse now used for temporary storage of petrol and other oils in drums was almost in the center of the area being searched, and the police were gradually closing in on it. As reports came in by telephone, radio and messengers, so flags of different colors were moved on the maps; and the precision of the raid was such that it looked like a continually narrowing circle.

Gideon was smoking his big pipe.

For once, this chase was the only job on his mind; obsessional. Deep down, he had the glum feeling that he might have made a mistake, that Benson might not be here. It was even possible that young Syd's disappearance and the attack on Small had been to fool him—Benson might be somewhere else, out on the outskirts of London perhaps, or at one of the ports, laughing his head off.

Only, Benson seldom laughed.

Three reports came in in quick succession from a Squad numbered, for the occasion, as South 21. They were coming up from the river, working their way through warehouses, and reporting each warehouse or large building that they had checked. Gideon, standing by the map, watched the Superintendent move a green flag from one warehouse to a line which showed another.

"That's near Rum Corner, isn't it?" he asked.

"Yes."

Gideon nodded, and drew at his pipe. Rum Corner was plumb in the center of the area being searched.

In London, not far away, Mary Rose was lying awake, tears stinging her eyes. Her brother lay asleep in the remand cell at Brixton Prison. Her mother lay, also asleep, in the next room. A mile or two away, Mrs. Edmundsun, so newly widowed, was looking at travel brochures, and every now and again at the scintillations from a pair of diamond earrings which had come to her only that afternoon. Detective-Sergeant Cummings, a bachelor who lived with a widowed mother, sat in his bedroom-cum-office at home, and smoked, and concentrated on everything he knew about Elliott, Edmundsun's manager. In another direction, Abbott lay, awake, feeling viciously angry with himself but a little easier in his mind now, because a message had come in—via Gideon, although he didn't know it—that Mrs. Benson had seen the attack, and had sent a message thanking him for helping to save her Arthur's sight. Arthur Small himself lay unconscious, under drugs, with a bandage round his head covering one eye. The two men who had broken into Kelly's Bank, earlier that week, were together in a room with some floorboards up, where a fortune in notes was hidden; they took some out and then replaced the floorboards—for the first time they were beginning to feel safe. Only half a mile away from them, Chief Inspector Lemaitre was looking at his blonde wife, and listening to her strident complaints. He was nearer revolt against her perpetual nagging than he had ever been; and one of the reasons for that was that he wanted to be on duty with Gideon.

In their different prisons, the other seven men who had escaped from Millways were sleeping; and the only one who would wake with a reasonably light heart was Matt Owens, who knew that when Gideon said he would make things easy, he would make them easy. At the Yard, the Information Room was a constant buzz of noise as reports of burglaries started to come in; Squad cars were hurtling round London, the Divisions were up to their eyes in work, and Sergeant Jefferson was quietly making notes, ready for the report that Gideon would want to see next morning. In his house, Superintendent Wrexall was very pleased with himself; for he was to go out to Guildford next day, about the accountant who had died an "accidental" death which might prove to be suicide. Wrexall had real cause for satisfaction, for one of the dead man's clerks had said that he thought that the accountant had been blackmailed; which proved that Wrexall's nose for blackmail was as good as ever. At Hurlingham, Kate Gideon was still up, and kept looking at the clock. It was a new, or at least a long absent feeling, to be worried about her husband; but after his narrow escape last night, she would be worried until they had caught Benson; and she knew how much the capture mattered to George.

The five Gideon children in the house were asleep.

Ruby Benson wasn't yet in bed, for the night held terrors for her. By the side of her bed, placed there with unexpected and touching solicitude by her son, were two white tablets. Soon, she would make herself take a milk drink, and take them.

Benson and Tisdale were awake.

Freddy Tisdale stood at the side of the window of the little office, looking sideways along the narrow alley toward a road which led to the docks. He had been there several times in the past hour, and when he wasn't standing there, Benson was. There had been no message of any kind for the past two hours; then, Charlie Mulliver had placed a lighted candle in the window opposite, a sign that the police had searched there and gone away.

In other words, all clear.

But it wasn't all clear.

Benson and Tisdale knew that, although they had not spoken of it. There

were too many noises. Cars coming and going, men walking, the *st-st-st-st-st*
of motorcycles which were being increasingly used by the police in London.
It was possible to sense when the police were out in strength, and, without
stepping outside the warehouse, these two knew it. Benson had seen one
little group of police move in a body past the end of the street in one direction; Tisdale had seen another group at the other end of the street.

And they had heard men walking about in a warehouse adjacent to this.

Benson went out, suddenly, crept down the stairs, and reached the barrels
of petrol. The screw cap of one filler hole was loose. He took it off, then
rolled the barrel over until petrol spilled out, the smell almost choking him.

He went back to the office.

Tisdale moved away from the window, and spoke in a hoarse, spluttering
whisper: "How do we know they're looking for us?"

"That's right," said Benson.

"Don't just sit there, what are we going to do?"

Benson said, "We're just going to sit here until they come. The streets
are lousy with them, we wouldn't have a chance out there. When they
start coming in, we go up to the roof. Then—"

"They'll search the roof!"

"Listen, Freddy," Benson said, "you wouldn't be losing your nerve, would
you?" When Freddy Tisdale didn't answer, he went on: "If we run for it
now we'll be seen, and we'll never get on board that ship. Now—"

"We ought to have gone earlier, we stayed too long."

Benson said coldly, "We stayed because I arranged it, and because the
ship doesn't sail until the morning tide. We go aboard at the last minute,
see, we don't hang around. One of the crew might recognize us, or there
might be some river police taking a peek. They don't leave anything to
chance, and you know it." In his harsh, clipped voice, Benson seemed to be
talking sense; and to be steadying Freddy. "Now, listen. We go up to the
roof. We jump across to the roof next door. It's a three-yard gap, and we
could do it blindfolded. They've been there, haven't they?"

Freddy muttered, "Yes. But if they leave a man outside, watching . . ."

"And what if they don't?" asked Benson. "Can you tell me any way we can
do it without taking risks?"

"If you hadn't seen your kid they might not have known we were in
London, they—"

Benson moved, swiftly, savagely. Freddy gave a startled squeak of alarm.
Benson gripped his wrist, so tightly that Freddy couldn't move his arm without risking a broken bone. In that moment they were at the level of beasts;
and Benson was deadly.

"That kid didn't squeal, understand? If you say that kid squealed—"

"I didn't say it! I meant if we'd left here last night instead of tonight . . ."

"The cops can get a warrant to search a ship any time they like, or they can send the customs men on board," Benson growled. He still gripped Freddy's wrist hurtfully. "If we'd gone aboard, we'd be caught by now, every ship in the docks has been searched tonight. If you used your brains you'd know that. You going to listen to me?"

"Ye—es," Tisdale muttered.

"Okay." Benson let the man's arm fall. "If they come in here, we go up to the roof and jump. We wait until they leave here, and then we jump back. They'll know we've been here, and they'll search everywhere else, understand? They won't expect us back."

Freddy muttered, "We haven't got a chance, and you know it."

"We've got a chance if you keep your nerve," said Benson. "Okay, let's . . ."

Then they heard footsteps coming along the alley. They stood quite still. The footsteps were slow and deliberate, of policemen. They could tell that there were five or six men out there, walking in single file, going toward the main doors of the warehouse.

Freddy began to shiver.

Benson said, "Okay, Freddy, let's go," in a soft voice, and he took Freddy's arm and led the way toward the stairs. It wasn't the first time he had known a thing like this: some men were as brave as men could be when they were on the run, but once they were cornered, they lost their nerve. Like Freddy. In these past few minutes, Benson had realized that Freddy's nerve was cracking, and that he would be a passenger from now on.

Benson couldn't afford a passenger.

But he did nothing yet.

They went slowly, stealthily, up the wooden stairs. They heard muffled sounds below. They opened the hatch which led to the roof, and looked about them. They saw the gaunt outline of the roof of the adjoining warehouse, shown up clearly by the glow from the docks, where a ship was taking on the last of its cargo before closing the hatches and setting off across the Atlantic for Buenos Aires.

No policemen were on the roof.

Benson said, "You go first." They had studied the spot, and knew exactly what to do. There were a few yards to spare, so that they could get in a short run before they leaped. Freddy, his teeth chattering now, made ready to run. Benson watched him, quite coldly, knowing exactly what he was going to do. Once on the other side, he would use his knife to silence Freddy.

He also had a gun, which Charlie had obtained for him; if he were cornered, he would use the seven bullets in it for the police.

He knew, deep down, that he had always intended to go away alone.

But he didn't want Freddy's body found on this roof; better leave it on the other, which had already been searched.

Freddy started to run. Benson could hear his hissing breath, knew that he was really frightened, his nerve quite gone. There was one good thing, he couldn't miss the opposite roof—anyone could clear ten feet even from a standing start.

He saw Freddy falter, at the last split second.

He realized that Freddy just hadn't the nerve to jump, and that was all about it.

He rushed forward, but he was seconds too late. On the roof of the other warehouse, two policemen had suddenly appeared. Freddy had seen them first, and Benson had been so busy watching him that he hadn't noticed. Now they were clambering toward the edge, and suddenly a whistle shrilled out in warning to the police below.

And Freddy Tisdale, trying to check himself, was so close to the edge that he slipped.

He screamed as he crashed down.

Benson swung round, as the scream rose to the night sky.

The glow of light showed the roofs of the warehouses clearly, and revealed policemen springing up on several of them, men who had stayed on the roofs of the warehouses which had been searched, so as to watch the street and to give warning.

Benson's only chance was to go down the stairs. It wasn't really a chance, probably no one else would have tried to take it. But he ran, drawing the gun from his pocket as he went.

In the room at the Divisional H.Q. Gideon saw the glitter in the eyes of a radio operator who was receiving a message from a Squad outside, and heard the shrillness of his voice:

"Tisdale's fallen off a roof! Benson's at the old Subra Warehouse."

"Come on," said Gideon.

Ruby Benson was standing in front of the gas stove, in a dressing gown which Art Small had given her, small feet in heelless slippers. She was watching the milk as it heated. The two white tablets hadn't been touched.

21 . Last Throw

BENSON reached the landing of the second floor of the warehouse as the police reached it from below. There were three of them, and he had a split second's advantage, because he was sidling close to the wall and they were rushing up, two men level with each other and the third just behind. Others were below. Whistles were shrilling, men shouting, someone fell over an empty barrel and the booming sound echoed clearly.

Benson jumped forward.

He fired three times, and scored two hits, wounding the same startled policeman in the leg and the waist. This man lost his balance and fell against the others, and as they were pushed to one side Benson leaped past them. He reached the half-landing, turned, and fired again as one of the men picked himself up and prepared to leap down the stairs. He didn't know whether he had scored a hit, but the man stopped. He went rushing toward the ground floor, and another policeman, clearly visible in the lights which were flashing from side to side, blocked his path. The man saw the gun and, without hesitation, flung himself to safety. Benson passed him, and then reached the big storage room, near the barrel which he'd partly emptied earlier, the reek of petrol still in his nostrils. He struck a match, and flung it at the pool of petrol.

The match went out.

Benson saw it go out, and knew that he hadn't a chance even of the vengeance he had wanted. So he stood close to the wall, watching the men who were momentarily wary of him, able to see those on the ground floor and anyone coming down the stairs. He slid his right hand into his pocket and took out a matchbox, opened the matchbox with one hand, then put it to his lips and tossed three tablets into his mouth. They were like the tablets he had sent to his wife.

That was the moment when the policeman who had lost his nerve found it again and leaped at the killer. He judged the moment to perfection and clutched Benson round the legs, clawing him down. The tablets spilled from Benson's lips, the gun went off and a bullet wasted itself.

Next moment, the cold steel handcuffs were on those sinewy wrists.

Gideon entered the warehouse about five minutes later, and already a lot had been done. Emergency lights had been rigged up from a car battery, the big ground floor was lit, not brightly but enough for everyone to be seen. A dozen uniformed and three plain-clothes police were standing about, and there was a stir as Gideon came in, with Trabert and Simpson close behind him; Simpson was a tall, bony man, and in this light he looked almost skeleton thin.

Benson was handcuffed to a burly detective-sergeant, and standing as erect as a man could be, feet firmly planted, shoulders back, eyes narrowed but glittering, mouth set tightly.

He didn't speak as Gideon came up.

Gideon said, "This was the way it had to end, Benson; why the hell didn't you have some sense?" His voice sounded tired; he wasn't tired, but fighting against showing his hatred for this man, determined to appear impartial instead of bitterly hostile. He paused, and looked at the killer for what seemed a long time, watched intently by all the rest. Then: "What did you say to your son this morning?"

He saw Benson start, and then begin to look incredulous.

Gideon went on: "The kid's young. If he goes on the way you've started him, he'll end up on the same place. Give him a break, Benson. What did you say to him?"

Benson said in a grating voice, "Did the kid squeal?"

It would have been so easy to say yes; to make him suffer this awful disappointment; to send him on his slow, laborious journey to the gallows with a new hate in his heart. Gideon knew all that, and could not bring himself to do it.

"No," he said, "he didn't squeal, but I happen to know children. What did you say to him?"

Benson didn't answer.

The light in his eyes was radiant.

Only a few hundred yards away, in the house in Muskett Street, Ruby Benson put the tablets into her mouth, and then sipped the hot milk.

When it was obvious that Benson wouldn't talk, and that Gideon had nothing more to say, the sergeant in charge started talking: How Benson had tried to take the tablets, two of which they had salvaged, one of which had been trodden under foot. How one wounded man was on the way to hospital, but not likely to be on the danger list. How a constable had defied Benson's gun, and collared him. All this, while Gideon looked about him, nodded at the policeman who had brought Benson down, in a way that he was likely to remember all his life, and looked at the tablets.

"Trying to kill himself, was he?" he asked. "What's in them, Benson?"

Benson's eyes still held that glow; that new, precious pride in the son who had not failed him. It was a form of exaltation. Gideon realized it, and felt a kind of nausea because it could come to this man and in this way.

"Come on, what's in them?" Gideon demanded.

Then Benson made his one mistake.

"Why don't you ask my wife?" he sneered.

Ruby Benson had been in bed for ten minutes, and was feeling a little queasy, when she heard the tires screech outside the house. She started up, staring toward the passage. A policeman was on duty in the front room, and she heard the door open, and heard his heavy footsteps. Next moment, a man strode in from the street, and spoke in a voice which she would never forget: Gideon's.

"Where's Mrs. Benson?"

"She—she's upstairs, sir, just gone to bed, she . . ."

Gideon didn't respond, except to start pounding along the passage and toward the stairs. Ruby clutched her silk nightdress tightly at the neck, and sat there, bewildered, feeling her heart race with heavy, throbbing beats. Gideon's footsteps thundered, the house shook, Liz and young Syd would be bound to wake.

Her door burst open.

Gideon drew up, at sight of her, gasping for breath. Then, more steadily, he moved toward her, and answered the question that was in her eyes.

"Yes, we've got him, it's all right. Did young Syd give you any tablets tonight? Aspirins, or . . ."

She raised her hands in sharp, stabbing alarm; and in that moment she told Gideon "yes" without having to utter the word. She saw the panic in his eyes as he went on urgently:

"Where are they?"

"They were aspirins! I've just taken—"

Gideon swung around toward the policeman behind him.

"Get some salt, mustard, make a strong emetic—and get a move on!" Now, his voice was controlled and calm, although it was obvious that he imposed the self-control with great difficulty. He was so big, so frightening, so full of menace. "It's all right," he told Ruby, "you'll bring them up and they won't do you any harm. Just a few unpleasant minutes. Benson gave them to young Syd—"

"Oh, no," she cried, "no, not young Syd, no!"

Gideon walked into his office, at ten o'clock next morning, and found Lemaitre and the Assistant Commissioner, Jefferson, Wrexall and two other superintendents all waiting for him. The morning report looked thick enough for a week instead of a day; Lemaitre had spread himself. Gideon grinned round, for a welcome like this could lift him out of depression, help him to forget the wounding of the evil things he fought.

Question and answer took twenty minutes until gradually the men left the office; and finally only Lemaitre, Gideon and the A.C. were there.

"There are about thirty newspapermen after you," the A.C. said; "I told them you'd hold a Press Conference!"

Gideon shrugged.

"Why don't we just give them a list of men on the Force? Then we'd all get some limelight." He loosened his collar as he rounded the desk, but he didn't sit down. "Benson won't say a word, of course; I don't think we'll get anything out of him now or later. Thank God his wife's all right, though."

"You say the tablets contained one of the opiates?"

"Yes. Mulliver says he got them from a ship's captain who sailed out yesterday morning. He'll be held when he reaches port. Mulliver supplied Benson with the gun, too. Still, Mrs. Benson's been lucky. She'll get over it all, of course; but she'll be a sight happier if we could prove that young Syd didn't know what was in them."

"Think he did?" asked the A.C. quietly.

"I don't know," said Gideon, "I just don't know. I don't want to think that he did; the thought that a kid of twelve would give his own mother— well, we'll have to work on him, that's all. Through the family doctor or his schoolteachers, or—" Gideon broke off, and shrugged. "Main thing is that Arthur Small will definitely be all right except for a scar which won't be too prominent."

"Good," said the A.C. "Good."

He went out, soon afterward; and Lemaitre, who was usually very subdued during the great man's presence, relaxed at once and jumped up. He squashed out a cigarette and started to take out another.

"Wish to hell I'd been able to get there, but you know what it's like with Fifi." Gideon not only knew what it was like, but realized that they must have patched up their latest quarrel, for Lemaitre showed none of the sourness that was too often in his voice when he talked of his wife. "Well, we can sit back and take it easy, now the whole bunch is caught."

Gideon looked at the report.

"Who's been kidding you?" he asked dryly.

"Oh, that's only routine," said Lemaitre. "Every man who can force a door must have been busy last night, but there was no big stuff taken. They picked up Jim Ree again, had his rope ladder ready at a place in Grosvenor Square. It's all there in the report, anyway. Three of those notes from the Kelly's Bank job turned up this morning from a restaurant in Soho; better get over there pretty quick, might be able to find out who passed them. Arkwright says will you spare him ten minutes, he wants to check a couple of points on the case coming up at the Old Bailey on Monday. Cummings has found out that Mrs. Edmundsun's been getting a lot of travel literature, and Elliott bought a pair of diamond earrings recently. Cummings is a sticker; if we ever pin anything on Elliott, we'll have to thank Cummings. Well, that's about the lot, and it's all there—oh, no, it isn't!"

"What else?" Gideon asked evenly.

"Smedd rang just before you came in, said would you ring him back. Wants to rub your nose in it, I expect."

"Hmm," said Gideon. "Maybe." He put the call in, and didn't have to wait long. He was already in as good a mood as he was ever likely to be in, because when he had got home last night he had realized just how edgy Kate had been about him; and just how deep was the new affection between them. So much was good.

But a girl who was lying bravely to save her brother . . .

"Good morning, Commander," said Smedd, in his hard, brisk voice. "I thought you would like to know of two new pieces of evidence in regard to the murder of Winifred Norton, and the charge against William Rose. A regular cinema goer who attended the Roxy Cinema last Thursday for the performance which Rose's sister states she and her brother also attended, has made a statement. This statement declares that Mary Rose was with a young man, whose description might possibly tally with that of her brother. Also, a clerk in the same office as Rose has stated that three days before the murder he tried to borrow Rose's penknife, but Rose told him he had lost it. Further inquiries about the evening of the murder have brought to light the information that an older man was seen with the murdered girl near the spot where her body was found. This man has not yet been identified, but I am of course making the closest possible inquiries. . . ."

As he listened, Gideon's eyes grew very bright and his hopes ran high.

Gideon's Night

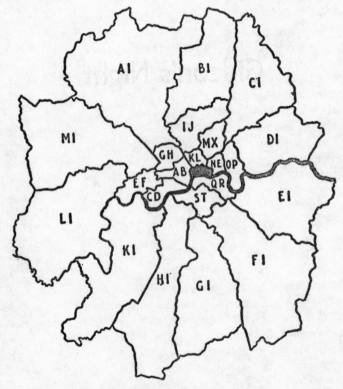

SKETCH MAP OF GIDEON'S TERRITORY. The map conforms only approximately to the boundaries of the Metropolitan and City Police Forces, and the divisional reference letters do not coincide with the real London divisional letters or boundaries.

1 . Night's Beginning

In the early, misty dusk, Gideon stepped out of his house and closed the door on brightness and music. It was not yet six o'clock. His family, except Matthew, who was out, would spend the evening gathered round the fire, the television, lesson books and, if Prudence could make the others sit back for half an hour, her violin. It was a happy family, happier today than it had been a few years ago, when he and Kate had drawn apart; and he was thinking about that. For when he had kissed Kate good-by she had held him tightly for a moment, not wanting him to go out into London's night. At one time she simply had not cared and neither had he. Now they were man and wife if ever two people were—and at this moment Kate was back in the living room, exerting her firm but often unsuspected control over the family.

It was chilly.

Gideon shrugged his big body inside the thick gray overcoat, a massive man with slightly rounded shoulders, a fine head, rather heavy features. He had a slow, deliberate walk, because he had trained himself not to hurry except in emergency, and he was in good time. On the nights which he was going to spend in his office at the Yard, or out and about on the Yard's business, he liked to arrive fairly early. Lemaitre and other daytime-duty men would wait to brief him with the day's happenings, and he did not want to keep them too late.

He walked toward his garage, round the corner.

This was Hurlingham, part of the London suburb of Fulham, where he had lived most of his life and all of his marriage, yet the night scene had freshness: the haloes round the street lamps, the lights at windows where neighbors lived with their troubles and their problems—and where, only a few weeks ago, a regular patron of the magistrates' courts had broken in, by night, and got away with three hundred pounds' worth of jewelry.

Gideon, Commander George Gideon of the Criminal Investigation Department of the Metropolitan Police, hadn't yet lived that down. He smiled dryly at the thought now. The thief was in jail, most of the jewelry had been recovered, and the men at the Yard had had their little joke.

He reached the corner.

A tall man was just along the street, beyond the garage, and looked as if he had been lounging against the wall and had just straightened up. Suspiciously? The thought was hardly in Gideon's mind when he recognized the "man" and his smile turned into a grin. This was Matthew, his seventeen-year-old son, thin and spindly although possessed of broad shoulders and big hips; he would fill out, but at the moment could hardly be more awkward or cumbersome. He was the ugly duckling, anyhow, with plain features and invariably untidy hair, but the greatest cause for worry was about his future. He was clever, almost brilliant in his studies, but had always been vague about what he wanted to do. He seemed to think that the world would fall into his lap.

Obviously he had been waiting here, so he had something to say to his father that he didn't want to say in front of his mother.

"Hello, Matt, just coming home?"

"Evening, Dad. Yes, I—I was kept in this afternoon. I'm a bit late."

"Feel sorry for you young hopefuls sometimes," said Gideon, in a tone which obviously had Matthew guessing; was this sincere or was it parental sarcasm? "In my young days school finished about four o'clock, and we had an hour's homework to do, if we had the sense to do it." Gideon was unlocking the big green doors of the garage, and Matthew stood ready to push the sliding doors to one side.

"I know," he said quickly and hurriedly. "I'm just about fed up with school. They don't really teach you anything worth while. What the dickens is the use of learning about algebraic problems and logarithms and Greek gods? Why, there are times when—"

He pushed the door and it ran easily on the runners; a sharp noise as it banged against the stop cut off his last words.

"I mean, do *you* know anything about Greek gods?" he demanded hotly.

"Not much," conceded Gideon. "It takes me all my time to sort out what's true of one." He was troubled, because he was coming to the opinion that Matthew simply didn't like work, and, if Gideon had a hate, it was of laziness. But nothing of this sounded in his voice as he went on: "Lend a hand with the car, will you?"

There was no room to open the door and get to the wheel while the car was in the garage, which was too narrow for it to be backed inside with any safety. So it had to be pulled by the bumper until the door was clear. At one time that had been a nuisance but now it was almost second nature; garages weren't easy to come by in London.

They pulled.

"Dad, *must* I stay until I'm eighteen?" Matthew burst out. "Why can't I leave at the end of this term? There's no law to make me stay, fifteen's the legal leaving age, and even if I did win a scholarship to a university, what use is it to me? It isn't as if I wanted to be a professor or a mathematician or—or—"

"A student of Greek mythology," Gideon completed for him. "Nip in the other side, while I get the car off the pavement." He got into the Wolseley and switched on the ignition, while Matthew scrambled in the other side as eagerly as he had when he had been a child. Gideon started the engine and reversed slowly. He seldom talked while he was reversing, or driving in traffic, and Matthew knew better than to expect conversation. He pulled in to the curb. "When's your mother expecting you home?"

"Oh, I'm late, but she won't worry how much—"

"You'd be surprised how much she might worry," said Gideon. "You'd better pop in and tell her you're back and that you're coming with me for the drive."

"Oh, *fine!*" breathed Matthew.

Two minutes later, the front door closed on Penelope, the youngest girl, and Matthew came hurrying back. He slammed the car door, and settled down.

"Dad, I *thought* you'd understand. I'm tired of school. I want to get a job and start earning some money, instead of sponging on you all the time. Tom left school at fifteen and he's done well for himself, hasn't he? I know he's much older than I am but—well, he's actually going to get *married*. He must by earning a whopping big screw. If I don't start soon, what chances have I got of succeeding?"

Tom, Gideon's oldest son, had lived away from home for several years.

"I see," said Gideon, as he drove at fair speed along the narrow street. "Know what you want to do for a living, Matt?"

"Yes!" The word came out almost defiantly. "I've decided."

"Hmm." Gideon managed to hide his surprise. Now that it had come, he wasn't sure that he liked the thought of Matthew with his mind made up in such a way that he didn't want to tell his mother; even defiant because he was sure that he would run into opposition.

"What's it to be?" Gideon made himself sound eager.

Matthew turned to stare at his father. As they passed a street lamp, Gideon took his eye off the road for a moment, so as to glimpse the eager face, the unusually bright eyes, one hand raised and clenched as a measure of the lad's intensity.

"I want to be a policeman, a copper. I want to start in the ranks and work my way up, just like you did!"

"Good God!" exclaimed Gideon.

"I know Mum won't like it. I don't suppose you will either. Mum's always complaining that she's never known where you'd be from one moment to the next—why, look at tonight. She hates it when you go out on night duty, and whenever you're called up in the middle of the night, well, you ought to hear what she *says* sometimes. I know she's frightened, but that—"

"Frightened?"

"Of course she is, especially since that time when you were looking for Syd Benson," Matthew rushed on. "She just can't stand it when she thinks you might be in danger, but that's just *like* a woman. Women simply can't understand that a man *has* to have some adventure. What would life be like if there wasn't any danger? And after all, you've lived to be pretty old, haven't you?"

Gideon slowed down at a junction with a main road.

"I'll give you old," he said roundly. "I'm fifty-one, my lad, and fifty-one's no age. So you really want to start as a copper, you think your mother will hate the idea, and that I'll tell you to stop talking nonsense. That right?"

"Well, yes, won't you?"

They turned into the main road. It was fairly well lit just here, and there was more traffic, but not enough to be troublesome. Matthew still looked as if nothing but this subject mattered even slightly. Two policemen stood at a corner, and one saluted as Gideon's car passed, while both of them watched.

"Well, *won't* you?" demanded Matthew.

"Do you know, Matt, I'm not quite sure," said Gideon. That was true. "I'm really not sure. In some ways I'd like to feel that one of my boys was coming into the Force. It can be a damned good career. You might be right about your mother, but if you want a thing like this badly enough you'll have to show her that it really matters to you; then, even if she doesn't like it, she won't be unreasonable. But you've a lot of time for thinking about it, Matt, and you've got a few ideas that won't do you much good if you want to be a copper. Unless that's *all* you want to be," he added dryly, "a chap pushing a bike around, with a possibility of becoming a sergeant if you'll wait fifteen years or so."

"Of course that's not what I want! I want to do detective work in the C.I.D., like you. After all, you're right at the top—"

"If you forget the Assistant Commissioner for Crime, that's right," agreed Gideon, smothering a grin. "But all you can see is where I am, not how I got there and what I learned on the way." He paused to negotiate three cyclists who were riding abreast, and then swept forward along a nearly empty road leading to the heart of London. Traffic coming out was getting thick. "If you do want to study for the C.I.D., the more you can learn at school and even the university—"

"But Dad, what use are—"

"Greek gods, I know," said Gideon, and he wasn't smiling. "The answer is that they might make or break you—certainly they might make you. It's about seven years since they dug up that statue of Minerva out of the ruins of the Barbican. It had lain under the ground for about fifteen hundred years. Funny thing, coincidence, but about a year afterward a lot of Greek and Roman pottery was found in France, caused quite a stir in archaeological and historical quarters, and some of the stuff was extremely valuable. Soon afterward it was stolen. You should have heard the screams that went up. It so happened that we had a youngish chap at the Yard who'd been interested about the stuff they dug up at the Barbican, and had learned a lot about it. We had a pretty good idea that one of several wealthy collectors had stolen the new discovery, or bought it from the thief. Our chap was able to mix with the suspect collectors, talk their own language, and find the stuff. One of the collectors had bought it, knowing it to be stolen—the thief got five years and the receiver three. That chap's got a lot to thank his interest in Greek gods for, Matt. He's a Divisional detective inspector to-day. If it hadn't been for that job he would probably be a detective sergeant at the Yard running around and doing what I tell him."

Matthew made no immediate response, and Gideon drove more quickly. In less than ten minutes they would be at the Yard, and he was falling behind time. Yet he didn't want to cut Matthew short.

Then Matthew said abruptly, "I suppose you really mean that *anything* a man knows might come in useful in detective work."

"Not might, Matt. It's bound to, sooner or later. It won't always be spectacular, but you've got to be a jack-of-all-trades, as well as knowing the ropes and routine. Know what detection is, really? It's patience, persistence, a good memory and a first-class power of observation. You come across some little thing in a case; let's take something simple like a foreign language. I've often heard you saying that you hate French lessons. Well, any Yard man who can speak and read French fluently is a step ahead of another chap who's just as competent in all other ways. Why? Because every week, sometimes a dozen times a week, we pick up a Frenchman or we have to question a French witness, and it can save a hell of a lot of time and trouble if we can do without an official interpreter. The more you know, Matt, the more chance you've got of getting on. Like to know something else? I didn't know a word of French before I joined the Force, but when I realized how much it might help I spent most of my spare time picking it up. You ought to have heard what your mother said about my nose being stuck in a book!"

Matthew grinned.

"I can imagine," he said slyly. "I think I see what you mean, Dad. General knowledge is very important."

"General knowledge is *all* important," corrected Gideon, "and all the special training, the routine, the walking the beat and taking your turn at traffic duty won't help if you haven't got it. Supposing we had trouble with a musician, for instance—the things that Pru can tell me about music would be as much use as anything else I know."

Matthew nodded again and was silent, but that didn't mean that he was subdued. They reached Parliament Square, where the yellow face of Big Ben was shrouded in mist, and where the lights of Westminster Bridge were clearly visible at this end, but vague and misty at the middle and beyond.

"Well, think about it," said Gideon more briskly. "Don't be in too much of a hurry. If I were you I'd wait a few weeks and then have another talk with me. There's no point in worrying your mother if it's going to come to nothing, is there? Now I'll have to look slippy. Got your fare home?"

"I—well, I *am* a bit short," Matthew said, and grinned. "You couldn't send me home in a prowl car, could you?"

"I could not! We don't have prowl cars; we have Squad cars and patrol cars, and the drivers are too busy to be running infants about." Gideon turned into the courtyard of Scotland Yard, from the Embankment, and pulled up, stopped the engine, and then took two half crowns from his pocket. "Here you are, and get that nonsense about sponging on me out of your head. What do you think I work for? Lot of use money would be to me if I didn't have a family to spend it on."

"Thanks, Dad." Matthew took the five shillings thoughtfully, and they got out and met at the back of the car. A tall flight of stone steps led up in front of them, and the tall, pale building rose high above their heads. "It's going to be a nasty night," Matthew observed casually. "Isn't this the kind of night that the Prowler gets around?"

There was a hint of excitement in his voice, after all.

"It's just the Prowler's kind of night, but when you get home you tell your mother there's hardly a trace of fog," ordered Gideon. He looked up as a plain-clothes man approached from the Embankment, brisk, heavily built, footsteps very firm. "Hello, Joe," Gideon greeted. "How about finding time to take my son Matthew down to the Information Room and let him see how it works? He has an idea that a policeman's life is full of excitement."

Matthew caught his breath, gazing at the newcomer as if willing him to say yes.

"Dullest place in London, this is," said the plain-clothes man, "but I don't think it'll be dull everywhere tonight. It's just the fog the Prowler ordered. All right, Matthew."

"Oh, *thank* you, sir!"

"Pleasure."

"Should've introduced you," Gideon said. "Matt, this is Chief Detective Inspector Whittaker."

Whittaker offered his hand, Matthew took it eagerly, and Gideon smiled but was a little uneasy as he went with them to the big hall, and then left them for the lift and his own office, his desk, the reports from the day men, the early reports of the night's incidents. It was quite dark now, and a lot of bad men were on the prowl—

Prowl.

Words came in spasms, sometimes, like varieties of crime. Get one report of robbery with violence and three or four were likely to come within a few hours. Hear of one racehorse-doping job, and there'd be a crop of them. They seemed to go in cycles, like playing with conkers, bowling hoops, spinning tops, tossing the yoyo and roller-skating. A week or so would pass without a smash-and-grab job, and then there would be half a dozen on the same day. At the Yard, and particularly in his job, you accepted the inevitability of crime which never stopped; you could never really get on top of it.

But you could stop some aspects of it, and usually you could catch a particular man if you really went all out. That was why he had chosen tonight to come on duty. The morning weather forecast had been "smoke and fog in towns and industrial areas tonight, clearing toward morning," and he wanted to know a lot more than he did about the Prowler, who always spread his terror on a foggy night.

2 . The First Reports

THE Yard was strange and even a little eerie by night, especially if you didn't come after dark very often. Now it was at its worst: dead, flat, drab, almost dreary. Young Matt had dreams of romance and adventure and there could be a little of both; a needle of romance and a pin of adventure in a haystack of routine and crime. Never mind young Matt. The passages of the C.I.D. buildings were fairly wide, and the cement of the floor and the walls seemed new—and also harsh and cold. The whole place struck cold, if it came to that. Doors were closed, and none opened, no one came walking along briskly, full of the next task to be done. The administrative staff was out and away, at home, the pictures, the theater, clubs, with girl or boy friend, mistress or wife, so the Yard was empty but for one or two key people, except in the C.I.D. section.

A door opened, brighter light shone into the dingy light of the passage, and a stocky man appeared, bustling, a sheaf of papers in his hand. This was an Inspector from Records. He wore pince-nez.

"Hello, George," he said. "You on tonight?"

"Yes, Syd, got to make sure I don't slip."

"You slipped as far as you ever will years ago," said Syd dryly. "Looks as if you've picked a good one." He fell into step as they walked toward Gideon's office. The Records man was half a head shorter than Gideon, going bald where Gideon had a lot of thick, wiry gray hair.

"What's on?"

"What isn't?" Syd asked. "Lemaitre will tell you. He's waiting, and—mind if I have a word in your ear?"

"Nothing's ever stopped you yet."

Syd grinned, but spoke seriously.

"Don't keep Lemaitre any longer than you can help tonight. He's having another basinful of wife trouble. And if you can keep your other ear open while I whisper in that, too, if you want to keep Lem from going crazy, persuade him to walk out on his Fifi. She gets worse and he gets—well, the truth is any man who marries the lush and sexy type ought not to be surprised if he runs into trouble."

They stopped outside Gideon's brown door, which had the word COM-MANDER printed on it, in black. Gideon had his back to the door and looked down at the Chief Inspector from Records.

"Got any facts?"

"You've got eyes."

"Any real reason to think it's any worse than it was, Syd?" Gideon asked in a quiet but insistent tone.

"As a matter of fact, I have," said Syd. "I was out in KI Division this afternoon, where Lem lives. The boys know all about Fifi and her goings on, and of late she's had one or two boy friends who didn't kiss good night on the right side of the door. Lemaitre got home early one night and saw one of these gentry leaving. There was a mother and father of a row. One of the local coppers heard it. That was a week ago—all's been quiet and peaceful since then, but if Fifi breaks out again—" Syd paused, and frowned. "Don't tell me that you hadn't noticed anything wrong with Lem. He isn't that good at fooling you."

"I knew there was something wrong," said Gideon, "but I couldn't get anything out of him. Thanks, Syd."

"Okay, Gee-Gee!"

The Records man went on, and Gideon opened the door of his office. It was like opening a door into a steam oven. The "steam" was cigarette smoke, which was thick and pale, and the heat came from radiators which had spasms of working as if made exclusively for the Arctic, and at other times were barely warm.

At one end of the long room with windows overlooking the Embankment Chief Inspector Lemaitre sat back in a chair, halfway through a cigarette, and a sergeant stood by him, glancing round. The sergeant, dressed in thick brown serge and wearing a collar and tie, looked too hot even to breathe comfortably, and his face was bright red. Lemaitre's was very pale, his eyes were a little glittery, he had his coat off, his waistcoat was un-buttoned, and the ends of his yellow-and-black tie hung from a collar which had been wrenched from its stud.

"Hello," said Gideon. "Sorry I'm late."

"Good evening, sir." That was the sergeant.

"S'all right," said Lemaitre gruffly. "It doesn't matter to me whether I get home tonight." That was an effort to be funny and it failed completely. "What's the fog like?"

"Nothing much, yet."

"Going to be just about right for the Prowler," Lemaitre remarked. "You take it from me, George, one of these days the Prowler's going to leave a corpse behind, not just a girl who's scared stiff and got a nasty memory. Seven times is too many times to get away with it." He stood up as Gideon went to his larger desk which was at the other end of the room. Gideon took off his coat and draped it over the back of his chair, then took a pipe out of his pocket. It had a very large bowl, and was rough on the outside; knobbly, too. He began to fill it slowly from a brown leather pouch.

"Tell you another thing," Lemaitre went on, while the sergeant stood and waited for instructions. "You're going to have one hell of a night. Never known so much to come in between six and seven o'clock. Having a bit of a lull now, but that won't last for long. What do you want first, the day's stuff or what's doing at the moment?"

"We got any leads?"

"Not really."

"Give me the day's stuff, will you?" Gideon said. "Sergeant, pull up a chair and make notes when I tell you to."

"Yes, sir."

"Oh, bring up a chair for Mr. Lemaitre."

"Rather stand, ta," said Lemaitre, and in fact sat on the corner of Gideon's big, shiny desk. Several piles of papers stood on this, with three telephones, two ash trays, pen and ink, a blotting pad and several reference books, in-cluding *Whitaker's Almanack*. "Here it comes. Only two big jobs last night which kept us on the go this morning: murder of that old woman out at

Ealing, and her missing lodger. He was picked up at Hammersmith and made a statement, all the usual stuff, he didn't mean to do it. I'd string him up without a trial if I had my way."

That kind of remark, made in front of a sergeant, was a clear indication of Lemaitre's frame of mind.

"The other job was the Milden Street jewel robbery, fifteen thousand quid's worth of stuff lifted, without a trace. We had every fence we know questioned today and haven't got a smell of the stuff. We don't even know who did the job. It had none of the usual trade-marks; it was just neat and tidy and anonymous. There are the hangovers, too. Then—"

Lemaitre talked for ten minutes, touching upon dozens of different crimes, all of them large and important enough to have been brought to the Yard's notice, ranging from pocket picking to shoplifting, smash and grab to soliciting, fraud, embezzlement, attempted suicide, and causing grievous bodily harm—a kind of everyday's charge list which might have been lifted out of any issue of the *Police Gazette*. Lemaitre added odds and ends of information which were in the official report, one of the piles of papers on Gideon's desk. He smoked all the time, lighting one cigarette from the butt of another. Now and again Gideon signaled to the sergeant to make notes; otherwise he didn't interrupt. And he didn't light his pipe.

Lemaitre paused. Then:

"That's about the lot," he declared. "Shouldn't think it will break any records."

"What's this business of a Mrs. Penn who rang up three times to say she was worried about her husband because he hasn't been home for several weeks?"

"AB Division job," Lemaitre said. "Shouldn't think there's anything much in it; they sent a man round to talk to her. She's only been married a year or so, and just can't bear to think that her husband got tired of her and walked out so soon. But that's what he did all right, although she can't bring herself to believe it."

"Didn't you say she said she thought he must be dead?"

"That's what she *said*."

"She give any reason?"

"If you ask me, she's right out of reason," Lemaitre opined. His one fault was his habit of jumping to conclusions; nothing seemed able to cure him. Before he could go on, one of the telephones on Gideon's desk began to ring. Lemaitre looked at it with disgust, squashed out a cigarette and immediately began to light another; the tips of his forefinger and middle finger were so brown that they looked almost black. His eyes were tired, bloodshot and a little watery.

Gideon lifted up the receiver.

"Gideon," he said into it. "Who . . . Oh, yes, put him through." He covered the mouthpiece with his broad hand and said to the others, "AB Division."

"Perhaps hubby's come back," Lemaitre said sneeringly.

The truth about Lemaitre was that he needed a rest; somewhere quiet, somewhere on his own or with a wife who would fuss over him a little; and he wanted to be free from anxiety. And the truth about Lemaitre was that he'd married a bitch and, in spite of it, had never really fallen out of love with her. Lemaitre had failings but normally he was a sound man; now, he wasn't seeing anything straight because he was picturing his wife in another man's arms.

This was the first time Gideon had been really worried about him; he would have been, even without the Records man's comment.

A man came on the line.

"Gee-Gee? Elliott here. Just had a job which looks as if it could become nasty. Thought you'd better know at once. Kid disappeared from his home, Trenton Street, Chelsea. Four months old. The mother left the baby in the kitchen while she talked to someone in the front room, and when she came back the kid was gone. Hell of a job."

"Any history?"

"That's all we know, yet."

"I'll put you through to Morley—he'll take all details—and I'll have a call out for the baby as soon as we can put it on the air and the teletype," Gideon promised. "That all?"

"Yes."

"Anything more about a Mrs. Penn and her missing husband?"

"Just another poor kid with a husband who thinks he's Don Juan," said Elliott, and he wasn't prone to jumping to conclusions.

"Sure?"

"As near as I can be. Why?"

"I was looking through some reports on her yesterday," said Gideon, "and she seemed pretty levelheaded, not really the type to bury her head in the sand. Lem doesn't agree with me, but—"

"If she comes through again, I'll try to see her myself," Elliott promised.

"Thanks," said Gideon. "Now I'll put you through to Morley."

That only took a moment.

Next, he called the Information Room, told them about the missing baby and had them flash radio calls to all patrol cars. Soon the teletypes would be busy, all the Metropolitan Police and many in the Home Counties would be on the lookout, for the one thing which always gave that little extra inducement to effort was the search for a missing child.

Gideon rang off, and another telephone rang promptly.

"Here we go," Lemaitre said, almost savagely. "Why don't they give us another pair of hands and ears?"

"Hello, Gideon here," said Gideon. "Yes, put him through. . . . Hello, Mike . . . I haven't been in long but I gather they picked up the lodger, a man named Grey. . . . Dunno how long he's lodged there, why? . . . Oh . . . *oh*. Yes, I'll see to it." He put down the receiver and motioned to the sergeant. "Take this down: Arthur Grey, suspect in the murder of Mrs. Sarah Allway of Giddons Road, Ealing, answers the description of a man calling himself Arthur Smith who disappeared from a house in Clapham three weeks ago after leaving his landlady for dead. Make a note that we want all details, and then telephone Hammersmith. Grey's still held there, isn't he?"

"No. Cannon Row," Lemaitre said shortly.

"Might be able to do it myself then," Gideon said. For the first time he lit his pipe, taking his time over it. It was cooler in the office, but just as smoky, and there was an acrid smell—the smell of smog—which rose above the smell of the tobacco. He nodded to the sergeant, who hurried out to type his notes so that Gideon could have them in front of him and copies could be sent out to other Departments and the Divisions. The smell, the smoke, the sight of Lemaitre's pale face and glassy eyes and the set of Lemaitre's lips did nothing to cheer Gideon up. When he had come into the office first Lemaitre and then the Prowler had been on top of his mind, but already there were signs that it might be a very bad night in a lot of ways.

A kidnaped infant, for a start.

A middle-aged man who lodged with elderly women and then attacked them.

Out in the dark city, within a radius of ten miles of this point, there were the professional criminals waiting to take their chance, there were people who had never committed a crime committing one now, there were the pros out in their hundreds, there was vice so thick that it stank, there was everything that would duly take its place in the crime statistics of the year; and there was Kate, the family—and young Matthew, probably still downstairs here with his eyes glistening, and Whittaker already so busy that he was wishing that he'd never set eyes on the boy.

There was the Prowler.

And Lemaitre.

For a few minutes the telephones were silent. Cars hooted outside as drivers became impatient with the fog, and on Charing Cross Bridge a train rumbled and a fog signal exploded with its mournful note of warning; the fog was really thick over the river.

Here, Lemaitre stood by his own desk shrugging himself into his coat.

"Lem, how are things at home?" Gideon asked, right out of the blue.

"Things at home are so good that one of these days you'll be charging me with murder," Lemaitre said. He forced a grin, fastened his collar and tie, and straightened his coat. His eyes were dark with shadows, his cheeks very lean; he had a bony chin. "Oh, forget it. Never has been a bed of roses—never been much bed at all, if you know what I mean! But there's no need for you to worry, George. Anything else I can do, before I go?"

"What do you expect to find when you get home?"

"A cold supper and an empty fireplace," said Lemaitre abruptly, "unless she's staying in because of the fog. She's taken to suspecting every man who looks at her on a foggy night as the Prowler. If she's home she'll tell me just what she thinks of me for leaving her all alone—oh, forget it, I said." But Lemaitre's smile was much too set. "Could get home and find her as sweet as honey, too. Sure there's nothing else?"

"No, Lem, thanks."

"See you the day after tomorrow, then," Lemaitre said. "So long."

Gideon said good night, Lemaitre went out, and the door closed behind him. It wouldn't be long before the night-duty inspector who would share the vigil with Gideon came back, but for a little while he had the office on his own. He lifted the receiver, put in a call to KI Division and, while he was waiting for it to come through, looked through the reports. Lemaitre had summarized them almost perfectly.

"Want me, Gee-Gee?" said the KI Divisional man.

"Oh, hello, yes." Gideon was so mild that he sounded almost disinterested. "Lemaitre's just left for home. Have a man in his street when he gets there, will you, and have someone find an excuse for calling on him in half an hour or so after he arrives."

"Sure," the Divisional man said, with complete understanding. "Any news about that baby?"

"No."

"Pity. If you don't find 'em quick you often don't find 'em at all, except in the river or under a foot of earth," the KI man observed; he was being factual, not callous. "Well, I'll fix that job in Lemaitre's street, and then see what's doing tonight. I hope the Prowler doesn't play any tricks on my beat."

"Let me know if he does," said Gideon dryly.

As he rang off, he warned himself ruefully that the Prowler was on top of everyone's mind. One reason was that no one was allowed to forget him. The evening newspapers had a paragraph about him whenever there was fog and there'd been a front-page story in tonight's *Evening Globe*, not much but just enough. It had repeated that the police had not yet caught the

man known as the Prowler who, on foggy nights, would lie in wait for
young girls, in the porches and the front doorways of their own homes,
springing out on them, throttling them to silence and . . .

That was anyone's guess. The *Evening Globe* also pointed out, as if more
in sorrow than in anger, that two things were known about the Prowler.
He had once left a handkerchief of very good quality at the scene of an
attack, and each girl who had seen him had talked of a "big shiny face";
presumably a mask of some kind. Neither of these clues had helped the
police; nor had the descriptions of the Prowler given by the girls, for one
had said "big and powerful," another had said "smallish" and several had
plumped for "average size." Even ordinary witnesses to the same incident
gave widely differing descriptions, and these girls had been cold with fear.
But that didn't help.

It was also anyone's guess whether the Prowler would be out tonight.
The fact that he'd been out seven times this autumn had been one of the
reasons why Gideon had decided to come on nights for a week. He didn't
expect to catch the Prowler on his first night, but he might see something
which had been missed, or, when he got the early reports, might be able to
suggest new moves against him.

A second reason for coming on nights was based on reports from the
East End of increasing rivalry between the gangs of youths. Such rivalry
could become ugly and create a serious situation, and Gideon wanted to keep
his finger on its pulse.

In London itself the gangs operated only by night.

Now there was Mrs. Penn and her missing husband and her fears. There
were dozens of Mrs. Penns and dozens of missing husbands, and only once
now and again was it a police matter; usually it was just a case of a man
who, like Lemaitre, couldn't stand living at home any more. Or else the
man was a callous beggar, who had no more interest in his wife.

There was the mother of the missing child.

There were dozens of other cases, some already reported and some still to
come. Perhaps all of them would be quickly solved, or else would peter out;
and perhaps one of them would become a sensation, perhaps a murder was
lurking, perhaps that child was already dead.

The police would be on the lookout everywhere now.

It was a quarter past seven. The sergeant would soon be back, and
Appleby, who was to work with Gideon for the night, ought to be here at
any moment. Appleby was used to night work, an elderly, thoroughgoing
man without much imagination but with a profound knowledge of his job
and of the underworld. The C.I.D. would come to a standstill without its
Applebys, but—

Gideon scowled, for the telephone rang.

As he stretched out for the receiver, he had an odd feeling, almost a premonition of bad news, and he did not reckon to allow himself the luxury of such things. Perhaps it was because it was night, and there was the smoky fog outside, silence on the road and on the river, and silence in the passages, too.

"Gideon."

"Inspector Wragg of GH Division would like a word with you, sir."

"Put him through," said Gideon, and relaxed and grinned. Wragg was the man who had won promotion because of his interest in Greek gods and Roman relics. What a lot of bull one said to one's children sometimes! Had he sounded unbearably pompous? He'd meant to talk as man to man, but looking back felt that he'd laid the moralizing on with a trowel. Still, facts were facts, and Wragg—

"That you, Gee-Gee?" Wragg had a crisp voice.

"Yes."

"Thought I'd get straight on to you about this," said Wragg. "Had a teletype about that kidnaped baby ten minutes ago, and then only a few minutes after, a kid was taken away from a car on my Division. Four-month-old boy. The mother's frantic."

As he listened, Gideon had the premonition again; this was going to be a night he wouldn't forget in a hurry.

3 . The Baby Snatcher

THE child lay in its cot, sleeping.

The room was warm. A faint glow of light came from beneath the door, and the sound of voices, which seemed a long way off, was just audible. Above it, soft and even, was the child's breathing.

Here was peace, with no knowledge of evil.

Sounds from the street came into the room from time to time: the beat of a car engine, the rattling of an old bicycle, three times in quick succession the staccato beat of a motorcycle engine which developed into a roar outside the window and then died away. Men and women walked, all briskly, in the cold night.

Then there came a sharper sound nearby, quick footsteps close to the window, followed by a clear ringing sound inside the house. Almost at once the distant voices stopped, a door opened, there were more footsteps, and these passed the door where the baby lay sleeping.

The front door opened.

"Oh, hello, Lucy!" a woman exclaimed, with obvious pleasure. "Come in a minute, dear."

"No, May, I'm not coming in," said the woman named Lucy. "Jim and me wondered if you and Fred would like to pop in for an hour. There's ever such a good program on the television. First there's Dobson and Young, *you* know—"

"Well, come in a minute, it's too cold to stand here," said May. "I'll ask Fred, and I expect he'll jump at it. Between you and me, dear, I don't think it will be long before we get the tele' ourselves. He's always moaning about not having it when everybody else has, but what with two children at school and now Baby, it does seem an awful lot of money." The front door closed. "How would you like to have a look at Baby while I go and ask Fred?"

"Love to."

"He's a *pet*," said May in a softer voice, and there was a faint sound as the handle of the door turned. "That's what he is, an absolute *pet*. I put him down at half past six and as sure as I'm here he won't stir again until seven o'clock tomorrow morning. What about that for four months old?"

"You don't have to tell me," said Lucy.

The door opened, and light fell into the room but not directly onto the child, for the cot was behind the door so that bright light from the passage could not fall upon its eyes. They crept in, whispering, one woman short and with a mop of frizzy hair which showed up like twisted wire against the light, the other of medium height, plump with untidy dark hair. They stood at the head of the cot, just able to make out the dark head and the face, until the child's mother stretched out a hand and adjusted the blue woolen shawl a little, feeling the warm patch where the child's breathing fell.

"Bless him," she said in a voice that was almost choky with emotion. Then she turned and hurried out along the passage toward the kitchen and her husband. There were voices from the kitchen, and then, clearly, May's voice:

"Oh, he'll be all right; he never *does* wake up. What's the matter with you tonight? We've done it before, haven't we?"

A gruff voice followed: "Oh, all right, if you really want to."

"If you'd rather stay here on your own with your nose stuck in a book, that's all right with me," said May, as if crossly. "I'll be just as welcome on my own."

"I said I'd come, didn't I?"

"You didn't sound as if you appreciated the kindness very much."

There was a pause; then a half-laughing "Oh, you," and May came hurrying, to have another look at her baby, and to draw Lucy into the passage.

"Fred's coming, dear. He always puts up this act. It's pride really; he doesn't like to think that if we want to see anything on the tele', we have

to come next door for it. Read him like a book, I can. I'm just going to pop
up to the bedroom and tidy my hair—"

"Oh, don't worry about your hair!"

"I couldn't let Jim see me in this mess; he'd start feeling sorry for Fred,"
said May, the dark-haired, younger woman. She turned and hurried up the
stairs, calling back, "You can wait, dear. No, you go back to Jim, and Fred
and me'll be along in a couple of jiffs."

"I'll wait," decided Lucy.

Fred came along, a stocky, gray-haired man with a smell of strong tobacco about him, and looked at the baby, smiling a gentle smile, and then
they waited in the passage a little awkwardly until May came hurrying. Her
hair didn't look much tidier, but she had dabbed on powder and lipstick,
and was licking the tip of her forefinger and running it along the length
of her eyebrows.

"Come on," she said. "All ready."

As she went out, she glanced round at the front-room door. As Fred
pulled the door behind him, he also glanced round. Then the door closed
with a snap, there was a clatter of footsteps as they went out of one entry
into another, voices, the opening and closing of the door.

All was quiet inside the house.

For some minutes, all was quiet in the street.

Then, from across the street, someone came walking.

It looked like a man of medium height, dressed in a big raincoat, a trilby
hat and rubber-soled boots or shoes, and making little sound while walking;
at most a soft, sliding sound. No one was in sight. It was a street with two
rows of about fifty small, terraced houses on either side, each of two stories,
and there were three lamps on either side. The lamp nearest the child's
house was clearly visible, but the others were almost obscured by fog, which
was much thicker now. A car passed the end of the street and its lights
showed vaguely, but clear enough to show the smooth skin of a woman's
face; this was not a man. The car disappeared as the shrouded woman
reached the doorway of the child's house.

She bent down by the letter box, put her fingers inside and then groped
gently, touched a piece of string, and pulled. There was a slight metallic
sound as a key came out, tied to a string. She inserted the key quickly,
pushed the door open and stepped inside, then closed the door without
looking round.

She began to breathe hard, hissingly.

She leaned against the door for a moment, then straightened up as if with
an effort, and walked toward the door of the front room, the passage leading

to the kitchen, and the narrow staircase. She hesitated outside the door, then went up the stairs, quickly but with hardly a sound. There was enough light from the narrow hall to show the four doors leading off a small landing. She pushed each door open in turn, and shone a torch inside and the light fell upon beds, walls, furniture, a bathroom, handbasin, a mirror which flashed the brightness back; but this was not what the woman was seeking. She turned away and went downstairs, and hesitated again at the foot of the stairs, then turned toward the kitchen. Obviously there was nothing there, or in the tiny scullery, that she wanted. Two rooms remained: the front room and a smaller one next to it.

She opened the front-room door.

After a moment, she saw the cot and the child.

Her breathing became very heavy as she slipped the torch into her pocket, where it fitted snugly, and went close to the cot. Obviously she knew exactly what she wanted to do, and did not waste a moment. She pushed the bedclothes back, so that the baby lay wrapped in a blue blanket which enveloped all but his head, and lifted the bundle. She held it against her shoulder, one hand in the middle of its back as if she was quite familiar with it, and then pulled the shawl off at the top of the cot and wrapped it round the baby. This took only a few seconds, and soon the woman was stepping out of the room and into the passage, closing the door with her free hand. She took four strides to the front door, opened it and peered out.

A man and a woman, or boy and girl, passed on the other side of the street, and a motorcycle roared by.

The woman with the baby stepped into the foggy night and closed the door behind her with a snap. The house next door was in darkness, for the television was in a back room, out of sight and hearing of the street.

The child's eyes fluttered, but it did not wake.

The woman lowered it now, so that it was cradled in her arms, but didn't carry it with any outward pretense of affection; in fact she walked quickly, bumping the child up and down a little. Although the shawl was wrapped about the head, the little pink face was completely uncovered, and fog swirled about the mouth and nose.

Suddenly the baby coughed.

In the distance, there were the noises of the city.

"Well, thanks ever so, Lucy, and you, Jim," said May Harris. "It's been ever so nice, hasn't it, Fred? I enjoyed it very much."

"Best show I've seen for a long time," agreed Fred Harris, who looked as if he meant it.

He was red-faced with the warmth of the little room, where the television screen still showed its picture, but the sound had been turned down so that there was only a ghost voice which might have been a million miles away. May Harris was as flushed as her husband, her eyes were bright, her face was shiny as if she had not put a powder puff near it that evening, and her hair was a dark untidy mop. But there was merriment in her blue eyes, and much more character in her face than in Lucy Fraser's. Jim Fraser was an elderly man, nearly bald, with sharp features and a lot of deep lines at the eyes and mouth; he and his Lucy were fifteen years older than the Harrises.

"Glad you could come," Fraser said. "Sure you won't stay and have a cuppa?"

"Oh, I couldn't leave my baby any longer," said May Harris. "It isn't that I think he'd come to any harm, but you do hear of such things don't you? Fred, if you'd like to stay for a cup of char, I'll go and finish off that bit of ironing."

"Never outstay your welcome, that's what I was always taught," said Harris. "They don't want us cluttering up the house."

He laughed, Fraser protested, May argued, Lucy went into the kitchen and put the kettle on. May was still protesting that they shouldn't stay when the tea was brought in, a large brown pot and white cups and saucers crowded on a small wooden tray.

"Well, now it *is* made we may as well stay and have a cup," Harris conceded. "Like me to pop in and have a look at the brat, May?"

"Don't you call *my* child a brat!"

There was another general laugh as Harris went to the door. The house was identical with his own, and he could have found his way blindfolded. Once in the passage, he took out his pipe and lit it, as if he couldn't do without it for another moment. Then he went out, leaving the front door on the latch. The fog was much worse than when he had come here, and even the nearest street lamp was only a patch of misty light. The footsteps of people not far away seemed a long way off. In spite of the weather, he stood on the doorstep drawing at his pipe and adding smoke to the fog; then he strolled to his own house, let himself in with his own key, and noticed nothing at all unusual. The key on the string banged gently against the door. He didn't go into the front room at first but along to the kitchen, where he put some coal on the fire which heated the hot-water boiler behind the fireplace.

Then he went to the front room.

He opened the door softly, crept in, saw the foot of the cot, let his gaze shift quickly toward the pillow—and caught his breath. For a moment, he did not seem to be breathing at all. Then:

"*God!*" he gasped.

He spun round and switched on the light, not knowing what he expected to find. There were the bedclothes, turned down as if his wife had lifted the baby out, but—nothing else.

He made a strangled sound.

He pushed the cot away from the wall, as if he feared that by some miracle the child in swaddling clothes had been able to climb out of the cot and had landed on the floor close to the wall. There was just a blank space. For a moment he stood as if he had lost the power to move, but suddenly he turned round, reached the passage and called in a loud voice:

"Jackie! Millicent!"

There was no answer.

He hesitated, his hands clenching, turning his head this way and that— and then, as if driven by some compulsion which he could not resist, dashed up the stairs. He made the walls shake and the staircase quiver in his fear as he called again:

"Jackie! Millicent!"

There was still no answer.

All the rooms were empty—his and May's, the tiny room where the child slept during the night, the room with two beds, which Jacqueline and Millicent shared. His daughters were out, he didn't expect them back until half past ten; there was a nearby school-and-youth club they went to every Tuesday.

He stood on the little landing, a stocky man with graying hair, a big face, his clenched fists raised at chest height, an expression of bewilderment touched with horror on his face and in his honest gray eyes. He licked his lips.

"It can't—" he began.

Then he gulped, and started down the stairs, and as he went he said in a hoarse whispering voice:

"May, what'll *May* say?"

"It can't have happened, I must be—"

He broke off.

He went into the front room again, where the light was so bright and the cot was empty, and he knew that it was coldly, cruelly true. He stared at the door, lips set tightly and pipe forgotten. He heard sounds, without knowing what they were. The dazed, horrified expression was still in his eyes as at last he moved toward the door.

"May," he said chokily. "Oh, God."

Then the front door was pushed open, and his wife appeared, still flushed and obviously anxious and alarmed. Fred stopped, quite still. He did not need to speak, for his face told her of reasons for great dread. Her expression, already anxious, changed to one of sudden alarm, but not yet with fear or horror. She moved quickly toward him, gripping his right hand tightly.

"Fred, what is it? I heard you shouting. What—"

He tried to speak, but could not.

"Why don't you say something instead of just standing there?" cried May. "Why—"

Then—and it was only a few seconds after she had entered the passage— the significance of the open front-room door and the bright light inside seemed to strike her. All color drained from her cheeks. She pushed her husband to one side and ran into the room. She stared at the cot, her hands raised, her mouth wide open, and the light from the ceiling shone upon her eyes and seemed to put stark terror into them.

She jerked her head round to look at her husband. She could not speak. There was a moment of awful silence, and then tall Jim Fraser spoke from the porch.

"Everything all right there?"

"Fred," May said, in a queer little voice, "it can't have happened. It can't, it—oh my *baby*. Where's my baby? Why did you shout—*Jackie! Millie!*" She swung round suddenly toward her husband, saying as if to herself, "They're home early, they've taken—"

"I've looked—" Fred began, and choked. "Looked—everywhere."

May didn't speak.

Jim Fraser appeared in the doorway, sparse and thin and old looking and puzzled.

"Everything is all right, isn't it?" he began, and then saw them and realized that horror was here. Quite suddenly he became a different man from the elderly, easygoing neighbor who was always ready to lend a hand. His voice became firmer and touched with authority as he moved forward, going on: "Here, what's up? What are you looking like that for, May?" He glanced toward the cot and immediately understood, and his voice became even more authoritative. "Say you've looked everywhere, Fred?"

"Y-yes. Y-yes, I—"

"My *baby*," said May Harris, in that queer little hurt voice. "Who's taken my baby?"

"Fred, nip next door and tell Lucy that she's wanted here," said Fraser. "Tell her to make it snappy. Then go along to the phone box at the corner of Grettley Street, and dial 999. I'll look after May while you're gone, don't worry. Looks as if someone just picked the baby up, doesn't it? No sign that anyone did it any harm, is there? Lot of funny things happen, and babies usually turn up. Come on, Fred, get a move on."

Thus he averted panic, then.

Appleby had arrived at Gideon's office, a clean-shaven man with gray hair which he kept short, a fresh complexion, rather bright, beady, glittering gray eyes, a thin-cheeked man with a long nose, a big mouth and, by reputation, a sense of humor; the kind of humor that puts tacks on chairs. He was a Cockney who spoke with a nasal twang he had never quite overcome, and he was reputed to know more thieves' slang and Cockney rhyming slang than anyone else in the Force. He had come in almost flustered, not realizing that Gideon would be in his own office, and expecting him at the office of the Chief Superintendent usually on duty at night. Now he had settled down at Lemaitre's desk, with dozens of papers spread out in front of him, looking much more like a busy bookmaker than a C.I.D. man.

"Sorry, old pal, I must be slipping."

"My fault, Charley," Gideon said. "I forgot to send a message saying I'd be here—could've come to your office, as far as that goes, but now you're here we'll call it a day. Or a night." He grinned as he sat back in his big chair and looked across at Appleby. "I haven't heard you say it yet."

Appleby looked puzzled.

"Say what?"

"Who it's a good night for."

Appleby gave a quick smile.

"Oh, the Prowler. Got the Prowler on the brain, some of these people, but I admit I'll have more peaceful nights when the swine's inside. Real trouble with the Prowler isn't the harm he does by scaring the wits out of these kids. Oh, it's bad enough, but—you want to know something?"

"Always ready to listen."

"One night last week we had *twenty-seven* blasted calls through 999 to say that the Prowler had been seen," Appleby said, "and we had to make *twenty-seven* bloody investigations on a night when it took every patrol car and Squad car we had twice as long as usual to get around in the fog. The Prowler does a hell of a lot more damage stopping us from getting on with other jobs than he does to these girls."

"You might sing a different tune if you had daughters of your own, Charley."

"Coupla sons have been quite enough for me and the old china to handle," Appleby said without arguing. "Funny business, these babies, isn't it? Two snatched."

"You know how things often run in pairs," Gideon remarked, more to get Appleby's reaction than anything else. Being close to his pension often seemed to blunt a man's approach to his jobs, made him fall back on routine and the conventional approach, which often saved a lot of trouble.

"I know how they run in quintuplicate sometimes," said Appleby dryly, "but these two babies were snatched within a few hundred yards of each other on the same evening. One from the southern edge of GH Division, one from the northern edge of AB Division. If you ask me, that's one for the curiosity stakes."

"I'm with you there," Gideon said. "Hope we don't get a third. Anything else look worth special attention?"

"Not yet," said Appleby, "but the night's hardly started."

"Don't I know it," agreed Gideon, and got up. "Been down to the Information Room lately?"

"Half an hour ago. Your young hopeful was still there."

"I'll nip down and have a word with him, and if he's still hanging around I'll send him home," said Gideon. "Won't be long, but I might pop into the canteen on the way back."

"Have one for me," said Appleby.

So he was alert, apparently right up to his job, and as zestful as a man fifteen or twenty years his junior; Gideon decided that, if there was a weakness in the night operation at the Yard, it didn't lie in any slackening of Charley Appleby's keenness.

At his normal slow, deliberate gait Gideon walked toward the stairs. The lift wasn't at this landing, so he walked down; it was only two flights. The ground floor had the deserted look which he didn't relish, but as he reached the Information Room it was like going out of the shadow into sunshine. The big room was well lit. The uniformed men with their long rakes, like croupiers at four green baize tables, were all moving little blocks of wood which represented the patrol cars in the districts they covered. Each table represented one of the four Districts of Metropolitan London, and each was an administrative area. There were small colored counters showing the spots where crimes had been reported that evening.

Several men sitting at the radio transmitter, with earphones on, were at ease just then, and lounging against the front of the transmitter was young Matthew, who hadn't yet noticed his father. Whittaker was in his small office, talking on the telephone. Teletype machines clattered busily, recording messages from magic, silent voices, and strangely disembodied sounds came faintly into the room.

A sergeant sitting by the receiver said:

"Here's a call."

Matthew straightened up eagerly, and still didn't notice his father. The big clock on the wall showed that it was nearly half past nine; the large second hand ticked round abruptly every second.

"May I—" Matthew began.

"Yes, put 'em on." The operator motioned to a spare pair of headphones, and then said briskly, "Scotland Yard." Matthew jammed the headphones on, his eagerness really something to see; how like Kate the boy looked sometimes!

Then, his eyes lost their brightness. His lips set. He made no attempt to get the headphones off, but obviously he didn't like what he heard.

The operator kept saying, "Yes . . . Yes . . . Yes," and made written notes, swiftly. Gideon stepped behind him and tried to read the notes, but they were in shorthand and he didn't know the system which was used.

"Yes, we'll send at once," said the operator. "You are Mr. Frederick Harris, of 27 Hurdle Street, Fulham, and while you were next door at a neighbor's house your four-month-old child was taken from your house. . . . Yes, Mr. Harris, we'll have someone with you in a very few minutes, and we'll do everything we can."

He rang off.

"That's *three*," he said, and the tone of his voice matched the look on Matthew's face.

Matthew had seen Gideon now, and was staring at him.

"Hurdle Street, Fulham," Gideon repeated, as if to himself. "That's CD Division and not far from the other two snatch jobs." He nodded at Matthew, and then moved toward a long counter and picked up a telephone. "Give me Mr. Appleby, he's in my office. . . . Hello, Charley, another baby's been stolen, CD Division this time. I think I'll go over myself and see how things are. Flash me if you want me."

"Righto," said Appleby.

"Come on, Matt," Gideon said to his son as he put the receiver down, "you can come with me as far as Wandsworth Bridge Road, and can walk home from there. Won't be a couple of jiffs." He moved his massive body very swiftly, and went to Whittaker's office. Messages were being flashed to patrol cars in the Hurdle Street area; in a few moments the Division would be called, then the teletype messages to the other Divisions would start going out. Here was a major task, and somehow that showed in the attitude of all the men down here, in the way the rakes were pushed about, in the attitude of the men sitting at the radio.

"I'll get everything done, George," Whittaker said.

"Thanks. And try this—send someone from GH and AB over to Hurdle Street. Each must be a chap who's been working on the baby-snatch job in his Division. We want to find out similarities and all that kind of thing. Who's on duty at AB?"

"Dixon."

"He won't lose any time," said Gideon. "Dixon and Wragg, hmm. Tell 'em I'll be there."

"Okay," said Whittaker.

"Come on, Matt," said Gideon. "I—"

He stopped in the middle of what he was going to say. A new message was coming in, a distant voice sounded clearly, and two of the radio operators glanced at each other in a swift, meaningful way which told its own story. Matthew watched. Whittaker was already on the telephone but was looking out of his office.

An operator said, "Okay, right away." He turned to look at one of the District map tables. "Smash-and-grab raid at Kilber's in Hatton Gardens. One of our men injured trying to stop the car's getaway."

"Okay," the patrol-car control said, and began to put out the messages.

Gideon put a hand on one man's shoulder.

"When Mr. Whittaker's off the telephone, ask him to call Mr. Appleby, in my office, to have Hatton Gardens checked. Seems a queer place for a night smash-and-grab job to me. Better have the street and district cordoned off."

"Right, sir."

"Come on, Matthew," Gideon said, and this time they got out of the room without being interrupted.

4 . Common Factors

IT WAS much foggier in the Yard than when they had arrived, and the Embankment lights were all invisible, little more than pale haloes in the murk. But it wasn't the kind of fog to keep traffic to a standstill; there was at least a fifty-yard visibility. Squad cars were on the move, engines roaring, the gas and smoke from their exhausts smelling strong and unpleasant on the fog-laden, windless air. Yellow fog lights shone on the fog, cars passed and Gideon got into his own, making the body sway to one side with his fifteen stones, and Matthew got in the other. Doors slammed.

"Listen, Matt," Gideon said, "I've got a lot on my mind and I'm not going to talk much, but don't let that worry you."

"No, I won't."

"You've had a quick look at what the job can be like," went on Gideon. "Sometimes it goes on like that right through the night, but often nothing very big comes of it. We've got this baby-snatching job tonight and we don't like it. It'll be all right if we get the babies back but hell if we don't. The job can be hell. There are times when I've hated what's happened."

"I can understand that," Matthew said gruffly.

"Good. Here's another thing you ought to bear in mind. That radio operator used shorthand. He can also speak Italian, Spanish, Russian, Greek and Dutch. There's bound to be someone with the Scandinavian languages and someone else in the building who knows others. You can't know too much, and you can always find a use for what you know."

"I could see that, too," said Matthew thoughtfully. "Especially about the shorthand. I thought the only decent job you needed shorthand for was journalism. One of them did hold a long conversation in a language I didn't understand, too."

"Well, you kept your eyes and ears open, anyway. On the whole, did you enjoy it?"

Matthew didn't reply at once, and so puzzled Gideon, but it was too difficult a drive to allow him to glance at the boy. He turned round Parliament Square as a bus loomed up dangerously close, and he let it push its way ahead.

"I didn't just enjoy it," Matthew said quietly. "I was fascinated, Dad. I want to be a policeman more than ever."

Gideon said, "Well, don't be in too much of a hurry." He was wondering what Kate would say and what he ought to do. Matthew had undoubted brilliance, and a scholastic flair. The Force wasn't exactly what he'd had in mind for the boy.

He couldn't think about it then, anyway.

Fifteen minutes later, Matthew got out of the car to walk toward Hurlingham, and Gideon turned into a narrow side street which took him to Hurdle Street and the disaster which had struck at Number 27.

It was never possible to tell how human beings would react under this kind of savage pressure and shock. The mother's reaction might vary from shrieking hysterics to cold, frightening quiet. The best reaction was tears developing into words which wouldn't stop. As Gideon approached the front door of 27 Hurdle Street he heard a woman talking so fast that it was difficult to distinguish the words. If that was Mrs. Harris, it was a good thing.

The street was crowded with police cars. Neighbors were out in strength, in spite of the biting cold and the fog. Front doors were wide open, light streamed from them into the street, and from windows also; yet there were places where it was impossible to see across the road. Policemen and the public made shadowy figures. People were coughing; someone gave half a dozen loud sneezes.

Inside the front room was Wragg, of GH Division, a man not unlike Appleby to look at, but with jet black hair smoothed down glossily over his smallish head, and a black mustache. In the room with him were photographers, fingerprint men and two others who were taking measurements of the position of the cot. There was a tall, bald-headed man and a short, stocky one—the stocky man had the hurt baffled look of a distracted father.

The woman was talking somewhere else in the house.

Wragg flashed a quick smile; he had very white teeth.

"Hello there," he greeted. "I thought you wouldn't be long. These chaps don't need telling anything, though." He glanced at a portly man standing by the window of the little, crowded room; that was Willy Smith, of CD Division. "We had a message just now that a chap who was on the baby job at AB will be here soon, too."

"Good," said Gideon. "Who's the father—stocky chap?"

"Yes. The other chap's a neighbor, named Fraser."

It was like Wragg to hand out information wherever he was, and like Willy Smith to let him; there was no false Divisional pride in Willy. He grinned at Gideon, but behind the grin there was anxiety for this man and his wife and the stolen child.

"How'd it happen?"

Wragg explained briefly and comprehensively.

"How'd the snatcher get in?" asked Gideon quietly.

"Well, they have a key on a piece of string just inside the door; you can hook it out through the letter box. Thousands of people do that. It doesn't help to tell them it's inviting trouble. Looks as if the key was hooked out, anyway. No prints on the door; no scratches, either. But the front-room window's open a couple of inches. He could have come in that way, too."

"I see," said Gideon, and stepped to Harris's side.

"Mr. Harris?"

Harris looked up almost blankly, and nodded.

"I'm from Scotland Yard," Gideon said quietly, "and I would like you to know that we shall do everything humanly possible to get the child back before the night is out. I expect the others have asked you to try to think of everything that might help us."

Harris nodded again. He looked rather like a man who was punch drunk, and didn't quite know where he was or what was going on. He wasn't likely to be any help to anyone. The chief hope lay in the neighbor or in the child's mother. There was no point in talking to her now—while she was talking nineteen to the dozen just inside the kitchen.

"Place to talk next door," Willy Smith volunteered. "I fixed it with Fraser."

"Let's go," said Gideon.

The room looked in turmoil, the street looked like the scene after an accident, but in fact the situation was completely under control, and no time was wasted. Gideon was used to the matter-of-fact way in which the men went about their job, the quiet questions, the unflurried search for fingerprints, footprints, anything that might give the slightest help. Plainclothes men were questioning the neighbors, too, trying to find anyone who had been in the street during the time that the Harrises had been out of their house. More policemen were on duty outside Number 29, and as Gideon went inside he had to duck, the top of the doorway was so low.

Here, the front room was better furnished, and obviously little used. The light was bright, and a gas fire hissed and glowed more yellow than red.

"I was on the snatch that we had earlier," Wragg said. "House in Field Street, much the same type as this. Young parents, named Dean. First child, four months old, asleep in a 'carricot' in the back of their little car. They were out shopping, and parked the car in a side street near their road. They say they weren't away for ten minutes, but when they got back the baby was gone. By the time I got there, the mother was in hysterics. Still is, probably."

"Any leads?"

"None at all, but—" Wragg stopped as there was a tap at the door and a big, burly-looking, youngish man appeared with a shock of gingery hair, red cheeks and bright blue eyes. He was wearing a new-looking overcoat and he stood at attention.

"Mr. Gideon, sir?"

"Yes," said Gideon. "You from AB Division?"

"Yes, sir. Detective Sergeant Hill."

"You were on the spot at the baby-snatching job, weren't you?" asked Gideon, and motioned Hill further into the room. He closed the door before obeying, and obviously regarded Gideon with awe. He had very large hands and long arms, and he looked astounded when Gideon offered him a cigarette from a fat silver case, kept for offering.

"If you don't mind, sir, I won't just now—never smoke except when I'm at home."

"Good rule," said Gideon. "Let's have the story, will you?"

Hill told it in detail yet with no waste of words. The AB Divisional case ran more parallel to the Hurdle Street kidnaping than the kidnaping from the car. A four-month-old baby boy had been asleep in the kitchen of a small house, and his mother had been in the front of the house, talking with the minister of a local non-conformist church. Entry had been through the back door, which had been approached through a small back yard in turn approached from a service alley. It had been the first of the three kidnapings, and had first been discovered at half past six.

"So what is there in common?" asked Gideon quietly. "Give me yours again, Mr. Wragg, will you?"

Wragg did, succinctly.

Gideon nodded at Willy Smith, who gave the details, as known, of the kidnaping here in Hurdle Street.

"Have a go, Hill, and see what common factors you find," Gideon said.

"I'd rather leave it to you, sir."

His deferential manner, very near to obsequiousness, was beginning to irritate Gideon, but he didn't show it. Nor did Willy Smith; but Wragg looked with obvious impatience at the sergeant from the neighboring Division.

"All right," said Gideon. "Each baby was male. Each was about four months old. Each was healthy. Each was in a room or a car, asleep. Each job was done between six o'clock and nine fifteen tonight. Each was in this part of London; the place of kidnaping was probably within the radius of a mile from the place where GH, AB and CD Divisions meet. Each was the child of parents in more or less the same social and financial position—each family has enough money to rub along with but, as far as we yet know, none of them is wealthy—not wealthy enough to pay a fat ransom, for instance." Gideon paused, and it seemed as if that was for breath as much as anything else. "Each appears to have been a happy family, and the father as badly upset as the mother. Each kidnaping might have been done with some knowledge of where the baby was likely to be at a certain time—it's not certain that these were all chance kidnapings, as they would have been if all the jobs had been by day, and the babies taken from outside shops or houses. No sign of violence in any case; all cots and bedclothes undisturbed. So far, no evidence in any case whether the kidnaper was a man or woman."

Gideon stopped, as if he'd finished this time.

"Another thing," Willy Smith put in dryly. "Only a madman would do a thing like this. Man or woman."

Gideon didn't comment. Hill was having difficulty in keeping his big hands still; obviously he was likely to be ill at ease all the time he was in Gideon's presence. Wragg said abruptly:

"Could be a looney, but—"

There was a flurry of movement outside, and after a brief pause someone tapped sharply at the door. Gideon, his back to the fire, was beginning to feel too hot, and was also feeling uneasy because so far there was nothing at all that could be constructed as a lead to the kidnaper.

"Come in."

It was a plain-clothes detective sergeant from the Yard.

"Hello, Jones, what's up?" asked Gideon.

"Thought you'd better know this at once, sir," said the sergeant. "Young chap outside has been riding round the block on his motorbike a lot tonight. He had it new—new secondhand, that is—yesterday, and meant to ride it, fog or no fog. He says he was pulled in at the curb with engine trouble just round the corner in Grettley Street—the end of this street, sir—when he saw a man coming round the corner carrying a baby. This was about twenty past eight."

"Ah," breathed Gideon. "Any description?"

"Smallish, and wearing a raincoat and a trilby hat, sir."

"That all?"

"The best I could get," Rasen said.

"Sure it was a man?"

"The motorcyclist says so, sir."

Hill's eyes were glistening and his hands stopped fidgeting. Willy Smith clapped his hands, and Wragg was eager.

"Now we're looking for a smallish man seen with a baby near the other two places," Gideon said. "Hill, use one of the radio cars outside to contact your Division, and put out that description, will you?"

"Yes, sir!" Hill went hurrying.

"Gor, where do they get 'em from these days?" Wragg almost exploded, but he was also on the way to the door.

"Hold it," said Gideon sharply. "We're looking for something else. Three baby kidnapings in one evening, out of the blue, add up to someone who isn't normal. Why should anyone take three in a row? We're looking for a motive, or else we're looking for a maniac."

"Where does that get us?" Wragg asked reasonably.

"Dunno," said Gideon, "but it's something to think about, and we might pick up a lead."

"Right," said Wragg. "Motive or mania!"

"Right," said Willy Smith.

They went out together.

Gideon felt a sense of frustration, even of anger with himself, because he could do so little, and nothing really quickly. He asked himself the questions again: why had the babies been kidnaped—three children of parents who were unknown to one another? It seemed certain that the three kidnapings had been by the same individual, and he didn't like to take refuge behind the "mania" theory.

The need for a motive nagged at him.

It would nag at Wragg and Smith, too, and one of them might get an idea. In any case, just by being here he had gingered them up, and they would be on their mettle—Division working against Division, too. A little competition wouldn't do any harm. He hadn't really wasted a journey, and had seen again the thing that he had seen hundreds, even thousands of times before, and which never failed to make him hopeful.

The police, at work.

Within half an hour policemen by the hundreds would be questioning people in the neighborhood of the three places from which the babies had been kidnaped. The motorcyclist's lead might be decisive. He'd talked to young Matthew about the uses of general knowledge, but hadn't mentioned the advantages of thoroughness for detail and Lady Luck.

He went out into the passage, then into the street, seeing the crowd, the cars, the wreathing mist, the pale yellow lights—and then hearing a voice quite clear above the rumble of conversation.

"Hear what he said? They found the kid, dead."

When he first heard that, Gideon was just outside the Frasers' house. By the time he had walked ten paces he had heard it a dozen times, sometimes whispered, often spoken in a loud, clear voice. It traveled from speaker to speaker and was taken up on the instant, as a cheer is taken up among crowds lining a street to see some great celebrity. Gideon's first reaction was to reject it, but he was in no position to reject or accept; so far it was simply rumor.

He came upon the Flying Squad man, Detective Inspector Rasen, and asked gruffly:

"Is it true? The child's been found?"

"Don't know anything about it myself, sir." Rasen looked about the crowd distastefully. "Lot of ghouls, that's what they are."

"Get the story checked, will you?"

"Yes, right away." The Flying Squad man called his car crew, and in turn they called the police who were questioning the crowd. In a few minutes Gideon felt better; it had been a rumor, and was soon tracked down to its source, a man who had said, "Wouldn't it be awful if they found the baby dead?" But the rumor and the speed with which it had traveled had robbed Gideon of any hope of peace of mind. He went back to 27 Hurdle Street, feeling bleak and depressed. All the photographs, of the fingerprints and the baby's cot had been taken; there seemed little hope of getting a line from anything found there.

The woman was no longer talking.

Gideon knew that he need not stay. He had come to see how the job was being handled, and couldn't really handle it himself, could only set the pace. He'd set it, and would be much more use back at his desk; yet he was hesitant about going, and stood in the little passage, big and massive and powerful looking, aware that several Yard and Divisional officers were looking at him and wondering what he was going to do.

Two men, Harris and his neighbor Fraser, were in the kitchen. The door was ajar. A man, probably Harris, was talking in a despairing kind of voice, protestingly. Gideon took a step nearer.

"I don't care what you say," a woman said. "If they don't find my baby, I'll do away with myself. Life just wouldn't be worth living."

Gideon turned to a man just behind him.

"Anyone sent for a doctor?"

"Not to my knowledge, sir."

"See it's done, will you—find out the name of the Harrises' family doctor first."

"Yes, sir."

"May, dear," another woman was saying anxiously, "it's no use talking like that, honestly, and in any case—"

"If they don't find my baby, I'll do away with myself," the mother said. "I shouldn't have gone out and left him, that's the truth. It was my fault. It wasn't anyone else's fault, it was my fault. *Fred* didn't want to come. It's no use saying anything, Fred. You were sitting in that chair with that book in your hands, and you didn't want to come out, so it was my fault. And all because of a rotten television program, too. I risked my baby's life all because of that; it's my fault."

Gideon pushed open the door.

He almost filled the doorway, and his very bulk made the others stare at him. The dumpy, frizzy-haired woman was startled; the dark-haired, taller woman with a masklike face and desperately glittering eyes looked as if it didn't matter if the devil walked in. She was sitting on an upright chair, with her husband just behind her. The neighbor's husband was standing by the window.

"Mrs. Harris?" asked Gideon quietly.

She stared.

"You haven't—" began Harris unexpectedly, and the tone of his voice seemed to transform his wife. She sprang to her feet and flung herself at Gideon, and in that shattering moment Gideon realized that he had done the one unforgivable thing; he had given the parents unjustified hope. The woman clutched his hands, and she was trembling; and he cursed himself for having pushed open the door.

"I just came to tell you that hundreds of policemen will be searching for your child within the next hour, Mrs. Harris, and that we shall do everything it's humanly possible to do."

He had meant to try and take her mind off despair; instead, he had cast her more deeply into it. She dropped his hands. She seemed to stop trembling. She turned back to her husband, who put his arms round her shoulders and stared at Gideon as if pleading with him to go before he did more harm.

All a man could do was try.

And within a mile of this house, two other families knew this same grief.

But now, facts were building up. Wax polish on the floor beneath the partly open windows had a shiny surface which hadn't been smeared that night, so the kidnaper had used a key—probably the one hanging in the letter box. There was a chance that the kidnaper knew that a key was kept there—and obviously many neighbors knew that. So all the neighbors would have to be questioned quickly and closely. The right way to deal with the Harrises was to give them plenty to think about, too, and to let them help with the investigation.

Willy Smith came up.

"Wouldn't be someone who'd lost a child, and was looking for him, would it?" he asked almost apologetically. "I've just been thinking about the Postlewaite case, when a woman lost her own child—natural causes, if you remember—and wouldn't believe it was dead. She went round taking other babies out of their prams, and when stopped with one, swore it was her own." When Gideon didn't answer, Smith went on: "Don't you remember? About seven years ago, and—"

"Oh, I remember," said Gideon. "I'm just wondering if you've got something there. Try it, Willy. Check with the Registrars of Births and Deaths, find out if anyone living near the Harrises has lost a baby recently. The weakness is that a *man* wouldn't be likely to be affected, but the mother—"

"We've been told it was a man."

"I know, but try it. That motorcyclist might have made a mistake in the dark."

"I'll send a man round to the Registrar of Births at once; that won't take long. If we have a bit of luck we might get a break soon. Any special way you want us to handle the job?"

"Your way," said Gideon.

"Thanks." Smith looked up at him with a half smile. "I'll see you get all the news as it comes in. There's a chap from the *Evening Globe* outside, by the way. Any special angle?"

"Don't think so," said Gideon. "The more publicity we get on this job, the better."

"Taking the very words out of my mouth," said Smith.

Gideon went to his car, and wasn't surprised to see another one just behind it, marked *Press*. No one stood near and he hadn't yet been recognized. He got into the car and drove off. Two policemen had to clear a way for him, there were so many people about. The fog seemed to have lifted a little just here, too; he could see the curious faces more clearly. Ghouls? If they started another rumor and it reached Mrs. Harris, they would be more than ghouls.

He flicked on his radio.

"Gideon here—any messages?"

"No special messages for you, sir, but we've just had a flash from Hatton Gardens."

"Go on."

"The smash and grab was a decoy raid, drew two of our chaps off a burglary a hundred yards away, but we caught the lot." There was deep satisfaction in the speaker's voice. "Two were involved in the smash and grab, two others were found on enclosed premises."

"Fine! Where was it?"

"Marks and Sanders," the man said.

The firm of Marks and Sanders was one of the largest diamond merchants in Hatton Gardens. The premises had an elaborate burglarproof system and a fortune in precious stones was usually kept in its strong room. Well, that was a score to him. Four men on a charge, a burglary stopped, and a success to give the men at the Yard an added incentive. It might all have happened in exactly the same way if he hadn't sent that message through to Appleby; but it might not. . . .

He turned a corner, and a few yards along found that the fog was even thicker than it had been earlier; so it was patchy, and was moving from place to place. What he wanted was a good steady fifteen-miles-an-hour wind that would shift the damned stuff.

He crawled along at twenty miles an hour. Two people passed, and he could hear what they said quite clearly. The radio kept crackling, but he didn't turn it off. It was after ten, but the night had hardly started. God knew what was going on behind this blanket of fog—how many people were frightened, how many people were in a kind of terror, how many were planning some crime, how many—

"What you want is a whisky and soda," Gideon said aloud, and he promised himself he would have one as soon as he reached the Yard. But he didn't go straight up to the canteen; he went to the office, and opened it to find Appleby and the brown-clad sergeant together. He didn't like Appleby's expression.

"What's up?" asked Gideon sharply.

"They found the body of the first baby in a Fulham garden, not far from where it was taken," Appleby said. "Suffocated."

This time it was true.

5 . The Prowler

GIDEON sat alone at his desk half an hour afterward. Appleby had gone down to the canteen for a cup of tea. The office was blessedly quiet, and the telephone hadn't rung for fifteen minutes, but it would soon. Downstairs there was little doubt that the Information Bureau was getting really busy. Every mean little crook in London would see his chance tonight, and it wasn't cold enough to keep them indoors.

The important, in fact, the essential thing was to keep a sense of balance. One had to. Most of the time it was easy enough, but when something happened like tonight, the sense of balance could be too easily disturbed; one could see life as one sordid tragedy after another, instead of getting a true perspective.

The telephone rang.

"Here it goes," Gideon thought, and lifted the receiver. "Yes."

"Mrs. Gideon's on the line, sir."

"Put her through," said Gideon.

If this had been by day, the call would have surprised him; Kate seldom called. Was there some kind of family emergency? His thoughts ran quickly, but evenly enough, over the possibility. Matthew hadn't been fool enough to stay out, had he? He was uneasy about Matthew, not sure that he had helped him.

"Hello, George."

"Hello, Kate." His anxiety didn't sound in his voice.

"I wondered if you'd be in."

No emergency, then. What was it?

"I know where I'm best off," said Gideon. "The office is as warm as toast, and—"

"What have you been doing to Matthew?"

"Eh?"

"You heard me," Kate said.

He could picture her sitting by the telephone in the kitchen, where there was an extension. She was probably on the arm of his chair, wearing a black skirt and white blouse, a full-bosomed, handsome woman with a gleam in her eyes, a good complexion and an air of great competence.

"All I did was to let him have a look round at the Information Room."

"If you'd given him a hundred pounds, you couldn't have pleased him more. He's been going round with his head in the clouds ever since he got back—it's the first night I've ever known when he didn't want any supper!"

Gideon chuckled.

"What I really told him was that I wanted him to go all out for that university scholarship."

"That I don't believe," said Kate. "I—just a minute."

She put the telephone down on the table by the chair; for a few moments he heard nothing. He smiled at the thought that Kate had called up just for a chat; for it amounted to that. It went deeper, of course, and Matthew had made the reason clear. She was edgy when her George was out at night, and needed a kind of reassurance, and—

Something seemed to hit Gideon a savage blow.

Years ago, Kate and he had lost a child, one about the dead baby's age. He had been out, after Kate had pleaded with him to stay. That had begun an estrangement which only the years had broken down; and tonight there were three babies, one dead and two in danger. Until this minute he hadn't thought of that.

"George?"

"Hello, I'm still here."

There was a note of laughter in Kate's voice.

"It was Matthew. He found that he was hungry after all. Apparently you didn't do him any serious harm. What did he talk about?"

"Where is he now?"

"In the larder, foraging."

"Well, don't let him know that you know yet," said Gideon. "This fancy might fade out. He wants to give up the idea of a university, and join the Force as copper."

Gideon paused, but Kate didn't respond immediately, and he went on more quickly and a little anxiously. "He has a silly notion that the life is adventurous and romantic, and I tried to make sure that he knows that it could be dull."

"I don't know what you tried to do, but you succeeded in making him think that our policemen are wonderful—even including his father," Kate said, quite normally. "I've suspected for some time that he didn't want to sit for the examination, but"—she was anxious after all—"can't we persuade him that he'd be more use at the Yard as a lawyer than—"

"A flatfoot," Gideon said dryly. "We'll have a damned good try. Anything else, Kate?"

"Not really," Kate said, and then added almost brusquely, "What kind of a night is it up there?"

"Bit misty," Gideon said promptly.

"I know you and a 'bit misty,'" Kate said roundly. "It wouldn't be thick here and thin by the river, but I didn't mean that. I meant are you busy?"

"Busyish," said Gideon, and hesitated, and realized more clearly and without the sense of shock that the reason that he had gone to Hurdle Street was because of the death of his own child so many years ago. Subconscious compulsion. In the morning, Kate would open her newspaper and read the headlines, and if he didn't tell her now she would probably think that he had deliberately kept it back from her. So: "One very ugly job," he told her.

"Oh."

"Looks like a psychopathic case," Gideon went on. "Three young babies have been kidnaped." He needn't tell her that one of them was dead.

She was momentarily quiet again. Then:

"I'm sorry it happened on the night you're there," she said, "but perhaps it's as well for the parents that it did." She implied: "You'll do everything possible, it matters so much to you." Then she went on with a spurious lightness of tone: "Any news of the Prowler?"

"It looks as if he's having a night off," said Gideon.

Another telephone rang and he glanced toward it—and, while it was still ringing, Kate said, "I can hear that. I'll ring off, darling," and she rang off. He smoothed his chin as he put the receiver back and stretched out for the other.

Kate had done him a world of good; he must find some way of making her understand that.

"Yes," he said, "Gideon here."

"Got a Prowler job," said Whittaker from the Information Room. "Out at Brixton."

This was it; the half-hoped-for and half-feared. Here was the deepest reason for Gideon being at the Yard tonight; here was the greatest challenge. By it, Kate, the kidnaped babies, Matthew, everything and everyone were bundled out of Gideon's mind.

"Bad case?" he barked.

"Usual, I suppose," said Whittaker. "This girl had been out to a youth club. She usually comes home with her boy friend, but the boy had hurt his ankle and couldn't walk, so she came back on her own. This swine was crouching just inside the porch of her house; she didn't see him until she was almost on him. He jumped at her and nearly choked the life out of her."

"Anything else?"

"The usual. Cut some of her hair off, but that's all."

"Fetish job," Gideon said, making that half a statement and half a question. "He take the hair away?"

"Yes."

"Got the color, some of the hair, and . . . ?"

"Chestnut, long wavy, and we've sent a few strands over to the lab."

"Fine," said Gideon. "How is the girl?"

"She'll be all right when she's got over the shock. It happened an hour ago. She wasn't found for twenty minutes or so, and her parents lost their heads. I say she'll be all right," went on Whittaker in a different tone, "and she will be, but he came nearer to choking the life out of her than any of the others. One of these days—"

"I know," said Gideon. "What've you done?"

"The usual. Flashed QR and ST Divisions and all patrol cars, and . . ."

"Wait a minute," Gideon said. "It's a nasty night and we've already one big job on, but we've got to go all out to get the Prowler, too. The two jobs overlap in places. So far they're in the central districts, mostly near the river. I'll call each of the outer ring Divisions and get some help. You call available patrol cars and have them block bridges and underground stations. We'll stop buses, too. We want a man with a lock of hair in his pocket, long hairs probably on his clothes. He—"

"You're really going to town," Whittaker broke in. "We can't start searching until—"

"We don't have to search; we only have to threaten to, and our man will panic," said Gideon. "Get a move on—stop all traffic at barriers on bridges, main roads and stations, and put a cordon round."

"There could be hell to pay—"

"There will be if you don't get started," Gideon said. "There won't be many people out tonight, so traffic will be pretty thin. It can be done. Right?"

"You're the boss," said Whittaker. "Right."

"Let me know how things go," said Gideon.

He had been aware of the door opening soon after he'd started to talk, and glanced up to see Appleby, brisk, fresh and rather startled. He put the receiver down but kept his hand on it.

"Hear all that, Charley?"

"Yes. Prowler?"

"Yes. Get on that telephone and call the outer ring Divisions—one for you and one for me, until we've done 'em all. We want a dozen uniformed men from each into QR and ST, quick—and we want our own chaps at the road blocks."

Appleby was already at Lemaitre's desk.

"Then what?"

"We want every pedestrian questioned about a baby seen out tonight, *and* about that hair," said Gideon.

"We need samples of the hair—"

"You may have a lot of trouble in the morning," warned Appleby.

"I'll take what's coming, and if we get the Prowler or those babies we won't have many questions. The fog is all the cover most crooks need; our chaps might as well concentrate on one or two."

"Right," Appleby said.

Both men were on the telephone without respite for twenty minutes. By that time the concentration of police in the Divisions directly concerned was nearly finished, bridge barriers were set up, and the great search was on.

Gideon made written and mental notes as he went on, checked and double-checked, and made sure nothing had been forgotten. If the Prowler and those two children were inside the cordon, they would probably be found.

When it was finished, he lit a cigarette and sat back.

"Anything else doing?" he asked Appleby.

"Not much, yet—only just turned eleven." Appleby smoothed down his brittle-looking, close-cut hair. Midgeley came on and said he'd told his chaps to lay off the pros tonight; anyone out for business in weather like this deserves a break.

Gideon grunted noncommittally.

"The Hatton Gardens chaps are over at Cannon Row," Appleby went on. "Got three at a warehouse in Smithfield, helping themselves to carcasses of mutton. Couple of back-door jobs in Park Lane. We called off two night-club raids; wouldn't be likely to get a big enough haul. Had a call from Paris; there's a Johnny on the nine-o'clock plane carrying about two hundred watches—we've tipped off the Customs. That chap Grey over at Cannon Row for the landlady murders has collapsed—he's been sent to the hospital, and old Gore thinks it's genuine."

"Something I needn't worry about now," Gideon said. "And what else?"

"That's about all."

"Enough," said Gideon ruefully.

He had come to get the Prowler, because the Prowler was doing a lot of harm. It was always the devil when one man seemed able to cock a snook at the police for any length of time, and there was risk that the Prowler would become more violent the longer he stayed free.

Would he kill?

That was an academic question. He would terrify, anyhow. Whittaker could say that his latest victim would be all right, but how did he know? What kind of shock to the nervous system was a thing like this? If it happened to one of his daughters he wouldn't be complacent about it; he—

A telephone rang.

"Gideon," he said.

"There's a Mrs. Penn on the line, sir," said the operator, "and she particularly wants to speak to you."

"Penn?"

"Yes."

"Got her address?"

"Yes, sir, she's at 21 Horley Street, Fulham."

"AB Division?"

"That's right, sir."

"Put her through," said Gideon.

Here was the harassed, worried, stubborn and courageous Mrs. Penn, the woman whose young husband had run out on her, and who was sure that something "awful" had happened. He wondered how she had got hold of his name, and wondered also if he could find out more than Lemaitre or the Divisional men had yet been able to discover.

He waited for a long time.

Then the operator came on the line.

"Sorry about that, sir, she's gone off—been cut off, prob'ly. Shall I put her through when she comes on again?"

"Yes," said Gideon, "at once."

There was nothing he could do.

In that part of southwest London covered by the ST and the QR Divisions, the police were not only out in strength, but they were in a much more angry mood than usual, for the Prowler had often struck on the borders of the two Divisions, and the Divisional Superintendents hadn't minced words when they had said what they thought of the men on the beat. That, of course, was unjust. The Criminal Investigation Department was fairly well up to strength, but the uniformed branches were short one man in three of full establishment. The Superintendents knew it, but they also knew that something was needed to get their men right on their toes tonight, and a few nicely chosen words to individuals for passing on through sergeants had that effect. There was more: if the Prowler was caught it would be a feather in the Divisional cap.

Above everything, Gideon was on the rampage.

The fog was not so bad in that part of London, but patchy. The Prowler might decide to call it a day, but the police would assume that he hadn't. Still, facts were facts. In that part of London there were nine times as many streets as there were policemen, and even when the reinforcements arrived there would still be many more streets than policemen. Some of the streets were so long that, even on a clear night, it was difficult to see from one end to the other. The Prowler might lurk in one street for an hour, and not run the slightest risk. He would hide in a doorway, too, or behind hedges or walls—always in the most unexpected place; but he only attacked from the front doors or the gardens of the houses of his victims. Only two certain things were known about him: the shiny face, probably a mask, and the fact that he always knew where to attack. He must study the places where he was going to work, being sure that a young girl lived there.

He usually chose girls in their late teens; pretty girls, too.

Jennifer Lewis was nineteen.

She was not usually afraid of the dark or afraid of the Prowler, for the Prowler, although familiar as a name, was someone out of a book—a creature one read about but who didn't really exist. She would not have worried about walking home on her own that night, except for the man who had sat on the bus opposite her and kept looking at her, and who had jumped off the bus just after her.

Her home, in Middleton Street, Brixton, was over ten minutes' walk from the bus stop, and part of the way it was along narrow, ill-lit streets. Because of the patchy fog, she couldn't walk quite so quickly tonight; sometimes, near street lamps, it was almost dazzling, at others she found herself on the curb when she thought she was in the middle of the pavement.

She was a pretty girl, with a nice figure and nice legs. Attractive in every way. She had a boy friend whom she felt sure she was going to marry in a few years' time, but he was away on his National Service, and Jennifer Lewis believed that, if your own boy friend couldn't see you home, no boy should.

The man followed her; or she thought he did.

She didn't even see him when she looked round, but she could hear his footsteps, and they always seemed to be exactly the same distance away. She turned two corners, rather slowly each time, and he still came on. By then she was breathing hard and hating her fears, quickening her pace whenever she could, dreading moments when she had to slow down.

Then the footsteps behind her stopped.

She listened for a few seconds, fearful that they would start again, but they didn't. She tried to convince herself that the man had reached his home, that he hadn't been following her, but her imagination began to play tricks, and she was almost sure that he was tiptoeing after her, making no noise. Could he be walking on his stockinged feet?

She strained her ears for the slightest sound, but there was none. The streets were deserted. Lights shone at the front of a few houses, but these were few and far between. The night was clearer as she neared her own street, and at last she came within sight of the lamp and the post box at the corner. For the first time since she had left the bus, she felt relief from tension, although she still walked quickly. As it happened, there was no street light near the front of her home, and, as the family lived at the back, there would be no light at the front windows. She passed the lighted window of one house, several doors away, and saw the shadows of a man and woman against the blind.

Now she walked more naturally, and without tension.

It was very nasty just here, the middle of a thicker fog patch, but there was no longer any danger of losing her way or wandering into the curb, because the gate of her house was painted a pale blue and couldn't be mistaken. She saw it, looking almost as if it were coated with luminous paint, and opened it quickly. It squeaked a little, but she expected that. The silence about her was so complete that, of itself, it seemed frightening.

Yet she was no longer frightened.

She did not think of the Prowler.

The porch of the house was narrow, and normally she could see every inch of it from the gate, but tonight the fog put it out of sight, as well as the door, which was painted black. She took three short steps toward the porch. . . .

A figure appeared in front of her, the figure of a leaping man.

Pain born of fear slashed across her breast; then came horror. But before she could scream, before she even tried to, the man's hands were at her throat. She felt the pressure of his fingers, suddenly and savagely brutal.

Her own arms were free and waving wildly.

She felt herself carried backward by the man's weight, and would have fallen but for his gripping fingers. She couldn't breathe, had no hope at all of shouting, of calling for help. His face was close to hers, a hideous, grinning face, a *mask* of a face.

Then she kicked him.

She wore sensible walking shoes with solid toe caps and felt the kick strike home and heard him wince, even felt him relax his grip. She kicked again with all her strength, and for the second time the toe cap struck home. This time there was a sharp sound; she had caught him squarely on the shin. Again his fingers relaxed but didn't let go altogether. She had time to clutch at his wrists, and dug her fingernails into the flesh.

All the time she saw that leering mask of a face and heard him breathing, felt his hot breath on her cheeks.

She could breathe.

She screamed.

"Help!" she shrieked, and the sound came shrill and louder than she had dared hope. *"Help, help, help!"* She pulled despairingly at the man's wrists, feeling them warm and sticky where blood came from the scratches, and in her terror she kept screaming and kicking and writhing—until suddenly he struck her viciously across the face. She went staggering, gasping as he leaped for her again.

She fell, but her hands were free for a moment and she struck out blindly. She caught her finger under the edge of that grinning mask, and actually dislodged the mask itself; when she struck again it slid off his face but was held by string or elastic in a grotesque position alongside him. He seemed like a two-headed monster—and the bared teeth and the savagery on his real face were worse by far than the false one.

"Heeeeeelp!" she screeched into the dark night, but could hear nothing, felt only the fingers of his left hand at her throat again as he knelt on her. She saw something bright and glinting in his other hand.

A knife.

Oh, God, no!

Then she felt a tug at her hair. She didn't realize what he was doing, but, as she fought, he banged her head against the cold stone of the ground, and she felt great pain.

She nearly lost consciousness.

Then footsteps sounded; of running men.

The Prowler raised Jennifer's head and banged it down three times, but at the third he peered upward into the murk, as if only then hearing the footsteps. He let her go, and jumped up. Men were coming in the same direction as the girl had come. The Prowler turned in the other as soon as he reached the pavement, and started to run—and his rubber-soled shoes made little sound.

Clearly, a man said, "Hear that?"

"Someone running."

"After him!"

"Never mind him; we want to find who screamed."

They were approaching more slowly now, and the beam of a torch lit up the wreathing fog. The padding footsteps of the Prowler were fading.

A street door opened, and a man appeared with a woman just behind him. The two men were almost level with the doorway.

"What's happening?" asked the man from the house. "We heard . . ."

"Someone screamed," said one of the two men abruptly. "Must have been near here. You look for her; we'll go after the swine who ran away." He started to move quickly, but already the slither of padding footsteps had faded, and not far along Middleton Street there were turnings to the right and left, and, not far beyond these, other turnings which led in several different directions.

The men reached the first corner, and hesitated.

The man and woman whose shadows had appeared on the blind of the house near Jennifer's were now walking toward the spot where she lay, while other doors opened, other neighbors appeared and called out.

The first neighbor saw Jennifer lying there, and his wife exclaimed, "Look!" He went to Jennifer quickly, shining the torch—on her legs, both bent, her skirt, which was rucked up, one hand, her face, her chestnut hair, which had come loose from the tight-fitting hat, and:

"Look, that's *blood*," the woman neighbor gasped.

6 . The Con Man

GIDEON lifted the receiver of the ringing telephone slowly, and before he put it to his ear he finished reading one of the reports which had just come in from NE Division, which covered part of the East End of London, and part of the riverside area. It did not really say very much, but the little was interesting.

London did not have gangs in the accepted sense, but it housed several gangs which worked all the southern racecourses, and they had been very quiet of late. Tonight, said the NE Divisional Report, the two largest, Melky's gang and the Wide boys, were out in strength, and it looked as if there might be a clash. There was no indication yet of the place of meeting, and no certainty that there would be trouble.

The irony was that the Divisional man asked if the Yard could find them additional men.

"Would happen tonight," Gideon grumbled to Appleby, who was reading a copy of the same report, and then he said into the telephone, "Gideon."

Appleby saw the way his great body seemed to gather, as if for a leap, and saw the glint in his eyes.

"Where?" he demanded, and wrote swiftly.

"Time?" He made a note.

"I've got it," he said. "You contact the Divisional at once. I'll send photographers, fingerprints and a D.I. Have the place ready for them; we want anything we can get. *Wait*. What color was her hair? . . . Chestnut color and wavy, good—tell the Division to send those scrapings over at once. . . . I don't give a damn how difficult it might be!" he roared. "Get it here! . . . All right."

He rang off.

Appleby looked across, grinning, as if about to make some crack; Gideon's glare stopped him.

"Who've we got in?" Gideon demanded.

"Piper's just back, from a false alarm in Grosvenor Square."

"He'll do." He lifted the receiver again, said, "Ask Mr. Piper to come in at once," and then rang off, but only to pick up another telephone. "Give me Laboratory," he said, and as he waited looked across at Appleby. "Who's on duty up there, do you know?"

"Gibb."

"Thanks, hello . . . Gibb? . . . Gideon . . . Fine, thanks, but busy. Listen: I've got a Prowler job and we want something quick. Girl seems to have scratched his face, and we're sending for scrapings from her finger-

nails. Have them put through the tests for blood group, will you? We might
be glad of it."

"As soon as the scrapings come."

"Thanks," said Gideon warmly. He put down the receiver again, and saw
that Appleby was writing with more than his customary speed, as if he was
anxious not to do anything wrong. Gideon smothered a grin as Appleby
glanced up but didn't speak.

After a moment of almost startling silence there was a tap at the door.
Chief Inspector Piper came in, big and fleshy and with florid skin—a man
on whom C.I.D. ex-ranks seemed to be indelibly stamped. He had rather
small, dark blue eyes.

"Hello, Piper," Gideon said. "Got a Prowler lead."

Piper's eyes lit up.

"Putting me on it, sir?"

"Yes."

"Thanks."

"Get two men from Fingerprints, two photographers for an outside job
and any sergeant you like to 51 Middleton Street, Brixton," Gideon ordered.
"A girl named Jennifer Lewis put up a fight. Fingernail scrapings are on
their way, but you might pick up a lot more to help."

Gideon paused and Piper looked as if he was bursting to get on his way.

"Anything else, sir?"

"Yes. A papier-mâché mask was found near the girl; one of those children's Guy Fawkes things. We've suspected that he wears a mask for some
time—either for disguise, to frighten his victims even more, or both. That's
the lot."

"Thanks," said Piper, and went out twice as quickly as he had come in.

Appleby looked up, smiling openly this time.

"Like offering a kid an ice cream," he said.

"Like offering you a nip," said Gideon, and bent down, opened a cupboard in his desk and took out whisky, a siphon of soda, and two glasses.
"Come and get it."

Appleby looked as if he couldn't believe his own eyes, but he got up.

Gideon called the Information Room again, and gave crisp instructions
as Appleby, at a motion of Gideon's hand, began to pour out.

"Get moving on this," Gideon ordered, while whisky was rippling and the
instructions poured out of him. "All available men to close in to points
within one mile of Brixton Town Hall. The Prowler attacked again near
there. Now believed to have been wearing a painted Guy Fawkes' mask.
He tried to kill this time; we don't know whether he's succeeded yet. Anyway, it makes him ten times more dangerous. Warn all women seen alone

in the vicinity, make them go in pairs or with male escorts wherever possible.
. . . Got all that?"

There was a pause.

"Okay," he grunted, and put down the receiver. When he looked at
Appleby it was almost a glare. "The swine will go to earth somewhere inside the cordon, or else he'll find a weak spot and slip through."

"Take it easy," Appleby abjured, almost spilling his whisky. "Not often
you take a gloomy view."

"Just struck me that we've already got a hundred men within easy reach
of the scene of attack. If we'd had another half hour to work in, we would
probably have had the cordon closed before he had a chance to get through
it. That looks like Prowler's luck to me." Unexpectedly Gideon grinned,
and picked up his drink. "You're right, though. When you've finished that
drink, how about a walk?"

"All right. I'll go down to the Information Room and make sure that
everything's being done," Appleby said dryly.

He drank up quickly and went out.

Gideon sipped again, lit another cigarette, and then picked up the telephone; this was one long series of talks and reports, and it wasn't possible
to give much concentrated thought to any one thing. That was the Commander's cross; and the cross of the Chief Superintendent on Nights, too.
From Superintendents down to detective officers, the men who went out on
specific jobs had one thing only on their minds; thus, they could concentrate
on it. They had to, or they would never get results. Sitting here like a spider
trapped in the middle of his own web, it was almost impossible to envy
Piper. Gideon could see everything that was happening, every fly they were
trying to trap, but he couldn't concentrate. He had to be dispassionate, too,
and so could sympathize if the NE Divisional Super cursed the Yard for
saying "no" to the request for extra help; to that Superintendent, the fact
that the gangs were out was the most important single fact of the night.

"Get me NE Division," Gideon said into the telephone.

"Yes, sir."

Gideon put back the receiver again and glanced through a number of other
notes and reports while he waited. The brown-clad sergeant came in, with
three short typewritten memoranda from Divisions. Gideon made more penciled notes, and wondered whether anything was happening at Lemaitre's
home, and how Lem was getting on with Fifi. If there had been any trouble,
word of it would surely have come in by now. He wondered about Mrs.
Penn; why she had asked for him, and then rung off—or else been cut off
but had not troubled to call again.

Why did it nag at him?

She lived in AB Division, and there was plenty doing there. Funny thing he couldn't get her out of his mind.

There was nothing new about the baby hunt. The other two infants were still missing, and the woman Harris in her little kitchen was probably saying exactly the same thing over and over again, still blaming herself; and if her child was killed she would always blame herself for going next door for an hour and leaving it alone, asleep. The sturdy husband of hers probably had exactly the same dazed, almost stupefied look.

It was an hour since Gideon had been told that the first baby had been found dead.

The telephone rang, and his lift of the receiver was automatic.

"Gideon."

"Your call to Mr. Hemmingway of NE Division, sir."

"Yes, put him through." Been a long time coming, he reflected, and began sardonically, "Hello, Hemmy, been having a nice sleep?"

Superintendent Hemmingway was one of the older men in the Divisions, and he preferred to work mostly at night, when his beat was always busier. Like Appleby, he was only a year or two off retirement. Like Appleby, he seemed to have more zest for his job now than when he had first taken over the Division. He didn't mince words, and he was as familiar with his beat as Gideon was with London's Square Mile.

He knew the names, addresses, ages, friends, relatives and habits of the hundreds of small-time and big-time crooks who lived in his Division. He knew just which of the stallholders in the Sunday markets would handle stolen goods knowingly, and those who wouldn't take a chance. He knew when a man was on the run and when one was having a rest. He was reputed to be able to say who had done any job in the Division or outside it, from the trade-mark left by the crook, and there were those who said that although fingerprints were not his special subject he could look at a print through the magnifying glass that he always carried and, if it was known to him, identify it almost as quickly as they could in Records. Even allowing for some exaggeration, there was a lot of truth in all of this.

On routine, and on general knowledge as well as specialized knowledge, Hemmingway was the best man in the Divisions. But he had a weakness, as they all had a weakness, and one of Gideon's difficulties was that of making sure that it did no great harm.

Hemmingway's weakness was that he always took the short view; the long view was something he couldn't see. He lacked not only imagination, but also the ability to look ahead and see what was likely to develop out of a crime or a series of crimes. He could tackle what had happened as well as any man alive, but he lacked the little something extra which would enable him to forestall the crook's next move.

"Sleep," growled Hemmingway. "How about those men I want, Gee-Gee?"

"Wish I could," said Gideon.

"Talk sense," said Hemmingway, his voice rising. "I've got to have them. There are twenty-five or thirty of the Wide boys out; thing like this doesn't happen more than once a year. Looks as if they're going to mix it. We've got to stop them from clashing."

"Hem, we've got two big jobs on—the baby snatching and the Prowler—and I've called every available man I can from the Divisions. Can't you handle your own boys?"

There was a moment of silence.

Then the door opened, and Gideon looked up and was startled to see Lemaitre come in.

Lemaitre was as pale as he had been earlier in the evening, and his dark eyes were shiny and very bright. His lips were set tightly, and he looked as if he would gladly punch the nose of the first man who got in his way. He let the door slam, which wasn't like him, and stood staring at Gideon, his yellow-and-black tie a little too bright and his shoes too light a brown.

"Look here, George," Hemmingway said at last, and it was obvious that he had been counting ten before speaking; his was not often the way of sweet reason. "You've got those two jobs covered, and if the worst comes to the worst you'll fix 'em in a few days' time. We *live* with the gangs out here. If we can't stop them from fighting tonight, every kid who's got the strength will be thumbing his nose at our coppers for the next couple of months. I want twenty more men than I've got, and that's half the number I really need. Fix it, won't you? Just five carloads—"

"I'll send two," Gideon said abruptly. "We're stretched too far tonight, but I'll send two."

"Listen, George—"

"Be seeing you," said Gideon, and added a mumbling "G'bye" before he put the receiver down. If he'd had his way he would have sent a dozen Squad cars, but far too much was happening. Whatever success they had against the gangs, there would be more trouble later; they were hardy annuals. The Prowler and the baby snatcher were much more deadly now.

Lemaitre was still standing there quite still, and his clenched fists were moving slightly, as if he was tensing his fingers all the time.

Gideon took out another glass, poured two fingers, splashed in a little soda, and stood up and carried the drink to Lemaitre. Lemaitre took it, and tossed half of it down, without saying a word.

Time was flying and time was precious, but this was a moment to take things slowly.

"Hello, Lem," Gideon said. "Everything's happening."

"You're telling me," said Lemaitre. "I want something to do, outside."

Gideon stared back as he sipped his own drink.

He could let it go at that and send Lemaitre out, with his Fifi troubles burning white hot inside him, or he could try to make Lemaitre talk. Given half an hour, given even a quarter of an hour in which he could be sure of no interruptions, he would probably be able to work on Lemaitre, and help him; but there was no such certainty and Appleby would be back any minute.

"Got two jobs," he said quietly. "Hemmingway's in a flap, Melky's and the Wide boys are out tonight and he thinks they're going to fight it out. He wants three times as many men as we can send him, and my name's mud. If you go, he'll probably think we're really doing everything we can, anyhow."

Lemaitre said flatly, "What's the other job?"

"That Penn woman who's worried about her husband. I want a man to go and see her. She called up again and then rang off before—"

"Women," said Lemaitre, between clenched teeth. "She probably drove him into the Thames. If I had my way—" He broke off, took out a fresh cigarette, lit it from the stub of the one he was smoking, and then moved to squash the stub out on an ash tray. "I'll go over to NE."

"Tell Hemmingway I'll send more men when I can," Gideon said, paused, then added in the same tone of voice, "of course, the real thing I want from you is an opinion on the situation over there. Hemmingway sees it just from his point of view, the biggest thing they have in the Division. But if you agree that it's really ugly, I'll get more men over there."

"Okay," said Lemaitre.

"What's it like out?" asked Gideon.

"Could be worse—still quicker to travel by car than tube, but it won't be if it gets much thicker," said Lemaitre. "Okay, George, thanks."

"Forget it." Gideon stood up. Appleby still wasn't back and it might be a good moment to speak personally, after all. "What did you run into, Lem?"

The reply came like a bullet.

"She's walked out on me."

"Oh, hell!" said Gideon, and for a moment he felt a surge of relief, tinged with understanding. "Sure?"

"Just packed up and walked out, clothes, knickknacks, everything." Lemaitre found a taut grin. "I know what you're thinking; it will be a good thing in the long run. I might agree with you when I'm used to the idea, but I always thought that in spite of everything, at heart she—"

He broke off.

There was a bright sheen in his eyes, his voice was thick, and he couldn't bring out the words "loved me." He was a man in his forties and men didn't come tougher; yet the wrong note now would have him blubbering.

"Lem," Gideon said.

"Oh, forget it. There's nothing you can say."

"Not so sure," said Gideon. Blessedly, the telephones were silent and there were no footsteps in the passage. "It isn't so long ago that I half expected to get home and find the same situation. Quite sure that the only thing that kept Kate home were the kids. When they were out of the puppy stage I thought she'd go. Instead, we're—well, it's in the past, Lem. This crisis could be the turning point for you, too."

Lemaitre's face was working.

"See what you mean," he said jerkily. "Thanks, George. I'll go and smack a few heads for Hemmingway." He nodded and went out, letting the door slam, and his footsteps sounded loud and clear along the stone passage.

Gideon moved slowly toward his desk and, without sitting down, picked up the telephone. He wanted a lot of time, but had very little; he had to be quick. He called for NE Division again and this time Hemmingway came through almost at once.

"Found me another copper?" he demanded abruptly. The tone of his voice suggested that he hadn't taken umbrage; he was too old a hand.

"Yes," said Gideon. "Hemmy, listen. Lemaitre's coming over. I thought I'd warn you that he's having some domestic trouble and he'd like to break a few bones. If it comes to a fight anywhere, try and get him into it. He'll be worth half a dozen of your chaps, and—"

"Not on your life. My coppers are as good as any who come from the Yard," said Hemmingway. "But I'll nurse him, George."

"Any change with you?"

"Just heard that they seem to be heading for the old Dockside Club and the Red Lion Gymnasium," said Hemmingway, "and if they do we can seal them off, let them fight it out, then nab them for breach of the peace as they come out."

Gideon didn't speak.

"Gone deaf?" asked Hemmingway.

"You did say this was the Melky gang and the Wide boys, didn't you?"

"Yes."

"Shouldn't have thought they would hand themselves to you on a plate," mused Gideon. "You know them better than I do, though."

"When they want to cut one another's throats they forget every bit of common sense they ever had, and it never was very much," said Hemmingway. "There've been rumors of trouble for a long time. The Wide boys have been working the Melky gang's race tracks. When it's like that, it's just a gang war, and all they want is to fight it out. They get like your Soho boys, George!"

"How do my Soho boys get?" asked Gideon dryly.

"So that they almost forget the police exist," said Hemmingway with a chuckle. "They think they can do what they like and get away with it. Take it from me, this is just between the gangs. Okay! I'll put Lemaitre in the front line but distrust his judgment for the night, that about it?"

"Right on the nail," said Gideon.

He put down the receiver, then slowly rounded his desk. He sat for a few seconds staring at the window, where the mist was swirling; it looked as if a wind was moving it. Then he turned back to the desk. There were notes about worried Mrs. Penn, who still hadn't called him again, and there was a note: *"Jennifer Lewis—dead?"* He'd know soon enough, and if she died it would put the Prowler right at the top of the Yard's list of jobs that must be done quickly. As it was, the morning newspapers would be pretty rough, unless the Prowler was caught during the night. There would be the usual questions loaded with innuendo—why hadn't the Prowler been caught long ago, he'd been active quite long enough, and so on. One or two of the newspapers would probably add that it was a scandal that the police were so far below strength, and imply that those who were on the strength weren't up to standard. So far as the Prowler was concerned, there was cause for prodding—he ought to be safe in jail. Was there any way of making sure they got him tonight? To Gideon, that was the most vital job of all.

7 . The Night Warms Up

IT WASN'T long since the cordon had been tightened round the Brixton area, but Gideon was already beginning to feel impatient. If they were going to catch the Prowler, it would probably be done quickly. Every minute he stayed free helped him. In an hour's time, they might as well call the whole thing off. An hour? It was nearly half past eleven and he didn't need reminding that the night had only just started.

Piper was probably just as anxious as he.

He had another worry in his mind, now—about NE and the two big gangs. Hemmingway knew them so well that he was almost certainly right, but the Divisional man had drawn the picture in overtones. The gangs did not ignore the police, and were usually careful to avoid tangling with them; but it looked almost as if they were ready for a tangle tonight. Perhaps they thought that in the fog they could get to their respective headquarters without the police realizing that it was a gathering of opposing forces. Hemmingway had been reasonably well pleased with the two Squad cars, after all; he had probably planned on the assumption that he would get only half what he asked for.

Gideon grinned.

Appleby came back, his footsteps brisk, his manner lively when he entered the office.

"Everything well in hand," he said, "and you've got the Divisions by the tail all right." Obviously he enjoyed saying that. "They'll get the Prowler tonight or bust. You know the kind of thing; Scouts' honor."

"Yes. Nothing in?"

"So far they've questioned about seventy men, none of them with the girl's hair on his coat, or any indication that he's used a mask," said Appleby. "Probably before the night's out we'll have twice the average number of false reports that the Prowler's been seen." He sat at his desk, a little smug and, for the first time, really irritating Gideon; it seemed clear that for some obscure reason he didn't really agree with what had been done. Behind any such attitude there might well be a consciousness that he and the usual Night Superintendent had fallen down on the Prowler, and he would be most glad if Gideon had a failure. The human reaction was the same in policemen as in anyone else. "Two warehouse jobs out at Stepney," he added.

Gideon said abruptly, "Stepney?"

"Yep."

"Whereabouts?"

"Near the river."

"Close to the QR and NE Divisional lines," remarked Gideon. "Big jobs?"

"One lorry load of cigarettes which should have been out of the warehouse at five in the morning, one lorry load of scrap metal."

"They get away?"

"Yep."

"Charley, you have a look at this," said Gideon, and got up and went across to Appleby's desk. They stood together, looking at Gideon's notes. "Hemmingway reports that Melky and the Wide boys gangs are on the move, heading for their headquarters, and I've sent him a couple of Squad cars—Lemaitre wanted something to do, too, so he's gone over. Now we get two warehouse jobs, right on the border of the Division, and we know that one of the favorite jobs of these gangs is shifting lorry loads of stuff that they can sell easily."

"It smells," said Appleby.

"Hemmingway didn't think so."

"Everything over there smells, so he wouldn't notice a little stinkeroo like this," said Appleby, his eyes brightening. "Want me to talk to the other Divisions bordering Hemmingway's, and find out what's on?"

"Yes."

"Right," said Appleby, and if there had been any resentment, even subconscious, it appeared to have faded completely.

Gideon went back to his own desk, pondered for a few minutes, then picked up the telephone. He noticed that Appleby was watching him, almost covertly, as if Appleby meant to study how he worked. Gideon was not conscious of any difference in his approach tonight, but possibly he was more on edge than usual because of the baby kidnapings and the failure to find the kidnaper. The Prowler job wasn't in the same street, was much more of a challenge to the Yard's pride than the baby snatching, but in terms of human misery the baby job won easily.

"Get me AB Division," he told the operator.

"Yes, sir. Just a moment, sir! The Division's on the line now, if you'll hold on a moment."

"I'll hold on."

The wait was longer than Gideon had expected, but that gave him time to think. He was going to tell AB to send a man to see Mrs. Penn, and he couldn't really explain why he felt that was so important. At least it wouldn't do any harm. He knew exactly what it meant, though. He was going to give an order in the guise of a request, and soon a man would leave Divisional HQ for half an hour or so, and go back and make his report—as hundreds of detective officers and higher ranks were doing at this moment. If you took the short view, there were plenty of police, thousands of them, all out tonight, each one watching, waiting and ready—and much more on their toes than usual because he had prodded them.

It was easy to forget the uniformed men and the detective officers, the men who did the chores.

"You're through, sir."

"That you, Ridge?" asked Gideon.

"Hello, George," said Jacob Ridgway, of the AB Division. "Just been talking to the back room about that baby job; wanted to know what you were giving the press."

"Everything."

"That's what they said. No luck yet?"

"No."

"Only child of the people here," said Ridgway abruptly. "Middle-aged couple, too. Wanted a kid all their lives and now they've got to order the funeral. Get him, George."

Funny, how even the most case-hardened copper could get soft and almost sentimental over a baby job, Gideon reflected.

"We'll try. Ridge, what do you know about that Mrs. Penn and her missing-husband worry?"

"Nothing, except that she's been round here once or twice by day."

"Can you send a man round to Horley Street to have a word with her? She rang me, but didn't wait to say anything."

"Using your sixth sense?" asked Ridgway and it was almost a jeer. "Okay, I'll send a chap round to talk to her, and if there seems to be anything to worry about I'll call you back. That all?"

"For now, thanks."

"Okay," said Ridgway.

That was about the time that Piper and the Yard specialists reached 51 Middleton Street. Divisional men had already marked off the area and prepared the ground, and had even thought to bring the injured girl's clothes back from the hospital. The parents and a brother were at the hospital, and the police had the run of the house.

In ten minutes, Piper was on the radio telephone to Gideon.

"I've checked the hospital for her fingernail scrapings," he said. "They shouldn't be long. Some hair on her coat. I'm sending that over right away. Wavy and chestnut brown places it." Piper was forceful and direct, exactly what Gideon wanted then.

"What else?"

"That mask: a good-quality theatrical one. It didn't come from Woolworth's after all. It should be a good line for the morning," said Piper. "After we've got the prints photographed."

"Man's prints?"

"Yes. Beauties."

"Anything else?"

Piper seemed exultant with his answer.

"Yes, sir! There's a little privet hedge between the approaches to Number 51 and next door, Number 53, and in the soil where the hedge is planted there's a heel mark, plain as we could want. Left heel, I think, worn down on the left side and with a mark made by a broken heel protector. No doubt about it."

"You'll get photos and then casts just as soon as you can, won't you?" said Gideon.

"You bet I will," Piper promised.

Within five minutes, the radio had carried the news to the men on the bridges and at stations, and the tempo of the watch seemed to quicken everywhere.

It was not Ridgway's man on his way to see the persistent Mrs. Penn, or any of the Yard and Divisional men concentrated about the Brixton area in the hunt for the Prowler, who came upon the next thing which reached Gideon's ear. It was a youthful policeman named Rider, who was on the borders of two of the outer ring Divisions, very near the outskirts of the Metropolitan Police district. He was on his own, patrolling a very different kind of beat from anyone in the heart of London, for this was a residential district for the middle-income group. Here, the roads and streets were wide and often winding, the houses were mostly detached and standing in their own small gardens, most of which were beautifully kept. The fog was not very thick, and in some places it was possible to see easily for several hundred yards.

P. C. Rider's beat was one of the most exclusive. The houses he passed were in the high price range, everyone had a garage, some of the families had two cars. Trees grew along the streets as well as in the gardens. Very few lights were on, for here the local authority economized by keeping only one street lamp in four alight during the night, in spite of protests from those people of the neighborhood who had been robbed in the past, and in spite of the strong protests of the police.

P. C. Rider walked more quickly than usual, because of the cold, but he did not consciously skimp any part of his job. His torch light flashed on doorways and windows as he looked for anything that was remotely suspicious, and when he even thought anything was unusual he went to try the door and the window, probably unheard by the people sleeping in the room just above his head. As he turned a corner, he heard a rustle of sound— it might be a cat, it could even be a dog although few dogs were nocturnal wanderers, it might be a cuddling couple or it might be—

Anything.

Rider saw nothing.

A cat, then?

Usually, if you scared a cat, it scampered and jumped, and you heard or noticed something else. By doing a lot of night work, you learned how to notice these things, but now all Rider noticed was the silence which had followed the scuffling sound. So, he played cunning. He did not flash his torch about the houses near the corner, but plodded on, and, a little way from the spot where he had heard the sound, stopped and bent his head, as if he was lighting a cigarette. A policeman who stopped on his rounds to light a cigarette seemed to be the most unsuspicious policeman in the world.

There was still no sound.

There were bushes in the garden of the house where Rider had heard the rustle, and he knew that a man could crouch there out of sight. But if he went back, it would warn any such man. So instead he stood and shone his torch at the window nearer him and, as if he had noticed something unusual, he walked toward it and opened the wooden gate, which made no sound at all. He reached the porch and shone the torch on the keyhole of the front door—and, as he did so, the rustle came again, this time much fainter.

He looked round quickly.

In vague silhouette against the corner lamp, a crouching man wheeled a bicycle out of the garden of the corner house.

Rider jumped into action.

He leaped one low wall, swung along a narrow drive, and reached the street simultaneously with the man with the bicycle, who had difficulty in keeping his machine upright and keeping the gate open.

"Stop a minute!" Rider called, and went running. "Here! I want a word with you."

The cyclist pushed the cycle free, then cocked a leg over it—but he didn't ride off immediately. Rider saw him turn, while on the saddle, and saw his arm drawn back, as if to throw something. Rider ducked. He heard the sound of the missile making a funny little noise in the air, then heard it crash on the ground behind him. It made the noise of stone on stone; if that had hit him, it would have made a mess of his face.

He blew his whistle and pulled out his truncheon in one and the same movement. The man pushed off from the curb, only a few yards ahead, probably more scared because he had missed but pinning his faith on the bicycle. Rider knew that he had too good a start to be caught by anyone on foot. So the policeman stopped short, slipped the strap of the truncheon off his wrist and hurled the truncheon. He aimed just in front of the cyclist, hoping to strike the handlebars or the man's hands. He didn't know what he struck, but the cyclist wobbled and, wobbling, swung the wheel so that he was at right angles to the rest of the bicycle.

Now Rider had a chance.

He took three long strides while the cyclist was trying to regain his balance, and was within arm's reach when the man fell heavily, the bicycle clattering and the bell giving a single clear ring which seemed to echo for ages. Rider reached the man as he struggled to get up, and promptly put a hammer lock on him.

"Now what's it all about?" he demanded without excitement. "What have you been up to?"

The man didn't speak, but shivered in the tight painful grasp. Lights appeared at several windows, several men who had heard the police whistle looked out, and one came hurrying from across the road. In less than five minutes Rider found that his captive had two thousand pounds' worth of jewels, stolen from the corner house, tucked in his pockets.

It was a long time before Rider began to realize what a stroke of luck he'd had, and how much good this might do him.

"Something's gone right," Appleby called across to Gideon, less than half an hour after the incident. "They've picked up Lefty Winn, out at KI. Red-handed, too, couple of thousand quid's worth of sparklers in his pocket."

"Luck's one word," Gideon said. "How'd they do it?"

"Copper named Rider kept his eyes and ears open."

"Must make sure I have a word with him next time I'm out at KI," said Gideon. He had been along to Fingerprints for a word with the man in charge, for the mask had arrived with a dozen strands of Jennifer Lewis's hair and had only just come back. "Anything new about Jennifer Lewis?"

"No."

"The babies?"

"No. Here's what's come in." Appleby handed Gideon a sheet of paper on which were several short paragraphs in an immaculate hand. Gideon read:

11:31. Two sailors, ages 19 and 20, attacked and robbed in train at Fenchurch Street, just been paid off, total loss £131.

11:35. Negative reports from GH and CD on baby hunt.

11:39. Three men sighted breaking into a warehouse in Chelsea, all under charge.

11:41. Negative reports from Information on the Prowler job.

11:49. Smash and grab in High Street, Ealing, by two men in an unidentified car. Window smashed, amount of loss not yet known.

11:50. Information Room reports that there have been nineteen reports of the Prowler being seen in eleven different areas.

11:59. Body taken out of the Thames at Rotherhithe by River Police —been immersed several days. Medical report to follow.

12:00. Hit-and-run accident in High Street, Wandsworth, woman of seventy-two severely injured, now on way to hospital.

Gideon sat back and then heard the booming note of Big Ben. The bell sounded very near, as if it were just outside the window, not a couple of hundred yards away.

"Warming up, eh? Notice anything that isn't there?"

"Sins of the old omission? No," said Appleby. He reached out for the list, frowning a little, showing his white teeth in the set kind of smile, as if he must look on the bright side at all costs. "No," he repeated, "what have you noticed?"

"Almost a complete blank in the East End—no warehouse jobs, no free fights, no drunk beating his wife up. Funny business about the East End tonight; somehow I don't like it. If we don't pick up the Prowler soon I'm going to get more men over to Hemmingway. Can't say he didn't ask for them. I—"

His telephone rang.

"I'll get it," he said, and went across like a great bear, plucking up the receiver and growling, "Gideon."

Appleby saw his expression change, and knew that this news hurt him. It hurt badly.

"They've just found a second baby," Whittaker said to Gideon. "Suffocated, like the first one, in the garden of an empty house near its home."

"Whereabouts?" Gideon demanded sharply.

"Quinn Street, Chelsea. 'Bout half a mile from the place they found the other one. That's—"

"I know where it is," said Gideon, and went on in the same sharp voice. "One was found about half a mile west of Hurdle Street, the other half a mile east. Close a cordon round the whole area."

"Right," said Whittaker.

Gideon rang off, and Appleby said gruffly, "The Harris kid hasn't much chance now, I bet."

8 . Tricks

"OF COURSE he'll be all right, May," said Lucy Fraser. "No one would do any harm to a little baby. You needn't worry; he'll be all right. I'll bet I know what it is, too. Someone has lost a baby and they've stolen yours to try and make up for it. I'm *sure* you needn't worry. They'll look after it as if it was their own, and the police will soon find them, and everything will be all right."

May Harris looked up at her blankly.

The two husbands were in the front room, talking to one of the policemen; most of the police had gone now, but two were on duty outside, and there were several people in the street, although it was well after midnight, and just here the fog was as thick as it had been at any time during the night.

"I should never have left him," May said drearily. "It was ever so good of you and Jim to want us to see the program, but one of us ought to have stayed behind; if we had this wouldn't have happened. I'll never forgive myself."

"But he'll be all *right*, May!"

"If he'll be all right, why haven't they found him?" Mrs. Harris asked in a lifeless voice. "It's nearly three hours now, and you'd think every police-man in London was here from the crowd outside."

"Mum," said Jacqueline Harris, who was sitting by her sister's side on the sofa in the kitchen, "I'm sure Mrs. Fraser's right, too; no one would hurt Baby."

"Of course they wouldn't," Millicent said in a scared voice.

They were fifteen-year-old twins, who had come home just before ten o'clock to find the street crowded and to discover with horror that disaster had struck their home. Millicent was fair and fluffy and rather plump. Jacqueline was dark and thin and very much like her mother, although much tidier in appearance. Each wore gym tunics of navy blue, white blouses and long black stockings, and they sat very close together, looking as helpless as they felt, and watching their mother in her blank distress.

For a few moments there was silence. Then Mrs. Harris said sharply: "What are they in the front room so long for?" She jumped up. "They've been there a long time. What are they saying to Fred?" She rushed into the narrow passage, with Mrs. Fraser after her and the two girls standing up and staring as if they had no idea what to do next; they were pale, they were tired, their eyes were glassy with anxiety and fatigue. This was the first serious emergency in their lives, and they felt so utterly useless.

"If we don't get Baby back, what will Mum *do?*" Jacqueline asked in a whisper.

"Don't even talk about it," Millicent said.

Then they heard their mother burst out as she entered the front room, "What's going on here, what are you so long for? I don't want you to keep anything from me, even if it's the worst." She glanced round at the four men—her husband, Fraser, Willy Smith, the Divisional Night Superintend-ent, and a sergeant.

Harris looked less stupefied now, as if he was beginning to feel again. There was a little color in his lips and a spark in his eyes as he moved to-ward his wife.

"They don't want anything, May, they've just been asking me a few ques-tions. They—"

"Why aren't they out looking for my child?"

"May, they've got to work their own way, and they're trying all they can to help us," said Harris with gentle patience. "It's no use worrying them too much. Did the girls make you that cup of tea?"

"I don't want any tea! I want—"

"You've got to have a cup, and two of those tablets that the doctor—"

"I'm not going to have any tablets from any doctor," his wife shouted at him. "What do you think I am, Fred Harris? Do you think I want to be drugged to sleep while anything might be happening to my own flesh and blood? I don't care if I never go to sleep again, I'll never rest until we've found him, and if we don't—"

"Now come on, Mother," Harris said, in a voice that was suddenly sharp and authoritative. "It's no use carrying on like this; it's time you pulled yourself together. It's all very well behaving like this with me, but what about the girls? Now stop shouting, and come and have a couple of aspirins even if you won't have the sleeping tablets." He took his wife's arm firmly and forced her out of the front room toward the passage, and, as if startled by his firmness, she went without any further protest.

"He'll be all right now he's got on top of himself," Fraser said to Willy Smith.

The Divisional Superintendent looked pale and flabby, even a little vague, and his smile seemed pointless. He watched the husband and wife go out of the room, and was fully aware that the neighbor, Fraser, looked at him impatiently, as if he couldn't understand the lack of results.

"How well do you know this baby?" Smith asked in a very quiet voice which could not be heard outside the room.

Fraser said, "Well enough to know that if they don't get him back—"

"I mean, to look at," Smith said, in the same soft voice, and his eyes were very hard.

Fraser caught his breath. "Have you found—"

"We found a baby wrapped in a blue shawl in Quinn Street, not very far from here."

"Not—dead?"

"Mr. Fraser, do you know the Harrises' child well enough to be able to identify it?" asked Smith. "I don't want to have to make one of them do it. If you don't, then will your wife—"

"I'll know the child," Fraser said abruptly.

"Then will you make an excuse to come with us for ten minutes?"

"No more?"

"We've got it in the car in the next street."

"Aye, I'll come," said Fraser. "No one will miss me. If anyone does you can tell them I've popped next door for five minutes."

"All right. See to that, Sergeant."

"Yes, sir."

"Come on, Mr. Fraser," Willy Smith said.

In a good light outside a police car, the child lay wrapped in its shawl, obviously still with death, yet not outwardly harmed, and with no outer evidence of violence. It had a very thin mat of fair hair, and Fraser looked at it only for a moment before he said hoarsely:

"It's not the Harrises' bairn."

"Sure?"

"The Harris bairn had black hair."

"Well, I suppose that's something," Smith said, and didn't add that, while it gave the Harrises a kind of reprieve, it was the sentence of grief on a newly married couple, who had been so happy in their love and with their first born a few hours ago.

Willy Smith left Fraser outside the door of 27 Hurdle Street, and then drove off. The child's body was on the way to the morgue, and Smith was glad that he didn't have to take the news to the parents. After a few minutes he told his driver to slow down, and then picked up the radio telephone. He called the Yard, and was asked to hold on; Gideon was on the telephone. Smith sat waiting as his driver edged slowly through the fog, and there was rather an empty look on his face.

Then Gideon came on. "Hello, Willy."

"Hello, George. Thought you'd want to know that the baby found in Quinn Street wasn't the Harrises', so it's the one from Wragg's Division. I've left it to you to tell Wragg."

"All right."

"I'm going back to the Registrar's office now," said Smith. "Nothing likely at Fulham, but two men are still at the Chelsea office; they might get a line. It's worth calling on all parents who've lost a child lately. I'll call you from Chelsea."

"Thanks," said Gideon.

"Didn't realize until tonight how many people get born and how many die in a few weeks," said Smith. "I had a twelve months' coverage done on the job; thought that if the loss of a baby had turned someone's mind it might have taken more than a few days."

"Could do, too," said Gideon. "Fine, thanks."

"Having a nice night?"

"Short of good coppers, that's all," said Gideon, and rang off.

Smith chuckled as he put back his receiver, and then switched off. His driver glanced at him but Smith didn't make any comment. Soon, they pulled up outside the office of the Registrar of Births and Deaths, where a uniformed policeman was on duty, as if those inside needed protection. Smith bustled out of his car and past the man, nodding, and then into the offices. A light shone from the first-floor landing, and Willy Smith went up, not too quickly, for he was a man who lost his breath very easily. He saw moving shadows, and, as he reached the doorway, the elderly, gray-haired Registrar and one of the Divisional men looked up.

"How you doing?" asked Smith.

"Fifteen infants died here last month," said his sergeant. "There was a nasty gastroenteritis epidemic." Smith remembered that as the man spoke. "Nineteen for the rest of the year ending this month."

"Thirty-four in all," Smith said, almost to himself. "Thirty-four." He felt the gaze of the other two men on him as he spoke, but he made no further comment except to thank the Registrar, and ask his man, "Got the list?"

"Yes."

"Good, let's go." Going downstairs was a different matter from walking upstairs, and he hurried and was only slightly out of breath when he reached his car. He slid into his seat and called the Yard again, asked for Gideon, and was put through at once. Gideon's voice was deep and it sounded un-flurried, like that of a man whom nothing could really disturb. That was perhaps Gideon's greatest strength, the confidence which he could put into other men.

"What have you got now, Willy?"

"Thirty-four babies within the age group we're after, and that's a hell of a lot to try to tackle tonight," Smith said. "I'd been banking on three or four at the most."

Gideon said, "Hmm."

"Want me to go ahead?"

"Willy," said Gideon quietly, "have another go at the Registrar, and blame me for it. Each death certificate will have the certifying doctor's name, and we'd better check the doctors. Find out from them if they know of any of the bereaved mothers—or fathers, if it comes to that—who went a bit queer. That might give you a lead to two or three names, without making it a major job."

"Good idea," said Smith. "Why don't I get one myself sometime? Got the Prowler yet?"

"No," said Gideon.

"How's that girl he bashed about?"

"Touch and go," said Gideon.

It was certainly touch and go, and Whittaker had been too optimistic.

Jennifer Lewis was on the operating table at a London hospital, with the night staff and the night-duty surgeon ready to operate, for X-ray photographs had shown a splinter of skull so dangerously lodged that unless it was quickly removed it would almost certainly pierce the brain.

At the hospital, her mother and father and brother waited.

At bridges, stations, bus terminals and other vantage points the police still watched and waited, too, but now the traffic had dwindled to a trickle; there was not work enough for so many men. They could go back to their own Divisions, and some could be sent to Hemmingway; Gideon had only to say the word. He didn't. He told himself that he would wait until half past one before giving up hope of catching the Prowler.

He went up to the laboratory, as much to see what else was going on as to check on the hair and fingernail scrapings. Up here, in the big, airy laboratory, it seemed a different world. Things might be in a hurry, yet everyone moved slowly and almost casually. Two Bunsen burners hissed, one of them with a small white crucible over it. A burette seemed to be blowing bubbles. Gibb, the night chief, was a tall, spindly individual with a pointed chin and a rather sour look which experience of him belied. He was peering at a slide on a microscope, and as Gideon came up, he said:

"These are the nail scrapings."

"Anything?"

"Blood."

"What group?"

Gibb laughed. "You guess! I'll tell you as soon as I can. The hair's dark chestnut brown, very healthy, naturally as straight as mine—she probably waves it herself."

"Thanks. So she scratched him for certain."

"I'm talking to the Commander, aren't I?" asked Gibb dryly. "Not a rookie. She could have scratched a pimple off the end of her nose. Okay, okay, probably she didn't."

"Corrected," Gideon said. "What are you cooking?"

"Sudden death by some gastric trouble this afternoon; we're testing for arsenic. Got the body of the woman taken out of the Thames coming up; that'll keep us busy. That arm they fished out of the Thames last week had been in the water three weeks, I would say. There was some green paint sent up, from the shoe of the woman run down in Wandsworth. We've analyzed it but I wouldn't like to name the manufacturer until there've been some further tests. Okay?"

"Let me know when you've finished; I'll send some work up," said Gideon.

He kept a straight face as he left.

In a smaller room nearby, two men were busy making duplicates of a plaster cast which had already arrived from Middleton Street. Piper worked as if he moved on wheels. Gideon inspected the imprint of the heel and the clear indentation of the broken heel protector, and felt a curious tension, a sense of excitement, a feeling that at last the Prowler's days were numbered.

He went down to Records, where the little man with pince-nez was standing at a desk with fingerprint sheets in his hand.

"Hello, Syd," Gideon said. "Any luck with those prints that Piper sent in?"

"We haven't got 'em on the file, so he's a brand-new criminal for you," said the Records man, as if absently. "I can give you all the dope in ten minutes. It's a tented arch pattern, with a double . . ."

"Thanks," Gideon said, five minutes later, and went down to his office, where Appleby gave the impression that he had just finished the greatest clowning act of his career, he was grinning so broadly. He didn't pass on his joke, and Gideon went to sit down.

It was nearly one when the telephone rang again, and with an automatic movement Gideon lifted it off its cradle and gave his name. Appleby, wreathed in cigarette smoke, was working at one of his minute-by-minute lists.

"Ridgway here," said the AB Divisional man. "Sorry I'm late with this. I thought it had been passed on. The Penn woman. She lives at Horley Street with her mother, but hasn't been home this evening—that's unusual. I checked the house where she lived with her husband. Mrs. Penn left the flat the early part of last month, a few weeks after the husband vanished. Hadn't paid her rent, so she was thrown out. The landlord's a so-and-so. My chap probed a bit, but didn't get anywhere. Can it wait until morning?"

"Oh, God," Gideon groaned. "If she hasn't been home, she might have decided to throw herself into the river, or—" He paused, knowing that he was being unduly gloomy and that, with all the bridges manned, there was a closer watch than usual on the river. Why did he want to dramatize Mrs. Penn, anyhow? "Yes, leave it," he said. "Thanks. Much doing your way?"

"Bit quieter than usual if it weren't for the two main jobs. Before you go," went on Ridgway, "I forgot to tell you earlier that Bigamy Bill's back in town."

Gideon said sharply, "Sure?"

"One of my chaps was at the Roxy Hotel—it's his son's twenty-first birthday tonight—and he called up and said the B.B. was there."

"Alone?"

"With a blonde."

"Young?"

"His usual style, bit bosomy but easy on the eye," said Ridgway. "It would be a kindly thing to whisper a word of warning in her ear."

"I'll see what I can do," said Gideon. "Thanks."

"Pleasure," Ridgway said, and rang off.

9 . Hope

IN THE background at the Roxy there was soft music, and, about the room, soft lights. Only a dozen couples were left in the night club, which was in a basement of the hotel, and three of these were elderly tourists, sitting it out on the edge of the tiny dance floor. The *décor* was African, with futuristic drawings of animals and Africans, assegais and tom-toms, and the music, though soft, had a tom-tom-like rhythm given by a dreamy-looking colored man who was playing the drums.

Two of the people on the dance floor were dancing cheek to cheek, the girl in her early twenties with fine, wavy, fair hair and a fair complexion, flushed just then with too much to drink. Her eyes had a glazed look, but she had complete control of her movements, and danced rhythmically. She was plump but nicely built. The man was half a head taller, dark, with receding hair and very fine features. He held her tightly and danced dreamily, and the music seemed never to stop.

But it stopped at last.

The man slid out of the girl's embrace, then twined his arm round her waist again, and they walked together to a table in the corner.

". . . years," the man said, in a whispering voice. "Been waiting years for you, Florence, that's the sober truth. I've been waiting for years."

"Oh, *Bill*," she said.

"Know what I want to do?" Bill asked, nuzzling her white shoulder. "I want to get married. Soon. *Tomorrow*."

". . . Bill," she sighed.

"Can't *get* married tomorrow," Bill said in a sad voice, "but in a day or two we can." He covered her right hand with his, and the hard surface of a beautiful diamond ring scratched the soft skin of his fingers. "Can't do without you," he went on, "just can't wait."

". . . *Darling*," she cooed.

"Why don't we—" Bill leaned close to her, and finished the sentence so close to her ear that no one else could possibly hear it. Three couples got up and went out, the women yawning. A Polish waiter yawned, too. Business was bad, tips were bad; if they could get rid of the couple in the corner necking, the rest would probably go. The band began to play again, but no more briskly, West Indian music in that African setting.

". . . s'go," breathed Bill.

He stood up, and the girl Florence put her hands in his and let him pull her to her feet. She swayed, apparently very drunk. The diamonds on her finger scintillated so brilliantly that one of the remaining women stared enviously, then plucked at her husband's coat to make sure that he didn't miss this evidence of some man's readiness to spend freely on his love.

Ten minutes later the couple went out into the misty night; the West End was still remarkably clear of fog. The blonde leaned heavily on Bill's arm as they waited for a taxi, which wasn't long in coming.

"Ensor Street," Bill ordered, naming a small street in Soho, and then he helped the blonde in, and climbed in beside her, close beside her.

The taxi vanished about five minutes before a police car pulled up, and a plain-clothes man got out and nodded to the commissionaire as he hurried down to the night club. He looked round, grimaced in disappointment, and then spoke to the head waiter. . . .

"Yes, sir, there was a man like that, and a young lady, but—they go, not long ago, they go."

The Yard man reported by telephone.

"Well, we can't do anything about it," Gideon said gruffly. "No crime to take a girl to your flat even if you've done it fifty times before in—" he broke off. "All right, you come back, nip over to the Grand Hotel, and look slippy. Fingerprints and Photography have someone on the way. Couple of bedrooms have been entered and it looks as if there's a lot of loot. The job was discovered ten minutes ago; there's just a chance you'll be in time to pick up the chap with the stuff on him."

Nine rooms had been broken into at the hotel, and a rough estimate of the valuables stolen was ten thousand pounds.

In spite of concentrated work of all the Departments, the police didn't find a single significant clue.

Gideon replaced the receiver just after one thirty, made a note about the Grand Hotel job, then leaned back and stretched—his arms were so long that he looked like a massive birdman. He yawned, then ran his hands through his hair.

"You young chaps," scoffed Appleby, "you can't take it half as well as we old men. Why don't you go and take a nap? I'll call you if anything blows its top."

"Not a bad idea," said Gideon mildly.

"Did we stop Bigamy Bill?"

"Missed him by minutes."

"That son of a gun has all the luck," said Appleby, as if with envy. "Only has to snap his fingers at a girl and she's ready to pop into bed with him, and after that he sells her the marriage idea so well she can't make over her cash and securities fast enough. You know, Gee-Gee," went on Appleby, leaning back in his chair and spreading his hands on the desk, and for once apparently wholly earnest, "human nature beats me. It does, really. Especially girls where a chap like B.B. is concerned. They read about it in the newspapers—once a week or so there's a big spread showing how a crook like Bill got away with it—they get all the juicy details in the *News of the World* and a hell of a lot of awful warnings from judges and magistrates all over the country, and what do they do? Fall for the first charmer they meet. Got any theories about it?" In fact Appleby was not interested in Gideon's theories, only in his own simple philosophy. "Look at the number of sweeties Bill's fixed, in more ways than one, too. He must be fifty-five if he's a day. I can remember when we had him in dock *for* bigamy. He got six months, but he also got wise to the situation—he could go to any length short of marriage, and get away with it. Since then he must have ruined thirty or forty kids and probably a hell of a lot more we know nothing about, because the poor sinners don't want to tell the world what fools they were and how much he sucked them for. You want to know what I think, Gee-Gee?"

"Yes." This new slant on Appleby interested Gideon; each man had his pet ideas, and some were worth sharing.

"We laugh at Bigamy Bill," went on Appleby. "You've only got to mention his name, and you get a grin. Why the first time I heard it tonight I was grinning like a Cheshire cat—half wishing him luck, too. You try it tomorrow. Just slip B.B. into the conversation with anyone, and see what happens. Always good for a horse laugh, like stories about ma-in-law and flatfoots on the beat. But the truth is he does a hell of a lot more harm than a chap like the Prowler. You may say I'm talking through my titfertat, but you could be wrong about that. Take the Prowler, now. We're bound to get him soon, or else scare him into being quiet, and at the most he'll have attacked a dozen girls and frightened the wits out of them. Maybe this Lewis girl will pop off, so he'll become a murderer. But B.B. now—he's ruined more girls than the Prowler's ever thought of, and all we can do is to try and warn each new girl before she's swallowed the bait. We've tried to get him on intent to defraud, and what happens? His counsel puts the girl up in the box, and before it's over she admits that she knew exactly what she was doing, and B.B. gets off and laughs at us. Now *there's* a man I'd like to put inside for the rest of his natural."

Appleby stopped, put his head on one side, then ran the length of his forefinger underneath his nose and sniffed with a noise like a distant bandsaw. "Hark at me. Always ought to have worn my collar the wrong way round, and no one ever realized it!"

Gideon said quietly, "There's a lot in it, Charley. The chap who first said the law was an ass had something."

"But it's the law and we're here to enforce it," said Appleby, wrinkling up his face in a rueful grin. "I know, I know, and I can see you're in training for the next Assistant Commissioner. That's the kind of ropey stuff he trots out when he gets a chance. I—"

One of his telephones rang.

"About time someone stopped me gassing," he remarked. "All aboard for the crime stakes; wonder what we've got this time? Anything from rape to murder and dear Mr. Policeman my pussycat's not come 'ome. . . . Appleby speaking."

A telephone rang on Gideon's desk.

"Gideon . . ."

Gideon pushed a note pad away from him as the operator said, "It's Superintendent Smith, sir." He felt himself tense. By now Willy Smith had probably finished his rounds of the doctors who had signed the death certificates of the infants.

"George?"

"Yes, Willy?"

"Got two possibles," Smith said, and there was a note of excitement in his voice. "There's a Mrs. Golightly across the road, at 42 Hurdle Street; lost her baby about two months ago, and she hasn't been right in the head since. The landlady of the place where she used to live had a baby a few months older, and this Mrs. Golightly used to take it out of its pram up to her own rooms. The landlady gave the Golightlys notice. We got this from a neighbor who knew her before she came to live in Hurdle Street—neighbor's only just heard about the missing Harris baby. That's the most likely. Then there's an unmarried girl whose baby was taken away from her and put into an adoption home a month or two ago. The girl signed the release at her mother's insistence, but ever since she's been a bit queer. She lives at Hill Street, Chelsea."

"That's nearer you than Hurdle Street," Gideon said crisply. "Go and check on her."

"Who'll do Hurdle Street?"

"I will."

"Right," said Willy. "I can get to my place as quick as any patrol car."

He rang off, and Gideon stood up abruptly. Appleby was scribbling a note and looking across at him as if he didn't like his expression.

"What's up?"

"Might be on the track of that baby snatcher," Gideon said. "I'm going to Hurdle Street. Tell Info to have a patrol car at Number 42, quick—No," he changed his mind as he reached the door. "There's a car round the corner from Hurdle Street; have the crew call at Number 42—a Mrs. Golightly."

"Gorblimey Golightly!" Appleby exclaimed. "Here's a chance to throw some weight about."

The door closed on his last word, and Gideon almost ran down the corridor.

The fog, thick but on the move in Parliament Square and on the Embankment, was much thinner a little way from the river, and at no time was Gideon slowed down to a crawl. The city was empty and it seemed dead. There was no sound from the river, and no lights showed across from the other side, not even the lights of Battersea Power Station, with its huge chimneys and its massive square block. Now and again another car came toward him, lights ghostly in the murk. There were few policemen about; too few.

He kept picturing Mrs. Harris's face when he had first given her hope and then snatched it away again, and was grimly aware of a kind of personal responsibility which everyone else would scoff at, but which was deep and immovable in him. He could keep in touch with the Information Room and Appleby from the car; there was no need for him to sit at his desk all the time.

He kept the radio on.

There was a cacophony of words and phrases continually spilling into the car as instructions flew to and from the Yard, to and from the Divisions. The dead night seemed to come back to life. There was no light but that of Gideon's headlamps, dipped toward the curbs, but the night seemed full of light—brightly lit offices, houses, clubs, hospitals, homes, police stations. With the radio off it was a dead or at best a sleeping city; with it on there was a pulsing throb of life, of bustling activity, a sense of swift, exciting movement everywhere.

Then:

"Calling Commander Gideon, calling Commander Gideon."

"Gideon here," Gideon said. "I can hear you."

"Message from Chief Inspector Lemaitre, sir."

"Let's have it."

"Good reason to believe Mr. Hemmingway right about the situation in NE Division, sir."

"Right. Give me Mr. Appleby."

"Yes, sir."

So Hemmingway had been right and he had been wrong; there seemed nothing particularly sinister about the gathering of gangs in the East End. Well, it wasn't the first time by a long way that he had been wrong. He wished Appleby would hurry, but the man was probably on the telephone, making his cracks, or writing down his notes in that immaculate handwriting, being bright and breezy and hiding—what? Theories about the almost criminal idiocy of the law?

In five minutes, Gideon would be in Hurdle Street.

"Appleby speaking, Commander."

"Charley, listen," said Gideon. "Take half the men we moved into the central districts for the Prowler, and have them go to NE at Hemmingway's disposal. Get 'em there quick."

"Okey dokey."

"Thanks," said Gideon.

"Don't run away," said Appleby hastily. "Something else here you ought to know about. Just had a telegram from the *Sûreté Nationale*." His pronunciation of that was almost perfect, Gideon noted with surprise; his French accent on that word at least was better than his English. "You know that Guthrie girl who was cut up and buried in the French Pyrénées last year?"

"Yes."

"They've dug up evidence suggesting that there was an Englishman named Forrester with her," said Appleby, "and they say Forrester's on the way from Paris by air—he got away before the Paris people could arrest him. Will we meet him at London airport?"

"Any evidence?"

"They say they've a basketful, but didn't quote it; they've a man coming over on the same plane to see us. The silly mugs saved a couple of hundred francs by telegraphing instead of getting us on the buzzer, and the aircraft's due in any minute. It's a special flight and had a few spare seats."

"Have the Customs detain Forrester and the Frenchman," said Gideon.

"That's a relief," said Appleby, "I have."

Gideon was surprised into a chuckle.

Appleby rang off, and now Gideon switched off his radio, for he was very near Hurdle Street and didn't want another interruption. He found that his heart was thumping with a most unprofessional anxiety as he turned into Hurdle Street. Where before there had been a crowd not far short of a mob, there were now only one or two people standing about, and a solitary police car. Lights showed at three places, one of them Number 27; that was at the second floor, so Harris had persuaded his wife to go upstairs. The other lights were at the front door and the second-floor window of Number 42—or what he guessed was Number 42.

A Mrs. Golightly had lost her child and had tried to find some solace in another woman's. The landlady must have been seriously worried to have made her leave. It was at least possible—

"Remember the motorcyclist said a *man* was seen carrying the kid,"

Gideon said to himself almost roughly, as if he resented the way his tension was rising.

He pulled up. Yes, this was Number 42; the black numerals showed on the fanlight. Outside the house a uniformed policeman waited, advancing as Gideon got out of his car. The night was quiet and the fog almost clear here; just a murkiness which gathered about the lights. There was a gentle but rather cold wind stirring what was left of the fog.

"Gideon," said Gideon. "Anything doing here?"

"Been a bit of shouting since the detectives went in, sir, but my orders were to stay right here."

"Shouting?" Gideon moved swiftly, with that pulsing, almost frightening beat of heart. Inside, this house was exactly the same as the Harrises' across the road. There was a narrow passage, the narrow staircase and at the foot of it an elderly couple who looked scared, dressed in overcoats and night clothes, the woman with gray hair in big curlers, the man nearly bald. With them was a plain-clothes man, saying patiently:

"I am a police officer, and all I want is the answer to a few questions." He recognized Gideon, and moved aside quickly. "Evening, sir."

"Anything?"

"Found a baby upstairs, sir," the man reported. "An ambulance is on the way. Don't know whether we've saved it or not. Half suffocated."

As he spoke, a woman screamed upstairs.

Upon the scream, an ambulance bell rang clearly in the street.

10 . Rescue

"Go across to Number 29, and ask Mr. or Mrs. Fraser to come over here at once," Gideon said to the man. "Don't let them waste any time." He squeezed past to the stairs, but found time and opportunity to glance at the old couple and to smile with heartening reassurance. "We'll need to know how often Mrs. Golightly has been out tonight," he said. "Is Mr. Golightly up there with her?"

The woman answered, "No, he's away during the week."

Oh, God, thought Gideon.

He hurried up a staircase so narrow that one arm brushed the wall, the other the banisters. The woman upstairs was screaming wildly, a man was speaking—then suddenly the man spoke more sharply; there was a louder scream. Next there came a sharp sound, as of a slap across the face. The ambulance bell had stopped ringing but the beat of the engine suggested that it was now pulling up outside.

Gideon reached the landing.

A bedroom door stood wide open, just beyond the landing. Two police-men in plain clothes were there, one standing close to an attractive young woman in blue slacks and a tight-fitting gray jersey. She had one hand at her cheek, as if she couldn't believe that she had been struck. Her eyes held a glitter which Gideon had seen too often before—the glitter which sug-gested that she wasn't sane.

As Gideon drew near, he saw the bed, another policeman kneeling in front of an infant on the bed and applying artificial respiration with enor-mous hands which looked large enough to break the baby into little pieces.

There was no sign of life in the child.

The pretty woman suddenly snatched her hand away from her face and flew at the man who had struck her, and so great was her fury and so wild her strength that she carried him back toward the wall. Then she turned and ran toward the door, as if she had not noticed Gideon in the way. Her lips were parted as though she were screaming but could not make a sound.

She saw Gideon.

She flung herself at him bodily, as if believing that she could force him back, but, although he couldn't stop a collision, he hardly budged, and she was flattened against him for a moment. Then she struck at him. He caught first one wrist and then the other, and held them tightly in his big fingers, making her helpless although she kicked wildly, stubbing her toes and hurting herself much more than she hurt him.

"Handcuffs," Gideon said sharply.

"Yes, sir." The man she had pushed aside slipped shiny handcuffs out of his pocket as if by sleight of hand and fastened one loop over Mrs. Golightly's wrist, one over his own. Perhaps it was the touch of cold steel, perhaps it was Gideon's massive figure; certainly something quieted her, and she turned away and covered her face with her free hand.

Behind the door were an old raincoat and a faded trilby. Wearing those and the slacks, it was easy to see how she had been taken for a man. Gideon looked at her without compassion.

The ambulance men and a young doctor came in from the landing, and the child lay there, still as death, with those great hands ceaseless in their desperate work of rescue.

Two minutes later, Fraser hurried in, shivering in an overcoat over striped blue pajamas, sparse hair standing on end, eyes watering. The doctor had taken over, saying simply that they must deal with the child here; the ambulance men had gone down to their ambulance for the portable oxygen unit.

"Sorry about this, Mr. Fraser," Gideon said, "but is this the Harris baby?"

Fraser took one look.

"Aye," he said, and everything but dread faded from his eyes. "Aye, don't say—"

He couldn't finish.

"I should say it's fifty-fifty," said Gideon, but in truth he had no idea whether the child had any chance at all. He did not seem able to keep his mind detached about this case, which seemed to be built upon unending tragedy. For there was no doubt that Mrs. Golightly had killed the other two children, no doubt that she should never have been allowed to move about freely until the doctors had made sure of the soundness of her mind.

Her husband knew how she had behaved before, he must have known that she wasn't normal, and yet he had left her alone.

What made men do such crazy, criminal things?

Criminal?

It wasn't legally criminal; just a moral crime. Appleby could say plenty about that. Whatever the reasons, Golightly had left his sick wife alone for days on end, making no arrangements for her to have company. As a result two babies were dead, and one might die, and two mothers might suffer a shock so great that the balance of their minds would be affected just as much as Mrs. Golightly's.

There was another instance of Appleby's example of Bigamy Bill. The greatest crimes could be committed *within* the law. This woman had cunning, she had killed, she would be put into an asylum at "Her Majesty's Pleasure." Her husband had committed the sin of ommission. Funny to be quoting and moralizing like Appleby.

Now there was the woman herself to deal with.

Mrs. Golightly was on her way to Scotland Yard, where a doctor was waiting for her; she would be given a sedative and put to bed in Cannon Row, the police station just across the courtyard, and in the morning she would probably wake up quite sane, but aware of what she had done and filled with new despair.

The doctor looked up from the child, only twenty minutes after Gideon had arrived, and brushed his hair back from his damp forehead. Willy Smith had arrived; more policemen were here, as well as a nurse for the child. Gideon saw the way each man stared at the doctor, and realized that he had not been the only policeman who had felt the night's sickening fear.

"He'll be all right," the doctor said.

No one spoke for several seconds, but all stared at the baby inside the plastic oxygen hood, its head on its side, looking peacefully asleep, and with a faint movement at its chest.

"Sure?" grunted Gideon.

"Quite sure."

"Can we tell the parents?"

"Yes."

"Good enough," said Gideon, and nodded to Willy Smith. "Thanks. Come on." He led the way downstairs and into the cold street, and felt as if the only thing in the world that mattered had happened now; that there was cause for supreme contentment, for easing unbearable tension.

Fraser was standing just inside the front doorway of his house, and his wife was behind him, bundled up in a dressing gown.

"Excuse me, sir—"

"The child will be all right," Gideon said quietly, and heard Mrs. Fraser's cry, "Thank God," and then heard her begin to sob.

Soon, he was upstairs at Number 27, where Mrs. Harris was still fully clad but, persuaded by her husband, had lain down on the double bed.

She didn't speak when Gideon told her, but so radiant was her face that Gideon believed he would carry the sight of it in his mind until his dying day, as he would the look of delight, so near elation, on the father's face.

Two babies had died that night, but theirs had been saved. They might feel compassion but they could not share the grief or the hurt.

Willy Smith and Gideon stood by the side of Gideon's car, and a gust of wind came along the street, making Smith clutch at his hat, and causing Gideon to shiver. For the first time, they could now see the outline of every house in the street, and the fog eddied about as if it were anxious to get away as soon as it could.

"Now all you want is the Prowler," Smith said, "but it doesn't look like our night for him, does it?"

"Still time, I suppose," said Gideon. "Did you hear that I'd moved men into NE? The Wide boys and Melky's gang look as if they're spoiling for a fight."

"I heard. Taking their time, aren't they?" Smith shrugged. "I hope they cut themselves to pieces." He paused, but obviously hadn't finished. "I know what I've been meaning to ask you for weeks, George—nothing to do with shop, but about my daughter Peggy. You know her; she danced a lot with your boy Matthew at that teen-age dance they ran out at the Sports Club in the summer."

"Pretty kid," said Gideon, remembering well. "Must have taken after her mother."

"I helped," Smith grinned. "Don't know whether I ever mentioned it, but she's quite handy with the violin. Not in the top flight like your Pru, but not bad for an amateur, and she's as keen as mustard. I wondered if Pru would give her a few tips, help her to find out if it's worth while taking up lessons and going in for it seriously. I shouldn't think it is," added Smith, with an airy nonchalance which didn't deceive Gideon for a moment, "but if she could find out, it would put her out of her misery."

"Shouldn't think Pru would like to sit in judgment," Gideon said. "She doesn't take after her father. But *if* she can help I know she will. I'll tell you what. Sunday afternoons or evenings, when she's not playing with the orchestra or at the BBC studios, we usually have a kind of musical evening at home. Kate plays the piano a bit and—"

"Dad sings," put in Smith.

"Not on your life. One verse of 'Old Man River' is my limit these days. But next time Pru's going to be in, I'll call you and suggest you come over for an hour or two. Have your youngster bring her violin, and let's see what goes on from there."

"First rate," said Smith. "Thanks, Gee-Gee. Now I've got you for a minute, there's another thing, too. You know I run a series of lectures over at Divisional headquarters once a fortnight. General police routine and special subjects, particularly anything that will help to make them think there's some fun in it. We get too many resignations from the chaps who come in full of enthusiasm, find it a bore and resign in their first year," Smith went on. "This is my way to try and get 'em to stay. I've always found out that if you can hold 'em for three years you've got 'em for keeps."

"S'right," agreed Gideon.

"Well, you won't believe it, and I did my damnedest to kill the idea, but a lot of the chaps seem to think that George Gideon is the Big Cheese. Would you—"

Gideon chuckled, a deep, pleased laugh, for that had come so unexpectedly and yet with such obvious sincerity.

"Yes, I'll come and talk to 'em," he said. "Any time you like, within reason."

"I'll fix it soon," Smith said. "Thanks, George. Well, it's time I went to see how crime's getting on in CD Division; been quietish except for that baby job until now. Hell of a relief that's over."

"I know how you feel," said Gideon.

Smith went off. Gideon got into his car, watched by the only two uniformed police who were now in the street. He didn't start the engine immediately, but adjusted his coat and told himself that he seemed to be taking up more room these days, because the car wasn't shrinking. He hadn't been on the scales for months. He flicked the radio to life, and the medley of London's night sprang into the car: odd phrases, odd words and, unexpectedly, a background of dance music. One of the Squad cars was probably near a place where music was being played, but at this hour it seemed odd.

He called Appleby.

"How are things, Charley?"

"You're a fine one," Appleby said. "First time tonight I get a chance of forty winks and you have to wake me up. Things have gone quiet, everywhere a deathly 'ush. If you really want the details—"

"Not if there's nothing big. I thought I'd drive over and see Hemmingway while I'm out."

"I'll hold the fort," Appleby promised. "That plane from Paris arrived, the French chap is on his way, should be here inside the hour. Still foggy out at Hounslow and the Great West Road, but not so bad."

"If the Paris chap really seems to have anything, have the airport police ask Forrester to come to the Yard with them for questions," Gideon said. "If you don't think it's strong enough, let him go and have him tagged."

"Oke."

Gideon hesitated, reluctant to put the receiver down until he knew for certain that there was no news in about the Prowler, but knowing that Appleby would have passed anything so important. The hiatus lasted only a second or two, but he was very conscious of it; then he asked almost too quickly:

"How's the Lewis girl?"

"Nothing new," said Appleby. "Piper's back; he did quite a job. The mask will be trotted round to London suppliers in the morning, telephotos of the heel print will go out tonight. If you ask me, you could take everyone off the cordon now. We're not going to get Mr. P. tonight."

"You could be right," conceded Gideon. "Give 'em a bit longer—if he's still out he won't be able to hide all night, so we might catch him yet."

"You're a sticker, you are," Appleby said, and then suddenly burst out laughing. "Stickier than glue. Three G's for you in future, Gee-Gee!" Still tickled by his wit, he rang off, and Gideon flicked the radio off ruefully. Anyone who lived or worked regularly with Appleby must need the patience of Job; he didn't think he could last a week without getting fidgety.

He drove to the Embankment and then over Battersea Bridge, less to test the police who were blocking the bridge at the other end than to drive in a roundabout way to the East End, covering the area where the Prowler had struck. There was one good thing: the Prowler wouldn't strike again tonight. His activities always finished soon after eleven o'clock. From now on the night should be one of straight routine, except the East End gang job, the tail end of the hunt for the Prowler, and anything he didn't know about.

That last affected Gideon as much as anything: the countless crimes be-

ing committed at that moment, cloaked by London's darkness. Four out of
five of the night's offenses would not be discovered until next morning, and,
as he drove, he was probably passing a dozen crimes actually being committed, yet was oblivious to them all.

Now, his mood was reflective and mellow.

A three minutes' hold-up at the far side of the bridge where two cars
in the other direction were stopped by the police, their drivers being questioned and their shoes examined, cheered him further. No one would get
through the cordon easily. Probably thousands of motorists had been
stopped, hundreds of buses held up; the old job of looking for a needle in
a haystack was on again. But they'd found at least one needle tonight.

So as he headed toward the East End his thoughts were easier than they
had been for some time. Willy Smith had high hopes for his daughter. Willy
and the lectures, too—good idea, those lectures, it wouldn't be amiss to have
them at all the Divisions. Might be a good idea to make them a bit more
interesting than the usual run, and pep things up a bit. Get a couple of
crime reporters to talk on the newspaper angle of crimes, for instance, a
pathologist or two for the grisly stuff; that always went down well, put a
bit of humor into it. Willy was right in one way; the uniformed branch
had a heavy rate of loss by resignation, and the Force's manpower position
was going to be really acute before long. The plain-clothes branch was always kept at full strength and there were those—including people at the
Home Office, who ought to know better—who thought that if the C.I.D.
was at full strength everything in the garden was lovely, and the conquest
of crime should be well on the way.

Idiots.

The conquest of crime wasn't the C.I.D.'s job. Conquest began before
a crime was committed—conquest would have begun with Mrs. Golightly,
for instance, if her husband hadn't left her on her own. The conquest of
crime was simply a matter of prevention, and the job of the C.I.D. wasn't
triumph over crime but a war against the criminals after they'd done their
job. The real fight to win began with the uniformed men out on the beat—
men like that chap Rider. And the uniformed branch was at least 40 per
cent understaffed because they couldn't get enough of the right men to
stay.

Was better pay the answer?

It might be part of it; that was all. The job wasn't really attractive yet,
there weren't enough youngsters who felt like young Matthew. That gave
him a warm glow. Here in the small hours, driving through the quiet with
his headlights behaving as if they were driving the fog away in writhing
defeat, he could feel the satisfaction at knowing that Matthew wanted to
follow him at the Yard. It ought to be possible to persuade him to sit for

the university scholarship, and make him realize that he would do much better for himself in the Yard's legal department, for instance; but if he did start out as a copper—

Gideon put the thought aside as he crossed Lambeth Bridge, was held up for a minute, then drove past the Yard. The radio kept silent, so there wasn't much doing; Appleby would make sure that he was kept informed.

He thought again, in that mellowed, untroubled mood, of the crimes that were being committed now and would not come to light until later, and he felt almost philosophical, so deep had been his relief at the finding of the Harris child.

He was quite right about one thing: about the crimes being committed within a stone's throw of him as he had driven through the streets of London.

Among the men who had seen his car drive past, and who had crouched out of sight until there was no danger of him being seen, was the Prowler. He was still inside the cordon, still in greater danger than he knew.

Among the women whom Gideon had passed was Mrs. Michael (Netta) Penn, until recently of 11 Lassiter Street.

When she had telephoned the Yard, she had simply been worried and distressed; when Gideon's car passed within a hundred yards of the cellar where she was sitting, she was terrified.

For a long time she had gone on searching for her husband, always desperately, fearful of the reason for his disappearance. She had never found the courage to speak of it to the police, but she was frightened in case her husband, her beloved Michael, had been murdered. She had believed that, if she could persuade Scotland Yard to look for him, they would find out the best or the worst.

That night, in the fog, she had telephoned Scotland Yard, asking for Gideon because Gideon's name had been in the newspapers several times recently and she had grown tired of talking to casual telephone men with indifferent voices, to officials who obviously thought that she was making a lot of fuss about nothing.

Two or three things that Michael had said before his disappearance had suggested that he was going to get some money; he had talked of "being rich." So she connected his disappearance with new-found wealth. She was absolutely certain he would not just walk out of her life; that if it was humanly possible he would telephone or write to her.

So—he *must* be dead.

He had been so happy, so confident in his love.

Among the people she had talked to about Michael had been the Rikkers of 11 Lassiter Street. She had called there tonight, before telephoning, to inquire for letters and messages—praying for one from Michael.

There had been none.

Rikker the landlord, a middle-aged man she had never liked, had been harsh and unfriendly, and his drab of a wife no better. Without realizing that it was the first time she had told them this, she had said that she was going to make the police look for Michael; that very night she was going to telephone Gideon.

Before Gideon had come on the line, while she had been awaiting a new sort of hope, Rikker had loomed out of the fog, opened the kiosk door, and twisted the telephone out of her hand.

"You come with me," he had said, and the night had muffled his voice and her fears had stifled hers.

Now she was in terror, because she was sure that they had killed Michael and that they were going to kill her.

11 . Night of Terror

IT WAS a small house. Sounds would travel from it easily. It was possible to hear the rumble of the buses from the main road which ran along one end, and the cars which passed, too. It was also an old house, and had a cellar deep beneath the ground, with only a round hatch leading to the pavement through which sound could escape. The hatch was covered, with boxes standing beneath it and sacking stuffed tightly between the top box and the hatch, so that no sound escaped.

Netta sat on an upright chair in the cellar, and she was tied to it with rope which she couldn't loosen, and which hurt her arms and cut into her thighs. One light burned above her head, but it was chance that it shone almost directly into her eyes, making them water, making her long to close them—although she dared not close them for long, in case she lost consciousness and so missed any sound or sight to indicate that the landlord was coming back.

She did not know how long she had been here.

There had been the telephone kiosk, the opening door, the landlord's powerful grasp, her fear, the way he had hustled her back to Number 11, with a scarf round her face so that, even if she had wanted to scream, she could not. The night had been thick with fog and empty of people, and she had been bundled over the threshold of the house where she had once had her home in two furnished rooms upstairs.

Then, she had been wildly happy.

Now—

Rikker had taken her downstairs into the cellar, his wife had followed

and, when the door at the foot of the stairs had closed on them, she had
realized how utterly silent it was down here. In part, that might be due to
the stillness of the night, but here were the bricks of the walls, whitewashed,
looking big and solid.

One big section looked new. The floor was of solid concrete. In one
corner, beneath the manhole, there was a heap of coke, for burning.

They had questioned her, first the man, and then his wife.

How often had she been to the police? What had she told the police?
Why had she gone to the police?

How often?

What had she told them?

Why had she gone?

First the man and then the woman had thrown the same questions at
her, the man roughly, the woman in a whining, pleading tone; and in a
way she liked the woman less and feared her more than Rikker, a thickset,
powerful man, wearing a heavy sailor's sweater of navy blue, who needed
a shave. All the time she had lived in the two rooms upstairs he had needed
one; occasionally he rasped thick, horny fingers over the gray stubble, and
on his breath lay the strong odor of whisky.

How often . . . What . . . Why?

At first her mind had been paralyzed by fear and she told them the simple
truth, time and time again. She had telephoned the police six or seven
times; she couldn't be sure how many. She had told them that Michael had
disappeared, and that she was sure that something had happened to him.
And she had telephoned them because she was certain that Michael
wouldn't just have walked out on her; he had been too much in love.

And he had.

She could picture him now, with thick, fair hair which curled a little and
the smile in his eyes and his rather snubbed nose and his gentle hands.

How often?

What?

Why?

"I've told you!" she burst out at last. "I keep telling you; why do you want
to know?"

They hadn't told her.

They had left her tied to the chair and gone out, letting the heavy wooden
door swing to behind them, and with the unshaded electric lamp just above
and just in front of her eyes, so that it hurt to look at it, and she could never
escape from the glare.

At first she hadn't been able to forget the questions. It was as if her mind
had received an image—as the eye received the image of the filament of the
electric lamp—and, even when the questions had stopped, she had echoed

them. Fear had been her dominant emotion then, and in a way it still was, but then she had not known the root causes of her fear; now she did.

They had killed Michael.

They would kill her.

There was no way of being absolutely sure, but she felt sure. They were frightened too; they had been frightened of what she might have told the police, and she had told them nothing—*nothing*. She had not dreamed that the Rikkers knew anything about Michael's disappearance. He had left for his office one day, and for weeks afterward she had lived on the memory of the way he had promised that before long he would get her out of these two furnished rooms into a real home of their own. It had been a blissful day, but—

He had not come home.

She had been out that afternoon, visiting her mother, who lived in Horley Street, Fulham, not far. She had not reached Lassiter Street until seven o'clock, and had quite expected Michael to be home, but—she had never seen him again.

She had telephoned his office, and been told that he had left at the usual time; that was all.

He hadn't gone back to the office, either.

When the Rikkers had told her that she must leave the two rooms, she had been alarmed because Michael wouldn't know at once where to get in touch with her. She had gone to stay with her mother, who knew what had happened. And she had got a job. Life had gone on, drably, emptily, and once a week she called at 11 Lassiter Street to see if there were any letters, or if Michael had come back. The Rikkers knew her new address, but she had sensed they had no liking for her, and she hadn't trusted them to forward letters or any messages. She had been right not to; several times she had found letters addressed to Michael. Nothing much, but—

All of these things went through her mind while she was alone in the cold, bare, almost soundproof cellar.

The cold bit into her.

Now and again she began a shivering fit which she could not control. Her feet were so cold that they ached, her fingers so cold that she felt as if they would snap if anyone bent them. The ropes round her arms and body, and over her thighs, made all movement difficult except that of her head.

Once or twice, she had fancied that she heard a sound, but nothing had followed it.

Now she sat terrified. Yet she was falling into a kind of stupor—the bright light, the lamp filament, the shiny glass pear shape of the lamp, the thick walls, the cold, the aching, the images of questions—*how often, what, why?*

Now and again her head drooped with exhaustion, but each time she woke in panic and moved her head about wildly, to wake herself up, for there was the great fear in her—that if she went to sleep she might not wake again.

Upstairs, in a small back room with a kitchen table and an electric stove, two old saddleback chairs and several wooden chairs, a big deal dresser and some prints taken from the tops of tradesmen's calendars, the Rikkers sat and drank—Rikker whisky, his wife gin. Looking at them and forgetting the white and black of the big stove, it was easy to imagine that a hundred years had passed this room by. This might be a thieves' kitchen drawn by Boz and peopled by Dickens. Rikker, barrel-like and massive with a flat head and a low forehead, his wife small and flat breasted, with greasy gray hair.

In a corner was a big, new television set. It had not been there when Netta and Michael Penn had lived in the two rooms above.

In a cupboard beneath the dresser were seven bottles of whisky; single half-bottles had been the rule before the Penns had "left."

The Rikkers had not said a great deal, and the television had been on most of the evening although they had not taken much notice of it; the noise was in the background, that was all.

Every now and again, Mrs. Rikker had said:

"What are you going to *do* with her?"

Rikker hadn't once answered.

Then, halfway through the evening, there had come a sharp knock at the front door, making Rikker jump to his feet, sending his wife cringing in alarm. The knock had been repeated. Rikker had told his wife to stay in the kitchen, with the door closed, and had gone out. His wife would probably have collapsed, but Rikker had answered the detective's questions gruffly but civilly enough. Yes, Penn had left months ago, Mrs. Penn weeks ago. Why? She couldn't pay her rent. Did he know why Penn had left her? Usual reasons, Rikker supposed; he got fed up. Had he seen Penn since he had left? No.

No, no, no, no.

After the man had gone, apparently satisfied, Rikker had returned to the kitchen and poured himself too much whisky and tossed it down.

"Who—who was it, Rikky?"

"Never you mind."

"Rikky, who was it?"

"Shut your trap!"

"Rikky, was it—was it the *police?*"

He'd swallowed more whisky. She had stood on the other side of the table, out of hand's reach if he should move to strike her, but with her eyes wide open and rounded, and her thin lips parted to show unnaturally even, white teeth; a young woman's teeth in an old woman's face.

"Rikky! Was it a copper?"

"I told you to shut your bloody trap."

"I want to know who it was. Was it a copper? What did he want, what—"

"I told you to shut your *trap*," Rikker hissed, and he leaned forward and struck at her, but she dodged and he missed. "So a copper came and asked some questions. So what? He came to ask if she still lived here, and I told him she didn't, we hadn't seen her for weeks. That was nearly the truth, wasn't it? What difference does it make?"

The woman's face looked much, much older.

"Why—why do you think the copper came, Rikky?"

"She called the cops, didn't she?"

"Do you—do you think she said anything—"

"I told you before, she didn't *know* anything, so how could she tell the cops anything? She was just worried because Penn didn't come back, that's all. If she'd kept her nose out of my business—"Rikker broke off, as if even he realized that the remark was the ultimate absurdity.

There had been a long silence. Then:

"What—what are you going to do with her?" Mrs. Rikker asked hoarsely.

"The same as we did with him, what do you think we're going to do?" Rikker rasped. "But I'm not taking no chances. I'm going to make sure the cops don't come back before I get the job done."

There had been another long silence, and then:

"She—she ain't done us any harm, Rikky, do you think—"

"If she gets the police looking for Penn she'll get us caught on a murder rap, that's how much harm she can do. Now shut your gob, you always talk too much."

Silence.

"Rikky."

Silence.

"Rikky, do you think the police will come again?"

"What I think is I've had enough from you tonight, I'm going out for a walk," Rikker said roughly. He stood up, finished the whisky in his glass, and then went out, taking a thick topcoat off a peg behind the door. His wife first watched and then went after him, but he didn't look round.

Then, the fog had been at its thickest.

Rikker had met a neighbor, coming home from the pub, and the neighbor had told him that the police were after someone in a big way; a man in the pub had been held up at a station, someone else in a bus on West-minster Bridge. Something about a baby. And something about a girl.

"Rikky," his wife had muttered when he had got back, "when are you going to do it?"

"I'll take my time."

"How—are you—"

"I'm going to do what I did last time," Rikker said. "I'm going to knock her over the head, see, so she won't feel anything. Then I'm going to brick her up in the wall, the same as I did him. Any more questions?"

"You—you won't *hurt* her, will you?"

Then he had struck her across the face before she could dodge, grabbed her shoulders and shaken her until her teeth rattled and her head bobbed up and down. When his rage had subsided, he had pushed her away and she had slumped back on the sofa, half crying. He had poured himself another drink, then gone to the cellar door.

Gideon passed within a hundred yards of the house, and drove with his new-found sense of quiet satisfaction toward the East End and the gangs. This led him through the deserted city, its dark buildings tall against the sky, the Bank of England squat and forbidding on its corner, the Stock Exchange looking as if the Greeks had built it there.

Along Throgmorton Street, two cars were parked, with their side lights on, and in the building by them a light shone out at the third floor.

"Fog's practically gone," Gideon said to himself, and drove on, thinking that someone else was working late.

In the room from which the light shone out above Throgmorton Street, two men were sitting. Both were young-middle-aged. One was portly and pale, the other slim and hardy looking, carrying the tan of long hours in the sun; this made his gray eyes seem very bright and gave him a hand-someness which made the other man look nondescript. Both were well dressed and prosperous looking. They sat in an office with paneled walls, near a large polished desk with a swivel chair behind it. For some time they had been sitting in large armchairs, whisky decanter and soda siphon on a small table between them, and papers spread out on the floor all around them.

It was very quiet.

A car passed in the street, making a purring note; the bright-eyed man didn't notice it, but the other looked up sharply.

The bright-eyed man said, "Not nervous, George, are you?"

"Nervous? Me? Don't be silly, Paul. I never was the nervous type."

George Warren gave a quick grin and picked up his glass a little too quickly. "If I've got anything to be nervous about, it's you."

"I don't get you," Paul Devereaux said easily.

Warren's smile became too quick and bright.

"Forget it. I only meant that I'll be down the drain if I don't get a hundred thousand out of this, and you're the strength of the deal. That's all I've got to be nervous about. I've done my part." He picked up some thick documents and rustled them as if they were massive five-pound notes. "Share certificates in uranium ore found in the Lombo district of East Africa, where we have exclusive mineral rights *and* cheap labor. The uranium's there, too; any test will show it." He gave a quick little teetering laugh. "After all, you put it there! No doubt you planted it well, is there, Paul?"

"I planted it so that no one could dream that it didn't belong," Devereaux said. His bright eyes flashed, but he still looked a little wary. "In a day or two we'll get the prospector's report with everything confirmed, then we'll go to town with the new company."

"That's what I mean by my share," said Warren. "I've been doing a little discreet whispering already—hinting that something big is coming out of Warren and Company in the near future. Whisper it, though; don't let a good thing pass on to the other chaps, you know. I've had a dozen discreet inquiries to deal with already. If I'd cared to I could have collected the hundred thousand before issuing the shares. That's how high the integrity of Warren and Company stands!" He rubbed his hands together. "If that prospecting report is fully substantiated, we'll offer the shares for private sale, without any publicity. And everyone concerned will think he's on a bargain! I'll warn them that it will be five years before they see any big returns, too."

"Sounds like a cakewalk," said Devereaux, and poured himself another drink. "There's one little thing you won't forget, isn't there?"

"What's that?"

"You owe me ten thousand pounds and expenses."

"My dear chap, you'll have it within forty-eight hours of the new issue being offered!" said Warren. "That's a first charge." He seemed to have overcome his nervousness, and had a little color in his plump cheeks. "What are you going to do after this?"

Devereaux grinned.

"I'm going to be a playboy for six months, and make as many girls as I can provided they don't want me to run to mink. After that—well, I'll probably go exploring again!" He stood up and went to the window, saying, "It's time we went, George. Belinda will be wondering where you are."

"She can wonder," George Warren said abruptly. "If it wasn't for Belinda I wouldn't have got so heavily into debt, but—" He shrugged a gloomy thought off. "I've bought five years' reprieve, anyhow, and anything can happen in that time. Why, there might even be uranium in the Lombo district!"

"George, what was worrying you just now?" asked Devereaux quietly.

After a pause, Warren said abruptly, "I was wondering what Belinda would do if this was ever found out. She'd rob anybody if she could, but if there was any risk of being put in jail—"

"The worst that can happen is that the uranium doesn't pan out so well. It won't be the first hush-hush proposition that fell flat," said Devereaux. "You'll only collect from the get-rich-quick boys, anyhow."

Warren nodded and they began to tidy up the office.

12 . East End

GIDEON received a radio message as he neared Aldgate, telling him that Hemmingway and Lemaitre were in a street near the gymnasium where one of the gangs had gathered. He knew the place slightly—as he knew nearly everything which had the remotest association with London's crime. The gymnasium had once been a genuine part of dockland, giving stevedores, sailors and the local inhabitants a place to show their paces, have a turn with the gloves, the rope or the wall bars. The then owners had made a grave mistake by arranging to get a license, and, soon after beer and spirits became available in the bar, the quality of the patrons began to fall, although some old habitués had continued to come in order to drink at prices slightly below that of nearby public houses.

Then the Wide boys had moved in.

The gymnasium had several advantages for a gang. It was on the ground floor of an old warehouse, plenty large enough for a crowd to meet, and the Wide boys had nearly fifty associate members. It offered, through the ring and the fixtures, a meeting place which was ostensibly a physical-training club, so that no one could object to it, not even the police. Although officially it was illegal to sell beer after eleven o'clock at night, there was nothing against keeping the club open all night, if the members wanted it. A piano had been brought in, there were half a dozen amateur musicians including a surprisingly good drummer in the club and, as the warehouse was not in a residential district, music and dancing often went on for most of the night.

Not a hundred yards from the gymnasium was the old Dockside Club. This had a similar history, except that it had been a youth club for the thousands of young people who grew up in the sprawling mass of tiny, crowded, airless streets which led off the docks. It had existed for years, sometimes flourishing, more often than not just surviving, until the Melky gang had taken it over.

They had done so quite legally, for the Melky gang was remarkable because most of its members were very young. Even Melky, the absolute boss, was only twenty-two—although he had been married five years and had three children by a sexy little Italian girl who was said to be the brains behind him. The members of the gang had joined the club at a time when it had been run jointly by a Church of England and a nonconformist church; within six months the church influence had vanished completely, but all the club facilities remained. These were indoor games, a movie projector and screen, a television room, even an arts and crafts room, but there was no license for liquor.

Although the law was broken frequently in both establishments, and although occasionally members of the rival gangs would clash and there would be a bloodied nose or two, the general behavior of the gangs in London was reasonably good. Certainly there was no plausible excuse for the police to close down either of the places. Melky's gang worked the racecourses within easy reach south of London, and the Wide boys went northwest. They both worked the crowds—picking pockets, stealing winnings, snatching handbags—and the usual protection method was adopted; one or two of the "boys" worked while half a dozen stood by to make sure that if there was trouble the others could get away. Occasionally a member of the gang was picked up for being in possession of stolen goods, but, if one was sent inside, his wife or family was looked after by the gang.

Each gang had boasted of its size and strength.

Each had grown stronger in the past twelve months.

Recently, Melky's gang had appeared on the same racecourses as the Wide boys. That seemed the end of the unwritten agreement, and that was why Hemmingway was so worried about what might happen. He knew —and Gideon knew—that if there was a running fight through the docks, enormous damage could be done to warehouses, stored goods and even to ships themselves. When gangs really got out of control, it was dangerous and could be deadly.

Gideon caught sight of a policeman in a doorway as he slowed down in the street where he was to meet Hemmingway and Lemaitre. He stopped just in front of the corner and got out, aware of being watched, but seeing no one. There was no other car in sight. Just across the intersecting road there was the tall wall of a warehouse, and a hundred yards or so away there were the lighted windows of the old Dockside Club, in another nearby warehouse.

A man approached.

"That you, George?" It was Lemaitre, who sounded quite brisk.

"Yes."

"Hemmingway's gone round the back way to have a look at things near the Red Lion Gymnasium," Lemaitre said. "He'll be back in a few minutes. We've got all the streets sealed off, but there are between a hundred and a hundred and forty louts in those two clubs, and they're all spoiling for a fight. You can tell it a mile off. We've got about forty men, and they're spread thin."

And a hundred or more were waiting at bridges and other vantage points in the nearly forlorn hope of catching the Prowler.

"We'll get some more," promised Gideon. "Got the entrances to the docks covered?"

"As far as we can," said Lemaitre. "Don't want to push you, George, but if you could send for those reinforcements you'd do me and Hemmingway a lot of good."

"Let's fix it," Gideon said flatly.

They went to his car, and he leaned inside and flicked on the radio telephone, ignoring the noises as they came crackling in. As he waited for the Information Room to answer, he recalled the way he had been stopped at the bridge, told himself that it was idiocy to believe that the Prowler might still be trapped inside the cordon. It was after two o'clock! He ought to have had the reinforcements here an hour or more ago; certainly he ought to have trusted Hemmingway's judgment.

Even so, he was reluctant to give the order.

He gave it.

As he moved from the car, another approached along the street he had come along; it stopped behind him and Hemmingway got out, bustling.

"You, George?"

"Yes."

"If you don't—"

"I have," said Gideon.

"'Bout time, too," said the NE Divisional Superintendent, although obviously he was mollified on the instant. "I've just been round to the east-side gates—or where they would be if there were any! They've taken the actual gates down to let in some of the big stuff that's due in by road, so all we've got up is a flimsy wooden barrier. The two night-duty gatemen have got the breeze up properly; they say they can smell this fight the way you can smell the eucalyptus a hundred miles away from the coast of Australia."

Gideon said blankly, "Can you?"

Hemmingway chuckled, yet gave the impression that he was very much on edge.

"I read it in a book," he announced. "How much did Lemaitre tell you? There are all of a hundred and twenty rats waiting to mix it."

"Any idea why they've waited so long?"

"One side's waiting for the other to move," Hemmingway said, "that's all."

Earlier in the evening, Gideon had wondered whether this situation was as simple as it had seemed, but first Hemmingway and then Lemaitre had persuaded him that it was. Now his doubts came back. There had been fights before. He couldn't recall that any of them had started in the small hours, although often the fights lasted until dawn, the protagonists splitting up into groups which grew smaller and smaller. Tonight's behavior was peculiar. Everyone on the spot seemed quite certain what was on foot, but—

"Heard one rumor that could explain it," said Hemmingway.

"What's that?"

"After Melky's boys wouldn't stop poaching, the Wide boys tried to kidnap his pocket Lollo. They failed, but they said that if Melky didn't call his men out of their grounds, they'd get her."

"Where is Lollo?"

"In the old Dockside Club."

"Sure?"

"She was seen to arrive, just before twelve o'clock, with an escort of six of the biggest members of the gang."

"Hmm," said Gideon, and scratched the back of his neck.

It was quite obvious that Hemmingway planned to seal off all the entrances and exits to the area, and then let the two gangs fight it out. If it worked that way, then probably each gang would be so weakened that the police could step in and finish things off, arrest the gang leaders on charges which should put them in jail for twelve months at least, and so put an end to their activities for a long time. It was the kind of clear-up that the police liked and which they were able to fix now and again on a comparatively small scale; but Gideon didn't feel at ease over this.

"What's on your mind?" Lemaitre knew him well enough to sense his doubts.

Gideon grunted noncommittally.

In the distance, he heard several cars, and realized that these were the first of the patrol cars which had come off the Prowler job; they hadn't taken long. Well, that was over and done with, for tonight, and this now seemed the only urgent issue.

"Give," urged Lemaitre.

"Dunno," said Gideon, and looked at Hemmingway's strong, big features.

"Ever known them to wait for as long as this to start something? Don't hear anything, do you?"

"Bit of singing earlier, but it quieted down," conceded Hemmingway. "But—"

"All right, I'm stubborn," Gideon said almost roughly, "but if there's going to be a schemozzle between the gangs we usually hear them getting warmed up first—they get tiddly, then they get tight, they start singing and banging the piano about. Then they send out one or two scouts, to call the other side a lot of so-and-sos, and soon they can't hold themselves in any longer and start with the razors and the knuckle dusters."

Hemmingway almost jeered. "You must have been reading a book, too."

"Anything wrong?"

"Elementary, my dear Gee-Gee."

"Why aren't they drunk tonight?" asked Gideon.

"Serious business afoot."

"As you said earlier, when they really get mad with each other they lose every bit of sense they ever had," said Gideon. "Hemmy, know what I'd like to do?"

"Listen, George, we can't start the raid; so far they haven't done a thing to give us an excuse. If we start it, they'll be fresh and they'll probably join forces against us, and our chaps—"

"I'd like you to go and talk to the Wide boys' chief, while I go and talk to Melky."

There was a startled pause. More cars sounded in the distance, for London at night was very quiet and no ships near this section of the docks were being worked. Some way off, floodlights shining on the spindly cranes on deck and the heavier ones alongside showed clearly.

Even the river was now clear of fog, and there was a freshening breeze. Two cars turned the corner and came along slowly.

"*You crazy?*" Hemmingway demanded at last.

"Nothing crazy about it," said Gideon. "We just tell them that we don't like what they're up to, and they're to go home."

"Goddammit, George, they're inside their own premises. You can't even pretend you think they're going to cause a breach of the peace; you wouldn't have a legal leg to stand on." Hemmingway stared up at Gideon, who stood still and quiet and yet somehow dominant, by far the largest man in the little group which had been enlarged by the men now arriving from the Squad cars which had been at the bridges. "You really mean it, don't you?" Hemmingway added in a resigned tone. "But I'm telling you that it won't make any difference."

"You may be right," Gideon said. "Let's go."

"Alone?"

"If they're fighting mad the sight of half a dozen coppers will just about set 'em alight, but we'd better go in pairs. Lemaitre can come with me, and you take a chap. Send for him and then let's go ahead," added Gideon. He walked on, while Hemmingway gave an order, then hurried to catch up. Lemaitre and Hemmingway's aide, a detective inspector, walked behind them through the gloom.

Hemmingway was breathing hard, as if fighting back antagonism.

"Got an idea I didn't want to talk about in front of the others," Gideon said to him. "If it's any good, it'll be better if it comes from you."

"It won't, if it's anything like the rest of your ideas tonight!"

Gideon chuckled.

Ahead, a little man who was watching from the corner moved out of sight, obviously to go and report to his boss that the two men were approaching. Gideon felt quite sure that the members of both gangs were fully aware that the police were concentrating, and that the little shadowy figure was one of several scouts. He didn't go on at first, but their footsteps were heavy and clear in the street, and seemed to echo off the high warehouse wall.

"All right, let's have it," said Hemmingway.

"What ships are tied up at these docks?" asked Gideon.

"*Norda*, registered at Oslo, *Marianne* from Antwerp, *Black Marquis* from New Orleans, and a thing with a name I can't pronounce, from Cairo. But what—"

"They discharging or loading cargo?"

"The *Norda*'s loading, ready to sail in the morning," said Hemmingway, "I don't know about the *Marianne*. *Black Marquis* has just arrived; so has the Egyptian ship." Hemmingway scratched the back of his head, and they slowed down as they neared the corner. A shadow was thrown across the road telling them that a man was just round the corner, probably judging their progress from the sound of their approach. "Don't ask me what they're carrying; I'm not a walking encyclopedia." He sounded aggressive, and that was probably because Gideon had made him uneasy. "What's on your mind?"

"Both gangs out in strength, dock gates off and unprotected, suspicious quiet and a motive for a row which doesn't stand up," said Gideon.

"You're wrong there. Melky's so jealous that—"

"If anyone made a pass at his wife he'd try to cut them up without having a cold-blooded, full-scale gang war," said Gideon, "and I think that this is a put-up job for us to swallow. I'd like to know what's in the holds of those ships, or what's going in."

"I can soon find out," Hemmingway said, very slowly and uneasily. "I

can call the dock police; they'll know. Let's get this job over quick. Sure
you prefer to take Melky?"

"Positive."

"You know he's got a reputation for—"

"He won't use a knife on me or anyone else tonight," said Gideon. "I'll
take Lemaitre, you take your chap."

They reached the corner. The scout just round the corner vanished inside
the entrance of the gymnasium, and along the street were the lights of the
other club. Not fifty yards beyond it, where a single lamp burned in the
archway, were the "gates" leading to the docks; the opening was very wide,
and the only sign of life was in a small gate office, where a light burned
yellow.

Just beyond this office a dozen policemen were out of sight.

Lemaitre caught Gideon up.

"Any special angle, George?"

"Just see how it goes," said Gideon.

So he went in.

At that very moment, some miles away, the Prowler hid in a doorway,
near a tube station which was still open. He saw a police car, which had
been standing there for over two hours, move off at speed.

At the same time, nearer to Gideon, Paul Devereaux and George Warren
got into their respective cars and also drove off.

At Scotland Yard, the Information Room buzzed with messages both in
and out, the blocks of wood which represented patrol cars were being moved
all the time, the greatest concentration being now about the East End and
the NE Division. But news of burglaries, two with violence, of fires, of
smash-and-grab raids, of streetwalking, of car thefts, of almost every crime in
the calendar came streaming in. Appleby and a sergeant were in Gideon's
office, sending out instructions, sorting out everything that had to be done,
assigning men to the various jobs on which the Divisions needed specialist
help.

Approaching Scotland Yard in a police car was M. Monnet, of the *Sûreté
Nationale,* with a small black brief case under his arm, a small cigar
between his lips, a Homburg hat at the back of his head, a smooth-cloth
coat buttoned tightly about him.

At London airport the indignant—and possibly frightened—Leslie Forrester argued with the Customs, who were making a thorough search of
everything he had brought with him, and yet were so pleasant and apolo-
getic.

And in the cellar at 11 Lassiter Street, little Netta Penn sat as if her body were turned to ice, with pain at her eyes and numb dread in her heart. She couldn't even wriggle her fingers now, she was so cold.

For the past hour, she had heard sounds of scratching and faint banging, and at one time she had thought these were a long way off. In fact they were close to her—and she knew that Rikker was doing something to the wall of the cellar, on the other side of the door.

She didn't know what.

In the space of fifteen minutes, seven Flying Squad and three patrol cars passed the end of Lassiter Street.

13 . Melky

As GIDEON stepped inside the doorway of the old Dockside Club, beneath a dirty, tattered banner which hadn't been taken down and reading YOUTH FOR CHRIST CRUSADE, he heard music—hot jazz probably coming from a radiogram or a record player. Two members of the Melky gang were in a doorway which led to the main room of the club, where the lights were bright and the music was loud, and a shuffle of feet suggested that a few couples were dancing. Someone began to sing the lyrics in a shrill flat voice. The two youths, dark haired, pale faced and wary, were dwarfed by Gideon as he approached them. They seemed ready to try to bar his way, but he walked as if he hadn't noticed them; either he would bump into them or they would move aside.

They moved.

Gideon went into the big room first, and Lemaitre followed, also ignoring the two doormen.

A few tawdry decorations including colored toy balloons, many of them deflated, hung from the ceiling. At the end of the hall on a high stage was a girl in a strapless "gown," which covered just about as much of her as a two-piece bathing suit, swaying in front of a microphone which obviously didn't work. By her side were a record player and a youth with a shock of ginger hair swaying to the rhythm. The smell of tobacco smoke was thick and acrid. Three couples danced, hugging each other. Sitting at small tables round the walls were most of the members of the gang—nearly all young and sallow, some obviously not English, others as native Cockney as Bow Bells. Most of them were dressed in old clothes, and not to kill, which by itself was an indication that they hadn't come simply for a good time. Most appeared to be drinking soft drinks, but in some of the glasses there was undoubtedly hard liquor. At one corner there was a snack bar, where a blousy girl wriggled and giggled with two boys who had come to "help" serve, and were being pretty rough. Underneath smeary glass covers were sandwiches and sausage rolls, and attached to the wall was a steaming tea or coffee urn.

About the middle of one wall, at the biggest table in the hall, sat Melky —or Antonio Melcrino—and with him was his Lollo. Her name was not Lollo—when Gideon had first heard of her it had been Maria—but she had a figure which matched the fabulous Lollo's, and so had taken the name. She wore a tight-fitting, shiny black dress, obviously drawn tightly at the back to pull her stomach as flat as it could be, and to make her bust jut out so much that she looked more caricature than a real person. She had a mass of dark curls, fine, dark, glowing eyes, and full, red lips; she was really something, and it was hard to realize that she was the mother of three children.

Melky sat beside her.

He was third-generation London Italian. His mother and father kept a small café in Kensington, and had only one sorrow: the fact that their son had gone bad. He hadn't visited them for years. He was short and thin, with a sharp-featured, sensitive-looking face. His hair was not particularly dark, and was silky and brushed straight back from a high forehead. If one saw him in the street and guessed what he did for a living, it would be easy to suggest that he was an intellectual or an artist. The only artistry he knew was with the knife. He could carve patterns on human skin and, when the mood took him, pieces out of human flesh.

Now he sat, not really truculent, not sullen, simply wary—like everyone else here. His knife wasn't in sight.

The music stopped.

Melky did not motion to the red-haired boy on the stage, but another record went on, and the singer swayed and rolled her eyes and began to sing again. This was prearranged, of course; they weren't going to let the police think they could interfere or scare them.

Gideon stopped in front of the big table.

He glanced at Lollo, then took his hat off, a completely unexpected gesture, and he nodded to her as he might to any woman whom he met casually.

"Tony Melcrino?" he asked.

"That's me," Melky said, hardly moving his thin lips.

"What's going on tonight?"

"We're celebrating," Melky said.

"Bit late, aren't you?"

"My mother said I could stay up late," said Melky, and there was a slight relaxation in the attitude of the people about him; one boy laughed. The dancing couples contrived to mark time near the table, and over by the bar the giggling girl was standing still, each boy with an arm round her, all three staring toward Gideon.

"You can make it funny or you can take it straight," Gideon said. "I don't care how you take it, but if you know what's good for you you'll break this party up."

"What am I doing?" demanded Melcrino, and glanced up at Lollo and thrust out his chest. "Minding my own, that's all. Pity other people don't follow my example."

Gideon just stared at him.

The man wasn't really at ease, but he wasn't worried either; he was completely assured of his position here, and he had sound legal cause to be. Hemmingway was probably having the same kind of interview with the leader of the Wide boys, and telling himself that it was all a waste of time.

"Close the door when you go out," Melcrino said, and this time half a dozen of his followers made giggly noises.

"Listen to me, Melcrino," Gideon said, and stood so that he could see not only the man himself but also his wife, who had pulled a chair a little closer. "If you start a fight tonight you'll bite off more than you can chew. I'm warning you. Tell your boys to go home." He paused, and he saw the glint in Melcrino's eyes, and saw the way Lollo squeezed his hand; they thought they were so clever and yet were such naïve fools. "Hemmingway's giving the Wide boys the same orders," Gideon went on. "If you two want to fight it out, choose somewhere else. This is my beat."

"And it's my business," Melky said sneeringly.

Gideon was quite sure that the glint in his eyes and the squeeze from his wife meant one thing: satisfaction, almost elation, and elation could only be due to something he had said. All he had said was that the police assumed that a gang fight was in the offing.

"Don't make us get rough," Gideon said.

"You couldn't hurt pussy," Melcrino sneered. "Think we're scared of a bunch of ruddy rozzers? Go and fry your face, Gideon, that's how frightened I am of *you*."

He moved his hand in a gesture which brought the loudest laugh so far. That was the moment when the music stopped, a moment when the situation could become ugly, but Gideon did not think it would be ugly just yet.

"All right," he said, as if frustrated, "I've warned you. I came myself because I wanted you to know that we're right behind Hemmingway. If you try to carve up the Wide boys, most of you will end up in the hospital or in the dock, and we'll make every charge stick."

"Peanuts," said Melcrino, and so elicited a roar of laughter.

There was a moment's pause; soon Gideon would retire with the jeers of the gang in his ears, and they would think that they had scored a signal triumph, that they could poke their noses at the police. It would really elate them and, when they came to act, it might easily make them careless.

Then Lollo Melcrino pushed her chair back, gave a broad, seductive smile, and stepped toward Gideon with her hands on her hips and her body swaying. She was the perfect subject for one of the illustrated tabloids, and in fact she was really quite beautiful; her shoulders and that part of her not covered by the dress were creamy and smooth and free from blemish. Her dark eyes glowed, and she just stood in front of Gideon, put her head on one side, and asked in a husky voice:

"Why don't you hit one of your own size?"

She stood lower than his massive chin.

The laughter seemed to shake the walls.

"Didn't get any change out of that," said Lemaitre. "If we don't slap them down after this our name will be mud." There was unspoken reproof in his voice.

"Thick mud," agreed Gideon. He didn't hurry back to the corner, for Hemmingway would probably be another ten minutes; he'd had further to go. The sound of music faded slightly. Above their heads the stars shone, and not far along the river there came the sharp blasts of a ship's siren; one of the smaller ships was about to leave the Port of London.

Gideon switched on the radio as he reached the car, and Lemaitre lit a cigarette and flicked the match moodily over the car's roof.

"Give me Mr. Appleby."

"Yes, sir."

"Hello, Cappen," greeted Appleby, obviously at his brightest. "Not forgotten the old folks at home? How are things out there?"

"Ominous."

"Well, we can't send anyone else," said Appleby. "We've had to rush the cars over to Hampstead; three burglaries on the Heath. Could be by the same man but it don't look like it. Bit of trouble in Mayling Square, too. Looks like a peeress has run off with a chauffeur, taking some of the heirlooms with them, and his nibs tried to shoot the lights out of them."

"Who is it?"

"Lord Addisal."

"Don't take any chances with that," said Gideon urgently. "Who've we got on duty? . . . Send Morley. He—"

"He's there. But we can't keep it quiet; the *Daily Wire*'s there too."

"Morley can handle it if anyone can," said Gideon. "We don't want a rap over the knuckles from the House of Lords, and—"

"Ever hear that fool story about one law for the poor and one for the rich?" asked Appleby brightly. "Ever hear such libelous nonsense? I've got M. Monnet here—well, not exactly here, but downstairs waiting. What time will you be back?"

"Say half an hour, but don't keep him waiting too long."

"No, sir. That's about the lot," Appleby went on. "We're getting all the routine reports from the Divisions now. I'm telling the sarge to go through them and pick out anything he thinks worth looking at."

"Good," said Gideon.

Appleby was making sure that there could not be any cause for reproach, and he was proving almost exemplary in handling his job. Well, why not? A man could behave like a clown and still be a first-class detective. Take away Appleby's schoolboy sense of humor, and you had a man who ought to have been in or at least near his, Gideon's, shoes.

Gideon rang off.

"How's it going?" asked Lemaitre.

"Quietish. Trouble out at Hampstead," Gideon said, and saw Hemming-way and his sergeant turn the corner, walking very briskly. They had been longer even than he had expected, although he hadn't thought Hemming-way would spend a lot of time with the Wide boys. The two men came up. Hemmingway quickened his pace as he approached Gideon; the other man dropped behind.

"How'd it go?" asked Gideon.

"They just gave me a bit of lip," said Hemmingway gruffly. "If you ask me, when I told them to pack up and go home because we wouldn't stand for any gang fight, he was laughing up his sleeve. And do you know what I found out, George?"

"What?"

"The *Marianne*'s only waiting for her last load of cargo; it's due here any time. Not very big," declared Hemmingway, "just a few bags of mail. But some of the bags will contain registered packages, mostly British currency for banks in Belgium and Holland, a few containing commercial diamonds on their way to Holland." The NE man sounded bitter. "Not surprising I didn't tumble to it. The truth is that I didn't know the Post Office had started sending notes this way. They were sent by air until two weeks ago, when there were those thefts at the Hook."

"How do you think the gangs will play it?" asked Gideon.

"Why don't you finish the job?"

"Don't be a blurry fool. How do you think they'll play it?" demanded Gideon.

Hemmingway repeated, "*Blurry* fool; didn't you ever leave Sunday school?" and then his natural good humor asserted itself, and he went on more easily. "I think they'll be tipped off as soon as the van's on its way.

They'll probably get a phone call. They'll start the riot then, but it'll be phony. They'll stop the van close to the *Marianne*, I should say, while we're sitting and waiting for them to cut themselves to pieces. At a signal they'll all pack it in and shake hands."

"Could be," agreed Gideon. "Well, it won't take much time to find out what route the Post Office van will take, and to make sure they don't get away with it. I'll have to leave it to you, though; I'm wanted back at the Yard. Going to stop and see the fun, Lem?"

"If you don't need me."

"Come and tell me how it goes when it's over," said Gideon. "Sorry I can't stop; there's a Frenchie here from Paris, wants us to extradite a chap who's just come over." He bent almost double so as to get into his car. "Mind Melky's wife," he said. "She'll cause more trouble than the rest of the gangs put together."

He heard their chuckles as he started the engine and drove off.

"If they come any better than Gee-Gee, I'd like to be there to see," said Hemmingway.

"If they come any better than Gee-Gee, I'd throw my hand in," Lemaitre said. "Better get cracking, hadn't we?"

A little over fifteen minutes later two more Squad cars passed the end of Lassiter Street, which was silent, like the rest of London.

Curiously, a little fog hung about here, although now there were very few traces. Not far away, Gideon drove for ten minutes through the empty streets, where every light seemed very bright, until he reached the Embankment. Soon he could see Big Ben, and gave himself a little personal eye test; he was able to pick out the time when he passed Charing Cross underground station, and rated that as good. He was even more comfortable in his mind than he had been when he had started out, and was resigned to the loss of the Prowler. There would be the East End mock fight to hand out to the press, the Harris baby rescue and two or three other successful jobs. There might be a few back-handers about the Prowler, but that was all. He turned into the gateway of the Yard at precisely ten minutes to three. Three Squad cars stood waiting, with their crews ready; when the reserve cars were down to three it really meant a busy night. He had a word with two of the detective inspectors in charge, then hurried up the stairs, up the lift, and along to his office. As he neared the door, he heard his name called from the corner.

"George."

He turned round, to see the lanky Gibb, from the laboratory, hurrying after him on his spindly legs. Gibb had taken off his white smock, and wore a baggy tweed jacket and a white collar which was several sizes too large for him. He had a theory that constriction of the throat by a tight collar and tie was a primary cause of early development of heart diseases.

"What've you got?" asked Gideon.

"That fingernail scraping, blood, Group O," said Gibb promptly, "and all the dope on the hair. How's the girl?"

"Don't know yet," said Gideon.

"Let me know," asked Gibb. "I'm just going downstairs for some eggs and bacon."

Gideon said, "Tell them I'll come down later if I can," and went to his own door and opened it.

His own French was fair, although he could understand others better than he could speak the language, but he wouldn't win a schoolboy's prize with his accent. As he opened the door two men were talking in French so fluent and flawless that it was hard to believe that they were not both Frenchmen.

One was M. Monnet, the other Appleby.

They were sitting on either side of Appleby's desk, talking nineteen to the dozen, the Frenchman's pale hands waving about all over the place, Appleby with one hand in his pocket. On telephone duty at Gideon's desk was the sergeant who had been in and out all evening—and in an odd way he surprised Gideon; he simply didn't register except as a piece of office furniture.

Neither of the men at the small desk heard the door open, but the sergeant jumped up.

Appleby was saying something; the Frenchman answered swiftly, then slapped his hands together and roared with laughter. Almost to Gideon's chagrin, the two men began to talk, one against the other, so fast that Gideon just couldn't pick out the meaning of what they said, only picked up a few words here and there. Then he realized that they were exchanging unfamiliar phrases—Monnet in Paris argot. Appleby translating Cockney rhyming slang fairly liberally, and trotting it out as if French were his native language. Monnet was capping every phrase.

Gideon found himself chuckling.

Appleby looked up, startled, and then scrambled to his feet.

"Hello, hello, didn't see you! This is M. Monnet—"

The Frenchman got up nearly as quickly and bowed, a tall, immaculate young man with a smoothly clean-shaven face and, now, no hint of the laughter he had shown when talking to Appleby. He held out his hand.

"I am very happy to meet you." There was a slight precision of phrasing; otherwise his English was as good as his French. "You are Commander Gideon?"

"Yes." Gideon gripped a small, firm hand and waved to the sergeant. "Bring me up a chair." He saw the wariness spring to the Frenchman's eyes, and suspected that the man was uneasily aware that he might have annoyed Appleby's superior. "Glad to see you, M. Monnet, and before we go any further I've got one request to make."

The chair arrived.

"Yes, certainly, Mr. Gideon," said Monnet, while Appleby watched also with a kind of apprehension. One truth about Appleby was that even so near the retiring age he had an inferiority complex.

"We're going to speak English," said Gideon. "Exactly one minute ago I stopped thinking I could speak French."

Monnet relaxed, and threw up his hands, delighted.

"But it is not true, I have heard of your excellent French, Commander! But you are very kind. I am anxious, because—"

"Give me a minute," said Gideon, and looked at Appleby. "Anything in from Brixton Hospital?"

"No change."

And no Prowler.

"Otherwise normal?"

"I should think so." Appleby slapped a hand on a sheaf of reports. "I haven't finished looking through the Divisional reports but if there was anything to worry about, they'd tell us."

"Good," said Gideon. "Now, M. Monnet . . ."

Among the reports on the desk was one from AB Division—Fulham. It said simply that a Mrs. Russell, of 21 Horley Street, had telephoned at two o'clock because she was worried about her daughter, a Mrs. Penn, who still hadn't returned home, although she would normally have arrived soon after ten o'clock. The report added that there had been no word at hospitals or police stations about a Mrs. Penn being involved in any accident.

14 . M. Monnet

SPREAD out on Appleby's desk were the documents which Monnet had brought with him. Most were in French, but all had translation notes attached, and Gideon read the notes rather than the originals. It was apparent that the *Sûreté Nationale* had long suspected Leslie Forrester of the murder of the English girl in the Hautes-Pyrénées, but there had been no firm evidence. At the request of the authorities at Pau, Monnet had been in charge of investigations. He had finally collected a number of statements and much evidence, including a photograph, that Forrester had been with the girl in Pau three days before her body had been found. Following that, there were some carefully prepared statements and documents showing a painstaking collection of the evidence. Through all this there were the indications that the *Sûreté Nationale* had made up its mind not to suggest that an Englishman was involved until they were absolutely sure. That evening, Monnet was to have charged Forrester.

The sergeant still acted as telephone boy, taking messages and not once interrupting Gideon.

Gideon looked up from the documents.

"Does Forrester know you're after him?"

"That I cannot say," said Monnet. "It is peculiar, pairhaps, that he should leave Paris tonight, but also, pairhaps not. He visits Paris on business four or five times a year, you see that, although only once had he been there this year, since the murder. His business, you will also see, is that of a commercial travelair; he represents a woolen manufacturair."

"Ever questioned him?"

"No, sir. But I have talked to the patron of the small hotel where he always stays, near St.-Germain-des-Prés, and it is possible that the landlord has told him of the questions. That I do not know. What do you considair, Mr. Gideon? Is it sufficient evidence for Scotland Yard?"

"On the strength of this I'd recommend extradition," said Gideon, "but we'd have to hear what the chap's got to say for himself first. You'd like to take him back at once, I suppose."

"If it is agreeable, yes, but I shall be quite satisfied if he is undair detention," said Monnet. His eyes were very bright; obviously he was delighted with his reception.

"Soon as I saw all this stuff I asked the airport police to bring Forrester up, under guard," said Appleby. "He should be here soon."

"That's good," said Gideon.

He could hear his name being spoken from behind him, and glanced round to see the nondescript sergeant looking as if he was willing his superiors to stop talking. The sergeant had the telephone at his ear, and now he covered the mouthpiece quickly and hissed across:

"Excuse me, sir, Superintendent Wragg on the line. He says it's urgent. Can you—"

"Coming," said Gideon, and heaved himself to his feet. " 'Scuse me." He lumbered across the office, a little stiffly, for something had given him cramp in his right leg, while the sergeant held the telephone out almost anxiously. In the back of Gideon's mind there were all the things he had learned from Monnet, and the probability that Forrester had in fact killed the girl and buried her body under the rocks in the Pyrénées, doubtless expecting it to stay there for years. The severe winter of the previous year had uncovered the body, for ice and snow had caused a small avalanche, and first a skull had been found, then all the bones and the odds and ends of the girl's belongings which the French police had painstakingly collected and pieced together. Forrester had probably thought his year-old crime almost forgotten.

Now Wragg.

Wragg of the GH Division had not sent in any special reports after that of the second baby. He was a self-sufficient type, and if he made a mistake it would be from taking too much upon himself rather than trying to shift responsibility; no time waster, either.

"Gideon," said Gideon into the mouthpiece.

"Thought you'd want to know this," said Wragg. "We've cornered the Prowler."

It was certainly going to be a night to remember.

Gideon put down the receiver, three minutes after he'd had the news, and grinned broadly. Monnet was staring from the other side of the room as Gideon rubbed his great hands together. Sometimes it all went wrong and occasionally—not very often—everything went right, and this was the night of nights. Wragg was sure the cornered man was the Prowler. He had been seen leaving a tube station in Wragg's Division, and Wragg had been extremely thorough; he had not taken all his men away after the official finish of the great hunt. At the approach to all the stations, main bus stops and bridges in the Division, he had slapped white paint, thinned down so that it wouldn't dry quickly, and his men had studied the footprints of every passenger.

One of the uniformed men had seen a heel print identical to that which he'd seen on a telephotograph.

"Our chap showed his hand a bit too early, and the Prowler realized what was on," Wragg had said, "so they had a game of hide-and-seek up and down the station. Then the Prowler reached the street, but we had half a dozen men there by then. He got into a little park near the station, and hasn't come out. The whole place is sealed off, so we'll get him, but I thought you'd like to be in at the finish."

"You get him; I'll come if I can," Gideon had said, and then rung off, still grinning and rubbing his hands together. "Looks as if the Prowler's in the bag, Charley," he added. "How about that?"

Appleby gaped. "No!"

"Wragg says yes."

"Must be personal magnetism," said Appleby. "You want 'em and they come. Perhaps I mean hypnotism. Look at the only known policeman who can mesmerize crooks, M. Monnet." Monnet, realizing that there was a cause for rejoicing, rejoiced with them with bright smiles. "Forrester's here in the waiting room," Appleby went on. "I said you'd be right down."

Gideon said more slowly, "Yes, I will." He hesitated, while Monnet watched with obvious anxiety, hoping that he was to be present. Going down to interview a frightened man wanted for inquiries about a year-old murder was a kind of anticlimax, and Gideon would much rather be on his way to see Wragg, but if ever there was a case for *entente cordiale* this was it. "M. Monnet, if you'd like to come down with me you can see and listen to everything from outside the room while I talk to Forrester. Would you?"

"If you *please!*"

"Let's go," said Gideon.

It wasn't going to take long.

Guilt was a thing which you couldn't take for granted, no matter how tempted, and it revealed itself in a variety of odd ways. Sometimes it was so apparent that it seemed too good—for a policeman—to be true. That was the case with Forrester. He was a man in the early thirties, well set up, well dressed in light gray. A diamond tiepin flashed in his tie; his hair was immaculate; if he could have kept his nerve he would have created a very good impression. As it was, he paced the floor of the small waiting room with the window through which no one could see, but through which watchers could see in. As Gideon entered, he spun round, snatching a half-smoked cigarette from his lips.

"Look here, what the hell is all this? Who are you? Why am I being held here? I demand my rights, do you hear? I demand my rights."

"And you shall have them," said Gideon, very quietly. "Don't worry about that, Mr. Forrester." Nine times out of ten the gambit he decided to use would fail, seven times out of ten it would be folly; but he had seldom felt more convinced that it would come off. His tone had silenced Forrester, and he went on quite casually. "What did you do with the money, the diamond ring and brooch which you stole from Miss Guthrie before you killed her?"

Forrester nearly broke down, but something stiffened his resolve and he spoke evenly enough. "I didn't kill her. I don't know anything about it."

"Why not tell us the truth? We shall find it out in the long run," Gideon insisted. "Where—"

"I know nothing about it," Forrester declared, his eyes glittering. "I want to see my solicitor, at once—that's if you won't let me go."

"I'm afraid it will take a few days, M. Monnet," Gideon said soon afterward. "I hope you can stay in London; we'll be happy to have you spend some time with us. Of course we'll get everything done as soon as we can, but unless we can break down Forrester's denials—"

"There is no urgent reason for my return," said Monnet, "but I do not want to go back without him."

"We'll break him down if we can," Gideon promised. "I'll detail a Chief Inspector to work with you; just the man to wear Forrester down."

Monnet was grateful, and Gideon took him along to a C.I. whose French was almost as good as Appleby's. Then Gideon went back to his office. Appleby would already know the result of the interview, and he ought to know also whether Wragg had yet caught the Prowler. But Appleby was sitting at the desk writing, no longer showing any sign of excitement. It was nearly four o'clock, and he looked tired.

"He's tough, then?"

"Yes. Anything from—" Gideon hesitated, and then added abruptly: "Hemmingway?"

"No."

"Couldn't slip up there, could he?" asked Gideon musingly, and found himself stifling a yawn. Appleby didn't volunteer anything about the Prowler, which meant that there wasn't any fresh news. It was hardly worth going to see Wragg now, though; inviting being met by a smug superintendent and a handcuffed prisoner. The office, still warm, was untidy, indicating the amount of work which had been handled in the past eight hours. Long shifts, these night shifts. The sergeant in brown who didn't register was not in the office, but the Divisional reports, with all of Appleby's notes and comments, were on Gideon's desk. He went to it, then realized that he was very hungry; he hadn't had anything at all since a meal with Kate at about five o'clock, except a couple of stiff whiskies.

He sat down, rather heavily.

"Thought you'd go and have a bite," said Appleby. "No use neglecting the inner man, Chief."

"Just thinking of that, too, but I think I'll send for a sandwich."

"Two minds," said Appleby, grinning. "I ordered ham *and* beef, tea *and* coffee." He waved a hand at Gideon's smile of appreciation. "You know your trouble, George, don't you?" It was the first time he had brought himself to say "George" and even then it was obviously an effort, for he paused for a moment before adding, "You *work* too hard. Know what they say about all work and no play? Digs a copper's grave next day. I don't know what ticks with people with a metabolism like yours, I don't really."

The door opened and a uniformed man came in from the canteen with sandwiches, tea, coffee, mustard and some cakes coated with sugar icing.

"Thanks," said Gideon. "Fine."

He munched and drank as he looked through the reports. As he knew well from past experience, this was the night's quiet time. If it followed custom, the telephone calls would become more and more infrequent, the sound of Squad cars returning from their different assignments would be clear outside, and soon the day would begin for the rest of London. The charwomen, the men on the way to stoke boilers banked up for the night, the workmen due to start as soon as daylight came would be on the move. As much work as possible would be done on the roads and on electricity, gas and water mains before the throngs began to descend upon the streets. Soon the first buses would approach Parliament Square from each direction, and all the tube lines would be busy again.

Most of the night's crimes had been committed.

Not all, thought Gideon, as he flipped the pages over. In the city or a suburb men might still be drilling the safe of a bank or warehouse, men might be loading lorries at this moment with stolen goods, crooks might have done their job and be sitting in comfort at the scene of it, perhaps having a meal, so that they need not leave too early and so furtively. Any man wandering abroad between one o'clock and half past four was likely to be questioned by the police; after that, the police were likely to assume that he was about his normal business.

So it was not all done.

There was still no word from Wragg, and that worried him; none from Hemmingway or Lemaitre, and that puzzled him. There were other jobs that he knew little about, some that he knew nothing about—one, although he did not realize it, under his very hand.

This was the report from AB Division, and the note about Mrs. Penn and her anxious mother. It was near the bottom of the pile, because it had come in near the end, and Appleby was as methodical as an automat. Gideon glanced across at him and saw, now that the night was well advanced, that Appleby looked tired and old, with deep lines at his forehead and his eyes, others at his lips. All the brightness and the vitality seemed to have been drained out of him, but he sat working doggedly, sifting papers, jotting down notes, suggesting which crook might have committed this job or that, assigning men to inquiries, deciding which case could be left to the Division and which one needed urgent following up by the Yard.

It was very quiet in the office.

Gideon turned a report over, and saw the AB form, typewritten, ran his eye down the first page, which carried a brief and concise report of the baby kidnaping, and two reports of shops being burgled. On the next page was the report from Mrs. Penn's mother. Gideon started to turn the page, seeing Appleby's note on the shop burglaries: *Looks like Pinky White, left-hand job, his usual means of entry: suggest pick him up.*

That would be done in the morning.

Gideon flipped the page.

Sharp and stinging, the telephone rang. It was the first time tonight that it had surprised him, and he glanced up. Appleby had been shaken out of his mechanical movement of hand and pen, too.

"Gideon."

"Mr. Wragg for you, sir."

"Put him through."

"Right away, sir. . . . Here's Mr. Gideon."

"What's on?" asked Gideon, in a voice which betrayed his fear of bad news.

"I hope there's a special bit of brimstone for the Prowler," Wragg said, and Gideon thought with a sudden weight of depression that the man had got away. Then: "Climbed up to a top-floor room of a house overlooking the park. There's a girl in the room. Says he'll kill her if we don't let him go. Sounds as if he'd do it, too," said Wragg, who in turn sounded the most depressed officer in the Force.

15 . The Desperate Men

LESS than half an hour earlier, Marjorie Hayling had stirred in her sleep, in her one-room flatlet at the top of an old house in a cul-de-sac in Earl's Court. Stirring, she had shifted the bedclothes, uncovering her white shoulder and a little of her arm. A street lamp just outside the house threw a shadow into the room—the shadow of a man who was climbing in. It appeared on the ceiling and then, as he drew further in, on the top of the wall, a dark, moving shadow.

There were sounds outside, footsteps, men calling out, someone saying clearly:

"There he is!"

Another light, that from a powerful torch, had touched the man's feet as he had hauled himself into the room. A small cabinet was close to the window, and he kicked against it and sent it rocking.

That woke the girl.

At first, all she knew was the fear of a fast-beating heart, and quick, almost painful breathing, as if she had waked from a nightmare; but gradually the sounds had come into the room. Her eyes had focused on the man coming toward her with his arms outstretched. She could only just make out his hands and his face, although he was so near.

She tried to scream, and he pounced.

She felt his icy fingers at her neck, and struck at him, but her arm caught in the sheet and she could do nothing more to help herself. She saw the glitter in his eyes, then felt the choking pressure at her throat. Suddenly there was a tightness at her lungs, becoming worse and worse until it seemed as if her chest would burst.

Then she lost consciousness.

The Prowler felt her go limp, held on tightly for a moment, then let her fall. For a fleeting moment his hand touched her hair, and there was strange gentleness in the movement, but he heard more sounds below, as of a car drawing up, and he turned to the window, which was still wide open. He stared down, desperately. Fifty feet below were a dozen men, half of them policemen in uniform, most of them staring up. One man held a torch, two pointed, someone exclaimed:

"There he is!"

Another called in a deep, carrying voice, "Don't give us any more trouble; you can't get away."

"*If you don't get away from there and let me go I'll kill her!*" the Prowler shouted, and his voice was shrill and clear. "*That's what I'll do, I'll kill her.*"

A man said, as if shocked, "There's a woman up there."

"I'll kill her!" the Prowler screeched, and then backed from the window and slammed it down so that the walls of the room shook. He darted across the room and switched on the light. The girl lay limp on the bed, her dark hair against the white pillow, bare arms and bare shoulders all uncovered now. He opened the door into the "hall," then the door leading to the landing, and, as he did so, heard a banging; that would be the police trying to get in at the street door. He spun round—all his movements were swift and darting—went into the bedroom and pushed an armchair on squeaking casters toward the landing door. It banged against the wooden panels. He turned the chair on end, then slammed the room door on it. He could feel the pressure; the chair was between the two doors, and he had barricaded himself in better even than he had planned.

He was breathing very hard as he turned round, went to the bed, tore a sheet into strips and bound the girl's hands together tightly.

The noises from the street were muted now, but he crept close to the window and looked out. More cars were in the street, and suddenly a much brighter light shone upward, making him dodge to one side. No one was attempting to climb up the side of the house, and he turned and studied the unconscious girl.

She was breathing very evenly.

He watched her, his eyes narrowing.

He was a slightly built man probably in the middle thirties, with fair, receding hair, a little, pointed nose and rather thin lips. Not bad looking

in a way; an ineffectual type if one judged by appearances, the nine-to-six
kind of office worker, except that the cut and quality of his clothes were
very good. His hands were very large in proportion to his body, and his
fingers looked very strong.

He glanced about the room.

In one corner was a small gas stove, and above it some shelves, curtained
off, probably containing pots and pans. Near this was a small larder, on a
table. The whole of this corner could be curtained off, too, leaving the bed-
sitting-room looking fresh and pleasant. It had been recently painted and
papered, and the carpet, a patterned green, was new looking. On the small
dressing table in the corner there stood a vase of carnations—six pink blooms.
The whole room had the look of one who was house-proud.

A small wardrobe stood against one wall.

The man moved to it, and began to shift the wardrobe, gradually pushing it until it was wedged against the door. Now the only possible way in
was through the window, and the Prowler seemed to relax when he realized that.

He went to the side of the bed, and touched the girl's hair.

Then a booming voice sounded, almost as if it were in the room, and
he made a darting move toward the window.

"*Listen, you there! If you open the door and come down, we'll give you
a fair deal. We won't hurt you.*"

He ran his hand across his forehead, and moistened his lips. Then he
went close to the window, but he couldn't see out properly, so he opened
the window a few inches. He was able to see much better. Five cars were in
the cul-de-sac, now, and a man stood by one of them with a microphone
to his mouth. The voice came again, loud and clear.

"*We won't hurt you. Open the door and come out.*"

He leaned down and put his face close to the opening of the window,
and called:

"*If you don't let me go I'll kill her!*"

"*Don't be a fool, you'll only make it worse for yourself.*"

"*I've told you what I'll do. I'll kill her!*" the Prowler screeched, and then
he slammed the window down.

Marjorie Hayling's eyes were wide open.

She had heard every word.

It was half past four.

A few miles away, across London, Rikker stood by the wall in the passage
leading to the cellar of his little house. It was cold, yet he was sweating.
His hair, face, shoulders, hands, clothes, everything was covered with a
thick film of dust. By his side were a small crowbar, a hammer, a cold

chisel and several other tools. Heaps of powder from the cement and the bricks lay on the floor, and the air was filled with the writhing dust.

He kept coughing.

A dozen or so bricks, some broken, some whole, were on the floor just behind him. Chippings of bricks lay about, and now and again, as he moved, he crunched some under his feet. He kept wiping the sweat off his forehead, and his face was streaked with damp grime; there was a crust of dirt on his short, stubby eyelashes.

Suddenly he flung a crowbar down. It clattered noisily as he strode toward the steps which led upward. He had to pass the door which led into the main part of the cellar, where the woman was, and he looked inside.

There she sat, under the light, and he could not tell whether she was awake or unconscious; whether she was alive or dead.

She was still alive, but barely conscious.

Rikker went upstairs. His wife sat in an old saddle back chair, her head back, mouth open, uncanny white teeth showing. She whistled and squeaked as she breathed, her eyes were tightly closed, and he knew that she wasn't pretending sleep. He made as if to wake her, but some whim changed his mind, and he went through into the scullery and washed his hands and doused his face in cold water. He dabbed himself dry, and returned to the kitchen; the running water and the sound of his movements hadn't disturbed his wife. Rikker opened the doors of a cupboard, took out a bottle nearly full of whisky, splashed some into a thick glass, and went into the scullery and filled the glass with water. Then he drank deeply.

Going back, he kicked accidentally against the door, and it slammed. His wife started, her eyes flickered, and she struggled more upright, her lips working as if she was as thirsty as Rikker himself, or else caught by sudden fear.

Her eyes were strangely round and brilliant.

"You done it?" she asked in a gasping voice. "Have you?"

"Lot of use *you* are," Rikker sneered. "I thought I told you to bring me a drink an hour ago."

She started to struggle to her feet.

"I'll get it, I'll get it!"

"Siddown. I helped meself."

She sat quite upright now, staring at him almost as if in horror.

"You—you done it?"

"No."

"I—I thought—" She glanced at a little alarm clock on the mantelpiece. "It's half past four! You said you'd be finished by three, you said—"

"Well, I ain't finished yet," Rikker said roughly.

"W—w—why?"

"The wall's like concrete, and I can't make the hole big enough. Can't make too much noise, can I?"

"How—how much longer will it take you?"

"How the hell do I know?" Rikker demanded. "All I know is I've been working all night, and I'm tired out, see?"

"Can—can I do anything?"

Rikker leered at her.

"You can have forty winks while I do the work," he said roughly. He picked up the glass and drank as if the contents were beer, not whisky. He looked tired, and the dust, now caked on his face and especially round his eyes, made it appear as if he had a mask on. "Yeh, you can come and help; I've got more bricks nearly loose now."

She got up eagerly.

"Got to get it finished quick," Rikker went on, almost to himself. "Got to get her inside and the wall patched up again, but—"

"What are you going to do if you can't—*can't* get it finished tonight?"

Rikker growled, "I'm thinking, ain't I?"

He nodded abruptly and then went downstairs, walking very slowly and carefully, so as to make no noise. It was the noise which drove him almost to desperation. He picked up the crowbar, and then his big, heavy boots crunched on the brick chippings. As he prized at some of the bricks he had laid bare, they moved much more easily than they had a few minutes ago, and his shoulders seemed to brace themselves and he worked with greater eagerness. His wife picked up a screwdriver and prized more bricks away, and she was able to work almost as quickly as he.

"Looks as if the worst is over," she said. "They're moving easier."

"Could be." Rikker began to chip at the cement between the bricks, and this was something which took more time and which really needed much more force; but too much force would make a noise which would be heard by the people next door, and that was the one thing which Rikker was desperately anxious not to do.

Then, cement began to crumble.

"Got another soft patch," he said, and there was a glitter in his eyes and he began to work more quickly. The piles of bricks grew, and the hole in the wall grew. It was a sturdily built cavity wall, as he knew from grim experience.

"Nearly got room already," Mrs. Rikker wheezed, and the dust which had now gathered on her eyes made them shine like polished glass. "How much *more* room do you want?"

"Not much. But I want a rest from this. I'll go and mix the plaster now," said Rikker. "There's plenty left over from last time. You start tidying up, and use plenty of water, or that dust'll be the death of me."

He went into the larger cellar. His victim raised her head very slowly, and looked at him with dulled, pained eyes. He scowled and averted his gaze, and went hurriedly toward the corner where there was a small bag of cement and a heap of sand. He shoveled some sand onto a plaster board, picked up the cement and a hand trowel, and began to work.

His wife was coming downstairs with a broom and a bucket of water.

"Get a move on," he called. "This job's giving me the creeps."

At half past four, Tony Melcrino got up from the table, where he had been sitting for so long that his legs ached, and looked down at his Lollo. She was lying back in the armchair, her legs up on a smaller chair, and his thick, belted overcoat round her shoulders. There was no way in which Lollo could look anything but beautiful, not even like this.

She was breathing softly, her lips pouting and quivering, pouting and quivering.

He beckoned several of his boys; they walked across the dance floor, their footsteps echoing. The music had been stopped for a couple of hours, and the members of his gang were sitting round the walls, many of them asleep, a few playing cards. The giggly girl at the bar was lying behind the counter with one of her two boy friends, both fast asleep. The garish room and the dingy festoons and decorations looked even worse. So did the sign that hung so low that it almost touched Melcrino's head.

YOUTH FOR CHRIST CRUSADE.

Melcrino didn't look his twenty-two years, and might easily have been taken for eighteen or nineteen, partly because he was so small.

Two guards were at the front door.

"See any cops?" Melcrino asked.

"They're quiet."

"Sure they ain't gone?"

"They're around."

"Spike still at the corner?"

"Yeh."

"With Widey's boys?"

"Yeh."

" 'Kay. Bert—" Melcrino turned to one of the men who had come from the dance hall with him—"go and tell Widey I want to talk to him."

"Sure, okay, Melky."

"What are you waiting for?"

"Okay, Melky!" Bert hurried out, and then ran toward the other club-house, which was so near and yet was often out of bounds, for the two gangs seldom mixed. Two or three of the Wide boys watched as Bert approached, and word was sent back to Jacky Wide, who was not only leader of the gang but had given it its name.

Bert sent a cryptic message, and the answer came promptly:

"Sure, Melky can come."

"He didn't say he'd come here, he said—"

"Widey'll talk to him but he won't come and lick his shoes," a Wide boy said. "You go and tell Melky that. If he wants to talk, okay, he can come."

Melky was still in the doorway when he got the message. Obviously he didn't like it; as obviously, it didn't surprise him. He put his hand just inside his trousers waistband, where he kept a knife with a sheath which was kept well greased to facilitate quick movement.

"You ain't going to let Widey tell you what you're going to do," Bert protested roughly. "You'd be crazy."

"So the mountain won't come to Mahomet, so what does Mahomet do?" asked Melky, and gave a little grin which many people had learned to dislike. "Two of you come with me." He stepped into the dark street, looked right and left, and then walked quickly toward the Red Lion Gymnasium. The guards at the door let him in without question. He and his two bodyguards were led across the dance floor in this club to something he hadn't got himself—a comfortable living room with easy chairs, a television set and a cocktail cabinet.

Widey had two men with him, small, thickset, very tense looking. Widey himself was taller than most of the members of either gang, not a badlooking man with a shock of black hair, pale features and a pointed chin; his head was shaped rather like a pear with a very flat top. His eyes were dark blue, and he watched Melky narrowly.

"Want to talk to me, Melky?"

"That's what I said. You know what time it is?"

"Four thirty."

"It's nearer five o'clock," Melky said. "You think that van's coming?"

"It'll come."

"Listen," Melky said, "you wouldn't have had that van stopped before it got here, would you?"

Widey looked so startled that his very expression carried conviction. Then he gave a quick grin. He could be very attractive when he grinned; there was a bold air about him, something almost piratical, and a swagger, too.

"That would have been a brain wave, Melky, only I never thought of it!"

"So long as you didn't."

"I didn't," said Widey. "So what's next?"

"Do we still wait?"

"You can go home, but I'm going to wait," said Widey, and his voice became harsher. "We've got the cops drawn off nicely; we don't have anything to worry about. We let the van go through the gate, and then we start the fight, and while the cops are laying for us we take the stuff off the van. That's the way it will be. If you've got cold feet, okay, my boys can fight among themselves. They'll make it look convincing."

"Who said anything about cold feet?"

Widey grinned. "Maybe you have good reasons for wanting to go to bed."

"Sometimes I wish I hadn't agreed to string along with you," said Melky, his lips drawn very taut. His right hand was moving close to the favorite spot at his waistband. "Sometimes I think I'll be glad when—"

"Listen, Melky," Widey said, suddenly quite earnest, "if the cops think we're going to war they'll sit back and let us fight it out, see? They'll expect us to cut ourselves up. So that's what we let them think. But you and me, we're too fly for that. A few of the boys are nabbed and maybe they'll get six months, so what do we do? We look after them when they come out, no one's any the worse off. The cops think we're going to sit back and lick our wounds, and that's how much they know, the flickin' so-and-sos. We'll have it all our own way for weeks before they get round to realizing that we ain't dead yet, and then we'll have a rest, see, and they won't be able to pin anything on us. That's the plan we agreed, Melky, what's the matter with keeping it that way?"

Melky didn't speak.

"But just say the word," said Widey, "and I'll go it on my own. I—"

A sharp ringing sound cut across his words, the ringing of a telephone. The phone was behind him, and he turned round swiftly, leaned forward and grabbed it.

"Who's sat? . . ."

"*Whassat?* . . ."

"Okay!"

He put down the receiver very slowly and turned to look at Melky, his head on one side, his lips twisted in a grin which told its own story. He didn't speak immediately, but seemed to enjoy keeping Melky on tenterhooks. Then he announced:

"The van's on the way. Okay?"

"*Okay,*" breathed Melky. "It'll be here in ten minutes. *Okay.* No knives, no razors, nothing to do any serious harm, that okay?"

"That's the way we planned it, and that's the way it's going to be," said Widey. "You ever known me go back on my word?" He held out his hand. "Shake on it?"

They shook hands.

"*Okay,*" breathed Melky, and turned and hurried out with Bert and the other member of his gang to start the mock fight. In five minutes the "battle" would be at its height, and in five minutes the Post Office van carrying a small fortune would pass through the gateway of the docks.

When he had gone, Wide grinned broadly and evilly, and very slowly took out a double-edged blade fitted into a handle so that it could cut nastily, but not go dangerously deep. Then he went outside to a big barrel by the door and whipped the cloth off the top. It was full of potatoes. His men came hurrying, each dipping into the barrel and picking out two or three potatoes. They looked like ordinary unpeeled potatoes, but buried in each was a double-edged razor blade. Many of the men had ugly, spiked knuckle dusters on their hands already.

"So Melky fell for it," Jacky Wide said. "He fell for it good and hard. After tonight there won't be any Melky gang left."

16 . Gideon Moves

GIDEON heard Wragg's telephone go down, and replaced his own. As he did so, he stood up slowly, and the button of his coat caught the Divisional report he had been reading, and pushed it to one side. The page above that which reported Mrs. Russell's anxiety about her daughter, Netta Penn, fell slowly, and so hid the paragraph from sight. As he moved again, he knocked the report off the desk and stooped down to pick it up.

"The Prowler's shut himself up with a girl and says he'll kill her if we don't let him go," he said to Appleby, quite flatly.

Appleby said, "Gawd, *no*."

"I'd better go over," said Gideon.

He didn't go to the door at once, but lit a cigarette and deliberated. Appleby pushed his chair back, his eyes brighter, the look of an aging man vanished for a moment.

In fact Gideon was trying to make up his mind about his own motives for wanting to go to Earl's Court at once. The Prowler was his primary reason for coming on duty tonight, and above everything else was the man he wanted—but was it necessary for him to go in person? He knew all the arguments. When a man barricaded himself in and had a hostage, it could be very ugly, for only desperate men did that. There was nothing to suggest that the Prowler had a gun, but he didn't need a gun to kill that girl. If the police had to lay siege, it could last for a long time, and that would mean real trouble in the morning, with the Home Office involved, big newspaper stories inevitable. If he didn't go, and if Wragg didn't get the Prowler while saving the hostage's life, then the Assistant Commissioner, the Commissioner himself and probably the Home Secretary would want to know why the senior official on duty hadn't taken charge.

This wasn't just a question of wanting to finish the job off himself.

"You'd better get over there, quick," said Appleby. "You certainly know how to pick nights, George."

"The Prowler was almost a cert," said Gideon, and he glanced down at the report which he had picked up, ready to throw it on the desk. By chance, the page which fell open was the one with the note about Mrs. Russell's report, and he glimpsed the name "Penn."

He read the paragraph quickly.

"What's on now?" asked Appleby.

"That Mrs. Penn," said Gideon. "Remember she rang me, but didn't hold on long enough?"

"Ridgway sent a man round to see her, didn't he?"

"Yes, she wasn't home. Now there's a report from her mother that she wasn't back by two o'clock," said Gideon. "What's worrying me is why she didn't wait to talk to me." He was scowling now. "If she took the trouble to ask for me, why didn't she hold on?"

"Don't ask me."

"It smells," said Gideon. "Charley, have a Squad car go round and see Mrs. Russell now, find out all they can from her and if she's got any idea where her daughter went. Follow it up. Tell the chaps in the car that it's a special from me."

"Gee-up, from Gee-Gee," quipped Appleby.

As he went outside, Gideon shook his head and through his clenched teeth said, "The blurry fool!" and then he began to hurry. The annoyance with Appleby lasted only for a few seconds, and he realized that his own hesitation about what he should do was due to one thing only: he was tired. His eyes were heavy and there was the feel of sandpaper in them, telling its own story. Except for a couple of hours that afternoon he hadn't slept since six o'clock yesterday morning, which meant that he'd been on the go for a straight twenty-four, and he wasn't used to it. Give him three or four such stretches in a row, and there would be nothing to worry about.

It seemed brighter out in the courtyard, and the stars were pale, but it was false dawn. Half past five. Gideon caught a glimpse of a bus passing in Parliament Street, its passenger lights very bright and glittering. Six or seven cars were waiting now, and one of them was beginning to move. Had Appleby been as quick as that, or was it another job? Gideon got into his own car and pulled out, and the Squad car drew level.

"You going to Mrs. Russell, at Fulham?"

"Yessir."

"Quick work, keep it up."

Gideon saw the driver's fleeting smile of satisfaction, and let him draw ahead; seconds weren't likely to make any difference at Earl's Court. Why the hell had they let the Prowler get away, anyhow? It was all very well to slap a copper on the back for being observant, but of all the men to let through their fingers!—a brute who had proved only tonight that he would rather kill than be captured.

That reminded Gideon of another job he'd meant to do. He flicked on the radio, and as soon as he was answered he asked:

"How's that Lewis girl out at Brixton?"

"Last we heard, no change," Whittaker told him from Information, "and with that kind of injury if they can hold on for a few hours it often works out all right."

"Yes, good, thanks."

"Pleasure. Going out to Wragg?"

"Yes."

"There's a man who's kicking himself," said Whittaker. "Don't tear him all to pieces."

"I'll leave a bit whole," said Gideon, and rang off.

Talking to Whittaker reminded him again of Matthew, and the boy waiting for him outside the garage, the only place where he could rely on having a word with him without his mother knowing. Bad thing to let him think that one parent might take sides without the knowledge of the other, but it had showed him more clearly than he'd ever seen before how little time he really spent with his family, except the Sunday "jam" sessions. He smiled. When he called them "jam" sessions, Pru immediately flew off the handle. To her, music was something almost sacred; her violin was a kind of altar. The thoughts flickered through his mind as he drove fast through the streets, which were gradually coming to life; the occasional bus, the occasional cyclist, here and there a private car. Probably he was passing men with their loot in their pockets, men who wouldn't get picked up for tonight's job, but sooner or later would end up in court.

He'd have a hell of a lot to do when he got back to the office, preparing reports for the men who would take over. The Golightly woman would have to go before the beak; she would have an eight-day remand, of course. Forrester would have to be tackled. The four Hatton Gardens men would be up at Bow Street; the hundred and one—

He heard a fire engine roaring, and it rang its bell, apparently for his benefit, clattered past him and then swung round a corner and went the way he was going. It soon disappeared from sight, although he was doing fifty. When he reached Earl's Court, he saw a crowd already gathering, and a policeman obviously on the lookout for him.

"It's a little complicated to find the place, sir, but you turn right here, and then—"

"Get in, and guide me."

"Yes, sir!"

"Anything developed?" Gideon asked as the man sat down, and he knew that this constable, like most who knew him only as a name, was surprised that he talked like a human being.

"Nothing new as far as I know, sir, but I haven't been at the scene myself."

"Hmm. See that fire engine?"

"Mr. Wragg sent for it, sir."

"Ah," said Gideon.

The route was complicated all right, but the journey only took a few minutes. He pulled up near the cul-de-sac. On the other side was a small park, with a single lamp burning in the middle of it. Two policemen were on duty there. Then Gideon reached a corner, with the constable by his side, and saw at least twenty men, six cars and the fire engine; the firemen were already running the turntable up toward the window of a house, but it didn't seem to be the house where the Prowler had been trapped. Wragg was on the lookout, and came hurrying, tall and supple and fresh looking although he'd been on duty just as long as Gideon; that was the difference ten years made.

Yet Gideon was desperately anxious.

"Anything new?"

"No, been waiting for you."

"Seen any more of him?"

"We use the blower every two or three minutes and tell him we won't hurt him if he comes down, but that's all. We've got men upstairs outside the girl's flatlet, but I don't want to force a way in that way. There are two doors and the Prowler's almost certainly got them both locked. While we were getting both doors down he could strangle her."

"Hmm," said Gideon. "What do you propose to do?"

"I think we ought to try to get in from the roof," said Wragg, and pointed. "That's the house—one with the white paint." Two mobile searchlights had been rigged up, and were shining toward the window from which the Prowler had shouted. "See the way the eaves hang? If we could get a nimble chap up there, with someone to hold onto his feet, he could hang over the edge upside down, and see inside. If he had tear gas—I've sent for some bombs and masks—he could fill the room with the stuff, and give time for the fire escape and some ladders to be run up to the window."

That was all sound enough.

"He might hear the noise on the roof," Gideon objected.

"We've got to take some chance," argued Wragg. "If you ask me, he won't let himself be captured if he can help it. Behaves as if he knows he's finished, and he might as well make it worth while. We can get up to the roof from the back. I've already had some ladders rigged up. Care to see?"

"Yes. If we go straight ahead with the fire escape turntable, you think he'll realize it in time to do more damage?"

"Sure he will," said Wragg. "Look at the position of that window. He can see nearly everything that's going on, and with a man on top of a swaying turntable, you can't judge the position to the inch *quickly*. Once we reach that window, it's got to be quick."

"Yes," Gideon agreed again.

As he spoke, the man who used the blower called out again, and down here his voice was deep and almost too vibrant. There was no response this time, and no sign of movement at the window. Wragg had given orders, and ladders were being placed near the wall, so close that they couldn't be seen unless the Prowler leaned right out. Once the police gained a few minutes to work in, the ladders would be run up to the window and the turntable moved into position.

"Let's go round the back," said Gideon.

Wragg led the way, and a man brought him two tear-gas pistols, rather larger than army revolvers but much lighter. Just round the corner there was a narrow service alley, with a cement path which led to a small back garden of the house. Police were in strength here, too, and neighbors were watching from lighted windows and back doors.

"All for one man," Wragg said, almost bitterly. "Twenty or thirty to one, and we still can't be sure of stopping him doing any harm. I'll have the pants off Cobley, the copper who—"

"Probably feels a damned sight worse than you do," said Gideon. "Tell me about the girl up there."

"All we know is what we got from the people on the ground floor—the owners of the house. They had it turned into one-room flatlets, and let them to business girls. The girl's named Hayling, Marjorie Hayling. Aged twenty-nine. Been here eighteen months. Her boy friend lives a few streets away; we'll probably have him on our rump when he gets to hear of it. The flatlet itself is reached by the top landing. It's a kind of attic room, the only one on that floor. There's the landing door and a tiny hall, bathroom on the right, bed-sitter straight ahead. I've seen a similar entrance downstairs, and the double door makes it the easiest place in the world to barricade. We wouldn't have time to stop the Prowler killing her. I've got the stairs lined with men; if he should try to get out we'll have him," Wragg added. "Trouble is that you can't be sure which way he'll jump. He's crazy."

"He knows what he's doing," Gideon said grimly. "He's frightened."

They reached the back of the house and the ladders which had been run up to the roof. A man in plain clothes was halfway up the ladder, and climbing down. He was a little out of breath when he reached the ground.

"What's it like up there?" asked Wragg.

"Not too bad," the detective officer said. "There's a chimney stack we could fasten a rope round, then we could rope one man to it and he could hold the chap who was going to break the window. Shouldn't cause too much trouble, but it's a long way to fall."

"Have a fire sheet hanging out," said Wragg.

"Tell the Prowler what we're up to," Gideon objected.

There was a pause before Wragg looked toward the service alley, where two men were approaching, one wearing a helmet, one bareheaded; there was sufficient light from the nearby houses to show that obviously he recognized the man, and he scowled.

"That's the copper who let him go. All right, all right, the one who spotted him, too! George—"

"Hmm?"

"We could promise the Prowler that we'd let him go; it might work," said Wragg. "We could withdraw the nearby men, and have the whole area sealed off."

"Yes," agreed Gideon ponderously, "we could. But we couldn't be sure that he wouldn't kill the girl before he left. I know we can't be sure she's alive either, but—" He broke off as the two newcomers drew up, the constable drawing himself rigidly to attention. He was obviously a youngster, and one of those who had barely scraped into the Force by the five feet eight inches height regulation. The light was just good enough to show his tension.

Wragg said to the plain-clothes man with him, "Well?"

"Cobley would like to speak to you, sir."

"He's got a tongue, hasn't he?" Wragg said nastily. "What is it?"

Bad, thought Gideon, very bad. It wasn't until they had authority that the best and the worst came out in a man, and for Wragg to talk to anyone like this in front of the others, especially in front of the Commander, was a clear indication that he had a lot to learn about handling men. Pity. This could so easily break this Cobley.

Cobley said abruptly:

"I would like to volunteer for the roof job, sir. I've had training in the army; I'm sure I could do it."

Wragg stared.

Gideon felt helpless. He wanted to whisper, "Don't turn him down, Wragg, don't kill everything he's got." The silence seemed to drag unbearably, but in fact it wasn't yet ten minutes since Gideon had arrived, not more than three since the report had come from the roof.

"What boots you wearing?" asked Wragg abruptly.

Ah!

"Regulation, sir, but I could take them off."

"All right," said Wragg. He wasn't gracious, but that didn't matter; obviously he'd seen the folly of smacking Cobley down too hard. "Where's that tear-gas bomb?" Another plain-clothes man handed it to him. "You say you've used these, Cobley?"

"Yes, sir, during my army training."

"Do you know what we want to do?"

"Break the window and fill the room with gas before he can do any harm to the girl, and give the others time to get in."

"That's right," said Wragg. "If you make a noise on the roof, or do anything wrong, you might make him turn on her. And if you fall you'll break your neck."

"I think I can do it, sir."

"Right," said Wragg, and turned to Gideon. "I'm going up to hold his legs. Feel like coming?" He didn't add that he thought Gideon was too heavy for the roof, just looked as if he hoped that Gideon would realize it himself.

"No," said Gideon, "I'm going round to the front and I'm going to talk to the Prowler while the ladders are put ready and you're on the go. Good luck, Cobley."

"Thank you, sir." Cobley was still very taut.

Gideon hurried round to the cul-de-sac.

In that room the Prowler was standing by the window, now peering out, now turning round to look at Marjorie Hayling. She was sitting bolt upright, and the fluffy jacket was loose round her shoulders. There were red, puffy marks at her throat. Several bruises were already discoloring, and her eyes still held the brightness of her tears, but she had won control of herself, and talked rationally and quietly to him.

A different voice boomed over the blower.

"Hello, Prowler! This is Gideon of New Scotland Yard. I want to talk to you. Open the window."

The Prowler didn't move.

"I want to talk to you; open the window," Gideon called. His voice was deeper than that of the first speaker, but it wasn't so vibrant.

The Prowler flattened himself against the wall as he looked down into the street, at the strangely distorted-looking people there, the cars, the fire escape with the turntable some distance from the window. He could not see close to the wall below, could not see the ladders being carried stealthily, almost flush with the wall. His hands were raised in front of him, the fingers clenching and unclenching.

"Open the window; I want to talk to you," came the deep voice.

"Why—don't you see what he has to say?" the girl asked huskily. "He can't hurt you from down there. Why don't you open the window and speak to him?"

The Prowler did not move or answer, but his eyes swiveled round toward her.

"We've got all the time in the world," Gideon called. "Just open the window so that we can talk."

"Why don't you?" the girl pleaded, and she did not stop even when the Prowler glared at her. "I don't know what you've done, but I'm sure they won't hurt you. You'd be wise to give yourself up."

"*I want to talk to you.*"

"Why don't you—" the girl began.

"Shut up!" the Prowler spat at her, and suddenly he pulled at the window with his fingers, straining and heaving to get it open; and he opened it an inch and put his face close to the opening and called: "*If you don't go away and let me go I'll choke the life out of her!*"

Then he slammed the window, and turned to face the girl, and she knew that he meant exactly what he said. Yet she did not flinch, just moistened her lips and said:

"It won't help you if you hurt me, will it? If you kill me, you won't have any chance at all, and they'll hate you. But if you give yourself up—"

Gideon heard the shrill note of hopeless defiance in the Prowler's voice, and he had a fair idea of what was going on inside the man's head. For a long time he had got used to having everything his own way, and for a long time he had lived with only one fear: of the police. Now all those pent-up fears were bursting out and he could not think beyond the burning desire to get away. Fear and tension bore at him. He had preyed on helpless girls for a long, long time, and now one was helpless in that room with him, and the only weapon he could think of was his power over her.

He was used to using such power.

He had used it murderously tonight.

He might again.

Gideon switched off the blower and spoke to a man standing by him, in a quiet voice which hardly carried.

"Tell that chap over there to start his engine."

"Yes, sir."

"Have him drive to the corner, and keep the engine going," said Gideon, "and tell two other drivers to start up, too."

"Right, sir."

The man went off, and a car engine broke the quiet. Now three extending ladders were in position, two men standing by each, ready to run the ladders right up to the window.

Dozens of people were staring up at the window, which was in the spotlight; many on their way to the station paused to look. There was a rumbling sound, of an underground train in the distance. The engines of several cars made more noise than there had been in the cul-de-sac all the time, but it seemed normal enough—as if several of the police cars were going away.

The noise would reach the Prowler, and would muffle any sounds made on the roof.

Then, Gideon saw the head of P. C. Cobley, edging over the guttering; and he saw the way his hands gripped the gutter. Gideon had passed the word that no one was to exclaim or point or draw attention to the roof, for fear the Prowler would notice what they were doing, and he had to guard himself, watching covertly, his heart sick with apprehension.

Cobley was much further over, his head and shoulders showing now. One hand disappeared; then he brought it into view again, holding a bomb. He wriggled forward inch by inch, and it seemed to take an age. The car engines were still warming up, and there was no sign of movement at the window of the room.

Now, Cobley was leaning right over, bent double at the waist. He was just above the window. A little further over, and he would be able to see into the room. Now the light shone on his fair head, and on the bomb, which looked almost black. Gideon could imagine the pain at his thighs as he put all his weight on them.

"For gossake get a move on!" muttered a man by Gideon's side.

He was clenching his hands and gritting his teeth.

17 . One Job Over

EVERYONE in the cul-de-sac was watching tensely, even though there was a risk that the Prowler would realize what was happening. There was no sign of movement inside the room, no shadow, nothing at all. Gideon moved toward the blower again, switched it on, and added to the almost screaming tension by saying quietly:

"You had time to think it over, now, so what about it? We won't hurt you; come out and give yourself up."

Silence.

Cobley edged still further over. He could not control the aim of the bomb yet; he needed another inch or two. The blood must have rushed to his head a long time ago. He might not be able to keep there much longer, might black out. Wragg would be stretched to his limit, too.

"Open the window and talk to me," Gideon called. "Don't be a fool. I might be able to strike a bargain with you."

Silence.

"If you're worried about the girl in Brixton, you needn't be," said Gideon. "She isn't dead. We want to help you, but we can't if you won't come and listen."

Still silence.

Cobley was edging himself toward his left side now. In a moment or two his head would be below the top of the window, and the important thing was to distract the Prowler's attention. There was no way of being sure that they could; a slight shadowy movement, even a rustle of sound, might be noticed.

Then the Prowler came close to the window.

"Let's be reasonable about it," Gideon said, and he kept his voice quite steady. "Let's talk it over."

He could see the Prowler standing there, as he had a few minutes before when he had opened the window and shouted defiance. Now he hesitated. Cobley was lowering his right hand, and he was also being lowered slowly; it would be only a moment before he could act.

The Prowler opened the window.

"If you don't let me go I'll kill—"

Then there was a swift flurry of movement, the savage thrust of Cobley's fist at the window, the crash of breaking glass. Cobley hurled the bomb as the Prowler backed into the room. Already the ladders were being run up, the fire engine and turntable were on the way; the little street seemed in turmoil as masked men stood ready to hurl themselves at the ladders.

Then a woman screamed.

Cobley was falling.

Two men rushed forward to try to break his fall.

And inside the room there was the cloud of gas, near the window; the girl on the bed, quite helpless.

"No!" she gasped. *"No!"*

She saw the way the Prowler swung toward her, and knew that if he could he would kill her. On he came and she screamed as gas bit at her eyes and nose and throat. He looked crazed as he reached her. She felt the grip of his hands, and did not think that she would ever breathe again.

Then a man came hurtling in at the window.

She felt the Prowler release her, saw him turn round, and saw the other man, blood streaming from a gash in his hand, leap bodily toward him. Other men followed, all masked and grotesque and moving swiftly.

The sharp pain at her eyes and nose was getting worse; she could hardly breathe; but there was no danger from the thin-faced man, no more danger from the Prowler.

"How's Cobley?" asked Gideon gruffly.

"Broken right leg, cracked ribs, concussion," Wragg said. "It'll keep him away for a month or so! Not much doubt that the Prowler would have killed her if he'd had a little more time. Well, the Prowler won't give the newspapers any more Roman holidays. The Hayling girl will be all right. There was hardly any need to send her to the hospital, but better to play safe." He was talking a little too quickly, almost garrulously. "That's the lot, I think."

Gideon looked down at the papers and oddments which had been taken from the Prowler's pockets, and which a sergeant was examining. He was putting the money and impersonal things to one side and pushing those which looked interesting toward Gideon and Wragg. They were in a downstairs room at the house where the Prowler had taken refuge and the things from his pockets were on the deal-topped table.

The Prowler himself, handcuffed to a detective, was already on his way to the Yard.

He hadn't said a word.

Gideon picked up a crocodile-skin wallet, felt it, looked at it, and said: "This isn't plastic; it's the real stuff."

"Look at that," said Wragg, and lifted a slim gold cigarette case.

"Monogram on the lighter," Gideon said, and opened the wallet. "Stuffed with notes." A curious kind of tension came back into the room, even when it had looked as if this would be a kind of anticlimax. He took some papers out of the wallet, and read in the same almost startled voice, "The Hon. Alistair Campbell-Gore, 29 Moniham Square, W.1. Hear that, Wragg? He's young Campbell-Gore, he—" Gideon's voice cracked.

"What do you know?" said Wragg weakly. "Chap inherits half a million quid one year, and starts going on this kind of prowl the next! It doesn't make any sense."

"It's going to make the biggest noise we've heard for a long time," said Gideon. "I thought I'd seen him before, that pinched little nose and—well, that's it, now I've seen everything. Get it all ship-shape, will you?"

"I will!"

"And let me have reports on Cobley."

"I will. Where you off to?"

"The Yard," said Gideon. "Home from home."

He left the house at once. A small car had just drawn up near the police cars, and he wondered if this was the press. He turned in the other direction and crossed the road without, apparently, being recognized. That way it took him more than two minutes to get to his car, but better that than to stand and talk to newspapermen; and if he just brushed them off, they wouldn't like it and it wouldn't do anyone any good. His car was far enough from the end of the cul-de-sac not to attract any particular attention, and he got in and drove off. Now a steady stream of people was heading for the tube station, and groups of three or four were waiting at all the bus stops. What time was it? Nearly six. Well, it hadn't taken long, but at one time it had seemed unending. It would be a long time before he forgot the way his heart lurched when Cobley had started his daring leap.

And the Hon. Alistair Campbell-Gore—

"I give up," Gideon said, and then flicked on the radio. They had caught the Prowler, but no reaction of triumph had come with it, and he realized that the tension of the last scenes had added to his tiredness. If he had his way he would put his head down for a couple of hours, and there wasn't a chance. The only big job outstanding was the gang trouble out at the docks, and he was half inclined to believe that it would die a natural death. In spite of the truculence, the gang leaders might have decided that it wasn't worth risking a clash with the police.

"Hello, Charley," he said.

"Strewth, you haven't half missed a birthday party, you have," said Appleby, and his voice seemed to be filled with genuine excitement. "It's still on, too, if you get a move on you ought to see the last act. All the world's a stage, and—"

"Never mind Shakespeare, what's happening?"

"The Melky gang and the Wide boys," said Appleby. "Dunno what went wrong, but something did. Hemmingway fixed the van. When Melky and Jacky Wide opened the doors at the back, half a dozen of our chaps jumped out, and they didn't mind using their truncheons. That was soon over. But the Wide boys were just tearing into Melky's gang. They were about even in number but the Wide boys simply cut them up. That Jacky Wide seems—"

"What else has come in?"

"Only unusual thing's from Willesden. Chap's dug up some human bones in his back garden. I sent Piper over. Nothing urgent."

"I'll go straight to NE Division," said Gideon. "Don't tell 'em I'm coming."

He had to drive past the end of Lassiter Street.

He saw a car standing halfway along it, and two heavily built men standing by the car; that was the Flying Squad, and they didn't seem to be in any great hurry or to have anything much on their minds.

Gideon was half a mile from the two clubs when he saw the first evidences of the fight: two ambulances, coming away from the scene of it. Driving through the little mean streets as a gray light filtered into the sky, he saw more. Here and there a man crept along the pavement by himself, one holding his arm up as if it hurt, another with a bloody head, a third limping. Two police cars, each carrying two of the "boys" and two policemen, passed. Nearer the clubs, there was the noise of shouting and scuffling. At the corner where Gideon had waited earlier, four men were struggling—two "boys" and two plain-clothes policemen. Round the corner and nearer the first club were three or four other struggling groups and several men on the ground, but the thing that worried Gideon most was that the police were involved in each of the struggles; there was no question here of the Wide boys fighting Melky's gang. He couldn't drive along this street, so he left the car in the middle of the road and hurried toward the corner, for the worst of the fighting would probably be in the street between the two clubs.

It was not.

There were signs of a fight, though. Battered hats, caps, sticks and, like a litter of paper, little pieces of potatoes, some whole potatoes, and, sparkling in the lights from the street lamps and the clubs, the brightness of steel. He only needed a glance to tell what had happened.

Two policemen were outside each of the clubs, and he asked the same question:

"Mr. Hemmingway here?"

"No, sir."

"No, sir," the second man said, "they—Mr. Hemmingway and Mr. Lemaitre, that is—they went to the docks."

"Right," said Gideon. "Thanks." It was a long walk from the gateway just ahead to the quayside, and he didn't want to tackle it, but there was no car in sight. He walked as briskly as he could toward the gateway, and saw several police cars coming toward him; three in all. He recognized Hemmingway in the first, but not Lemaitre. Hemmingway slowed down; he looked bitter and angry.

"Room for me?" asked Gideon.

"Hop in."

Gideon got in.

"How'd it go?" asked Gideon.

"First time I've ever felt like throwing my hand in," Hemmingway said roughly, and he looked vicious and angry. "This is my beat and I ought to know how their minds tick, but Jacky Wide fooled me." He glanced sideways at Gideon. "He fooled you, too, and he fooled Melcrino. We picked up *one* of the Wide boys—one, out of that mob—and got bits of the story out of him. Widey was after the stuff from the van all right, but it wasn't his first objective; he didn't mind if he let it go. He made a deal with Melcrino to stage a mock fight to fool us, while some of the gang was holding up the van. Melcrino thought he was on the level, and started to fight with the gloves on. Jacky Wide didn't. His boys used razors, knives and knuckle dusters, and the Melky gang didn't have a chance. I don't mind telling you that for once I felt almost sorry for them. We've picked up about twenty of them already, and sent them to the hospital, and there'll be as many being nursed at home. Take it from me, George, the Melky gang doesn't exist any more. The few who didn't get hurt will rat on Melky and go in with Jacky Wide. And the *Wide* boys—"

He broke off. This was the thing that really hurt, the thing that Gideon wasn't going to enjoy hearing.

"Well, let's have it."

"The Wide boys had it all laid on. That's the truth. They'd pretty well finished the Melky gang before we weighed in. They knew we were coming, and what did they do? They went through this gateway here like a lot of rats. They'd chosen a night this week because the gates were down. They went straight to the docks, where four old motorboats were tuned up and waiting—pleasure boats being prepared for next summer; the dock police didn't know that the men working on them were Wide boys. They did a darn near perfect job, George—even had two fake warehouse raids up the river that held the River Police while they headed for the Surrey bank. Made it, too. We could see 'em scrambling up on the other side; the tide was pretty high and they didn't have any trouble. They'll all get home without a scratch, and Jacky Wide will be cock o' the walk for a hell of a long time to come—and ask yourself where *we'll* be?"

"Take it easy," Gideon said quietly, "and get the word put round quickly that the Post Office hold-up job was Wide's idea, and we stopped him and drove him and his boys across the river. That might help a bit."

"Oh, it will help," agreed Hemmingway, "but the truth's the truth, George. Jacky's ten times as strong as he was, and we're going to have a lot of trouble with him in the future."

Of course, he was right. Not only in the Division but in the neighboring Divisions, there would be a time of tension and setbacks. The police would make as big a smoke screen as they liked, but wouldn't be able to hide the truth.

"Any news of Melcrino?" Gideon asked.

"We've got him, and he'll cool his heels for six months or so," said Hemmingway. "Funny thing, though—they didn't touch his Lollo, just told her she wouldn't be hurt, and she could go home to her kids. She went, too. That's what I mean about Jacky Wide," the Divisional man added bitterly. "He's smart, and I *mean* smart. Letting Lollo go free is just the right touch. Wide would put most people against him if he'd hurt her, but now he'll be a kind of white-headed boy."

"You'll find a way to black his nose as well as his head," Gideon said. Then he yawned.

On his way back, along roads which were much thicker with traffic, and where every other vehicle coming toward him seemed to be loaded with vegetables, fruit and flowers from Covent Garden, he told himself that this was one of the worst setbacks Hemmingway had ever had, and he, Gideon, couldn't escape blame. They hadn't given Jacky Wide enough credit for being smart. A really capable organizer in the East End could be a Divisional and a Yard headache for years. Well, you couldn't have it all ways. When he'd got the Prowler and saved the Hayling girl it had looked as if practically everything had gone right that night; but it seldom worked out that way.

Anyhow, the night was over.

It was turned half past six. The light in the sky was the real dawn, although it took a long time coming, and there was a haze overhead as if the fog was coming back. The wind had dropped. He was glad that driving wasn't difficult, and found himself looking forward with something near repugnance to the task of getting all the reports signed and prepared for the fresh men in the morning—but he would have to make a good job of it. He and Lemaitre usually took over together and, if they had poor or patchy reports from the night-duty men, the air was always blue.

He didn't switch on the radio.

He went by a different route, missing Lassiter Street this time, and driving along Throgmorton Street where the light had been on at the window last night. It would be months, perhaps years, before he had the slightest suspicion of the crime being planned when he had driven past that night.

It was a quarter to seven when he reached the Yard. The atmosphere was quite different now. More cars were about; several of the day men were already in, men who were fresh from their night's rest and walked with enviable briskness. Gideon squared his shoulders and put a spring into his walk, and played with his pipe as he went into the lift with two Chief Inspectors, who wanted to know what kind of a night it had been. He told them about the gang fight, and that the Prowler was now being questioned, then hurried along to his own room and Appleby.

Appleby looked every week of his age now, thin and gray and pale, but his eyes were still bright and he gave a ready grin as Gideon stepped into the room. By his side was a mammoth pile of reports, and he slapped a hand on them and said:

"All ready and correct, sir, just want your okay. Only one job outstanding as far as I can tell, and I don't mean the NE fiasco or the Prowler."

"What is it?" asked Gideon.

"That Lassiter Street inquiry," said Appleby. "Mrs. Penn called there last night, it seems, and she hasn't been home since. Neighbors say there's been a lot of noise going on. Shall we have a go, or wait until the day staff arrive?"

He looked almost longingly at the clock on the wall.

18 . Night's End

HERE was the thing which people forgot, Gideon thought tensely as he looked at Appleby: the human factor, the fact that coppers got tired. You could get over physical tiredness, but if you got a touch of mental fatigue it could lead to serious trouble. Probably that was the reason for Hemmingway's failure to grasp the full significance of what was happening in his Division; as likely, it was the reason why he himself was so dispirited. He, George Gideon, had been ready to sleep on his feet when he had walked along the passage, but that feeling had gone, and he knew one thing for certain: mental weariness hadn't yet caught up with him.

He wanted to send Appleby home, he wanted to go to Lassiter Street, and he didn't want to leave anyone else in charge here.

There were footsteps outside, the door opened, and Lemaitre came in briskly. He raised a hand in greeting, took out cigarettes with an almost automatic movement, put one to his lips and said perkily:

"All ready and correct, sir, reporting for duty."

"What's cheered you up?" demanded Gideon.

"Got mixed up with a couple of Melky's boys and proved to myself that I'm still as good as any three of them," said Lemaitre. His eyes had a rather hard, shiny look, but he was fifteen years younger than Appleby, and a night without sleep wouldn't do him any harm. He had been able to work off his despair, too, and probably it wouldn't hit him so hard again in future; when his Fifi had walked out on him, she might have done him a lot of good.

"All right, you take over from Charley," said Gideon promptly. "I'm going to Lassiter Street."

"That Penn business?"

"Yes."

"Ten to one there's nothing to it," said Lemaitre airily. "Ready to go, Charley?"

"Won't take me long to hand over," said Appleby, "but I want to nip along to the end room for a minute." Odd thing, thought Gideon, Appleby could be as coarse and vulgar as any man, but always used the euphemism "end room." Gideon clapped his hat on the back of his head and went to the door, where Appleby joined him quickly, and they walked briskly toward the lift and the head of the stairs. "As a matter of fact," said Appleby, "I just wanted a word in your ear, George."

"Eh? Well, go ahead."

"Until tonight I always had a bellyache about still being a C.I.," said Appleby very slowly. "I always thought you Supers were damn lucky, you most of all, and that I was passed over because of my accent, not lack of ability. This is where I want to say I was wrong. Been a pleasure working with you, George, and I couldn't get anywhere near the standard you set even if I had my time over again."

He was staring straight ahead.

So was Gideon.

They went on for a few paces in silence, and then Gideon said gruffly:

"I've got fifteen years here yet, Charley, if I don't get pushed out earlier, or get knocked over by a bus, and what you've just said is one of the things I'm going to remember as long as I'm here. Thanks." He could have said that Appleby had opened his eyes too, showing unsuspected qualities, but this wasn't the moment; it would look like words for words' sake. There was a much better way, for they reached the lift, and he stopped and said, "Good night, Charley. Like to come on to day duty?"

"Just between you and me, I wouldn't mind," said Appleby. "These jam sessions at night take it out of me."

"I'll fix it," promised Gideon, and then held out his hand. "Good night, Charley."

They gripped.

Then Appleby grinned and turned toward the door marked GENTLEMEN, and said with a waggish air of flippancy:

"Thanks, Gee-Gee. Now I'm here, I might as well pop in for a Jimmy Riddle."

Gideon chuckled as he vanished, and as the lift came up. He was still smiling when he reached the Yard. Different men were on duty in the hall, more men were about, a little group of girls on the office staff was coming in, there were charwomen in the passages and in the offices where doors were propped open. He went hurrying to his car, throwing "Morning," "Morning" right and left, and drove out into the brightening day. He had a fairly clear run to Lassiter Street, and on the last five minutes he wondered exactly what "a lot of noise going on" implied. With luck he would soon know. He turned into Lassiter Street and now found two Squad cars waiting, a uniformed man on duty, and a little crowd of early-morning watchers. A milkman was rattling his bottles and a newsboy came cycling along, whistling, and as he drew level with Gideon he shouted:

"Better look out, lot o' coppers along there!"

Gideon drew up behind the cars. The front door of Number 11 was open, and he could see the broad shoulders of a Flying Squad man just inside, and thought he heard a woman's protesting, whining voice. In the distance he heard the ringing of a fire engine or an ambulance. The constable recognized him and stood aside, and he went hurrying.

"I tried to stop him," the woman was saying in a thin, nasal voice. "You can't blame me, I tried to stop him, that's Gawd's truth; everything I could, I did."

Stop *what*?

"What's on?" Gideon asked sharply.

The Squad man turned round. The woman, with her wispy gray hair and thin, dirty face and drab clothes, was cringing back against the wall. There were sounds from below Gideon, and a door below the stairs—the door leading to the cellar—was wide open, and electric light shone out.

"Found the woman—Mrs. Penn, that is—down in the cellar, sir," the Squad man said. "They were going to brick her up in the wall."

"What?"

"You can't blame me, I tried to stop him," the drab whined again. "I did everything I could, I swear I did."

"How long's she been dead?" Gideon asked, and he felt as if he was being choked, for only he could have made sure that more was done here during the night; he should have followed that hunch much earlier.

"Not long," said the Squad man, "no sign of *rigor* yet. Strangled. She was tied to a chair. I'd hang this pair so high—" He broke off abruptly, and then added, "There's the ambulance. I'll go get the men." He hurried past Gideon, while the drab clutched at Gideon's sleeve with skinny fingers. Gideon shook her off, went through the doorway with his head lowered, and went down the flight of stone steps. There were brick chippings, thick dust, the floor roughly wiped over; and there was the hole in the wall and everything that it signified. Two Squad men were in the little passage where the hole had been made, and they were knocking at some bricks a little way further along.

"Found anything else?" Gideon demanded.

"Her husband disappeared, and a hole's been bricked up here," one of the men said ominously.

"Keep at it." Gideon went through into the main cellar, and still had to keep his head low, or he would have touched the ceiling. There, lying on the detectives' coats, was the body of a slight, dark, pale-faced young woman whose eyes and mouth were slack; by her side were two silent Yard men. In a corner was a short, stocky, gray-haired man, with a low forehead and a brutal face, a thieves'-kitchen character in real life. Two more Squad men were with him. On the floor near them were a bag of cement, some sand, a pail of water—everything needed to cement the wall.

"Charged him yet?" asked Gideon. He had to speak, to say something.

"No, sir, waiting to see what else we find."

"Right. Who is he?"

"Name of Bartholomew Rikker, sir, owns the house."

"He admitted anything?"

"Won't say a word."

"He will," said Gideon harshly, while Rikker stood there in flat defiance. Then men came hurrying down the stairs, carrying a folded stretcher between them, and it wasn't long before the body of Mrs. Penn was lifted gently onto the stretcher and then carried out. Gideon had one look at her face, and felt a surge of anger which made him clench his hands as he looked at Rikker.

He'd hang him high, too.

He went into the passage.

The men had prized some of the bricks loose. He tried to persuade himself that the girl's husband's disappearance had nothing to do with this bricked-up hole, but at heart he felt sure what they were going to find. It was five minutes before they started the "new" hole. That was all they needed to know; the smell was evidence enough before they found the body.

Rikker refused to say a word, except to demand his "rights"—free legal aid—but his wife didn't take much persuading to talk.

On the night when Michael Penn had come home earlier than his wife, he had been in high spirits and carrying presents for his Netta, and he had told the Rikkers why. He had won nearly two hundred pounds on the weekly pools—for which he always used his office address—and the check had reached him that morning. He had cashed it, spent a little on luxury, and taken the rest home to gladden Netta's heart—one hundred and ninety pounds in one-pound notes.

And the Rikkers had barely enough money to subsist on.

If the woman could be believed, Rikker had wanted to borrow some of the money, Penn had refused and told him that the first thing he would do would be to get out of the two dingy rooms upstairs, and there had been a fierce quarrel.

"I'm sure he didn't mean to kill him. I'm positive he didn't," Mrs. Rikker said drably. "It was really an accident."

"Like the accident to Mrs. Penn," said Gideon.

He didn't say so, and probably wouldn't say so to any but his closest friends, but this was the kind of job which made him curse the names of the Members of Parliament who had fought to put an end to hanging. Hadn't Rikker forfeited all right to live?

The Rikkers were at Cannon Row, and would come up at West London Court later in the morning. The preparing of the charge wouldn't take very long; it was the last thing Gideon would do at the office. He walked across to the Yard building, in broad daylight. He felt as if he had failed utterly, but sheer tiredness overcame depression. He yawned two or three times on the way to his office and, when he reached it, yawned more widely.

Lemaitre looked up alertly.

"Hello, George, tired?" He leaned back in his chair and tapped the pile of reports which Appleby had left. "Well, you haven't much to worry about. These are all in apple-pie order, hardly any need to do more than initial them." He paused. "Bad show, the Penn murder."

Gideon grunted.

"Don't start blaming yourself. If it hadn't been for you Rikker would have got away with it," Lemaitre said. "The only other thing that went sour on us was the Wide boys' job. There isn't much we need worry about. The Prowler's illustrious ma and pa are downstairs but I wished them onto the secretary's office; no need for us to tackle them yet. The Prowler can thank his lucky stars his wasn't a capital charge, too."

"Jennifer Lewis all right, then?" Gideon was eager.

"Good chance of recovery, according to the hospital."

"Thank the Lord for that," said Gideon. "All right, let me see the reports you think I ought to see."

Lemaitre handed a bunch of reports over, and Gideon was about to go through them when he heard a commotion outside. Then a man began to laugh uproariously. Another joined in. Two more came toward the door, their footsteps almost drowned by the deep-bellied laughter. Lemaitre glanced up, his head on one side, and Gideon said irritably:

"Well, that's one way to start a day."

He expected the men to pass; instead, the door was flung open without warning, and Appleby, wearing his hat and coat and all ready to leave, came striding in, still laughing and looking as happy as if he'd won a fortune. He held his flat stomach until he was able to speak coherently.

". . . never believe it," he said at last. "Greatest joke I've heard in years!" He burst out laughing again, while a C.I. in the passage was grinning broadly, and Gideon clenched his teeth. "You—you know Bigamy Bill had a blonde—"

He couldn't go on. Lemaitre and Gideon exchanged glances as they waited.

"He thought he was on—an easy picking," Appleby went on, his voice husky, "but do you know what she did? She—cor, strike a light! she absolutely cleaned him out! Loose money, watch, cuff links, took everything she could lay her hands on, she did. When he woke at half past six, she wasn't in bed with him, she'd gone."

Lemaitre began to chuckle, and even Gideon grinned.

"Don't tell me B.B.'s reported to us—" Lemaitre said.

"Not on your life; he wouldn't dare show his face. But he kicked up a hell of a fuss, and got his landlady out of bed. Take it from me, *she'll* talk. George, there's a problem, what do we do if he does report it? Do we try to catch that blonde?"

One thing was certain; this had made Appleby's night.

He left soon afterward, still grinning and chuckling, and Gideon turned back to the reports, the depression eased. He couldn't fault anything which Appleby had done or recommended and left behind, so he initialed what had to be done, yawned again, stood up, and took his hat and coat off the peg again. Lemaitre, talking on the telephone, looked up and waved, but Gideon didn't go. Lemaitre would probably find the lonely nights the worst time, for a while, and here was the chance to kill two birds with one stone.

Lemaitre finished, and banged down the receiver.

"Copper conked at Camberwell," he said. "No great harm done. Don't you want to go home?"

"Lem, how'd you like to give Appleby a break?"

"Eh? How?"

"He's had all the night work he wants for a bit."

"Oh," said Lemaitre slowly, and looked surprised. He frowned; then his face began to clear and finally he smiled rather tautly, and nodded. "See what you mean. Good idea if I don't have to go home every night. Okay, George, ta."

Gideon nodded and went out. . . .

Soon he was driving homeward, his stream of traffic very thin, the inward stream thick and fast, and a lot of the drivers in too much of a hurry. That was normal. He was checking everything that had happened and trying to make sure that he hadn't forgotten anything significant; certainly there was nothing that couldn't wait. He would spend the rest of the week on night duty, and get back on days next week.

Meanwhile, Kate would be cooking breakfast for the kids, if she hadn't finished already, and it would be good to see her bright eyes and fresh face, her spotless white blouse and—

He slowed down.

At the corner where he turned off the main road, there was young Matthew, leather satchel slung over his shoulders, school cap at the back of his head, obviously waiting for something and not for a bus, for that was further along the road. He recognized the car, and waved eagerly. Gideon hoped that he wasn't going to ask for a lift to school, and a continuation of the discussion of last night. Here he was, round face scrubbed, teeth shining, a little pimply although he seemed to be over the worst of those troubles.

"Morning, Matt."

"Thought I'd catch you," greeted Matthew eagerly, and he leaned against the window but showed no desire to get into the car. "Just wanted a word, Dad. I thought you ought to know. When I got back last night I couldn't help talking about where I'd been, and I thought I might as well strike while the iron was hot, so I told Mum what I'm going to do for a living. She didn't seem to mind as much as I thought she would. Do you know what she said?"

"No, what?"

"She said that she'd be a happy mother if I ever turned out to be half as good a copper as my father! So I told her I'd have a damned—I mean a darned—good try."